THE SWORDS OF THE GODDESS

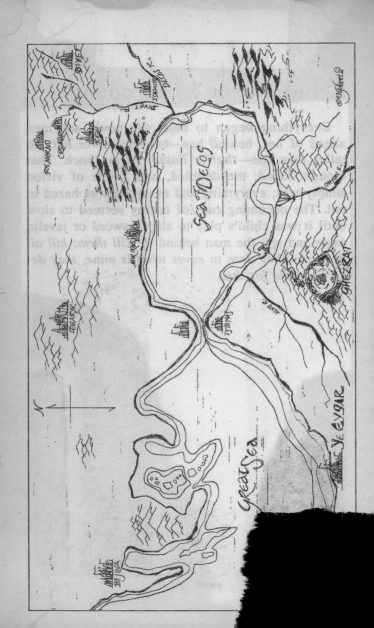

THE SWORD

AND

THE LION

ROBERTA CRAY

DAW BOOKS, INC.

DONALD A. WOLLHEIM, FOUNDER

375 Hudson Street, New York, NY 10014

ELIZABETH R. WOLLHEIM
SHEILA E. GILBERT
PUBLISHERS

First Printing, June 1993

1 2 3 4 5 6 7 8 9

DAW TRADEMARK REGISTERED
U.S. PAT. OFF. AND FOREIGN COUNTRIES
—MARCA REGISTRADA
HECHO EN U.S.A.

PRINTED IN THE U.S.A.

For Dhugan—of course

And for all those I know who did—

and those who didn't

you were both right.

Thanks to my sister for the maps.

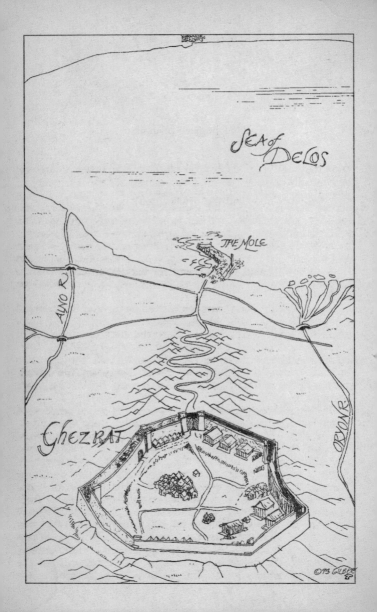

1

Atos the sun finished his crossing of a cloud-strewn sky and slid into the distant sea, marking the end of the chief day of planting for the Spring Festival of the Earth Goddess. All across the plain, men and women set down their plows and tools, left ships sitting at the mole and goods waiting to be loaded, and went to bathe and oil themselves and put on their finest garments; young girls prepared bundles of grain and flowers for door lintel and gate, to honor Denota. In the fields, a few chosen boys walked by light of sunset and torch to plant the sacred circle of grain that on harvest would go to Denota.

In the east the first stars came into being and light edged the distant mountains where Atelos the moon would soon begin his long climb. The gates to the temple were opened and people streamed in, bringing offerings of fruit and flowers, seeking the blessing of Denota for the coming year. The line of waiting supplicants stretched far down the broad, cobble-paved avenue, nearly to the square before the main gates.

On the outer walls, only the first rank of night guard kept watch, and on this night the great bronze gates stood open, and would remain open until the last offerings and final blessings were given. Along the many inner walls of the city, other people stood so they could look down into the goddess' courtyard, or took the night air with their families.

Away from the temple, the streets and avenues were nearly deserted, for many people worshiped Denota in their homes and courtyards, and had already prepared the bread and olive oil that would be eaten in Her honor, the wine that would be drunk; they had marked the doors with grain and barred them from inside. An occasional guard made his way home or to the barracks, other men who worshiped in the House of Warriors or the Temple of Atelos gathered at the wine and bread merchants for gambling and gossip. A lone woman hurried home with the last loaf of flat bread from a bakery, and two fresh flowering branches to cross above the lintel and call Denota's blessing upon her household; she had to flatten against a door on the alleylike little street as a skinny, barefooted messenger boy pelted past her.

Just behind her, a door opened for two young girls in the blue robes and tiny brass bells of the virgin goddess Xelas and the servant who would accompany them to the temple of the river goddess where they would sing and dance until moonrise.

The Sacred Ground of Denota, which shared highest ground in the city with the prince's many-storied palace, blazed with lights in honor of the Mother of All, First-Goddess: On this night, the goddess would bless the planting and newborn beasts; Her hand would touch pregnant women, women wed during the past year, and girls in their fifteenth year. The smooth stone courtyard bustled with activity: priests who carried the baskets of grain from the last harvest, bread made of that grain and the last pinch of seed saved to plant at sunrise on the morrow; priestesses bearing jugs of water and thick sheaves of spring flowers. A small boy clad in fresh green and crowned in new leaves stood at the foot of the goddess' shrine, flanked by two very young priestesses; he held a short garland-wound rope attached to a newborn foal, also crowned in new leaves. The child shifted fretfully; the foal lay at his feet and nibbled at the flowers.

Away from the joyful bustle in the courtyard, nearly lost in shadow at this hour, stood the small, windowless hut that led down to the cavern underlying much of the upper temple. The hut itself was windowless, stone which had been coated with red clay from the river Oryon, and incised with a bas-relief of Denota blessing the newly-created Ghezrat. Within the hut, a similarly intricate carving covered the floor: Denota creating olive trees and grape vines; blessing downy birdlings emerging from eggs, skinny-legged young beasts and two fresh-faced children. To one side, a steep and narrow stairway went down along the inner wall of the temple, past raw stone and damp dirt, ending in a high-ceilinged cave. It was ordinarily kept dark here, except for a single oil lamp kept burning in a deep niche. Tonight, there were four other lamps to represent the four corners of the year; they cast black shadows of stone icicles and many people across a smooth limestone floor.

Silence held here, ordinarily, except for the distant drip of water; tonight that was lost under the rustle of fabric, the sound of many people breathing. The air was fragrant with crushed thyme and citrus; it blended oddly with the metal-smell of steam rising from the Cleft of Denota.

The Cleft itself cut across the center of the cavern, a long crack, narrow at both ends and wider at its midpoint than a man could span with his arms. Steam issued from it in faint, foggy tendrils all the year, but on this one night in spring, it swirled upward, a double spiral of pale green and darker green, lit from beneath by the goddess Herself, perhaps, or by Leros her son, god of mountains and earthquakes.

A net woven of vines and seaweed, interwoven with straw and olive branches had been stretched across the spiral of steam. Tephys, High Priestess and Seer lay upon the net, swathed in a robe of fresh green. The pale oval of her face and her blue-black, flower-twined hair stood out in sharp contrast to the robe; she lay quite still, eyes closed, her breast moving as she deeply inhaled the steam and awaited the goddess' words.

At her right shoulder knelt Eyzhad, senior of the few men who served Denota; opposite him, the aged priestess Meronne who had been Seer: two to hear the words of the goddess and, if need be, interpret what the priestess said.

Prince Pelledar sat cross-legged in the place of high honor, eyes closed, head bowed, his hands cradling the head of the priestess. Of all those present, only he was black-clad, by tradition; his face stood out pale against a thick black beard. His eyes were lowered, fixed upon Tephys' face as Meronne had told him to do.

Thirty-six women stood in a loose half-circle a distance from the Cleft; dimly visible in the uncertain light: Twelve green-clad priestesses with offerings of flowers and slender grape branches just come to leaf; then the twelve older women who came to this place four times a year only, wearing their finest garments and ropes of new leaves and blossoms around their throats; last of all, twelve young women in white sashed in bright green, girls chosen by Tephys at the last midwinter to serve the goddess for a year and of them were some who would serve her for life.

Prince Pelledar sat very still and tried to ignore both the half-circle of women facing him and the growing discomfort in his hip joints, the dead weight of Tephys' head which rested on his outstretched hands. He tried instead to concentrate on this—so he had been told all his life—great honor, this vital ceremony. *And yet, how important is it, truly? For does not the grain grow and the herds increase in other lands, lands where the goddess is not worshipped?* He dismissed the thought as unworthy—indeed perhaps dangerous where he presently sat—and rested his eyes on a point just above his fingers. It was said a previous Holder, long ago, had entertained impure thoughts on such a night, and Leros had set the cavern to shaking so he had fallen into the Cleft.

His tutors had told him that tale when he was a boy, and he had scoffed at it then. He had since heard Meronne threaten her novices with it to still their giggling and thought it foolish; just now, perhaps it would be better to not upset the goddess *or* her son. Leros was slow to anger, but he was a fearsome god when roused.

Concentrate upon the priestess, he reminded himself sternly. Tephys' hair was nearly buried under a riot of purple and white blossoms. He could smell the cloying scent of flowers, the new oils they had combed through her hair—above all, the dizzying steam rising from the Cleft. The priestess stiffened slightly, drew a deep breath, relaxed as she let it out. Pelledar became aware he was holding his own breath, and made himself exhale quietly.

When the goddess spoke—but what did she ever say, save such things as Tephys herself might choose to say to these waiting women? Blessings upon the crops, upon the babes, and the increased herds. She had not spoken any other words, not in all the years Pelledar had been prince. The son at his side and a little behind him—his heir Septarin—had not yet been born when Pelledar's father had held Tephys' head and been party to the prophecy warning of the coming of Bejina with war and siege. *But my father's generals warned him the Bejinis were ambitious, even before Tephys spoke of war,* the prince reminded himself.

How is it, that of all the gods and goddesses, it is the mother of growing things who speaks of disaster and war? He had asked that after the Bejinis had finally been driven away, just as Denota had said. His father had no answer. The priests had none that made sense to him, then or now, but priests ever spoke in riddles. And Tephys—he had asked that of her once he was prince, and she had laughed at him. He could feel his cheekbones turning red, remembering that jeering laugh even after so many years. But Tephys spoke with a goddess and knew herself to be above the reprimands of a mere prince. And a woman with her temperament clearly felt no need to soften her speech for such a lowly being.

Pelledar sent his eyes toward Eyzhad, then Meronne. She was old, he thought possibly the oldest woman in all Ghezrat; her face was, to his thinking, repulsively lined and puckered. She had been the mouth of Denota all his grandsire's reign, part of his father's. The phlegmatic Eyzhad had been one of the last chosen by Meronne before she gave over her role and her robes to Tephys. Pelledar had been tutored by Eyzhad for a time and liked the quiet and self-effacing priest, but he had no notion of what the man thought of him—or of anyone or anything else. Just now, the priest sat back on his knees, within hand's reach of the priestess' near shoulder; his eyes were closed and he had not moved, had not even seemed to breathe since helping Tephys onto the net. Meronne's little black eyes were fixed intently on her former pupil, her concentration total. The prince cautiously tensed and relaxed his leg muscles. Meronne cast him a warning look. She pursed her lips and turned back to Tephys, and Pelledar restrained a sigh. *If my legs cramp and I move because of it, she will blame me, especially if Denota does not speak this night.* At least Meronne would not snap at him as Tephys did, though she could be fierce indeed when she instructed her novices. Eyzhad, of course, had respect for royalty; if anything went amiss here because a prince shifted his weight, Eyzhad would never show displeasure by so much as a reproachful look.

Tephys drew his attention once again; her head rolled back and forth on his hands and she mumbled something under her breath he could not understand. Eyzhad opened his eyes and leaned a little forward; Meronne's lined cheeks were suddenly flushed.

Pelledar lowered his own eyes, fixing them on a yellow-centered, pale-blue flower. He felt uncomfortable, something that came to him often during these ceremonials: Chief goddess Denota might be—she was still a *goddess*, mistress of fields and births, and growing things. Whatever a man had to do with these, it was peripheral—he planted seed, in fields or in women. This spring rite was for the newborn, the seedlings, and girls of an age to wed or those wishing to quicken. It had nothing to do with men; only three men served the goddess and most of those coming to her shrine this night would be girls and women, farmers or herdsmen the only men. In the homes where the spring was celebrated in private, the rites were prepared by women and mostly for and in honor of women.

Denota's words during these equinoctal ceremonies had always been to praise the planters, to extol the cheeses and vines, now and again to choose life-priestesses from among the green-sashed novices.

Of all the four festivals, this spring ceremony was the one to which a prince might send his wife, or his unwed eldest daughter. But Pelledar had no daughters, and Tephys had insisted upon his presence this night, with that of his son. *She becomes arrogant,* he thought resentfully. *There is no purpose to my being here, save that she orders it.*

There were no men in all this cave tonight, save himself, his heir—Eyzhad, who as Denota's priest was virtually sexless. And his nephew—but he would not think of Hemit, just now.

Men who sought a temple this night would go to the House of Warriors, particularly those older men who had held out against Bejina, or those who had more recently battled to take back the forts flanking the western isthmus between the Sea of Delos and the Great Sea.

But the House of Warriors was no place for Ghezrat's current prince. Pelledar had gone there often as a boy after he came of age at fourteen, but never since he came to manhood and then to power. In a temple filled with warriors and retired soldiers, he felt even more out of place than here. *My father fought for his land, and his father and his before him, back through all the generations of Prince of Ghezrat, seven hundred years. And I—* He had participated in battle only once, and even then had not actually fought against the pirates who had come from the Great Sea to take or sink the city's small fleet; his father had not let his youngest son join in the fighting. *I was of age, I had the training. It was wrong for him to deny me, and set me apart from other men by that act.*

There had been no other fighting in all the years since, and he was acutely aware of it: No full war in twenty-two years; there had been a skirmish or a brush with some enemy along the borders, and great deeds done—but none by him. *There are men under my rule who fought every day for a hundred days, who swam from fort to fort across storm-tossed straits to take back the narrows while I stood at my father's hand and watched him plot pointless strategies with his generals. Men who fought and died of wounds before the city's walls, and of plague and hunger within them, when Bejina set upon us.*

He closed his eyes briefly, shifted his legs so as to rest his wrists against the long shinbones. The woman lay utterly limp and her head was heavy; the ropes pressed against his hands. Hands, he thought sourly, that had never been hardened by a sword hilt or a long spear.

He opened his eyes, glanced sidelong at Eyzhad once more. The priest's hands were softer than his, but the thought gave him no comfort. The House of Warriors would have given him none, either, this night or any other. *Whose fault—my fathers, that of the gods? Whose, that I rule warriors, who am myself no true warrior?* At least those in this cave did not look at him with *that* thought in their eyes: "We have fought for Ghezrat, but he has not. How can such a prince lead us should our enemies rise against us once more, as they surely will?"

But he was wrong. Everyone else in the cavern with its lamps and underlit steam gazed at Tephys, whatever their own thoughts. But at his father's back, five paces behind him, Septarin held himself rigidly still and straight, keeping his face expressionless with an effort that would surely have pleased his tutors. His eyes moved in the gloom, seldom still, darting from Tephys to each of those flanking her, to the circle of priestesses before returning to his father. *That he brought me here; that I must participate in this women's rite!* He was just old enough at fifteen years that he could have gone by himself to the House of Warriors, though the old men who filled that house bored him terribly. Better yet, his chief tutor could have taken him this night as a secret initiate to Atelos; he had been pressuring the man for nearly a year, and if not for Tephys, he might have managed it tonight. Because he was Pelledar's heir, he was bound to this place and time, standing by while big-bellied common

women and dirty pregnant peasants and gawky girls waited
for some sign from the Mother of Earth! He could feel the
blood burning his cheeks, feel the anger sealing his throat.
*Show nothing. Remember what Etimos has taught you, the
correct conduct and bearing of a warrior.* Septarin clenched
his fists at his sides until the nails dug painfully into his
palms, and briefly closed his eyes. He burned with shame. *If
there is a Leros here, in that place below, hear my plea! Let
me not become like my father, sitting as groom to a priestess
who serves the goddess of earth! Let me not grow old and
die, soft like my father!* The glorious tales of war Etimos had
told him, that the bards had sung: What better life could a
man live? What greater reward than to die young and still
beautiful and strong, a hero—unless a man might live and be
such a hero? With an effort, he unclenched his fists, brought
his chin up, and schooled his face to a complete lack of expression once again.

His resentful gaze touched upon the line of women
briefly, fastened on the seated man who leaned against his
mother's shins, her hand on his shoulder the only thing
keeping him upright. Septarin swallowed and looked away
hurriedly, tried to fix his thoughts on visions of battle and
heroes once more.

Hemit, eldest son of long-dead Prince Perlot and the
Mirikosi Princess Khadat, sat at her feet, his head lolling
heavily against her. He had been a hero of the battle of the
Isthmus and they sang of Hemit's deeds each winter when
that victory was celebrated. They also sang of his father—
brave Perlot, who had been run down by a Yeveki long-ship.
But Hemit and what few were left of his father's company
had evaded the Yeveki ships and reached land, coming by
surprise against those who lay siege to the fort and breaking
them utterly, though with fearful loss. Perlot was never
found; Hemit returned to his family's palace upon a shield,
his head broken and his legs ever after useless.

Khadat stood behind him, head bowed and eyes fixed
upon her son. He did not know where he was this night;
more and more, he retreated into some private place of his
own. She bit her lip, tried to keep the anger inside but as always it was too great to contain. *It was your word, Goddess,
that told of the battle that took my husband and all the good
in this my firstborn! Is there no pity in you, to steal from me
my Perlot and my Hemit both? At least give me back bright*

Hemit, as exchange for condemning Perlot to wander ever between day and night, because I could not perform the rites over his broken body?

She trembled; the woman next to her took hold of her arm to steady her. She swallowed, inclined her head slightly. The hand was removed at once. She scarcely noticed; her eyes fixed on the wreck of a man of perhaps thirty. His legs had once been golden-brown and as well muscled as the finest statues in the Mirikosi palaces, but now they were withered, pale sticks with no meat on them. His hands plucked endlessly at the hem of his garments. Hair once blue-black and crisply curled like his father's, though they kept it well tended and freshly oiled, now showed thick strands of silver and it lay flat against his head, thinning back from a brow as unlined as a babe's. Khadat swallowed. He resembled her, this once-fair son—or he had in his glory: Hers, she had always thought him, and none of Perlot's, unlike her younger son who might have been Perlot come back to life at the age when he had crossed the Sea of Delos to court her and bring her back to Ghezrat. *Is it a fault in me, Denota, that you do not take pity upon my son? Tell me what sacrifice I must make, what rite I must perform—tell me, gentle Denota, order anything you will, and I shall do it!*

No answer. There was never an answer.

At the other end of the half-circle, last of the initiates, Breyd, second daughter of Menleus, kept her hands folded together before her, her eyes fixed on Tephys and tried to keep her face straight. Such a *solemn* place, this cavern. She was aware of Denira, childhood friend and fellow initiate, standing at her elbow, but she didn't dare look at her; Meronne's bright eye had fixed on them earlier, daring either of them to giggle, or even to smile. *How foolish Meronne is! This is Spring Festival, a time of joy, and they behave as if it were a funeral pyre for the entire city! After all, Denota is goddess of the young. Surely she takes pleasure in laughter, fresh grapes, lambs romping in the pastures?* Meronne would tell her *that* was different and give her a horrid, squelching glare. All the same—such a *very* solemn ceremony.

Breyd tried to fix her thoughts on Tephys' still form, as she had been instructed, to blank her mind to allow the goddess entry, should she wish. *As if a mere novice could deny Denota that entry if she wished it. I wonder if Mother made the bread with dates and honey? And if Grandmother had Father bring branches from her vineyards in time? She promised me oil and hot peppers if I survived this dull ceremony. I think I might, but I wonder if she has had time with everything else to prepare it?* Her mind chattered on until Tephys shifted in the prince's hands and moaned loudly. Meronne edged forward to look at her before casting a warning glance at the initiates for whom she was chief instructor. *Beloved Denota,* Breyd thought as her eyes moved from Meronne to the glowering Septarin, skipping quickly beyond him to the lamp and the two children guarding it. *Goddess, surely you know my heart is yours. But truly, is all this dull ceremony of your choosing?*

At her side, Denira shifted and Breyd heard her swallow something suspiciously like a giggle. She bit the corners of her mouth and tried to think of nothing.

The little, niggling fear came into that nothing. Surely Denota would not choose her for lifetime service, condemning her to a narrow, rutted circle of rites, and learned responses, and the companionship of other virgin women until death many years on. And yet, that might serve better than the alternative: with her elder sister Niverren to wed at midsummer, there was no reason why Breyd should not have a husband; Nevvia her mother would press Menlaeus to find her one. But no man had spoken for her, save Laius, and what other man would, between her odd, dark little face and the bride-price Menlaeus could afford? Laius. Nevvia simply could not understand what was wrong with the massive, swaggering, and bluff Laius. But the thought of preparing meals and bearing children for Laius, sleeping nightly in his bed for all the rest of her life—*Goddess, better anything than that!* Better a lifetime of the boring rites here than a life that might end a year hence in childbed, if not sooner at Laius' hands. But Nevvia saw him only as the closest friend of her beloved only son—and Tarpaen sang Laius' praise. Better the eternal feast prepared for women who died giving birth than a lifetime of such a husband, to sitting aged and drooling long years from now, propped daily in the doorway by a grandchild—

She bit the inside of her cheek, hard. *You swore to yourself you would not pursue this thought; it accomplishes nothing. Father knows what Laius is; he would never give me to Laius.* At least this year of service to Denota had given her a respite; her brother had to quit pressing his friend's suit.

A high-pitched wail echoed from the walls; she caught her breath as light spilled from the Cleft and rose in a fountain of green and gold to the ceiling, falling back in a near-blinding shower of sparks. Tephys cried out; the prince gasped and let go of her head. Meronne snarled out something and snatched at his wrists, shoved his hands back under Tephys' head before she leaned across the net, brilliant light turning her old face bright green. Eyzhad blinked rapidly and his mouth sagged open comically as Tephys began to speak.

Sparks still skittered across the stone floor. Above the hissing and the still audible whine from below, Tephys' voice came—lower than normal yet strong enough to fill the cavern. "My blessing to the crops, and the first harvest. My hand shall protect those women who have quickened, let My love guide the young, that they grow wise in My ways.

"But take heed, and let the people of Ghezrat tread carefully when they walk in the fields, lest they trample the grain and waste it; let them choose wisely do they sacrifice a beast to my chosen Lord the sun, or to those Our children who bring rain or send the fishes swimming into their nets. Let nothing be wasted, let all be carefully tended, and that which is brought in, let a greater portion of it be stored. Let the diggers of clay and the makers of charcoal be diligent at their tasks, and honor those who make and fire storage pots; let them not falter in the days to come." Breyd saw Pelledar's face, and then Meronne's, his white and stricken, hers grim as it had never been before. *What does She mean by this? What among those words had frightened them so?* As if in answer, she felt a sensation through the soles of her feet as though the rock heaved and then a prickling up her back and into her fingers that was distinctly uncomfortable; warmth rapidly became heat. She gasped, turned to look at the girl on her right and then at Denira; both were staring blankly at Tephys.

She couldn't move, couldn't speak; Tephys' voice droned on, terrifying in its very lack of expression. "For in a little while, will come the Diye Haff, and riding before all, their warlord and Emperor Haffat, and they shall make dreadful war upon Ghezrat. Let my people ready the walls, prepare the stores, set the smiths to smelt metals and cast weapons.

Send the children out to gather stones. For two-score of days there will be hard battle and great deeds. Then will come a time for other deeds of valor, of a kind unknown in Ghezrat. Prepare the city and gird yourselves, who have not fought for all that is yours in a lifetime of men. Ready the companies and prepare the captains."

Meronne's harsh whisper broke a small, stunned silence. "And shall Ghezrat prevail?"

"After a time, and a hard time, and great battle." Tephys' head rocked wildly back and forth; the prince fought to capture it between his hands and hold it steady. Blood splattered across his hands; the priestess had bitten her lip. "Let word go forth; in three days' time, thirty-four men shall be chosen in the House of Warriors. Let all those trained with sword and spear come, all those men with grown and unwed daughters, that I may choose thirty-four Primes for Dyaddi to protect the city's walls. In two days' time thereafter, let those thirty-four Primes come to My courtyard and bring their unwed daughters, that from among these I may choose the thirty-four Secchi to complete the Pairs." Tephys' mouth moved a little while longer, but only Meronne, bent low over her, could hear words if any were spoken.

The priestess fell utterly silent and lay so still she might have been dead; all around the cavern, women and girls began to whisper, and one wept.

Breyd heard none of them. For one terrifying moment, she was still herself, aware of a frightened Denira turning toward her, Denira's touch and a hiss of pain as she snatched her fingers away. Breyd felt stone beneath her feet and then—nothing.

Menlaeus stood before her in full panoply, but what he wore was unfamiliar. His cloak was red and the armor brightly polished bronze, well fitted to his sturdy, rather stocky frame; red cloth covered the graying hair he kept cut short. The face was his: squarish and handsome; crinkly lines under his eyes and beside them because he smiled so much; neatly trimmed beard and mustache. His mouth was like hers—small for a man, her mother said. He was looking at her, both proud and afraid. Her legs were cold—bared to the wind. People in the street stared at her, silent and awed. Heavy bronze shielded her breast, and suddenly she saw her father old, feeble—helpless. *Will you protect him?* a harsh voice demanded; she couldn't answer it.

Blackness. When she could see once more, she had a sword in her hand, a shield upon her other arm, Menlaeus at her side. *No! I did not ask for this! How can I protect my father? And I cannot—I can't use a sword, I cannot fight!* Pain and exhaustion, hunger and constant fear everywhere, and people who stopped in the streets to gaze at her or back out of her way. Constant whispering: "She is Secchi, the goddess chose her." *No, I cannot be Secchi! Goddess, look at me, I am half my father's size! What armorer could fit me? What enemy would see me and not laugh?*

And then an explosive burst of smoke and stench and hard stone beneath her; she was cut and bleeding in many places, her vision was blurred; she knew men lay around her dead, or horribly injured. The smell of blood was going to make her ill. Her body had been driven to such exhaustion, she wasn't certain she could move, but there was something else which kept her where she was. *Find it, important*—That faded; her hand slid across the rock, unrecognizable under dirt, cuts, and dried blood. The cries of men in pain and shrieks of fear and dread rang in her ears; thick black smoke filled the air and she could smell pitch and burned wool, burning flesh.

Blackness. She held her father's hand, gazed down into his face; Menlaeus lay quite still. His armor was dented, his face smudgy with mud, his beard filthy and tangled, his eyes gazed into hers intently, as though he must tell her something, and then they closed. *Oh, Goddess, no; not dead, please not dead!* There was no visible wound upon him, but his face was thin, drawn, and utterly white. His fingers rested on his sword; next to it lay another—smaller, lighter, plainly made. *My sword.*

She could not move, it seemed, but there was no time anyway: A crashing, deafening roar, flames and smoke everywhere, and then many hands were dragging at her, pulling her away, and Menlaeus was gone.

Breyd gasped for air and with unnerving suddenness the cavern was all around her once again. Denira was staring at her anxiously, her face very white. She shut her eyes tightly, opened them at once; the vision was still there, waiting for her; it would take her again if she let it. In that one moment, she had felt the smooth bronze hilt of the sword against her palm and the extended shoulders of her father's armor digging into her wrist where she had cradled him, the weight of

metal hanging from her own small shoulders and the crossed
leather straps that kept it in place. She stuffed the palm of
one hand against her teeth to keep them from chattering and
prayed she would not be ill.

Pelledar sat very still, the muscles of his arms corded in
his effort to keep his hands still, to hold the priestess without
hurting her. His palms felt scorched where she had rested
against them; his fingers tingled painfully from secondary
contact with the goddess. *I thought my father exaggerated
when he spoke of pain. When he said I would know, if it was
the priestess choosing her own words, or the gods speaking
through her.* It was not until long after Tephys had been
taken away and he himself brought dazedly to his feet,
guided back into his many-storied palace and into his own
apartments, until his anxious queen had sent servants for unmixed wine and pressed him to drink deeply of it, that he remembered what Tephys had actually said.

War was coming to Ghezrat, the dread Diye Haff coming
to steal his city. Traders warned of the Diye Haff, though
once Diyet had been so distant a man scarcely knew the
name, let alone where it lay. Letters came from other rulers
to warn of Haffat—his ambitions, his armies, and the prophecies of his lion god. Haffat rode at the head of a vast army,
going where and when he chose, and lands fell to him almost at his asking.

The goddess had no delusions about the strength of the
Diye Haff and their lion god. She had never in all Pelledar's
thirty-five years ordered the naming of Dyaddi.

Septarin followed his father from the cavern in a daze. *I
must believe there is a goddess, to answer my entreaty so!*

Khadat waited until Hemit's two massive servants were
able to come for him, then followed them up the stairs. She
was trembling violently. *There cannot be a war, cannot!
Denota, are you mad? Already you have cost me a husband,
a son—and what have I left now to spend as coin in your
wars save my baby? Will you take Apodain from me as well?*
She let herself be handed into the sedan chair, sat stiffly as
the chair was lifted and carried toward the fine palace set in
the hill just below the prince's palace. A little while, the
goddess said. Enough time to create and prepare Dyaddi.
Such training was not accomplished overnight, however

much of herself the goddess gave to the Pairs. Or so they said.

And so, there would still be time for a desperate mother to find a way to save her last son.

The temple emptied slowly; Meronne brought Tephys awake and gave her small sips of pale wine. Finally the priestess was able to walk, though she leaned heavily on Eyzhad.

No one was left in the cavern save the two young protectors of the flame, Breyd and Denira.

"Breyd?" Denira's whisper trembled. "Breyd, the ceremony is over! Let us go!" Breyd swallowed, tried to speak; no sound came. "Breyd? Breyd, what's wrong? Are you all right?"

She finally managed to nod. "Fine." The word didn't even sound like her voice.

Denira peered at her anxiously. "You aren't fine! You frightened me. I think my fingers are burned where I touched you—"

"I'm fine, truly. Go on home, Denira."

"I can't leave you—"

"You can, go on. I want to find Meronne, anyway." Breyd held out a hand and felt a dreadful sinking sensation as Denira backed away. "We can talk tomorrow."

"Tomorrow," Denira echoed blankly, then turned and sped off across the cavern. Breyd leaned back against the cool stone and closed her eyes tightly; she was shaking violently as if with cold. It subsided finally, leaving her face sheeted with sweat, the hair plastered to her skin. She looked around cautiously. Go, she thought, before Meronne comes back to check on the lamp; Meronne would know what was wrong with her at once, she would demand to know what vision Breyd had been given. *I cannot talk to Meronne about anything, and this—! Don't think.* She shook herself, drew a deep, shuddering breath and forced herself to cross the open floor, to climb the narrow steps. They would be waiting at home, to hear what had happened. *What I have to tell them, though—oh, Father, no!* She didn't dare think about it.

Haffat

Several long days' ride northeast of the Sea of Delos, a vast army camped on warm sands; the wind even at midnight was dry and still hot. The moon edged into the sky, outlining ragged bluffs. Wind whined through brush, bringing with it the smell of burning—the city of Idemito lay in ruin, its buildings still smoldered.

The emperor's plain felted pavilion stood in the midst of other, similar tents, its only mark the banners of the Diye Haff, of Emperor Haffat, and Axtekeles: Lion, Guardian, and God—and Haffat's Guide in his apparently endless quest for new lands. Despite the late hour, fires and torches burned brightly, illuminating a line of men in the black robes of lion-priests. The first held a low table, and another at his side a red cloth to cover it; after them, a small boy who was naked but for a red loincloth. Behind him walked two more priests. In the distance, at the edge of the light, a woman fought the restraining hands of yet another priest.

The child's eyes were glazed and fixed on a point just in front of him; he stopped as his knees touched the table and allowed a priest to set him on it.

Two more men strode toward the table: One was tall, pale, and rather gaunt; his eyes were black and very intense. He was as plainly clad as his soldiers except for the gold-leaf lion upon the breast of his armor. Haffat glanced toward the tent where banners flapped in the wind; a fire burned in a deep pit there and behind it stood his male relatives who had not already been given kingdoms to rule for him. He looked down at the table, gazed into the eyes of the child, and finally laid a long hand on the boy's hair; the mother cried out his name, and was abruptly silent.

The boy smiled; Haffat smiled back at him, then looked back the way he had come as the high priest Knoe made his way into the open. He was as tall as Haffat but broader, and at first he seemed clean-shaven like the emperor and head-shaven as some of his lesser priests were. But Knoe was completely hairless, even without eyebrows. It startled most men; Haffat had long since ceased to notice it.

Knoe bore a part-grown bull calf in his arms as though it were no burden at all. Another priest came in his wake, bearing a golden bowl and a lion-hilted knife.

One of the priests knelt before the child and said something to him; the boy sighed as though suddenly tired, edging himself back upon the table obediently and lying flat, hands stiffly at his sides, eyes wide and staring. Then with another little sigh, he let them close.

Knoe met his emperor's eyes across the table. Haffat glanced at the child, across his shoulder at the moon, or perhaps at the smoking ruin of Idemito. He nodded abruptly, took up the sacrificial blade, and walked around the table. Knoe set the young bull on its feet and held it steady. Haffat thrust; the beast collapsed and the bowl filled to brimming with its blood. Knoe let the bull fall, dipped his finger in blood and laid it upon his tongue, then dipped it in the bowl a second time and touched the child's eyelids and his lower lip.

The boy whimpered faintly, licked his lips; from his mouth came a deep roar of a voice. "Say to my son Haffat, well done. Idemito of the Hot Sands is his, her trade routes his. From Diyet to Idemito and all the land between, it is all his.

"Now comes the route to the sea, and to the Great Sea. Let Haffat leave here his brother Heplo, so Heplo may bring about the peace and set the terms of it. Let Heplo rebuild the walls and make Idemito safe, and let him swear the great oaths this night, that he does not forget to whose grace he owes his lordship of so great a city, and to whose coffers he owes tax, to whose flag allegiance—to whose honor a sacrifice of young bulls upon all feast days.

"Let there be celebration among the army, and then let my son Haffat take horse and nine parts of his army. In nine days time, let him ride south to Mirikos of the bright ships, and let him take Mirikos. They will make no resistance, having heard already of Idemito and how deadly Haffat is to any who deny him. And when Mirikos is his, and her ships his—and his cousin Herric left on its throne, let him take the city's ships and bring with him again nine parts of his men, and so come to Ghezrat.

"Let him plan his battle against the Ghezrathi well; they have been long a warlike folk. Let him beware; when two are made one, the way will be hard."

Silence. Haffat touched a finger to the blade of the knife and set it against the tip of his tongue, and only then spoke. "Great Axtekeles, then Ghezrat is to be mine also?"

"Ghezrat shall be yours, Haffat. It is to you, to see that it remains yours."

"I shall take it, Dread Axtekeles," Haffat said steadily. "And, having taken, shall keep what I take."

Silence answered him, then the faint whimper of a restless child. Knoe gestured; the priests who had brought the boy took him back to his mother, who received him with loud wailing, and the child, shaken from his odd tranquillity, began to weep with her. The priests led both away.

Haffat seemed unaware of anything—unless it was the prophecy just given to him. Knoe laid the dead calf upon the table, took the knife from his emperor's hand and knelt to cut up the beast in the proper manner. When he rose once more, the bundled hide held the organs and long bones. He set that in the emperor's fire, and other priests wrapped the rest of the meat in the red cloth and carried it away.

Most of the onlookers went with them and some of Haffat's kin went into the pavilion to escape the wind and sand; only two of Haffat's sons stood talking outside. Knoe folded his arms, nodded once. "So."

Haffat seemed to come back from a vast distance. "Mirikos, and Ghezrat—and once beyond the straits, what else could be mine?"

The lion-priest shrugged. "All the world, do you continue as well as you go now."

Haffat laughed suddenly, and the laughter eased the gauntness of his face. "All the world! Ah, Knoe, with Mirikos and Ghezrat, I shall have all the world coming to *me*, bringing all the best goods! And eventually, I shall run out of trustworthy governors. But—what is this of two becoming one?"

Knoe shook his head. "No doubt the god will make that clear in time." But it teased his mind; something he had heard, something spoken of in whispers? Years before, perhaps, when he was yet the lion's novice—it eluded him.

Haffat passed the two men standing outside Haffat's tent,

watching the sacrificial meat roast and clapped both on the shoulder. Man and boy, Knoe thought grimly; Haffat's sons by his two youngest wives were nearly of an age, but Hemyas was very much Haffat's son—clever, and brave, born to rule, loved by the men he commanded. Hadda: Hadda drank too much; he dressed too finely for a man on the road to battle; he liked to play the reed-pipes and to keep company with other young fools. Unfortunately, Knoe had not been able to persuade Haffat to leave the boy—this beloved bauble of a child—behind.

Hadda himself had wanted nothing else than to be left, for all his friends and particularly his beloved Jerred remained in Diyet—the emperor's chief scribe who could not be spared from his duties merely to keep the emperor's son company.

Knoe then handed the sacrificial blade to one of his priests, dipped his bloodied hands in a bowl of water held for him, and dried them on a soft cloth. The air reeked of burning: the city and villages, the sour spined wood they used for cooking in Idemito, the charring hide.

"Priest." Knoe turned. Hadda stood at his shoulder. His chin bore that arrogant tilt Knoe hated, though it was true most men had to look up to meet the high priest's eyes. *He tries to look as though he does not fear me; does he think the priest of a Lion does not read men's hearts?* "How much of that just now was *your* doing, priest?"

"My doing?" Knoe folded his arms. "You still doubt the god rides with your father, after all this time?"

"I sometimes think the god speaks—conveniently," Hadda snapped. He bared his teeth in a mirthless grin. "My father is a brilliant general. Of course he wins cities!" The boy must be in the grip of temper, Knoe thought, and was amused at the thought; Hadda would never confront him unless he was drunk or furious, and there was no smell of wine about him. "But each of these sacrifices takes us farther from Diyet, and you said after Righ that you would press my cause. Priest."

"You cannot think I deliberately choose to bring you with us!" Knoe laughed. "Or do you believe that your father conquers half the world merely to keep you from your—?"

Hadda shot out a hand, clamped it around the priest's forearm. "I have told you before Jerred and I are not lovers, and I do not like the way you look down upon him. Choose your words with care. Priest."

Knoe detached his arm effortlessly from the Prince's grip. "From, let us say, your dear friend." Hadda eyed him for some moments, then turned on his heel and strode into the emperor's tent. Knoe cast his eyes up and went over to the fire to tend the meat.

2

Breyd climbed into the clay-floored chamber which was stuffed ceiling to floor with flowers. She jumped convulsively, caught hold of the entry; it always caught her by surprise how little sound from the outside filtered down into the cavern or even into the small room; and the courtyard just now was ablaze with light, filled with laughing women. Her knees were threatening to give way and there was a vile taste in her mouth; she gripped the rough doorframe hard and tried to still her face. *If I go out like this, I must look awful, people will stop me and ask what*—She didn't dare think about it; but it wouldn't leave her. *It wasn't real; the goddess would never give such sign to a mere novice who was only chosen in midwinter! I must have imagined*—She wouldn't let herself remember it; her fingers felt cool bronze, her legs the dead weight of her father's head. *He will be named Prime, and you Secchi; and he will die because of you.* She bit her free hand once more and the pain cleared her mind. For the moment, at least. Her eyelids sagged shut, and there was Menlaeus, standing before her in red and bronze, afraid and proud both. She stuffed the fingers in her mouth and bit down, stepped away from the little building and began to work her way around the courtyard.

Perhaps she had imagined all of it, even Tephys, for there was no sign of fear or talk of war in this main part of the temple, where bright-faced priestesses held hands and danced by threes around low pillars crowned with flowery offerings, or jars of grain or wine. Near the gate, two boys played pipes and a third sang a high, sweet song in praise of growing things.

But now she could hear shrill voices in the street beyond, frightened women's voices higher on the hill where the nobles and the prince lived. Breyd edged along the wall, skirting a pile of cushions where a small boy and a newborn foal slept together. She bit her lip and hurried past them. *If war comes*—Tears tightened her throat painfully.

Somehow she made it all the way to the gates without drawing attention to herself. But by the gate, a lump of a woman pushed slowly to her feet, stretched her neck and shoulders and held out a bundled wrap. "You'll need this, there's a wind along the street."

Breyd averted her face and took the wrap from her grandmother's servant, shook it out, and obediently dropped the length of lightweight, deep blue wool across bare shoulders. She didn't feel cold, she wouldn't have anyway. "There is always wind in the streets, Ina." Her voice sounded a little tight, nothing more. "But you should not have waited for me."

The older woman shook her head, drew a wheezing breath and led the way into the street. "I don't often have the chance to sit and watch the blessings. But you know *she* asks it." Ina always referred to Nidya so, her own odd way of voicing affection for her mistress. "Because your mother worries when you or Niverren stay gone too long, and *she* grows tired of all the fuss." Ina gave her a would-be stern look, then turned down the crowded street.

Breyd sighed and took refuge in the blessedly ordinary. "I know." Nevvia was probably already wearing down a path between the courtyard and the outer steps, waiting for her youngest child, and no vision of horrid doom was too farfetched. Nevvia had always been something of a fusser, of course, but in the past year or so, since her youngest daughter reached woman's years, she had begun to create causes for worry where Breyd was certain none could possibly be. *Remember she was a small girl when the walls were nearly taken and horrors inflicted upon the women who were not inside the city; that she was a young woman with a beloved young husband when the Bejina attacked.* She swallowed; not a good thing to remember just now, not any of that. *Father, please, no.* She bit her lip, somehow managed to stay with the older woman down a crowded, narrow avenue, past an open wine merchant's shop that was full, past a warm, fragrant bakery where a few women stood close together, speaking in hushed voices while they waited for loaves.

Ina edged sideways through foot traffic and turned down a cobbled, narrow street. Breyd had to slide between a gossiping clutch of old men and the wall of a shop shuttered for the night, then lengthen her stride to catch up; Ina moved quickly for all her bulk and her years. All along the street, she heard nervous whispering and high, excited voices. People were blocking the middle of the street, others could be seen only as shadows on darkened steps and in black doorways; men and women stood on their flat roofs, to talk with their neighbors. The goddess had spoken; there had not been such news in many years. After a long peace, war again came to Ghezrat.

An ancient stone wall loomed ahead, one of many left inside the city when it expanded beyond them. Ina turned into a crooked little alley between small, one-storied houses, pushed through a clutch of people to pass by the fountain and pool under its sheltering porch. The usual cheerful tinkle of water dripping from a clay pipe and falling into the shallow pool was drowned under the shrill voices of anxious women, far too many of them crowded into the deeply shadowed little porch, all talking at once. All about, lanterns and shielded oil lamps, a street crowded with familiar faces: neighbors who fell abruptly silent and glanced furtively or in speculation at the young novice priestess; three elderly brothers who blinked at her then put their heads together to whisper; women and men who broke off conversation, waiting until she had passed by to resume. One of the worst gossips on the entire long alley nudged her sister meaningfully as Breyd came near; both stared openly.

Whispering broke out as soon as she passed; Breyd set her teeth and lengthened her stride once again. *Gossips. Busybodies. Rumormongers. Why do they act as though Denota's sash has turned me into something unclean, or an enemy like the Diye Haff? If they want to know what was said tonight, they could ask me, instead of staring.* No one asked her anything, though; no one had since the day she'd been chosen to wear that green sash. She felt herself flush angrily; one of the rare times she had confided in her sister and Niverren had laughed at her, told her she spent too much time worrying about herself and what others thought of her. *But I don't! It isn't that, I'm not like that! It's as though a change of clothing changed me—and it didn't. Why can't any of them see that?*

Even Niverren couldn't; but then, Niverren didn't see much that wasn't herself and Creos any more, her approaching marriage.

Breyd had asked Denira if people treated her like that; but Denira was no help—she ran to temple and from it and got home to her mother as quickly as she could. *The way she looked at me, tonight. Oh, Father—*

She knotted her hands into fists and swallowed, pressed her way through the silent, gaping neighbors; made herself concentrate on walking normally so old Misso and her sister wouldn't have the pleasure of thinking they'd scared her, as they'd so often done when she was a child. Ina stood on the low step, waiting for her; she ushered the girl in before her, pulled the door tightly to, and set the bar across it.

The door must have been shut ever since sundown when the Festival began; the shutter was still in place over the tall, narrow window opening and the square, low-ceilinged front room was stuffy and warm. Menlaeus entertained his infrequent guests here; he and Nevvia slept on the wide, curve-legged couch near the doorway into the courtyard. The room contained nothing now but the couch with its single woven cover and beside it the chest that held spare bedclothes. It smelled like Menlaeus' old, oiled leathers and Nevvia's favorite body oil. *Familiar. Safe.* She always felt a little like a child in this room, even now; those smells were among the earliest she remembered.

The family would be gathered in the sheltered courtyard after a private celebration of the equinox. They would be waiting to hear what Tephys had to say, too. Breyd pulled the shawl from her shoulders, handed it to Ina, and stepped onto the rough-surfaced stone tiles.

The courtyard was only a few years old; Breyd could easily remember when the house had consisted of the main room across the entire street side of their building, the kitchen, storage and privy all together at right angles to the main room; a small chamber hard against the old section of city wall beyond the privy had housed her and Niverren. Tar had slept in the storage in bad weather and, like their parents, moved to the flat roof under woven leaf shelters for the hot, dry season. When Nidya had let her vineyards to tenants and moved in with the family, though, Menlaeus had been able to buy the house next to theirs and added the paved courtyard, a room for his daughters across from the kitchen and, parallel to the old wall, more storage and a separate area for Nidya.

During the dry months, most of the family gathered in the

courtyard morning and evening: Nidya or Ina cooked over the brazier; Nevvia and her daughters did the washing in the shade near the kitchen; Tarpaen brought his friend Laius and they played a board game. Her mother's slender-legged chair and its pile of cushions was kept near the brazier; Niverren's close to it but usually occupied by someone else these days, since she had set up her loom in the courtyard next to the low, flat wall left from the previous house. Tar preferred it to a chair, and so did Nidya.

She had not expected to find Tarpaen here. He scowled as she came into the light, but Tar frowned at most things. Menlaeus looked up from the low brazier and smiled. Nidya had waited up for her, and sat on the low wall with a cushion between her and hard stone; she held one of Niverren's shuttles and was using it to point out something in the warp threads.

Niverren sat cross-legged on her padded, woven mat, peering intently at whatever Nidya was showing her. A basket piled high with spun and dyed wool or linen thread and a few small hanks of imported and very expensive Gryptiosi cotton sat close to her right knee, an oil lamp on the edge of the wall illuminated her work. She was using a long-toothed wooden pick to pack the last rows of fabric down tight. Her back was to them all, but Breyd thought she could guess at the expression on her sister's face: the tip of her tongue would be just exposed between small neat teeth, a faint smile would turn the corners of a bow-shaped, full mouth, and she would be so close to the loom that her nose nearly touched the threads.

Nevvia had been sitting right on the edge of her chair, clasping and unclasping her hands; she sighed faintly and held them out. "Darling child. You know how I worry when you are abroad so late. I began to wonder if you had decided to walk the entire outside wall before returning home!"

"Ina went with her, Mother," Niverren broke in, her voice edged with the good-natured irritation that marked all her speech with her mother since her betrothal.

Nevvia laughed, and the sweet bubbling laughter, as always, erased years from her lovely, fragile face. "Oh, Niv, it was a jest, can you really see Ina walking all the way around the city, even to humor Breyd?" She smiled at Menlaeus and then at Tarpaen, finally at Breyd. "You know I really do try not to set you apart from your friends, Breyd," she added

gently. "But after all, when I was a girl, we weren't permitted to walk around the city quite as freely. Of course, we had
war then—" She frowned, shook her head. "After all, you
are such a tiny, lovely little thing; and not all men are trustworthy."

Niverren primmed her lips as she cast a glance over her
shoulder in her younger sister's direction, "Yes, we know,
Mother. Breyd is the pretty one. All right, truly, she is, but
Ina was with her and after all, she is Denota's for now. No
one in the city would dare think impure thoughts of a virgin
priestess, let alone lay a hand upon one." She managed a
smile. "Well, anyway, I am glad tonight was the planting
festival and not the summer games, Breyd; Denira would
have beat you at the foot races handily, I've done at least
seven rows since she came back. And such a fuss! Tar said
she nearly flew by, making so much noise one almost expected enemy soldiers to be on her heels." Nevvia looked
distressed; Niverren had turned back to study the loom and
didn't notice. She pressed here and there with the pick, then
dropped it in her lap and slewed around so she was facing
the courtyard.

Breyd swallowed, forced a smile, and spread her arms in
a wide shrug, then walked over to hold her hands above the
warmth of the brazier. Her father touched her arm. "It's all
right, Father, I was at the end of the line of priestesses tonight, farthest from the stairs," she said. Not quite an apology, or an excuse, though it could be taken for either. "And
Khadat brought Hemit, it takes them so long to bring him
down and even longer to carry him back up the steps and out
of everyone's way."

"Oh, Khadat," Nevvia said dismissively. "Wrapped in
swaths of widows' brown, no doubt."

Breyd turned her head to meet her mother's scornful look.
Nevvia nursed some ancient grudge against the foreign,
wealthy, and noble Khadat, who supposedly had little use for
even the women of her own class—little use for anyone outside her immediate family, it was said. There was no one
claimed to care for Khadat. Whatever personal grudge
Nevvia had, she never spoke of it—but she never let the
woman's name pass within the family walls without some
unpleasant and very uncharacteristic remark. Breyd shook
her head. Khadat wasn't important. But she was a safe sub-

ject, compared to— *No! Don't!* "I don't know what Khadat wore, Mother, I wasn't near her."

"I should hope you were not!"

"No. But—well. She's a different class of priestess, of course." Breyd knelt to push a half-burned block of charcoal back into the fire. Her mother sniffed. She glanced up at her father, who seemed mildly interested. "Hemit is worse than last time, they say he never speaks any more and he looks dreadful."

"We weren't waiting to hear about old Hemit," Tarpaen announced impatiently. "*I* wasn't. The streets are full of people screaming about war, and about the Diye Haff. You were there when Tephys spoke, after all, what did she say?"

I can't— "*Denota* spoke, through Tephys," Breyd managed. Her lips felt numb, her hands were trembling; she wrapped them around her so Menlaeus wouldn't see, but he must have thought she was cold. He edged over and put his arm around her shoulders.

"Never mind all that, what was said?" Tarpaen demanded. "Besides war, and Diye Haff?"

"War—" Her voice faded away.

Tarpaen snorted angrily, bringing her back to the present. "Yes, well, when?" Nevvia caught hold of her son's arm and murmured something too low for anyone else to hear.

Breyd fixed her eyes on the coals, leaned into her father's warmth, and repeated everything she had heard Tephys say.

"That's *all?*" Tarpaen asked, and added suspiciously, "You're not keeping anything back, are you?" She shook her head. "I could have heard all that if I'd gone to the wineshops with Laius tonight! But if that is all she said, why didn't you just tell us?" He snorted; Nevvia made distressed little noises. "Well, Mother, I'm sorry." He didn't sound at all sorry. "But truly! Ever since Tephys named her, she's been acting so strangely, you have to practically twist her arm to get two words out of her and now, you'd think she'd spoken the prophecy herself! It's not as though she's been sworn to silence or secrecy—though anyone would think she had."

It was an argument she had heard all too often from him lately; Breyd felt her cheekbones redden and she turned to scowl at him. He was sitting at their mother's feet, one hand clenched at his side, the other on her knee, his eyes fixed on her, even if he couldn't see her clearly. "Don't be silly, Tar," she said acerbically, "even a part-time priestess has secrets. And I have more to do than put on airs for *you*."

He snorted. "No, you put them on for everyone, don't you? But that stuff wasn't a secret, and this is your family. You shouldn't pretend to have secrets among your family."

"That isn't for you to say—" Breyd began automatically.

"Children, please." Nevvia rested one hand on her son's shoulder. He sighed, sounding rather petulant and more than a little like his friend Laius, but he looked up at his mother and smiled. Tarpaen resembled her more than either daughter did; he should have been pretty himself, with those wide-set, deeply fringed dark eyes, that full red mouth, and all those curls. One had to look closely, closer than Tarpaen ordinarily let people come, to see the clouded right eye, result of a fever years earlier. Ordinarily, the beautiful face was marred by a sardonic twist to his mouth and an overall expression of dissatisfaction, like Laius'. Only rarely, as now, did the beauty shine through as he took his mother's hand in his and laid it against his cheek.

"Tar, you really must not fuss at your sister so much; if the goddess speaks to Her priestesses, She may not want them to tell anyone else and, of course, you are a man so Denota's mysteries aren't for you anyway." To Breyd's relief, Tar seemed to find this amusing; he grinned abashedly at his mother, who smiled fondly and shook a finger at him. But when she looked up again her eyes were anxious. "You said Pairs, Breyd. You did hear Tephys say Pairs? It's very serious, then, and much more dangerous than you just said, if they want Pairs. Really, truly war, not just fighting at the straits or the docks." She appealed to Menlaeus; her free hand tightened on the chair arm and Breyd could see her knuckles go white. "Husband, they will call you!"

He smiled a little, shook his head. "I'll be called to the muster tomorrow morning," he corrected her gently. "I know. It doesn't really mean anything, of course."

"If they—oh, no, She can't choose you!"

"Don't worry about it, wife, please don't. I know, I am a member of the heavy infantry, and have been for years, and I have unwed daughters. But that doesn't tell the whole tale, does it? There might be worse spearmen, but probably not very many. During that skirmish to take back the mole, I was put in the fourth rank of spear, don't you remember I told you? And—well, I suppose I'm competent with a sword but not much more than that, certainly not in the best class—not even near it, really." He spread his arms in a wide shrug and smiled. "The goddess won't name a poorly rated foot soldier as one of the elite who guard the walls and the gates."

Nevvia opened her mouth, closed it again without speaking; she still looked very distressed. Menlaeus let go of his daughter's shoulders to go to her; Tar came up onto his knees and whispered something against her ear. She shook her head, eyed him sidelong, and laughed. "Oh, both of you, you *men,* you're just trying to distract me." She considered this and the laughter vanished. "But none of that matters, does it? Because of what Pairs are, and because you have— have daughters—"

"Oh, Mother, you do borrow trouble," Niverren interrupted her briskly. "One of those daughters is about to be wed, the other is a priestess. I cannot imagine why the goddess would choose Secchi from girls who already have callings. She never has in the past, has she?"

"Niv, you don't know, and it has been so long since She last chose Pairs, who can say what She wanted then, or that it will bear on what She wants this time?"

Niverren shook her head and turned back to her loom. "Well, by this hour tomorrow, we will know if she wants Father. Worry all night and most of the day if you must, but it won't change anything, will it?" She glanced back at her mother and her eyes softened. "Oh, Mother, please do think before you work yourself into a knot. Think how many foot soldiers there are in our entire army. And how many Primes are to be actually chosen—thirty pairs, wasn't it, Breyd?"

Her throat hurt and her vision was blurry. *Thirty-three others.* Breyd let her head fall forward, closing her eyes tightly to keep tears from spilling. "Thirty-four," she whispered.

"Is something wrong with your voice? They keep you down in that smelly steam too long, I think. Oh, well, if it is only thirty-four men from all those thousand, I would never toss the knucklebones at such odds." She turned back to peer closely at her loom and made a vexed little sound. "Oh, no! I knew it was too dark out here for this, and now, with all the fuss, I shall have to unpick the last two rows. Niddy, it's very late, poor Ina must be nearly asleep on her feet waiting for you."

Nidya settled a dark shawl across her shoulders and set down the shuttle she'd been holding and spoke for the first time. "Ina knows full well she can go in to bed any time she chooses." Her face was deeply lined but held more than a trace of the unusual southern looks—the oval face, narrow nose and bow-shaped mouth she had passed on in certain measure to her daughter and grandson and in full to Breyd. Her voice was unexpectedly low and rich, particularly for a woman of her years. "But yes, it is late for an old creature born in the vineyards and used to a farmer's hours." She shook off Niverren's arm, stood with only the least aid from the wall behind her. Breyd came across to hug her, Niverren leaned over and kissed the old woman's cheek. Ina came out of the main room and crossed the little courtyard, lighting a small oil lamp at the brazier. At a nod from her mistress, she went on through the doorway to light the way and ready Nidya's couch.

Nidya wrapped her arms around Breyd, then Niverren. Tarpaen got to his feet and came over to briefly clasp her close; Nidya gave his arm a pat, gazed into her younger granddaughter's eyes intently, then turned and followed her servant.

Did she mean me to understand something from that look? But Breyd couldn't decide what Nidya thought she was communicating.

Tarpaen had gone back to Nevvia's side and was wheedling softly; his mother argued with him in a low whisper. She finally cast up her eyes, smiled and nodded; Tarpaen was on his feet at once. He kissed her cheek and strode across the courtyard, through the door into the main room. A moment later, Breyd heard the sound of the bar being drawn back and suddenly loud voices as the door opened. Nevvia looked at her husband from under thick lashes and said, "Laius was expected him, and the boy is of age, you know, it is nice of him to ask my permission when he no longer needs it."

"I know." Menlaeus gave the two words no expression at all. He knelt and shoved half-burned charcoal into the dying fire with the tip of a cooking skewer. Into the silence, Nevvia laughed that bell-like, chiming laugh of hers and everything was fine once more. She let her husband hand her to her feet, went over to hug Niverren while Menlaeus set the ladder against the wall, knelt to hug Breyd. "Don't stay out here long, promise me. We have the washing tomorrow, don't forget. Oh, dear; your face is so cold, Breyd, it isn't good for such lovely skin to let it take the night air like that, you can't possibly be warm enough. There's a shawl next to my chair."

"Oh, Mother," Breyd replied softly, "I am all right, honestly. The coals are still plenty warm. But I won't be out here for long, anyway. Good night, Mother. Father."

Menlaeus held the ladder steady while his wife climbed onto the roof above their daughters' room, turned back with his foot on the bottom rung. "Sleep well, both of you," he said, and went on up.

She had hoped to have the brazier to herself, a little time to herself to simply think, but Niverren came over and sat by her. Breyd stifled a sigh, pulled the sandals from her feet so she could warm them against the heated rocks, and moved over a little to make room.

"Mmmm, that is lovely." Niv wouldn't simply sit and enjoy the quiet, of course; she chattered. "My hands are cold."

"Too many hours sitting and weaving."

Niverren smiled, shook her head. "No choice. Not if I want a full bride-box." They sat and watched the red fade from the coals, Breyd nodding now and again as her elder sister described in detail the new pattern, the wool, the way her pick had been catching threads until Tarpaen found and rubbed down the rough edge for her—on and on. Fortunately, Niverren hardly ever expected an answer, and never when she was engrossed in something the way she was with this. It made thinking utterly impossible, of course. *Perhaps it's just as well,* Breyd thought, and once again plaited her fingers together to stop them from trembling.

Tarpaen spent too much time with Laius; why could Nevvia not see beyond his family wealth and the trade connections, and the breezy adoring manner the man put on for her? Tar's accusations sounded like purest Laius, she had never kept any secrets from her family. But this: How could she blurt out what she had seen tonight?

Perhaps it wasn't true prophecy, she thought suddenly. Perhaps Denota chose that way to warn a novice to pay heed and give Her ceremonies the proper respect. *No. She would not do that, it was horrible: I could smell, hear—I could feel everything, it was just like something real.* She blinked, nodded and made some small noise as her sister paused in her headlong, one-sided conversation for some comment, then went on again.

The coals began to cool. Breyd stirred, cast a glance toward the now quiet roof. "Thank you," she said as Niverren finally ran out of things to say about her evening's work. "For settling Mother down tonight."

"Well, someone has to," Niverren said practically; she pitched her voice so low Breyd had to lean against her shoulder to hear her. "Niddy hasn't much patience these days because Tarpaen nags at her and she indulges him so that of course he acts like a spoiled boy. And then, someone else I could name simply worries her," she added with a mildly accusing look. "And Father's always so calm, I think it makes her *want* to fuss. Sometimes even I feel like shaking him because he never reacts to anything."

Breyd shook her head. "You make us all sound like dreadful people, Niv. We aren't—we're a family. But Father can't help being the way he is. I can't imagine him wringing his hands and get excited." *I cannot imagine him dead—* She turned her head and bit her thumb.

"You should know," Niverren was saying pointedly. "You're altogether too much like him." She pulled back a little to gaze thoughtfully at her younger sister. "And that isn't good, you know. You aren't a man, Breyd. The goddess may not want you after this year, and no husband would want a wife who's as emotional as—as a stone wall."

Breyd shrugged, fixed her eyes resolutely on the brazier. "Denota may want me, though."

Silence. "Well?" Niverren prompted finally.

"I haven't thought about it." She could feel her elder sister's disbelieving stare, didn't look up to meet it. "You say it yourself so often. Why should I worry about something, if I can't change the outcome by worry?" *Why worry about anything? If what I saw tonight comes to pass, then I've seen Father's death and likely my own.* She was suddenly irked by Niverren's all too familiar remarks, unhappily aware she'd provoked the conversation herself.

"It's not the same thing. If Denota doesn't keep you, Mother will want Father to find you a husband before you're too old. You're already seventeen, you had better begin to think about it."

"Why? Did Mother have any say when her father and his gave her to our father? It isn't my business, you know that."

"Nonsense. I chose."

"Well, but you've always wanted to marry Creos, and they knew that, didn't they? And so did his family. And you have money from Nidya's sale of wines to the Mirikosi and Creos has a portion of his family's fields—and it all worked out for you."

"All the same—"

"I don't have anyone like Creos, Niv. And I have another half-year of this." She lifted the ends of the green sash, let them drop to her lap again. "I'll think about it when—if— the time comes." Her mouth went dry; she forced the words and they sounded strangled. "If there's truly to be war, it probably won't matter anyway."

"Oh, nonsense," Niverren said again. If her sister had sounded odd, she didn't notice, as usual. "Things like that always matter." Breyd merely shook her head, felt around for the brazier lid and covered the coals, caught up her sandals in one hand and got to her feet. Niverren stood up too, rubbing her fingers and wrists. "Half a year isn't so long, you know."

"I know it isn't."

Niverren sighed, mildly exasperated. "I never do know what you're thinking, it's maddening."

"I'm sorry."

"Oh, no, you're not. You'd change if you really meant that. It was like picking meat from a nutshell tonight, getting words out of you, and Tar getting Mother all fussed, and for what? A prophecy, nothing closer to you than to anyone else in the city! I wanted to tear my hair. Or yours, better yet."

There's nothing wrong with being like Father, Breyd thought angrily. Better than being like this common-sense, aggressively outgoing sister who half the time wanted to know everything she thought and the rest of the time didn't notice anything outside her own wants. Much as she loved Niverren, she had been glad when Niv was betrothed, even happier that she would live with Creos' family. Nevvia fussed, but it was gentle and provoked by love—and it could be ignored or teased out of her. It was nearly impossible to ignore Niv when she got in one of those moods and tried to drag from people how they felt, what they thought. She had never been that way until she and Creos were pledged, Breyd thought, and remembered how Niverren had gone on and on about Creos wanting to know everything she thought, or felt. . . . *How can they? Niv must drive Father mad when she picks at him.* Her eyes filled with tears. *Oh, Father.*

The tiny room she shared with her sister was mostly taken up by bed; Niverren curled up against the wall and fell asleep almost immediately. Breyd listened to her for a while and finally slid into an uneasy doze herself.

She woke sometime later, brought gaspingly awake by some horrid nightmare she couldn't recall. She tried to calm her thudding heart, then tried to sit up. The old gown she slept in had wrapped around her legs and Niverren had rolled over and now lay facing her, an arm thrown across Breyd's shoulders. *Probably what caused the nightmare, being trapped like that. Not facedown on hard stone, with the smell of burning everywhere, and tiny sharp stones boring into my face, and Father—* She slid from under Niv's arm with a convulsive jerk that would have wakened anyone else and got to her feet, stood against the door frame until she had quit trembling, then leaned partway out to listen. Still nothing. She rubbed her eyes, stepped into the courtyard, and looked around. No one in the courtyard; the ladder her brother used to reach to the roof where he slept, over the entry room, still lay on the ground. She looked up. By the position of moon and the few stars visible, it was late, much nearer dawn than middle night.

Furtive noise from the entry room brought her around, heart thudding wildly, but it was only Tarpaen, swaying a little as he paused in the doorway to the courtyard. Moonlight picked out a stain running down the white cloth of his good tunic from shoulder to waist, glittered in his narrowed eyes when he saw her—or at least, saw someone in the doorway, she could never be certain how bad his vision was. Breyd turned from him and walked back indoors to lie down next to her sister; she listened to Niv's soft, even breathing, to her brother cursing under his breath as he strove to put the ladder quietly against the wall and then climb the rungs to the roof, and at the moment envied both. She was afraid to close her eyes again.

Somehow she fell asleep anyway but came sharply awake what seemed only moments later. The air was cooler, however, and she could see the gray light of false dawn.

And then a stealthy sound she finally recognized as the creak of her parents' ladder. She eased herself off the bed, took the small step that brought her to the door and looked cautiously out. Menlaeus, fully clad, crept down the last rungs and stepped back into the courtyard as first horn rang out across the city. He turned toward the entry, Breyd came into the open; he stopped short, blinking, then held a finger to his lips, beckoning her to follow with a small jerk of his head. She nodded.

Just inside the entry room, he stopped and turned back to whisper, "You should not be awake at such an hour."

She wanted to cling to him and weep; only the certainty that it would upset him to no point kept her from doing just that. "Nor should you, Father."

He smiled ruefully. "I couldn't sleep. It's unexpected, after all these years, for the goddess to take Pairs. I remember the last time, but only barely. And it seems unfair to upset your mother, so I thought it would be best if I left before she woke." He touched her shoulder. "After all, it won't come to anything. And my panoply is in the company messes anyway. There might be further word, where to go and what to do, and what is going on. Don't worry, little Breyd. There might be war, but it won't touch you, you'll be safe."

She swallowed, nodded, and tried to sound as calm as she ordinarily would—copying her father's way of speaking, she suddenly realized. Did that mean Menlaeus could be worried, under that easy-going exterior? "I won't worry." The little sleep she'd managed made that true for the moment; it set a barrier between herself and the real world, and the horror of that prophecy. She had always told Menlaeus everything; she could never tell him *that*. Never burden him with it. Bury it deep, keep it to herself—*I will have to.*

He gave her a quick, hard hug. "Tell your mother—" He considered this, shook his head. "Never mind. I should be back before the morning is very far gone, and she has the laundry today. I will return before she has time to think about it. Don't look so, Breyd, I promise everything will be all right." He turned away before she could say or do anything—fortunately, she thought—and let himself into the silent street. She set the bar in place and went back to bed. Her dreams were all in red, and when Niverren woke her, just after sunrise, it felt as though she hadn't slept at all.

Nevvia was worried and doing her best to put a cheerful face on it, though Breyd thought she hadn't slept much either, and her eyes were suspiciously red-rimmed. Niverren brought out a dish of dried figs and a loaf of flat bread, which she set atop the brazier to warm. She pressed her mother into her usual chair and wrapped her hands around a cup. "Niddy had Ina heat some of the winter wine, I added more hot water to yours, Mother." And she stood and waited, hands on hips, until Nevvia sighed and reluctantly drank it down. Niverren took the cup back, replacing it with a hunk of warm bread, and held out the bowl of figs. "Eat, please, Mother, you know how long the day is when you don't, and how ill you get. Father will worry if he comes in to find you sick."

"You're bullying me," Nevvia protested faintly. "It's just this thing with Pairs—"

"Darling, silly Mother, are you still worrying about that?" Niverren knelt beside her mother's chair and laid a hand on her arm. "Hasn't the goddess always taken good care of us? Our family, and this city? She won't put us through that, will she?" Nevvia patted the hand absently but obediently ate a bite of bread. Niverren eyed her critically. "You're all tangles. Let me fix your hair, Mother, while you eat. Breyd, if you're finished, you'd better get one of the jugs and begin fetching water."

It was the last place she wanted to be, out in the street, among curious neighbors, right in the midst of the gossipers at the fountain. Ordinarily she would have argued that with Niverren, but Tarpaen came down the ladder, feet feeling for the rungs he had trouble placing with only one good eye. His face was set in the angry lines reserved for a morning after too much wine and too little sleep. Breyd glanced in his direction, thinned her lips, and went into the kitchen for a jug. Maybe by the time she brought in enough water, Tar would have eaten and be in a better mood. Better yet, he would take offense at something as he did so often of late, and gone out. But as she hurried through the entry room and onto the low stone step he was there, waiting, shoulders against the door frame, blocking her way. Startled, Breyd dropped the jug; it hit the step and shattered. The street was nearly deserted at the moment, but two passing women paused to stare. Tarpaen glared challengingly back, and they hurried on. "Oh, gods, Tar!" she gasped finally. "You gave me a fright, don't do that!"

Tarpaen ignored the jug, folded his arms across his chest

in an excellent impersonation of Laius, and continued to block the doorway. "What business had you checking on me this morning?"

She stared at him. "You scared me for *that?* I was not— Tar, I do not have to answer to you!"

"You don't answer to anyone," he said flatly.

"That isn't true." Breyd drew a deep breath, let it out in a gust. This was an old and, as far as she was concerned, stupid argument that proved nothing. "Tarpaen, I was not wasting good hours for sleep waiting to see when you came back, *or* in what condition. If Mother and Father don't care, why should I?" She glanced back into the house; through the entry into the courtyard where her sister was combing her mother's long, dark hair. She lowered her voice. "I had a bad—" she swallowed that, and said instead, "I thought I heard Mother crying."

"Well, why wouldn't she be upset?" Tarpaen still looked angry, and as though his head ached but he lowered his own voice. "And you did nothing last night to help, did you?"

"Tar, what? What could I have done? Changed Denota's prophecy, or denied it ever happened?"

"You could have—ah, Atelos curse it, *you* could not have done anything."

Breyd sighed loudly and turned from him. "Then we've nothing to talk about, have we? Niv and Mother are going to wonder why I'm not back with water, and I have to go get another jug, thanks to you. You might pick that up, since you made me drop it."

"Men don't pick up broken pottery," he replied loftily. "But I had another thing to say to you, before you started all this silly arguing." He caught hold of her wrist when she would have left him. "Laius asked about you again last night, about what dowry Father would provide for you."

"Laius?" She stopped trying to pull free of his grasp and stared up at him in shock. "Tar, we had this out even before Tephys chose me for this year! I will not under any circumstance marry Laius! But he has no right to speak to you in such terms, not while I serve Denota!"

Tarpaen's mouth twisted and he made a dismissive gesture with his free hand. "That's a convenience for you, nothing more. I'm your brother, I know you better than you think."

"You don't—"

"You *listen,*" he hissed and tightened his grip on her wrist.

"The priestess won't keep you past this year, you don't fit. Especially if you have already showed a preference to marry. Now, Laius—"

"Tarpaen!" Breyd wrapped her fingers in his hair and yanked at it, hard. "You let go of me, right now! I am not going to stand here in the street while you go through another of your long lists of what you see as virtues in Laius. If you think he's so wonderful, wed him yourself!"

"What is this?" Nevvia had come up behind them unnoticed by either, and stood in the doorway staring from one to the other, to the ruin of pottery around their feet. Tarpaen caught his breath in surprise and let go of his sister's wrist. Breyd more reluctantly loosed her grip in his hair and he stepped back to rub his scalp. Nevvia looked shocked and then looked into the street and flushed a bright red. "Fighting in the street like horrid, scrubby little urchins, where everyone can see you?" She caught hold of her son's near arm between both hands and tugged urgently. "Come into the house at once and change, Tar, you look utterly dreadful! Disreputable, as though you'd spent the night carousing! Is that wine down your front?" He winced as her voice rose. "That fabric was expensive, go take it off at once, so it can be washed!" She turned back to frown at her daughter. "And you pick up the pieces of that jug, then go get another and do it quickly, the fire is ready and there's no water for it."

"All right, Mother." Breyd knelt and made a well in her skirts to hold the shards of broken pot; Nevvia's voice faded only slightly as she pulled Tarpaen into the courtyard. "Fighting like that in public! Oh, Tar, you might as well have gone right down to the fountain for all that everyone on the street could see and hear you!" Tarpaen muttered apologies which Nevvia ignored.

Breyd bent low to gather up the small, sharp pieces that could cut a bare foot, scowled at the red mark circling her arm just above the wrist bones. That was going to bruise, curse Tarpaen for an arrogant, impatient wretch. Laius had a lot to answer for.

Curse Tar anyway. Nevvia was angry with him just now, of course, but that wouldn't last long; she would be making excuses for him by the time Breyd came back with the first jug of water, if not by the time she went into the kitchen to exchange the broken pottery for whole. Tar was getting out of hand, though he always had been impatient. Nevvia might have spoiled him anyway as the only son, but she stood between him and everything she could because of his eyes. He'd been a difficult boy at fourteen, the age when all boys took the obligatory tests to determine what military training they would receive, what company they would join. Tarpaen had no sense of distance beyond what he could reach, and he had failed everything.

Breyd had thought then she couldn't really blame him for being singled out so terribly. All his friends, everyone he knew being chosen for the slingers, or the light infantry, to drive a common chariot or fight from one. She had understood less when Tar had remained angry after Menlaeus called back a favor from a boyhood friend to get his son a trumpet and a place among those who blew the calls for the companies. Tar had risen in rank so quickly, Breyd supposed he must have proven himself deserving. But he showed no pleasure in his company and never spoke of it, other than in passing when he was talking about his best friend Laius, who drummed in the same company. Since he'd become friends with Laius, Tarpaen had changed and not for the better. Breyd made a face, picked up the last bits of jug, and got back to her feet.

Turning to go back into the house, she nearly dropped them all again; Nevvia had come silently across the room and stood just inside the entry. "He says you were spying on him early this morning." More of a question than an accusation; Nevvia was not good at confronting anyone in anger. Breyd shook her head. "I told him you had no reason to spy on him."

"Oh, Mother; so did I. He wouldn't listen to me."

"Well, but you're younger than he, after all. And a sister." Nevvia stepped back into the room so Breyd could come in, pushed the door to behind her. "He's insulted and angry because you refused Laius again."

"I can't—" She would have gone on into the courtyard but Nevvia touched her face.

"I know. I reminded him you're in service. But your brother is right, too, Breyd, it's not a life calling. You aren't like Tephys or any of those who serve under her, the goddess won't keep you. Laius is young and strong, he's of good enough family, he is wealthy, and he'll have you. What more could you ask?"

"No, Mother, please. You know how I feel."

Nevvia sighed. "You know I would never force you, but another year and men won't ask about you, not with your dowry. Why not Laius?"

"Because I've seen him drunk, Mother, and I've heard him talk." If she had more sleep, perhaps, the words that she would have kept to herself might not have tumbled out. "He wants a woman to cook for him, to warm his bed, and to be there to beat when he comes home full of too much wine—like your father." Nevvia's hand dropped from her elbow as though it were a heated coal. She swallowed and brought up a forced smile. "I had better fetch the water."

"Don't take the blue jug," Nevvia reminded her automatically, but her face was utterly white. "I don't want it leaving the house, it cost a fortune."

"I know. There are still two cheap ones in the corner." She tipped the broken stuff onto the rubbish heap in the far corner of the kitchen, caught up another jug, and hurried back out, aware of her sister's mildly curious glance, her brother's angry one. Her grandmother's dry voice: "What long faces this morning!"

It took her half a dozen trips to fetch enough water to let them begin; Tarpaen was gone by the time she came back with the first and stayed gone all morning. She passed him, still scowling but combed and in unstained cream-colored linen, when she went out at midday for more water.

The courtyard of the Temple of Warriors was narrow, taking up a long space between the outer wall and the inner, with the back wall of its temple hard against the Goat Gate. Menlaeus walked through the gates and bowed his head toward the temple, then moved off to one side where he could stand and watch. His company commander Frewis had not yet come; his boyhood friend Olmand was not far away, talking to Bechates. Beyond those two, other men he knew. In fact— *How curious,* he thought. *I suppose anyone who has soldiered all his life and reached my age should know most of the men here, but I have served or fought with everyone I see so far.* His neighbor Rophan, who had served a year in his heavy infantry. *He was the first to bring me his problems—how many years ago?—a dispute with old Mirso over some chairs. And now all the people around us do.* His thoughts drifted. He was not worried about this choosing of Primes. *I told Nevvia the truth. I can fight, but I am not a great fighter. I have no rank—except that of company ear because the men confided in me.*

Mibro came in with Frewis and several other men; Mibro and he had spent plenty of night-watches together. *Bechates—fussing as always.* Duplos was right behind him, white to the lips and all but wringing his hands. *But he has only the one child, and he has always worried about Xera because she was so ill when she was a baby.*

He stepped into the open, barren courtyard finally, smiled at men or spoke to them as he worked his way through the crowd. A hundred—two hundred men? More than that, at least a thousand by now. But he knew them all. A profound unease brushed his mind. *I know them all, I have fought with them, or served with them, or settled disputes for them. I know the fears of many, or their hopes—I know that Lotro is one of the most accurate with a javelin in all the light infantry, and that he wept with joy when his first daughter Eriana was born.* Bechates, who drove men mad with his fidgeting and mumbling about all the things that could go wrong before a battle—but when the time came to fight, he was as brave as any, and more skilled with a sling than most.

How will Nevvia manage if I am chosen? Poor, beloved Nev; he had been so pleased when the two fathers had joined them. She had been an exotic beauty then: adorable, fragile, utterly charming. She still was; he loved her almost beyond bearing. But his own warrior father's practical blood told, and he knew there was no more real strength in her than the surface showed. Breydos had stripped that from her and all his other children—deliberately, Menlaeus often thought; no one could have been that callous to his own family by accident. It still amazed him that Nidya had so much strength after all those years as Breydos' wife. Though he was grateful for it. Nevvia might—Nevvia *would* need her in the days to come. *I do not want to see the pattern here, but I see it anyway. Of all those here, I think I am the only one who knows all of them so well, who knows so much about them.* But if the goddess chose him, then She would also name one of his two girls Secchi. *Niverren is about to marry. But Breyd— she's a child, will the goddess send even children to fight the Diye Haff?*

A horn blared out once; silence fell. Tephys stood before the steps of the Temple of Warriors and held up her arms. "In a little, I will ask you to form ranks by the gates. But you must know first what the goddess asks of us, and what I must do to satisfy Her request. You know what the Dyaddi are: Fighting Pairs, father and daughter bound together by Denota to guard the city's gates against any enemy who might overcome all other barriers. They are that, but they are more.

"Those who are chosen are no longer two when they fight; they are one—one being, the goddess herself among us, if you like. She fills you, and if you must fight you fight with Her anger, Her strength. Your present weapon-skills will be enhanced beyond any ability you could command alone; your daughters will know all that you know.

"She will not take those who cannot withstand the burden She asks them to bear for all the city, know that. Those of you who are named Prime today and named by Her, She knows the heart of each of you, the strengths and the weaknesses—just as she knows each of your daughters.

"Pray with me now—for clear minds and hearts, and for Ghezrat."

A little later, Menlaeus found himself in the second rank of men, between Frewis and Bechates. He felt light-headed, the way he had after he'd lost blood. *As if she spoke to me personally. To the man with a fragile daughter and no great talent at weapons.* It had frightened him very badly. But the fear had left him as Tephys prayed for them and then for guidance in making her choices. And now, he simply waited. *In a way, she did speak to me. But I think she touched something else at that same moment.*

Tephys was suddenly there, asking a question of Duplos who stood on the other side of Frewis. She took his hands between hers; Duplos squared his shoulders and finally nodded. The priestess spoke again and he knelt. She said something else in that same soft voice, then bent low to kiss his brow. Duplos got awkwardly back to his feet; Tephys had already come to Frewis. "You already serve your city and Denota. Would you give her this new service?"

"If she asks it," Frewis said; his voice sounded tight, Menlaeus thought. The corners of Tephys' mouth turned up a little.

"Of course you would. But you already serve Her in an important way, and who would replace you as a captain with so much knowledge of the plain and so many companies, if She took you?"

"I—there are men who could be trained, priestess," Frewis managed finally. *It is difficult for him to admit how good he is at what he does,* Menlaeus knew. "But none who have done it for so many years, and none who would be able to act without thinking about what he must do. It could cost us too many lives."

"And to you, any lost life is one too many, isn't it? No, Captain. Denota will ask nothing different of you; care for the men who serve you and do your best by them. It will be enough." Frewis glanced at her and nodded rather shyly.

She stood in front of him, eyes searching his. *What will she ask me?* Menlaeus wondered. *What did she ask Duplos, or the others, how will she test me?* Not by weapons, or knowledge of tactics, but perhaps questions about his daughters?

She took hold of his hands and her first question caught him completely off guard: "Who can speak for the Primes?" she whispered. "Who will speak for the men who will take up this terrible burden, who will leave familiar companies and join together—who will bring daughters to be trained as warriors and who will serve as channels for the wrath of Denota? They must be strong for all of us and bear the greatest weight of any company. Of course they will have a captain, but a captain's only business is warfare and the fighting. Who will understand the fears of Bechates, or how deeply Duplos cares for his child? Who will settle debate between Loros and Prosean? Who will do all of this because he has the skill to lead men, and because he cares for them?"

Her fingers tightened on his and they were much too warm, all at once. Her eyes were compelling. The goddess gazed at him through those eyes, he realized; that was her warmth burning his hands. Menlaeus wanted to deny her, but he could not lie to her. *Denota, it is only me, Menlaeus! I am no leader—* But he was, in his own way.

Tephys stood, and waited; and Denota waited with her. He could see what both wanted—what both saw in him, and it surprised him that so many simple things he did should be so worthy in the goddess' eyes. He swallowed, bowed his head. "I speak for them. I, Menlaeus."

Haffat

The midday sun shone pitilessly on vanquished Idemito and the burned rubble of the city's gates. Within the walls there was little sign of damage, only leafless, long-thorned branches hung across many doorways to mark a house of mourning.

Two red-robed priests hurried on foot from the city; a third followed with a small cart, pulled by a hill pony.

The gaping hole where the gates had been was guarded by enemy archers. The priests hesitated; the Diye Haff came alert, but one nodded and waved the cart and its companions on. The priests hurried on. The multitude of dead would not know release until the final rite was performed, the sacred bowls of wax set at the twelve points of the pyre, until fire reduced to ashes Idemito's bravest young men and her king, and those ashes sealed into the niche being prepared in the Warriors' Cave.

The dead High King's palace had been taken by Haffat and his elite guard; his brother Heplo had already sworn fealty oaths, taking the crown and throne in a brief and businesslike ceremony attended by the city's nobles, the remaining members of the royal family and priests of Idemito's lone temple. Heplo dismissed them and went into the king's personal garden with his brother, two of Haffat's scribes, and his own secretary; the lion-priest Knoe came with them.

The garden was pleasantly cool. Overhead trellises were covered in grapevines and headily fragrant jasmine. A broad, shallow pool lay half hidden under flowering bushes; benches flanked the ends of the pool. A low couch and many cushions lay scattered across a fine blue carpet beneath a trellis.

Heplo looked drawn and pale in the uneven light, and

seemed unaware of the beauty around him. He dropped down among the cushions, watched as Haffat paced the narrow, graveled path, his steps quick and his turns decisive. The emperor's face bore little sign of the past days of hard fighting with little or no sleep. As he walked back and forth, he enumerated on his fingertips. Heplo tried to look grave and attentive; the three men wrote busily. "Unless you find serious sign of revolt, let the people go about their business as they always have, and leave the priests and their temple alone. You have the army's weapons. Idemito's only true military leader was their king, and Lysenan is dead. You have a good eye for such things, Heplo. If you sense trouble, an uprising or men plotting against you, do not doubt what your sense tells you." He paused, turned to look at his brother, who nodded. Haffat laughed suddenly. "You look like a man about to step from a precipice! Heplo, the god chose you to rule Idemito, you heard his words last night! But I did not need Axtekeles' assurances to know that you were capable."

Heplo spread his arms, shrugged; a rueful smile briefly turned the corners of his mouth, but his thoughts were somber. *How does he hold to this pace? He wears out men all around him, and yet he continues, and has enough mind and energy to remember these least details, to oversee everything himself.* Drawn by a god's promises, Heplo reminded himself, and was uncomfortable with that thought. Knoe and his lion-god: who knew what the foreigner and his foreign god really meant for Haffat, and for Diyet?

Haffat grinned at him widely, then went back to his pacing, another finger turned down, briskly all business once more.

"I shall leave you a mixed company, mostly spearmen and archers, also two messengers; you should not need a large company, the people are broken and you do not want them to remember that we came by conquest. Given the opportunity, simple people quickly forget such things, so long as they are left in some familiar comfort.

"Remember, when you set the tariff and the new taxes, to keep the amount secret from the people as long as possible. They expect to lose a large share of their crops and coin, so learn all you can first, find out what they expect before you set the rates—if you delay as long as possible in letting them know what the rates are and set them as low as you can, they will be the more relieved and pay with better heart." He paused to consider, shook his head. "You are my brother, you know as well as any man what will please me, and how best to govern. Knoe?"

The priest came forward and raised his hands in blessing over the bowed head of the new High King of Idemito; Heplo felt the hot wind on his face that Knoe called Lion's Breath. It was meant to give a man strength; he was not certain it had worked for him. He looked up as Knoe walked off, and his eyes went wide with sudden alarm. "You are surely not leaving!"

"The city, yes; it is yours now, and you know I prefer my tent, in the middle of my army. Also, it pleases them—my men and your people. There may come a day when I have need of the morale I build among them now. It should also please your people, that I hold to my promise not to interfere with their city beyond this minimal level. You should rebuild the gates at once; pay the same rates to the men who craft new gates and install them as their former king would have paid." Haffat sent his scribes ahead, then turned back at the doorway. "Remember also to send down the two wagons of grain and all the rice that can be spared, as soon as the jars can be loaded and secured; we will need it to reach Mirikos."

Heplo sighed very faintly, nodded and struggled to his feet. "I'll see to the grain. I shall miss you, Haffat."

Haffat came back across the little garden to embrace his brother. "And I shall miss you. How many days have we shared campfires, drafty tents, and hard ground?"

"Two hundred and forty."

"Listen to my brother, he keeps a count! And all the years before that, in palatial comfort. Think of me, brother, when you sit here and sip cool drinks, and when you sleep on a king's couch between fine, soft sheets." He gripped Heplo's shoulder, turned and strode from sight.

Heplo sighed; Haffat would miss him, as he missed all those he left behind, but it would not turn him one finger's worth from following Knoe's god, wherever Axtekeles led.

3

Prince Pelledar's throne room was also his favorite room: high in the palace with many windows to give a commanding view of the plain, the two rivers and many bright canals that crisscrossed it, and the sea. The walls had been painted in his father's last years: bright flowers and birds on the wall behind his throne, dolphins and waves, octopi and fishes opposite the ancient high stone seat that had been the throne of twenty-seven Ghezrathi kings, and had been moved from the ruins of four successively sumptuous palaces. Deep windows flanking the throne looked out across the courtyard of Denota's temple, the deeply textured city to the broad inner and high outer walls, beyond to a steep and forbidding southern plateau that faded into purple, sandy distance.

Just now, Pelledar, Prince of the City and Great King of Ghezrat, stood at one of these windows, watching as thirty-four men escorted eighty-seven young women into the temple courtyard, the chosen Primes bringing their daughters for the goddess to choose. The sound of muted weeping just reached his ears, though here and there he could see a young woman who strode upright and seemingly unafraid at her father's side—unafraid, or more likely, simply unwilling to publicly shame herself or the man who had sired her. *Or unaware of how grim the possibilities that face her—but these young women are not alone in that.*

He turned from the window, and the preparations for the making of Dyaddi. In a little while, his presence would be sought by the priestesses, to seal the bargain between city and the common families which supplied these very necessary fighting pairs. *People are such hypocrites,* he thought sourly. *They welcome any protection in war, even a Dyadd against the gates, so long as the daughter who strides about with the men, in men's armor, fighting with men and with men's weapons—so long as that daughter is not their own, or any of any class worth naming.* His grandsire had said that, long years ago. Pelledar watched the goddess' court-yard fill, and wondered whether it was truly as the priests said: that Denota took her Primes from the larger ranks, those soldiers who would not be missed because there were so many of them—or if She was simply practical, knowing she would get less cooperation from noble and well-to-do trading families.

The rich and the high-ranking would never tolerate it, for such young women to be chosen from their ranks, whatever the goddess said, his grandsire had told him and there had been scorn in his voice. *Though, for a price, they allow their sons to wed such young women, once Denota no longer needs them.* Pelledar wondered how near Eyzhad was to fin-ishing his present task: For two days and a night, the priest had been shut in the small antechamber next door, working with the prince's chief clerk and a scribe, making lists of el-igible and acceptable men, then narrowing the choices and setting against the names a series of trade and tax conces-sions that would be given the families of those matched to the Secchi this day. *And so, honor of a sort is preserved, the city reassured that it is not breeding a nest of Amazons, and at the same time, the families of the Pairs given reason to quietly accept the goddess' choice of their daughters: that they will be mated to a man above the size of their pockets, and above their station. How foolish people are.*

And emotional. Someone down there was having hyster-ics; doubtless she was only the first of many. He could ex-pect outrage from at least one father of a prepromised boy, hysteria from their mothers. Probably there was no family in Ghezrat boasting of rank, wealth, and an unwed son which did not count its chances this morning—and quite possibly pray earnestly to be passed over.

What a dreadful fuss, and over what—when yet has the city ever actually depended upon the Pairs? Just now, he would have given much to set aside the entire, ugly ordeal, but memory of the goddess' presence and the surge of power that had numbed his hands to the elbow stopped that thought at its inception. Denota ordered Dyaddi; She would have them, whatever foolish contortions Her children must go through to deliver them.

A voice interrupted increasingly gloomy thoughts, and replaced them with others, equally unpleasant. "Husband's brother."

"Khadat." He had almost forgotten the woman was there, so quiet had she been this once, and for so long. Just now, she sat in one of his fine new chairs, stiffly upright, seemingly unaware of the pleasant odor of the ruddy wood, the silken fabric of soft cushions at her back, the water-beaded cup of fruit juice, fresh from the chilled jugs kept down in the palace well. "Your servant said it was a matter of great urgency." He gestured toward the window and the courtyard three floors below. "You must know I have little time today."

"Then I shall be brief." Khadat's usually low voice was harsh, as though it came through an overly tight throat, and her words were clipped. She sat forward, hands clasped together so tightly the knuckles showed white. "This war: I have decided that Apodain will not have any part of it, and you must help me."

Pelledar stared at her, groped for the second of his new chairs and dropped heavily into it. At a gesture, a servant brought another cup of chilled grape, which he drank down at a gulp. Khadat sat motionless, eyes fixed unblinking on him. "I—Khadat, what can I say to you? This is most—most unexpected." He held out the cup for the servant to refill, then blotted his upper lip delicately with a proffered cloth. "And what does your son say to this—request of yours?"

Khadat compressed her lips. "Apodain? He does not know of it. He will not know, until it is too late." She leaned forward, fixing him with intense eyes. "Husband's brother, you know all too well my plight! My firstborn killed in battle when Apodain was yet a babe, my husband dead, and my Hemit—my Hemit—"

"Yes, yes," Pelledar murmured hastily. It would not do to let the dreadful woman dwell on her wreck of a son. Khadat swallowed, shuddered madly, and closed her eyes. When she went on, her voice was again under control.

"The goddess knows what I have suffered. My sister, all her children dead of hunger or plague when the Bejinni encircled Mirikos, and then, my husband, two of my sons— Shall I lose the last hope of my old age?"

"But—but brother's wife, Apodain is one member of a very large company of chariot, and a skilled fighter. If he goes to battle, does this mean necessarily that he will die?"

Khadat laughed mirthlessly. "In a full war against an enemy so deadly the goddess calls for many Pairs, do you dare predict he will return to me alive and with his limbs and wits intact? I have heard as much as anyone about these Diye Haff, and I know my son. Of course he is skilled; he is his father's son and guardian of his family's honor; his horses and his chariot are the best I could buy, his weapons and armor new since his father's panoply rots at the bottom of the sea and I will not permit him to use Hemit's while Hemit— Hemit yet lives." She turned away from him to sniff discreetly and blotted her eyes with the back of one hand. When she turned back, her face was set. "However I strive to protect him, he is still rash Perlot's son. Apodain will attempt such deeds as to be named hero, and cast a path between the sea and the goddess for his father's shade."

Silence. Pelledar sipped at his second cup of grape to gain time. "Khadat, I cannot deny the boy—"

"You can! I will pay, a gold bar—two! Any amount you ask!"

"But without a good reason to keep him within the city—"

"You are Ghezrat's king," Khadat broke in flatly. "And the boy has royal blood, he is eighth in line—and he is underage."

"Because I am king, I could deny you and send you away, at once. But who treats a fighting man of nineteen as underage in this day simply because of royal blood?"

She shrugged that aside. "I will do what I must. And you will not deny me. I am dead Perlot's wife and a woman of vast holding and wealth, a daughter of one of the greatest trading families in all of Mirikos and owner of ships in her own right. It has always been to your best interests, husband's brother, for us to remain in good stead each with the other. And by the goddess' own words, there will come an end to this war."

Pelledar got to his feet and walked across the chamber to gaze northward to the inland sea, across the new-planted fields; he walked back then, slowly, leaned against the deep sill and gazed down at the top of Tephys' dark head as she walked along the line of Primes and their gathered daughters. *If I give in, there will be trouble—from Apodain, who will one day take Perlot's place in the councils, and who will then hold the power and wealth Khadat now controls. From others, who resent the interference, or who want such a two-edged gift for their own sons, or the commanders who will not take kindly to my interference. And yet, if I simply tell her I cannot, then I will have a very bad enemy in Khadat, who vastly understates her power in Ghezrat and beyond its borders, and who knows it. Were she any other woman, with less strength and intelligence, I swear I would have had her poisoned five years ago. And she surely knows that, as well.* What, he wondered gloomily, was the point to being prince and Great King, if a plain woman of middle years, graying hair, and imperious disposition could order him about—and she not even his own wife?

A faint cry from below brought his attention back to the courtyard; Tephys was speaking to the young women now, and apparently she had said something to distress one of them. Pelledar smiled faintly, squared his shoulders and said, without turning from the window, "I shall order Apodain removed from the company of noble chariot on one condition: That his name be added to Eyzhad's list for those young women, down there. You will need to tell him sooner than you would like, of course. But we can devise some trade concession to disguise the real reason he weds a Secchi, if you like."

That would settle her, he thought in some satisfaction, but before he could even savor having bested the woman, Khadat replied, "Done." Pelledar turned slowly to stare at her; she gazed levelly back. "Did you think I lied, when I said I would do anything to keep my son alive?" She stood abruptly, and brought her arms across her chest to give him a full and formal bow. Pelledar stood, rooted in shock, and watched her walk away.

The corridor that led from the throne room to the broad stairway and down to the family apartments was as brightly painted as the throne room—this with fantastic beasts and birds. Loosely woven drapes were hung to cover the deeply set east windows, and Septarin only just had time to hurry away from his usual listening post outside his father's throne room to duck into one of these deep alcoves as his aunt emerged and strode briskly down the steps. He pushed the drape aside to watch her safely out of sight, then slipped back into the hallway and hurried after her.

He was plainly clad this morning, in a short linen kilt and

close-fitting sandals, but as he watched Khadat pass through the outer gates and turn toward the temple, he smoothed the fabric with visible pride. Young fighting men of high rank wore such simple garb to train and to practice; there would be no one in the city by nightfall who did not know Pelledar's heir was such a man. *How fortunate for me that Father has that softness, that he has never fought.* It had not taken much wheedling on Septarin's part to persuade his father to grant the special dispensation that would allow him to join the royal chariot. Captain Brysos had been angry, because he had never before allowed drivers or fighters under seventeen, and he preferred his men older than that—but what choice had a mere captain, faced with his prince's direct order? *I will show them all, they won't be sorry they let me fight for them.*

He glanced up as he emerged in the horse-forecourt; the sun was short of midday, he had plenty of time before his favorite tutor Etimos came to escort him to his first serious lessons in weaponry. *Spears, javelin, a short thrusting sword, bow; How often have I had to bear old Khadat bragging of my dead uncle who was the best with three of those four? But I shall command all four, and then my cousin Apodain will have to acknowledge that I am his better as well.*

Apodain. He cast another glance at the sky, grinned suddenly and unpleasantly. "I wonder," he murmured softly, "how my beloved cousin will react when he hears what his mother has done? But *she* will not tell him any sooner than she must, and does he not have a right to know?"

And Khadat had gone left at the gates—no doubt to give thanks to Denota for what she herself had done. *Etimos is right,* Septarin thought scornfully. *Women pray to their goddess for help when She turns events against them, then thank Her when there is no need. What fools.*

But knowing how this weakness worked—that could indeed be useful to a man. Just now, it allowed him time to spend a little time alone with his cousin. Septarin laughed aloud and hurried across the courtyard.

The palace which had been Perlot's and was now Khadat's was only slightly less sumptuous than the prince's own; it had been built on the same plan, with the same deep windows and brightly lit rooms, two stories high instead of three. In Perlot's day, there had been exquisite murals and many fair gardens about the walled grounds and upon the roof. Khadat had paid little heed to such things since her husband's death, though, ordering them tended so they were neat but no longer the wonder of Ghezrat.

There were only two servants in the horse-forecourt when Septarin passed through the gates; both came over to him at once and, he saw with pleasure, took notice of his new kilt. But Apodain was not at home. "He went to run the circuit of the outer walls, lord," one of the servants said. "But he should return before long. If my lord would care to wait? And perhaps wine?"

Septarin glanced at the sun. "I will wait, a little while," he said airily. "But no refreshment." The servant ushered him into the cool hall, but as they reached the outer door, he turned back. "My lord, the young master has returned. I will let him know you await him."

Young master. Septarin's mouth twisted. *That* was surely Khadat's doing, and he wondered briefly how Apodain liked it, that the servants spoke of him so. Doubtless, being Apodain, he either did not notice or did not care; Apodain never showed concern for such details. The prince's heir watched as his cousin strode across the courtyard, grinning widely; saw the smile fade as the servant spoke to him. But Apodain had a smile in place once again as he crossed the threshold. "Cousin. An unexpected pleasure." One of the household servants brought him a cup and a damp cloth to blot his sweaty face and throat. "Come, it's too close down here, my rooms are better. Inyat," he addressed the servant, "bring wine and water, please." He draped the cloth over one broad, bare shoulder and led the way, down the hall and up the steps two at a time. Septarin eyed his cousin's superbly muscled back and legs resentfully; he nearly had to run to keep up. It was truly unfair that a mere four years should make such a difference in men's bodies, he thought, and was uncomfortably aware of his own thin chest, of legs that were properly long but sticklike. Of the ease and smooth strength with which his cousin always moved, even now, when he had just run all the way around the outside of the city—a long and tortuous path, and in such heat.

At the head of the stairs, Apodain stood aside, ushering his younger cousin into a large, plain room, its only furnishings a chair, a low table, and a narrow couch, the only decoration a tall black pottery jug encircled by a gold-painted ship and dolphins. Apodain dropped to the couch, indicated the chair with a casual wave of one hand and blotted sweat from his face, then squeezed it from the blue-black curls that hung over his brow. He waved the cloth at Septarin, at the linen kilt. "I had heard you were to join the company, cousin. Congratulations." He didn't sound enthusiastic, but then, Septarin thought, the two of them had never been fond of each other.

He smiled, a mere twist of his mobile mouth. "Thank you. But that is not why I came." He smoothed the fabric with both hands, drew a deep breath and plunged on. "Did you know your mother had an audience this morning with my father?"

A very short while later, Septarin clattered down the stairs. Khadat might return any moment; Etimos might well be waiting for him. At the gates, he paused to glance over his shoulder and up. Apodain stood motionless, leaning against the window sill, just as Septarin had left him. The prince's heir turned away and hurried into the street.

Apodain was unaware of him, unaware, too, of the chip of stone digging into his shoulder. He stared out across the city, out past the plains toward the distant sea with bleak eyes. *Dear gods, my mother. What has she done to me?* Before all his company, before all the city, she had named him coward as surely as if he himself had petitioned Pelledar. *Desert my men, disgrace my father's name—and then wed with a common Secchi!* He swallowed; in a moment he would surely be ill. He swallowed again, turned blindly from the window and buried his face in his hands.

In a short while, Khadat would return home. She intended to tell him nothing until it was too late, or so Septarin said. *Ah, the pleasure in his eyes when he told me! What I would have given to smash that nasty smile from his lips!* But it was too late for Apodain once she sealed the bargain, and the men prechosen for the Secchi would be named tomorrow at sunset, made to stand upon the palace steps with the Pairs in full sight of the city while the oaths were taken: Primes and Secchi to each other, Pairs to the City and the Prince, the prechosen to Secchi.

People would begin to whisper at once—Denota chose Her Secchi but no goddess chose their future mates, that was all money, trade, politics. The entire city would wonder what their prince could possibly have offered Khadat, who had no need of wealth, or power. Or Apodain. How long would he have after the ordeal of tomorrow's public oath, before word went about that brave Perlot's son had left his company to hide behind his mother's walls while others fought to protect him? *And how will they finally weigh it—that I asked the boon myself, that I begged my mother to ask it for me, or that I let her?* Septarin would help spread the word, though, and he had little doubt what his cousin would say.

The normally airy and cheerful room that had been his for so many years was suddenly a stifling, narrow cage; he couldn't breathe. He flung the towel down and strode across the room, ran down the stairs and through the small room that had been his father's, into the tiny walled garden where Perlot had entertained guests, out the narrow side gate, and into the city. Once the gate closed behind him, though, he leaned against it, irresolute. There was no place he could go, no escape. At least, he would not have to face his mother just yet. He drew a deep breath and for the second time that morning set out for the main gates of the city.

Across the wall from the prince's horse-forecourt, Denota's temple grounds were crowded indeed. Priests and priestesses stood in a silent and watchful group near the central shrine and two large priest-guards kept watch at either side of the closed gates. Through the thick wood, and over the walls, came the low murmur of many voices: family and friends of those within the temple and the curious, waiting. Tephys sat on a low stool under a thatched roof, waiting for the men to arrange themselves in a ragged line along the still-shaded wall. Their eligible daughters—anywhere from one to four— clustered before them, and many were openly weeping.

A hundred or more anxious thoughts touched her. *Goddess, guide me well in this,* she prayed, then rose and walked steadily across of the courtyard. Sudden silence, broken only by Tephys' clear voice and scattered, muffled sobs.

"The blessings of Denota upon each of you, who come to offer her such service. It is not often She sets such a task for her children, seldom she deals such high honor to any. And it is an honor, there is none higher—never forget that. You who are made Dyaddi are last and innermost guardians of the city's walls. You who are chosen will find the days to follow grueling and you may think now that you are incapable of what is asked of you. But Denota will give you Her strength and the strength of your Primes. You will learn to fight—to use killing weapons with speed and skill. This knowledge will come to you from your Primes. Once you are chosen and the goddess joins you as Prime and Secchi, you will feel only a little of that bond, and you may find it strange. You will know from close contact with your Prime how the weapons are used, how held. Only later, when the final bond is made between you and the goddess, will you become true Dyaddi: Two who are One, the wrath of Denota come to life, to slay her enemies. And when those enemies are slain or fled, She and your city—and your city's prince—will not be ungrateful. To each of you, the goddess' bride-price, and the respect and honor of her people."

She raised her hands over her head. "Beloved goddess, judge us well, and grant us strength in the days to come!" A disjointed mumble answered her as the Primes and their daughters repeated the prayer.

Well along the wall, Breyd stood in front of Menlaeus and held Niverren's hands. Niv had not spoken all morning, ordinarily a blessing, but Breyd missed her cheerful chatter. Niverren's face was still half muffled under the scarf she had worn to shield her from prying eyes along the street. Tephys finished her few remarks; Breyd wondered if anyone had actually listened, then realized she herself had little idea what the priestess had said. Something about the prechosen husbands, something else about wrath— But with Duplos and his only daughter at her right elbow, it would have been difficult to hear much anyway. Xera had come into the courtyard weeping steadily and showed no signs of stopping. Niverren glanced past her sister at Xera, drew a shuddering breath and let her eyes close. Breyd squeezed her hands and Niverren nodded once but kept her eyes closed; she was utterly white about the lips and she claimed not to have slept the past night.

That wasn't true. Breyd knew, because she herself had gone sleepless, unable to close her eyes without nightmare and vision overwhelming her. In one way, that had helped, though; she was too exhausted to pay much attention to the staring crowds. And now that the moment was at hand, she could stand with head high and keep quiet. Whatever she felt. *I could never do that to Father,* she told herself, and tried not to look at Xera.

Tephys was pausing before each Prime to speak to him, then to take his daughters by the shoulders in turn. Breyd half-turned to look up at her father. Menlaeus smiled, squeezed her shoulder. His eyes showed his worry. That of itself unnerved her; Menlaeus never let worry about anything show. *He cannot know. Can he?* She swallowed. She had never thought of him as anything but strong; until the goddess' vision she had never even thought of him as growing old—never old like *that*.

Her stomach ached dully. She had been unable to eat any of Nidya's rice this morning; but Nevvia had fussed the entire time, hovering over them, tears spilling down her cheeks while she talked brightly and reassuringly—or what she must think was reassuring. *Even Mother cannot believe the goddess made some mistake; that she will let Father go this morning and send us home with him.* Niverren, roused from her brooding misery, had finally snapped at her; Nevvia had retreated to the kitchen and not come out again.

She hoped she would not shame her father before his fellows, and before all the silent priestesses. Breyd shifted her weight cautiously to ease tired feet and legs, watched as sunlight touched the opposite wall and began to move across the courtyard, held Niverren's chilled fingers, and watched Tephys move slowly toward them. Xera shuddered as the priestess' hands came down on her shoulders, but at that touch, she brought her head up and suddenly, blessedly, stopped crying. The priestess spoke against her ear. Xera inclined her head, Tephys spoke again, so softly the words did not carry beyond father and daughter. Duplos took a step forward and placed his hands on those of the priestess, his daughter set hers upon his. "Denota's blessing upon Her Pair, Her honor to you both." Tephys withdrew her fingers and moved on.

Niverren's hands were trembling as she freed them from her sister's grasp. The priestess passed by Breyd and paused before the elder sister. But Tephys barely touched Niverren's arms, then shook her head and stood back. "Wed your beloved, Niverren," she murmured, "but do not wait to finish your linens. War comes and many lives will be lost; make new life between you." And then the priestess' hands were heavy on Breyd's shoulders, vibrating gently with the goddess' power, Tephys' thought strong in her mind, presenting a vision of herself, her father, a man with a sword threatening Menlaeus who lay unarmed upon the ground. *He has guarded you all his days and will protect you with his life. But the child Breyd saw her father as invincible and perfect. He is no brash boy, to seek the hero's way, but a man of middle years: a man of deeper thought than a boy has, of longer training, but he does not move as quickly as he once did, and he no longer has the endurance of youth. He could be hurt, or killed in the fighting to come. A child—an unthinking daughter—will not see this, or will not accept it, and will be the death of him.*

She was trembling violently, as though she had a fever; Tephys tightened her grip. "I can't—priestess, I can't, I am not—I cannot do it, please—"

"What is this?" Tephys hissed furiously against her ear. "That is no response, how dare you give the goddess such trouble?" Her eyes went suddenly wide and angry. "A vision— You did not tell me of this! Why was I not told, at once?"

"I—I could not—and there was no time," Breyd replied helplessly. Niverren turned to stare at them.

Tephys shook her head. "Hush! Others will hear you, is there not enough trouble here today, without that? Again; and think well how you respond to Denota's call. Do you think you will save him by a child's whining?"

Breyd bit her lip, swallowed. Tephys was waiting for an answer, her mouth set in a furious line, spots of color on her normally very pale cheeks. "No, priestess."

"Do you think to change his fate by your child's tricks, or turn our enemies aside with this silliness? Again!" Once more the inner question. Breyd was aware of Menlaeus behind her and terror threatened to swallow her whole: How much had she heard, or understood of that? Tephys' mental shout tore into her: *Pay heed, you willful creature!* Fear: for Menlaeus, of Tephys; it vanished under a wave of pure fury. *How dare she or the goddess play with my father's life?* "No!" she whispered angrily. "His strength, his knowledge, my youth and endurance and quickness, joined together. No man—*nothing!*—shall harm him while I can prevent it. While I live." Tephys glared at her, then took Menlaeus' hands and set them on her shoulders. Breyd reached up to cover them and Tephys set hers upon both to seal the bond. The surge of warmth that was Denota's power flared through them; she could feel not only her father's hands, but the concern for her that was surely in his eyes.

"Protector and protected, both of you, to guard each other and safeguard the city," Tephys said quietly; she looked merely worried, all at once. She still sounded angry when she learned close to whisper, "You should have told me at once. Come before Atos retires tonight; Merrone will speak the sun to rest. You and I must talk of this." She moved on to the next Prime before Breyd could reply.

Niverren was looking at her curiously. She could ignore that, but not this new thing that was between Menlaeus and herself.

Father. What had she done? But what *could* she have done, to deny Tephys? Protector, and yet in need himself of protection. *I cannot protect him, this is my Father! Why doesn't she understand that?* Too late, now. Child's tricks, Tephys had said. *How dare she? She saw what I did, my vision, and she still insists that—?* Tephys clearly cared no more about the fate of one Pair than the goddess did, to name Menlaeus Prime and then set Breyd at his shoulder. *But I owe him everything, my life, and I cannot let him die if any act of mine could prevent that.* She wondered suddenly if Menlaeus could somehow tell what she had been thinking. But she could not tell what his thoughts were; she turned her head to look up at him. He smiled reassuringly and let his fingers rest on her shoulders. She thought the fear that had tightened his face for so many days was gone. Perhaps the goddess' bond had taken better with him than it had for her; she could only hope so. One of them should be able to take comfort in it.

The Pairs were all chosen, but that was not the end of it. The sun rose high and fell from midday. The Secchi were separated from unchosen daughters and Niverren was gone, doubtless home to tell the family what had happened, to let Creos know the goddess had not taken her, what Tephys had said to her. Had that been a prophecy for Niv? Her mother would be busy the rest of the day trying to interpret what Tephys meant by those words. *Worry about Mother later,* she ordered herself.

A short, bulky man in dusty and well-worn fighting garb came from the direction of the gates and stood before them; Menlaeus straightened and tightened his grip on her shoulders to make certain he had her attention. "That is Grysis," he murmured against her ear. "Weaponsmaster and, I suppose, our new captain."

Grysis waited for complete quiet, clasped his hands together behind his back and strode slowly along the line. "You men know me; you Secchi will come to know me. The goddess has provided the bond to make you Pairs, I will give you the training you need to become *fighting* Pairs. In a little, we will go to the main barracks, where the Secchi will be given armor. Many of you will find it uncomfortable, they tell me, to wear men's garments and bear weapons. You will become accustomed to it, just as you will become accustomed to the weapons themselves, though I know each of you will doubt that at first, and think old Grysis is mad." A few nervous giggles. "Many of you will find the attention given you difficult at first, but that does not matter. Ignore it, and you will find it ceases to bother you." His eyes swept across the line of men and young women. Finally he nodded, stepped back to converse briefly with Tephys, then faced his new company once again. "Dyaddi," he said commandingly, and turned to lead them through the temple gate.

There were people clustered all around the gate, blocking the street; they fell back whispering and staring openly as the pairs came out. Fortunately, Grysis had brought men with him to clear a path so they could pass unimpeded. There were men on both sides of the gates leading to the fighting ground and the various barracks and messes set around it. Men on the fighting and training grounds stared and whispered, but there were blessedly few of these, and Grysis had his company moving so fast, it was difficult to pay much attention to the watchers.

At the low building that served as messes for the common foot soldiers, the Secchi were taken aside and shown into a large chamber where Meronne stood surrounded by priestesses; men came in with several brass-bound chests, which they set in the middle of the room. Grysis left; Meronne waited until all the men were gone, then held up a hand for silence. "Pay attention to me, and do not waste any time with silly questions or foolish ditherings! You will find new linens in that chest." She pointed. "You will take what you need and put it on now. The panoply of Secchi you will then assume is old, worn by your sisters many years ago when the last Dyaddi were named. We will aid you into the fighting gear. You, in turn, will care for them and honor them.

Each of you will be fitted for a new panoply before the Diye Haff come. The other boxes contain swords and small shields; you will each choose from these, taking the weapon and the protection that fits most comfortably." She folded her thin arms across her chest. "You will wear these things at all times of the day and night except when you sleep; you must become used to them, and unconcerned by them. You will not put them aside until the Diye Haff have turned and run and the Pairs are disbanded. Your families will have to do without whatever help you have given to this time, whatever tasks were yours now are not. You are fighting women, Secchi; you will concentrate upon learning to fight and accepting the goddess' will. This will be explained to your families, but if any of you have difficulties, you will come to me or go to Grysis, and we will deal with them.

"For now, concentrate upon dressing yourselves and arming yourselves, and do it quickly. There is much yet to be done before this day ends!" She stepped back and sat, her face grim and her entire mien unapproachable. Thirty-four young women stared at her, looked helplessly at each other and at the chests.

Breyd looked around the chamber. No one was going to move, it seemed, until someone else did. And now several of the girls were looking at her, as if for guidance. Because they knew she had been a priestess and had dealt with Meronne before? *Secchi to first Prime, more likely.* "Well." Her voice came out too high and she cleared her throat. "Well. That *was* an order. Let's get changed and at least have this part behind us."

"Sensible of you." Tall Lochria, Bechates' daughter, nodded briskly and walked over to throw back the lid of one box. She drew out a pleated linen kilt, held it up, shook her head. "Not for me. Xenia—it is Xenia, isn't it? This looks more fitted to a girl your size, don't you think?"

Xenia took the cloth and held it against her waist, then flushed a painful red. "I—I cannot wear this!"

"I do not think we were given the choice," Lochria said dryly. Breyd came across to pick another from the box. Even her mother had not thought of *this*. Nevvia would have a fit. But Lochria was right.

Besides— She swallowed. "Remember what Tephys said; what the goddess asks of us. This—well, it isn't much. Is it? Compared to everything else?" She glanced at Lochria, saw understanding in the other young woman's eyes; they were going to have to take charge of the other Secchi. *Lochria looks and sounds like a leader. As for me—well. At least I can try. For now. Until they learn better.*

No one was paying much attention; they looked as scared as she felt. Or simply overwhelmed. It had been so different when Tephys tapped her to serve the temple for a year. So— ordinary, really. This, though— "Think of it as a new fashion," Lochria said; her laugh sounded almost true, but when Xenia turned to stare at her, she turned bright red. She picked up a kilt, held it against her waist, and tried again. "Haven't you ever envied your father, not having all that cloth to gather dust and mud, and wrap around his legs when he walks?" She leaned close to Breyd and added in a low undertone: "*I* never have, but Xenia will not know that." Breyd smiled, then went over to find herself linen.

Once all thirty-four stood before her in bare feet and short linen undertunics, Meronne clapped her hands once more. The eight priestesses each went to a girl and took her from chest to chest. One held leather belts and pockets, and hardened leather caps; another contained the hardened leather breastplates and shin-protecting greaves. Others were full of swords and shields. The priestesses drew their young women from place to place, choosing armor and helping the Secchi into it, fastening straps for them, picking out a cap that would fit closely enough not to fall off; they finally left them at the chests of weapons and went back to arm yet another eight. Breyd and Lochria went last of all.

Breyd looked down at the expanse of exposed leg and bared knee. Vision threatened; she ran her hands across the leather breastplate and it faded. Lochria was still on her knees in front of the box of weapons. Someone well back in the room moaned, "I cannot go into the barracks yard like this."

And then, surprisingly, Xenia's voice. "But you have such good legs, Eriana." There was a shocked little silence, followed by an explosion of nervous laughter. Breyd glanced toward Meronne, but the old priestess didn't seem particularly affronted by any of the strained horseplay.

Lochria had set out two swords and was concentrating on choosing between them. Breyd took one from the box, then another. A third seemed to fit her grasp somehow. "I feel—I don't know," she said. "Like a child playing with Father's things."

"I know," Lochria said quietly. Breyd knelt to look at her; Lochria nodded. "It's all happening so quickly, isn't it? It's very strange, my being here. We all assumed my youngest sister would be chosen, she's always done so well in the games and she's even hunted with Father. You?"

Breyd bit her lip, tried to find herself one of the round, leather shields small enough to stay on her arm. "I think—I knew it would be me. Niverren—"

"Oh. You're Niv's sister." Lochria nodded. "My family lives near Creos' family, I've known him for most of my life. There was talk once, his father and mine, you know. But nothing came of it. I saw your sister when he brought her home; she's very pretty." Breyd slid her hand into the straps of one shield, set it aside and tried a second for comparison, then went back to the first. *Talk to her,* she thought in sudden panic. *Find something to say. She will think you snobbish otherwise, and you need at least one friend here. One other person in all Ghezrat who understands this new thing.* Denira would not, she realized with a sudden pang. How could she?

"You don't seem upset—about all this," she managed after a moment.

"Well." Lochria picked up a sword, held it away from her to gaze at it consideringly. "I'm not the kind to weep or tear my hair. But it's—I think it's more that I'm afraid I won't be good enough. Who could ever be good enough to please a goddess? But I don't think we'll have to actually fight anyone, not if they put us against the city gates. The Diye Haff will be stopped long before that. And of course, as poor as my family is, there might never have been a proper husband for me. But now my family will have ties with the Erinos, and they own two trading ships." She set aside sword and shield, returned the rest to the box, and glanced at Breyd. "You don't seem very upset, either. You must be very sensible or better than most of us at controlling your face."

Breyd got to her feet, pulled the baldric over her shoulder the way Menlaeus wore his and guided the plain short sword into the sheath. "A little of both, I hope," she said. Lochria laughed and stood up, brushed off her knees.

"Practical. I think we'll get along well, you and I." And before Breyd could respond, Meronne got to her feet and spoke. "You had better hurry, all of you! The Primes and your captain await you here, and the High Priestess awaits you at the temple!" She clapped her hands together; the priestesses fell in behind her as she walked between the Secchi, straightening a tunic here, a shield there, tugging someone's cap lower on her forehead. "Come," she commanded the women with her, and strode into the sunlight. The priestesses followed.

Lochria nodded at Breyd and the two walked down to the doorway through their very uncertain and nervous-looking companions. "All right!" Lochria said finally. "Let us go outside and be done with it. The first time will *surely* be the worst, don't you agree?"

From the back of the room came a high voice: "Until my mother sees me!" Shrill, tense laughter and giggles greeted this.

Most of the Secchi were visibly shy of walking onto the training ground. Duplos looked nearly as embarrassed as his daughter. Breyd was almost afraid to look at Menlaeus, but unlike Bechates, he was not red-faced at sight of his man-clad girl. *He knows it is not my choosing, after all.* Grysis merely nodded and clapped his hands together once, then led the way down to the far end of a bench and table-littered room. He stopped and waved at a pair of benches near the back wall. "This will be your area, for eating and when we need to sit and talk. For now, you will eat in this room only when there is practice; later, you will live in the barracks and take all your meals here unless you are on duty, outside the walls." He gestured toward the far end of the room, and everyone turned to look. "The food hatches are there; yours is the righthand one. You will go always to Logus or his aides, at that hatch." He paused, and in the silence someone's stomach grumbled loudly. Grysis chuckled. "Did any of you eat this morning? You Primes, take your young women up there, there will be bread and fruit at this hour. You Secchi, eat. Learning how to use weaponry will be an arduous enough task without trying to do it on empty stomachs."

Breyd swallowed hard. *I can't eat; I think I'll be sick if I try.* But Menlaeus stepped aside and let her precede him between the long rows of benches to the hatch; a lean, narrow-faced man looked at her wide-eyed and handed her a flat wooden bowl of bread and dates. Menlaeus took one and a jug of wine and two cups, gesturing for her to lead the way back. It was a little awkward sitting with that hard leather covering her chest and stomach, but she was finally able to tear the bread in half and bite into it. She chewed for a long time; it seemed all right. Her stomach wasn't actually threatening. She finally swallowed and took the cup her father handed her. The wine was sour and fortunately very well mixed.

"Better?" Menlaeus asked quietly.

He looked so anxious, so worried, she dredged up a smile somehow and nodded. "Much better. The wine is—"

"I know it is. The barracks well is sulfur-flavored. Fortunately the level is high and there aren't many men drinking it. You're certain you're all right?" To prove it she took another bite of the bread and then most of the dates. Suddenly, it *was* a little easier, as though the simple act of sitting together and eating removed some of the strangeness from their surroundings. Grysis sat and ate with them, washed his bread down quickly with a cup of the sour wine, got to his feet, and signed for silence. "I had better return you to the temple, there is very little time left to us today and none to begin anything. Tomorrow, you will gather here at second hour and be prepared for a long day.

"Before we leave, though, you will take the rest of your weapons: Each of you will be issued a case of javelins and a spear, which you will keep with you at all times. There are also cloaks distinctive to your company. You will wear these at all times in the city, with your fighting gear." Many of the women were visibly relieved as men came in with folded stacks of dark red cloth; the fabric was edged in deeper, figured red, held at the throat by a round bronze pin and long enough to cover at least the backs of bared legs nearly to the ankle. *Red.* Breyd had to force herself to touch the cloth, and it was only when Menlaeus looked at her oddly that she realized she must be worrying him once more. She draped it quickly across her shoulders where it hung like a dead weight.

There had been whispering all along the streets when they went to the barracks; on the way back, total silence. *They look at us as though we had become the goddess ourselves— look how they step back the way women did in the Cleft at midwinter, when Tephys brought out the goddess' scythe. But*

I am still Breyd, only Breyd—can't they see that? The crowd had at least doubled in size.

The afternoon passed in a daze: She later remembered prayers and more prayers; one of the novice priestesses sang a blessing song. Mostly she remembered Tephys and another priestess standing under the thatched roof with her and her father. Tephys' eyes were still black whenever they touched on her, as though daring her to create another scene. *You cannot fight the bond, the goddess will not hear you and Tephys will not let you,* she finally decided tiredly. *Give in to it, use it—at least take what weapon they give you to fight for him.*

But at first it seemed like so much outward show: Tephys made Menlaeus sit and set out his weapons before them. She pointed to Breyd then. "Sit at his right side. Now take hold of the sword hilt. Menlaeus, set your hand over hers and guide what she does." It took them longer than most of the other Pairs, even nervous little Eriana. *But each time I touch that sword, and I see my hand covered in dirt and blood, and Father—* She couldn't decided if Tephys thought she was still fighting the bond. But Menlaeus was patient and each time she faltered, his hand took hers and went through the motions again. *It is pantomime; how can I understand a sword this way?* But all at once, she did; her muscles understood between one turn of the blade and the next what was asked of them, how his muscles moved and why. The strangeness faded; her anger grew. "Do as your Prime shows you," Tephys murmured. *This is my father!* Breyd thought furiously. But she could no longer sense Menlaeus, and the sword once more was an awkward lump of bronze with a wickedly sharp blade. *And—and my Prime.* She looked up into her father's eyes. The little line between his brows vanished and he nodded; his thought—the least sense of approval—warmed her. *That is right.* His grip shifted; hers matched it exactly.

Atos was nearing the end of his day's journey when Tephys finally released them all. "Go in honor," she said. As Breyd passed her, she whispered sharply, "Wait a little, I will talk with you as soon as the others are gone." Breyd nodded, aware of her father's sharp glance. She looked at the priestess blankly. *What do I tell him? Or does he already sense, or know?* But Tephys had already turned her back and was striding toward the red clay hut.

She walked as far as the gates with Menlaeus, still trying to think what to say. But just outside the gates, Niverren was waiting for them, Creos at her side. "I thought you would never be done, we have been here for hours," Niverren said fretfully.

Creos patted her arm and said, "Your weaving will keep a little, Niv. Sir, are they going to let you go home?"

"Yes." Menlaeus pushed damp hair off his forehead. "It was thoughtful of you to wait."

"Well." Niverren smiled. "Creos suggested it."

"All the things we heard when I took Niverren back to her mother, you would think people were ashamed of you," Creos said.

"Their own families! So he said we had better come back to wait for you. So people would know we aren't like that—like those others. Afraid or—or whatever they are. And—oh," she sighed vexedly, shook her head, "I couldn't work anyway."

"Why not?" Menlaeus asked her, but she merely shook her head once more and Creos answered for her. "Your son and his friend Laius came in just after I brought Niverren home, both reeking of wine and very unsteady. I—I think, sir, it was Laius who began it all, but Tar was in an ugly mood."

"All I did . . ." Niverren began.

"I know, love," Creos assured her. "Nevvia was upset about the Pairs and Niverren was trying to make things easier, so she said something about tiny little Breyd clomping around the city with a man's armor hanging down to her ankles, and Tar just—he got so furious, even his mother couldn't still him."

"It's that awful Laius," Niverren said indignantly. "You know how Tar is, everything Laius says might as well be words straight from Atos' lips. He was shouting that Father had done something to cause his illness so he could never fight, and then he was yelling that Breyd had bribed Tephys to—oh, I don't know, it sounded just like something awful old Laius would say. Why would Tar think it was all Breyd's fault that you were chosen Prime?" Niverren drew a deep, steadying breath. "Tar had Mother in tears, it was awful, and even Ina was crying when we left."

4

"People *stare* so," Niverren fretted. But then she stared herself and Breyd fought the urge to wrap the red cloak tightly around her. *How odd,* she thought. For the past hour or so, she had forgotten the short pleats of the underlinen, though she had been certain she would die of shame when the first company came out of the barracks. Niverren blinked. "Oh, dear. Mother will faint, seeing you in public like that. And Tar—" She shook her head helplessly. Menlaeus stepped forward, took his eldest daughter's arm.

"You said there was trouble at home. Hadn't we better go? Breyd?"

Breyd shook her head. "Tephys—"

"You're all right," he said, a little anxiously, more than half a question. "She isn't angry with you, is she?"

"No." She managed a smile for him. "It is—was a minor thing, the night of the Festival, a priestess thing. She had no time to ask the—the ritual questions before this."

She couldn't remember having ever lied to him before and she could feel herself turning red; surely he would realize. But perhaps he would assume it was part of Denota's mysteries, nothing to do with a man. Niverren was eying her in mild curiosity. Menlaeus said, "Yes, I heard some of that earlier, what she was saying to you, and I wondered at the time. I had better go home and sort things out. I will come back and wait for you, though, if I can."

She shook her head. "I remember the way home, Father."

"Yes," he said dryly, "but you know you would hate coming down our street alone, looking like that."

"Father," Niverren broke in impatiently, "really, we had better go, now, Tar is in a terrible state. Can you believe, he and that awful Laius wanted to pick a fight with *Creos?*" Menlaeus met his youngest daughter's eyes and shrugged, then went with the other two. Breyd fetched a little sigh and went back into the temple courtyard.

Tephys was seated amid cushions before the small clay house that held the steps to the subterranean temple; one of her young girls had brought her a dew-beaded jug, a clay cup and a little tray of soft white cheese, bread, and a few leathery looking dates. The priestess indicated the tray with a wave of her hand. "Eat a little. We can share the cup." She patted the ground next to her, waited while Breyd settled down next to her. "I apologize for my harsh words this morning." She didn't sound very apologetic, Breyd thought sourly. "But a prophecy of your own—and touching such a matter!" She ate some of the crumbly cheese. "You have known from the first that you would be Secchi, and you never said anything. Did you think you could avoid it by keeping it secret? Never mind, let it wait a moment, eat." Only when the tray was empty and the contents of the jug— more water than wine—half gone, did she return to the subject. "Sit back—so. Rest your head in my lap, close your eyes. Relax." Tephys' fingers were light on her temples, the sense of her a mere tickle at the edge of thought, gone almost as soon as sensed. Conscious awareness of the temple grounds, of old Meronne leading the ceremony bidding nightly farewell to the sun, of the usual muted city sounds beyond the temple walls—all that faded. Replaced by vision: Menlaeus in the red cloak, bronze armor, fear and pride both in his face; herself, at his side, fighting with him against a horde of huge, bearded men with deep blue eyes; a dreadful burst of sound and fury and death everywhere, a dead man pinning her to the ground, her father dying with his head in her lap, and then gone. . . . She would have fought it if she could, but the priestess was stronger than she.

The sky was a much darker blue when she opened her eyes once more. Tears ran down her cheeks; she rolled over cautiously and sat up. Her head was pounding, her back stiff. Tephys sat before her, head bowed over cupped hands. Breyd opened her mouth; no sound would come. She swallowed, ran her tongue over dry lips and tried again. "Will my—does my father have to die?"

Tephys brought her head up, and replied crisply, "We all will die, one day or another, young Secchi."

"I meant—"

"I know. My anger was not for you, or your question. But

I cannot give you a certain answer, and I am sorry for that. It did seem to me I saw something beyond what your memory of vision held: Three fighting to drive the enemy from the city walls. One was you, and one a young man. The third—the third wore the red cloak of a Prime, though I could not see his face."

"Then that will have to do," Breyd replied steadily, but her heart sank.

Tephys shook her head. "For now. Remember that there are many days left to you to learn how to fight; Denota will bind you and him more tightly together. You will not be helpless *or* alone, out there!" She spread her hands. "I know it is hard for you; it is hard for anyone to be given such a task. But believe this: If you are not there for him, then no one is."

"All right."

"If you do not fight with him, then he *will* die, and you will have to know you could have prevented his death and did not. Is that easier for you to face, Breyd?"

She shook her head. "You know it is not! But to have seen that—"

"Yes. Well, you are not the first or only one to have a vision in time of dire need, and not the first who must find the courage in herself to act in the face of such foreknowledge. Remember that Denota does not always show the literal truth to her children; that she does not carve a man's fate in stone, or a woman's. I don't tell you there is no cause to fear," Tephys warned. "Just less than your lack of training and preparation make it seem now. The goddess may grant you further vision, and you will tell me at once, if she does," she added sternly, and Breyd nodded. "At *any* time."

"Yes," Breyd said meekly, and Tephys laughed.

"Go home," she ordered, but smiled as she said it. Breyd scrambled to her feet, smoothed the short kilt self-consciously and settled the several leather straps and cords into place. Tephys sat back to watch her go. The smile faded as Breyd hurried through the gate and it shut behind her. *How could such a simple child as that one speak against Denota's bond? It is unheard of!* She sighed and let her head drop into her hands. The girl had a hard time before her. *Should I have told her, warned her—or would it do anything save to increase her fears?* She dismissed the thought; even the strongest could break under a load of prophecy, and surely Breyd was not one of those. *And it is my task, to carry that weight.*

It was an hour when most would be inside, eating, or walking along the inner walls; there was hardly anyone outside the temple when Breyd emerged, and no one standing and staring. No Menlaeus, either. She drew the red cloak around her and walked quickly, looking only straight ahead, not letting her eyes fix on anyone. On her own street, a few women stood near the pool; Misso came into the open and stared, but others stepped back into shelter and had someone actually bowed? *As if I had become—* But she hadn't become anything yet! Not—not really.

She wouldn't look; wouldn't look at Misso, either. She brought her chin up and stepped around the old woman and hurried on. Where was Denira—what did she think? *Why hasn't she come to talk to me? It isn't my fault, I wasn't given a choice!* She lengthened her step, pressed the wooden sword case against her hip to keep it from banging into her leg, hesitated only briefly at the door before raising the latch and stepping inside.

It was quiet within. She pressed the door closed, crossed the outer room and paused to glance around the courtyard. No sign of Nevvia, no sign of Tar, either—except that the usually neat pile of cushions had been scattered in all directions and left to lie where they fell. She bent to gather them up, froze halfway to her knees—Tarpaen, in the kitchen, had just spoken her name. *I can't face him,* she thought in despair. *Not after everything else today, not after what Niverren said. And if Laius is in there, with him—* But then she heard her father's voice; Tar was talking to Menlaeus, not her. She straightened up, letting cushions slide from her fingers, stepped quickly over to the near wall, and edged along it.

Tarpaen's voice was tremulous and thick with too much drink, shaking with an occasional sob. "It's—all this, you and Breyd, it got worse and worse as the day went on, and then Niv came back and she was so—you know how Niverren is. Sometimes I feel that nothing touches her, she always acts like I'm only pretending to be upset, as though nothing I feel is important, that nothing anyone feels matters, except what *she* feels. And I—I don't remember all the things I said. I never meant to upset Mother."

"I know."

"But it's—it's so *unfair*, Father! All I ever wanted, just the chance to fight for Ghezrat, to gain honor and rank because I did, and because what I did counted for something. In the streets, the barracks, the wineshops, it is all they talk about now, the old men: The pride you feel when people watch your company pass and you go out to protect them, the strength you gain from each other."

"I know, my son." Menlaeus spoke so softly, she could barely hear him. "I wish—"

"All those men who've fought before—the things *you* never talk about," Tarpaen added accusingly. "All those other men speak of nothing else and I must hear it, constantly—how the city depends upon its men, the joy in weaponry and the pride in forming a shield wall the enemy cannot break through, the bond that makes all such men brothers ever after. It was—I thought when I was a boy, how wonderful it would be, to be a hero, to wield a sword and slay men, or turn aside an attack, or lead the charge that broke an enemy, and then for people to watch when I went by, to say, "There goes Tarpaen, there walks a hero!" Silence. "That was a only boy's dream, I know that. Was it wrong to want that? Was that why—why my eyes, this—" And then he did begin to weep.

Breyd stopped. She could just see her brother now, crouched in the room that served as winter kitchen and storage, his shoulders shaking and face buried in his hands; her father on one knee before him, holding him close. She could sense the compassion he felt for his troubled son, and it made her extremely uncomfortable; he was uncomfortable himself to be faced with so much misery—Menlaeus who never voiced his own fears and concerns. *I never thought he had any, until the night of the Festival.*

He must have also felt her presence; he looked up, met her eyes, shook his head slightly. She nodded and stepped back out of sight as he began to speak. "Tar, remember how many years it has been since the last war fought before the city's gates, how long even since the last skirmishes. So often, men forget the discomfort and pain, and recall only the excitement. I do remember the fierce pride I felt when we were paraded from the barracks through the city, and through the main gates. But I also recall the three days we were pinned at the end of the mole, with no food and only dirty water to drink, and the pain in my guts. The men who died of wounds, the friend who lost his leg and bled to death in my arms. I never saw any reason to share that with anyone; it would only upset them, to no purpose."

"But—"

"I am not sorry I fought; had things been otherwise, though, I would have ended my days without another war, and been pleased for that. Or, I would have gone forth with my old company, had it been asked of me, and I will fight the Diye Haff before the gates as the Prime in a Dyadd, if it is asked of me. I understand that pride you are talking about, Tar. I feel the pride in what skills I have to protect my family, my prince and my city. I feel it. You—know how difficult it is for me to say such things. I do not live only for that, though; there is more in my life that matters than war and fighting."

"You confuse me," Tarpaen said.

"I don't mean to. Tar, there is nothing wrong with wanting to protect what is yours, nothing wrong with wanting to gain honor and praise by such deeds, nothing. No god of Ghezrat would punish you for wanting to fight, not even for dreaming of becoming the greatest hero Ghezrat has ever known. Who has not dreamed such things, at some time in his life?"

"I know." Tarpaen sniffed loudly. "I mean, I suppose I do. But to stay behind the city walls, to hide behind my *sister!*"

"It isn't like that, Tarpaen," Menlaeus said sharply. "Your sister didn't ask for this."

"I know. I said that earlier, I think, but I never meant it. I was—"

"I would never have asked this, either, that a daughter of mine be placed in the fighting." A brief silence, broken only by the sounds of Tarpaen trying to gain control of himself. "I understand your anger, son. If there was anything else I could do, beyond what I have done, I would do it for you. You know that."

"I know." His voice was muffled by his hands. "I—all those things I said, earlier, whatever Nidya told you, I didn't mean them, truly, Father. Sometimes I simply cannot bear it, that all my strength and this one thing I want above all others, it means nothing because I cannot *see* well enough to fight!"

"There is honor in what you do, son—"

"To stand upon the walls all safe, while others move and die according to the trumpet calls I make?" Tarpaen demanded bitterly. "I know it was the best you could do for me."

"It was. And it is not necessarily safe, Tarpaen, two men died with their horns still strapped to their lips, the day we took back the docks. And the walls—even our walls—are no guarantee of safety."

Tarpaen seemed not to have heard him. "Just—to stand there," he went on bitterly, "while my *sister* fights! Father, I'm *sorry*, but I cannot seem to think of anything else." He groaned; Breyd moved silently and swiftly across the courtyard and stepped back into the shadow of her own doorway.

"That is the wine, setting you to brooding. You have more sense than this, Tar. Stay away from the winehouses, if the drink and the talk upset you so. Particularly," he added flatly, "if you will then come and vent your anger and frustration upon the household, and upon your mother."

"Mother—"

"Your mother needs your strength, and will depend heavily upon you, you must know that. She is easily enough upset just now, without you adding to her burden. Think of that, before you do this again. For now, go, forget this day, get some sleep." A moment later he came into the open, arm wrapped around his son's shoulders. Tarpaen moved unsteadily and partway up nearly fell from the ladder. Finally, he pulled himself over and vanished from sight. Menlaeus sighed, walked back across the courtyard and stepped into the room his daughters shared. "Are you all right?" he asked.

"Yes."

He leaned against the door frame, folded his arms across his chest. "Tar and Laius were gone when we got back, your mother asleep; Nidya had ordered them to leave and gave valerian-dosed wine to her servant and Nevvia both. She says neither will waken before dawn tomorrow. Niverren was worried for Creos, afraid Laius might return and cause a fight. She's gone with him and will sleep with his sisters tonight." He spread his arms in a wide shrug. "A very long day."

Breyd laughed quietly at the understatement. "Yes."

"You're certain you're all right? Tephys was angry with you earlier."

I don't think I can lie to him again, Breyd thought uncomfortably. *This new thing between us—he won't know what the lie is, but he'll know it's there, and whatever else I do, I can never tell him the truth about this.* "That night, down in the temple, when Denota spoke through Tephys—I saw something, too. I should have told her at once." She shrugged, a wide spread of arms that matched his earlier gesture. "That's all."

"You saw—?"

"Fighting. A lot of dust, mostly, and a sword." She swallowed and went on in a small voice, "It frightened me, I could feel and smell it—I thought it must be like that, to be suddenly thrown into a battle." Menlaeus seemed to relax. *He believes.* She drew a deep breath, went on. "And then I felt—well, foolish, and I knew it would upset Mother. I—I didn't mean to make so much of such a small thing."

"Yes." He looked at her, thoughtfully, for a long moment. "She is no longer angry?"

"Tephys? No." *Change the subject, now,* she thought. "When—when did Tar come home?"

"Not long before you did. Poor foolish boy, he must have been drinking hard all day and he has no head for it. Laius was with him, of course, urging him on; I think Tar might have come home to quietly sleep it off long before otherwise, but Laius had taken in enough wine to turn brutish and, of course, he is as frustrated as Tar, that they will not let him down from the walls to fight. Tar wasn't very clear about events after Nidya chased them away, but I gather there was another shop or two, more wine, and Laius tried to fight with some other patrons, then turned on Tarpaen when the boy tried to get him to leave. Tar's good eye is swollen nearly shut, and the guard had to bring him home. He was terribly ashamed of the whole mess, but Laius is locked in the barracks for at least this night—possibly longer."

Breyd sighed heavily. "Well, one good thing has come of it, if Laius is closeted." She let the overly warm red cloak fall open.

"More than once, I hope," Menlaeus said. "Your mother has spoiled Tar, and he's taken advantage of that. I think he may realize finally that he can't simply do whatever he wants and get away with it." *For the moment, anyway,* Breyd thought, but she merely nodded. It made her a little uncomfortable, listening to her father talk that way—as though she had somehow become his equal because of the bonding which would occur. She bent down to work at the knots holding the greaves against her lower legs. The thick leather came free finally and she rubbed damp shins. Menlaeus pushed his shoulder away from the doorway and stretched. "Your grandmother has a lotion for that." He turned away, hesitated, came back and put his arm around her shoulders. She wrapped both her arms around his chest and leaned against him. "I would never have chosen this for you."

"I know, Father."

"For either of us. Not for what your brother sees as the honor, not for my comparative safety so far behind the lines."

"No one would think that about you!" Breyd pushed away to look up at him wide-eyed.

"Ah. Perhaps not."

"It was Denota's choice, none of yours."

He laughed quietly, shook his head. "People like us would not think so, but there are people in Ghezrat who do not live as close to the goddess, you know. There will always be those who think the choice can be influenced, or that it is all decided by Tephys, or the prince, who might be somehow swayed."

"I won't believe that. Whoever says it."

"Some also say that some of the choices were fixed in other ways. I would not have asked us to be made Dyadd, even for the man they chose for you."

She shook her head. "Of course not! I know better! Who would say that but Laius? Of course I won't believe it, Father!"

He smoothed the hair back from her forehead and kissed her brow. "Get some sleep, child. Tomorrow will be long and difficult." She nodded, and he was gone; the ladder creaked and she heard him crossing the roof above her. She went back to undressing, fighting strange garments and stiff knots in the near-total darkness.

"The one night I could use Niv," she mumbled. Just as well Niverren wasn't here, though. Niv would go on for hours about Tar and Laius, about what Creos thought, what he had said to them, and to her, how she felt about it. Niv would fuss about her sister's new clothing and weapons, too, and want to know how Breyd felt about it all—Tar's outburst, what she could feel and sense of the goddess, her father, about the chosen husband. . . .

Breyd paused, the heavy, hardened leather breastplate in her hands and the night air suddenly cool against her sweaty skin. Her father's words came back to her: "Not even for the man they chose for you." *They named me a husband—they must have. And yet, I can't remember any of that.* She hadn't even wondered about it in the barracks when Lochria had spoken with such pleasure of her own newly chosen. *What man did they name for me?* But that was not important, would not be important for some time to come. *Might never be important. The Diye Haff will kill my father, and me as well, and Tephys simply chooses not to tell me.*

The thought, squarely faced, was oddly steadying. *I will not let them kill my father, they will not touch him.* But that was Denota's bond shouting defiance, not Breyd. Kill—she drew the sword and ran a finger along its honed blade, then shuddered and let it fall. To cut a man with that; he would bleed horribly. *I cannot.* It would make her violently sick just to think about it. She had to force herself to pick up the weapon and put it back in the baldric, which she set atop the rest of her panoply. She drew the familiar old blue robe over her shoulders, curled up on her side of the bed, and fell asleep between one breath and the next.

There was a chill wind blowing along the ground outside the city walls, whining through the loose rubble of stone that lay strewn down the steep slope. Apodain sat with his knees drawn to his chin, still wearing only the sweat-stiffened loincloth he'd run in earlier in the day; he was oblivious to the black sky and the cold. *I cannot stay here, I must go home,* he thought dully. He had thought this any number of times, over the past hours. He couldn't find the strength or the will to move, and knowing his mother would be waiting, increasingly upset with him as the day wore on, made it more and more difficult to consider. He built pictures in his mind, now and again: Sliding unseen through the back gate, through his father's private garden, and mounting to his own room unnoted, discovering the next morning it had all been a particularly foul joke on Septarin's part; coming into the horse-forecourt and his mother standing there, tall and forbidding as she had seemed to him all the years of his childhood. Throwing himself from the walls, or from the roof gardens, leaping from here, where the ground dropped off steeply not far from his feet. Getting to his feet, finding the narrow trail that led nearly straight down from the walls to meet with the main road, traveling along that until he came to the mole, somehow sneaking into the lower decks with the rowers, or bribing the shipmaster to let him sail with them, leaving Ghezrat behind forever. . . .

But there was nowhere to go, nothing he knew beyond Ghezrat. *And how would you bribe anyone, whose mother keeps you poorer of coin and ornament than the sons of impoverished merchants?* She still treated him like a small boy, as though time had solidified around the household when Perlot died. He was not of age—but neither were two of his cousins and they were not ruled by a mother. *How dare she?* But before he could gain his feet, the anger drained out of him; he sighed and let himself down again. There was no point to anything, no future that did not hold shame—there was nothing.

He brought his head up, peered uncertainly into the dark; a stone clattered downhill, not far away, and then another. There was movement in the shadow, perhaps. Men or beasts, what did it matter? He shrugged, let his chin onto his knees once more.

And then, beyond any doubt, he heard the sliding, crunching sound of men walking hurriedly across the uneven ground, nearly upon him. There was little light here, but enough that he could make out the familiar bulk of Reott, one of his brother Hemit's servants. "Um—young master," he began tentatively. "The Princess Khadat grows worried, and has sent us looking for you. You aren't injured, are you, sir?"

His throat was dry, his voice harsh because of it. "No."

"Then how dare you frighten the household and your mother so?" That was Emyas—Khadat's poor young Mirikosi cousin; the slight aristocratic lisp was unmistakable and deceptive: Emyas could carry Hemit up the stairs by himself.

Apodain shook his head, and then, uncertain how well they could see him, said again, flatly, "No."

"The princess sent her sedan chair. In case you had fallen out here." Emyas had never liked Khadat's youngest son, and secure in the blood tie and her need for his skills attending to Hemit, he had never troubled to hide his dislike. Apodain liked most people, but he loathed Emyas. "It waits upon the road. Since you are not injured, you will get up and come with us, on your own feet." Apodain set his jaw; Emyas broke the silence. "This is the *order* of the princess, and you will obey it at once. Tell him, Reott," he added impatiently.

"Sir—by her charge to us," Reott began unhappily; Emyas made an impatient noise.

"Never mind—just do as you were ordered!"

A cage to bear him home to yet another cage—Apodain had never known panic in all his life, but he felt it now. He scrambled back, somehow gained his feet and would have pelted headlong down the slope, but he had sat so long and in such cold that his legs would not respond and the blood rushed from his head. A hard hand clamped around his biceps, fingers dug into muscles as he tried to pull away. Blackness teased his eyes and his mind, he swayed, felt himself pulled along, stumbling over stone and loose shards of rock. Reott caught hold of his other arm and bore him up. "Let go of me," he said, but the words were faint, the two men likely did not hear them. They would not have listened anyway.

He drew a deep breath, another; the horrid light-headedness receded. He stumbled, gasped as he was dragged sharply up and pain flared in both shoulders. And then the road was solid under his feet, the enclosed sedan chair and its two bearers a darker shadow on the wall-shaded road. Emyas let go his arm. *How dare he drag me about, like a sack of millet or my witless brother!* He had never been so angry in his life; he tore his other arm free. "How dare you, Emyas?" he demanded. "Keep your hands from me!" Emyas snatched at him; Apodain slapped the hand away and stepped back, away from both men. "If my mother wishes to see me, I will come—in my own good time!"

"Will you?" Emyas said softly. "Reott!" Reott looked very unhappy but he took one long step forward and his fist caught Apodain a hard blow just below the ribs, driving the air from his lungs and doubling him over. Apodain coughed, drew in a pained, wheezing breath, tried to stand back up; Reott's forearm slammed across the side of his neck and into his collarbone. Everything went blue-white; he fell.

There was pain everywhere: in his belly, flaring outward

from his shoulder and all down his arm. In the other arm,
pinned between his body and the road. Loose stone dug into
his ribs and his hip, cut his cheek. And then, for a blessedly
brief while, there was nothing. When he could again sense
and feel, he was securely trussed, hand and foot, a thick
cloth tied around his mouth and the sedan chair jolting up
the road toward the city gates. The cushions were soft, yield-
ing so he could get no purchase on them with his aching
shoulders or already numbed fingers to push himself upright;
the interior of the chair smelled strongly of his mother's favorite scented oil. With a sob that was anger and frustration,
equally mixed, he fell back into their clinging embrace, and
gave himself up for lost.

She was waiting for him in the courtyard, arms folded
across the formal dress she normally wore to banquets or to
deal with matters pertaining to Perlot's holdings and her
own vast trading company; she had thrown a cloak of his father's over, as she often did, either for warmth or the comfort of a thing once his. Apodain never dared ask such a
thing of her. The effect was daunting, as she had surely intended. She watched impassively as the two massive servants lifted him from the chair as though he were only
another of the pillows, waited until the bearers had taken the
chair away, then turned to lead the way into the house, and
into her personal accounting room. She indicated a low
stool, stood silently while Emyas thrust him onto it and lit
lamps from the low-burning fire.

"Shall I have your word to behave," she asked crisply, "or
will you sit there like that, bound and gagged, with these
servants to guard you, until I am done speaking to you?" She
leaned against the wall, eyed him closely, waited. Apodain
let his eyes close and sagged. Finally nodded. "Untie him,"
she ordered. Emyas undid the knots, pulled off the gag. "Go,
see to Hemit." They hesitated and Emyas frowned. "I have
his word, and the word of Perlot's son *should* have some
worth. He will not defy me any more this night. Go."

A long silence; Apodain heard the whisper of sandals on
smooth floor as the two men went by him, a draft and then
the door closing behind them.

He felt Khadat move away from him, heard the faint creak
of wood as she settled into her usual chair. "They tell me
Septarin came to see you today. What did he have to say to

you?" He shook his head. "You have behaved very badly, Apodain, particularly for a man who is of prince's blood and claims to be among the city's fighting elite. You have frightened me, upset the household—all because of whatever your young cousin said to you. Not even knowing if what he said was the truth."

He looked up. "And do you tell me he lied, if he says I am removed perforce from Ghezrat's fighting elite and made to wed with a Secchi?"

The silence was so complete, he could hear his heart pounding. Khadat looked at him for a very long time. "If he told you that, then he did not lie."

He swallowed. "Why?" It took a terrible effort to get that much out, a stronger one to continue to meet her eyes.

"Because I seek to save the life of one son," Khadat said. "This matter of the Secchi—it will be necessary for you to go through the formalities tomorrow, of course, but there will be time for me to change that part of the bargain later. I would not have agreed to that, had Pelledar been reasonable." She paused, waiting for comment, and when he made none, she added crisply, "You are acting very foolishly, Apodain. All that I have done for you—"

"All?" His voice rose alarmingly; he swallowed, licked his lips. "You have named me coward before the entire city!"

"You exaggerate," Khadat said flatly.

"I do not!"

"If that bothers you, we will concoct an acceptable reason why you have left the chariot company, and see it spread."

"Who will believe it? That Perlot's son coincidentally left his company just as the Diye Haff threatened? No man leaves his company with war looming, Mother, and once I swear troth to a Secchi the tale will be complete, and enough for anyone." He tore at his hair; the pain of that kept him from weeping.

"Why should you care what common men think? You are Perlot's son, as you constantly remind me. Does nothing else matter to you? Do *I* not count as much as the man who got you on me, and then threw his life away for a narrow bit of water and two small patches of sand and rock? Perlot's son," she went on bitterly. "And so, you want to fight the Diye Haff, so everyone will know you are truly Perlot's son."

"I want to fight as Father fought, to protect those who cannot protect themselves, to keep Ghezrat whole and safe!"

"Do not dare interrupt me," Khadat snapped. "And do not mouth the words of your commanders and your father at *me!*" Apodain looked at her bleakly, watched as she got to her feet and went to the table piled with scrolls, thick sheets of papyrus weighted down by a clay tablet. Watched listlessly as she poured wine, dipped water into the cup and brought it over to him. "You did not eat all this day, did you? Fool of a boy, here, take this, drink it all. Think as you do what I went through, abasing myself to your uncle, letting him even *link* our name with that of a common soldier's daughter!"

He drank; the liquid was cool, the alcohol eased the tightness in his throat. "Mother, I will try to appreciate what you went through, I know it cost you. But please consider my side of this! Think of the shame I feel, knowing men will name me coward whatever story you put about later. That shame will cover this entire house."

"Again, you exaggerate," Khadat said. She was standing over him, watching him closely. When he finished the wine, she took the cup, refilled it, and handed it to him.

"I do not exaggerate. Father would have understood."

"Your *father,*" Khadat exclaimed sourly, and the word sounded almost like a curse. Apodain, startled into silence, stared up at her. "Of course, he would have understood, he that died for no true cause at all. The city was safe, other men could have taken back the isthmus, if it was necessary. He threw his life away, and Hemit with him!"

"What they did kept a hundred or more men from dying, and who is to say that once the isthmus was in enemy hands, they would not have gathered strength, brought an army, and attacked the city itself? Mother, if men do not fight, if they don't do such deeds as Father did, do you think no one will die?"

"Do you believe that if *you* do not fight," Khadat said, even more bitterly, "the city will fall and all of us will die?"

"I did not say—"

"You said enough. More than enough. Be silent, and drink that." He closed his eyes, drank. Looked up finally to see his mother seated once more, studying him through half-narrowed eyes. "You are not resigned to this, are you? I know you, as I knew your father; you will try to find some way to circumvent me."

"I—" He closed his mouth. She had come altogether too close to the truth, just then.

"That will not happen. Because you will swear to me now, Apodain, on your dead father's lost spirit, to do nothing against this. You will go tomorrow and stand upon the prince's steps, and speak the vows with this wretched, common child, and you will show no sign that it is other than an honor, and of your own free will. Your chariot and your horses, the weaponry that was kept at your barracks has already been brought back here, your captain told you will no longer serve him or the city. You will let that stand. You will swear all of that, to me, now." She folded her arms across her chest, waited. He let his gaze drop to his feet.

"I—Mother, please." The words were the faintest possible whisper, nothing else would come.

"You will swear this," Khadat said, her voice implacable, the words falling on him like blows. "At once," she thundered. Silence. He had no strength left to fight her, only one last despairing thought. *She cannot force me to swear; I will not swear.* But he had underestimated her. "Swear," she said softly, "or I will give it out that I came home from Denota's Cleft with word of the coming invasion, and that you wept with fear and begged for any aid I could give, to keep the city walls between you and dread Haffat." His head came up and he gaped at her in openmouthed disbelief. Her face was hard, the voice was gentle by comparison, the words— "That you are brave Perlot's son only when the chariots fly across the plain in practice formations, as though such maneuvers were an extension of the games, an amusement to you. That once faced with true warfare and the threat of a bloody, painful death, you blubbered like a babe and soiled yourself, for fear of battle." The cup clattered to the floor and rolled away, spilling the remnants of mixed wine. Apodain wrapped his arms around his belly and bent over, moaning. "Do you think I would not do even this, in order to save you?" And, when he made no reply, she thundered, *"Answer me!"*

"I know you would," he whispered.

"Why?" Khadat knelt before him, hands cupping his face, her breath warm on his face, eyes searching his. "Why would I do this? Tell me why I would do this," she insisted softly.

"To—to save—to save me," he whispered.

"From dying foolishly," she prompted.

"Foolishly." His teeth chattered. Khadat released his face, sat back on her heels.

"Swear," she said.

"I swear—" he swallowed wine and bile, evilly mixed. "Swear—"

"By your father, by his lost soul, that you will remain compliant in this matter," Khadat said inexorably. "Swear."

He was sweating freely, shivering. He nodded violently. "I—I swear it." And, as she gripped his shoulders, "By—by my dead father, by his lost soul, I swear." If her hands had not held him, he would have fallen from the stool. Khadat gazed at him for one long, searching moment; Apodain saw her through a blear of exhaustion, tears, and utter defeat. And then she leaned forward and wrapped her arms around him, pulling his face onto her breast.

"Beloved son," she whispered. "I will keep you safe, whatever comes. I swear that, by the goddess, by all else holy to me—by Haffat's lion god itself, I will keep you safe." Apodain breathed in warm flesh, his mother's scent, the smell of linen and the stuff she used in her hair. *Stifling,* he thought dizzily. *Cannot—breathe.* He barely heard Khadat's concerned exclamation as he slid from her grasp and crashed to the floor.

Nevvia was still sleeping when Breyd woke the next morning and began the laborious task of climbing back into the leathers. Her fingers were a little swollen, making it hard to tie the knots. A shadow crossed the open doorway; she looked up to see her grandmother standing there, a steaming cup in her hands. "Let me see," she ordered. Breyd stood, tugged uselessly at the short skirt and felt very nervous. If Niddy acted like those women by the fountain—! But Nidya merely walked all the way around her and handed her the cup without comment.

Breyd wrapped her hands around the warm clay, inhaled deeply: unfermented grape, seasoned with honey and mint. "Thank you, Grandmother."

"Your father has been up since the gray hour." Nidya settled on the edge of the bed. "He said today would be as long and difficult a day for you as yesterday. I thought perhaps you should have something to warm you this morning, since yesterday you went off without. Ina has gone out for bread, she should return any moment." She watched as Breyd finished her drink, set the cup aside and went back to fastening leather greaves on her lower legs. "Yes," Nidya said finally. "I can see why Menlaeus would want you gone before your mother wakens."

Breyd shook her head, straightened the narrow baldric and settled the leather-covered sword sheath over her left shoulder. "She will need to see me some time." Nidya laughed quietly.

"Yes, certainly! But would you not prefer that I have some time to prepare her for this change? Has the boy seen you yet?"

"Not me, at least, not here," Breyd said. "He may have been in the streets yesterday when we came from the barracks, or later when they sent us home." She tugged at the waist of the leather cuirass, pulling it straight. "Niv did. I think she was just as pleased when I went back into the temple, so she didn't have to be seen with me."

"She isn't ashamed of you, Breyd, just—even Niv can see the change in you. You aren't just our little one any more. You're—a symbol for people. Don't look at me like that, I remember the last Secchi and I *know,*" Nidya added tartly.

"Oh." Breyd caught up the red cloak and after a few moment's confusion found the throat edge and fastening pin, refolded it, and set it across the end of her bedding.

"And of course, Niverren worries what Creos' family will think; they don't follow Denota's way very closely."

"I know."

"She is very fond of you, though," Nidya went on. "In fact, she and Creos will come to the presentation. They said they would come home early enough that I could also attend." Breyd shook her head in confusion. "The formal naming of Pairs, before the palace," Nidya reminded her. "And the formal swearing of the prechosen."

"And Mother. Will she come, too? Is she upset, Grandmother? I—I heard a little last night, Tar and Father, enough to guess some of what must have been said. I didn't ask for this, she can't think—"

"She is not upset with you, just generally upset," Nidya said flatly. "Certainly she does not believe you somehow bribed Denota to make you Secchi, but she isn't happy just now, and you know she would hate to weep in public. I don't think many of the mothers will come for the naming, though, do you? She will come to see it in better light, as time goes on—that Menlaeus is no longer in the fore with the other foot companies, but against the walls and so in less danger."

"Perhaps," Breyd said doubtfully. She shook her head. "I'm— Oh, Niddy, I wish it was all over, or that it wasn't happening. If only Tar could be in a real company!"

"Wish he'd never met Laius, while you make wishes," the older woman said dryly. "At least Tar has an *honorable* reason for not fighting—unlike Laius, who cannot be trusted with weapons lest he forget in his blind rages who is the enemy."

"Like his father, and his father's father." Breyd sighed. "I suppose one good thing comes of all this: Laius can no longer pressure Tar for me."

"Cannot honorably do so," Nidya said. She picked up the empty cup and got cautiously to her feet. "He expressed more outrage than your brother, before I sent them both away yesterday, and most of it because of your prechosen. I would avoid him, were I you." She walked over to the door. "Here is Ina, finally."

Breyd settled the cloak across her shoulders, fastened the case of javelins around her waist, and picked up the long spear. One end was caught under the chest that held her clothes and her sister's, and the winter bedding. *How did I get this wretched thing in here last night?* she wondered in mild irritation. Nidya turned to watch, her face impassive; Breyd finally freed the weighted end, eased the point along the floor. "Thank you, Grandmother."

"For what? The tea?"

"For everything," Breyd said. She wrapped her free arm around the old woman. Nidya's still-strong fingers dug into her forearm briefly, before she pushed away.

"You are all sharp corners and points, and the leather smells musty. I have a salve, somewhere, for the odor, we'll rub it in tonight." She leaned against the doorframe and folded her arms. "Do not let your brother upset you. Or your mother, her actions or her words. They both love you, remember that."

"I know. I will try."

Nidya leaned back a little to study her. "Yes, it will not be easy, will it? But you'll manage, I think." She smiled suddenly. "You know, when I was a girl, there were Pairs created. I was never in the way of being made Secchi, of course; Father had been lamed when the chariot he drove turned over, years before, and anyway he had the vineyards. I remember thinking how wonderful, that women should fight with the men and walk among them as equals, and I envied them the right to do that, to become heroes. Instead, we had to come and live within the city walls for—oh, it seemed a very long time, though it could not have been as long as it seemed, I suppose. I remember watching the companies go out of the city, one after the other, the Pairs last of all. And I thought then, how strange: one day a girl, with all a girl's household chores and daily routine; the next, striding through the gates with a sword and a long spear, to kill men." She sighed, sat quietly for a moment, then sighed again. "I do not remember that any of them did kill; probably not, since the enemy was kept far enough away that we were allowed to stand along the outer walls and watch the fighting, though all I ever saw was dust. And then, we went home, and everything had to be rebuilt because it had all been burned or torn down, and most of the crops had been trampled flat. Father was very annoyed." She shook herself and stepped into the courtyard. "Enough of my ramblings, come and eat."

Menlaeus came into the courtyard from the kitchen as Ina portioned out bread. He glanced cautiously toward the roof, and Nidya followed his glance. She nodded. "There will be plenty enough to do today, do not worry about either of them."

"I was going to go out and check on the vineyards this morning," Menlaeus said. He tore his bread into fourths and stuffed part into his cheek. "Tar will have to do it for me. We will need additional storage jars in there," he gestured toward the kitchen. "Whatever spare ones were left from the last shipment of wine to Erinion, he can load into the cart and bring. There might still be grain in the main storage, mostly millet, if I recall."

"Tar will manage," Nidya said. "Nevvia and I can sort out what we will need to fill the jars, and where and how to acquire it, she needs something to keep her busy and you've enough to worry just now. We have Niv, and I've sent for my grandson's son Xhem, they have enough children to take care of the herds. The boy's small but strong, and old enough to be of some use."

"Good. Yes. In your hands, then." Menlaeus finished his bread. "Daughter?" Breyd nodded, put the last of her bread in the leather pouch and got to her feet. He walked around her, tugged at the leather cuirass and shifted the javelin case so it hung down next to her leg instead of across her thigh, then stepped back to study the result. He smiled, shook his head. "I remember when you first were chosen by Tephys, and came home all in white and green, with ripe wheat encircling your hair. I thought, how strange it was, you looked like a child playing priestess, but not really a child." He cast a glance skyward. "We had better go now; I know Grysis, he will be very angry if we are late."

Haffat

The city of Mirikos sprawled untidily along the northern shore of the Sea of Delos. Unlike Idemito, its walls were low, in many places crumbling with age and neglect, or the city had long since outgrown them, but Mirikos had for long depended upon its excellent trading relations to serve as protection.

To the east sat the vast army of the Diye Haff, a sea of tents, and before all, clearly visible from the city and its harbors, the banners of Haffat and Axtekeles. A statue of the lion god cast or coated in gold gleamed in the early morning sunlight.

At such an hour, Mirikos normally bustled; today, she lay silent, and her people hid within their houses and ships, or stood staring and waiting upon the walls. The small Mirikosi army had gone out in the black hour before dawn, and stood, four deep, across the eastern road.

The wind blew steadily from the ocean, bringing welcome relief after the heat of the long desert march, and the mixed smell of salt, drying weed and fish.

Haffat sprawled in his high-backed throne before his tent, oblivious to everything but his next prize. At his right hand Knoe knelt, eyes closed, lips moving in silent prayer as he prepared for the morning ritual; two live white marsh birds lay crosswise before him, long legs and wings bound, eyes hooded. Haffat paid no need to Knoe, either; at his other elbow a scribe sat, cross-legged, writing as his emperor dictated.

"Say also to my brother, the Great King of Mirikos, that he shall not lose face by my offer, for how should he have the right, strength, or will to stand against Haffat and the will of Axtekeles? He will retain his birthright and the throne of his city—subject to the government Haffat brings—and all trade agreements as are his or the city's shall remain as they are. And he shall surely have the gratitude of his people, that Haffat did not fall upon Mirikos with death and fire and pillage, to leave her a leaderless and half-empty shell, as he was forced to do in Idemito, and in Pos Merno, and in Lebaryk.

"Let my brother think upon this, and ask himself if he will carry the deaths of his children into the afterlife, if he will see the end of his bloodline and the loss of all that is his before he himself dies. Or if he will live long and in peace, and accept his brother Haffat into Mirikos. Let him take counsel and pray if he will, but let him send back word before the sun retires from this day." Haffat paused, thought a moment, nodded. "Say all of that," he ordered the scribe, "and set my name upon it." The scribe came to one knee with his writing board upheld a short time later, the long document flattened between his hands, a puddle of blood-red wax at the bottom of it. Haffat removed the seal ring from his middle finger, set it carefully in the wax, making a large rectangular impression that contained his name, the ancient family glyph, and a beautifully detailed representation in the foreground of himself in profile, crowned; behind this, a war chariot, drawn by springing lions.

The scribe took back the writing board, touched a corner of the wax cautiously to test it, rolled the letter and tied it with cords, then got stiffly to his feet. Haffat nodded, gestured toward the silently waiting city. "Take this to my cousin Harunn, who waits with his escort to deliver it to my brother in Mirikos."

A long silence, which Knoe finally broke. "If you wish a reading," he began. Haffat shook his head.

"For Mirikos? I do not need it, Knoe." He rubbed his chin. "How long do you think it will be, before Harunn sends back word that the city is mine?"

Knoe chuckled grimly. "That, my master, depends only upon whether your *brother* Khoryios chooses to see his wives and young children strangled before he runs onto his sword, or if he chooses poison." He glanced at the sky, shrugged as Haffat turned to look at him impassively. "He may already have done so, knowing there is no other way for him and his."

"We were overlong on the march from Idemito," Haffat said. "Word doubtless reached him by other means, what happened to Idemito when they tried to refuse me."

"If not, he will have heard of Pos Merno, and Lebaryk, and each of the other lands you have made yours, between here and Diyet." He leaned forward to stroke soft white feathers.

"Tell me," Haffat said, "of this vision, and why you would have us remain here so many days." His deceptively mild gaze touched upon the priest, went back to the city walls. "I admit this last march was hard on many of my men, and difficult for all. But if most take ship south, they can rest as well on the sea as in this place, and even those who march will find the road easier than the one which led here." His gaze flickered across the priest, out across the camp where only a few men moved, aside from those ranked before all, where Mirikos could clearly see them. "Why give Ghezrat more time to prepare against us?"

Knoe sat back on his heels. "Because of a thing touching their goddess Denota, and their beliefs," he said. "It is said, Denota mated with Atos, sun god and brought forth the minor deities: those governing the fishes, the seas, rain—well, there are many of them, doubtless their own priests can put names to all of them. They also say that, on a time, Atelos the moon desired her, and he rose during the day to creep full across the sky, covering Atos and sending darkness to cover the earth, and during that dark, he ravished Denota. The next winter solstice, when Atos was well to the south and hid much of his light and warmth, Denota gave birth to three: Strife, Famine, Discord."

Haffat made an impatient noise in his throat. "And you believe all this?"

"My master," Knoe said evenly, "It is not necessary that I believe it, the Ghezrathi do. And it came to me in a dream, two nights past, that there will be such a day to come: the moon at full will rise during the day, and cover up the sun, and a momentary darkness will fall upon the city." He bent forward to stroke the birds again. "I spoke with your astrologer at once, but it was only this morning he could tell me what I wished to know."

"And this day will come—when?" Haffat asked.

"In forty-four days and four," Knoe said.

Haffat considered this in silence for some time. "The Ghezrathi will make good use of whatever days we give them."

"And so shall we. But it will still avail them nothing."

"And the other thing?" Haffat said. "Two who become one?"

Knoe indicated the birds before him. "For that purpose did I have these brought to me, to mingle their blood and learn what I can of it. But that thing, whatever it is, will also count for nothing. Axtekeles has promised you Ghezrat." He looked up, stood suddenly and gestured broadly, a sweep of hand that took in the city walls and the banners of Mirikos' young emperor. They were being brought down, and above the palace rose the white and gold lion of Haffat. "Just as he said he would give you Mirikos." He bent down to gather up his birds, and walked away. Haffat sprawled in his chair, eyes fixed on the distant city, but now the least of smiles curved his lips.

5

Tarpaen let himself out of the house and stepped into early afternoon shade. There were few people about, mostly women who congregated as usual under the porch sheltering the neighborhood source of water. He ignored them—easy enough since the pool was on his right, and his right eye the worse one. Those people on the street itself, he strode straight past or through, his expression forbidding, and they gave way before him.

Horrid, shrill-voiced gabbling and interfering women, sending me upon their women's errands. He growled a curse under his breath, broke free of the narrow alley and turned toward the barracks.

His last thought left an uncomfortable feeling in the pit of his stomach; it wasn't normally in him to think of his mother, grandmother, and sisters the way Laius spoke of women—those exact words, he recalled with even greater discomfort, Laius had used to describe his own mother, dead the past winter of the wasting disease. Nevvia had every right to be upset just now, with Breyd parading around in men's garb (though Nevvia hadn't actually seen her and those bare legs yet). Nidya had been nice enough to him this morning. *Be fair,* he told himself. *They've already apportioned Breyd's tasks among themselves.* The storage jars and extra grain were things his father would ordinarily handle, as he did all things concerning Nidya's vineyards.

Ten-year-old Xhem might even prove to be useful, picking up some of Breyd's chores, but Tarpaen really did not want to go fetch the boy. He avoided Xeric's poor farmstead and its milling pack of grubby brats and only vaguely recalled Xhem as one of the dirty-faced, howling little monsters. *Nidya might have waited for Father. I heard him offer to handle all this after the night meal, but no, she must send me instead—as if I were a nurse, to care for a small boy!* Both

Nevvia and Nidya had better remember that he was also a member of a distinguished company, a man with outside duties and not a wiper of young noses. *Hah. You send horn cries from the walls, what is distinguished about that?*

At the gate into the barracks, his feet slowed. His head still pounded with the previous night's wine, but unfortunately it hadn't been enough to let him forget the fighting: Laius trying to fight with him, him shouting wildly at his poor weeping mother. *But she should have seen my side, she wouldn't listen to me!* Then Laius baiting Creos, Creos' shouting back; Niverren's shrill voice as she tried to separate the two, until Nidya shouted them all down and threw her own grandson from the house. The rest of the evening was even more of a blur. He thought he remembered two wine-shops, or had it been three? His anger had vanished when Nidya slammed the door on his very heels, to be replaced by deep gloom that threatened to turn to tears at any moment. Only the certain knowledge Laius would openly jeer at him on the streets had kept him from *that* humiliation. Somewhere, much later, when the night air had turned cool and damp, he had a fuzzed memory of the fight Laius finally managed to start, smashed winejugs and shrieking patrons everywhere, then grim armsmen pulling Laius away and someone grabbing his arms, the captain of the horn and drum company glaring at him.

He didn't remember anything of the journey home, only that Nabid had handed him over to his father, and he had a vague memory of weeping copiously on Menlaeus' shoulder. He did not recall at all Nabid warning him to come to the barracks around midday, or that Laius was being held there; Menlaeus had to wake him at sunrise to tell him.

Nabid. Of all the evil fortune, that someone had called Nabid when the fight happened. The captain would be properly furious, he'd warned Laius against fighting, more than once.

Tarpaen's stomach dropped. If Nabid forced him from the company, what was left for him?

Despite the heat of midday, the barracks grounds were covered with fighting companies, many seated or standing in shade, tending to their weaponry, but most in full sun, honing their skills. In the case of the Dyaddi—at least, the Secchi—learning them. He could see young women clad in short tunics and dark, worn leathers, some near the wall of the common foot barracks, throwing javelins or thrusting with the long, counter-weighted spears at man-sized bundles of straw; he couldn't make out individuals and was not sure if Breyd were among them. Beyond those Secchi, more targets and first a few Secchi, then boys who stood farther back from the wall and loosed arrows from deeply curved horn bows. Farther down the courtyard still, separated from the company of common archers by a small distance for everyone's safety, the newest slingers wrapped cast iron stones in long linen bands and whirled them overhead, loosing them against a square drawn on the bare wall.

He slowed, reluctant to confront his captain just yet, peered toward the Secchi. It wasn't just his eyes, it was the clothing: Any of them might have been Breyd—any of the little ones, at least. He compressed his lips, turned away.

Several of the common chariot passed him, young and in many cases inexperienced drivers guiding horses at a walk across the courtyard and through the gates; most of the fighters here were older men, graying hair escaping from helmets, thicker bodies braced two-handed against the movement of the chariots. A thicket of javelins mounted on the outside of each car rose above the heads of driver and driven.

There was a large empty space on the fighting ground once they were gone. Tarpaen aimed for the messes where many of his company ate and slept, and where Laius was being held. Movement in the shade caught his attention as he passed; the royal chariot fighting company were grooming their horses, while the drivers went over newly reassembled cars. He checked his stride momentarily, caught by surprise. Unless his eyes deceived him more than usual, that was Prince Pelledar's skinny heir not five paces away, his loins covered by a short pleated kilt, a brightly colored bowcase strung across his back. The boy turned just then, to shout something at another of the company a distance away. Unmistakably Septarin, doing his best to draw attention to himself. *But he is at least two years under age!* Tarpaen realized he was staring; he dragged his mouth shut and hurried on.

Nabid was seated at the signal company's bench, talking to his second; as Tar hesitated in the doorway, Mip gestured, and the captain turned, then got to his feet and came across.

Tarpaen swallowed, touched his fist to his breast in salute and bowed, setting his head to pounding furiously. "Sir?"

"So you're about at last, young hornmaster," Nabid said sternly. "If you have come looking for Laius, he's yonder, in seclusion, and there he will stay for two more days. You are fortunate you weren't locked in there with him."

"Sir," Tarpaen said humbly, and swallowed once again. "Sir, I appreciate that."

"Do you? A man might wonder if you do." Nabid glanced over his shoulder. "Considering the company you keep and how you keep it. But I will not ask true sense of you, that you give over this carousing friendship with mad Lorus' son. No—you would not, would you?"

"Sir—sir, he's my friend. If I desert him—" Tarpaen shrugged helplessly.

"Yes. Well, I cannot fault loyalty. Ordinarily! However, I will accept your apology, and as proof that you mean it truly, you will swear to me I will never again find you as I did last night—drunken and fighting such a battle within the city. The Diye Haff are coming to kill as many of us as they can, we have no need to murder our own. Swear that."

"I swear it, sir." Tarpaen inclined his head once more, winced. Relief left him weak-kneed; if this lecture was to be the worst of his punishment, he could easily bear it.

Nabid studied him silently for some moments, finally shrugged. "Well. There is plenty for me to do today, you can go now. But remember my words! Because next time matters will not go so easily for you. Another thing," he added as he was about to turn away. "If you have any influence on your friend, persuade him to a course that involves less wine and fewer fights."

"Um—sir." Tarpaen blinked. *Influence—with Laius?* For the first time, it occurred to him that he had no such thing. Laius did what he wanted, and anyone who would be his friend went along with Laius, or went his own way. "I . . . will try," he said. The next words wanted to stick in his throat. "Thank you, sir."

"Ah," Nabid clapped him on the shoulder and actually laughed. "You're young, you'll learn, boy. Go, do what you can to make Laius see sense. I will not give him another such opportunity; he will find himself without a company next time. I told him as much; you tell him also, will you?"

"I'll tell him, sir."

"Yes. Do that. He's there, go, I'll let you have a little while with him. Remember the company meets here late this afternoon, third hour. After last night, you would be wise not to be late."

"Sir." Tarpaen saluted gravely, turned and sought the cell where Laius was held. Sweat ran down his temples.

As he had feared, he found Laius at least as hung over as he and in no good mood. Tar leaned against the door, watched as his friend paced back and forth; two steps each direction only brought him against the wall, for Laius was a long-legged bull of a man. Black eyes met Tarpaen's briefly; Laius collapsed on the bench set into the wall and growled, "Here, sit. Talk, tell me what our noble captain plans, or has he even told you?"

Tarpaen sat next to him, a boyishly lean figure against the older, solidly built Laius. Laius combed his thick beard with stubby-fingered, very hairy hands, settled his shoulders against stone, and listened impassively while his friend described the meeting with Nabid. Finally he shrugged. "He won't take me from the company, whatever he says; my family has a little influence, and they one and all prefer to keep me here, rather than have me a man of no company at all. And so does Nabid."

Tarpaen swallowed past a dry throat. "Are you certain of that? Because—well, I just remember the look on his face last night, and he was really very grim just now."

Laius considered this briefly, shook his head, and chuckled. "Ah, well. I myself recall nothing of last night, after your grandmother chased us away, and most of that was a blur. Personally, I believe Nabid will keep me here another day or so and pretend I've learned a lesson; I for my part will pretend I have, and both of us will know both of us lie."

Tar shifted uneasily. "Laius—"

The other clapped his shoulder. "Never mind, I'll be circumspect—at least until the Diye Haff come and they don't dare release me. Will that do to ease your mind?"

"All right," Tarpaen said. It wouldn't, really; it was still better than he'd hoped from Laius, who had made one of his sudden shifts of mood, from blackly ready to settle slights to cheerful lack of concern for anything.

"Good. Then tell me, what have you heard about these new rumors? The boy who brought my breakfast was full of them—that the prince bullied Brysos into taking his beardless son into the royal chariot. Not as a driver, mind you, as a fighter! Because, the boy says, Septarin is to take Apodain's place."

"Apodain's place? *Septarin?*" Tarpaen protested automatically. "But Apodain is Perlot's son—"

"—and the man trothed to your sister," Laius reminded him. Tarpaen waved that aside for the moment.

"Perlot's son; everyone says he'll have command of the royal chariot when Brysos goes."

"Not now, will he?"

"Without any warning? What—was he taken ill?"

"I thought that, at first. Now I think on it, I remember someone last night saying he'd seen Perlot's boy staggering from the gates yesterday, looking as though he'd drunk tainted wine or taken a spear in his guts. But there was nothing said today of sickness or injury." Silence. Tarpaen stared at Laius, uncomprehendingly. "The boy says all the talk in the royal chariot and across the courtyard is that no reason whatever was given. There was a request, properly approved by the prince, and ffft—" Laius spread his hands wide, "no more Apodain!"

"You're saying he simply left? But Apodain would never give over his place!"

"The boy knows for fact that his horses and panoply were sent for yesterday evening, and that the company was told this morning when they arrived that he was no longer one of them. No reason spoken, but, of course, he's noble," Laius added, as though that explained everything. Tar shook his head again. "Did you see him out there just now?"

"You know how well I see anything," Tar said gloomily. "But I did see Septarin, all kilted and armed and making certain everyone was aware of him."

Laius snickered. "Yes, I don't doubt that. I want to knock the feet from under him when I see him swaggering about. I wager even you could count his ribs from ten paces away! He'll kill half the men in his company, trying to fill his own sandals. But Apodain—" he prompted.

Tarpaen shrugged. "I didn't see him."

"I wonder which of the rumors is true. The boy said some say his mother sent for his things, but she runs that household as if she were Perlot himself, come back to life; others say he came with the servants, to make certain all his armor and weapons were piled neatly into the pretty chariot his mother bought him." Laius rubbed his shoulders against rough stone, cast his companion a keen glance. "And this is the man your sister has been prepromised to? He's a filthy coward!"

"You don't know that, Laius. Father wouldn't—"

Laius clapped his shoulder, and Tarpaen fell silent. "No. Menlaeus would surely never permit such a joining," Laius said thoughtfully, after a long moment.

"Permit?" Tarpaen looked at his friend incredulously. "Laius, Father has no say in the matter, least of all against one as powerful as Khadat!"

"Why would Khadat want a match with a lowly Secchi for her last precious baby?" Laius smirked. "You know the stories about Khadat, Tar, the woman is a monster. She will never allow Apodain to wed anyone, lest any part of him be taken away from her."

To his annoyance, Tarpaen could feel himself blushing. "But that's not— Laius, you can't think that—"

"I have drunk enough wine with Khadat's household servants, and it seems to me," Laius went on flatly, "if Apodain *has* left the chariot, his mother is behind it. Though if she is half the monster they say, doubtless the lovely exterior *he* presents to the world is mere shell. To me, he has always looked too good to be what he seems anyway. Now, why would the nephew of our city's king ask to be put on the prechosen list?"

"How would I know?" Tarpaen asked sourly. "And why does it matter? It has been settled by the prince and the priests—and, they would tell you, by the goddess herself."

"Bah. It matters because I would know what Apodain has done, and why." Laius flung his arms wide. "Because I do not like Apodain at the best of times. Even less, now he has been trothed to your sister. Besides, I have nothing else to occupy my time for a day or so. Well?" Tarpaen shrugged. Laius cast his eyes up. "So. There is nothing Prince Pelledar could give Apodain or his mother that they need—unlike others on that list. No reason for Apodain to choose it, what man would have that much charity in his heart? Unless you will say he sees it as an escape from Khadat. Better, perhaps he saw your sister on a time and conceived desperate longing for her." He snickered; Tarpaen managed a faint grin in response. *He* thought of Breyd as a beauty, even Laius did, though most did not; Khadat would certainly see her as small, dark, skinny, common and foreign-looking, particularly when compared with her handsome, beautifully molded Apodain. "No reason, then, on his part. On Khadat's, even less. Unless he is indeed coward, and he or Khadat, or both together, had to make that bargain."

"It doesn't follow," Tarpaen began.

"Ah? But the boy who brought my food says he has already heard the prince's gangly heir say Khadat's household was all upside down after the prophecy, what with Apodain puking and wringing his hands and weeping." Laius looked at him. "Have I not always said the man had no substance?"

Tarpaen could not recall Laius having ever said any such thing; he had always thought Apodain an upright and handsome figure. But Laius—Tarpaen shrugged, and took the course of least resistance. "Of course. But this is merely rumor, and such ugly rumor. Um—what if Septarin likes Apodain no more than you do, and takes this as an opportunity to smear his reputation?"

"Hah." Laius turned his head and spat against the wall. "A man would think you liked Apodain."

"No, I don't like *or* dislike him. But I do not like that kind of rumor, either, Laius. Remember the stories we heard against you, the last time you sought to change companies?"

"Ah. But none of that was true; this may be. No matter. It will come out eventually. If Apodain does nothing, says nothing, and takes no part in his company," Laius sat up, touched his friend's knee, "then I say Apodain is a coward, and no mate for your sister."

Tarpaen gazed at him, perplexed, finally heaving himself to his feet and beginning to pace the cell himself. "I—Laius, truly there is nothing I can do in the matter! Father considers it done, all the family does."

"Even though it so badly upsets your mother? I thought there was nothing he would not do to keep his household from her upsets."

"Well—well, yes. But this!"

"There are ways around such things, even for a common soldier. I know. Of course," Laius went on sarcastically, "*you* still believe Denota chose all thirty-four Pairs Herself, don't you? That there was nothing else involved besides the goddess picking those who would best serve?"

"Well, of course I don't! But Laius, we are talking about Breyd. You can't believe she deliberately forced the choice, can you?" Laius grinned hugely and shrugged.

"Why not? She is a favorite of the priestess, and you tell me so often how she dotes on her father's company."

"But if that is so, why do *you* want to wed her still?"

Laius considered this very briefly, shrugged again. "Because I know her." He met his young friend's eyes and grinned once again; his teeth were very white against the huge black beard. "Because I find her very pleasant to look upon, and acceptable company for the few hours a man spends in the house, and because I know she has been well trained to run a household. Will you have me say as well I am fond of her? All right, then, I am fond of her."

"But she—"

"You will say she does not care for me. But since when has that mattered? Once she realizes what manner of whining infant she has in Apodain, she will surely be willing to sever that bond and contract to me."

"Well—" Tarpaen temporized helplessly.

"And, of course," Laius went on, his voice dropping from its usual booming, carrying level, "if something were to befall Apodain, before the Pairs were dissolved and she *must* marry him—" He tipped his head onto one side, watched Tarpaen.

Tar stared at him blankly; as the other man's meaning sank in, he fell back against the wall and gaped. "Laius! You don't dare say such things!"

"Say them? What did I say?" He leaned to one side, gazing beyond Tarpaen. "Here comes someone, you had better go. Take that silly look from your face," he added impatiently. "I never suggested *you* kill the man, did I?"

"I—" Tarpaen turned on his heel and practically ran from the cell, brushing past the boy who stood near the doorway, bread and a jug in his hands.

Once outside, he stopped and leaned back against the wall of the barracks to wipe damp hands down his tunic. He squinted, sent his eyes across the companies scattered around the yard. The royal chariot company was nearest him; Septarin stood next to a fine blue and yellow car, a spear topping his dark hair by at least an arm's length, the butt trailing the ground, impatience twisting his young mouth as an older man tried to explain something to him. Laius had the right of *that* one, at least. Septarin wouldn't take well to instruction and would be more dangerous on a battlefield— *Than I would,* he thought bleakly. *But I could*

*at least throw straightly; I could use the eyes of my driver
to see for me, where to throw. They know this, and they take
a skinny boy into the fighting companies but not me.* He
swallowed painfully and turned away.

To his other side, some of the Secchi, with their Primes
behind them, were learning to throw javelins; other Secchi
stood in full sun with swords in hand, practicing very basic
crossings with their Primes. No sign of Breyd among those,
but looking along the nearby line, he could make out his father. And then, the small figure before him drawing back
and releasing her short spear, and a delighted laugh, undeni-
ably Breyd's. Tarpaen shoved away from the wall and
stalked across the grounds, heading toward the exit. She was
enjoying herself. Enjoying herself! *I nearly felt sorry for her,*
he told himself bitterly. Septarin swaggering about the field
while he was doing errands for his grandmother, and his sister played at soldier! Whichever of those two men she finally wed, rough Laius or cowardly Apodain, she deserved
what she got. Tarpaen paused in the gates to send one last
black look in her direction; from so far across the ground, he
couldn't even tell if the Secchi were still at practice.

The main road was crowded for the time of day: Laden
carts and donkeys heading in packed with grain and other
dried goods in case the enemy went to siege; companies going out to practice maneuvers on the sandy plain away from
either river and the farmlands, or returning from those maneuvers. Other carts bore raw ore and wood for the weapons
makers. Tarpaen wove in and out of the traffic, walking rapidly in spite of the heat, and arrived at Nidya's vineyards in
short order. The hired family who lived in the little hut next
to the canal and saw to the vines was out working; Tarpaen
found one of the daughters minding her younger brothers
and sisters, told her he was taking things from the barn, and
left before she could say more than a startled, "Sir." He
loaded the cart with long, pointed jugs, hitched the donkey
up, and led it away.

The boy next, he thought. Better to return to the city with
the boy in charge of this cart, rather than himself. Better to
make one trip of it, in any case; Nabid had sounded quite serious that he shouldn't be late, though ordinarily the rules
for trumpet and drum company practice were lax, and Nabid
seldom enforced them. Remembering Nabid's anger the

night before, and his set face an hour earlier, Tarpaen thought it might be an excellent idea not to press his luck.

At first he wasn't certain if he could find his cousin's small plot of land, so seldom did he come this way. There was no cause. He and the much older Xeric had little in common. Tar was a city man, member of a company; Xeric had been wed for nearly as many years as Menlaeus, with seven older children to tend his goat herds and weed his garden plot and help care for his wife Lyra's doddering parents and for the babies. The land itself had come through Lyra's mother: a dry, sloping parcel with a well that went dry on odd years. Their sustenance was a few huge olive trees that kept them, most years, along with the grapevines that Nidya had given them on Xeric's marriage, though they had never flourished as they did on the fertile plain between the rivers. As Tar led the donkey onto the narrow path that led to his cousin's hut, he could see the pitiful small clusters of purple, dusty fruit through thin ranks of leaf. At the far end, a child was calling for help, trying vainly to pull two skinny goats away. Tar hesitated, shook his head, and plodded on; goats were something he knew nothing about.

As he drew close to the hut, he could hear voices—too many of them, too shrill. Down the hill, the child was still calling for help; sound assaulted his head from both sides. He winced, clutched at his temple with his free hand. A face appeared briefly in the doorway, another voice was added to the cacophony within—and then, sudden silence.

A stick of a boy, all thin arms and legs, long feet, and a head seemingly too large for narrow shoulders and the over-large, still damp tunic draped over him, stepped into the sunlight. He stopped short at sight of Tarpaen, then bowed very deeply indeed. The tips of his ears went red, curly dark hair fluffed wildly, and the back of his neck was much paler than the rest of him—as though someone had just washed his hair and hacked it short. *Poor boy,* Tarpaen thought in sudden and unexpected sympathy. *Everyone in the city will know him for a peasant, and the other boys will ridicule him.* He knew all too well how that felt; he dropped the donkey's lead rope and came across the hard-packed dirt to clutch the boy's shoulders.

"Here, that's the respect you give a noble or a prince, not a cousin," he said roughly, and gave the boy a shake and—when Xhem glanced up, startled, what he hoped was a friendly grin. "You are Xhem, I take it? You're so tall, I wouldn't have known you."

"Everyone says that, this past year," Xhem said ruefully, and cast up his eyes, but the thin shoulders relaxed briefly. "You are my cousin Tarpaen?" Before Tar could answer, a heavy, graying woman emerged from the house, her expression grim. She caught sight of Tarpaen, blinked, and Xhem turned. His body tightened under his cousin's hands. "Mother, it's my cousin Tarpaen, come to fetch me."

"Earlier than we had thought," Lyra managed after a moment. "I intended a meal, at the least, for your trouble."

A meal? Here? Tarpaen brought up a smile, and manners he must have absorbed from his father, somehow. "My apologies, dear cousin, I haven't time, my company meets today and there wasn't anyone else to come, no other time for me."

"Ah. Yes." Lyra was clearly hungry for gossip, uncertain how to pursue it. "I would have thought Menlaeus would come for the boy, since we see him most often, him and your sister Breyd." Avidly curious eyes met his. He gave her another smile, kept the sudden surge of anger from his own face. "Since of course this—this *other* matter has claimed his attention, and then Grandmama Nidya's message only came yesterday evening, when I was at the milking. But of course we can manage without Xhem, and Nidya says both Menlaeus and Breyd no longer help in the household." She considered this, added quickly, "And yourself, of course, you are busy upon the walls, aren't you? Tell Nidya we will come into the city only when there is no other choice, lest others take our harvest and our olives. That happened when Xhem was a baby, you know, and Xeric insisted the Bejini might murder us all and fire the hut." She cast a resentful look toward the interior of the hut, then turned back and settled her chapped fists on her hips. "You, son, a few last words to you: You will keep your face and your ears clean, yourself neat and quiet. You will do all that Nidya and Nevvia order, and with a smile and good manners, and you will—" She droned on and on. Xhem, after one brief, red-faced glance at Tarpaen, fixed his eyes just in front of his bare toes and would not look up; moved only his head, to nod when his mother paused in her headlong speech. "You will not shame us, in any fashion," she said.

She embarrasses him, Tarpaen thought. *As if he does not*

*look old enough and clever enough, both, to know what is
expected of him, without his mother's words. As if he has not
already heard all of her words twice since sunrise.* Or more,
judging by the speed and ease with which the words ran off
Lyra's sharp tongue. He took hold of the boy's shoulder and
drew him over to the cart, stopping her in mid-sentence.

"Cousin Lyra, I truly beg your pardon, but I have little
time left to return home and still reach my company. We
must go now. Have you," he asked Xhem directly, "any bundle to bring with you?"

"A small one, a moment," Xhem said woodenly, and
darted into the gloomy little hut. Xeric came back out with
the boy a moment later, patted him on the back, and said
merely, "Greet your grandmother and the household for us."

"Father." Xhem hugged him quickly, then tossed the
woolen pack in among the jugs—probably a single change
of tunic, Tarpaen realized, for what else would a child of
such a poor household own?—took hold of the rope and
tugged, bringing the donkey around so they could head back
down the track. At its end, he turned and waved, then followed Tarpaen out onto the road.

They reached the main road in silence: Xhem glanced
over at his older cousin now and again, more often at the
great walled city still some distance away and high above
them on its rocky promontory. The rest of the time, he
seemed to be concentrating with an unnecessary intensity on
leading the donkey and high-piled cart. *What,* Tarpaen wondered wearily, *did awful Lyra tell the boy about me, to make
him ashamed of my company?* As they moved from the
dusty track onto the wide main way and the crushed stone
surface, the boy winced. Tarpaen touched his arm to get his
attention. "Let's stop; I need to shake the dust from my feet.
Have you sandals?" Xhem nodded cautiously. "Put them on,
you'll cut your feet on the stones otherwise." He knocked
his own sandals against the cart wheels, dislodging a cloud
of dirt. *Did she say I was weak, or incapable of fighting? A
drunkard, or simply no man at all, that I do not carry weapons?* He swallowed. *Find out.* "Why have you gone so quiet,
boy?" His voice came out harsh, overly loud and he jumped
at the sound of it.

Xhem was sitting on one of the dressed blocks of black
rock that edged the south border of the road. His ear tips had

gone red once more, and when he looked up, so were his cheekbones. "Um. My mother said that if I was a bother, didn't do what was asked, if I chattered, you'd send me home at once." His eyes moved up the city wall. "I don't want to go home without seeing *that* from inside," he mumbled, then looked up, eyes wide and frightened, as Tarpaen leaned against the cart and laughed.

"Ah, never mind, boy," he said finally, and wiped his eyes. "You won't be sent home on my account. Certainly not for talking to me as we go. And I promise you, I need your help to get these things into the city." Xhem bent low over his sandals, fixed the knots and got back to his feet. The shoes were too long for him, and he walked anxiously as he tugged at the donkey's lead and got him moving again. "We can do better for you than those," Tarpaen added. Xhem mumbled something that sounded like, "Thank you." "You'll need something you can run on hot stone streets in. Or carry water."

Silence, but a companionable one. A small group of common chariots came thundering down the hill, heading toward the mole; Tarpaen took the donkey's lead and pulled him from the road until the horses and plain cars were gone. Xhem stared after them, eyes and mouth round with amazement; his cousin had to take his arm to get his attention and it took both of them to get the suddenly stubborn little donkey back onto the road. "Oh," Xhem breathed. "I never saw such a thing!"

"Never saw chariots?"

The boy shrugged. "Well, from a distance, now and then, but all we can see is the shape of the car and the horses. Never like this, so close I could see men's faces and their armor!" He transferred the wide-eyed look to his older cousin. "Does your company have chariots, and horses?"

Tarpaen drew a deep breath, expelled it in a loud rush, and explained briefly about his eyes, about the signal company. The road tilted up, began to work back and forth across the face of the steep cliff toward the gates. "It's not," he finished reluctantly, "a fighting company. At least, some of us go into the midst of battle, but a few like myself cannot." He glanced over at the boy but the look of disenchantment he fully expected wasn't there.

"Oh, but, your eyes, that is Fate, isn't it? My father says so, when such things happen. At least you have a company, my father never would, nor any of his kind. And—and at least you appear like a warrior." Tarpaen scowled at him in surprise, and Xhem reddened, fumbled for words. "I mean, that, you are tall and muscled, and you wear a long dagger on a baldric, not a short knife at your waist the way a farmer does. You stride—" He shook his head.

"I walk fast because I fear to be late," Tarpaen said as dryly as Laius would have, but his young cousin's words touched him. *Who has ever looked up to me? Yes, it's only a rough child, a farm boy; once he's had some days in the city, he will see me as others do—only half-blind, useless Tarpaen.* But an idea struck him. Xhem, busy gazing at the troupe of slingers being marched single-file down the road, didn't notice his companion had gone very quiet.

They passed through the main gates, were stopped briefly at the inner ones. Tarpaen took hold of one side of the donkey's halter, gestured to Xhem to take the other. "There's little room, keep a close hold on him." To his credit, even with so much distraction all around him, the boy kept his attention on the beast and cart, and on getting through the heavy traffic of the outer city. Tarpaen glanced up at the sky, at the shadow cast along the tower that stood before the barracks, recalled the last horn he had heard, and made up his mind. "We'll go this way first. Come on." Xhem looked bewildered but obediently tugged at the donkey. "There won't be time enough to unload first." He led the cart into the broad street that ended at the barracks, located one of the messenger boys he knew by sight and fished a three-sided copper *klept* from his belt. "Here, Ilyon, mind this for us, will you? Another *klept* when we return." He nodded to Xhem, who had been exchanging wary glances with the messenger; he came away from the cart, looking around curiously. "How," Tarpaen asked mildly as they crossed the road, "would you like to see my messes? And my company?" A look of speechless delight was his only—and gratifying—answer.

He held out his hand and the boy took it. *This is how it would have been if I'd had a little brother,* Tarpaen thought. *Someone to look up to me, someone to care about and show things, teach things.* He'd go back to Xeric and Lyra once the war was over, of course. But that could be a long time. And for now— "Tell you what," he said impulsively. "You know, you and I will be together a lot from now on—like brothers. If you like, you can just call me Tar, instead of cousin."

"Tar," Xhem said thoughtfully. "My brother Tar."

"I never had a brother," Tarpaen said. "So I just thought—"

"I have brothers," Xhem replied. He smiled again, and Tarpaen felt his face grow warm. "But never an older brother. I would like that, Tar, very much."

Some time later, with the sun slanting deeply toward the Great Sea and shadow thick on the streets, they retrieved the cart and moved through the maze of streets. Tarpaen stopped finally at the end of his narrow street. "Wait here, I'll bring someone from home to watch this while we unload it." Xhem nodded. He still looked like a peasant, Tar thought critically—even with the bronze badge Nabid had pinned to his tunic, as the company's mascot and runner. That mangled hair, those sandals. The wide-eyed astonishment at everything around him.

But the hair would grow, they could find him other sandals, Nidya could afford to buy decent cloth to make the boy a better tunic that wasn't handed-down, undyed and poorly spun wool. Eventually, he'd learn his way around the streets and become used to them. In time, he might even find spending his few spare hours running messages and errands for the horn company to be commonplace.

He might decide that Tarpaen—whom he now adoringly referred to as, "my brother Tar" was unworthy of such hero worship. But Tarpaen felt an unaccustomed warmth under his ribs as he skirted the crowd at the fountain.

Atos' final rays lay upon the broad, white steps of the palace, turning them to fire. The gates to the horse-forecourt had been thrown wide to let in as many of the people as could fit; more blocked the broad avenue, and still others had climbed onto the inner walls to watch the public investiture.

The Pairs stood along the top two stairs, Primes behind, Secchi before, clad alike in fighting gear and fully weaponed. Atos touched bronze armor and points, silver pins, iron buckles, sent shards of light back among the crowd. Prince Pelledar stood to one side, Denota's priests and priestesses at his back, Tephys before him; he gestured. Silence.

"I give to you, Ghezrat, your innermost ring of safety against the Diye Haff. Welcome them, who sacrifice much to protect us all, men who leave their companies and a way of fighting long known and familiar to learn another; maidens, who forsake mother and hearth and the gifts which are women's, to put on men's gear, take up men's weapons, and slay the city's enemies. Welcome these, who bear the love of Denota and the strength She instills in them, the mysteries with which She surrounds them that no enemy has ever broken their ranks."

Breyd stood before Menlaeus, trying to ignore stiff muscles and pain along the inside of her right arm that flared down into her shoulder blades. *My face must be so red; look at all those people, the way they look at us.* She couldn't find a single familiar face in the enormous crowd below them. Pelledar stopped speaking; the crowd roared its approval of the pairs and Lochria leaned close to her, speaking softly under cover of that cheer: "All those people, the way they look at us! You would think we were glowing, or something." Breyd glanced at her in surprise. "Or heroes from the old tales come to life. Of course, it may be merely relief, that we are not *their* daughters."

"Well," Breyd said doubtfully, but just then, she found a familiar face: Nidya. And next to her, Ina. Niverren and Creos stood just behind the two women. *I thought they were too ashamed of me to come.* No sign of Tarpaen—well, she hadn't expected him, or the farm-boy cousin who'd looked at her so warily when she and Menlaeus finally came home from a long day's weaponry workout, and so adoringly at Tar. It bothered her, and she wasn't certain why: after all, why wouldn't a farm boy gape at her? Everyone else did. At least she wouldn't have much to do with Xhem.

Tephys came forward to invoke the goddess and her blessing upon the Pairs, and then another blessing upon the prechosen and the marriages which would eventually come of these. *I forgot about this,* Breyd realized with a guilty start. Lochria had brought it up, Menlaeus had, and Niverren had said something; she hadn't thought about her eventual husband otherwise. *Well, but, with everything else—and because I know I will never live long enough to marry him or any other man. But what does it matter? I have no more say now than if Father chose.*

Menlaeus laid a hand on her shoulder, gentle reminder to pay attention. Tephys finished her prayer and walked partway down the steps, halting several stairs below the Secchi and directly in the middle of the line. Young men, clad all in white and each bearing a formal sheaf of three ripe wheat stalks, three poppies and three cornflowers, came from the palace; the first of them halting on the step below the First Secchi, the rest made a compact group behind him. Breyd eyed them sidelong, brought her eyes resolutely forward again. Her young man would be at the end of that line, and suddenly she was frightened. *Will they expect me to give him the welcoming kiss—before everyone?* Had anyone said? She couldn't remember.

Meronne walked the length of the stair, touched the first prepromised on the brow, then turned to walk back; the boy followed. Meronne placed his hands upon the shoulders of the first Secchi in line, said something in a voice too low to be heard by anyone else. The boy nodded and spoke, the Secchi said something. He handed her the sheaf and stayed where he was, facing her. Meronne went around them, back along the stair.

Oh, no. Breyd swallowed. At least she would not have to stand like that for very long; Eriana must be ready to sink through solid stone, with everyone including a strange young man staring right at her. Secchi to First Prime would be the last of the women; very few people were looking at her just now. She shifted her weight cautiously. Aching muscles were trying to freeze up, she would surely fall when she had to walk again. Her eyes sought Nidya; her grandmother would know how this bothered her. Niv was talking to Creos, of course, probably something to do with her own bride-box. *Am I becoming like her, my thoughts fixed upon myself?* Uncomfortable notion. But she had cause just now.

The line of prepromised was diminishing, the line of young men on the step nearing where she and Menlaeus stood. And then Meronne stood before Lochria with a short, softly overweight young man in very finely woven silk, who stuttered as he spoke the binding words and turned a brilliant red when he handed his prechosen wife the sheaf. Lochria's response bore no trace of her dry humor, and Breyd risked a glance at her. The two could not have looked less suited to each other, but she would have sworn both were pleased. Menlaeus touched the back of her arm, reassuring presence as much as warning to pay heed.

She swallowed, blotted her palms against an inner fold of red cloak, and brought her chin up. *Remember what Niddy said; if you cannot at least pretend pleasure, manage a little polite interest.*

She went still with shock. Apodain, dead Prince Perlot's son stared at, or possibly through, her. *Apodain?* Everyone knew him, of course; his skill in the games was as legendary as his physical beauty. No bright smile—she would not have expected it; but the vitality was gone, too. *What has happened to him?* He looked almost worse than Hemit, as though something had burned out the core that was Apodain. His jaw was set, his eyes wide, expressionless, and she wasn't even certain he saw her. *I—is it because of me that he looks so awful?*

Meronne's face was thrust between them; Apodain started and Breyd caught her breath in a gasp. The old priestess gave her a grim look, lifted Apodain's hands and set them on the Secchi's shoulders; they were heavy and limp, and hurt muscle already painful from overuse. "Speak the words after me," Meronne ordered softly. "I, Apodain," she paused; after a very long moment she nudged him and he repeated the words, "do swear to the Prime and to the Secchi, that when this Pair is dissolved, by end of war, or by injury that prevents further fighting to the Prime, or death to the Prime—" Breyd flinched at that; Apodain snatched his hands away. Meronne glared at both of them, grabbed his hands, put them back on her shoulders and continued. "I shall take the responsibility of this woman from this man, and wed with her, that she shall thereafter be my wife and that such dowry as the city and my prince grant me—" She had to pause there for a long time; Apodain could not seem to force the word 'dowry' between his lips. "And I shall keep her safely, for all her days." Meronne waited for Apodain to finish speaking, finally hissed, "The bundle—give it to her!" Apodain let his hands slide away; Breyd tried to ignore her aching shoulders and concentrate on finishing this dreadful and humiliating ceremony. He held up the sheaf and she reached for it and her fingers brushed against his; his hand jerked, the bundle fell to the steps. Meronne retrieved it, mumbled a prayer over it, and thrust it at Apodain. He managed to keep his arm steady this time; Breyd clutched it tightly. Her face was burning; everyone must be staring, whispering, wondering why Apodain—why they were taking so long. They would attach significance to the bundle; Niverren certainly would. *A simple trader, a merchant—it would have been enough, how dare they put me in people's eyes this way?*

Tephys' voice pierced her thoughts. The prechosen turned to face the crowd, but Apodain shifted only after Meronne prompted him with a sharp-fingered poke and a hissed warning. She had another jab for Breyd and the words, "Pay heed, irreverent child!" *Irreverent!* That was so unfair! Apodain's thick curls were on a level with her nose; the scented oil he used on them expensive and pleasant, a change from the cloying stuff her mother rubbed into her hair and skin. His shoulders were dark with sun, all smooth muscle. He was trembling, she realized, as though so exhausted, he could only remain on his feet by will alone. *What has he done to himself? I saw him last year, when he ran from the gates to the sea and back, he had strength left to smile and wave at the crowd when he was finished!* Was he ill? *But—it must be me, the shock of seeing what was chosen for him, he is noble and beautiful, and I—* She could feel the blood making bright spots on her cheekbones. There was nothing in her or about her to warrant such a mate; he, in turn, would be so ashamed of her he would never speak to her, or look at her if he could help it.

The crowd began to disperse, but those on the steps remained where they were. Breyd turned her head to look at her father, then leaned out a little to gaze down the lines. Meronne was at the other end talking to Tephys.

And then she saw Khadat. The woman was standing on the first landing, arms folded; she looked very angry. Breyd drew back hastily. Apodain's head turned; he went absolutely rigid and she heard him swallow. *It becomes worse; I forgot about Khadat.*

The horse-forecourt was empty once more, the gates closed. Tephys raised her hands. "You managed that quite well, all of you. Go now." All along the line, young men turned to speak with their future wives; she heard Lochria's merchant stutter out a friendly good-bye. *He must say something now.* She was wrong; Apodain walked away without a backward glance, straight down the stairs. Khadat moved to intercept him. He slowed; she stepped back so he could precede her. She did not look back, either.

Breyd could feel herself trembling. Menlaeus came around to her side. "He acted like I was unclean!"

"No," he replied. "I think he must be unwell, and Khadat merely worried about him."

"But—why Apodain?" she whispered.

"They did not say." Menlaeus shook his head. "Some matter between Khadat and the prince, I suppose; they do not tell us such things, you know."

"But—why me?" She was blinking rapidly to keep angry tears at bay.

"Secchi to the First Prime," he replied automatically. She turned to look at him; he shook his head.

"The way he looked at me—"

"No. Don't distress yourself, child. There must be something wrong with him, it isn't you. Come, everyone else has gone. We don't belong here any more."

6

Prince Pelledar stood in the west window of his throne room, staring out toward the sea. Two Ghezrathi ships were tied along the inner edge of the mole and another stood off in deep water awaiting its turn; men worked furiously to unload them. A constant stream of carts went back and forth between mole and city; the main gates had been thrown wide and so had the Sheep's Gate, the Shepherd's Gate and the Goat Gate. The square just inside the main gates was clogged with people, carts, and donkeys at the moment, blocking the phalanx of light infantry trying to make its way down to the plain for drill. All along the wide avenue leading uphill, he saw carts: men selling storage pots, women crowding around to buy. Men and women fought their way through the square and along the wide streets hurrying to and from the markets in search of whatever storable food was available, and outside the main gates farmers and villagers sold bags of dried grains, rice, and lentils, baskets of dates and raisins, long strings of peppers and figs, laying birds in woven cages. *Anything that will keep people alive if there is a siege; also, whatever will fall into the hands of the Diye Haff should we lose the plain,* Pelledar realized. There would be no herders or farmers left outside the city's walls once Haffat came; they would be crammed inside the city's walls. The morning reports said many villagers were already coming in to seek shelter. Before long there would be nothing left for the outsiders but canvas strung across the ends of narrow alleys, or ancient, crumbling clay huts built for families of five or six which would house twenty or more.

He turned away from the window. *My father must have managed such matters, surely Grandfather did. How did they do it?*

He turned around and sighed. It could never have been with the aid of such a divisive council as his. Today it would be even worse, for the usual seven noblemen and women had been joined by the priestess Tephys and Eyzhad, who knelt at her feet, by the sun-priest Vertumnus, and General Piritos. They sat on the long semicircular bench facing the throne, and Pelledar knew they must be impatient with him for wasting so much of their time, though even Piritos had kept his grumblings to himself this once and listened with the others as Pelledar's chief secretary read yet another of the mass of messages brought by the master of the Luccerosan trading ship presently docked at the mole. The shipmaster stood near the back wall, and beside him a Selgozi trader. Two of the ships still waiting offshore were his, he had come ashore with news and messages.

Khadat, seated at one tip of the hard stone bench, shifted cautiously and tried to show nothing as the scribe read in his flat voice of more atrocities. Her dead husband's brother must know she would rather be anywhere but here. *He does this to get even with me because of Apodain, I am certain of it; his conscience is making him uneasy and he seeks to share the misery.* He knew she must be certain her family's ship was unloaded correctly and the goods sent only to the storage vaults within Perlot's palace, something she could only accomplish if she were down there with the ship and its captain. And that ship had to be gone with the evening tide.

Then there was Apodain. She could not decide what to think about him, save that he had no sense whatever. He spoke to no one and avoided her. *I told him I could undo this marriage before the time ever comes.* It had to be the shock of that dreadful little common Secchi; after ten days he could not possibly still be moping over the royal chariot. *He has always been sensible—like me instead of his father. Or so I thought.* She did not trust that he would keep his sworn word to her, she realized, nor fully trust Hemit's servants or her cousin Emyas to keep him from—*from what?* She didn't know what Apodain might do. At least he could not regain his place in the royal chariot, or fight in any other company. He was royal, thank the goddess, and therefore three years too young to make his own decisions. If Perlot had been merely noble—! But Khadat's father would never have contracted with a mere foreign nobleman for his precious child. *Apodain is acting the fool. Let him have sons of his own, and he will understand why I acted as I did.*

But he might not. Perhaps only a woman would see that her children must live, whatever the cost to foolish pride.

That Secchi, that common child— It infuriated her, remembering the ceremony and Apodain—having to hand the bundle to that dreadful little commoner. Pelledar must have chosen the smallest and plainest girl of the lot to deliberately shame her. In his childish, sulking mood, Apodain would not have cared if she had been squat and ugly as a frog or fair as virgin Xelas. He would not have noticed had the Secchi been four-footed and long-eared, and drawn a cart. *She looks like a peasant, one of those skinny-nosed, dark little southern women my uncle brought to tend the Mirikosi flax fields! She will never wed my Apodain, I will not have it!*

But Haffat must lose, the goddess said so. If he did, he might well lose Mirikos also. And there were noblewomen in Mirikos far better suited to providing the wife of a prince with grandsons. *Wait until this war is over,* Khadat reminded herself grimly. *Wait, until Pelledar can no longer threaten to unmake the bargain, contending that I broke it first.*

A chill touched her: the ruling family of Mirikos was dead or missing. And no one knew how Haffat's puppet emperor might proceed against the Mirikosi nobility. She had already lost a certain amount of power. Then again—according to the captain who waited with that ship out there, they still had the family ships and the trading company had not been touched. The family flax fields and the olive grove—oldest of any on the north shore of the Delos—were as they always had been, though there was rumor of a new tax. *A tax. What is that, if the lands themselves and the possessions are intact?* She let the secretary's droning voice fade, let her eyes rest on Pelledar's back, and began enumerating her remaining strengths.

Eyzhad had long since ceased listening to the letters; he was worried about only one thing: *Why does Haffat not attack us now? Mirikos fell into his hands like overripe grapes; he lost no men and suffered no dead or wounded. The city is his and her ships are his to command.* But Haffat remained encamped before the city gates; he was said to be buying or simply taking ships but none of them were being readied for carrying men or war supplies.

There must be an answer. Haffat did not do things by whim. And he traveled with lion-priests, possibly with priests of Diyet's gods. *They are nothing like our gods, they do not move in the same world beyond this world. And yet, the world where their worshipers dwell is also our world. They do not call the sun Atos, but he rises in the east and sets in the west; the stars move in the same patterns across the night sky for them. Perhaps their priests study the movement of the heavens as do we.* It was worth considering; he could think of nothing else. He rested his hands on his knees and closed his eyes. A priest of Denota did not spend much time studying the skies, but if he could not find an answer, Vertumnus might.

Pelledar had turned back to the window. He could listen as well while his eyes moved from the docks to the gates, along the crowded main road with its constant stream of people, carts, donkeys and camels. And this way, he did not chance meeting Khadat's eyes; Khadat was furious with him and making no secret of it. *I had nothing to do with the choice, beyond telling her the price of Apodain's commission. How was I to know she would accept that? Let her glare at Eyzhad, he put them together!* Eyzhad would not much care if Khadat glared at him; he had Tephys and the goddess to protect him. Besides, it looked as though he had fallen asleep against Tephys' knee.

The scribe finished a short letter from the queen of eastern Ykrit, who was politely refusing to sell him wheat—like the rulers of two other eastern nations, who feared Haffat might turn their way next. *Once we have fallen. They do not believe even Ghezrat can hold back the Diye Haff.* The scribe cleared his throat inquiringly; Pelledar waved a hand for him to go on.

"From Mirikos, brought by the Locchrean ship,

"To my Brother and Great King, Pelledar, from his Brother, Greetings. To him, long life and honor, and many strong sons; to him, the favor of the goddess, that Haffat may be turned from his quest, or that he fall before Ghezrat as so many have. Know, my Brother, that Mirikos will not stand against such Haffat. Her walls were never meant for siege, even before she outgrew them. Let my brother see to his own walls and his gates; let his armies be fearless and without number, and let thought of war sit warm in their bellies. Let them slay so many of the Diye Haff that none shall wage such war again.

"Let my brother especially beware the lion god Axtekeles, and his priest Knoe. Knoe's fame precedes him and it is dreadful." Silence. Pelledar bowed his head, closed his eyes briefly. When he opened them again, he could see seven chariots on the plain, practicing maneuvers. *My son goes there,* he thought, *and the thought still dismayed him. How could I have been so foolish, to let Septarin play upon my feelings?* Septarin was over-young for his years, and those too few for a company in any case. *And yet, he would have won his pleats eventually, and in the meantime kept my attention from important matters. Perhaps it is his fate; if so, he may prove himself out there. If not—well, he is my first-born, and I am truly fond of him. But I have two other sons, and Ye Sotris carries what may be the third.*

And poor Apodain. A truly great king would have thought of a way to flatly tell Khadat no, without making an enemy of her.

The room had gone quiet. The secretary's voice came. "Sire, that is the last of the messages."

Pelledar turned. "Return after the council goes, I will have answers to certain of those. Meantime, prepare a proclamation, to be called from all the fountains, three times this day and three tomorrow. From tomorrow at first horn, there will be no more large carts and no beast-drawn carts of any kind allowed beyond the main gates and the open square. The main avenues must be kept clear enough from now on that an armed phalanx marching three abreast can walk without obstruction. Also, let those men too old to fight who would still serve the city go to the barracks with whatever armor they have. General Piritos will appoint someone to send them to the main crossings and all inner gates, to see that the proclamation is honored. Prepare that," Pelledar added as he came away from the window, "and as soon as it is ready, return for my seal." He waited until the secretary had gathered up spooled and flat parchments and the archaic-style clay tablet the Kredonyi still used, then took his seat before the council. He settled his shoulders against stone smoothed by generations of Ghezrathi kings and nodded; his steward brought the two foreigners forward. They carried messages and their own accounts of tents before Idemito and Mirikos, but nothing new. They had also brought copper and tin, an entire hold of grain and oil. Pelledar sent his steward and one of the general's aides to settle the bargain so the ships could be unloaded and the captains sail on the night tide.

Polyos, an elderly noble, spoke up as the merchants left.

"You heard them. All these conflicting tales, and we still do not know whether Haffat thinks he intends a league of nations or spreads the horrors spoken of in the written messages."

His son Potro nodded as Polyos nudged him. "And how do we sort out the truth? Does he gather in lands to hang about his throat like beads on a string, or is he another common lout, pillaging and murdering his way across the lands?"

The councillors looked at each other, at their king; no one seemed willing to speak first. "Sire," Polyos said finally, and at his thin, elderly voice, Khadat jumped and so did his son. "I tell everyone here the same thing I said to you two days ago, in private. The letters, these men just now—they have not changed my opinion." He kept his eyes fixed on a spot just above the throne. "I do not believe anyone can say what this Haffat will do when he comes to conquer Ghezrat. *If* he comes to take the city, though, we may not need to fight him. I think there may be some way to convince him to leave us alone. He is far from Diyet, after all, and that Selgozi merchant tells us he has been gone for at least a year. Surely he is tired of so much fighting!"

"If he is," Piritos growled, "why has he not taken his army and gone home?"

"How should I know? I am no soldier." Polyos replied peevishly. "But—if everything we heard here is true—he does not actually fight very often, and only when those he would conquer do not surrender at once."

Piritos leapt to his feet. "What do you suggest? Shall we grovel before him and let him crush our faces into the dirt?"

"I did not say that!" Polyos snapped. "And yet, what if we fight and lose? What will he do to us then?"

"The goddess," Tephys began, but Polyos loudly overrode her.

"Oh, yes, Denota! But I do not worship her, I never have done so, and do I not prosper? Haffat rides with a god at his elbow, and that god has not yet failed him. What if this lion is stronger than Denota, even here in her own city? This lion god has already defeated gods in other lands. Many of them. And Denota is revered in Mirikos, if I recall, so why would she turn her face from Mirikos and still protect us? How can we be certain she can hold against Axtekeles here?"

"That is not for us to ask," Tephys replied sharply. "We are not gods, to have that right."

"No. We are mortals, and our lives are playthings for those gods, if we let them be." Several of the council began to shout at that, but he topped them all, answering his own question. "He will wreak such slaughter within our walls as we have never seen! We have gold and silver aplenty, let us offer him—"

"And now you say, offer him tribute before he even comes to our shores?" Piritos looked down a formidable nose at him; his hands were balled into loose fists. "Do that, merchant, and he will believe we are weak; he will press an advantage that I, for one, do not believe he has!"

A silence, which Khadat broke with a nasty little laugh. "Ah. But I would expect *you* to say that, General. You are a man, and so you think with a part of you which is not your brain. You want to fight this Haffat, to see which of you is stronger and therefore the better man. You want the soldiers who follow you to kill and maim those who follow Haffat, and the other way about, until the man who has fewer dead is seen as the greater man! Do not dare look at me like that!" she shouted furiously. The general glared down at her; a vein throbbed in his temple. "I will not have it! I have already lost all of my men but one to such posturing!"

"Ah. And perhaps you think Perlot would agree with this foolish woman's speech of yours—could he come back from the dead to answer it?" Piritos snapped. "Or that Apodain would?" Khadat paled; her jaw was set.

"Apodain is yet a child, and for all I loved Perlot, he was a *man* like you, a fool because he saw in warfare a way to earn glory for himself. And like you, he cared *nothing* for the living or the city he left behind, or else he would never have gone!"

"If you think that, you did not know him at all," Piritos said flatly, and turned his back on her. "I beg that my prince remember what those letters said, that he recall the words of those two shipmen: Only in Croatar did Haffat leave the throne in the hands of its prince, and he pays ruinous tribute. Shall Ghezrat pay tax to a foreign king? We have never done such a thing in seven hundred years, never! Shall we let our old people and our babies starve, while our coin and food and goods are sent to Diyet? Perhaps Mirikos is untouched, perhaps Haffat's army remains outside—but its ruling family is dead and which of us truly believes that was suicide?"

"You cannot prove—" someone murmured doubtfully. But Piritos shook his head.

"Of course I can prove nothing! But I do not care about that. They are dead and knowing if it was suicide, murder, or sacrifice will not make them live once more."

"I come of Mirikos," Khadat said. Her voice was again under control, but she twisted her hands in her lap. "As you all know. And my father was stepbrother to the old king and uncle to Khoryios who is now dead. I was fond of Khoryios, and I weep for him. But don't you see what he won by not sending his army to fight? Are you all so blind as that? I say we must *not* resist if Haffat comes! And, after all, we have strong walls and many soldiers. We can use them as the shield Mirikos did not have while we bargain to make certain no harm will come to our prince and his family. He can have no reason to hurt Ghezrat, if the city can increase his wealth."

"Yes," Piritos said flatly, "let us give him the means to grind our neighbors in the dirt also."

"Do not *dare* interrupt me, Piritos. Remember who and what I am, and what you are," Khadat snapped. She drew herself up, looked along the bench, and tried to temper her anger. "Please, all of you. Let us at least try what I suggest. Offer him coin and precious stones, and if we must, give him trade concessions as well! Must we all die so this—this general can prove which of us is the stronger—the more foolish? Is it not better to live than die a useless death? Or a fool's death?"

"Shall we listen to you instead?" Piritos demanded furiously. "You would have us live in shame and poverty, reft even of honor! But how can you say that once the gates have been thrown open, this Haffat will not kill us all anyway? This is Ghezrat, woman! There is no greater land about the Sea of Delos! We hold rights to trade routes south and east, we hold the isthmus and so control the route to the Great Sea! Or do you really think Haffat cannot distinguish between a land of herders and herds such as Righ—and mighty Ghezrat?"

"Foolish!" Khadat began, but Piritos overrode her.

"Shall we show Haffat a better reason for taking Ghezrat than he already has? He wants the isthmus, the trade routes, a bountiful sea and land blessed by the goddess, and now you say we must also persuade him that we sit upon a mountain of coin and stones? My prince," he swung back to address Pelledar, "do not, I *beg* of you, pay heed to this fool's notion put up by women and the enfeebled old men, that we grovel before Haffat and his army—or his god!—before dire need demands it!"

"Besides, who can say there will be such need?" Polyos' son spoke up. He had been a novice priest under Eyzhad and many suspected the rather gaunt young man with fanatic eyes would have been happier there than in his trader-father's business. "Father, please," he added stiffly as the older man stirred and mumbled under his breath. "You know quite well how I feel about this! Ghezrat has not fought a real war in many years, but we are surely ready. We have an army, we even have red-clad Dyaddi. I myself serve with the royal chariot and they are matchless, as this Haffat will learn. Denota has warned us against the Diye Haff, but she also vowed we shall see an end to the fighting, *and victory to the city*. I would not offer Haffat a single copper *klept*, or the least granite pebble from our streets, but that he must come through the gates and wrest it from us! Which, knowing our strengths, I say *he will not*."

"Oh, such a very pretty speech," Khadat sneered. "I shall comfort your mother, your young wife, and your babes when you waste yourself in battle! When your mother tears her hair and weeps, she will need someone to remind her that, after all, her son died a hero and his name will be sung by Ghezrat's bards for a hundred years. What could possibly make her happier than that?"

"It is a better thing," Potro hissed, "than to cower in my mother's house so others may die in my place!" He sat back on the bench; Polyos gripped his arm and whispered furiously into his ear. Potro finally nodded, and stiffly said, "My apologies, Princess." It was quite clear that he did not mean it and Khadat made no answer; she was utterly white and for once beyond words.

"But," Anchris spoke into the silence; he was a solidly built noble of middle years who often served as the council's peacekeeper. "We are straying from an important point, and no one has yet addressed it that I can recall. Haffat has crowned yet another of his many brothers King of Mirikos— Great King, as he calls the wretched little upstart. But why does he not strike his tents and march against us? That is not at all usual. What does the man wait for? *Why* does he wait?" Anchris looked up and down the bench.

"Perhaps he is tired. His men may be exhausted from the long march across the desert," Tephys said. "He may hope to create a puzzle to catch us unawares. But if you truly ask my opinion, Haffat follows a logic of his own as he has from the first, or he obeys the whims of his lion god. And if that, then who can say what he does, or why? Axtekeles and the ways of his priests are hidden from me."

"Dear goddess. I have it." Eyzhad sat up straight, so suddenly the back of his head struck her knee. "The skies and stars are the same everywhere, are they not? Haffat's priests would know nothing of Denota's mysteries, but there must be men among them who have heard of our beginnings, when Denota and Atos mated. After all, I know the myth of Axtekeles and the priest who saved a lion cub from floods in the first days of the world, sealing the bond between the lion god and those who follow him."

"There is a point to all of this?" Piritos asked, but mildly for him.

"Oh, yes indeed!" Eyzhad replied eagerly. "For if they know that much, then they must also have heard of Atelos, and how he stalked the goddess and came between her and Atos—and unless I have misfigured, the Moon will step between us and the Sun once again in—in, I think, thirty-eight days. Vertumnus?"

The sun-priest nodded. "You reason more quickly than I did. There will be such an eclipse in thirty-eight days."

"And you think that Haffat knows this?" Polyos laughed. "What, do you believe he will wait to set upon us at such an hour, thinking the city will fall into his hands because of it?"

Eyzhad shrugged. "He may see it as an advantage, or he may think we cannot gauge when such an event will occur, or simply that it will strike superstitious fear into us because he knows our ways and attacks on that day."

Polyos laughed again. "And you do not think so?"

Tephys stirred; her eyes narrowed. "Why should it? I think most men will perceive it as a sign of weakness, that he thinks he must use such tricks to assure his victory. But it will not change the final outcome." Khadat pounced on that.

"The *outcome*. But the road to victory?" She leaned forward, gripped her head briefly between long, white hands, then sat back up and fetched a deep sigh. "Why does no one listen to me? We must at least try to bargain with this Haffat! After all, he is a peasant, of peasant stock, surely he is amenable to bribery! But what have we lost, other than a *man's* notion of face, if he does not accept our offer and simply turn aside? And what is that worth to dead men?"

"You serve as a priestess at the four corners of the year, and you still must ask that?" Eyzhad demanded angrily. At Tephys' touch, he subsided, but his eyes were still hot.

Khadat's voice was higher than usual and it trembled. "I ask it, I have the right to ask it! I have lost nearly all a woman can lose to war!" Silence. When Khadat spoke again, her voice was flat and utterly without expression. "I do not expect this council to take the path of sense. I have sat on this bench and listened to all of you make fools of yourself for all the years since my Perlot died. I have listened to you with pain and sorrow today, and pity for your lack of vision. All right, then. But when all is over, and you mourn your dead, remember which of us urged the better course."

Pelledar dismissed all of them except for Tephys, and walked over to the window so he could look out toward the harbor once more. Tephys sat where she had all morning, hands clasped together in her lap, and waited for him to speak.

"This eclipse," he said finally. His fear showed in his voice; he swallowed, cleared his throat cautiously. "You knew of it?"

"That a full eclipse was coming? Of course I knew."

He swung around to eye her in alarm. "But—but in your prophecy—!"

"The goddess did not speak of the eclipse, or," Tephys corrected herself carefully, "if she said anything about it through my voice, Meronne has not told me. I do not recall it." A brief silence, which the priestess finally broke. "My prince, do not worry about the eclipse, Denota has never lied to her people. Haffat is a dire enemy, but we have faced dire enemies before and not yet fallen to any of them."

"No," Pelledar said doubtfully. He hesitated, glanced at her, and turned back to the window before he spoke again. "And yet, Haffat is emperor and warrior both; I am not."

"Perhaps Axtekeles demands no more of his emperor. There is more to Ghezrat than mere war."

"Well, of course," Pelledar said immediately. "And yet, my ancestors were warlike kings. They won battles. Always before this, a prince knew what Piritos knows, and *he* led the way into battle, but I must let Piritos lead. *Never* has Ghezrat been ruled by a prince who has not fought with his armies, who has not even fought in a single skirmish."

"Does it really bother you so much?" Tephys sounded as though she really wanted to know.

Pelledar bit back the sharp retort he might ordinarily have made. "Sometimes. It—all right, yes, it bothers me to see the common soldiers on the fighting grounds, and know that the least man of them has blooded his sword, but I have not."

"That is not so. Only those men who served your father and his father may have killed enemies before this, and not all the men who fight ever killed anyone."

Pelledar turned away from the window long enough to give her an abashed smile, but it had slipped before he went back to his study of the city below. "Of course, there have never been so many fallow years between battles."

"Of course. But Denota warned us in time to prepare for Haffat; She does not see peaceful years as a flaw in the city, the people—or Her prince. She promised us victory." He gave her a dubious look. Tephys shook her head. "And you know full well it has been a very long while since the man who rules Ghezrat led his armies into battle. Your grandsire did not, nor his father—even this Haffat does not, if what I have heard is true. Nor does your own general.

"But why should you compare yourself to Haffat? He is merely a general with an emperor's helm; he moves from place to place, and lives in the midst of his army. He does not know how to care for his people. It must be he is not needed to see to the everyday tasks which face most rulers, or perhaps he does not know how to do these things."

"Trade, taxes, the petty day-to-day business of keeping a city in good health?" Pelledar eyed her in patent disbelief. "That makes me greater than a Haffat?"

"Such things are not petty," Tephys said mildly. "Ask any of your people—the commons who do not suffer disease and hunger, the merchants who wear silk and gems, the nobles who prosper, the farmers and herders who supply the city

with sufficient to eat and drink, and who themselves do not
want, because they are allowed to live in peace and quiet.
They may not think about such things, any more than you
do, but there cannot be a Ghezrathi who would prefer that
you set aside all these *petty* details to put on a war helmet.
Ask any man in the streets, these next days, how good it is
that he can walk where he must—to the barracks, to the
docks, to the marketplace to fill his storage pits. Or ask any
woman who finds her way without danger of being crushed
in the streets because you saw so much overcrowding, and
dealt with it. Ask anyone who prepares to fight for his city
how he appreciates that the prince works within his walls to
find the raw materials for weapons and sends them good
generals."

"Hah," Pelledar said, but the tension went from his shoulders and the smile he gave her this time was genuine enough
to warm his eyes, even if his color was high; he was unused
to such praise, particularly from her.

"Is there anything else you need of me?" Tephys asked finally. "There is the final ceremony of binding for the
Dyaddi, and other things I must tend to."

"I am sorry, I keep you from important matters," Pelledar
said immediately.

Tephys walked to the doorway, turned back to look at
him. "The city's prince is also important."

He listened to her sandals clicking on the steps, fading
into nothing, then sighed. "It is all very well for her to say
such things; it is in her best interests to keep me happy." He
had to admit she had never bothered before. But he could
not believe what she said. "How much will people really
care in the days to come that their prince keeps them happy
in peaceful times, if he cannot keep them safe from war? I
know nothing of the business of war. Piritos knows, but
surely *he* already looks down on me because I am useless to
him."

He knew the main reason his mood was so dark: Eyzhad's
certainty that Haffat's lion god knew to wait for Atelos to
come to earth during the day, and to block Atos' light. A
shiver ran through him. "Polyos was right. Who is to say
Denota is stronger than Axtekeles?" His stomach contracted;
he did not dare say such things aloud, it was probably dangerous to even think them. Tephys had no doubts, but she
would never tell him if she did. *My grandfather hunted*

*lions. I remember what he said when I was very young, that
lions are strong and dangerous beasts, and only a strong
man dares to seek to kill one.* He closed his eyes. He had
never felt less a strong man in all his life.

In the cavern below Denota's courtyard, it was cool and
dark save for the ever-burning lamp. Tephys stood before the
Cleft, watching her young novice priestesses distribute the
red cords that would serve as the physical sign of this final
seal to the bargain between Primes and Secchi, and between
the Dyaddi and the goddess. The girls were treating the
cords with proper reverence, she thought; Meronne must
have given them a stern lecture before sending them down
here. She let her eyes close as the last girl placed cords
across the palms of the First Prime and his daughter. There
was still a strong aura of discontent around Breyd. Tephys
reminded herself that Breyd was not actually causing trouble, then turned away from the Dyaddi, so she could cleanse
herself of the improper emotion and seek her own bond with
the goddess.

Denota came into her at once, calming fears she had not
realized she felt—until they were gone. Denota's Voice
soothed the remnants of her irritation: "The child is fearful
and angry because of it, but still she does not falter. Do not
be hard on her, My Own. The cords will seal the bond between them; she will be Secchi and nothing else, as the rest
of them are Secchi."

Tephys sniffed. *Secchi and nothing else! This is Breyd,
Mother of All!*

"Yes, I know it is Breyd; her reverence is not strong for
the ancient ceremonies, but her love for Me is honest, deeply
as it is buried just now under anger and fear. She has a great
burden to bear, My Own, and she knows it; do not add to
that burden."

I will try, the priestess managed. Denota's gentle laugh
tickled the hairs on her forearms.

"All Ghezrat does Me honor, My Own, each in his own
way—or hers. Even the child who laughs at My rituals. She
laughs, My Own; she does not jeer. Remember that, in the
days to come."

Her Voice faded; the sense of Her within was still very
strong. Tephys sighed and turned toward the waiting Pairs.
"Let the Dyaddi pay close heed to Denota's words, as I give

them to you: The three strands will be knotted together, overhand, so." She fished a three-part green and yellow cord from her sash and laid it across her palm, then walked along the line so they could see how the three knots were made, and how spaced. She stepped back, held up the cord and pointed to each knot in turn. "This central knot for the Dyadd, this for the Prime, this the Secchi-knot. Tie them as evenly apart as you can, then hold them in your sword hand, and wait." She shoved her cord behind the sash and knelt before the first Pair. Eriana watched anxiously as Tephys took her cords and her Prime Lotro's and traded them, Prime to Secchi and Secchi to Prime. Tephys closed Eriana's fingers around the cord and frowned at her when she would have snatched her hand away; the stuff had suddenly become warm.

"Seal the bargain, and complete the bond between you," Tephys said softly; she waited for Lotro to fasten the knotted cord about his daughter's brow, for Eriana to tie the knotted cord around her father's brow. "This final knot you have tied is Denota's, sign that she will protect you both." She held out a hand to each; the goddess' will flowed from her to Eriana and to Lotro and then from Prime to Secchi and Secchi to Prime. Lotro caught his breath; his daughter cried out, but both sounds were muted; Tephys withdrew her hands, Eriana clasped both her father's hands in both of hers and a red mist rose from their hands to swirl around them. Tephys moved quickly to the next Pair. She had to nudge Jocasa, who was staring in wide-eyed fear at the just-bonded Pair to her right—or what she could see of them. Her Prime Mibro patted her arm reassuringly, but he had gone pale.

Breyd and her father were again the last Pair. Something was happening, down there; she could see Tephys working her way slowly along the line, a faint red glow behind her like distant fire reflecting on clouds. She held the knotted cords loosely, gazed toward the flame without actually seeing it. It must have been another girl who stood in this cavern—in very nearly this same spot—and bit back laughter at the solemnity of the spring planting ceremony. Another lifetime.

She was weary from long hours of weaponry practice; her arms and legs ached from the unaccustomed work, her fingers hurt constantly. The sword felt heavier each morning, and it never felt comfortable; she could not remember all the sequences of strike and parry Grysis made them practice so often.

She hated the sword, with its long, sharp edges and wicked point. *They chose wrong. I could never push that point against a man's body and shove it into him; I could not cut anyone.* She had better not think of that here; it had already made her physically ill more than once.

Despite exhaustion, she slept poorly. Niverren was restless most nights, and that would have kept her awake anyway. Now and again, she heard her mother weeping out in the courtyard, where she had crept to keep from waking Menlaeus. Niverren would have gone to their mother, to at least try to comfort her. Breyd could not. *If I said the wrong thing, somehow, if Mother somehow found out about my vision, about my nightmares—she would have true cause for fear. She simply could not bear it.* She felt so helpless, anyway: Her mother had always soothed *her*, when she was afraid. *She was strong for us; I can be strong for her, now, but not her way.*

Her knees hurt from the hard, sand-strewn floor of the Cleft; the cold of it was seeping into her bones.

At least Tarpaen had settled down for the moment, and even Laius seemed to be sober on the rare occasions he came home with Tar. Of course, messhall gossip had it that Captain Nabid had been absolutely livid. He must have been, to frighten Laius.

She shifted her weight, trying to ease the discomfort in her knees; Menlaeus touched her arm, gave her a worried look when she met his eyes. *Let it go,* she told herself. He could sense her moods often, as she could his; he could tell she ached just as she knew he had been stiff early, but the walk here had eased his tight muscles. She still wasn't certain how much of this was the closeness that had always been between them, how much goddess. *The muscles on either side of his mustache show, when he hurts, as if he is holding the pain in.* They didn't show now.

It was becoming difficult to remember how things had been before the initial bond.

This final ceremony—she glanced down at the cord, then down the line to where Tephys knelt, only four Pairs away from them. Beyond her stretched a line of bonded Pairs, and that ruddy glow seemed to envelop them. Aroepe knelt just this side of the priestess; her hands were shaking, and the ends of the cord trembled.

She turned away, brought her eyes back to the cord she had knotted. Meronne had told her she must contemplate the knots and their meaning. *But Denota has already named me, named Father; She will not set us aside because I did not follow the ritual closely enough.* She might withdraw Her protection from them though. Breyd closed her eyes and tried to remember: Central knot for the Dyadd, Prime and Secchi knots flanking it. Very symbolic—the kinds of simple symbols they put in children's songs. *I see them; I see what they mean. What else can I gain from this? Will this ceremony make us one cord, knotted together as it is?*

It would be another box, like serving the goddess or marrying Laius; this one would not be for life, though. How would she feel to be so much a part of her father, then lose that closeness?

They would marry her to Apodain at once; how would that be—to lose the goddess bond and gain such a husband—and Khadat? *Does She punish my lack of reverence by linking me with a coward?* She had not wanted to believe all the barracks rumors; after all, she had often cheered Apodain at the midsummer games, or seen him, proud and handsome, in his chariot on his way to maneuvers.

But that Apodain was gone; in his place was a white-faced, silent creature who stammered out the binding words and fled to his mother once the ceremony was done. Or maybe that shining Apodain was no more real than one of the pottery statues in Denota's: gold-covered and beautiful, but hollow and easily shattered. Laius said much the same thing, and he was only repeating what many of the men in the barracks said.

She shook her thoughts free; Tephys now stood before Lochria as her Prime bound her brow—near enough that Breyd felt the edge of Denota's power as it flared around the Pair. She felt her stomach tighten and swallowed cautiously. The priestess knelt between her and Menlaeus and held out her hands. Breyd held out the cord she had tied and blotted damp palms against her cloak.

Tephys frowned at the delay, then handed them switched cords and said, "Take them, and complete the bond between you."

The cords were warm, but she had expected that. Breyd came up onto her knees, so she could tie the knot at the back of Menlaeus's head and bent her head so he could fasten the cord around her brow. Tephys said something as their hands fell away, but she could never say later what the words were: Denota's power wrapped around them both, dizzying and warm—different from the vision-power. She opened her eyes and gasped: She saw Menlaeus and then herself, but not the self she saw in a mirror. *I see through his eyes—not a small and too-thin child with odd features but a strong young woman, with his strength, her mother's beauty. He thinks me beautiful. He is truly proud of me,* she realized and the thought surprised her. But she could feel his pride, just as she could feel the shift in his leg muscles when he sat back on his heels, and the bunching and flexing of his upper arm and the long muscles down his forearm as he reached for her fingers.

It was knowledge she could never have expected. She knew when he moved, how he moved, almost as though something of Breyd inhabited his body. With the weapons-training and this, she would know how to direct an attack to protect his flank, how to deliver a killing counterblow as soon as he struck. *I can strike that blow.* She met his eyes and smiled. *It is not wrong to want to fight, to feel the fierce joy of fighting, to protect what is yours, to kill men who would kill you and your loved ones.* That was male sense, male perspective, the male being practical in time of need. Not Laius' crazed desire simply to kill. She no longer dreaded the edged weapons; the dreadful pictures of men killed by her sword or her spear were not gone, but her perspective had changed. *They will die, and I will gladly kill them, if they threaten me or him, or what is ours.*

Menlaeus stared at his daughter in astonishment. He had felt the movement of her strong hand muscles when she gripped his fingers; for that moment he had felt *her.* It unnerved him and embarrassed him both to realize how she still saw him: Tall and infinitely strong; handsome, still young. Very brave. *I am no longer most of those things, if I ever was. That is a daughter's love clouding her eyes.* She had relaxed in some way he couldn't quite define; the binding had given her strength to accept the weapons and the burden they brought. But he could feel something of her thoughts, too: *It is not wrong to be distressed by death; to be sickened by killing.* That was female, surely; the mother, wife, sister, or daughter who sat home and waited for word of the men who fought to keep them safe, or because some prince said they must fight. She no longer held that belief above all else; his own belief had taken its place for now. *That is good, daughter; even a man can be distressed by death and sickened by the killing, but if he must kill anyway, it is dangerous to let such soft feelings sway him.*

Her fingers tightened on his; she might not be able to sense all his thoughts, or his exact thoughts, Menlaeus realized with relief. But she could tell their direction, just now. And she accepted it.

Breyd felt the movement of his hands, felt her own muscles respond. His thumb ached at the base because his father's sword hilt was so broad he had to stretch his hand to hold onto it; she knew that because it made her own thumb ache.

It should have terrified her, such impossible closeness— but even the vision-fear that had gripped her for so many days had let go. Menlaeus would not die; the goddess had shown her what might come to pass, if she continued to fight against this bond. Surely that was it. She drew a shaky breath. *We are two who are one, as She promised. No one will overcome us!*

Grysis was pacing impatiently back and forth before the messes. "You are all late—well, much you could do about it, eh? We will work an hour with the swords and then with javelin, to test the new bond and seal it. You and you," he jabbed his forefinger at the first Prime and Secchi, "go to the smithy, return once you have been rearmed. Now!" He turned back to the other Pairs and clapped his hands together. Cloaks were shed, swords drawn, Primes formed a line facing their Secchi; one loud clash of bronze swords rang out. Breyd could hear Grysis' bellow all the way inside the end of the stable where the weaponsmith worked.

Grysis merely pointed them back to the head of the line when they returned and sent Lochria and Bechates. Breyd felt shy in the polished bronze breastplate, greaves, and forearm bands; the double layer of stiffened linen *ptroges* which hung skirtlike to cover most of the linen undertunic. It was more impressive—more soldierlike—than the older panoply. *Something to live up to; a day ago, I doubt I could have made myself put it on and walk back into the fighting grounds.* The new panoply was completed by a smooth-fitting, hardened leather cap covered in overlapping little brass plates and that in turn covered by a bright red cloth tiara that could be wrapped around the face to cover everything but the eyes.

The cloth might be stifling on a hot day; it was still better than those old-fashioned, solid brass, full-head helmets, the ones the older men still wore. *Those* had nothing but narrow slits for eyes, nose, and mouth. *They need us to hear commands, hear each other, particularly we Secchi.* Many of the older and more experienced phalanxes prided themselves on needing nothing but hand signals from their officers to execute the most complicated maneuvers.

She now carried a crescent-shaped bronze shield, smaller than the old one and painted—black points along the edge surrounding two heads of wheat bound in three red cords. *Real armor is heavier than leather.* Her legs felt leaden after only two full repetitions of practice patterns; the sword was also heavier, longer and single edged. *Father shines like a mirror; so do I.* They contrasted wildly with the rest of the Pairs and would be clearly visible to the enemy against the plain armor, black leather, and dark cloaks worn by most of the phalanxes. They would stand out sharply against Ghezrat's pale stone walls.

Even this morning, the thought would have unnerved her. It bothered Menlaeus a little, still, to be made into such a bright symbol, she could sense his unease. His discomfort went deeper than appearance, though. The weight also bothered him, though it was not slowing him as it had her. The armor he had inherited from his father was a padded and quilted shell reinforced with strips of leather, and it had covered all his chest and back. He felt vulnerable; her back twitched whenever he had a moment to think about his unprotected back and the muscles between his shoulder blades tightened. *It is hard for his body to accept what his mind accepts, that the other half of the Pair is the armor that shields his back.*

Lochria and Bechates came back. Lochria was tugging at linen bunched inside the arm of her breastplate and Bechates would not look at anyone. Lochria grinned at Breyd and shrugged; Breyd sent her eyes heavenward. Grysis shouted at them both: "Pay attention! Laprio, Aroepe, go! The rest of

you, two more sets at this speed and then we will increase
the tempo for two more, and *then* a rest, if you have earned
it!" He clapped his hands ringingly. Breyd brought her attention resolutely back to the task at hand and tried to ignore
the shield hand that was trying to cramp from the unexpected weight. Up, down, parry right, counterparry left,
slashing right, slashing left—repeat, finish with a twist
meant to disarm the unwary. It had never yet come easy, but
this time it did. *So that is how he turns the blade! The wrist,
not the forearm!* Menlaeus smiled encouragement; she nodded and pressed the next attack. It really was just the way
Grysis had said, but now she *knew* it.

Once the entire company was reclad, Grysis called a full
halt and led them into shade. "Go ahead, sit; you have
earned it. To those of you who have not fought in this kind
of panoply—which is most of you and all the Secchi—
bronze will turn a sword point, an arrow, and even a spear,
but the plate does not cover all your body, so do not rely on
it for total protection. And if this Haffat brings siege engines
for hurling stones, remember bronze will buckle or be
crushed by such missiles, and that *might* prove ill for the
body wearing the bronze." He paused; nervous laughter answered the rather grim joke. "You have done well so far today. Ready javelins, and let me see how well you Secchi
now hit the marks!"

Breyd went last this time; she gripped four javelins in the
hand that ran through the shield straps, held a fifth loosely
in her right, and bent over to stretch out a stiff back, rest her
elbows on her knees and consider the sequence. *Grip the
throwing strap with the fingertips only. Release as the right
foot comes down on the fourth step, snap the wrist for speed,
follow through with one last step, and pull up.* It had confused her terribly the first time she tried it and never got
easier; there were too many things to remember and it hurt
her shoulder, her elbows and her wrist every time she let the
long shaft fly. *Father is right there behind me and he is worried. Worried I will fail again, or simply worried because I
am worried?* She turned her head. He squatted down next to
her. "It's not so difficult, daughter, it's only a little complicated."

"Complicated, he says!" She laughed. She could almost
hear Tephys hissing, "This is no time for laughter!" But why

not laugh? It was familiar, comforting—her father, teaching her things the way he once taught her how to drive Niddy's cart back from the vineyards.

He ran it with her; as she came back with the javelin, she demanded, "When did you put that hop in the second step?"

Menlaeus smiled and tugged at a lock of hair that had escaped her helm. "It was always there; you were so worried about the snap you forgot it." He looked down the line. "He is only halfway down, try it again."

Grysis eventually released the Dyaddi when it was growing dark. "You women will be stiff come morning. Return tomorrow at midday, we will eat together and talk about the gates you will guard, and after that walk the circuit of the walls. Any fighting you do will not be on even and easy ground such as this!" Several Secchi groaned; Grysis grinned evilly. "Go home and rest."

Lochria and her father lived two narrow streets beyond their own. Bechates, a tall, overly thin man with a querulous voice, had been a slinger; he still kept the linen sling around his right wrist and a wallet of cast metal stones at his waist. He fingered the sling now and grumbled, "This breastplate—look how they stamped the mark of Denota. It could catch a point!"

"Father, it won't," Lochria said confidently. "Because I will never let a point near you, and you will protect me, remember? Besides, if some enemy caught his point on your armor, he would be close enough that one of us could run him through while he was trying to free it."

Bechates glanced at her sharply. "Yes, I know; I thought of that."

"I know you did," she replied softly. She looked at Breyd and Breyd saw the same knowledge in her eyes: surprise at the way the bond had taken, surprise that it no longer made her sick to think of such things.

"All the same," Bechates said. He was still coming up with unpleasant possibilities when the two Pairs parted company.

Niverren and Creos were sitting in the main room, heads close together, when Menlaeus opened the door. Niverren jumped to her feet and hugged her father and sister. "Ah, you're cold!" She leaned back to look at them and laughed uncertainly. "New armor! You both nearly shine in the dark. Nidya is reorganizing the small storage and sorting out food for the wedding feast. We thought it better to stay out of her way because she and Ina fill that room between them and you know how Niddy is when she's cleaning; she is in no mood to be crossed by a mere granddaughter."

Menlaeus touched her cheek. "Ah? Not even a granddaughter two days from her wedding?"

"Particularly not," Niverren said, and laughed again, this time happily. Creos wrapped a long arm around her shoulders, but Niverren leaned away from him long enough to murmur against her father's ear, "Nidya's cross because Mother is so worried and none of us have been able to do anything about it." She let Creos pull her close once more.

Breyd could feel her father's sudden surge of worry as clearly as if it had been her own. Perhaps it mirrored her own, but it was uncomfortably different, too: Fragile, sweet little Nevvia; he still saw her as he had when he first wed her, that young, that delicate. Almost *afraid* of him because she had not known men other than her uncles and her father. Her father. Breyd followed Menlaeus reluctantly into the courtyard; she had no right to know *that* about her mother and her grandfather. *How did Niddy remain so—normal, after such a terrible man?* And then she remembered what she had said to Nevvia, the reason she would not marry Laius— her face was hot. Menlaeus had stopped to let her catch up; he wrapped an arm around her shoulders and squeezed her reassuringly. She brought up a smile, nodded to let him know she was all right—nearly all right, anyway.

The courtyard was warm with the afternoon heat and Atos still touched the upper wall. Tarpaen and Xhem sat close together where Niverren's loom had been set up for so long; Tar was working on something small he held between his hands. Breyd saw him glance up under his eyelashes for one brief moment before he murmured something to the boy. Xhem looked at them and his mouth fell open, his eyes went wide, and his face turned very red. Tar was nearly as red and he looked furtive.

Nevvia sat in her favorite slender-legged and low-backed chair, pale peach-colored cushions surrounding her. Her mouth trembled and so did her hands. "I'm sorry," she whispered. "I've made a fool of myself again, I swore I wouldn't upset the family so. But you were gone so long, all the day, and then, all the awful things T— that they say about this final bond." She pressed her lips together firmly and blinked;

Menlaeus knelt next to her and took her hands between his own. "I wondered if you would even come home again, either of you." She patted the cushions on her other side as Breyd hovered uncertainly. "Here, come and sit next to me. Oh, baby, you're so bright—what have they done to you?"

She didn't need Menlaeus' obvious worry to remind her to hide her normal disgust at being called baby, even managed a warm smile as she knelt and wrapped her arms around her mother's shoulders. "It isn't so bad, Mother," she whispered. "I don't have to sleep in it, anyway."

"Sleep in—? Oh." Nevvia laughed shakily. "One of your dreadful jokes. You're all right, though? This last thing, this final ceremony?"

"Everything is all right," Menlaeus assured her. Breyd patted her mother's cheek and got back to her feet. "They didn't feed us much, though; not for as hard as we worked. How nice you look, and how cool. I have not seen you wear that yellow in a very long time, did you bring it out to see if it would suit for Niverren's wedding?"

Breyd got to her feet. "I think I should see if Niddy—" She turned hastily away as her mother wrapped too-thin arms around her father and buried her face in his shoulder. What was between *them* was not her business and she was horribly uncomfortable. If Nevvia ever found out, she would die of shame. Fortunately, the goddess bond was less by the time she had taken a few steps, and across the courtyard was an assurance of his presence, awareness of niggling pains and stiff joints, blessedly little else.

One of them would have to move for the night, to put a decent distance between Prime and Secchi.

She stopped short of the kitchen doorway; Tarpaen was grinning at her in the insolent fashion that never failed to make her angry.

"Why, little sister. What have *you* done lately, catch Niv and Creos kissing? I can't tell where that cloak ends and your face starts."

"That isn't your business," she snapped. "But I really do wonder who has been repeating all the old stories about Pairs to *somebody* here, where Mother could hear them?"

Xhem's face was as red as hers felt and he wouldn't look at her. Tar's smile vanished. "I didn't mean to upset her, you know I wouldn't—but why am I explaining myself to *you?*" he demanded rudely. "Just because you wear greaves now and carry a sword doesn't mean you're better than I am, you're still a nasty-mouthed little—!" Nidya loomed behind him in the kitchen doorway and cleared her throat—softly, but Xhem still heard her. He caught Tarpaen by the wrist, sent his eyes sideways. Tarpaen glanced in that direction himself, bit his lip, and went back to whatever he was doing—reworking an old dagger sheath for the boy, Breyd thought. She glared at both dark heads and brushed past them.

Nidya took her arm and pulled her into the kitchen; the old woman's eyes were dark with anger, something rare. "Because my grandson is acting like a fool does not mean you must also behave like a fool!" she hissed. "You will not upset your mother any more than she already is!"

"No, Niddy," Breyd murmured meekly. The older woman studied her face, then, to her surprise, smiled and patted her cheek. "I know you didn't start it. You look tired, child, like they've worn you to a thread. I spoke to Tar earlier, he won't upset your mother like that again. At least he hadn't told the boy any of the nastier rumors about Pairs, or the bloodier tales."

"They aren't true," Breyd said wearily, but her face was hot again.

"I know that," Nidya snapped. "I was of an age when they were last chosen; I had a friend who was made Secchi. Do you suppose your father is as hungry as you look?"

"I think so. He has a little headache and his stomach is tight enough that it will probably start to growl any moment."

"He said that, or you know it?"

"I know it."

"If you think to unnerve an old woman by that kind of showing off, you won't do it," Nidya said. She smiled to take the sting from the words then. "Not this old woman, at least. Go, shed what of that you can or simply sit and wait, I will tend to you when I've fed your parents." She caught up the blue luster jug and set it on the good tray with flat bread, a small round cloth of goat cheese, and a bowl of figs. Breyd hovered in the doorway, watching as Nidya set the tray on the claw-footed tripod table that was Creos' present to his new family.

"Where is Breyd?" Nevvia's fretful voice reached her. "Is she—she is all right, isn't she, Mother?"

"She is fine. She spent the day learning how to fight, she's tired. Don't fuss at her, girl."

"I'm not—all right, I suppose I am fussing," Nevvia replied. "But my little girl, my baby—"

"Don't let her hear you call her that," Nidya grumbled. "She is old enough to wed and begin babies of her own, and at just the age *you* fussed horribly when I called *you* baby. You had better eat, both of you. Breyd will be right out. She is helping Ina shift some jars."

She didn't want to go back out there, she suddenly realized. She was exhausted and the double burden of her own thoughts and her father's worries was nearly too much for her. But Nidya gave her a shove on her way back into the kitchens; Tar would see her hovering there and make fun of her. She wouldn't let herself think about the scene that would surely follow; she walked slowly across the courtyard, ignoring Tar and Xhem, piled more cushions onto the low, leopard-footed chair that had been Niverren's as a young child, and dropped into it, her head against the low back and her legs stretched out before her.

Nevvia looked over at her and her eyes went wide with distress. "Oh, Breyd, no! You can't sit like *that!* Those skirts are just indecently short, I can see—" Tarpaen's muffled giggle interrupted her; Menlaeus came up onto one knee and gave his son a stern, warning look over Nevvia's hair. Breyd hastily pulled the sides of the cloak across her knees; Nevvia cast her eyes heavenward but laughed in resignation. "You're a dreadful child, sprawling about like your father does; why, I'd beat you if I didn't think I would hurt my hands on all that metal!" Breyd sat up a little straighter; her mother merely smiled and shook her head. "You cannot loll in chairs like a man once you are wed; that dreadful Khadat will never—" The smile vanished. Menlaeus broke off a bit of bread, dipped it into the bowl of figs to sop up the sweet juice, and held it to her lips. "Oh, all right; I promised I would not mention that name again."

"It upsets you to no good cause," Menlaeus said mildly. He held up another bite; Nevvia shook her head and pushed it toward his mouth.

"I am not nearly as hungry as you are; I distinctly heard your stomach just now. Eat that."

Nidya, who had come back with the plain wooden tray, eyed her granddaughter, but she merely set the tray on

Breyd's knees. "Here, drink this, we put the jug in the cistern this morning so the wine would be cool for you. And eat," she added tartly. "I made this especially."

She gestured toward wedges of cut bread, cheese—and a dish of dark olive oil in which strips of hot red and deep green pepper floated. "Oh, Niddy," Breyd whispered, and to her horror felt tears in her eyes. Menlaeus turned partway around to look at her; she blinked rapidly, smiled, and shrugged in his direction, then fished one of the red strips out of the oil and ate it. She drank to wash some of the burn from her mouth and the tightness from her throat, dipped a wedge of bread in the oil, smeared it with cheese and ate.

"Better?" Nidya asked finally. Breyd, her mouth full of the last bite of cheese and bread, nodded. "Good." She glanced toward Nevvia and Menlaeus, and lowered her voice. "She won't be awake much longer; I dosed that last cup with valerian."

"What is this?" Nevvia asked suddenly. "Oh, husband, it is too tight, it is cutting into your brow!" Menlaeus stiffened and Breyd came halfway to her feet. Her mother was reaching for the red binding cord, and before either of them could say anything she had hold of the dangling ends.

Menlaeus slapped her hand away, then went so white Breyd thought he might faint. He held out a trembling hand, Nevvia flinched away from him. Nidya's fingers had clamped down on Breyd's wrist. "Let him deal with this, child."

She couldn't answer, she was trembling violently. *They might have warned us!* Menlaeus shifted to catch her eye and shook his head very faintly. Nevvia fell into his arms and wept as though her heart had been broken. Probably, Breyd thought bleakly, it had.

Nidya's wine eventually took effect; Menlaeus let Nevvia gently down onto her cushions, laid a thick woolen wrap over her, then came back to pull his daughter to her feet. "I will stay with her here, in case she wakens. I think you might—sleep better if you take the roof over your grandmother's room."

"I know." It was as far as she could get from him.

"Remember that they did not tell us to sleep in the armor."

"Practice," Breyd said and dredged up a smile from somewhere. "For the day they put us outside the walls and lock the gates until we have won. You Primes can tell us all you like they won't do that, we Secchi know better."

Menlaeus laughed quietly, hugged her hard, then turned away to undo his cloak. Breyd went stiffly up the awkward ladder, gathered up one of Nevvia's light wraps and a pillow from under the woven screen on her way around the roof. It took her quite a while to free herself from the new armor—unfamiliar straps, fingers stiff from so much practice, her whole mind stupid with exhaustion.

Her dreams were all dust, fire, and blood, her body forced beyond simple exhaustion, the horror of searching among dangerously loose stones for something she could not find; crawling through dark holes for someone who was not there.

Haffat

It was very dark outside Mirikos; only a few fires still burned in Haffat's camp, and the moon had set hours before.

The tent Knoe used for divination was small and unfigured, plain black cloth, with no banners to mark it. The inside was equally plain: a long table with unfigured, sturdy legs in the center of the tent; a clay lamp the size of a small orange which hung from the midpole, its wick cut short so it only occasionally cast enough light to cast the shadows of three men against the cloth.

Haffat stood unmoving against the rear wall of the little pavilion and tried to keep his mind clear. Difficult, when there was so much work to finish before they could leave Mirikos. Knoe sat cross-legged before him, his back against the near legs of the table, eyes closed. The third man lay upon the table, head toward the other two; Knoe had cut the prisoner's throat at precisely the peak of night.

There are ships to be loaded; food and weaponry to be checked and I must again assure the captains who are fretting over the distance between Mirikos and Diyet, lest their disease spread to all my captains. He was letting his thoughts intrude once more; he bit his lip, glanced down at the priest, and again cleared his mind.

Knoe could sense the emperor's restlessness—his initial anger at what he saw as waste of life. *Dread Axtekeles, give me the words that will best persuade him. We have brought Your way to so many lands already, thanks to Haffat—the beginnings of it, at least. I will gladly spread Your worship to all corners of this earth, but Haffat grows restive and his rages have struck twice in the past fifteen days. Return us soon to Diyet, give me the prophecy that will direct him, and before two winters are gone, all men in that land will bow to the lion.* And the lion-priest would live out his days in wealth and splendor, for Axtekeles was not a mean god. He rewarded those who served him well and spread His Word. *You know I have served you well, all my days. I will not fail you, whatever other man proves faithless.*

Warmth filled his belly; Axtekeles's warmth that preceded the Lion's Breath. Soon the god would speak to Haffat, through him. *What greater honor than this, to be the vessel for a god?* The conquerers, the kings—they came and went, and after a while no one remembered who they had been. Perhaps no man would remember Knoe's name a lifetime on. *But I will have done this service to Axtekeles; he will remember Knoe.*

The air was turning red above the lamp. Haffat fixed his eyes resolutely upon Knoe's hairless skull and the handprint he had himself put there. His palm was still sticky where he had pressed it in the dead man's blood.

It was quiet, save for the distant barking of a dog, and then totally still again. Knoe's chin came up; his eyes opened and met Haffat's, but there was nothing of Knoe in that level, fierce gaze. "Say to my son Haffat, well done. You have performed each thing I asked of you, and because of that I give you Mirikos. You will again leave behind two of My priests with the city's new prince, and he will build for them a shrine to My honor, where men may worship.

"Let my son prepare well for the Ghezrathi, who await him with new-edged swords and a forest of spears."

Haffat licked his lips, reluctantly asked the question Knoe himself had insisted he ask. "And—two who become one?"

There was no answer; the hint of red above the lamp faded. Knoe stirred and blinked, and was again Knoe. When Haffat would have spoken, Knoe held up a hand for silence and led the emperor out of the tent and through the quiet camp and out onto wet, hard sand. To their right was the sea, a little starlight reflecting on the low-breaking waves. The sand was cool under bare feet, the air still. "The god is pleased with the sacrifice; He knows you do not find it easy, that your people have not bled men to their own gods in long years."

"I do not find it easy," Haffat said quietly. "I accept the god's will." Knoe glanced at him sharply but was apparently satisfied by what little he could see of the other's face. "What did you learn—that you can tell me?"

"A little of the city walls and the plain, but nothing of the city and nothing of two becoming one. Even with such a strong sacrifice, that remains hidden—from me *and* the god." Knoe shrugged. "Some trick of their earth goddess, I suspect, but she will not prevail. The gates will fall, the city will be yours. I saw you standing upon broad steps in a high place, your brother Heliar at your side and the crown of Ghezrat in your hands." Haffat started to say something, stopped abruptly. Knoe glanced at him curiously, but Haffat was gazing across the water. "I had hopes we might learn something from that Ghezrathi sailor. The man's heart must have been weak, I sent only my most skilled priests to question him. I suppose it would have been better if I had done that myself, but a man cannot be two places at once." This brought him up short. *Or can he?* "I have put forth a reward for information about this mystery, but no one in Mirikos has claimed it."

"Because they don't know—or because they are afraid?" Haffat asked.

Knoe shrugged. "Who can say? They worship Denota here also, and surely the mother of plants and lambs is no vengeful goddess. Still, it is of no great matter. A puzzle, only, but I do not like puzzles." They walked in silence most of the way back to the camp. Haffat waded out a ways and squatted down to wash his hands.

"Tomorrow as soon as it is dark, I shall send the next companies out—most of the baggage and supplies, the rest of the cavalry, the remaining third of chariot. They should quickly catch up to the infantry I sent two days ago."

"You really think this secrecy necessary?" Knoe asked.

"Of course, or I would not bother. That is my realm, and I tend to it carefully, you know: How many to send ahead and how to rearrange the camp so that any spies in Mirikos do not know men are already on their way to Ghezrat." He stood, stretching hard. "If any Mirikosi has seen anything, my own listeners have not heard of it. The Ghezrathi must know my army could never fit aboard all the merchant ships in the Sea of Delos, let alone those still in the harbor here. They will know what I have done as soon as the men who patrol their borders encounter mine. It is merely a delaying tactic."

"The god—" Knoe began. Haffat shook his head.

"I know. He says Ghezrat will be mine. But He told me to plan well, Knoe. And so, I seek whatever advantage I can, even such a simple ruse. They are old in war, the Ghezrathi, and they know what I am. They will not expect me to attempt such a simple trap. Or perhaps they will see the trap and think I am not so clever as they say.

"But that is unimportant. Whatever they think, or believe, they will still be trapped between two deadly forces." He bent over to dip his hands in the surge once more, pressed his palms against the short robe. Knoe stood a little back, out of reach of the water, watching him. Haffat took one last look at the water, then trudged back to dry sand. "Do you still advise me to take the Ergardi magicians?"

"Against Ghezrat? Of course." Knoe spread his hands. "You yourself talk of advantages. I cannot yet pierce the city walls, but they may be able to do what I cannot."

By inhabiting another man's body, and taking him over utterly. Haffat swallowed dread. "But Axtekeles—"

"They serve Axtekeles, in their own way." Knoe glanced at him. "Why do you look surprised? It is no secret, though ordinarily He does not deal in magic and spells. The Ergardi remain a separate cult, but they serve Him as passionately as they once served their chill northern gods; they bring Him men's bodies and men's souls as sacrifice. But I see this distresses you, so we will not talk of it. They also form and control Gryptiosi Fire, and you may need that in the battle to come." Silence, as they passed between the first tents. "He is a practical god, you know."

"I know that *you* are practical," Haffat said, and the lion-priest, surprisingly, clapped his hands together and laughed.

"Of course I am! But lord," he added earnestly, "you have followed Axtekeles for so short a time! I have served him all my days. A man new-come to the god's service often follows His ways strictly, and that is good. But I know the god well; Axtekeles did not turn from me for first bringing the Ergardi to His service; within this past hour, knowing they sleep in your camp, He again promised you the victory."

Haffat seemed reassured by this; a few moments later he left the priest and went in search of his bed and sleep for what was left of the night. Knoe sighed faintly. *Who would have thought a mere earth goddess so strong? How is it she still defies Axtekeles and hides her city, her priests, and the men who fight for her! How do two become one and why, and what has a goddess mystery to do with battle and warfare?* Perhaps Denota is toying with us all; it may be a ploy to distract me from more important matters.

The Ergardi were important, though he did not really understand them. *Though no man but I could have tamed them and brought them to the god.* No other man had seen their real worth; he had found them on a Diyet noble's estate harvesting grain, bought them for a pittance, and brought them to Axtekeles, and then to Haffat.

Haffat was afraid of the Ergardi; well, most men feared such power—to put on another man's body as though it were clothing. Another *man's* body. Knoe himself was not always certain the core of an Ergardi was as human as his own. Axtekeles welcomed them; it was all he needed to know. *But they were not uppermost in Haffat's mind tonight. Nor was his infantry or those ships—it was something else, something he thought of or remembered when I spoke of Ghezrat.*

Something to do with Ghezrat—but what?

7

Atos had just cleared the eastern ridges to warm the roof gardens of the prince's palace when Tephys sought audience with his queen. Ye Sotris sat in the deep shade of an arbor, smiling fondly at the two youngest princes who were dabbling in the shallow pool, giggling and trying to capture the small fish. Septarin stood on a long bench at the northern wall, back to them, gazing out toward the sea.

Tephys knelt to kiss the young queen's extended hand, then sat next to her. Ye Sotris patted her very swollen stomach and let her eyes drift back to the smaller boys. She was from Ye Eygar and therefore foreign, but Tephys thought her exotic-looking even for an Eygari. Dark freckles dusted prominent cheekbones, barely visible against warm brown skin darker than that of most Ghezrathi, but her eyes were light brown, nearly tan, and they held unexpected green flecks. The smooth brown hair looked nearly red in full sun. "I think this time I will give Pelledar a daughter; she feels different from the other three."

"Possible," Tephys allowed. "Denota has not given me any foreknowledge of that."

The queen raised her voice a little. "Children! Not *into* the water, please!" She sighed. "We will all know by midsummer. It is not—a good time to bear a royal child, is it?"

Tephys shook her head. "I would lie to you, but to what point? You are stronger than that, Ye Sotris."

"Yes. But I would know if you did lie, any of my house would." She shook her head and was quiet for a moment. "This coming war worries me. Not just the fighting, we Eygari have seen enough of that. But my husband draws away from me; does he think I care he has not killed men? I am pleased he does not go out to kill men! Any man can become a warrior, but the good Pelledar does for his people—that is not something a man learns, he is born with it."

"I know. It is a pity the men of Ghezrat see it differently—at least, once they all did," Tephys said. "Now some see these past twenty years and think, 'What is twenty years? Why can we not continue for all our lives and those of our sons in such peace?'"

Ye Sotris nodded, cast her eyes in Septarin's direction, and lowered her voice even more. "My son—our son. I think it is the worst thing of all for Pelledar, to have Septarin look upon him with such open contempt. I am his mother, and I cannot even guess what Septarin feels; sometimes I wonder how he can be *my* son, or Pelledar's."

"Having no sons of my own, I can hardly advise you," Tephys said. "Knowing who his tutors were, however—"

"Yes. Well." Ye Sotris sighed. "I held out against Etimos, you know. I wanted Septarin to have a master of music—but Septarin has known from his first steps how to wheedle whatever he wants from his father. And even Pelledar thought Etimos better for him. Not to mark him as so different from other noble boys, you know."

"Of course," Tephys began. Septarin's high, shrill voice overrode hers, and both women wheeled around to stare as he shouted.

"I see them, *I see them!* Ships, there, just coming past the point, ten—no, fifteen, twenty! More!"

"My son." Ye Sotris struggled to her feet and raised her own voice; Septarin, who had actually been jumping up and down on the bench like an over-excited child, spun around and blushed painfully. "Yes, you had forgotten where you were, and in what company, had you not? Take your news, my son, to those eager to hear of coming war and death. Your mother is not one of them."

"But—!"

"At once, I say," Ye Sotris' low, resonant tones overrode his petulant voice with the ease of long practice. "Go to your father, his council, the captain of your company—any or all of them, as you choose, but do not alarm your brothers, and I do beg of you, do not brag of the Diye Haff to me." She remained standing until her eldest son leapt from the bench and hurried from the roof, sparing her one sideways, furtively embarrassed look, and a narrow glare for

Tephys. But they could hear his joyous shout as he clattered down the steps: "The ships! Haffat is come!"

Tephys helped the queen back to her seat. Ye Sotris gazed blankly at the pool and the two small heads once more bent over it. When she finally began to speak once more, her voice was thoughtful, her eyes fixed on the distance. "Ye Eygar is a coastal land, you know. Pirates have always harassed us, so we always kept watch for their sails, and fighting men and ships were always ready to battle them. And yet—" She fetched a small sigh. "And yet, a boy Septarin's age would know nothing of spears and swords. A boy of fifteen plays pipes or lyre, composes verse or dances or performs those of his friends, or others composed by the ancients and handed down to us." Tephys stirred and Ye Sotris turned to look at her. "You need not say anything. What was there is not the same as what is here; it is foolish to compare such things, or try to change one to another. You did not come to argue such philosophies with me, anyway, did you?"

"No. I came at an hour you would be apart from your husband, his council, even your servants. Not," Tephys added hastily as the younger woman frowned, "because I do not trust any of them. Listen. Often, even in the most complete prophecy, there is the chance of shift, or change—"

Ye Sotris' brow cleared. "You try to tell me, I think, that it is possible Ghezrat will not win this war."

"I do not. Denota promised victory, but much can pass between first attack and victory."

"Yes."

"You are sensible, Ye Sotris; thank you for that. It may be that the Diye Haff will threaten the very gates. I do not *know* this, only fear the chance, because of certain things I have been shown."

"Yes." Ye Sotris nodded once. "I have thought about that myself: or that they might even occupy the city for a while. But there are many secret ways beneath the palace, where the children and I can hide."

She stopped uncertainly as Tephys shook her head. "They are secret from outsiders, but known to your husband, your eldest son and his tutors, and all your servants. A secret spread so thin is no secret at all. And any man can be made to reveal even the most vital secret." Ye Sotris' eyes were momentarily filled with fear, but she merely nodded again.

"There are also hidden places beneath Denota's ground," Tephys went on. "I know of certain of these from Meronne, who had them from her predecessor, and they are inviolate." She paused, looked at Ye Sotris, who glanced at the children and then brought her steady gaze back to the priestess. "If there is need, or danger, or any cause whatever, Ye Sotris, I shall come for you or send Meronne in my stead. You and the babes will come at once, I beg, without stopping for anything or to leave any message—for any cause. But you must not go with anyone who is not myself or Meronne. We will see the prince knows you are safe, but he will know nothing of who keeps you safe, or where you are."

"Yourself and Meronne, only," Ye Sotris said. "But I would tell my husband this day, in private, that my well-being is seen to. That much only, if you will permit it. It will ease his mind, and save him grief later if I were to simply vanish."

"Tell him," Tephys replied. She got to her feet. "It is a pity Septarin has none of your good sense," she said quietly. Ye Sotris smiled up at her ruefully.

"Yes. Children are not always what one hopes they will be. But Septarin is my son, and I love him for all his flaws." The smile faded. "I wish only that Pelledar had been able to withstand his plaints and keep him safe within the walls, but Etimos has filled him with heroes and he would not have safety at any price." She started convulsively as the morning peace was again shattered: distant horns, blowing a warning that came ever nearer, passed from messenger to messenger until the city was filled with their harsh cry, and all the horns in the city broke into a warning shout. The small princes began to wail in fear and fled to their mother, who held out her arms and gathered them close. Above their small, dark heads, her eyes were wide, but her voice, when she spoke, was still steady. "Before you go, High Priestess, your blessing upon me and my children. All," her voice faltered, steadied once more, "all of my children."

Tephys rested both hands upon the queen's head, briefly upon the two curly heads. "Denota's blessing. With Her aid, you will come through this, Ye Sotris." She saw the question in the other's eyes: *Every one of us?* But Ye Sotris did not ask it, and Tephys turned away, leaving it unanswered.

* * *

Septarin clattered down the stairs from the roof, slid on the last step, and nearly fell. He gripped the wall and tried to catch his breath. "Which way?" he muttered to himself. "The council." But *they* would knew soon enough. Besides, the throne room was crowded just now, he could hear them arguing and snarling at each other in there. His father would be displeased that he broke in with such news, and besides— there was Khadat.

It had been a mistake to tell Apodain about that bargain, he thought. Khadat had gone at once to Pelledar and complained bitterly. He knew, he had heard her. *And of course Father rained complaints on me for days after. Why does he not tell her to go away? He is prince and she nothing but a dead brother's wife. She is wealthy, she owns ships—but is that enough that he lets her do whatever she wishes?* Septarin gave the throne room entry a cautious look, then started down the next flight of steps. They might come out at any moment and he would really rather not see old Khadat. *Give her a chance to forget she is angry with me, she claims to be so busy, that should not take so long.* In the meantime, a sensible prince would be careful about crossing her; Khadat was surely not as dangerous as she believed, but she could be decidedly unpleasant.

Still . . . the look on Apodain's face when I gave him the news. . . . Septarin skidded to a halt halfway down the main stair. He had nearly run down his tutor. Etimos held up a warning hand. "Be careful, my prince. You will be injured. And a warrior does not hurl himself down steps the way a child does."

Septarin was trying to catch his tutor's arm. "Haffat—the Diye Haff—I saw the ships, out there!"

"Ah. The ships." Etimos merely nodded. "Then you should go to your company commander, I think. But with dignity. You are a warrior now, remember." He paused on the next step. "Does your father know?"

"No. I must go." Septarin descended the rest of the steps and stalked across the hall. *Does he think I forget my dignity? Does he forget who is in command of those ships?* Once he reached the outside, however, he pelted down the great stair and raced across the horse-forecourt. *I thought Etimos was fond of me! But he showed no interest in my news, just now, and he knows what it means to me.*

He was bursting with the news, but there was no one out

here at this hour except servants—and who cared what they knew? He could tell Apodain, but Apodain didn't care about anything any more; it wasn't any fun to taunt him. Besides, if Khadat found him there ... Septarin sighed, murmured a curse under his breath and ran out the gates, down the avenue and past Denota's temple. He was only halfway across the square when horns blared out the warning.

Breyd and Menlaeus were eating a late breakfast with Niverren and Creos—twenty-five days wed and still living in the main room of Menlaeus' house, as they probably would until after the war was over. Or, at least Niverren would; two days after the marriage, Creos had been chosen as a peltast for the special division of light infantry that would occupy the mole and the shore surrounding it, to harry the Diye Haff and keep their ships from landing as long as possible.

Creos held Niverren's hand and kissed it often as they ate—at least, he ate. Niverren was making a brave show, but Breyd could see most of her bread was a pile of crumbs in her lap.

"They don't want to lose any of us, beloved," Creos assured her once again. "We are out there solely as first wall, a mere diversion."

"I know. You said." Niverren's voice wavered a little; she swallowed, picked up her cup, and drank deeply. When she set it aside, she managed a smile for him, though her eyes remained anxious. "It is just—not knowing how long you may be gone, the uncertainty! And there are so few of you out there, and you know how many men they say Haffat brings."

"They say," Creos mocked gently, and kissed her hand once more. "Niverren, you know how long and narrow the mole is; an entire company would make it impossible for any of us to move, and that would be more dangerous. They did choose us for skill with throwing weapons and bows, and for our knowledge of that stone harbor and the land on both sides of it. Besides, there is a full company behind us, archers and slingers all there to back us at need and cover our retreat. And they send a ballista with us. Just think, we may do Haffat enough damage out there that he will not be able to land at all. Think of what a hero your husband shall be then!" He laughed at the vision; Niverren brought up the corners of her mouth once more, shook her head. "We will have a house of our own, well up the hill, if this comes to be, and I shall dress you in blue silk." He poured from the jug, took up his cup, and held it out. "Drink with me, beloved, a toast to us, and to the outermost and innermost ranks who protect the city," he added as he looked at Menlaeus and then Breyd. "To swift victory."

Niverren sighed, nodded, and held her cup against his. "Yes, I will drink to that: swift victory, and a safe return for all of you. But—" She was silenced by the wild warning cry of many horns. After what seemed forever, the horns were briefly silent, then began a new series of calls. Creos leapt to his feet, shoved the cup into his wife's hands, and bent down to catch hold of her shoulders so he could kiss her full on the mouth.

"No, Niverren, don't get up, don't move. Wait here." He stood back, looked into her eyes, then bent to kiss her once again. "I will come back to you, beloved, I swear it by Atos himself." He turned and ran; Niverren stood, cups and crumbs of bread sliding from her lap, the back of one hand pressed hard against her teeth and her eyes brimming.

A moment later, Nevvia cried out, "No! No, not yet, not now!" She came running into the courtyard from the storage, then spun around, arms outstretched, but Tarpaen caught her hands together, kissed them in turn and pressed her to one side.

"Mother, I must go, they call for the entire horn company! Xhem—come with me, little brother. Mother, I'll send him back as soon as there is word for you." He slowed as Menlaeus came to his feet, gripped his father's shoulder in passing. "Take care." Xhem slid between Tar and Breyd, ran to open the door. It slammed hard behind them.

Menlaeus set aside his cup, picked up the baldric, and pulled it over his head. Nevvia made a wordless, wretched little noise and came toward him, blindly, arms outstretched and tears spilling down her face. "Husband!"

He wrapped his arms around her, then leaned away to look down at her. "We must go also, little love. I just heard the call for First Prime and Secchi." He blotted her eyes with a corner of his red cloak, kissed her brow.

Breyd pinned the red cloak at her throat, hesitated, then hugged her mother carefully. Menlaeus included her in his own embrace. She kissed Nevvia's cheek, then whispered against her ear, "Mother? Darling Mother, please don't, we have to go and if Father's so worried about you—"

"I know," Nevvia whispered. She swallowed, blotted her face on her husband's cloak and gave her daughter a tear-stained, shaky smile. "I don't mean to. I told myself I wouldn't."

"I know, Mother. It's all right, we won't be anywhere but the barracks today, I'm sure of it. And Tar's safer on the wall than anywhere else."

"I know." She drew herself up, gave Menlaeus a little shove and said, "You had better go now, quickly. I have Niv, and Niddy will keep us both busy, go. Bring me news." Menlaeus kissed her again, and turned to gather up his javelins and the shield. More horn signals rang across the city, calling in the various companies.

"Oh, *Mother!*" Niverren came running. Nevvia gave her an abashed little smile; tears were running unchecked down her face.

Niverren wrapped her arms around her younger sister. "Nidya is right, you're all edges and corners, difficult to hug," she murmured. For a moment, she wasn't certain Breyd had even heard her; then, with a faint, shuddering little sigh, the girl's arms went around her, hurting her ribs. "Gently! Creos won't like me all bruised, you know." Niverren glanced over her shoulder; Nevvia hadn't moved, and Menlaeus hovered uncertainly, hands moving automatically to move the shield up on his left arm and position the javelins behind it. Nidya came from the kitchens and walked over to pull her daughter close; Nevvia turned and buried her face in her mother's shoulder.

Menlaeus settled the red cloth tiara atop his helm and gathered up his quiver; his eyes went toward the door. Breyd walked ahead of him and let them into the street.

Etimos had just brought the council Septarin's news when the horns began calling the warning; Khadat cried out, and Polyos leapt to his feet, a fist pressed hard against his breast. Pelledar waved a hand. "Go now, you each have your tasks and you know what they are. Meet me at the main gates, at the call, for the passing of troops."

As soon as the last of them was gone, he ran from the throne room. Tephys was just coming down from the roof; she stepped aside to let him pass. "I need you, tomorrow,

Prince Pelledar. This eclipse—it will take strong intercession if we are to avert disaster. I will send Eyzhad for you." Pelledar merely nodded and hurried up the steps. The sound of horns followed him, echoing in that narrow passage. He stopped near the top to catch his breath; Ye Sotris must not see him so panicked and he would frighten the babes.

Ye Sotris sat upon her favorite bench under the awning, her face pale but composed. She had an arm around each of the boys and was whispering something to them that made them giggle. *What have I done to deserve such a brave queen?* he wondered. He tried to look calm as he walked across the garden. She looked up, smiled at him, murmured to their young sons again; both boys turned to look up at him. *She makes herself appear calm for them; I can do no less.* Pelledar smiled at his sons, then knelt and took all three of them in his arms.

Khadat walked swiftly from Pelledar's palace to her sedan chair and drummed her fingers impatiently against the wooden frame as the servants bore her the short distance to her own broad entry. There were, she was pleased to note, no signs of hysteria *here,* though she had heard plenty of shrill-voiced panic in the streets. She stepped from the chair and automatically glanced toward the second floor windows. Apodain was standing where he usually stood these days, in the window of his room—staring across the city or, more likely, at nothing. *Sulking, still.* Khadat set her lips in a thin line and strode into the hall, hurried up the steps. Reott stood at the head of them. "Hemit?"

"He is well, Princess."

A well-meant lie, since Hemit had made no improvement in so very long. But at least he grew no worse. "Apodain?"

"He sent out word he would speak with you, Princess, when you came."

"Before or after the horn call?"

"Before. Not long after you left for the council meeting."

"I see." Khadat nodded. "Remain here, in case I need you."

"Yes, Princess."

Her son didn't turn from the window when she came in, though she was certain he must have heard her sandals on the hard floor. "Apodain?"

"Mother."

"Apodain, you will look at me when I speak to you." She folded her arms across her chest, waited as he sighed wearily but finally turned. "That is better. What is it you have to say to me?"

He looked at her blankly for a moment. "Oh. That you need not keep a guard in the hall, to assure that I will not try to rejoin the royal chariot—or another company. I will not."

"I see." Khadat considered this, finally walked across the room to take the only chair. "You at least see the sense of my course?"

I see people in the street who would tear me limb from limb, for forsaking my company, Apodain thought bleakly. *And a company that would not have me back, even if Septarin had not been given my driver. But I also see that she will not give over or give me my freedom before I come of age, though most mothers of my rank do. That I will go mad if I remain much longer confined to this room.* Three more years until a young nobleman was counted a man, with a man' rights. "I see the sense of it, Mother."

Khadat gazed at him, that unblinking, hard stare she had so often used on him and Hemit when they were boys. *I thought then that she knew my thoughts, that she could read me like a scroll.* It was still unnerving. She finally nodded, apparently satisfied. "All right, then. I have not yet had the opportunity to speak with Pelledar about this dreadful, common little girl, but that can come later. This afternoon, the companies will pass through the main gates, and I must be upon the wall before the gates with the rest of the council. You will stand at my side." Her eyes narrowed and she tilted her head a little. Apodain merely nodded. "You will do this, my son?"

"If you wish it, Mother."

"I wish it. I must visit your brother. You are free to move about the house and the courtyards, without interference."

"Thank you, Mother." He smiled, came across to help her to her feet, and kissed the cheek she turned toward him. The smile faded as she walked from the room. *A larger cage, but a cage nonetheless.*

And another ordeal. The bonding ceremony had been bad enough—or would have been, if he had been able to take any of it in. Just now, he could barely recall the girl—just that she was exquisitely small and dark, rather exotic-looking; and that her eyes had been wide with shock when she first saw him. *What does she think of me, I wonder? She will fight for the city, but her husband-to-be does not.* She would doubtless be one of the many who looked at him with contempt this afternoon. He had seen enough of that lately from his window, men who stopped in the street to stare up at Perlot's palace.

There have been enough curses uttered out there to send my soul to join Father's between the worlds, he thought bleakly. It would be better than an afterlife with his mother. The goddess knew *this* life loomed long and dreadful enough. But what choice had she left him? Suicide, of course—he had thought of that often enough, especially that first day. Perhaps he might have done it then, if the surprise hadn't left him stunned beyond acting. In cold blood—no. He would not risk Denota's wrath by such a desperate course unless there was no alternative; no warrior would. *And I was a warrior, even if I am not now.* A clean death at his own hands to avert torture, and the resulting deaths of other men should he talk; suicide to avoid his sacrifice to alien gods or for evil purpose—the goddess blessed such men. She would not bless one who sought to escape personal shame and a mother's clutches.

It is not the end of everything, an inner voice assured him. *You are only nineteen, you will outlive Khadat. There will be a chance to redeem yourself.* Just now, it seemed a very remote chance indeed. Apodain stared at the door. He could pass it now; it didn't seem to matter if he did or not.

Men, women, and children stood several deep on both sides of the street leading to the barracks, all around the square, and along the steep avenue that went to the palace, waiting for the companies to emerge.

The fighting ground was crowded but quiet, and well-organized. Near the gates, a company checked its weaponry and men tested the straps on each other's armor—Creos and the other peltasts readying to march out to the mole. Three horses stood a few paces back, and hitched behind them, a long ballista, mounted on wheels and covered in hardened hides. Another cart held jugs of pitch and covered, smoking pots of hot coals; a third carried men to work the ballista. Moments later, the company was gone, on its way toward the main city gates. A cheer went up from the waiting civilians.

A company of common chariot moved up to fill the space left by the light infantry; their captain moved down the ranks, stopping here and there to test harnesses or speak to a young driver, to check weaponry. Beyond them, in the center of the fighting ground, two full phalanxes of spearmen sat cross-legged in the dirt, listening to their officers run through the hand-signs one last time. Upon the low wall above the barracks, horn and drum signalers were gathered; someone up there was tapping his drum, adjusting the hoop. An officer on the ground raised two fists over his head; the first spear phalanx rose as one man. Two men in plain, dark cloth, horns in hand, jumped down from the wall to join them.

Five riders rode into the courtyard on steaming, sweaty horses—watchers from the small forts east of the great ridge who had sent on the first warning of ships. Boys ran from the stables to see to the animals and the men hurried into the main messes. Several of the officers broke away from their companies to follow. Grysis looked up from last-minute instructions to Menlaeus. "Wait, I'll return." He ran after them.

The common chariot clattered through the barracks gate and down the street to another cheer; the two companies of spear moved up to take their place.

There was open space before the barracks and a momentary hush. Breyd and Menlaeus stood where Grysis had left them and watched the spearmen form into long lines, three abreast, to march through the streets and the gates. More men came in from the streets; the phalanx of slingers and archers who would back the company on the mole. Menlaeus took his Secchi's wrist and drew her a little to one side.

Her skin felt cold, yet hot where Menlaeus had touched her, as though she had fever; it was hard not to wrap her arms around herself. Menlaeus must know how furiously her blood was pulsing; that her hands would tremble if she held them out. She could feel his worry; she felt the effort it took him not to hug her reassuringly. *He is right. If he does that, or if I hug myself men around us will see a Secchi afraid. They would jeer or laugh at me—or perhaps be afraid because one chosen by the goddess is openly fearful. Some might even say aloud what they now only whisper: that no girl has the right to bear weapons, whatever the goddess says. Those who believe we have some mystic power would fear I foresee what they cannot.* She bit her lip, clenched her fists. In a way, she did. *No. I know better now; the goddess warned me with that vision.* She had not had those horrid dreams since just after the final binding; that must be proof she was right.

She looked up at her father; she could tell he was not really afraid, but nervous; more uncertain how the first day would go, very worried about Nevvia, a little concerned for her, wondering where his son was, how Niverren was managing at the moment. Worrying about the various Primes on their way here, which of them would be worried, which afraid. None of that showed on his face. She looked past him, toward the constant stream of men moving in and out of the messes, across the fighting grounds. Most of them were expressionless, many had grim faces. No one looked afraid.

Menlaeus gripped her shoulder, smiled when she looked at him again. "Your face is fine."

Of course he knew the direction of her thoughts; she smiled ruefully. "Thank you. I didn't want to—" Someone called her name; she jumped and spun around. Tarpaen, his horn already mounted in its face strap and clutched tightly in one hand, was working through the crowd to reach her.

"Breyd!" He caught hold of her, hugging hard enough to drive the breath from her. "Breyd, I—" He shook his head and she felt him swallow. "I didn't want you to go out there thinking that I—I mean—"

"Tar, it's all right." She freed her arms from his crushing grasp, hugged him hard in turn. Another moment, she'd be weeping or worse yet, he would and she with him.

"I was—it hurt me, that's all," he mumbled. "And Mother has been so—"

"I know. Tar, it's not your fault," she urged. "You aren't the only one upset by this."

"You mean Mother. I didn't—I wouldn't have said any of those things, truly—I thought she would realize I was joking, and then, when she didn't—I'm sorry."

She eased her grip on his ribs, leaned back to look up at him. "I know you didn't mean to upset Mother, silly. I meant other families, it's set all thirty-four families upside down. How could it do otherwise? Tar, don't. Please."

He swallowed, nodded after a moment. "I'm sorry. I just

wanted to say that. And the other—about the fighting, that you can and I can't—all that. I didn't want you to go out there thinking I hated you, because I was jealous. I don't hate you, honestly. You're my sister."

She managed a careless-sounding laugh that sounded unnervingly like Niverren. "Oh, Tar. I never thought you hated me."

"Hah." Tarpaen gave her a shaky grin. "You never *could* lie. Father!" He turned to grip Menlaeus's arm, glanced up as someone shouted his name. "I've got to go, Mib's put me on first watch, by the Goat Gate. They let me send Xhem home so Mother would know. Take care of each other. Please."

"Yes, of course." Menlaeus pulled his son close, then let him go and watched him clamber back up the ladder and feel his way onto the walkway across the barracks. "I had better see if Grysis has any new word in there, if there is any new instruction for us. Wait here." Breyd ran a surreptitious hand across her eyes and nodded, sniffed discreetly as the slingers and archers moved across the fighting ground and out the gate.

A half-phalanx of royal chariot came up from the stables, horses led by their drivers. Their captain came from the barracks to hold his hands together, palm out and fingers spread, above his head. Men dropped the horse leads and came to gather around him. Breyd sniffed again and swallowed the last threat of tears. *Tar—if I didn't know you better, I would say you did that on purpose, to undo me before everyone.* But his emotion had been genuine, his distress real. Her eyelids prickled again; she swore between clenched teeth and tried to concentrate on something—anything—else. Brysos was giving the drivers some final instructions; a name caught her attention. "All of you, remember *who* rides with Loros now! He is no Apodain, with strength and skill and two years of hard work behind him."

"Thank the goddess he's not Apodain! Filthy little coward!" someone deep in the crowd grumbled. Brysos folded his arms and glared the drivers into silence.

"There is more to *that* matter than the princeling or anyone else has told you, but that is no matter. You will not, any of you, downspeak Apodain in my hearing!" He folded his arms, waited until a subdued chorus of, "Sir," and nods answered him. "Loros, *you*, at least, will not forget who occupies your chariot."

"Goddess, as if I could," someone—apparently Loros—replied fervently.

"Yes. Well. The rest of you will *not* allow the princeling to ignore orders. You will pay *no* heed should he try any maneuver not ordered by me and verified by an *officer*, by voice, hand sign, or horn!" He glanced over the company and lowered his voice cautiously. But it was a reedy, carrying tenor, and Breyd heard him easily. "Septarin has spent all his young life giving orders to his father's servants; he sees anyone who is not a prince's son as servant, even men such as us. And you have all heard him, he has made it clear often enough that he has a higher personal purpose than simply serving as part of the army that protects Ghezrat. He wants to push the Diye Haff into the sea by himself, and be cried a hero by all the city. He has no intention of obeying the orders of a mere captain if they do not serve his purpose."

"Send him home," called a resentful voice.

"Do you think I wouldn't? Which of *you* wants to tell our prince that his son is a danger to everyone around him? Septarin would deny it, and claim jealous men were out to get him, and where do you think the prince would side?" Silence. The captain heaved a sigh. "All right, then. Royal Chariot will not be out until sixth horn, unless the Diye Haff somehow find a way to land."

"Sir, they won't," one of the drivers near the front spoke up. "Not today, with the sea as rough as it is and the wind from the west. My father sailed the Delos all his life; it would be impossible for even a very skilled sailor to land a ship in such seas, and the inner side of the mole will be as unprotected from surge as the outer."

"They won't land out there," someone else said. "There are already men down there along the shore and on the mole to stop any such attempt."

"They won't land today anyway," someone else muttered. "Didn't you hear the priests in the Warriors' House? Atelos walks the sky tomorrow and steps between Atos and Denota; the Diye Haff will use that black hour against us."

The captain shook his head. "They *seek* to frighten us, that is all. Even the priests said as much, remember? Go, ready your horses and the cars, they want us to parade for Ghezrat, we may as well be pretty for that."

Laughter. "For the last time in a long time!" someone shouted back. The men went back to their horses and chariots.

More to that matter than you know. No one had seen Apodain since the sealing ceremony, but Breyd had certainly heard enough about him—rumors in the street, in the barracks, particularly among the Secchi. She could hate the man simply for making her the center of so much attention. *Some of the Secchi are worse than Niverren—wanting to know how I feel about Apodain, about his mother, about the things Septarin has blurted out in the messes loudly enough for half the city to hear.*

Unlike Niverren, her fellow fighting women paid attention to her answers, and pried even deeper when they thought she was hiding something, or lying to them. But he really didn't matter, Khadat didn't matter. "Well, of course he's pretty to look at," she'd finally told Xeria. "And rich. I would be a fool not to find such a man attractive, wouldn't I? But there is the small matter of a war to fight before any of *that* business counts." She'd done her best to ignore sidelong looks between Xeria and Jocasa that said, *well, some of us have a war to fight.*

Perhaps Denota did warn of Father's death and mine, so that I may prepare for it, and meet it with honor. If so, then Apodain really won't matter. She ground her teeth and swore at herself. Why weren't there any true answers? What good was a frightening and vague vision of the future, with no key to what it meant? If it meant their deaths, why didn't the goddess also warn Menlaeus? Surely *she* wasn't more suited to bear the weight of such foreknowledge than her father! But he might have had a vision of his own and not told her.

That would be like him. But she didn't dare ask him, she had to keep it from him. So far as she could tell, even with the impossibly close bond between them, he didn't know.

She watched the royal chariot drivers walk back to their cars, watched another phalanx of archers settle into a tight, crouched group nearby, checking their arrows, their bows and strings, the straps on each other's padded armor. She felt very alone. *Goddess, why have you done this to me?* The other Pairs had completely succumbed to the training and the rites, as was surely intended; the Primes strong and supremely self-assured, the Secchi quick, skilled, and completely matched in movement and ability to their Primes—deadly, also supremely assured. *I fight as well as any of them, my eye and aim are as good, the match with my Prime as perfectly fitted—but I alone lack that goddess-granted assurance that blinds the others to anything but complete and total victory.*

At times, it felt as though the whole thing was a rock, stuck in her throat: Even if she had wanted to talk to anyone about it, she simply couldn't force the words. *Once, I could talk to people—to Niddy, to Denira—to Mother, about most things. Those first days after Tephys made me novice, I could talk to her, or even Meronne. Father, always and above all. He understood, he could make the most dreadful things seem unimportant. But now—*

Now, there was, literally, no one. Tephys had no time to talk to her, and Meronne was at least as busy. She could never share such a terrible thing with Lochria, even though she and Lochria had become fast friends.

Menlaeus and Grysis came out of the messes; Menlaeus gestured for her to join them. Several of the Dyaddi had just come through the gates but had to step back as more horsemen came from outside. Breyd had to move aside herself or be run down. Menlaeus and Grysis hesitated; Grysis shrugged and sent Menlaeus on to the gates, turned himself and hurried back to the messes. Breyd skirted a few archers who stood in a worried-looking huddle, her eyes on the horsemen and her company commander, and fetched up hard against someone standing just beyond the archers.

Winded and startled, she fell back a pace and brought up an apologetic smile; it faded as she looked up into a familiar, heavily bearded, glowering face. Laius folded his arms across his chest. A few more archers passed, separating to stream around them.

"Your brother told me you were here, and I saw your father just now, over there. Good. I prefer to speak to you alone."

Breyd looked past him, then up at him. He was at least half again her size and even in the midst of so many, it made her almost as nervous as it always had, knowing Laius was between her and where she wanted to be. This time, she was angry, too. "Speak? Look, I haven't time for this, Laius, my company—"

"My company," he mimicked savagely, silencing her. He took a step forward; Breyd fought the urge to turn and run. *He would like that, wouldn't he, knowing for certain how much he frightens me?* His breath was hot against her brow, and then rough-skinned fingertips scraped at her chest, across her jaw, came to rest heavily on her shoulder.

"Take your hand from me," she said; the words came out breathy and too high. Laius grinned.

"Why? I call Tar my brother, you are therefore my sister, are you not? May a brother not lay his hand upon his sister without so much fuss? Or is it that?" His thumb jerked toward her forehead. "A dirty bit of knotted string, what does such a thing matter? Tarpaen said your father beat his wife for laying a hand on his."

Breyd stared up at him. "He did *not!* How dare you, Laius?"

What—will you now beat me?" He laughed; his other hand came down on her shoulder and dug into muscle when she would have retreated. "Will the goddess curse you—or me? Both of us? Perhaps merely unmake the bond if I pull that cord from your brow? And then what—will you go and wipe Apodain's pretty nose and lick his mother's sandals? I can offer you better than that, and you will not need to play soldier for *me.*"

Breyd gaped at him, momentarily stunned into silence. His fingers continued to dig into her shoulder; she twisted suddenly, ripping free of his grasp. "How dare you still speak to me of marriage! You have no right!" He glared down at her, she glared back; fury warmed her belly. "Do you think I would welcome *you?* I would leap from the walls before I shared your bed! Or share one with Apodain *and* Khadat, preferable to you!" His eyes went black, he bared his teeth and the free hand became a fist. Somewhere close by someone shouted out a warning.

Her vision blurred, everything was hazed in red and suddenly she could see Laius—from behind. Not so tall, not nearly so massive—his hair was thin at the crown. *Father,* she knew at once. Menlaeus had stalked up behind him, unnoted by either; his anger and hers blended and flared through her. *There are more enemies than those who come today in ships; how dare he choose this moment to threaten me? He thinks I will falter before his anger. He thinks me female and so weak—foul, dirty bastard, to threaten a woman so! To try to shame her before all the barracks! I will kill him, I will cut his—*

She blinked: Menlaeus stood directly behind Laius; Laius had gone pale and his jaw wabbled, his eyes were wide enough to pop from their sockets. Her dagger lay across his throat, her other hand was wrapped in his hair, he could not move. "Swear, here and now," she said softly, "that you will not ever again even *speak* to me—or I shall cut your throat and laugh as you die."

"You would not dare!" he whispered, but he sounded uncertain. She bared her own teeth in a mirthless grin. He edged back a little, but Menlaeus stopped him; she went with him, blade held hard against his throat.

"No? You have heard the tales about Secchi, Laius. We aren't safe, you know, we fighting women. We kill at will, as men do; we kill merely because we hold blades." They were surrounded, she suddenly realized. Laius sent his eyes one way and then the other and his shoulders sagged a little. Breyd stepped back. "That is the last and only warning you will ever get from me, Laius," she said, so softly no one but Menlaeus could possibly hear her. "Next time I shall use the knife. You do not ever say such words to me. Or touch me, in any fashion. *Ever.*"

"Don't wager on it," Laius hissed furiously, but his eyes wouldn't meet hers. He tugged at his padded tunic and straightened his shoulders, then cleared his throat and spoke aloud. "My apologies, little sister. I did not mean to startle you." He inclined his head; the flat, black eyes that met hers as he straightened showed no sign of apology.

"Accepted, friend of my brother," Breyd said coolly, but as Laius turned away, she rubbed wet palms on the red cloak, and her legs wanted to tremble. *I would have killed him, without thought or remorse, just as they say of Secchi! Unstable*— No. Angry, certainly; but with cause. And that Laius could drive her to such a brink surely did not make her a general danger—that was Menlaeus' thinking, surely. She carefully restored the dagger to its sheath, pressed down on the hilt to make certain it was tightly in place. Laius was gone when she looked up; she nodded curtly to the men standing around her and staring. Menlaeus caught hold of her shoulders and drew her across the grounds toward the gates.

All at once, she wanted to laugh. There was no doubt the

training had taken. *And—compared to Laius, what are the Diye Haff?* Menlaeus looked down at her. She grinned at him. "Only Laius, you know—no great matter."

"Only?" Menlaeus looked at her doubtfully, but Grysis was urgently calling them over to the gates, and he let it go.

Atos rose to midday before burrowing into thick cloud; wind kicked dust clouds all across the plain to rattle vines in untended vineyards and whine through the city as small companies emerged from the barracks and marched down the steep road. City people and those who had come in from villages and holdings outside lined the streets and filled the squares. The prince's special guards did not have the heart to disperse them so long as the armed had room to go where they were sent. Dutifully, people cheered as each company or group appeared, but once they had seen the soldiers pass, they lapsed into nervous silence again. Many looked at the sky as though they expected Atelos to emerge from where he had risen not long before, just above the eastern walls, and snatch Atos completely away.

As the day wore on, clouds grew thicker until no man could say for certain where the sun hid, and now there was whispering and the word men whispered was, "Omen."

Behind the barracks walls, they could hear the clash of weaponry, a cacaphony of sound as many horn calls went up at the same moment—chaos there, surely, by the sound of things. And yet, the single horn cry rang out at each hour, as it always did. And the men marched from barracks to the plain surely and confidently.

Xhem pelted back to Nevvia at top speed and passed on Tarpaen's message, as well as everything else he could think of that might reassure the women. His grandmother, of course, showed as little emotion as his cousin Breyd. Which was fortunate, since he must spend so much time with his great-grandmother. Nidya couldn't possibly *frighten* him the way Breyd did—and she had frightened him with her stiff, chill manner even before Tarpaen told him all those stories about Secchi. *Possessed by demons, indeed,* he thought indignantly as he eased through the crowds on his way back to the barracks for he had messenger duty shortly and he had also been sent by the tear-blotched Nevvia to gather more information if he could. *My brother Tar has a wicked sense of humor.* He grinned then; think of the tales he could pass on, when he returned home, to leave his younger siblings wakeful all the night.

The smile slipped. *Home.* He had been so grateful from the first, being brought into the city. Having Tarpaen to treat him like a loved and wanted little brother, instead of simply a strong back and a useful pair of hands, someone to shout at the way his mother always did when something went wrong. Having tasks to do for his grandmother and his aunts that would assure his place in their home, at least until the Dyaddi were dissolved—and then, to be taken as a messenger for the horn and drum company! *I am too young by four years even for the trials that decide what company a man will join; another three years from joining such a company. And yet, if my brother Tar still stands for me, and Nabid and Mib, if they are pleased with me—* He couldn't finish the thought. But to remain forever inside the city—what more could he ever wish than that?

His own family was inside the walls now; thank Atos there were too many of them to house with Nidya and what he increasingly thought of as his *real* family. He knew vaguely where they were; he hadn't been to visit them yet. His mother would think he gave himself airs. *Perhaps I do.* Tarpaen had sent word that Xhem was too busy managing Breyd's share of the household tasks and his duties as a company messenger—which really was the truth—to spend any time with them. He would be grateful forever for that. *Father will understand. He will be glad that I have such a chance, Mother will see it only as an excuse on my part to not return to the holding with them.* He felt guilty, knowing both were partly right, knowing that he did in truth want to avoid his family. Not that he was shamed by them. But that he wanted better for himself than a short and hard life working barren dirt—that could surely not be wrong.

Sixth horn sounded; Xhem darted across the square just in time. When he turned back to see what the outcry was, and to catch his breath, there were guards everywhere—men in the prince's blue, in white and red, in yellow and red—all surrounding the sedan chairs being borne toward the main gates. Xhem drew one last deep breath, expelled it in a rush, and edged through the crowd to find his way to the fore. A moment later, the sedan chairs were set down, and from one emerged a grim-faced woman. The crowd went utterly still as she turned to the chair, waiting until a pale young man with a haunted expression followed her.

Apodain. Xhem heard the name whispered all around him, but he knew Apodain by sight anyway; he'd seen him upon the steps the night his cousin was trothed to the man, and he'd heard plenty about him since then. Apodain appeared deaf and blind both; he simply stood until his mother gestured and turned to walk toward the steps that led up the inner wall, next to the gates. Apodain followed. Xhem lost interest, turned back as those around him began to whisper once more. The second chair had held a small, round man who was as white as his tunic, and who trembled so it seemed impossible he could walk as far as the steps, let alone climb then. A younger man, enough like in the face to be his son, came to his side from somewhere behind the chair and took his elbow.

Others came forward: the priestess Tephys and the priest who served under her. Four young women followed, clad in green and crowned with flowers, bearing long, deep baskets filled with bright-colored petals; then General Piritos came from the barracks, stern and lean, clad in shining bronze armor and muscled greaves; the sun-priest Vertumnus was resplendent in yellow which made his face look almost green. They stopped behind the last chair and from it, Prince Pelledar emerged.

Xhem gaped and only just remembered to kneel as everyone else did; his thin chest swelled with pride. He had seen many of these great ones before, of course—on the night of the public trothing when he and Tarpaen had finally found a place upon the inner walls. But they had been so far away. Today, Tephys passed so close to him that he could smell the flowered oil she wore and see individual petals in the baskets the young priestesses carried. He could see the deep lines in Prince Pelledar's brow, see how the man's brilliant smile did not reach above that flash of white, even teeth. The prince turned and held up a hand, smiled at the people, then let himself be put into the midst of the procession which went up the steep flight of stairs and onto the inner wall next to the main gates.

Pelledar turned to gaze out across a sea of faces and raised his arms for silence. "People of Ghezrat, behold those who go to fight for you and for this city! Give them loud praise as they march from the gates, and send after them your prayers for their safe return!" Somewhere deep in the crowd, a woman began to weep.

The prince sent his gaze toward the barracks; he could as yet see no movement from this vantage. The horns were silent. The woman stopped crying.

What else shall I say to them? Pelledar wondered, but at that moment, Eyzhad came to take his arm and gesture urgently with his head toward the outer wall. A single horn cry, sharp with warning, went up from the far side of the outer gates. A low, worried murmur filled the air behind him as Prince Pelledar swallowed a dread of heights and followed the green-clad priest across the narrow, temporary walkway that crossed between inner and outer walls; the faces of his council waiting for him looked no less anxious than those below had.

A low, lightweight chariot pulled by two dark horses was coming up the main road at some speed. Two yellow flags fluttered above the rear corners, and the horses' harness was also bound in yellow. The driver wore a streamer of yellow upon his helm, but the dark man beside him was clad in unrelieved black. "Truce color," Piritos said tersely; of all those on the wall, he at least outwardly appeared unworried by sight of an enemy so near.

"How did they get all that off a ship in such seas?" Polyos demanded shrilly. "And where did it come from? There is no ship at the mole, our men hold that!"

"They—it just *appeared*," Eyzhad replied; he sounded shocked. "The guard just now said—it was just *there*, this side of the Oryon and already on the main road, no way to tell where it came from! But no ship has put in, how could it, a man can see white on the waves from here, it would be sure death!"

Piritos held up a hand. "What matter how it came?"

Tephys pushed to the front and peered at the rapidly approaching car. "I think you will find it is very important, general. There is something—unpleasant—out there. Eyzhad, come here," she ordered. She leaned into him, closed her eyes and let her head fall back against his shoulder; his hand steadied her.

The general's mouth tightened. "Well, it is here, and we must prepare to deal with those men." He was peripherally aware of Apodain at his elbow, gazing down at the oncoming chariot, his face expressionless, hands bunched into fists,

then Khadat, murmuring angrily against his ear, drawing him
back away from the outer wall. Interesting, the way she
treated her grown but still not legally-of-age son. Who in
this age tried to restrain a royal young man when others his
age had the full freedoms granted all free men? *Only
Khadat.* But he dared not let his thoughts be turned just now.
"My prince," he urged, "we must bar the gates."

Pelledar had gone very pale when he first saw the car; he
was still pale, but his voice was under control. "Yes. Let
them earn their way in."

"And they will not," Piritos finished for him. He turned
away from the outer side of the wall to shout down into the
space between walls: "Bar both gates, and keep them barred
until your prince or I tell you to open them, and no other
man! Order the people to keep quiet down there." He
glanced at the signaler stationed next to the gates and added,
"To the companies waiting in the barracks, hold." The signaler blew a four-note horn cry; in the street below, sounds
of panic and nervous voices, all abruptly stilled.

Tephys drew a sharp breath and Piritos turned to glare her
into silence. But she was staring down the road in absolute
horror and her face had gone as white as her tunic. "Beloved
Denota," she whispered. "It is an Ergardi in that chariot! No
wonder they were not seen!"

"You speak in riddles, woman," Piritos snapped. "I
haven't time for this!"

"No. Speak with them if you will, but *do not* let that chariot inside the walls! Beware that driver, general!" She pulled
away from Eyzhad, turned back to Piritos and said, "Dyaddi.
Two Pairs, veiled, prominently on this wall where he can see
them—do it now, general!" Piritos glared at her but she had
already found Khadat and snapped her fingers at the woman.
"Your cloak—at once!" Khadat stared blankly; Eyzhad took
it from her shoulders, spread it on the sand and dirt-strewn
stones and Tephys knelt on it, stretched her arms heavenward and prostrated herself. Eyzhad edged cautiously between Khadat and Tephys; the noblewoman would surely be
furious. But Khadat was still staring at the priestess. Steam
or wisps of smoke rose from the cloak, then faded, replaced
by a very faint greenish light that enveloped Tephys.

Piritos signed to one of his aides. "You heard the High
Priestess, get two Dyaddi up here immediately!" The aide
pelted down the wall to the barracks. Moments later, out of

breath, he came back and nodded. Just behind him, two Pairs came up the ladders and across the wooden bridge. One of the Primes slowed as he edged around Tephys; the general clapped his hands lightly and indicated a place near the front of the wall, between and just back of him and the prince.

Pelledar eyed the priestess warily. When he turned again to look out, the horses had slowed to make the final, steep straightaway. The passenger wore plain priest robes but of fine, expensive cloth, and the prince thought he saw gold upon the man's forearms and at his throat. He stroked a hairless chin thoughtfully, gazed for a while at the shining bronze gates, at the smooth, high walls. Finally he looked up at the stone arch over the gates, and only then at the people standing next to it.

He knew we were here, Breyd realized. *He is playing games with us, to show how confident they are.* The faint blood-red haze of full bonding wrapped around the four. *They all play such games,* she realized—Menlaeus' knowledge. *How dare they make a game of this?* she thought, and the rage began to fill her. *They kill men, steal lands, murder women and babies—and that creature dares smile at us?* She saw him with that other vision then—Menlaeus'. *Dangerous; more dangerous than he seems, for he is crafty and he will lie with great skill. That driver—* Alerted, Breyd took her eyes from the priest to look at the other. *Wrong.* Something about him was wrong. But the goddess bond made it difficult to reason and the unthinking fury that cloaked all four in the red haze filled her to the exclusion of any other thoughts.

The prince fixed his eyes on the priest's hairless face and tried to keep his own expressionless. *Is that priest an Ergardi? No,* she said the driver. *But—what is Ergardi, to frighten Tephys so?* And that driver—but there was nothing special about him; he was an innocuous-looking, dark little man. Skilled at driving a team, obviously, but that was no particular sorcerer's talent. The man he had driven did not seem that unusual, either, save for his silk robes, but not all gods asked a simple life of their servants. There was something odd about his face—Pelledar blinked as the priest's eyes met his. They were black, intense eyes, and as he shoved the hood back from his brow, Pelledar saw with shock that he was not simply head-shaven as some religious—he had no hair on any visible skin: dark, hairless brow and brows, hairless skull, hairless lip and chin.

He will not make me speak first, Piritos decided. He sent the prince a warning look, but Pelledar was still staring blankly at the messenger and did not see him. The silence stretched. Finally, the priest shrugged and his lips made a little smile that didn't reach those intense eyes. "I am Knoe, servant to Axtekeles and priest to Haffat, Great King of Diyet, Emperor of the North and of many lands. I bring from my master a letter, which he commands me to deliver into the hands of his brother Pelledar, King of the Ghezrathi and Great King of this broad and fertile plain."

Piritos touched the prince's arm, minutely shook his head. Pelledar sent his eyes sideways, nodded even more minutely. He didn't need the general's warning; he didn't even need to remember what Tephys had said. Just a glimpse of the furnaces behind those black eyes—he would not willingly approach that man, not for any cause. He set his hands against the stone of the outer wall to stop them trembling, and called down, "I am Pelledar, prince of this city and Great King of Ghezrat. I will send out a man to collect this letter."

"I must put it into your hands, or it stays with me, and I return to my master at once," Knoe replied flatly.

Pelledar could just see Eyzhad out of the corner of his eye; the priest was urgently shaking his head. *As if I would let that strange creature set anything into my hands, so that he must come near me and perhaps touch me,* Pelledar thought indignantly. *Do all of them think me as foolish as that? If he were a sorcerer, he might kill me at a touch, but a hidden blade would serve as well.* "No. I will not come out, and you will not enter. Set it against the gates and I will have a man come for it. Or read it to me from where you stand, for the gates are closed to any we count as Ghezrat's enemy."

The dark man lowered his head and stroked his chin thoughtfully. Khadat, who had worked her way past the priestess, came over to gaze down at the truce-chariot. But when she would have spoken, the general caught hold of her elbow and glared at her. "Be still, woman," he hissed. "You will not show any division among us—not to the Diye Haff, and not to this Knoe!" Khadat tore her arm from his grasp and glared back; Piritos had already turned away from her.

Knoe looked up, as though he had heard his name spoken.

"My master will not be pleased with me. He would be even less pleased did I return with his letter unopened and unheard." His eyes went to and stayed fixed for some time on the Pairs. Finally, he murmured something to the driver, who turned the chariot so it faced away from the city, then reached into the sleeve of his black robe and drew out a thin, folded parchment. Once it was flattened between his massive hands, he began to read.

8

"To my brother, Pelledar, Prince of Ghezrat and King of the fertile plains, the deep isthmus, and the southern sea, greetings from his brother Haffat, Emperor of Diyet, Great King of Mirikos and all the lands between. My brother has doubtless heard of the path I travel, binding together the many small lands into one great land, that together we may stand against the threat any choose to bring upon us. Shall Ghezrat face such enemies alone? For the times change, and the world with them, shall Ghezrat keep to the old ways of skirmish and battle, alone, and see her fields laid waste and her commons murdered, all her fair young fighting men dead?" Knoe paused, looked up. Pelledar's face showed nothing, that of Piritos even less; at the prince's gesture, Knoe shrugged, returned his gaze to the parchment, and went on.

"Let my brother also take council, if he will, and let him remember the fates of other lands and kings who were willful and proud, who turned from the path of sense to the will and the fate of Haffat: The King of Idemito is dead and his ashes mingle with those of his army—because he was foolish, and threw those lives away for his own vanity, and because he must prove that Idemito grows men of stronger flesh than does Diyet!" A commotion on the wall somewhere behind the prince; he looked up expectantly and waited. But neither prince nor general had moved, and the four intriguing red-clads were still wrapped in that bloodcolored mist. Knoe finally shrugged and went back to the letter.

"Let him recall Mirikos, where there was no such dreadful loss. In Mirikos, young men walk upon the streets without fear. Let Haffat assure his Brother that the Prince of Mirikos lives but is confined to his chambers, since Haffat has heard ugly rumors which have no doubt reached this shore by now. The prince remains in seclusion only until the agreements between him and Haffat's governor are finalized. Also, there have been threats made by a very few foolish Mirikosi; when these men are found and arrested, Khoryios will again resume his throne.

"Let my brother Pelledar take all this into consideration when he decides how to act, but let him do so before another full day passes. Let him send up yellow flags when he is ready for parley, that we may live together, in peace." Knoe refolded the letter and slid it up his sleeve. Silence. He waited. "How say you?" he asked finally.

Prince Pelledar sent his eyes sideways: Khadat, who would have surely spoken and caused lasting grief for everyone—Apodain's strong young arm was around her and another hard across her mouth, and Eyzhad was speaking urgently into her ear. Beyond that unnerving, ruddy fog surrounding the two motionless Pairs, Piritos cast him a warning look. Pelledar bowed his head briefly and tried to gather his thoughts. *Does Piritos really think I will yield and order the gates opened? Or that I will bid Knoe bring his upstart emperor into my city to give me the kiss of an equal? A man whose father was a soldier, his mother a strumpet, and his Diyet a land of thin sheep and no more lineage than he himself has?* His head came up and he looked down thick stone walls toward the chariot, but he was suddenly so furious he could barely see the car, and could not make out the face of the man awaiting his response. *He will have an answer to take back to Haffat, and may his master cut his throat for bringing it!*

"Say this to Haffat, who calls himself emperor: He shall *not* name me brother, Haffat whose blood is no richer than that of his own shepherds and farmers! That he took to himself the rule of Diyet and made her strong, I commend him; that he wrested away from others the rule of many lands, I say he was the stronger soldier, and may call himself an emperor if he chooses. But he—is—no—Great—King! Khoryios who ruled across the sea was a Great King *and* my brother! And I say further that if this Haffat says my brother the Great King of Mirikos lives, then he lies!

"As for Ghezrat, say this to the *Emperor* Haffat: I had this crown from my father, who had it from his, and he from his father, and back for seven hundred years, father to son. Never has it gone to an invader; never has an interloper touched it. For all our history, Ghezrat has fought and has kept her own—the fertile plain, the sea, the isthmus, this city, all her people. Everything he now covets.

"I say this also to your emperor: If he will have Ghezrat, let him come and try her! Does he think because he threatens us with war and death, that we will fling aside our weapons and our pride and crawl before him? Because he covets our vineyards, shall we cower before him? Does he think we sit inside our walls weeping with fear of the armies he will hurl against us if we do not call him master?" Pelledar drew a deep breath. "He is not the first to desire what we have. Nor will he be the last. For we who are Ghezrat will not give over to him, not now, not after long battle. Not *ever!*

"Say this final thing to your Emperor Haffat: Pelledar, Prince of these people and Great King of Ghezrat bids you gather in those lands you have already taken, and seek no more. You have enough for any man: lands and trade routes, cities and farms and beasts, and all the northern shore of the Sea of Delos. Take pride and comfort in so much, and do not seek to add Ghezrat to your empire, for we will stop you— whatever your force, whatever god guides you. Say to the emperor, go home, and leave us in this peace of which he makes so much. We had peace in plenty before Haffat took the trading ships of bright Mirikos and made them into war vessels.

"Go back to your emperor, and tell him what I have said. And do not dare return with other terms of peace. Having had so many years of peace and so little of war, Haffat may think we are weak, soft, and ill-prepared to face him. But he will learn otherwise. Men who have known peace, even for a little, will fight the harder to regain it—and we will die Ghezrathi, rather than live as slaves to the Diye Haff!" The anger was suddenly gone; he began to tremble and without the wall against his legs might have fallen. He shut his mouth, dug his fingers into the stones, and waited.

Knoe had gone very still; for another very long moment, he gazed at the prince or perhaps just beyond him, then abruptly turned and said something to the driver, who whipped up the horses.

"Well spoken—oh, *well* spoken!" Piritos said softly. He slipped a hand under the prince's elbow to steady him. "Here, come, where all those who heard you speak can see you."

"See?" Pelledar said blankly. But he could hear it now,

below him, echoing across the city: people cheering wildly and crying his name.

Tephys stirred and Eyzhad ran over to help her to her feet. She clung to him briefly, then looked at those around her as if dazed and unable to remember who they were, or why she was here. At her gesture, the priest helped her over to where the Dyaddi still stood, though the goddess bond had faded. "Go," she said softly. "Back to the company, ready to pass before the city. But you have already performed a great service this day."

Breyd sent her eyes toward Menlaeus. *What did she do, just now—and why?* she wondered. *And what of that driver?*

Menlaeus touched her arm, nodded toward the barracks ladder. She nodded, went ahead of him. *Ask him later, what he thinks; ask Jocasa.* She cast Apodain a sidelong glance as she passed him and Khadat. He hadn't known her, of course; nothing had shown of her but the eyes and her hands, and he had clearly had his hands full. *They say I will marry him once this is all done—how odd that seems now.* They said, anyway. Her mood had swung once more. That priest. All those ships, waiting to land. Haffat would be angry when he heard the prince's words, if that priest dared repeat them. He would not rest until all of them were dead, and an empty city his. She could see nothing in her own future—and her father's—but death. *But they will pay in lives for us.*

Apodain gingerly removed his hand from his mother's mouth and then, even more cautiously, released his hold on her body. Khadat pulled sharply away from him and brushed at rumpled silk. Tephys indicated them with her chin and Eyzhad helped her over. "Khadat, thank you. You made my task a little easier just now."

"Task," Khadat spat. Tephys looked at her sharply, then at Apodain, who was hovering uncertainly behind her.

"What has happened here?" the priestess asked finally.

"A mere nothing," Khadat said stiffly.

"She was going to speak to Haffat's emissary," Eyzhad put in. Khadat glared at him; Eyzhad ignored her. "With what intent, I cannot say; Apodain prevented her."

Khadat glanced at Apodain. "I wanted to—well, what matter?" She threw up her hands. "Our prince has gone mad, baiting the man with such a speech."

"I see." Tephys folded her arms. "Khadat, you would do

better to thank your son. Do you realize what was in that chariot?"

"I only—"

"Listen to me, Khadat. Why should Haffat send his lion-priest with this message? I think he came to search for hidden weakness among us."

"And instead he found men eager to bait him with insults, and words of war! I have said all along—"

"Shut up, woman!" Tephys snarled; Khadat gaped, then set her jaw and glared at her furiously. "Pelledar is prince here, do you forget yourself so much? But do you really believe you could offer bribes to *that* priest? And now that you have seen this Knoe, don't you realize what he is? He is a man of war! He serves an emperor and a god, and both of them fatten upon war!" Khadat opened her mouth, closed it and compressed her lips sourly. "And the other," Tephys went on very softly. "Did you not hear me say what that driver is? Have you never heard of the Ergardi, Khadat? Why do you think I was down there, flat on my face all this time? So the goddess could use me to prevent that—that magician from sending his spirit across the wall and into one of us."

"My brothers told me about Ergardi when I was a child," Khadat replied coldly. "To frighten me. I thought better of you, priestess."

A nasty little silence. Apodain broke it; his voice was very weary. "You really don't understand, do you? I had to do what I did. The general would have thrown you from the walls himself!"

"He would never have dared!"

Apodain shook his head. "It was in his eyes. He would have."

Khadat paled; her eyes were black and all pupil, her voice a trembling, furious whisper. "Horrid, common man. I will have him—!"

"Have him—*what?*" Tephys asked, as quietly. Piritos had gone with the prince to the inner wall, but several of his aides were still nearby. "Khadat, do think what you say, and speak with caution. In time of peace you have power, but this is war: Piritos wields more strength than anyone save the prince himself—perhaps more than *anyone* else."

And there is no Perlot to speak for me, Khadat thought bleakly. *Much of my family in Mirikos is dead, those who live have no power to protect me. How it must please Apodain, to see me in such straits!* But when she glanced at him, she saw no sign of such satisfaction. He had turned away from her and was staring out across the plain, where twenty or so black-sailed ships rode a rough sea.

Tephys sighed. *Goddess, we stopped him this time. But what can we do to make certain the circuit of the city is proof against an Ergardi?* She was light-headed with fatigue; Denota had taken deeply from her to turn both lion-priest and magician back. *A ring about the walls—difficult, time-consuming, and there were many things I needed to attend to tonight, to ready for tomorrow's eclipse.* And the ring would not hold that long—well, but it need not, if the city's other, human defenses did their job. She turned to gaze out across the plain. Apodain glanced at her, his face expressionless, then sent his eyes toward the ships once more. They stood side by side for a moment or so; Apodain finally broke the silence.

"Could that—that man have really sent something of himself into one of us?"

"You don't know about the Ergardi?" she countered.

"I am—I *was* a soldier," he replied softly. "As my father before me was, and my brother. My tutors instructed me from the classics, and taught me the greater bard's songs, priestess. I was sworn into the House of Warriors. I may have heard the name, Ergardi, but I do not recall it."

"You are more than a simple peasant who can do nothing without an order. But you are still a soldier," Tephys said evenly. She felt his eyes on her, felt his shrug as he turned back to look at the sea. "Whatever foolish thing your mother has done, whatever foolish things you think because of her act. The Ergardi come from the north, where they served cold and remote gods; when their land and those gods were conquered, they escaped south, and came finally to the western deserts. Or so it is said."

"They *look* like the nomads from beyond Ye Eygar," Apodain said doubtfully. "Not northerners. I saw a few northerners once, at the port in Mirikos. They had pale hair and blue eyes, fair skin—"

"Perhaps the Ergardi also once looked like that. We know very little about them, besides this one thing: That if an Ergardi desires he may touch an ordinary mortal, cast out the spirit, and take the body. It is said also they can do this from a distance. This may have been one of the fables your uncles told your mother, but I chose to take no chances."

Apodain turned to look at her. Tephys gazed steadily back. "We know *two* things," he said finally. "At least one Ergardi serves Haffat."

"Or they serve Axtekeles. But if there is one, then there are at least three—and possibly more," Tephys said. "They do not willingly travel singly." She shook herself. "The prince waits for me upon the inner gates." She walked across the narrow, temporary wooden bridge that linked inner and outer walls. Apodain scooped up his mother's cloak, shook the dirt and sand from it, and followed.

Piritos and Pelledar were standing close together just to the side of the gates, Piritos still visibly proud of his prince—the prince himself surprised and gratified as people continued to cheer him.

Tephys took her place above the gates themselves as horns cried out the warning; the crowd fell silent. Guards began to press people back from the middle of the avenue and the square, and a column of men issued from the barracks.

Xhem had been as bewildered as anyone when the order was made for utter silence. Nothing then, except for Knoe's foreign-sounding voice, but no one at street level could make out anything the man said. *What is happening?* What he could see up on the walls was no help: the prince and his general hurrying toward the outer gate and then sounds of a fight and someone else running toward that. Xhem, shorter than most people around him, could see even less than his neighbors.

After a long and nervewracking time word came from the gates, whispered from man to woman to man: "Truce flag." And then, all around him, men and women, murmuring to each other: "Haffat sends to the prince terms of surrender." "They say he did that in Mirikos." "And in Idemito." "He has offered surrender everywhere, it is what he does, but then he kills the people anyway." "Shhhh! No such talk here!" one of the street guards growled softly. *Surrender!* Xhem's heart dropped into his sandals; all around him, people looked at each other warily. More whispering, then, "The prince—" "—won't do it." "He can't give in!" Another hissed, angry warning from the street guard and this time the people stayed quiet.

But Prince Pelledar's first ringing, challenging words to the unseen messenger dispelled their fear; from his high vantage, the prince's voice reached them easily. The man behind Xhem whispered piercingly to his neighbor, "Told you he wouldn't sell us to that butcher!" Word came back from the soldiers at the gate finally: the truce-car had fled. Men cheered and shouted and clapped each other on the back; women hugged each other and wept, or hugged their men or their children. The prince himself came forward to acknowledge the wild cheers. A sharp, warning horn cry topped them.

The prince raised his arms for silence. "People of Ghezrat, behold those who go to fight for you! Give them praise!"

The uneven hair on the back of Xhem's neck rose. All around him people leaned as far out as they could, to be the first to see the companies. Xhem had to squeeze around or past people several times until he could see again.

Thanks to Tarpaen and Nabid, he had already learned most of the company calls; he knew before he saw them that the first men would be a *ghrad* of spear—the common foot soldiers who created a tight shield wall that could block a road, protect slingers and archers, or form a deadly thicket of bronze points. Most were young, barely of age to fight, and older officers marched at the end of each rank.

People cheered loudly; the older men smiled to acknowledge the crowd, but most of the younger men looked abashed by the attention. The cheers faded a little as the company passed, and somewhere behind him, Xhem heard a woman's sharply indrawn breath, a whispered name. Beyond her, a child wept and another woman's trembling voice said: "Your father marches there, smile for him, child. Wave to your father, Keris."

The next call brought forth one of the lightly armored companies of slingers who wore no armor and soft runner's shoes, deep-brimmed hats to keep the sun from their eyes, and bulging pouches of cast metal stones at their hips. Slings were bound to their wrists and as they passed through the square, they waved the slings. People cheered; the four young priestesses standing on the stone arch above the gate sent down a cascade of petals as they passed. Somewhere nearby, Xhem heard a man: "My son, Ebrido." And a tight-voiced girl: "Oh, Father—my father, Ebrido."

The gates were finally open and the heat which had built up, scarcely noticed by the tense crowd, vanished in a blast of harsh wind. Half a company of common chariot passed by, closely followed by two more *ghrad* of spear and a phalanx of heavy infantry soldiers. These were mostly middle-aged men, veterans who bristled with weapons: spears, bundled javelins, bows and cases of arrows. Old-fashioned slashing swords. All carried shields, but they varied from long bamboo-woven ovals to small rounds of bronze that had been painted with hideous Atekis-faces or curses for the enemy. More common chariot followed, and a boy's too-deep voice murmured, "My uncle Ifreyo."

Xhem's blood was racing, his heart thumping wildly as men marched by and the complex and stirring horn cries that were the battle songs of each company preceded them. When the royal chariot came from the barracks gates, drivers and fighters alike sang, the people cheered them, the priestesses sent flower petals cascading around them. But all about him, Xhem could hear the pained voices as the chariot passed, as the phalanx of light infantry came after: "My son, Jadaed." "Ah, Father!" "Husband and brother both, to the same company." "There goes your father Potro, see how his car shines in the sun?" *They will come back, how can you doubt such brave men? Look how wonderful, how shining they all are, hear their songs!* He felt that, but he could never have said it aloud, and he felt suddenly shy. *If I spoke, they would say I am only a boy, an outsider among these city people. No one I know has died in fighting.* Some of these had lost friends or family before, he could hear it in those fearful and tear-filled voices all around him.

They do not let their soldiers see that pain and that fear, he realized. He had heard the tales and songs in the barracks about women who wept and clung to their men before they went out to fight, he had half-expected that today. But the only loud sounds were the horn calls, and the cheering.

Apodain finally walked over to the inner wall as the companies began to march by, but he kept aloof from the others. Particularly his mother. *She has had too many years of ruling Father's household and her share of the family ships; she thinks herself above everyone, a law unto herself.* But she had been just as arrogant when his father still lived.

She would never forgive him for shaming her in public—

she would see what he had done that way, at least. *Perhaps I should have let her say whatever she chose. What matter to me if one of them threw her from the walls? I might have been free of her.* He considered this, but only for a moment. Denota would charge his soul with her death, as if he had thrown her from the walls himself. *Too late now. Too late for everything. Mother is still alive—and Denota knows I scarcely care what she does, or what the consequences.* He gazed down at the company of royal chariot, watched as Loros, who had been his driver, fought to control the magnificent pair of nervous, matched white horses pulling Septarin's blue and gold chariot. His heart sank. That was *his* place; his driver—his right. Men like Piritos eyed him sidelong when they thought he was not watching; a child went to fight in his place. His hands tightened on the stones. Septarin looked ridiculous among the royal chariot with his skinny, half-grown child's body. And he was acting like a child just now—waving to the crowd, smiling and laughing.

Apodain glanced over as Pelledar raised his hand in blessing. The company passed beneath him, and the prince's eyes closed; his lips moved soundlessly. *He does not expect the boy to live. But—why does he let Septarin go, then?* But Septarin was surely the one at fault: Apodain knew his young cousin's whining, wheedling ways all too well. The prince must have simply worn down. *And how well does that wretched boy's whimpering sit with Brysos, I wonder?* Or with one or two of the older royal cousins who were also in the chariot company and who were notorious for their short tempers?

His palms stung: He turned his hands over and saw with surprise that he had cut them gripping the wall.

More companies followed: another of common light armor and one of heavy; slingers and a long line of archers; men mounted on sleek, unarmored horses, armed only with a javelin or two—the messengers between the companies and the city for matters too complex for a horn call. Half a dozen horn. Apodain blotted his hands on the hem of his mother's cloak, watched the army pass, and ignored the people in the street. No one looked in his direction, anyway. *As if I had ceased to exist.* Perhaps, in a way, he had.

Xhem craned his neck anxiously as the small company of horn signalers came into sight; he sighed as they went by. It was not likely his brother Tar would have been among them, but Tar still hoped, whatever he said. And Xhem had loyally hoped for him, even thought he knew all too well how bad Tarpaen's eyesight was.

Two drummers marched with another *ghrad* of young spearmen, to keep them in step. Tar's friend Laius was not either of those, but Xhem did not expect that. Laius made him nervous, with his changeable and often black moods, and Laius had made it quite clear he did not like Xhem, did not like sharing his friend Tarpaen with a mere peasant boy. But no one liked Laius—and Nabid had made it clear enough none of them *trusted* Laius, either, and with reason.

Well, Tar was loyal to his friend. He'd surely be pleased they were to remain together upon the walls.

More archers. Another five mounted messengers, another half-company of common chariot. Silence, and a little space, and then the horn call of the Dyaddi. A flurry of whispered speculation all around him and across the square, and then people fell utterly quiet as the first red-clad Pairs came into sight.

"My uncle Menlaeus, my cousin Breyd," Xhem found himself saying, quite softly. There was a lump in his throat. He *knew* these two, one of his earliest memories was his cousin letting him drive the small cart with its cargo of grapes; another was Menlaeus showing him how to use a sling to drive birds from his mother's vines. If Haffat killed them, out there. . . .

The woman at his side turned briefly to look at him, then gave him a smile that did not touch her very worried eyes. "My husband Duplos, my only daughter Xera." She turned away to gaze anxiously after the Pairs before the boy could think of anything to say.

They shone in the afternoon sun, the Dyaddi: brilliantly polished bronze armor and greaves, shining bronze shields and the hint of bronze shining through the cloth of the red tiara. Each of them carried a tall spear in one hand, shield in the other; a slender red sword baldric was slung sideways across the chest and at the waist a low cord to hold a long knife, another for bow and a sheaf of red-hafted arrows or for a bundle of red-shafted javelins. The end ties of the ti-aras had been thrown back, to reveal the faces kept hidden from the city's enemy: Older man's face, most thickly bearded and next to each, young, smooth woman's face. Dif-

ferent, each Pair from the other, and yet alike in the set of
jaw, the determined, squared shoulders, the level and fearless gaze. They had trained no longer than the least experienced company of spearmen, and yet these marched with
only one captain, and no drummer, and when they neared the
inner gates, they halted at no signal any of the onlookers
could see.

The air around them began to glow, softly—the faintest
hint of red colored the gates, put a flush upon pale cheeks
and fell across the nearest onlookers, many of whom stepped
quickly back. Tephys came forward and held out her arms.
Xhem looked all around him. Men and women had begun to
kneel; he flushed deeply and knelt himself, buried his chin
against his breastbone.

"Holy, beloved goddess, Your blessing upon these Pairs,
upon Your city and upon all who battle to save it."

All around him, people responded immediately: "Bless
these, and protect us, Goddess." Xhem felt more untutored
than ever. He rose only after his neighbors began to get up.
The Dyaddi cried out as one: "Goddess aid us, and bless this
city!" They drew their swords as one; the blades flashed in
the sun and the ruddy light surrounding them; sixty-eight
voices shouted: "For Ghezrat and Prince Pelledar!"

A great cheer answered them. Pelledar gazed down on the
Pairs and his face was very grave. At last, he held out both
hands in blessing. Tephys came to his side to lay her hands
across his; her voice rose over the cry of the people: "The
blessings of Ghezrat and her prince and the goddess upon
you all!" Light flared, unbearably bright green spilling like
a waterfall from the arch, flying up in blinding red sparks
from the upraised swords.

"Ghezrat and Prince Pelledar!" the people echoed. The
priestesses threw the last of their flowers, emptying the baskets.

The Pairs lowered their swords and as one resheathed
them; Tephys stepped back and the prince let down arms
which had suddenly become unbearably heavy. The Dyaddi
marched through the outer gate, onto the road, then began to
spread out in twos and fours around the city's outer wall.
The gates closed behind them. A few last petals drifted
down to the street. The nobles and the prince came down
from the wall, reentered their covered chairs and were borne

away. People looked around uncertainly and began to disperse.

Night fell; heavy clouds blanketed the sky and Atelos would not rise until late the next morning. Many people stood upon the inner wall and other bits of old wall inside the city, and many of the nobles gazed out from their high roofs; there were few lights upon the plain and none across either river; none that could be seen where the ships had been all day.

Creos' company had made fires on the jetty to cook an early evening meal and to heat spiced water to mix with the wine, but the fires had been doused before full dark, and now half the company sat or stood on hard stone at arm's length from one another. They could see little or nothing seaward for the extreme darkness; they listened intently, but the sound of waves slapping the stones drowned nearly everything else. The rest of the company slept. Wind blew constantly and hard from the west, whistling through cracks in the stone. Now and again it tossed spray high above the mole and along both its sides, so only those fortunate few who were closest to the shore were even partially dry.

Creos was wet, cold, and very stiff. He was unnerved by the darkness, trying hard not to let it show. *After all, a ship makes a great creaking and rattle, I have been out here in the great storms that come from the east; we still could hear ships above the storm.* He shifted his weight yet again; his backside was soaked, his legs numb from sitting so long in one place, but his knees ached if he tried to put weight on them for long. The man next to him cleared his throat cautiously and quietly and leaned over to touch his shoulder. "The captain said to pass word, a cup of wine along the line shortly, and then we'll exchange places."

"Good," Creos replied softly. Was it really late enough for the next watch? But it already seemed two lifetimes since he had left Niverren, a full lifetime of crouching miserably in place, waiting for some move by the Diye Haff to bring those ships in despite the west wind that made even the inner side of the jetty unsafe. But they might try to land nearby, on the sand. *What can we do to protect that, though? They did not put enough of us out here to protect all the shore between the rivers.* But it would take a madman to attempt such a landing, in such seas, in such total darkness.

Oh, Niverren, beloved. He sighed faintly and leaned over to touch the next man in line and pass the whispered message—hot wine, and changing of the guard.

Within the city, many now tried to sleep, knowing there was nothing to be seen anyway. In the house of Menlaeus, upon the roof over the main room, Tarpaen dozed uneasily, his ear ready for the horn cry that might order him back to the barracks or the outer walls—though it was very unlikely Nabid would use him at night, barring dire need. Xhem slept hard, curled against his back; he had spent the entire day running errands for the company or for his aunt. He had barely managed to stay awake long enough to eat.

Directly beneath them, in the room she had shared these past twenty-five nights with Creos, Niverren slept heavily, her breathing long and harsh, and a little fast; knowing she would otherwise not rest at all, she had let Nidya put valerian in her final cup of wine, and retired at once.

Ina was exhausted from helping clear more room in the storage for the twenty large clay jugs of new wine from the vineyards, stiff from the heavy work, and plainly terrified of all the tales she had heard of the Diye Haff. Nidya finally persuaded her to take a small dose in her wine and she, too, slept heavily. An occasional snore came from the room she shared with her mistress.

Nidya sat in Nevvia's favorite chair and leaned forward to wrap her arms around her daughter, who knelt on the cushions at her feet. They had been sitting like that for a full horn; Nidya's arms had long since gone numb. Nevvia rested her dark curls on her mother's knee, and now and again fetched a shuddering little sigh. She had said nothing since Tarpaen went up to sleep.

"A sensible woman," Nidya said softly, "would go and at least get some rest, knowing she accomplishes nothing sitting here and worrying."

"You sound like Niverren," Nevvia whispered fretfully.

"Yes, she has been asleep for at least two horns. The boy told us they would not return home tonight, they will sleep in the barracks in case—well, in case."

"In case of some sudden attack by those horrid, evil demons," Nevvia whispered. "Oh, Mother, I can't bear this."

"Yes. I know. You must try, for all their sakes, child."

Nidya stroked her daughter's hair; Nevvia shook her head and blotted her eyes with a trembling hand.

"I *hate* it! We were all so happy, you here and Ina, this lovely new courtyard and all the space, and Tar grown to manhood, and Niv about to wed with Creos and live in his mother's house, and—and now—now everything is so *awful*, and I hate it! As though—" She shook her head, thrust her fingers into her hair, dislodging the band that crossed her brow. Black curls tumbled across her ears and shoulders. Nidya made a "tching" sound, tugged at her daughter's wrists, and pressed the band firmly back into place. "We were such a happy family, all of us! Why did this Haffat have to come here?"

"Who can say?" Nidya replied softly. "They tell us a god drives him. We had war when I was a girl, you know."

"I know, you have told me."

"Of course. The Gletiusi came up from the south, across the desert; they had drought and famine, and thought they would have our lands and our sea. They were a dire enemy, but we defeated them; we will defeat this Haffat." Silence. Nidya stroked her daughter's hair. "Denota herself said so. She said that when the Gletiusi threatened us, and she also named Dyaddi then. The first days of war are always hard, Nevvia. They tell you very little, and you can see nothing, even if they let you onto the walls to look. What you can see makes no sense anyway. The people are confused and worried, the soldiers often seem to be confused and uncertain what to do. But it is not so bad as it seems at the time, and after a little, things become easier. The goddess will not let the Diye Haff so near the city that your son and your daughter and your husband are in danger."

"I could not—" Nevvia swallowed and shook her head. "If anything did happen," she whispered finally.

"Don't. Please." Nidya took her daughter's face between her hands and shook her head. "You make it difficult for them, child; they have enough to think about, without worrying about you."

"I know. Oh, Mother, I try! You know I do!"

Nidya sighed. "I know you do. I know you do." Nevvia sat back on her heels and began to straighten her hair. Nidya pressed worn hands onto the arms of the chair and got herself upright. "I do wish you would show some sense and at least try to get some sleep. Drink some wine; I have enough

valerian that a dose for you tonight won't empty the jug."
Nevvia laughed weakly. Nidya's herb garden was tended by
her tenant farmers, along with the grapes; she grew flavoring
herbs but mostly medicinal ones and one entire corner of the
kitchen was taken up with large clay pots of dried arrow, valerian, and other leaves. "If you won't, you won't, I suppose,
but an old woman needs her sleep, and I am exhausted.
Good night, daughter."

"Good night, Mother." Nevvia watched her go, then
turned away and settled her chin on her knees once more
and closed her eyes. A tear slid down her cheek. They were
out there, somewhere on that narrow ledge between the wall
and the drop that was almost sheer in places. *My beloved
Menlaeus is out there. And my baby.* But the bonding had
changed Breyd and Menlaeus both so much. *What if the
goddess cannot change them back, or she does not? If war
changes them so much, they cannot return to what they
were?* War could do that. Everyone knew it.

She held out her own hands and stared at them, turned
them over to look at the palms. They were not a noblewoman's pampered hands; they were tiny like Breyd's. *If the goddess asked me to take up weapons and—kill men—* She
couldn't complete the thought. *My Breyd is only seventeen,
just of an age to wed, a child, really. Denota, to ask her to
fight, to be part of battle, to kill—* It would not be her giggling, sweet, joyful child who came back to her, it could
never again be. Menlaeus—but he had fought before; he was
strong, brave, he could take care of himself and he would
guard Breyd. He would not be changed by another
battle—or would he? As changed as he already was—those
red cords—

She bit back a sob, blotted her cheeks carefully with the
backs of her hands, and got to her feet. Better, perhaps, if
she did try to sleep a little. If Menlaeus and Breyd were allowed to come home tomorrow, they would see her wan and
tearstained. *Mother is right, I cannot upset them so. I must
be brave for them. Somehow I must.*

All but four of the company that had been sent out with
the ballista early in the day slept; four men walked back and
forth on the hard-packed, damp sand just inland of the jetty
and peered into the darkness. The rest of the company slept
in dryer and softer sand above the tide line; the ballista

stood on the edge of the road where it widened to allow many carts access to ships. An enormous pyramid of stones had been built in the sand. Now and again, one of the guards cursed softly as he stubbed his toes on them; it was still so dark a man could barely make out the outline of the ballista against white-edged waves.

Farther inland still, a phalanx of heavy infantry camped on both sides of the road. Most men slept, or tried to, while a few walked up and down in the short grass to keep warm and to listen for warning of an attempted landing from those on shore or on the mole.

In a deep hollow to the east of the road where there was some shelter from the constant wind, someone had built a small fire. A few men sat around it, watching the heating pots of wine and water. One of the older men leaned forward and tested the liquid with his finger, nodded and rummaged around for his cup and a dipper. "Ground seems to have gone hard out here since I last sat on it," he said, and other gray-bearded men laughed with him. They froze, then, and some of the younger men leapt to their feet. A horse galloped down the road from the city. "No problem," the older man told them. He hadn't moved and he was cautiously sipping from a steaming cup. "There won't be any news up *there* yet. Now, if a rider came from *that* way," he gestured toward the sea, "then there might be cause for alarm."

"They won't land tonight," one of the younger men said. "In such dark, and with such a sea—"

"Lions see in the dark, it's said," one of the others broke in. "What if their lion god also does?"

"Keep such talk to yourself, Grenis!" One of the other older men shook a finger at him. "Say an evil thing and see it happen, don't you know the saying?"

"There are no lions in Ghezrat," the neighbor said, after a small and comfortable silence. "They say Denota would not stand for lions to dwell in her land. Surely she will not allow that lion god to come here."

"She was not proof against Atelos," a boy so young his beard was a scanty thing, murmured. The older men turned as one to glare at him; he bit his lip and sat back out of the firelight.

The cup was passed silently from man to man. An older veteran with the shoulder mark of a minor officer finally broke the silence. "Well, we have all heard enough about these Diye Haff, haven't we? Haffat has conquered everything between here and Diyet, and now he and his lion god have chosen this particular day to begin battle, knowing Atelos will rule the day sky for a time. That might cost a man sleep, did he let it. But remember what they told us in the Warriors' Temple: Atelos has caught and covered Atos many times, but he only set his seed in the goddess the once, and *never in all the ages since*. She knows him now, and she has turned him away every time." He turned and spat into the darkness. "And we shall do the same with Haffat, his priests *and* their lion." No one spoke for long after that, and the cup went around the fire once more. A horn called tenth hour from the city walls. Men left the fire and others came in from guard duty.

The first company of royal chariot had been separated into four smaller companies, and placed along the inner banks of the rivers, protection should Haffat decide to send men against the deserted villages and fields, to fire them. Here it was very dark, so dark a man might not see the deep cut of the banks until he had set foot on air and rolled to the stone shore. Water gleamed now and again when clouds separated and let the light of stars through; there were no fires along the banks and only very small ones well back within the trees and groves.

Around one low fire, several noblemen clustered, as did the soldiers of the heavy infantry company, but here, each man had his own ornate cup; drivers who often shared company with those they drove this night had their own fire, a little distance away.

Septarin sat shoulder to shoulder with two cousins, and sipped warm, spiced wine, and was momentarily content. The ground was hard, particularly for a boy who had never slept anywhere but his own fine couch, and it was strange—and a little unnerving—to be out so late in such impenetrable darkness, particularly with enemy so near. He took comfort that even those few men in the circle who had fought before showed no sign of concern. They were fairly quiet—partly to be certain of hearing any warning or any advance, certainly; partly, Septarin thought, because they were still uncertain how to treat with him. Well, that was reasonable—after all, they were one and all nobles, but he was the heir to a Great King and Prince of Ghezrat.

* * *

The royal chariot drivers huddled about their own fire and passed a single cup, more for the companionship of it than because they must share one vessel; they sat with heads close together so that Loros could pass on the words of the company commander, since some of those here had not been present at the briefing Brysos gave them in the barracks courtyard. Silence for some moments, after Loros finished speaking, as men drank and digested his words. Finally, one man stirred. "I was against it from the first—"

"We all were," Loros said flatly. "But Brysos was right: When the prince puts forth his heir and says, 'My son will fight with your company,' what man of us dare say no?" He shook his head.

"We had been better with Apodain," someone else mumbled. The man next to him gave a shove and laughed sourly, but when he would have spoken, Loros leaned across the fire to grip his wrist.

"We had been better. Whatever is said—whatever that *boy* says—I drove Apodain for two years. You all know me, I drove Brysos' son into battle when we fought the pirates, and I held him as he died that day! Do you think I cannot tell a brave man from a coward?"

"Huh. Perhaps. What man can be certain how he will test in battle, until he is there, though? Or how he will face it, until it comes?"

"Think that," Loros said, "and you will tell me next that Septarin will single-handedly drive Haffat back into the sea, and his lion god with him!"

"Shhh!" his neighbor said urgently, with a sudden glance toward the other fire.

"Well," the man across the fire said gravely, "you cannot say for certain that he will not, can you?" Dead, astonished silence; the man grinned, then spluttered with suppressed laughter, and those around the fire joined him.

The wind was strong and constant before the city walls. Breyd squatted down in a small jutting of the wall near the main gates, wrapped the heavy cloak around her legs and pulled her arms inside. Menlaeus had gone over to peer down the cliff; she could sense him coming toward her even before she heard his feet crunching across the shattered rock and dirt. *Sense of presence, not that enveloping—other thing from this afternoon.* She had seen that strange lion-priest with the slightly overlapping vision and it had touched her prince, too—how Menlaeus knew him: a young man unlike his harsh-tongued father and very different from the fierce warlord grandfather who had been prince when Menlaeus was young. The soldier's anger, partly trained into her these past hard days but mostly spilling over from Menlaeus; the outrage that other men should come to take what was theirs. *If Haffat had ridden through those gates just then, I could have cut his throat myself.* When Tephys had blessed them, though: *I felt as if we were all one, just then: Part of each other, a whole and greater thing than sixty-eight men and young women bound together by the goddess.* It had hackled the hairs on her forearms and filled her with a truly magnificent and pure fury, as it had upon the walls. *We have the right to kill them, all of them we can; Denota has given it to us; she asks it of us and we will bring her bodies.* Then, it had seemed right and honorable to think such thoughts; just now, she wondered at the dizzying strength she had felt in those moments, such unmixed hatred of the Diye Haff.

And a little wry gratitude that Denota did not keep them constantly so close. One could starve to death, she thought, in the grip of such a bond. Just now, she knew where Menlaeus was, that his sword hand was still tight across the palm from the previous day's long practice. That he was concerned about her. *Not just for this moment; something deeper.*

He bent down to peer at her. "Are you all right?"

"Cold," she admitted.

"We haven't much longer out here," he assured her. "Walk with me, that will warm you more than sitting."

"All right." She took his hand and let him pull her upright, let the fingers of her other hand trail against the wall. She didn't like to think about the fall either would have if they strayed very far from that wall; there were a few torches up on the wall, but it was quite black around the main gates and in one or two places the ledge was quite narrow. *How foolish I would feel, falling my first night out here and breaking a leg.* Break a leg, dissolve the Pair, perhaps save Menlaeus. But she knew better than that before she could even complete the thought. The goddess would punish them both for her failure. And if the bond were dissolved, Menlaeus would be put into a regular phalanx again.

Besides, that the Diye Haff come to take Ghezrat from us, that they seek to kill us, my family, my friends, my fellow warriors! She shook her head; her own thought, Menlaeus', the pool of anger that fed all the Dyaddi—she couldn't be certain. She could not sneak back inside in such a fashion, though.

There would have been a better answer for Apodain; break an arm or a leg. Probably he had feared he would not win the midsummer games ever again if he did that.

"Moving does help, doesn't it?" Menlaeus asked finally.

"Moving helps," she agreed. "But this—this night-watch is boring." He laughed quietly.

"Yes. I always did hate night guard; you know someone is out there somewhere, and it can make you nervous, especially on such a dark night when you can't see anything. Mostly it's long and cold and boring." He sighed. "It is better than the last battle I fought in, though; dust everywhere, enemy everywhere—we could hear the horn signals coming down from the city, see our captain interpreting them for us, shouting for us to go this way or that way. We couldn't tell for certain if anyone knew what was happening. This time—at least you will be spared that kind of battle, up here." He fell silent. Breyd sent her eyes sideways. He was tense, as though he could not quite think what to say next. "Daughter. Why don't you tell me what is wrong?"

Her mouth went dry. "Wrong?"

He stopped and leaned back into the wall; she wrapped her arms around herself and waited. His voice sounded so normal that without the bond she wouldn't have known how much it cost him to go on. "I know there is something very wrong, that it dates from the night Tephys spoke of war, that it has to do with this—with the war, the Dyaddi. Our Dyadd, in particular."

"Our—?"

"You can lie to me, but I will know."

She sighed, very quietly. "I know you will."

"You had a vision of your own, I do remember that. The day Denota named you Secchi. Even then I felt something— what you said wasn't quite true. And that whatever it was upset you terribly. Daughter, please. If you have been trying to protect me, all of your family from some sign of disaster, thank you for the thought."

She shook her head. "Anyone would—"

"No; your young friend Denira would not, unless she has changed greatly. Once you would not have done so, either, or at least, not as well as you have." She felt him turn his head in her direction, sensed the smile she couldn't see in the dark. "You are too much my child, I suppose."

She laughed very quietly. "Well, Niverren tells me I am."

"Understand that I don't *know* precisely what secret you keep, just that you do. Please, tell me." He paused, and when she didn't immediately respond, added, "I am not your mother or your sister, who might be unable to take the burden. I am the one who must fight at your side or at your back. I am also your father."

"Yes." She found it hard to get even that much out. She drew a deep breath, let it go, drew another and nodded. "Yes, all right." She kept the words flat and as emotionless as possible, told him as tersely as possible. It sounded very unreal, all at once. But Menlaeus would know; he must feel what she had felt, the fear she still felt. "I kept hoping I was somehow wrong, that it wasn't really a vision. Tephys couldn't tell for certain what it meant. I—I couldn't just *tell* you, not when I didn't really know. But I couldn't have said—"

"No. It's all right, I understand."

She swallowed and said in a small voice, "I'm sorry."

"For what you saw, or for hiding it from me?" He touched her shoulder.

"Both. For telling you now."

"No, it's done, let it pass. But the goddess does not grave a man's fate in stone when she gives prophecies. It may be a warning."

"I know."

"Well, then. You have told me, now two of us can think about it, and find a way to avoid this—death." *He sees I might die, also. Oh, Father, what if I have done the wrong thing in telling you?* If he worried excessively about her, and did not watch out for his own safety— She blinked rapidly. Menlaeus was still speaking. "The goddess surely has provided one way at least around your vision. Wouldn't it be better for us to find it together?"

She nodded. To her relief, her voice sounded normal; he could tell she was upset, of course. *Keep up the appearances, it is easier for everyone,* she thought. "Of course, Father. You see why I couldn't. Anyway, we can at least fight it together."

"Of course," Menlaeus said. "Isn't it what we were made a Dyadd for, after all—to fight together? Don't worry so much, though; everything will be all right." Breyd felt a little of the terrible tightness leave her throat. *That is so foolish, though. I am no longer a little girl with a scraped knee, to be reassured by those simple words.*

High above them, a horn sounded the hour. Menlaeus stirred. "First horn. Day will break soon, and we are done here." As the echoes of the horn call faded away, they could hear the creak of the postern gate. A faint flicker of light came toward them: Jocasa and her Prime Mibro were edging toward them, a small clay oil lamp in Jocasa's hands to light their way to their post and then light the way back for Menlaeus and Breyd.

"Father," Breyd said as they neared the postern. "Thank you."

She wasn't entirely certain what she thanked him for: for dragging the secret from her, for the way he took it—for waiting until they were alone and in full dark, where it was easier to tell him, or all of it together. Menlaeus merely nodded and said quietly, "Of course."

Pelledar stood at the edge of his roof garden and gazed out toward the sea. There were only a few lights out there, probably the various companies trying to stay warm. The wind had died away and a late fog rose from the sea and the rivers; he could not see the water or the ships out there, awaiting daylight and smoother seas. His eyelids felt gritty from lack of sleep the past several days, but he knew he would not be able to sleep if he went down to the couch he and Ye Sotris shared, and she slept so poorly the last months of her pregnancies, he would waken her with his tossings and turnings.

He felt very much like a fool, just now. "All that heroic, fire-and-glory speech; I actually said all those things to Haffat's chief priest. I must have been mad." Behind him, startled fish splashed down into deeper water; he himself jumped at their noise. "And all those people who cheered me, all those soldiers who fight for the city, they will die anyway. More of them than if I had kept my mouth shut, and simply told the priest to go away, and bid his emperor leave us in peace." He sighed. "And all the men who die tomorrow and the day after—and the days after that. Will all my rantings mean the least thing to men who are dying?"

"Do you think they would die easier if they had not heard you today?" Pelledar caught his breath and swung around; Tephys had come onto the roof and stood not far behind him. "My apologies, I did not mean to startle you, my prince. I thought I might be of use to you for a little while."

"I—perhaps you might. I could bear company besides my black thoughts," he admitted.

Tephys came up to lean against the wall; for a long time they looked out across the city in companionable silence. "You did the right thing today," she said finally.

"Piritos said as much."

"Do not sound so uncertain. I happen to agree with him, and you know how rarely that happens. You did not choose this war, it has been thrust upon you. Your soldiers and officers did not ask for it, and it is theirs, through no fault of theirs or yours, or any of ours. If you give them a sense of worth and pride, even for a little while, that is not wrong." Silence. "You must not listen to Khadat."

Pelledar laughed quietly. "Hah. How do you *not* listen to Khadat? But I know she is warped by my brother's death, and by Hemit." He shook his head. "I did wrong there. She has ruined Apodain—and I aided her."

"She has not ruined him," Tephys said. "She has certainly caused trouble, and he has been badly upset. I am very angry that I did not realize how deeply this matter of husband and sons and war cut through her, or I might have prevented what she did to the boy." Silence again. "Did you see the driver of that chariot?"

Pelledar shrugged. "I had eyes only for the messenger. That really was Knoe? Haffat's dread lion-priest?"

"That is Knoe, and do not underestimate him because he looks odd. He is stronger than I had thought, or his god is. But they are not as strong as Knoe thinks."

"That is good, then—isn't it?"

"Of course. Denota has promised us victory, remember. But the driver—" But Pelledar was staring out across the city again; Tephys closed her mouth. There was no need to burden him with Ergardi, and what danger they might be. *He will never be where one might invade him anyway; his general and I will both see to that. But Meronne and I will*

strengthen the goddess' protective ring about the walls to-
morrow night—if we have any strength left from tomorrow.
She went on briskly, "You seem almost relaxed. Better than
when I first came."

"I think so. It was good after all, having someone to talk
with. Thank you, priestess."

"Of course. There is nothing you can do between now and
day. Why not go and sleep?"

He began to shake his head, felt a yawn swelling in his
chest. "I—your pardon, priestess."

"Go, sleep. I shall go seek my own couch. Remember that
I need you tomorrow." He nodded, fought another yawn as
she bowed formally and left. *Can she do that somehow?*
Make a man tired by her mere use of the word 'sleep'?
Whatever the cause, he was exhausted, all at once.

I shall need you tomorrow. What would she do, to counter
Haffat? He shuddered as he remembered the last time
Tephys had needed him.

Haffat

The sea was still running high at middle night. It pulled at boats anchored off shore, trying to drive them into the jetty or the shore; tried to shove them eastward onto sand or into the mucky, swampy lowland where the Oryon River broke into runnels short of the sea. Farther to the east, the great ridge that paralleled the Oryon descended steeply to the shore as black, ragged cliffs and enormous stones that lay just under the surface well out to sea. Only a suicide would try to land a ship in such weather or on such a night.

It would have been just possible for a skilled captain experienced with Ghezrat to come into land several places west of the mole. But any such flat beach was well guarded.

East of the ridge, there was a small indentation in the shoreline, where a normally small stream fed into the sea. It lay in a steep defile between hills, overshadowed by trees, brush and cliffs and the entry itself was both narrow and shallow during the dry season. Once beyond that treacherous entry, the stream broadened into a gravel-bottomed bay, just capable of holding three ships if they were narrow-hulled and their captains true masters who knew the Ghezrat coast-line. Because it was so small and difficult to reach even in good weather and full daylight, also because only the local fishermen used it, just a small company of guard had been left near the bay.

Knoe had sensed them earlier in the day, when the Ergardi first drove him to the city with the Emperor's letter. They had not seen him, of course, any more than those on the city walls had until the driver willed it. It had been the work of a moment to stop short of the stream on the return journey and send a warning signal to the long, low boat holding off-shore eastward, and for the men in that boat to signal the infantry company making its way along the shore toward the city.

By full dark, the Diye Haff held both sides of the stream well into the hills and down to the shore, and had already taken forty-seven prisoners.

Knoe watched the faint lights bobbing straight out to sea and he shuddered. *They can all have such travel, for all of me. I would be in terror out there; the lion is not a god of water, and all the while we voyaged aboard that ship, I could feel the fingers of Denota's son tapping upon the hull. One mistake by any of those captains—*

But the Mirikosi who was master of all Haffat's newly annexed fleet was a master sailor who claimed to know this coastline, its wave patterns and the depth of the water all along this shore. More importantly, he had gone out with the Ghezrathi fisherman who used this hidden stream; he knew how to find it from off shore, how to negotiate the stream itself. *Or so Haffat believes,* Knoe thought gloomily as he waited for the lanterns to be unveiled back from shore, to draw the ship into the bay. *It may be he is not so willing to change sides as I believed.*

That was partly the sea travel giving him such black thoughts; he himself had examined the captain and found him honest about his motives and true to his oath. "It is what I do, all I know how to do," he had said. "Better to serve the emperor for coin than to sit in Mirikos and starve, or go back to fishing."

Haffat's imminent landing was high in his thoughts, too, and he was not looking forward to passing on the prince's reply. There would be no way to sweeten that astonishing speech, and it would infuriate Haffat. *Who would think a man of his talents and his empire could be so touchy about his forebears and his right to be called Great King? Why should he care if he has the right to call men he has vanquished his brother?* His temper was a chancy thing at best, and Knoe thought it had grown more erratic since Idemito. *If he kills me, then it is because Axtekeles wishes me to die.*

It made him a little angry, all the same, not being able to predict how Haffat would react. *I am Axtekeles' priest, after all, I should be able to read him better than that. He squirms at mere thought of sacrificing men to our god, yet I myself saw him snap his cousin's neck before Idemito because the man baited him over—I cannot even remember—something utterly stupid. And they tell me Hylso is not the first. Little* wonder Hadda eyed him sidelong and wished himself fervently elsewhere.

Hadda is not your concern, he reminded himself flatly. *Haffat is. Think, how best to present him with this answer.*

And he had better do it soon; someone had just unveiled a lantern down by the shore and now men who had waited the last hours of daylight deep in the brush moved along both sides of the stream to hold up oil lamps, and mark the path of the stream for the incoming ship.

Haffat's stomach still roiled from those last hours aboard the ship, waiting before the mole, watching the company camped there, trying to decide how good their ballista might be; then waiting for Knoe and his car to appear. The reaction of all those men had brought a smile to his face; they had not seen the chariot and the Ergardi's trick had frightened them badly, he thought. He could actually see little of the delivery of the letter; they hadn't been allowed inside the gates, but Haffat had not expected that. The chariot had come flying down the hill, and horn cry had followed so quickly, Haffat wondered if the Ghezrathi had decided to ignore the truce flags and take Knoe. But ranks and companies and phalanxes had moved through the gates and down the road to take up positions on the plain.

After that, he had endured what seemed like an eternity of dreadful seas, until the ships could slip away under cover of full dark and find that stream.

How curious to think this is the same water as that before Mirikos. He had taken almost a child's joy in the feel of salt water rushing past his ankles to tug at his knees; the smell of it, the chill tang to the air. How wonderful to walk upon cool, wet sand. *So much water going as far as the eye would see, stretching to the very skirts of the sky.*

He had never set foot in a boat before, other than one of the round ones used for fishing the deep, chill Diyet lakes. The sea lost most of its charm when viewed from aboard a ship. And the man who commanded the ship told him the sea had been calm, compared to how it often was. Haffat shuddered, remembering the captain's vivid descriptions of winter waters. *When I return to Diyet,* he told himself firmly, *I shall ride my horse around the sea.*

When he next came this way. *I am tired, I must be to even think of Diyet.*

The ship's rowers were working furiously, the ship rocking even harder than it had before the jetty; all at once, the motion ceased and the wind fell away. When he looked cautiously out, he could see lights. And then one of the captain's aides came running over. "Sire—Emperor. We are safely in; the captain says he will be able to set you ashore very soon."

A very short while later, he sat before a small fire under a stone overhang. Somewhere across the high ridge a horn call rang out; the hour call, one of the Mirikosi said.

He sighed faintly; one of his soldier-servants came from the fire with a hot drink, and warm scented water to bathe his hands and face.

"Have they begun the unloading?" he asked. Jemaro, one of his captains, walked down to the bay and came back shortly.

"Fourteen ships still sit out there, three have been unloaded and gone back out, three more are being unloaded, and it is not yet middle night."

Haffat wrapped both hands around his cup, inhaling the warm steam. "It is a start. Make certain the work does not slow; we must be in position and ready to attack at first light. Has the company of heavy infantry arrived yet?"

"Not yet. They cannot be far, since we saw them on the march near midday."

"The Ghezrathi will not have left their eastern border unprotected," Haffat said.

"No. But would they send a company large enough to overwhelm five full phalanxes of experienced troops? It is very dark out there, lord, they must have had to stop."

"Yes." Haffat sighed again, roused himself enough to drink. The servant sponged salt water from his arms, dried them, and held up a pottery dish of small loaves warmed next to the coals, runny cheese, and a cloth bag of figs. Haffat took a chunk of bread and scraped it across the cheese, then looked at the men sitting with him, two of his captains and several aides. "Eat if you can. This is the first time all day I have been able to look at food; none of us can afford to be weak or ill come sunrise." He looked around the fire and finally found his logistics officer. "Wilus, what do you think? Can we still hope to put two companies of infantry upon the west shoulder of that slope, this side of the—"

"River Oryon," somone supplied as he hesitated.

"River Oryon, yes, can we hope to do that?"

"It's already begun, lord," Wilus said. "They'll be in place and ready on this side of the river by first light. But we cannot move the cavalry into place tonight."

Haffat nodded, took another wedge of bread, and ate it dry. "I know, the horses would scent their horses and give us away. As to the rest of the ships, unload the first twenty, here, before dawn if you can. The other thirty can wait until we take the mole or find places where they can be beached."

Footsteps crunched on broken stone; Knoe came into the light. "The Mirikosi mercenaries—where will you put them?"

Wilus turned to look up at him. "You still do not trust them, do you, priest?"

"They fight for coin—just as those Idemitans, the few men from Croatar and Righ. I do not trust any man whose loyalty is earned with gold."

Jemaro shook his head. "They are soldiers, priest. It is not so much that they did not love their own lands, or have loyalty to their captains, their kings, and their companies. This is what they *know*. They have no other trade, and wish none. Perhaps they will eventually be ashamed they set aside former oaths to take ours—but never while there is a war for them to fight." Knoe shook his head, clearly still not understanding but dismissing the matter at the same time.

"I have provided for them," Haffat said. "They are my worry, priest."

"Of course, lord," Knoe replied softly. *He took your news in fairly good humor, do not anger him with trifles.*

Men ate quickly; Wilus went down to see to the unloading, two of the aides to find the emperor's pavilion and another for more bread and fruit. One of Jemaro's messengers came running up; Jemaro went with him.

Haffat drew the cloak close around his shoulders and cradled a warm cup between his hands; Knoe sat across from him and toyed with a last bite of bread. They could just hear the furtive sounds of ships being unloaded in the near-dark, a man tripping and landing in the water with a loud splash, low voices.

"It is going well," Haffat said finally, breaking a very long silence between himself and the priest.

"Fairly quiet, speedily, no one lost but the company afoot," Knoe agreed. "And I myself was shown them a little while ago; they did well today but will not reach you before midmorning tomorrow." The lion-priest sighed. "This afternoon—at the gates. I am sorry we did not accomplish more."

"What?" Haffat held his hands out to the fire. "Sorry you were not able to gain entry to the city—or to Pelledar personally?"

"In all honesty? A little." Knoe shrugged. "I know, it was never likely the prince's advisors would let us near him. I thought at least the Ergardi might be able to tell us more about the prince and those who serve him. I thought at first there was a chance of touch on my part or the magician's— but that went so suddenly and the barrier came up so quickly, it must have been Denota's priestess, somewhere out of sight, up there." He rubbed his eyes. "I do not think they knew what they were guarding *against*. Someone on that wall surely saw us simply appear mid-road, though." He considered this, shrugged again. "So it was a trade. They are not quite certain where we came from or how we got there; I believe at least one person up there thought we had somehow put one of the ships in unnoticed, long enough to set a car and horses ashore."

"There is still no company this far east," Haffat pointed out. "It was a good trade. They were too wary to let you close, but they do not know which way you came. But if they were as wary as that, I am glad the Ergardi did not manage the exchange of body. They would probably have killed him at once."

"They will die for Axtekeles if they must," Knoe said. "But I would prefer to lose none of them. They may prove useful here."

Haffat squared his shoulders; his eyes were black and his face set. "Let them aid us in killing Ghezrathi, then," he said flatly. "After hearing the message my *brother* Pelledar sent me, I will not allow him a simple surrender. I want long and brutal fighting, I want bodies from that mole all the way to the city gates. I want soft and unblooded Pelledar to see the suffering *he* has caused; I want him to feel each of those deaths deep in his gut. I want him to beg me for death, for an end to guilt and grief too great for any man to bear." Knoe met the emperor's eyes with an effort; Haffat's breath came quickly and his color was high. But he finally drew a deep breath, expelled it in a loud gust and the moment passed. "Go, priest; I know you have things to attend to before dawn. But if you have time, pray for Haffat. This one victory above all, this city—this land—I *will* have it, at whatever cost."

Knoe bowed and left him, but sleep was far from his mind. *Those four upon the wall today—what were they? What duty is theirs? And why were they there?*

9

The wind died away late and a few stars shone faintly through the clouds. Guards paced up and down the long stone jetty, stopping now and again to stare toward deep water. "They aren't where they were earlier; they must have drawn back into deeper water for safety," one man muttered to his neighbor. "I can see nothing out there against the horizon."

"Not surprised," the neighbor whispered. "There is still cloud to the north, and fog will be thick out there before daybreak."

"Fog—but no clouds anywhere near," the first man said softly. "It is an omen, I tell you."

"Tell me, but don't say so around the captain. You know how angry Frewis gets when any of us talks about omens or fate."

"Aye. Well, I wish they'd lengthen the watches."

"You know why they kept them short." Creos came up behind them. "Shorter watches means more men alert."

"What, Creos," the first man jeered quietly. "You think Haffat will come in and take the mole from us in the dark? With the seas like they are?"

"He might try to," Creos replied. "But the sea is calmer than it was. A strong swimmer could just manage out there."

"Oh, thank you very much!" the second man whispered sarcastically. "Why don't you go jump in and spare the rest of us such thoughts?" Creos grinned, patted his shoulder rather heavily and walked on.

Tenth horn had been sounded a long time earlier; no one challenged the company and no one could see any sign of ships. Creos rested briefly, walked up and down the mole twice more, then settled cross-legged close to the north edge of the mole. It was utterly still out there, except for the splash of waves against stones and that had become noticeably more quiet. Water no longer splashed them and now he could occasionally hear the creak of leather and armor along the mole, or a horse whickering somewhere on shore. Someone off to his right snored loudly; Creos jumped and his heart thudded erratically. Someone close to the snorer swore sharply and shook the man awake. The sea dropped further and became a gentle, whispery, *sploosh* of small waves slopping against the rocks.

A very distant horn call; Creos stiffened, but it was only the hour call. "First horn," his neighbor whispered. He shifted, gestured with his spear; Creos saw the faint light of stars reflected on metal as the man pointed eastward. "It's getting light at last, isn't it?"

Creos squinted. "I think so. First horn, though—we should see something soon." Someone to his left made shushing noises. Captain Frewis walked slowly along the mole to the very end and back again; the second time he passed, Creos could see his head outlined against the eastern sky, then black hills and ridges tipped in deep red. Creos' neighbor shifted his weight, turned to speak. Creos frowned at him. "Don't you dare say it! It's the storm warning, red dawn! One word of fate, or omen, or any such thing—" he added softly, then broke off as footsteps came up the mole. The captain passed them and now Creos could make out his expression; he was looking out to sea, turning from west to east, trying to make out where those ships were. A low fog lay across the water, as it always did on windless mornings; it would not completely fade until Atos rose.

But it was not as thick as usual, either. Creos leapt to his feet and clutched at his neighbor's shoulder. "They—the ships are gone!"

"But why would they leave?" someone asked; his voice was lost in a wild, unfamiliar pattern of horn call coming from the east.

"Left?" Frewis was staring in the direction of the Oryon, just above her treacherous delta where the eastern ridge rose steeply toward a sharp peak. "But they didn't go very far, did they? Look!" Men surged to their feet. The light was poor, Atos still below the horizon—but the long eastern slope beyond the river was occupied by a camp many thousand strong. In its midst stood a large pavilion and before it limp banners. All along the eastern shore between the camp and the river were several waiting phalanxes of heavily

armed foot soldiers. These were flanked by a long double
file of chariot, and they in turn were protected by cavalry.

Someone at the end of the jetty called out: "There are
ships west of us! Four of them!"

"I see the ships! Ignore them!" Frewis called back. "They
are too distant now to be our concern."

"They are no threat anyway," Creos' neighbor muttered.
"We have a half-phalanx of heavy infantry out there, behind
the tall stand of bushes. My brother is with them."

Creos clutched his arm, pulling him back around. "The
captain is right, they are out of our range, now. Leave them
to your brother. But look over there." He pointed. Someone
near the land end of the mole cried out a warning at the
same moment. A full company of cavalry rode at full gallop
along the west bank of the Oryon and up the shore road toward the mole. Atos rose, casting golden light impartially
upon the sea, the ridge, and the plain; light sparkled on
spears and swords.

"Ready the company!" Frewis bellowed, and raised his
spear high; but the horse company had already turned inland
just short of the main road, and rode straight for the heavy
infantry camped there.

At the same moment, with a horrid yell, the first phalanx
of Diye Haff light infantry raced across the river to bear
down on perhaps a hundred very confused-looking men who
had apparently been separated from their phalanx. They
drew themselves into ragged formation, set the butts of their
long spears into the ground and waited.

"The horsemen are passing us by!" someone on the mole
shouted.

"Hold your position!" Frewis bellowed. "We were told to
hold this jetty at all costs, and by Atos, that is what we shall
do!"

The company of horse drove into the Ghezrathi infantry;
the men on the east side of the road retreated across it, into
the other half of their company. In the dusty, furious confusion, Haffat's horsemen spurred toward them; the infantry-
men still on the road turned to run.

A moment later, the officer carrying Haffat's banner
reined in and shouted a warning to the men behind him, but
it was too late. The infantry had retreated but only until they
surrounded the horsemen on three sides, two men deep. And

twenty royal chariot cut straight across the road, trapping half Haffat's riders.

More chariot came to attack the rest of Haffat's horsemen; dust rose thick, obscuring the fight; men shouted and swore, horses screamed. "I cannot tell who is winning!" someone beyond Creos shouted.

"The cavalry outnumber our men—" someone else began.

But Frewis bellowed, "Watch for ships or men trying to take this mole from us! That company out there is not our business!" But some of the men who had waited the night on shore with the ballista broke and ran to the aid of the heavy infantry. Frewis swore and screamed threats, to no effect.

The Ghezrathi infantry broke free first; men ran awkwardly under the weight of full panoply, splashing through a shallow, muddy canal and up the opposite steep bank where they turned and sent a volley of arrows back into the cavalry to cover men dragging or carrying their wounded. The cavalry officer reined in and seemed to think better of pursuit, for he dipped his flag and the company turned to gallop back toward their camp. The royal chariot were already halfway to the Oryon, chasing the rest of the broken company. A few men lay still and bloody on the road, or along it; somewhere in the ditch next to the canal a horse screamed steadily until someone slid down the bank and across the water to cut its throat. The men who had deserted the ballista ran in a ragged line, pursuing the Diye Haff who limped toward their camp, leading or leaning on lame horses. Frewis swore and screamed furiously, but they were too far away to hear him now.

"What are they doing out there? Why didn't they retreat when they had the chance?" Creos stared aghast at the small spear company; the Diye Haff cavalry had turned aside but their light chariot were about to run them down. At the last possible moment, most of the boys simply dropped their spears and fled.

Enemy horn call blared; the light chariot turned to pursue them. The boys reached the west bank of the Oryon, hesitated at its very edge. But the river was no safety. Diye Haff were already wading into the stream. The boys huddled close together, facing out, waiting.

Someone on the jetty groaned, and another whispered, "It will be slaughter, I cannot watch this." But Frewis walked by just then and heard him. "It is a ruse, I was with Lodis the night he thought of it." He laughed aloud, suddenly; men stared at him in shock, or looked at each other in rising fear. If he went mad out here, now—"Look at that!" Creos raised his head cautiously as the captain added, "It actually worked!"

The supposedly terrified boys were no longer cowering; as heavy infantry came slogging through the water and the light chariot raced up to drive the boys into their hands, the Ghezrathi tossed back short cloaks and brought up linen slings already loaded. The head chariot was turned sharply and its driver shouted out a warning, but it was too late. The first rank threw and most of the heavy metal pellets found targets. Horses screamed and plunged wildly; a driver was thrown from his car and trampled. Other cars, too light for such rough terrain, tipped over and were dragged. Men hip-deep in the Oryon lost their footing and were carried off by the current or drowned by the weight of their armor. The first line of slingers had already knelt to reload their slings and let the boys behind them throw. Some men fought their way desperately back to shore while others floundered downstream after their fallen companions. Ten of the light chariots had been crushed to splinters and their horses ran wild; the few riders who were still able to stand got out and fitted bows with long arrows or readied javelins, providing a guard for others who gathered up as many of the injured as they could, to take them back to camp. The company of slingers ran back toward the road; none of them seemed to have been touched.

"Bah," Frewis said, "I owe Lodis a new dagger after all. "Who'd have thought that would work?" The men nearby laughed and Frewis laughed, too, but to Creos it sounded nearer hysteria than relief, and Frewis' eyes were very worried indeed.

Frewis kept the smile in place; the joke had been a poor one but it seemed to relax some of the younger lads. His mind was working faster than it had in years. *Those fools left the ballista nearly unguarded; four boys are not enough to keep it safe. But we will not be of any use down there, I will lose these few men guarding a machine none of us can use. How long have we before the city sees us—or will the enemy come for us first?*

* * *

Piritos stood upon the wall next to the outer gates on a flat stone, arms folded across his muscled bronze corslet. He smiled grimly. "It goes well, thus far." His aide nodded. "But we have no more tricks to use against them—and Haffat would not be taken in by anything else."

"It was meant mostly to give the green soldiers confidence, wasn't it, sir?" the aide asked doubtfully.

"Mostly," Piritos said. "But the men they've killed out there are that many less to fight us later." His eyes moved constantly, along the east ridge, along the Oryon as far north as the narrow bridge and the delta; down the main road that led to the harbor and the mole. *Something is not quite right out there,* he thought, and frowned. But he could see some of the company that held the jetty and just make out the top of the ballista through the trees. *That should not be there; I thought I made it very clear I had to be able to see them from here.* But there were no enemy close by and he had other urgent matters to deal with just now. He gave the horn signaler a sign to ready himself, then said, "To the light infantry under Lodis, ready to engage."

"Sir." He could almost hear the boy's mind turning as he put together the patterns. *It is the first day, but he should be more prepared than he is; I will not have this boy back.* The signaler finally drew a deep breath and sent the complex call naming the company and its commander, delivering the general's order. The call was repeated from the base of the cliff. Piritos watched for Lodis' banner to dip twice, to let him know the message had been received; he waited a moment longer, to be certain Lodis had interpreted the call correctly, then turned his attention elsewhere.

Inside the city, old men, women, and young boys stood wherever they were allowed atop the old inner walls and anxiously watched what they could of the battle. But there was little to see except companies and individual men and horsemen racing back and forth across the plain between the Alno and the Oryon, or clouds of dust whenever they met. It was nearly impossible to tell which company fought for which side. The royal chariot stood out brightly for the first hour or so, but mud and dust covered the cars long before midday.

Both markets were open, but many of the shops in the old market were empty, their owners and craftsmen standing on the roofs to see out; in the green-market, food was laid out but all attention was for the boys who stood upon the old tower that had been part of ancient outer fortifications from when the city was smaller, and called down to the people below what they could see of the fighting.

There were no ships in sight, though guards upon the southwest wall above the Shepherd's Gate could just make out Mirikosi colored sails several *ciph* west of the mole, possibly on their way to attack the isthmus.

Haffat's companies were everywhere. "The ships were a fake," one of the guards over the Goat Gate told his companion flatly. "Wager you they were only here to draw our attention from the east road."

"No wager," the companion said gloomily. "My brother was with the company at watch along the eastern flank of the ridge. They should have returned last night, but no one has seen them."

Atos cleared the palace and began to heat the city and the plain; the ground shimmered.

Piritos watched, his face grim, as the first wagonload of casualties started up the steep road. He beckoned to his aide. "Send word down there to clear the street, the square, and the avenue all the way to the barracks gates. This is no time or place for civilians." The aide turned and ran. The general held up his hand and ordered the signaler, "To the barracks hospital, be ready."

The dead had been laid neatly in a row across the bottom of the cart, muddy cloaks laid across their faces. Piritos closed his eyes very briefly. *How long before these boys are hardened to death?* It was always like this: the first days or hours such men were wept for and covered, their bodies treated with respect and possibly a little fear. *As though by touching the dead, a man is marked for death himself.* But Piritos remembered his first dead all too well, his own fears. And the later dead, as the fighting went on and on and the living grew weary and the numbers of dead mounted, the bodies would be gathered in haste and set quickly in the carts by men numbed to bodies; they would grieve later, when there was time and quiet for it.

There were not half as many injured in this first hour of battle as he had feared. *With an unblooded and green army fighting the battle-hardened, I could well have already lost a full phalanx by this hour. They are doing well, my boys.*

* * *

The Prime Duplos and his Secchi Xera had been standing near the main gates since first horn and were nearly at the end of their watch when the cart came slowly toward the gates. Duplos knew what it was even before the cries of men in pain reached them. He caught hold of his daughter's arm. "Do not look. It will do you no good and is no help to them." Too late. If the fighting bond had held them, she would have known what he knew and turned away; but Xera was only aware of his concern, not its cause, and by the time he touched her the cart was already rolling by. She stared, aghast: one man drove the cart and another had just jumped out to lead the nervous horses through the gates; a third man sat facing backward, waving a long palm leaf over the cart. But there were still flies everywhere, dodging the leaf to hover in clouds over a man who clutched his mangled, bleeding hand against his chest and land on another whose forehead was bound in a strip of linen torn from someone's undertunic. The cart lurched and someone out of sight below the sides began to scream. Two men leaned against each other wearily, their backs to her. There were others, but she couldn't look; Xera closed her eyes tightly and turned away. Duplos caught hold of her elbows to keep her from falling, then drew her close and held her tightly. She finally shook her head and said, "I—I am all right, Father."

He looked down at her measuringly. "You aren't. No one is, seeing that for the first time. But you managed at least as well as I did, the first injured men I ever saw." She let her forehead rest against his breast for a moment. He looked over her head, down the road. "Another is coming."

She pressed her hands against him and he cautiously let go of her. "I really am all right, and I won't look at them. But I can stand now, Father. I do not want them to think I am not fit to be out here." Another cart passed, and again the gates were closed.

"The wind is picking up," Duplos said finally. "We won't be able to see much of anything out there soon."

"Oh. I can't make sense of any of it, anyway."

How different she is, Duplos thought. *She wept in terror when I was made Prime, and she was still my sweet, timid little Xera until we tied the cords. And now—look at her.* She was aware he thought of her, of course; she looked up to give him a brief smile, then went back to keep watch on the road. *How will she ever set this hour and such sights and*

*deeds aside to marry the second son of a gem dealer? How
can they expect her to do what she must here, and then put
it from her and be a simple wife and mother?*

By midday, unseasonable heat had been pushed across the
city and all the way out to sea by a hot southern wind. On
the plain, there was still fighting everywhere, but not as
many men were out in the heat. Any companies which could
pulled back into shade whenever possible, while heavy infantry broke into smaller units to allow men to rest more often.

Piritos remained beside the gates; he had eaten there and
finally his aides rigged a canvas square over his head to
keep him out of the sun. The wind had picked up so during
the past horn, he had to rely almost entirely upon horn call
from below to tell him how the battle was going.

Many of Haffat's men had pulled back beyond the Oryon
around midday; the Ghezrathi who would have chased them
halted at the water's edge only when horn signals ordered.
"To the phalanx under Evrikos," Piritos instructed his new
signaler. "Hold the west bank, fight only if engaged."

He cast a glance skyward. Atos had passed from his peak
and begun his slow, steady descent to the western sea, but
now swollen, pale Atelos was stalking his enemy and rival,
and had nearly caught him.

Piritos brought his eyes back to the plain with an effort
and called himself an uncouth name. *Let those who believe
in such symbols deal with them,* he ordered himself. *We who
live by our weaponry, let us show these northerners that
there is more to taking a city than the replay of an ancient
myth!*

Upon the roof of the palace, Ye Sotris sat alone; the two
younger children should have just eaten, and were probably
about to nap with their nurse. The unborn—she laid a hand
across her belly and felt a strong kick. Soon, soon—but not
yet. Pelledar was already gone when she woke to sun
streaming onto their bed, a message left with her servants
that he was with Tephys and did not know when he would
return.

Septarin. Ye Sotris bit her lower lip, tugged at a string of
long wooden beads that had been a gift from her mother.
They never left her throat and usually she tucked them inside the throat of her gowns, out of sight. They were Eygari

and so she could now and again use them to see or sense at a distance. She could not bring herself to do that today. But they were also a link to the gods, a focus for prayer and a proof of piety. "Denota," Ye Sotris whispered. "I know these beads were not fashioned for You, and I know that You have many people to watch over this day. But if You will, if You can—have an eye, or a guarding hand over my foolish, beloved son. Send him back safely to me."

Deep under the temple grounds, just short of the Cleft, Pelledar stood still, a bowl of water balanced between his hands. They had given him no instruction save to stand and wait, and not spill any of the water himself. His legs ached. Tephys lay stretched at full length on her belly, almost at his feet. Eyzhad had just sprinkled her head, her wide-flung, cupped hands and bare feet with water from the bowl. The priest's hands shook; his face was pale and there was sweat on his brow, despite the cool air in this cavern. Meronne, who crouched at Tephys' head and energetically wielded a fan, glanced up at him and the Prince thought he saw contempt in that look. Meronne herself showed no sign of concern, but Pelledar could not remember ever seeing any expression on the old priestess' face except sour disapproval.

The rock under the high priestess was splattered with water; her robe was damp along the hems. Tephys' forehead was pressed into stone, and Pelledar thought she occasionally prayed, but her voice was so soft he could not be certain. Eyzhad prayed; his voice was too high and it trembled.

Pelledar sighed. He was tired, and very worried: Septarin was out in that melee. Ye Sotris had tried to keep her own fears from him but not succeeded. *What is happening out there, how goes the battle?* How long before Tephys finished this ritual, and he could go to find out?

If she kept him here much longer, he might need men to carry him out as they had his nephew Hemit. *Tired, so very tired,* he thought, and wondered how much of that was exhaustion from too much worry and too little sleep—how much due to Tephys, who was somehow drawing upon his strength to put forth the petition to Denota's son, Eyiddi the wind god.

Meronne hissed; someone in loose sandals was clattering down the narrow stone steps. One of the green-clad novice priestesses came flying across the cavern; Eyzhad jumped and in turning nearly fell as his bare foot slid on wet stone. Meronne came halfway to her feet, but Tephys gave no sign of awareness outside herself. The novice's face shone with excitement.

"Mistress Meronne, the wind has again shifted and heavy cloud has risen in the west!"

"Has it yet shrouded Atos?" Meronne asked calmly. The girl shook her head.

"It had not, when I was sent down, but it was so near—" She held up a hand, brought her thumb and forefinger nearly together. Meronne turned her around and gave her a shove.

"Then we are not yet done here, go! Return when we have accomplished our goal." But just then another girl came down the steps, halting as soon as she could see down into the cavern.

"Mistress Meronne, Priestess! Thick cloud now muffles all the sky, and Atos is visible only as a pale yellow light, Atelos not at all."

Silence. Tephys stirred, sat up and pressed wet hands to her eyes. "Then we have prevailed—at least upon this one, very small matter." She let Eyzhad help her up and leaned heavily against him, eyes closed, her breath coming quick and harsh for several moments. With one last heaving breath, she opened her eyes again, held out her hands first to Meronne and then to her prince. "My thanks to all of you. I must go and rest, and prepare for the next emergency. I suggest you all do the same." But as Prince Pelledar gave the water bowl to Meronne, Tephys touched his shoulder and held him back until everyone else had gone. "I saw this much for you last night: Your son Septarin will survive the fighting—though perhaps not beloved by his company."

Pelledar swallowed. "That does not surprise me, I fear; my son is too young and full of himself for that. Alive, you say. Unharmed?" Tephys shrugged.

"Not badly injured in the fighting, if at all."

In the fighting. He glanced at her sharply, but there was nothing in Tephys' expression to tell him if she meant more than what she had said. "I will give your message to his mother; she will be very pleased to hear it."

"Yes." Tephys blotted still-damp palms against her forehead. "And you, my prince?"

"I? I am quite pleased. Of course. But I knew he might

die, that there was always a chance of it when I let him join that company. I do not forget it."

"Sensible of you. I shall come when Piritos does, after dark when the fighting is finished for the day. We must take stock."

Tomorrow. And another day after that, and yet another. . . . Pelledar let his eyelids sag shut for a moment, then shook himself and let his servants come to escort him from the cavern.

Frewis strode the length of the mole and back again, seemingly tireless, now and again calling down colorful curses on the men who had deserted them and the ballista. They had not returned. In their place, a half-phalanx of Haffat's heavy infantry sat possessively by the ballista, and many of them jeered at the pinned Ghezrathi. Frewis returned their curses freely; no one else dared.

Most of them watched their captain moving back and forth, and some of them showed no emotion at all, but many of the younger men were visibly afraid.

"If we had a horn and a signaler," someone just beyond Creos mumbled.

"Horn," Frewis growled, and spat into the sea. "We *had* a horn, do you forget? We had one, and he is gone with those other sons of goats!" He drew a deep breath and let it out in a deep growl; when he next spoke, he seemed to have let a little of his fury go with it. "Hold yourselves ready, lads; surely before long someone will see us pinned out here." He shook his head angrily. "With all this unexpected cloud, who could possibly tell what hour it is?"

"The cloud—" Creos began tentatively. Frewis spat, silencing him.

"I know why the cloud is there—or why the priestess will say it is," he added, and several of the more devout young men nearby gaped at him, while some fumbled for goddess-blessed, or Warrior-priest-blessed charms. "Which of you has good enough ears to hear the hour bells?"

"Over such noise?" Fedin, his son, laughed sourly. "And all that distance?"

"I but asked." Frewis walked on down the mole, turned slowly at the end to gaze across the sea in all directions, then pivoted so he could look back over the plain, toward the city. Out here it was difficult to see the walls and the main road. The general might not be aware of their peril yet. Someone would eventually notice the unofficered young men and realize what had happened.

"We'll die out here," Creos' neighbor whispered. Creos shook his head and one of the older men leaned over.

"They chose Frewis for this task because he knows things down here, but also don't you know how good he is at getting out of impossible situations? Back when the pirates came—"

"Yes," Creos' neighbor whispered sharply. "We know! But that was years ago in a skirmish, this is *now* and those men are—"

"Shhh!" Creos urged. He could see the fear in the eyes of the boy next to him: *We will die here.* "We'll be all right," he went on, as much to still his own rising fears as his neighbor's, and to keep the older man behind him from starting an argument. "They aren't attacking us, are they? No ships are close enough to be a danger, and our people will come for us. At least we aren't out there." He jerked his head in the direction of the plain—or all they could see of it which was largely dust.

But Frewis was thinking as rapidly as he ever had and the results were daunting. Even if someone saw their peril, it would take a full company to rescue them. *This was not supposed to happen this way.* He felt sick. So little to turn a simple delaying operation into disaster. He spat into the sea and began to walk slowly back toward land. Every few steps he paused and asked the same question of each clutch of nervous, waiting men: "How well do you swim?"

At fifth horn, a little after midday, the sky went night-dark for a long moment, and all fighting stopped until men could see the thick clouds overhead and the land around them once more. Septarin had been in the thick of fighting and he was still in the thick of battle a horn later. *This is what war should be; this is good,* he told himself repeatedly, but he couldn't make himself believe it. He couldn't see anything beyond the next men to be chased or killed; he couldn't tell where they were, or what was going on. No one challenged anyone else to single combat as they did in so many of the bard's tales and no one had ever told him how frightening it was to be so confused and uncertain what was going to come at him next.

Perhaps they had; he had listened to Brysos and his cousins as little as possible because they talked about such unheroic, boring things. *There are so many of them! I never thought there would be so many of them!* He reminded himself this would mean more enemy to slay, a larger tally, a greater hero's welcome for Septarin. His head was starting to pound from all the dust, the way it always did, and he was furious with his older cousin Ryllan for ordering the riders to descend from their cars at one point and fight. *Only the common chariot fight afoot!* But the cousin had not listened to his protests; he had shouted him down and actually threatened to send him back to the city. *Even Brysos is not as rude as Ryllan.* Or as distrusting: Ryllan stayed close to him the whole day.

Enemy came at them from the side, barely seen for all the dust and without warning from any of the signalers. Septarin's driver brought the car around sharply and drew the horses to a halt. Septarin threw one javelin and a tall, skinny man in padded cloth armor fell, the point had gone right through his throat; Ryllan swore at him. "You almost killed one of my horses, you young fool! Get out of there, we're advancing on foot again—now!" Septarin made a face; that had been an excellent throw, and he'd killed his man. Ryllan sounded like Khadat. He snatched at the quiver of javelins and ran into the open to choose his next target. Not so good, this time; the man screamed and bent double, then fell, still shrieking in mindless agony. The sound cut into his head like knives, and he was grateful for the enemy who dropped his own weapons to drag the wounded man away. He turned back to raise his eyebrows at his cousin, but Ryllan pointed with his short spear and shouted, "The enemy is there, *prince*. Prove to me that was no mere accident!" A flight of arrows sang over their heads; Diye Haff fell and the rest turned and ran.

Septarin ran back to his car and braced himself for pursuit; hampered as those men were by full armor and the long metal shields, they would never outrun chariot. Horn signal rang out somewhere nearby; Loros turned the car toward the sea and Septarin drew in a shrill, horrified breath. "What are you doing? We can't go that way!" He grabbed the driver's arm, and then snatched at the reins. Loros slapped his hands away and wrapped the straps around his own hands. "They are getting away from us, you fool!" The matched white horses were younger and less experienced than Apodain's, and Loros had his hands full.

"Did you hear the horns? The mole has been cut off, we are needed there!" He finally got the car turned and lashed at them with the free ends of the reins.

"But those men are getting away!" Septarin's voice cracked. "We cannot let them cross the river and regroup; if we pursue now, we can cut them off!"

Loros was fighting near-hysterical horses with all the strength he possessed, cursing furiously under his breath. *Where is Ryllan? He said he would stay close in case I had trouble with this—this—* He set his teeth and took another turn of straps around his hands. *Stupid, stupid beasts. Septarin chose his match, didn't he?* "Our orders are to attack the company out there! Hold on!"

"No!" Septarin flung himself upon the driver and fought him for control of the car. Loros shrieked and staggered back, then suddenly let go of the reins. Septarin nearly fell out the back of the chariot as the horses lunged forward.

He glanced down at the fallen driver. *What is he doing down there? I need him!* "Loros, get up!" he shouted; but Loros didn't move. *He must have hit his head on something. Just as well.* Septarin's chest swelled. He wound the reins around his left hand and yanked so hard his shoulder burned with pain, but the horses finally came around the right way. He loosened his grip and let them run.

He was nearly within striking range of the fleeing infantry. *Wait. If I hold the reins, I cannot use even the spear; if I let go, I'll lose control of the chariot!* He looked down at Loros, who had not moved, then off to his left and behind him. *Black Atelos, where are the rest of my company?* The enemy had reached the Oryon and was turning back to face him.

They'll kill me! The headache was forgotten; so was everything but getting away from here. He gripped the reins in both hands and fought to bring his matched beauties around.

He was closer to such men than he wanted to be. One grizzled man was baring his teeth in a hideous grin; blood trickled from a long slash cut down another's cheek. *Not like this, I can't die like this! Ryllan, how dare you let me die?* But two chariots raced across in front of his and Ryllan leaned perilously out of his car to snag Septarin's harness while his driver turned both chariots and sent them flying from the river. Septarin closed his eyes and held on to the rails; jeering laughter and taunts followed them. *They are baiting me. Wait, all of you. I am not done with you yet!*

Ryllan was sweating freely, but his face was utterly expressionless as the driver brought the horses to a walk, and then stopped at the edge of the main road. Septarin looked down at him angrily. Ryllan shoved him aside and knelt beside Loros. "It's bad, someone will have to take him up at once or he'll die." He got to his feet, but before he could say anything else, Brysos' second, Naxis, came racing up the road from the sea. He looked utterly furious and Septarin bit back a smile. *That will show Ryllan to leave me in peril,* he thought.

Naxis came storming over the moment his driver stopped. "I knew it! I knew all along—I warned Brysos! I will take this—I will take the prince's son, you bring Loros." He dragged a stunned Septarin from the car. Septarin looked away from him, but there were men everywhere—drivers, a messenger, more chariot—and they all looked just as angry. *At me! Why are they angry with me, because the driver got hurt? I did nothing wrong. What is the matter with them? Didn't they see the danger? And now those men have escaped after all!* Naxis pressed his prince's son into his own chariot and put him next to the driver. He was pinned between the two men. *What are they doing? They cannot lay hands upon me, I am a prince!*

"To the city, as fast as you dare," Naxis told his driver. Only then did Septarin remember his driver. He looked back; the matched white horses stood with their heads down, and men were gathered around the rear of the car. He could see nothing else.

Atos escaped cloud cover near the end of day, casting ruddy light across the sea and shining levelly in the eyes of Haffat's men. Wind blew from west to east, kicking up dust and sand; Haffat withdrew most of his men across the river and into camp; other companies stayed in the positions they had won during the day. His infantry now stretched across the sand and his men held the mole. The ballista had been hauled across the Oryon and presented to Haffat.

As soon as the eclipse began to significantly darken the clouds, Creos' company had thrown aside weapons and armor, stripped down to their undertunics and jumped from the end of the mole into the sea. A few fortunate men managed to reach land quickly, but most had been caught in a strong side-current and carried some distance; many men who could not swim well drowned. A few hesitated too long and were taken prisoner. Many were simply missing: Creos was one of those.

As night fell, fires were lit in the enemy camp and across the plain. In the last moments of dusk, companies came down from the city to replace those who had fought most of the afternoon.

In the streets and the markets under the canvas shades and in winehouses and bakeries, people gathered to pass on gossip or to learn anything they could from the few soldiers who had leave. A large crowd waited in the square before the main gates—General Piritos' aide had come out at sunset and promised a list of known dead and wounded by eighth horn.

Tarpaen had been released from duty at sunset and permitted to return home until eighth horn; Xhem had already had his leave and had eaten the evening meal with Nidya and the rest of his new family, but he was on late messenger duty between the barracks and the palace. Tarpaen found Menlaeus and Breyd getting ready for a late watch at the south postern near the Shepherd Gate. "Son, I hoped we would see you before we went on duty. What news?"

Tarpaen knelt with them. "Mother sends her love. She was smiling when I left and she laughed at my jokes. Niverren is horribly worried, she wouldn't even eat. She heard at the bakery the mole was taken."

Grysis leaned out of the messes and called for Menlaeus. Breyd poured her arrows onto the ground and ran her fingers over each shaft before replacing them. "We were out there, Tar—next to the main gates, when a few men were brought in. They were soaking wet and reeked of salt water; I didn't see Creos, though."

"He wasn't with them; they have him listed as missing," Tarpaen said. "Niverren looks terrible."

"Small wonder." Breyd shoved the last arrow into her case, ran practiced fingers over her strung bow, the string, then fished into the side of the case to test the spare for damp. "You know how she cares for him." She glanced over her shoulder, Menlaeus stood by the entry to the messes, talking earnestly with Grysis and Lochria's Prime Bechates. Lochria herself was nowhere in sight. *She is probably still inside, trying to finish that gritty loaf.* There was no one anywhere near her and Tar, no one paying the least attention to them. She lowered her voice cautiously all the same and her brother put his head close to hers. "Did you see the prince's son brought in?"

"No. I heard wild rumors before I went home. They say he was brought back in an officer's car."

"He was. I saw him and I could hear him clearly, out there." Breyd had her javelins out now, and was checking the shafts and the points, shoving them rapidly and neatly into the case one by one. "Naxis was so angry he was absolutely purple, and Septarin—well, you've heard that self-righteous whine of his. I think he was saying the horses got away from him."

"Goat droppings," Tarpaen said rudely.

Breyd laughed. "Just so." She pulled the javelin case over her head and got to her feet. "His car came not long after, just before Father and I were relieved, but it wasn't his regular driver at the reins."

"His driver—of course, that's Loros," Tarpaen said. He got up, a little slower and more cautiously than his sister since he tended to lose his balance and hated losing it here. Breyd watched him closely but made no effort to steady him, and he was glad of that. "Remember about Creos," he said. "If you hear anything—so Niverren knows."

"Of course."

"Are they letting you go home tonight?"

She shrugged. "Maybe for a little while tomorrow, unless *they* come up with surprises later. Here comes Father."

Tarpaen looked behind her, then stared at her blankly; Menlaeus had turned away from the messes, but Breyd wasn't looking in that direction at all. "Please don't do that, Breyd," he said. "It's unnerving."

"Oh." Breyd considered this, looked at him in mild surprise. "I suppose it is. But I forget it's not really normal."

Eriana came running across from the main gates, her father just behind her. "We aren't late, are we? Father broke a sandal strap, and the streets are simply awful, so many people everywhere. Lochria is on her way, but she was stopped outside by someone's father—one of those men on the mole, he's heard any number of rumors—the father—and cannot get any straight tale from anyone. Hello, Tarpaen," she added as a brisk afterthought.

"Hello," Tarpaen said warily. "Father," he said as Menlaeus came up to join them. "Mother sends her love. I have to go, there's a meeting."

"Your captain's second is waiting just inside the messes," Menlaeus said, and Tarpaen left. Eriana giggled.

"Your brother is afraid of me," she said. "I cannot think why. Chrosin is pledged to me, after all. Did I tell you he's sent Mother a bolt of yellow silk?"

"You told all of us," Breyd replied dryly. "Several times."

"Oh." Eriana considered this, added, "Sorry." She didn't sound it. *How wonderful,* Breyd thought wistfully. *She and her Prime have the goddess bond, the training Grysis gave us—but she is still Eriana when she is not half of a Pair. I could never have been as giddy as Eriana, but I remember giggling like that, and it's gone now.* Eriana's silly chatter could become irritating, but more often it eased the tension among the Secchi. And on the wall when Knoe read his letter, Eriana had been as fierce and furious as Breyd or either Prime.

Lochria came panting up, nodded in Menlaeus' direction. "Eriana—aren't you supposed to be with your Prime in the messes?" Eriana gave a startled yelp and fled. Bechates came looking for Menlaeus; Lochria stayed with Breyd. "We are with you two at the south postern tonight."

Breyd had freed a length of leather strap and was unwinding the frayed handgrip and strap from her spear. "Good. You make better company than some."

Lochria laughed. "I am glad to hear it."

"I mean it. Here, hold the end of my spear will you?" Breyd knelt and fished a strip of leather from one of her bags. "The old one was fraying when I got it and it's useless now." She dropped the old grip and began to rewrap the shaft while Lochria steadied it.

"You heard that Creos is among the missing?"

"From my brother—but he learned it from Niverren when they let him go home."

"No different news for his father, then." Lochria let go the spear so Breyd could test the balance.

That was Creos' father outside the barracks; I forget Lochria knows the family. "The Diye Haff may have taken him, but if they did, Father says there will be a prisoner exchange tomorrow or the day after. It's easier than feeding all those extra men, and if they kill them—well, we hold some of their men."

"He may be drowned and halfway to the isthmus by now," Lochria said flatly.

"Perhaps. I doubt it, myself. He swims in the games each midsummer, remember?" She changed the subject. "Have you heard the new gossip, about Prince Septarin? They say he's in very deep trouble indeed."

Lochria grinned broadly. "I haven't heard! But how wonderful to think such virtue might be suitably rewarded after all!" Breyd clapped a hand across her mouth to keep from laughing aloud. Lochria's eyes were wicked and she was grinning once more. "Tell!"

"Don't know much," Breyd admitted. She told what she did know. Lochria wasn't smiling when she finished. "That's horrible. And Loros was Apodain's driver, you know. They say he is one of the best."

"I—didn't know," Breyd said faintly. She suddenly remembered him and the grim words he'd exchanged with Brysos over Septarin.

"Of course you didn't know," Lochria retorted. "For all of *you,* lovely Apodain might never have been born—never mind his driver. Look, there's Father, with Eriana." She groaned. "Pray the goddess Grysis did not just change the pairing for the watches!"

Grysis had not; he had come to pass on a very quiet order. "You will all be very careful these next days, what you say of the prince's heir and before what man. Better yet, do not speak his name at all. Captain Brysos says he ignored orders out there and put his company at grave risk. His driver is very near death. General Piritos, the prince, and his council are meeting to decide what to do with the young fool."

"I'll pass that on," Menlaeus said. "It should be enough to quell most of the gossip. Did he hurt the driver himself?" Grysis shrugged. "They'll ask, you know."

"Carelessness on his part, apparently. The arrows are not ours. But they tell me Loros will not live the night." He went back inside the messes.

"Look!" Eriana whispered excitedly a moment later. "By the gates, there!" She would have pointed; Lochria caught hold of her arm and pressed it down. Breyd turned to see a grim-faced, pale Apodain stalking across the fighting ground.

Men fell silent and stared as he passed them but Apodain seemed not to notice. He slowed near the messes, hesitated, came across to where the Dyaddi stood. His eyes touched Breyd, hesitated, moved on. "I am told the driver Loros was brought in earlier. Is—do any of you know where he is?"

"Brysos is inside, he would know," Lochria said. But Apodain glanced toward the doorway and shook his head.

"No. I haven't any right—I cannot go in there." Breyd stepped forward.

"Wait here, then," she said. "I will find out for you." She came back moments later, pointed toward the low building that took up most of the east wall. "They took him there, the door nearest the gates."

"Thank you." He was already gone, striding quickly across the fighting ground. Breyd gazed after him, realized she was staring and turned back to her companions. *He didn't even know me.* Why would he, though, even if he had not been so visibly upset? *For his sake, I hope Loros is not already dead, or that he won't turn from him. It must have cost him dearly to come here.*

Grysos called to her and gathered the Pairs together for last-minute instructions, then sent them out on watch. Breyd glanced toward the hospital barracks, but there was no sign of Apodain.

Outside the south postern, it was very dark; the wind was a constant, chill presence that went through every garment she wore, and deadened her ears to everything but itself.

10

The Diye Haff had pulled back across Oryon at full dark; the Ghezrathi retired into the ravines and ditches across the Alno and lit fires. There was not much purpose to secrecy now, and besides, men needed hot food and wine; the wounded needed to be tended so they could withstand the long, rough journey by cart back to the barracks.

Small lights moved slowly back and forth across the plain, marking the men and wagons who sought the dead and wounded. The enemy dead were taken to the Oryon and left by the west bank, along with the more seriously wounded. Prisoners were bound and taken up to the city to hold for exchange.

Around eighth horn, when it was fully dark, fresh companies came down to relieve as many of the worn as possible. Their captains stayed behind long enough to pass on anything useful they had learned during the day's fighting, then went back to the barracks to meet with General Piritos and to sleep, if possible.

Men and women waited as near the gates as they were permitted. They lined the avenue and the square in hopes of catching sight of their loved ones, or word of them. Each time he ran this way, Xhem thought, their numbers increased, until he wondered if all the houses in the city had been emptied. The silence was unnerving. On his way back from the Temple of Warriors, where he had been sent to ask for a priest to speak with the dying, he slowed, then stopped and stared. Niverren was standing between two older women, a dark scarf thrown over her hair and shoulders. She stared right over his head, intent on the gate. Xhem hesitated, then turned and sped toward the barracks. He did not talk to her much anyway; he would not know what to say to that white-faced and clearly suffering woman. He sprinted into the barracks yard, found the officer who had sent him on this last errand and told him the priest was coming, then went in search of his brother Tar.

Tarpaen was sitting with Laius just inside the messes, Tar polishing his horn, Laius flipping a drumstick and catching it and glaring at nothing in particular. When Xhem came running up, he turned and glared. "What do *you* want? This isn't a place for boys!"

Xhem took a quick step back, out of reach, but Tarpaen snapped, "Leave my little brother alone, Laius! You know Nabid finds him useful—and I won't have him harassed."

To Xhem's surprise, Laius simply stared at his friend for a long moment, then finally shrugged. "All right; you only needed to say you didn't mind him, you know." He got up and said, "There might be some bread left from dinner and I'm hungry. I'll be back." Tarpaen stared after him, then shrugged.

"Sorry, Xhem. You know how Laius is."

"I know. I had to find you, though. Niverren is out in the street, standing with the others. She looks—she looks awful, Tar."

"Oh, dear Atos," Tarpaen got to his feet. "It's Creos; his company hasn't turned up yet, she'll be frantic. I'd better go, she doesn't belong out there and I should go to Mother anyway. You—how long do they want you tonight?"

"Another horn, maybe two. Captain Nabid said I might be needed."

Tarpaen gripped his shoulders. "Of course you will. I will see you later, then." He got up, spoke briefly to Laius, and then went into the night. Xhem watched him go, then carefully worked his way farther into the messes. Out of Laius' sight. Just, he thought, in case.

"Niv?" Niverren came out of a long, cold blankness to find Tarpaen's anxious face close to hers, his hand on her arm. "Niv, you should not be here."

"I—" It was hard for her to speak. "Creos—"

"I know. They say it was all confusion out there today; the men jumped into the sea, they weren't set upon, you know. They just haven't found transportation back here yet, that's all." He looked at her; she stared dully back at him. "Creos swims better than anyone else in the city, Niv; you can't worry about him. But you know how you hate it when people stare at you; Creos knows it, too. He would hate it if he came and saw you here, with everyone watching you."

"I—I can't—"

"You can, Niv. Xhem is still on duty; he will know the moment Creos comes, and he'll let us know." He wrapped an arm around her shoulders and drew her away from the gates. When she would have resisted, he shook his head. "Poor Niverren. You look terrible. If you stay here any longer, you will faint in the streets. There are enough ill and wounded to tend to without you, don't you think?"

"You sound like Father," Niverren muttered fretfully, but allowed him to take her home. Once there, though, she turned stubborn again and when Nevvia offered some of Nidya's sleep potion, she refused it. "Creos might come home, and if I am asleep, and they send him right back out—or if he was wounded, and I wasn't awake for him—no, I can't."

She was too worn and upset to hear anything Nevvia and Nidya said to try and persuade her. Tarpaen thought it would have driven him mad. He finally climbed the narrow ladder and felt his way across the flat roof to the low, woven mat of reeds that protected the pile of cushions and loose-woven blanket that constituted his summer bed. He stripped off his sandals and the baldric with his dagger, the horn, and settled into the soft bedding, sighed and closed his eyes resolutely. But sleep evaded him for a long time. His legs ached from the unaccustomed hours spent standing in one place, his head spun with the constantly shifting patterns he could see from his vantage on the outer wall. With his eyes it was mostly dust, though he could just make out an occasional charge of chariot or enemy cavalry and the red tiaras and cloaks of the Dyaddi directly below him.

Horn calls replayed in his mind. And then, the terrible anxiety of that exacting hour when he had been sent up to General Piritos to send out the signals for the companies below, while an aide stood on his other side to translate those coming up from below. At first he had been utterly terrified of making a fool of himself, then of making the wrong call; it had gone from that to something that raised the hair on his neck—the general calling out companies and orders almost nonstop, himself translating words to signals. No one had ever challenged him so intensely, never had so much been on the line, never had it *mattered* so much, what he did, and how well he did it. He was astonished when his replacement tapped him on the shoulder—it could never have been a full horn!—but Piritos had actually gripped his arm and said, "Good work, lad! Very good job."

There had been men everywhere, milling around the fighting grounds or forming into their companies when he finally came down from the walls, making it difficult to get back to the table used by the horn and drum company—even harder to get anything to eat and drink in the short time allotted before he went back on duty, this time along the north wall with the over-captain of all the heavy infantry companies. He had only had a few moments to spend with Laius. But that was just as well, since all he'd done was grumble about being stuck inside the walls, then about all the people in the street, all the village cousins and old uncles crowding his dead mother's house. *I never dared shout at him before; I wonder I am still alive—or Xhem. But he cannot bully the boy, I won't have it.* Thinking back on that, he wondered at Laius; the man had simply shut up and walked off. *Maybe Nabid was right, and I have a little influence over him after all.* Maybe Laius was beginning to realize how few friends he had left.

He could still hear his mother worrying about things down there; Nidya trying to soothe her, telling her how things had been when she was young. That really *had* surprised him, how often she was right about the way things went on the first day of fighting. The warrior-priests who came to the barracks often said they must revere the old men for their knowledge; they forgot about the old women, he thought. But he had always thought of her as just Niddy, the old woman who came in from the fields, who brought money to enlarge the house and stayed to boss everyone around. Well, and to occasionally side with her grandson, or praise him when no one else did.

Somehow, between one thought and another, he fell asleep.

Ninth horn—midnight. The guard changed on the walls; the Dyaddi changed guard at all the gates. Another cart of badly wounded men came up the road—slowly to avoid jarring broken bones and dreadful wounds that were barely staunched. Men passed them on their way down to join the companies waiting for daybreak, and tried not to look at the carts, but the smell of blood and sickness followed them; the moans of men who tried to keep pain behind clenched teeth as the cart jounced up the road rang in their ears.

Wounded men filled the long barracks; physicians and priests moved between the pallets and here and there company comrades or family crouched beside the injured, waiting anxiously for the physicians, often working themselves to staunch wounds or hold down their men while wounds were cauterized or broken bones eased back into line and bound.

Well back in one corner, royal chariot driver Loros lay among the dying. His face was utterly gray in the dim torchlight. The ragged wooden stub of an arrow protruded from his upper arm; another was sunk deeply in his shoulder. His armor had been left in place, the second arrow untouched even to cut it short. Apodain's heart sank when he saw that; there were men who could be saved, but Loros had not been counted among them even when they found him. His throat and his near arm were black with dried blood, his face drawn and gaunt from trying to hold in the pain. Apodain knelt and took his other hand; Loros opened his eyes a little, and somehow managed to dredge up a thin smile. Apodain tried to smile back reassuringly. "Sir," Loros whispered. "I knew you would come."

"For the best driver in all the royal chariot? Of course I came. But do not talk," Apodain urged softly.

"Doesn't matter, sir. Won't have—long to talk anyway." Loros' fingers tightened on his; his lips thinned. "Septarin—I knew—"

"Oh, Loros, I'm sorry. It's my fault—"

"No, sir, never your fault. No one's—fault, really. My fate. . . ."

He had to swallow before he could say anything else. "If I hadn't—"

"If any of us hadn't." Loros coughed and blood ran down his chin. Apodain pulled the cloth from his belt and blotted it gently. Loros' grip was hurting his hand. "Sir—" He coughed again, his face twisted in pain and more blood came. Too much. Apodain blotted it. He turned his head long enough to rub his eyes, then leaned forward and kissed his driver's brow.

"The gods bless you, my friend," he said very quietly. Loros smiled, opened his eyes very wide, and died. Apodain withdrew his hand from the relaxed grip and closed his eyelids. *Dear goddess.* He bent forward, let his forehead down onto his knees, and stayed that way for a very long moment.

Finally he got to his feet. Men stared; a nearby priest came
halfway to his feet; somewhere behind him as he walked
through the rows of wounded, a woman made an explosive,
rude comment. He ignored them all, concentrated on walking through the long room of wounded without thinking, and
let himself out into the torchlit fighting ground.

There was no one he knew nearby—fortunately. He
walked blindly toward the gate until he found a patch of
shadows between torches. He leaned into the wall and closed
his eyes. *Waste. Stupid. Stupid, stupid waste. Why could it not have
been Septarin who took two arrows, instead of Loros?*
Septarin—what would they do with Septarin for such a
senseless death? *Nothing, most likely. After all, he is
Pelledar's heir, the royal brat—ah, damn-all, Loros!* Tears
ran down his face freely and he let them go. After a little
while, he straightened up, blotted his face carefully, and
started toward the gate. Better if Khadat did not find he had
left the house, though he scarcely cared at the moment. He
would need to send word to Brysos though; Loros had an
aged grandfather, all his family. The old man would have no
money for food without his grandson's earnings. *I haven't
much, but I can put together enough coins to keep the old
man alive.*

Someone was blocking his way. He fell back a step: Reott
stood there, irresolute and visibly unhappy. Emyas stepped
between them, then, so near he could smell the herbed wine
on the man's breath. "You were warned not to leave the
household, young cousin," Emyas said softly. "Tell him, servant," he added a little louder.

"You are to come with us at once, sir," Reott added.

"The princess orders you to return home with us, at
once," Emyas corrected him impatiently. "Go, ahead of me,
now."

Apodain shook his head. Men shouldered past them and
stared—at him and at the two bulky men facing him, particularly Emyas who stood with his arms folded, legs astraddle,
and an extremely disagreeable sneer on his lips. A Secchi
paused to gaze at one and then another of them, then hurried
on. He could hear her excited voice somewhere between him
and the messes.

"I am not yet finished here. I will come when I am done,
and not before," Apodain replied evenly. Emyas laughed unpleasantly and snatched at his arm. *To shame me before*

Mother's servants and poor Reott is one thing—but to come here! Has my mother not done enough already?

Something snapped. Apodain stepped back and spun full circle, slamming his fist backhand across his cousin's jaw as he came around. Emyas reeled backward, flailed his arms wildly and fell.

Reott's face was utterly crimson and he averted his eyes as he held out a hand to help Emyas to his feet. Emyas swore and slapped it away. But as he tried to rise, Apodain shoved hard, and he went down again. Reott knelt behind him and hissed urgently; when Emyas looked at him, the servant sent his eyes warningly sideways. Emyas looked. There were men all around them, most showing nothing but mild curiosity. But there were a few unfriendly faces, and two men had hold of their swords.

Apodain stood above his cousin, a dagger in his hand. "I said I would come when I have finished here, not before," he repeated evenly. For all the attention he paid them, the silent, gaping crowd didn't exist. "But you had better listen to me, cousin. You were brought here to tend to my brother; you are paid by Khadat, my mother, to perform this task. You are *paid.* You are as much a servant as Reott or any other man or woman in my mother's household, Emyas, not my equal or my better, whatever Khadat has let you pretend. Do not dare, ever again, give me orders of your own or orders from her mouth."

"You—" Emyas began, but Apodain shook his head and raised the knife so he could see it better. "Remember this, cousin: One day, Mother will die and the palace and all things hers or Father's will be mine. Men who are *servants* and who wish to live beyond that day would think long and hard how they treat Perlot's heir, and a nobleman—and the man who is eighth in succession to Ghezrat's prince. Men who wish to live beyond this moment will recall that they are not in Khadat's household just now; they are in the military grounds. There are men in this compound still friendly to me. And it is a place where men live by the proper order of things: Common soldiers do not order their officers about; servants do not order their masters. Servants who would survive to return to care for my brother would quit this place at once, while their blood is still inside their skin."

"You don't dare." Emyas' voice was so thick with fury, he

couldn't go on. Apodain shifted his grip on the knife and went into a fighter's crouch.

"I do dare, *servant*. It is you who do not dare, ever again. Whatever orders my mother gives you, whatever you think, whatever airs you have taken to yourself—you will not touch me in any fashion, unless I order it, or ask it. You will not order Reott against his proper inclination, and you will address me from this hour in the proper manner." He straightened up, deliberately turned away from them to sheath the dagger. "You will go, now. If the Princess Khadat asks my whereabouts, you will tell her that I came to visit a dying friend, and to arrange for the care of his kindred. You will tell her that I shall come as soon as that is done. That is all."

He brought his head up, folded his arms and waited. Reott bowed and softly said, "Sir." He had to kneel and whisper against his companion's ear before Emyas would move. Emyas' eyes were black with fury and his mouth set in a hard line, but he finally inclined his head in a sharp gesture, and let Reott pull him away. Apodain watched them go, and only when the two vanished beyond the gate did he realize men had formed a ragged half-circle behind him. Those nearest him all at once were members of the royal chariot, drivers and fighters both.

They blame me for Loros' death, he thought warily. The momentary pleasure he had felt at silencing Emyas deserted him and he felt merely a little sick and very tired. *Because I left him to Septarin. And I have no right to be here; they know that. And so do I, even if I forgot for a moment.* "Sorry," he mumbled and turned to leave. But they were all around him, close around him; and to his stunned surprise one man and then another gripped his arms or touched his shoulder, and all he could see in their faces was sorrow. Men who had been his companions in arms for two years spoke his name, and someone said, "I am sorry for your loss; he was a good driver to you." It all nearly undid him, and for a very long moment he could do nothing but stand in their midst, eyes closed. When he dared again trust his voice, he said, "If—if Brysos is here, I must speak with him."

"He is still in the messes," one of the royal cousins said.

"Would one of you bring him to me? Or, if he will not come, at least tell him I would like to help Loros' grandfather?"

Another of the royal cousins shook his head. "No man will deny you access, my good friend. Come, all of you," he added, just loudly enough to include the rest of the company. "We will take him." Apodain shook his head, but the men of his company moved in close to him to shield him from the unfriendly and the merely curious, and brought him through the messes right to the company commander. They stood shoulder to shoulder around the two, and when Apodain was ready to leave, walked him safely to the gates.

He turned back and managed a smile for them. "Thank you. All of you."

One of the drivers came forward to clasp his arms. "Brysos told us you weren't what they said. I admit I doubted, even when poor Loros defended you. Now—well, there may be some men in there who wouldn't welcome you back, sir. But I would."

Apodain shook his head helplessly, dredged up another brief smile that fell short of reddened eyes, and turned and left. There were people waiting along both sides of the street as he passed, but their attention was for the city gates and the barracks, not for him. The streets were mostly darkened beyond the first avenue and the square, but ahead and high above this first level of city, lights blazed from the palace windows.

The prince's council was busy in the throne room, going over lists of supplies and hammering out final plans for rationing, in case of a siege. They worked without Pelledar. The prince had moved down to the small throne room which he had decided to use as a judgment chamber. It was a long, low-ceilinged room, and Pelledar did not care for it: it was too dark and there was little to see but the walls of the horse-forecourt. His household men liked it for the enormous round brazier where they could sit and cook skewers of meat, and for the long open balcony next to it, and ordinarily he let them make free with it.

Tonight, the brazier was cold and there were only six people in the long, dimly lit chamber. Pelledar sat upon his high-backed black throne, flanked by Tephys and General Piritos. All three wore unrelieved black. Pelledar wore the ancient crown of judgment: two tall golden horns with the god of death suspended between them.

Septarin faced them. His hands had been bound behind

him, and long chains fastened around his neck, the ends held by two massive guards who gripped drawn swords in their free hands. Septarin looked very small and young but his cheeks were blotchily red and his face defiant. "Father! These men must be punished. Look at me, at what they have done to me!"

"In this place and at this hour, I am not a father to any one boy," Pelledar replied severely, and Septarin stared at him blankly. "I am father to all this city: the people within her walls, and those who fight for her. We three are chief mourners of today's dead. In this place and at this hour, I am prince, and you a prisoner." Septarin stared at him, slack-mouthed and stunned into silence. Pelledar held up a finger and beckoned Piritos forward. "General Piritos will give the charge against you."

Piritos rose to his feet and gazed expressionlessly down at the boy before taking up a narrow roll of parchment from the table before him and examining it. His voice, when he spoke, was also expressionless. "That you, Septarin of Ghezrat, are a sworn member of a fighting company and have taken the oaths of that company, to obey the orders of your commanders and your prince, setting aside all personal judgments in battle for the better judgment of the city's captains. That you did knowingly and deliberately defy orders in the midst of battle, thereby risking the lives of all your company and causing the injury of your driver—who may even now be dead—and the injury of three other men of the royal chariot who may be kept from battle at a time when every skilled fighting man is above price. That you did knowingly and deliberately risk your own capture by enemy, who could thereupon hope to use you as a bargaining chip to breach the city gates. That you did knowingly and deliberately risk the loss of horses and chariot, weaponry and your panoply, all of which could have become the property of the enemy and so used against your own people, to come against them and slay them." Piritos looked up from the length of hide; Septarin's eyes fell at once before that cold gaze. "Any one of these charges could be cause for your execution, this same night. Have you any answer, Septarin of the Royal Chariot, why you should not be put to death?"

The words froze his blood. Septarin looked up, gazing wildly from one to the other of the triad before him. "Father, have you all gone mad? I only meant—! There were—Have all of you gone mad? I am royal, a prince, that driver nothing but the son of a sandalmaker! We could have taken an entire company of enemy, if the others had followed me! It isn't my fault they wouldn't listen! If they had come at once when I called, we could have overtaken those men before they crossed the river, I told them that, but you know how my cousin is!"

"Your cousin knew to follow orders," Pelledar said.

"He is jealous of me! You know he is!" Septarin shouted. Silence. "I didn't mean for the driver to be hurt," Septarin mumbled.

"Loros," Piritos corrected him gently. "His name is—or was—Loros." He beckoned the prince and Tephys close. He spoke softly for some moments; Septarin couldn't hear anything he said. The anger left him all at once, and he had to fight to keep his knees from buckling. Piritos gestured and said something. Tephys shook her head; Pelledar said something else and she reluctantly nodded. Piritos straightened and turned back to face Septarin.

"You guards will take the youth Septarin and close-quarter him. We will take further council once you are gone as to what will be done with him."

"Father—don't—you cannot—!"

"Enough!" Piritos thundered; Septarin, who had never in all his life been shouted at in any fashion, gaped at him. "Silence the youth, however you choose, if he will not hold his tongue. Take him away." Septarin screamed and swore, and dug in his heels to fight them but he was vastly outsized by even one of the men flanking him and against two he would have had no chance at all, even if he had not been bound. They lifted him with no effort at all and bore him from the chamber.

The door closed behind them; Septarin drew in a deep breath to scream for his tutors or his mother—for anyone who would come rescue him from this waking nightmare. One of the guards clapped a large, square hand across his mouth; the second produced a length of dark cloth and bound it across the boy's eyes. They picked him up again and carried him down the hall.

They turned right, then right again, went down steps, along a close-feeling place. Still within the palace, Septarin thought frantically. More steps, two turns—they must be beneath the palace now, in one of the passageways that honeycombed the upper reaches of the city; he could smell wine. They stopped for a long moment.

The lack of sound was the most frightening thing thus far; Septarin concentrated on trying to sort out exactly which way they had come and how far, where they might be—anything to keep from being sick. They would laugh at him and spread the word throughout the city that Pelledar's son had wept and vomited, that Septarin was, after all, no braver than cowardly Apodain. *Common men, wretched commons daring to laugh at a prince!* The thought would ordinarily have fired him but not now; they had already demonstrated his strength was nonexistent so far as they were concerned. Both were armed—and if his father had given them some secret sign for execution, or if Piritos had—! They might murder him here and now, who would ever know what had happened to Pelledar's heir? Something creaked very close by and his whole body jerked; the ropes cut into his wrists painfully. His arms were untied, but one of the guards dragged them in front of him and fastened cold metal bands around them. The metal squawk came again, followed by the echoing slam of a door, and then dead silence.

Septarin stood very still where they had left him. Finally, when he was certain there was nothing to be heard but his own panting breath and a distant drip of water, he fumbled at the cloth over his eyes and tore it free.

There was a little light, perhaps a low-burning oil lamp, but it was far enough away that he could neither smell it nor see it through the hand-sized, shoulder-level opening in the door. It was just strong enough to let him see a little of his surroundings. The door itself was thick, solid wood and seemingly barred from the outside; at any rate, it would not move, but that scarcely mattered since the metal shackles on his wrists were fastened to the wall by a thick staple and he could not have gone two steps past the doorway.

He stared out the small opening for some time, but it was no good. There was no one in sight, and as often as he had explored the underground passages below the palace as a child, he had never seen this place. He might be anywhere. And no one, save those grim-faced guards, and the even grimmer three in the chamber above, knew where that anywhere was. Septarin wheeled away from the door and crouched down, buried his face in his hands, and burst into tears.

* * *

A distance above him, Pelledar slumped in his chair, eyes closed, and listened to Piritos and Tephys arguing over what must be done. "Leave him in seclusion for a night and a day," Tephys insisted, "and he will either have learned patience and a proper respect for orders or he will never learn those things. But you cannot still hope to return him to that company, general! He has proven himself as young for his years and irresponsible as we all feared. How many more men will you let die because of the boy?"

"Who is two years under the proper age for any fighter," Pelledar said wearily. "I know, and I am sorrier than either of you can know. It is my fault, for letting the boy badger me. And yet—" He spread his hands wide.

"And yet," Piritos rumbled, "not truly all your doing that the boy is what he is. What man ever trains up a son exactly the way *he* chooses? Call down fault upon the boy's blood, his mother's blood, and his tutors also."

"And my father," Pelledar said, with the merest ghost of a smile, "who after all trained me in such manner that I might raise such a spoiled son as Septarin. Or blame Ghezrat's enemies, who stayed their hand for so many long years."

Tephys made a distressed little noise, but Piritos merely nodded thoughtfully. "Just so. He is right in that, priestess: There are entirely too many boys on that plain tonight, or asleep in the barracks who see only the joy of battle and the hero's welcome from the bards' songs, too many older men who have fought in one or another of the skirmishes these past years but recall only that war made their hearts beat faster, that it bonded them to other men as fast friends the way no other thing ever could. And all these think us fools, those few men who remember times of battle and recall first blood and pain and the loss of good friends." He shook his head and changed the subject. "Forget blame, there is no point. Or blame the gods, for quickening Haffat's mother with Haffat. Blame the priest Knoe for bringing his lion to Haffat and setting him upon this quest. Since we are not gods, all such making of blame is without point. But if you simply shove Septarin into a prison cell to punish him for today, he will never learn anything. Just now he may be afraid or contrite, or both, but that will not last long. He just as likely already calls down curses upon our heads for daring to judge him and hold a prince responsible for the death of a mere common driver. Leave him where he is for long and that attitude will only harden. And since he *is* your heir. . . ." He let his voice trail away. Pelledar groaned.

"Set him loose at once and he learns nothing; he decides what he did was right and that we have let him have his way because of his blood. Keep him close-penned and he grows self-righteous and certain he was right and we are fools. Whatever I do is wrong, then!"

"Not entirely," Piritos said. He was pacing the narrow chamber, hands clasped behind his back. "I do not think he is a lost cause and Brysos tells me the boy has undeniable skill with a bow, even in a moving chariot. What he did to-day was wrong and foolish, but it shows me he possesses quick wits and the ability to act at once upon a decision. That is a rare talent which is only useful when tempered with good judgment, of course; but it may come in time. If we let it, and if we find a way to guide him. But above all, considering what our losses may be, I fear we might need him again before all is over." Tephys stared at him, and he turned on her impatiently. "Well?"

"You are mad," she said evenly. "To send him back out there? How many more men will die because of that boy?"

"I did not say we will or must, only that we may!" Piritos snapped. "If I must, I will send forth those old men who wear ancient panoply and patrol the streets; or the beardless young company mascots—even that half-blind horn signaler who stood upon the walls with me today! I will spend them if I must, to save us from Haffat—and I dare not spend a mere boy who has only his blood to mark him as better than any company mascot. And the prince knows it."

"I know it," Pelledar said, and closed his eyes. "Do you think I did not know my son might die when I let him go to the royal chariot company?"

"I did not, my prince," Piritos replied. "But if Septarin fights again, priestess—against the Diye Haff or any future enemy—we will not make the same mistake of underesti-mating him. And consider this before you simply condemn me out of hand: That boy will one day be ruler of Ghezrat. Will you have him swear the oaths and take the crown with such a dangerous fullness of himself intact?"

"And you think this will be stripped from him in battle?"

"Bah! You and Khadat—and all women!" Piritos replied

with sudden heat. "But you of all people should know better, Tephys, having seen battle forge men out of rough boys."

"I have seen it. I have also seen it break them without touching their bodies. And so, by your own words, have you, general." She let her eyes close briefly, shook herself. "Are we finished here? Meronne awaits me, we have much to do before the night is over."

"Go," Pelledar said. He waited until she was shown from the chamber and the door closed behind her, then fixed his gaze on Piritos, who was again pacing the room. "You and she are agreed upon this other matter, at least?" he asked finally.

Piritos shrugged gloomily. "That we also use the Dyaddi on the road, instead of keeping them all close to the walls? I fear we must. Denota does not keep them fighting-bonded at all times, only when there is need for it; there is no need where they are. Tephys swears the Secchi will not grow doubtful of the bond and their training if they are given so much time to stand and watch the fighting before they must join it—I do not completely believe it will not matter whether they doubt themselves, because of the bond. But she does not insist they remain against the walls—and the Primes are one and all seasoned veterans."

"To spend young women," Pelledar said. His voice trailed away.

"The chance was there from the beginning. Secchi have died for Ghezrat before this. I would prefer to spend none of the city's young, or the old." Piritos laughed grimly. "Tephys would say that proves me human; I fear it means I am growing old myself. But there is no more reason to assume the Diye Haff will assault the road than that they will attempt the walls. Grysis knows his Pairs well to choose those whose Secchi can deal with the responsibility, and those who will do best if the fighting actually reaches them."

"And—you think it will?"

"My prince," Piritos replied, "I cannot tell what may happen tomorrow, save that tomorrow comes all too soon. Do not worry overmuch for your son."

"All of my sons," Pelledar corrected him softly. "When I said that to Septarin, I meant it. I grieve for that driver who died of Septarin's foolishness, for all of them."

"Grieve, if you will—but for those who live and mourn Loros and the other dead," Piritos said. "The dead no longer care." He bent his head, turned and left the chamber. Pelledar pushed wearily to his feet and paced slowly after him.

Well to the west of the mole, a small clutch of light infantry and slingers—all that remained of a much larger company—gathered around their fire and passed a cup. Their captain finally shook himself as it reached him and held it up. "To those who await us in Denota's fields," he said. It was the first thing any of them had said since full dark, when the last of Haffat's cavalry pulled back and crossed the river.

"We need a company of fighting men mounted upon horses," someone across the fire murmured. "Such as they have."

"Oh, really?" the man next to him growled. "Who would have thought how well such a thing would work? To sit upon a galloping horse and accurately shoot arrows, or throw a lance? But why should we have thought of it? After all, we have used chariot and foot for a hundred years, what could possibly be better than what is well known?"

"All right, enough," the captain said flatly. He came partway to his feet and peered out into the darkness, chopping a hand for silence when someone else began to speak. "Wait—ho, the guard, Irlean? Is it you?"

"Myself and company," a prudently low voice came from a short distance away. "It's some of those from the mole."

"Frewis?" The captain peered uncertainly at the draggled, dripping man who led a dozen or so equally wet men into the light. "Here—make room at the fire, you men—find them some dry cloaks or blankets, they're soaked!"

Frewis chaffed his bare arms with white, puckery fingers. "Small wonder since we have only just dared come from the water, a little ago. Is it you, Alton?"

"None other," the captain replied. "Here—we haven't much food but enough to share and we've warmed wine and water."

"Good." Frewis let one of the slingers drape a blanket over his shoulders; he dropped down cross-legged before the fire and leaned forward. Water dripped from his hair to sizzle on hot stones. "I've fifteen men with me; if more made it in, I haven't seen them. Some didn't even try to jump into the water. But it was ugly out there, there's a long-current running. Even a strong swimmer like myself had trouble."

"It isn't that far from the end of the jetty to land, though," Alton said. He dipped wine and water from the pots tucked between warmed rocks and passed the cups.

Frewis spat. "We couldn't just swim in close by; those fools on the sand went running off and left us! I lost track of most of my men after I jumped, I had all I could do for a while to keep my nose above water. And farther down— past the mouth of the Alno a good four *ciph,* you know the old olive grove surrounded by willow?"

"I know it."

"There are Mirikosi ships anchored there. I knew for certain we'd lost it then; there were men lining the stern of the nearest, shooting arrows and flinging spears at us, and precious little a man could do with the water carrying him right into them." He drank deeply, wiped his mouth with the back of his hand, and passed the cup on. "Ah, bless it, I did need that!" He drank again, shook his head. "I can't say who else is left, damn all the bad luck. An arrow dropped Beryon, and poor young Evlo slipped and hit his head."

"Some of them may already have come ashore, or maybe they were carried past those ships," Alton said. "These ships, though: I wonder if word was passed to the city? You can't really see old Khneria's grove from anywhere on the walls and none of the ocean along there until you get well out into the deep." Silence. "No one knows. One of you, then: someone with good night eyes. There's a messenger over by the fork in the road, or supposed to be, in with the common chariot. We saw them settling in there, remember?"

"I'll go, sir." One of the slingers jumped up.

"Good. Three Mirikosi ships, and men here from the mole who are soaked and some hurt. Possibly others wandering about." The boy nodded and ran off into the darkness.

Frewis huddled in his blanket, alternately blowing on his hands and holding them to the fire. One of his boys lay with his head in another's lap, utterly still, eyes closed. Blood oozed from under a broad strip of cloth wrapped just above his elbow and dripped from limp fingers. Another cradled a rough-wrapped and braced arm; a boy with a thin wisp of beard lay moaning softly where his friends had put him, his broken left leg bound between two heavy branches. "Wandering," Frewis said very softly. "More likely they went into the water like Evlo, and won't ever come out. And no one will ever know what happened to them."

Khadat returned from the council meeting very late and went directly to her accounting. Before she could even take the list of supplies from her steward, Apodain walked in and quietly waited for her to look up. When she finally did, he said evenly, "I do not know whether it was your cousin's decision, or if you sent Hemit's servants men to find me this evening."

"I know you left the house, as you swore you would not. Emyas was at the gates just now, and he told me." Khadat began, but Apodain held up a hand and, surprised, she fell silent.

"I went to the barracks to see the man who was my driver. He died this night."

Khadat made a show of patiently waiting to be certain she was not interrupting him, then said, "We were told Septarin is charged with the death of his driver. But what is all that to you now?"

"It was important to me that I say good-bye to Loros. I do not expect you to understand," he added quietly. Khadat stared at him. "But I don't care whether you do. I only came to tell you this, Mother: If Hemit's men do not have enough to occupy them in tending to my brother, you should find them other tasks. You took me from my company, and I swore I would not try to counter what you did. I see no need for you to watch my every step, and I will not tolerate that such men as Emyas follow me." He gazed down at her with a stranger's face. "I also came to wish you a good night; I am going to bed."

"Good night," Khadat echoed blankly. She watched with bleak eyes as he turned indifferently away and left the room without the kiss he had always given her. *I tried to save him—and I have lost him anyway.*

Haffat

It was very dark indeed along the outer reaches of the Diye Haff camp; there was no moon, but thick cloud still covered most of the sky, muffling even the light of stars. There were no fires permitted except well inside the camp, and men hand-picked for their keen night vision patrolled the perimeters of the camp by twos.

Knoe worked his way along the river bank, going from tent to tent and searching as he had ever since sundown for the sacrifice Axtekeles must have this night. He walked briskly, well muffled against the chill wind blowing from the sea, slowing only now and again to peer at huddles of sleeping men, or to speak briefly with others who sat in the dark, talking in low, exhausted voices.

"A ram," Knoe said to any he spoke with. "Perhaps a bullock or a he-goat, but it must be horned." Haffat had forbidden his men to steal or kill abandoned beasts, as he always did, but there had been the usual "accidents"—animals men swore they had found dead or dying, pierced by Ghezrathi spears or arrows. Thus far, no one could tell him of such a living animal anywhere within the camp—or so they said.

The god must have virile blood, the meat and hide and long bones wrapped all together and set upon the fire, to please him and grant our cause better ground tomorrow. It worried him, and because he was worried, he was also very angry—who would think a mere earth goddess could command the heavens? *They only make fruit on vines and babes in women!* But he had been a fool to underestimate Denota; after all, she had kept that city safe for seven hundred years—and she had kept him and his Ergardi at bay. He realized now that he had counted more heavily than he realized upon that eclipse to spur Haffat's men, and that, too was disturbing. The sky had gone dark, of course, but not as dramatically behind clouds. And now he was hearing rumors that a phalanx waiting in the woods to join the fighting had been overflown by an owl during that brief night. *Omen, they call it. What do bloody-handed men know of such things—or of anything but how to kill other men?* And yet—

Yet. He was starting to see sidelong looks directed his way; no one had dared look at him so in all the days he had served Haffat. He could almost hear what they thought: *He has lost the god's ear, we are too far from home, the war could easily go against us.* There were even men daring to whisper behind his back, words too softly spoken to catch, the meaning all too clear: *He and Axtekeles are not of Diyet. What have they to do with us?* No one spoke aloud— yet. But single grains comprised the sand that buried a house. He would counter them, now, before Haffat's soldiers dared to scoff at him openly.

And so—"A ram, a bullock, a male herd animal of whatever years, but horned." He was growing cold and his fingers had long since gone numb, and still no one had seen or heard tell of such a beast. A horse would serve just as well, of course: It might prove a more worthy sacrifice. But Haffat, who squirmed at spilling human blood to the lion god, would flatly refuse his priest a stallion. *Well, he has a point; his horsemen have proven themselves in battle.* But that was not how Haffat would reason. *To put horses above victory, above deaths in battle—above his own empire! There is some of his son Hadda in him after all.*

He had nearly encircled the camp when he stumbled onto a small company that had thrown down its blankets under a screen of brush, two of the men trying to persuade a goat down into the little ravine behind them. "Ah." He clapped half-frozen hands together; men jumped convulsively at the sudden sound and the one holding the tether rope nearly dropped it. Knoe came across and took the end from nerveless fingers, tugged. The goat hesitated, resisted briefly, then came after him. "I see you have found another of those poor, wretched beasts slain by the Ghezrathi," he said bitingly.

"Um—it wandered into the midst of our mats just now, sir," one of the men said quickly. "We were—just taking it back the way it came, to release it." His voice faded as Knoe made a rude noise.

"It's truth, sir," another said.

"Truth! Of course it is," Knoe said. "And so you will not mind if I take it away myself? The lion god needs a sacrifice this night." Silence. "You may have back the strap that bound its jaw and kept it from calling out."

"Oh." The soldier who had held the tether shifted uncomfortably.

"Yes. Oh," Knoe replied. "You will give me the beast, and I will forget the condition in which I found it. I will also pray that Axtekeles continue to protect you during battle." He tugged hard at the rope. "Come to the priests' tent, purify yourselves at the sacrifice smoke and there will be meat once the god has taken his share." He walked away, the goat at his heels. Behind him, someone muttered, "Aye, a half-mouthful each, if that." Someone else shushed him quickly. Knoe smiled. The smile faded as he concentrated on finding his way into the center of camp without tripping over anything. *Even two nights ago, none of them would have dared grumble aloud within my hearing! And Hadda smirks whenever I come across him tonight. Stupid boy; if I fail here, we all do. Pray the sacrifice pleases the god, or I myself may not survive this battle.* Unpleasant thought.

He left the goat to be readied by his priests so he could sacrifice it at midnight, and went to inform Haffat.

The emperor sat studying a map of the plain with his captains; his brow was deeply furrowed as one of them finished reading a list of wounded. He gave his lion-priest a nod and waved him to the stool next to his own.

"You look cold, Knoe. There is bread and the wine has been warmed." He went back to the map. "We lost too many chariots this afternoon, when the Ghezrathi lured them into deep mud. Wilus, we need one of their cars; I want some as sturdy as those."

Another officer asked, "Sir, with the mole now ours, should we bring in the rest of the ships?"

"Do we need supplies of any kind? Wilus, find out if anything is low. If not, I would say wait until we control the plain also. Otherwise, check with the Mirikosi to see if it will be safe. Jemaro, how many of the third horse were taken?"

Jemaro spoke with his second, then said, "Fifteen for certain, but seven were badly wounded. They also took twelve heavy infantry and six of the light. But we hold fifty-two of their men, all told. We will exchange tomorrow?"

"If they agree," Haffat said. "And the Ghezrathi are not savages, to kill their prisoners. Besides, the men we hold are

their sons, they will exchange. Jemaro, you will go with the
yellow flag just before sunrise, to set the terms." He looked
around the table. "I think we are done for this night." The
captains rose, saluted, and left.

Haffat poured wine and drank deeply, then looked at Knoe
across the rim of his cup. "You are upset by something.
What?"

"Choose for yourself," Knoe replied sourly. "That the
eclipse was obscured, that I was of no more use to you today, and we still have not taken the city—"

He stopped; Haffat had begun to laugh. "Why not take the
blame for the way this river breaks into a hundred runnels
near the sea and that the ground is a knee-deep swill of
mud? Knoe, please! Do you really think I blame you for all
that? Things always go wrong in war!"

"I fault myself. It is seldom that I make a promise I cannot keep, for any reason. And then, to have warned you not
to underestimate these people, and to underestimate them
myself—"

"Don't be so hard on yourself, my friend," Haffat got his
mirth under control with an effort and finished his wine.
"We made gains this day. Even those officers who grumbled
at putting the Sea of Delos between us and Diyet seem satisfied we will win. We knew this would be no Mirikos; I do
not expect victory tomorrow, or even the next day. But it
will come: Axtekeles promised it, and I trust you—and I
have faith in my captains and my men. Now." He sat up, put
the cup aside and turned to business. "Did you find what
you went to seek?"

"They prepare the animal even now."

"Good. Do you need me?"

"I can do without, but we would be better served if we offered the beast the way we did in Idemito."

"Then I shall come." He hesitated. "About the Ergardi—"
Knoe shrugged. "For now, we are blocked from using
them; the goddess has wrapped the city in some barrier. It
would be easy for one of them to inhabit a prisoner tomorrow morning, but dangerous. At best, he would be turned
away at the gates, and at worst—either flung from his new
body by Denota's will, or the body killed if the priests suspected him. I have left them seeking some way to breach the
walls. Once we take the city, of course, things will be different: The people may continue to worship Denota and all her

kin, but Axtekeles will have cast them out. If Her priests are sensible, they will raise no more outcry than the red priests of Idemito did."

"And if the prince proves difficult, he will no longer be Pelledar. But someone will surely suspect?"

Knoe shook his head. "Why? Did anyone suspect the other two? He may be thought odd or a little mad, but after all, he would have cause for that. The Ergardi can still be useful in the meantime, though. That ballista—have you men who can work it?"

"Of course."

"Good. Will they work it for the Ergardi, though?"

"If I order it, they will." Haffat drained his cup and set it aside. "You look better than you did earlier."

"Better," Knoe said bitterly. "My emperor, I feel utterly useless! In all the years since I was taken from my village and my family, to serve the lion, I have never been so frustrated! I am high priest of Axtekeles, and a mere earth goddess thwarts us both! All I have done thus far has not given me the least glimpse into Her strengths or let me find her weaknesses." He sighed heavily. "Perhaps this sacrifice tonight will provide the key to Denota's mysteries."

"Mysteries?" Haffat snorted inelegantly and explosively. Knoe eyed him sidelong, startled into momentary silence. "My dear high priest, this place has seen seven hundred years of warfare! We fight, but they practice an art, my friend. You worry too much about two becoming one and this goddess. Remember that those who deal in mysteries are still flesh and blood—and that blood can be shed."

But he did not see those red-clads upon the wall, Knoe thought. He would have spoken, but high-pitched laughter brought him around; Hadda almost fell into the tent. Tears of laughter ran down his face.

"Father—priest! I am so glad to find you both here!" Hadda wiped his face, drew a deep breath and broke into laughter once more.

"Yes?" Haffat inquired mildly.

"I was drinking just now—"

"Oh, really?" Knoe muttered. Haffat cast him a sharp glance and he subsided.

"Drinking with some of the Mirikosi mercenaries; they play a most delightful game of chance and their wine is better than ours. And I forget what I said, but they were telling me how the defenses are set up here—you know, circles within circles, protecting the circle of wall?"

"Yes, yes," Knoe said sharply. "We know all that, your father learned that a long time ago. Well?"

"Control yourself, priest." Hadda giggled, got momentary control over his mirth, but burst into spluttering laughter once more. Haffat laid a restraining hand on his lion-priest's arm, frowned and shook his head. Knoe bit back a sigh. Hadda spoke shakily, through laughter. "Along the walls—all those guards in red? You will *never* believe what the Mirikosi told me!"

"Try us," Haffat said mildly.

This nearly set Hadda off once again. "It's—it's old men and—and girls, together. *Girls!* Father, can you believe it? They've sent their girls out to fight us!"

11

At first horn the next morning, Grysis gathered the Dyaddi together in the long, low room set aside for the captains and waited until they had settled on the benches, the few chairs, or on the floor. "I asked you here for the privacy," he said. "The General has ordered Pairs to the foot of the road with Kroserot's phalanx, and the High Priestess has something to say to you all. I will bring her here shortly; meantime, listen to Menlaeus." He went out, and Menlaeus got to his feet and faced them.

He looks—almost shy, Breyd thought. There was too much color in his face, and he was combing his beard with his fingers, the way he did when he was uncomfortable with what he had to say or do next. *He does not like this, acting like an officer, giving orders or explaining them. Leading.* He finally clasped his hands behind his back and waited for silence; the discomfort didn't show in his voice or the level gaze that moved from Pair to Pair. "They asked for five Pairs for the first watch of the day, though later they may also want Pairs for later watches. Grysis asked my help in the choice; the Primes are Laprio, Akeros, Prosean and Bechates. And myself, of course.

"My understanding is that they want to make us more visible to the Diye Haff, and they want the additional guard at the foot of the road. We wanted men who have fighting experience with a heavy infantry company: you know how things are during battle, and you know the maneuvers and the signals, so your Secchi will be able to move with you. I am told they do not expect the fighting to come so near the city today or tomorrow, but of course they can't be certain.

"I tell you this mostly so no one feels singled out, or slighted." He looked up. "I think I hear Grysis. One last thing. Kroserot is talking to his men this morning. Now, a few men might feel we're down there because their captains think they aren't good enough; there may be bad feeling, and there is still some discomfort about us. Let no one provoke you. If there is a problem, tell Grysis, so he can deal with it." He sat down next to Breyd again.

Breyd looked up as Tephys walked past her. The priestess looked very tired; there were dark smudges under her eyes and fine lines at the corners of her mouth. But her voice was clear as ever. "Four of you were on the wall when the lion-priest came with his emperor's letter, and in enhanced bond." She looked around the room. "Because of that, the rest of you may have felt a little something of what they sensed out there; I know they will have told you about the driver of Knoe's chariot. That driver was an Ergardi magician. Most of you have probably heard about them. They are very powerful, and they have many—talents.

"Most people cannot sense their presence; without the Dyadd bond, I doubt any of you would. I doubt any of the phalanx at the base of the cliff could tell an Ergardi." She paused. "Particularly not if he has taken up another man's body. One of our men." Breyd felt the blood drain from her face; Menlaeus caught hold of her near hand and squeezed it. She glanced at him, nodded very faintly, then looked past him to Lochria, who was as white as she felt. "They cannot simply exchange bodies during the fighting—like *that!*" She clapped her hands sharply and several people jumped; Eriana let out a breathless little scream. "And the city is protected, they cannot enter. But they may try something when we exchange prisoners—putting one of theirs in a wounded Ghezrathi, perhaps. And that is why I want Dyaddi down there where any exchange will take place. A priestess could tell, but they do not fight. You can tell, and you are as protected by your fighting skills as any out there; more than anyone else by Denota's bond. If you feel anything wrong, at any time, you have the general's orders to stop the exchange and find the Ergardi. And you will kill him."

She waited; only worried whispers and sidelong looks answered her. "All right," Menlaeus said finally, and the room was quiet again. "How do we kill such a magician?"

Tephys laughed sourly. "How do you kill anyone? The magician may be powerful, but the body is human." She turned and strode from the room, but at the doorway she turned back. "And you will keep the body where it is and send word to me at once."

Grysis let them talk only a moment, then clapped his hands once for silence. "Kroserot goes out at third horn; any of you who go with him, if you need anything—water, bread, anything at all—go and get it now. Meet outside as soon as you are ready."

Menlaeus helped Breyd up. "I'll go with them, in case anyone wants to talk. You're ready?"

"Ready," she agreed. She had sat next to him and listened as he and Grysis chose the other four Pairs; she had even contributed what she knew about the Secchi. *Aroepe is stronger than Eriana; she'll do better out there.* She understood much better how Menlaeus felt, though—sitting apart from the others and judging them, as if she were any better or had any more right. *Putting four other Pairs down there, in danger. They can say it's all safe if they like; we'll be much farther from the gates than we have been, and it will feel very strange.*

Bechates was already talking rapidly as he and Menlaeus walked toward the barracks. Breyd filled her two small water gourds at the cistern and patted the sack at her belt. A few dates in the bottom, half her bread from this morning—that was more than enough. She checked the straps on her greaves, the shield; there was nothing else for her to do but wait. *Maybe I can find Tarpaen before we go.* She took off the helmet and stuffed the red cloth inside it, then walked out into the open.

Over by the ladder to the inner wall, some of the horn and drum company were gathered close together; Tar was there, his back to her, but Laius was standing right next to him.

She turned away from him. Laius no longer mattered, not since that night here. But she avoided him whenever possible. If her brother looked up, she'd wave.

Her stomach was tight and her palms sweaty. *They're sending us down to fight. Father said all along they might. I had begun to wonder if we were only something for show against the walls, and up there when that priest came.* That priest. And his driver. *How do they think we'll kill an Ergardi?*

Lochria was the first back out; she came over and sat down next to Breyd. "I left Father biting his lip and frowning over a handful of stone shot."

"Father will take care of him."

"I know. Menlaeus is wonderful with him. He's all right once we're in place anyway. I—hope I will be."

"There's a phalanx going with us, remember, not just five Pairs across the road," Breyd reminded her.

"I know. It's just—never mind. I heard the Diye Haff sent a messenger a while ago; they want an exchange of prisoners." Lochria drew a shaky breath. "That driver—you saw him."

"I told you about it."

"I know; so did Eriana. Ergardi!" She swallowed, tried to smile. "I am glad Tephys says the old scare stories aren't so: You know, they can fly like birds and swim across the sea with the fish."

At least, Tephys says as much, Breyd thought. But Lochria didn't know the priestess, and there wasn't any point in both of them worrying about that. "Is Depradis coming to see you this evening?"

"If we get leave to go home, he'll walk me." Lochria smiled and this time it warmed her eyes. "He's very nice, not like most boys of his class I've met. Not nearly as beautiful as your Apodain, of course."

"Not my Apodain," Breyd said flatly. "I am not marrying him, you know that."

"I know you've said so. I still can't think how you'll get out of it."

"I will find a way."

Lochria looked past her. "Here comes your brother."

"Oh. Is Laius with him?"

"No, the boy is. I'll leave you; Father must be looking for me anyway." Lochria gripped her hands. "You're all right?"

"As all right as you are. Worried, because it's a new thing, that's all." She got to her feet as Tarpaen came up; Xhem trailed a little behind him.

"Breyd." There was a line between his brows and he was biting the corner of his lip. "Someone just said your company is going down to the plain, to fight!"

"No—a few, just to help block the road. How is everyone at home?"

The frown deepened. "No better or worse. Poor Niv is frantic with worry, there still isn't any word about Creos and Mother clung to me and wept when I had to go this morning.

Thank Atos for Nidya, she stays so calm; she got Mother to let go and even got her calmed down a little before I left."

"If she hears the rumors you heard—"

"She won't; only Ina gets out to hear the rumors, and she never passes them on. You know Niv, she never hears the gossip, but she's not leaving the house in case word comes."

"Good. Are you on watch this morning?"

He nodded. "First, two hours on and two off."

"They just said the Diye Haff are bringing men they took yesterday."

"I know, I heard. Maybe Creos is with them." Menlaeus came up; Tarpaen clasped his forearms. "Father. Is everything really all right?"

"Everything is fine," Menlaeus assured him.

"I told him," Breyd said.

"Well, she's right. They want the Pairs to get used to low ground and to let the Diye Haff know we aren't just for show, if they try the road. It's just a precaution, really."

"Oh? Well. If you say." He still looked doubtful; Menlaeus smiled and gripped his elbows.

"Yes. We will come back covered in dust, hot, thirsty and horribly bored. How is your mother?"

"Fine, sir," Tarpaen lied, and managed a smile to go with the lie. "So far as I know, she slept the night."

"Good." If he knew why she slept, that she was dosing her wine every night now, Menlaeus kept his worries to himself. "Where are you today, son?"

Tar's face lit up. "I came to tell you. Nabid sent me to the general, yesterday late—and he asked for me again, by name!"

"Now, there is good news!" Menlaeus smiled broadly and clapped his son on the back. Breyd gave her brother a hard hug.

"Good for you!" she said. Tarpaen winced as bronze plate dug into him, but he hugged back. He looked up as Laius shouted out his name.

"I must go. Take care."

"Of course we will," Breyd said. "And you."

"Yes. Yes, coming!" he shouted as Laius yelled his name once more. "Xhem can take any messages for the household."

"I have a little time at second horn," Xhem said softly.

"Good," Menlaeus said. He dropped to one knee so he

could look up at his nephew. "Tell your aunt Nevvia that we are both fine, that I miss her and Breyd sends her love. We'll come when we can, but not to worry if we don't come today."

"I'll tell her, Uncle." Xhem sped off. Menlaeus watched him go, then touched Breyd's arm and pointed.

"Kroserot is over there; we'd better go."

She nodded and followed him, settling the helmet and fitting the red cloth over it. Long red ties fluttered in a brisk, presunrise breeze; she wrapped them loosely around her throat and tucked the ends into her cloak. Lochria and Bechates came across to join them; the other three Dyaddi stood near the phalanx. Breyd gave Lochria a sidelong look and Lochria rolled her eyes. Twenty or more heavily armored and armed soldiers stood in loose ranks, waiting with their officer. "They don't look pleased to see us," Lochria muttered.

"No," Breyd agreed. Most of them were scowling openly and the rest looked decidedly wary. The short, thickly bearded Kroserot hissed something under his breath as the Dyaddi came up; his face gave nothing away as he returned Menlaeus' salute and he merely said, "Take positions along the right side of the phalanx, a Pair to each file." Third horn rang out as Menlaeus put himself at the outside and Breyd between him and a frozen-faced infantryman; the rest of the Pairs took places behind him and the company marched from the barracks.

Tarpaen settled next to the general's stone and waited anxiously. A messenger came in; the common chariot rode out. Messengers rode out behind them, followed by several royal chariot, and finally four ranks of heavily armed men in black armor and dark cloaks, the two ranks of red-clad Dyaddi on their right. No one could miss them. His heart sank. *Like targets.* Laius was mumbling; Tar turned away from the wall, but his friend was fiddling with his drumstrap.

Tarpaen turned back to watch the phalanx go. He hadn't even been able to tell from this odd overhead angle which of them were his. But he couldn't worry about them any more, because he could hear the general's voice giving some last-minute instructions to one of his aides.

Laius was muttering again. Tar wondered if he should go

talk to him. But Laius had already snapped at him down in the barracks this morning.

A jingle of harness caught his attention: two wagons full of fettered and wounded enemy waited just inside the gates. *It's a simple exchange; it's always done this way.* He looked out across the plain. Not much movement out there, except on the road, but he could just make out ships. Probably already inside the mole, with the Diye Haff working hard to unload them. *Plenty of other ships to unload, after all,* he thought grimly. Twenty or more out there this morning, Laius had said.

The phalanx was nearly in position already; the Dyaddi stood out like blood against their dark-clad companions and the near-white rock.

Gods, but you are morbid this morning! Laius hadn't helped, though; he was decidedly strange this morning. He reminded himself Nabid kept a close eye on Laius; if there was anything wrong, Nabid would know it. *But if he is too busy?*

He shook his head and knelt to rub fingerprints and dust from his horn. Laius was kept on the walls—trapped, he would say. There were officers everywhere up here, and he stood very near the general's aide. Behind him, Laius growled a low curse and tapped furiously at the drumhead. He looked up and met his friend's eyes, and rather unnervingly grinned. He glanced around, then came across to the outer wall and squatted down. "I had such a dream last night, I think I must tell you of it. Or perhaps it was a vision, granted by Atelos, for I was again in that moment when the sky went night-black, and then I was somehow *before* the wall, down there, with a sword in my hand and enemy everywhere. And I slew so many of them." He spread his hands wide and grinned. "Laius the hero, eh?"

"Laius the Lion Slayer," Tarpaen said, but the man's words chilled him. Laius merely laughed, got to his feet, and went back to his station as Piritos came over and mounted the stone block.

The phalanx reached the foot of the road and at a shout from their captain formed into a tight box six across, five deep, that went all the way across the road. "All right! Spears out, hold ready!" He walked down the road a ways and gazed out toward the enemy camp.

Breyd eased red cloth away from her mouth and took a sip

of water. Her mouth was still dry. *That's fear.* There were
men on three sides of her, but the city wall at her back had
been more of a prop than she'd realized. There were huge
boulders down here, piles of slag shoved aside when the
road was refinished—ruts and folds in the ground deep
enough to hide men. They could be anywhere, the Ergardi
with them. She took another small sip of water, restored the
gourd to her belt, and glared up at the soldier to her left; he
had eyed her warily all the way down. *A wonder he didn't
trip.* "It's all right," she snapped. "I won't attack you, we
aren't that unstable."

"I never thought so," he replied stiffly.

"Be quiet up there!" Kroserot yelled at them; Breyd set
her lips in a tight line and turned back to face forward.
"They're coming," he added, and came back himself to
stand in front of the phalanx. "I can just see the yellow banner heading this way. Remember, watch for tricks! You
Dyaddi have your own orders."

"Oh, goddess," Breyd whispered. Her vision blurred; she
blinked rapidly and clenched her hands on her belt to keep
them from trembling. *What Xera saw yesterday—I don't
know if I can take that. But if an Ergardi comes with them—*
How were they supposed to kill a magician? *Can he take
over me, or Father if we get near enough to kill him?*

Menlaeus touched her hand and when she glanced his
way, shook his head minutely and he silently shaped the
words, "Don't worry." She grimaced, looked forward again
as Kroserot walked along the front rank. *Don't worry. How
does he help worrying?*

Horn call sounded high above and behind them. *That is
Tar, standing at the general's side and translating his orders.*
She was suddenly, fiercely proud of him.

Kroserot walked back across the rank. "That was the signal. Our wagons are on the way down, theirs nearly here."
Breyd balanced her spear in the crook of her elbow and
tugged the red cloth across her nose and chin, then stood the
long shaft straight. It towered above her; the leather handgrip was dark with sweat and unpleasantly wet.

I can't see anything, she thought in sudden panic; dust
blew across the road, obscuring it now and again. She could
hear shouting in the distance, someone screaming, and a
steady drumbeat close by. *Ours? Theirs?* She couldn't tell.

Kroserot can tell; Father knows. He was tense but not really worried; it had to be all right.

Two wagons came down from the city; the company stepped off the road to let them by and moved back into position behind them. Moments later three enemy wagons rolled up from the northeast. Kroserot signed to his company to hold position, then went over to talk to the driver of the lead wagon. Breyd looked at the men sitting behind him. Most of them sat very stiffly and stared into the distance. *They are ashamed, because they were captured.* But there seemed to be no one badly injured—a boy with a wide, bloodstained bandage around his forehead, a thin, gray-haired man she had seen before clutching a heavily wrapped hand to his breast. It was very quiet out there. In the nearest wagon, someone moaned and fell silent when another cursed him.

Kroserot came back to his company; their own men got down from the near wagons to help the Diye Haff out and the Diye Haff drivers stood back to watch as their prisoners walked or limped over to the city's wagons; they were openly curious about the red-clads, and Breyd was glad she had the tiara to cover everything but her eyes.

Father told me our badly wounded were left on the field for us to rescue; they don't want to care for our men. She drew a relieved breath. No dreadful wounds, no dead men—no scent or feel of Ergardi on any of the men who had filed past them just now.

Two more Ghezrathi came slowly up the road, carrying a third between them. Menlaeus caught his breath and gripped Breyd's wrist, hard. *Warning. Oh, goddess, what?* An unpleasant mix of odors hit her as they came near: pitch and something else. And then she could see the lolling head, the unconscious man's face.

At first she didn't recognize him. This could not possibly be Creos! His mouth sagged open, his hair was plastered to his skull, and one arm swung loose. Someone had removed his armor, and his tunic was stiff with blood. Menlaeus kept his grip on her, fortunately, or she might have fallen. *Creos—oh, no! If Niverren sees him like this!* Men came down from the city's wagons to take him, and as they turned him around to set him headfirst in the wagon, she found herself staring at his bandage-wrapped legs. Something wrong with them. Her heart lurched. The left was much shorter than the right; it had been cut off at the knee.

The enemy wagons turned and went back toward the Oryon. Breyd moved blindly aside with Menlaeus to let their wagons pass across the road. Tears smeared her vision and ran down her cheeks, soaking the red wool ties. *You can't be sick, not here! You won't shame your Prime, or the Dyaddi!* She swallowed repeatedly, finally dared to draw a deep breath. Menlaeus squeezed her wrist again and let her go. She glanced up at him; sweat sheened his cheeks and he was blinking rapidly. At her other side, she heard a ragged, harshly drawn breath. *It isn't only me. But when they tell Niverren—*

Sharp, urgent horn call brought the company alert; Kroserot spun around and raised both fists. "Enemy chariot coming along the base of the cliff from the river," he snapped. "Ready the phalanx!" Twenty weighted spear ends slammed into the road in answer; Menlaeus held up his spear and brought the end down hard; the other Dyaddi followed. Breyd set her teeth together to keep them from chattering. She could hear the horses and the creak and jingle of harness beyond a screen of distant boulders, and then the chariot swept into sight and were drawn to a halt; forty or more men leapt down and ran up the road. More chariots came up, and more again. She gripped the spear and stared, stunned. There must have been a hundred at least, and still more came. *They think they have us—they think they caught us by surprise, and now they will kill us all and take the road, and the city, they will kill my father.* The goddess' fury filled her. *You will not touch him!* The man at her side gasped and drew sharply away from her. Ten abandoned spears clattered to the road as one. Menlaeus/Breyd drew sword and ran toward the enemy.

Everything began to blur: she could see men ahead of her, behind her—towering over her, no taller than she—*that is Father at my back.* That thought faded; the doubled, near circle of vision simply was; everything and everyone was hazed in red. The oncoming rush of enemy seemed to slow until it was child's play to slap a sword or javelin aside and spit the man behind it. *Kill them; kill all of them. They dare to covet what is mine, they deserve to die for that.*

Men had circled around them to attack the phalanx— Menlaeus' vision—others tried to slip around and catch her from the side or behind, but she/he saw each of them. Men everywhere, cursing furiously, shrieking in pain—blood running down her blade, but she didn't hear them very well. Menlaeus' vision or her own prevailed as needed; she blocked with her shield, spun and lunged, swung back the other way. Her sword was a blur and she could have laughed at all those dream-slow, stupidly gaping faces. *Fools, stupid, frightened fools; I will kill you for your fear, for daring—* Menlaeus drove his blade into another body and another, and she slashed out one way, back the other. The Diye Haff were frantically falling back, but there were too many others behind, blocking them.

Someone well to the rear finally bellowed out an order. She stared blankly at the men running toward the chariots, drivers whipping their horses back toward the river.

The bond dropped away like a stone; Breyd staggered back into Menlaeus, two swords fell from numbed fingers. He turned and clung to her, and she could feel how terrifyingly weak he was, how hard his heart was thudding. Somehow, they held each other up, but she saw Lochria fall to her knees, her chest heaving. Bechates stared down at her blindly. Between Bechates and Menlaeus, the ground was littered with Diye Haff dead. Breyd drew a sharp, pained little breath and forced herself to turn and look. Men everywhere. Dead, bloody men in a circle all around them. "We did that?" she whispered. "All—all that?"

Kroserot came up and looked at them in astonishment. "You killed all those men. All those—I killed a man and wounded one and in that time, you killed—" He shook himself. "Are you all right? Hurt?"

"I—" Menlaeus wet his lips and tried again. "I don't think we can move. Any of us."

"We'll get a wagon sent down. Stay there, we'll guard you. You'll be safe, the Diye Haff won't be back in a hurry." He stared down at the dead. "Not after that." Breyd was staring at her outstretched sword hand. It was red, wet. *It is not my blood.* Kroserot's eyes went wide and he backed away from her.

Menlaeus' knees buckled and he sat, bringing her down with him. "Daughter—child. Are you all right?"

"Not hurt," she whispered. "You?" He nodded and with a little sigh let his head down on his knees. *All right?* Breyd bit her lip and pushed away from him, tottered back to her feet. *All right? I did that. She filled us both, but my hand, my sword—I did that.*

A dead man lay almost at her feet; she stared down at him. *Man? He's a boy, he's younger than Tar!* Light brown, springy curls fell over an unlined forehead, one hand pillowed his cheek and distorted his lips. His eyes were open, staring as if in surprise across her feet. *Almost as if he had been resting, and had just wakened.* Just beyond him a man sprawled on his back, his white beard clotted with blood; a puddle of it filled his cupped hand. *His throat is cut ear to ear. Someone's father. I did that.* She spun around and everything swirled around her dizzily; there was no escape from them. Bodies everywhere: behind Menlaeus, beside her. Someone's sword in the dirt, all by itself—her stomach heaved; a hand still clutched it. She clapped both hands across her mouth and shut her eyes tightly, but it was there, inside her eyelids: sword, hand. Somehow she got herself off the side of the road before she was sick. Menlaeus dragged himself over to her; his hands were trembling with exhaustion and she thought he might be ill himself. She turned and huddled against him.

When she dared open her eyes again, some of the phalanx had moved down the road to guard them, while others cleared the road. She could see men carefully avoiding them; men eying her nervously while others stared in horror at the dead men or those who had killed them. An awed whisper somewhere behind her: "There are forty-seven dead where they stood—two killed forty-seven."

A high, trembling voice came from where the phalanx had stood. "Trepion—I couldn't stop the blood, he's dead!"

One of those close to her paused, a dead man's legs in his hands and said flatly, "We'll avenge him, lad."

"Avenge? What does that matter, he's dead! Avenge him and he'll still be dead!"

At least four men began to shout all at once. "Silence!" Kroserot shouted. "And you, Nellos, control yourself! He's not the only one of our company to die, just the first!"

"He has plenty of company for his journey," someone just behind her said; the man near her dragged his burden away by the legs, dropped them alongside the road and turned back. His eyes met hers. He started and began looking around for more bodies.

You are afraid we will kill you next, Breyd thought wearily. It should have infuriated her, but there wasn't enough strength in her for that. She let her eyes close, shutting them all out.

Kroserot came over and knelt beside them. "The wagon is here. Don't do anything, don't try to walk, we'll carry you to it."

Menlaeus nodded and whispered weakly, "I think—you will have to."

She lost most of the trip back up to the gates, rousing a little only as they came through the gates. Word must have preceded them; people fell back from the wagon as though afraid it would contaminate them and some looked at the Dyaddi in open fear. Menlaeus pulled her against him and wrapped his arms around her. "It's all right, don't pay attention. Don't let them upset you. They don't know what it was really like, child."

Yes, she thought bleakly. *But I know.*

She woke some time later in the barracks. The air was hot and still; her hair clung damply to her throat and her head pounded. She rolled over and cautiously sat up.

"Breyd?" Lochria's voice was very weak, hardly recognizable. Breyd pushed hair out of her eyes and rubbed them with her palms. The room had finally stopped swimming when she looked up once more. Lochria sat on the cot across from her, elbows on her knees, hands dangling limply between them. "You look—"

"I know," Breyd managed. "I feel worse. We didn't just dream that, did we?" Lochria closed her eyes, swallowed hard.

"Your father—Menlaeus said to tell you he's gone to find out about—about Creos." Her voice broke; she drew a shuddering breath, shook her head angrily. "About Creos. Whatever he could learn."

She couldn't think of anything to say. *Creos.* A shadow fell across her; Tarpaen dropped down next to her. "I saw them bring you, I thought you were all dead! But they said—said—I came as soon as I was free. I had to go home first. They sent me so I could tell the family, warn them about Creos. I brought Niverren." Breyd wrapped her arms around him and clung fiercely. Tarpaen reached out to Lochria and pulled her over so he could hold both of them.

"All those men—the phalanx. They're afraid of us," Lochria whispered. "And they have a right to be afraid."

"They aren't," Tarpaen protested.

Breyd sat back and looked at him. He was pale and he looked as if he'd been sick. But he didn't look afraid of her. "Didn't they tell you? How many men ten of us killed?"

"They told us. They've told everyone; the whole city knows by now. Ridlo said he thought they were all dead when you dropped those spears, and ran straight at the enemy—ten of you against so many, he was waiting for you to be cut down. And then he said no one could possibly move that fast."

"I know." Breyd leaned against him once more.

"The general was very pleased. He said they won't try that soon—not against Dyaddi."

"Pleased," Lochria echoed blankly. She shuddered, pulled away and covered her face with her hands.

She sees dead men, Breyd realized, *bodies everywhere— dead who were fresh-faced boys this morning, someone's father before he came here to fight. And our own men looking at us as though we were indifferent to what we've done.* She looked up as Menlaeus came into the barracks. Tarpaen stood up and helped her to her feet and she clung to her father.

Tar kept a hand on her shoulder and laid the other on his father's. "Did they tell you anything?"

Menlaeus sighed. Breyd looked up at him and went cold all over. *He looks old, all at once. So helpless. Weak.* But then he shook himself and when he spoke, he sounded simply tired, the way he did after a long afternoon of weapons-practice.

"All right," he said and Breyd found herself absurdly comforted by that calm voice. "It's not pleasant, but not as dreadful as I would have thought, seeing him down there earlier. One of the Mirikosi ships fished him out of the water late yesterday; his foot and ankle were crushed, they aren't certain how or when. He passed out when they pulled him aboard and he hasn't been awake since. No one in Frewis' company was anywhere near him, so probably we'll never know. The Diye Haff told the men who sat by him in the wagon this morning to say they had no choice but to remove his leg to the knee. The physicians over there said it is ugly, but all such wounds are; they said the Diye Haff made a good job of it, that he had been given numbing powders and a strong soporific. He will sleep for at least a full day, and he stands a good chance of surviving this."

"Like that!" Tarpaen sounded very near tears. Breyd forced herself from Menlaeus' comforting grasp and hugged her brother; she could feel his heart thudding wildly.

"Surviving—like that," his father replied firmly. "Now, listen to me, carefully, all of you: This is a dreadful thing; Creos may still die of blood loss or fever or the shock. But he is young and strong, and a sensible young man who deeply loves his young wife. That will all figure into whether he lives or dies. If he lives, he will have a wife who loves him, a family that will not care that he must walk with sticks so long as he is still alive—and a pension from the prince. And he will be removed from the fighting, for all time." Tarpaen stared at him; with an effort he pulled his mouth shut. Menlaeus nodded. "Yes, I realize it sounds terrible to you, put so bluntly. All the same, it could have been much worse. He could have died, or come back like Hemit did. He could have vanished and Niverren never known whether the Diye Haff had kept him or if he had died out there, and how he died. They will both be relieved he cannot fight ever again, and grateful for that stipend."

"Yes," Breyd said. *To never fight again. How can I force myself to go through those gates another day, knowing what I did out there?*

Menlaeus touched her arm. "Your mother expects us."

"I know."

"They gave us leave until eighth horn, full dark. Do you want to come with me now—or can you stay here for your sister?"

If Mother sees me like this— "I—I will stay. Niv may need me."

"What of his family?" Lochria asked suddenly.

Menlaeus shook his head. "I don't know if they were sent for; his father was here all morning and was here when they brought the boy in. It's all I know."

"I'll go to them. Father, I know you're awake." She edged back onto her cot and leaned across it to catch hold of his fingers.

"I'm awake," he said faintly.

"Come. They'll all be frantic at home." Bechates groaned and sat up slowly, then got to his feet. He and Lochria made

their way between the mats and cots and out the door.
Menlaeus kissed Breyd's brow and followed them.

She gazed after him blankly. Tarpaen wrapped an arm
around her shoulders.

"Here, let me, you look ready to faint."

"I—I won't."

"All the same. A brother can hold onto his sister, after all.
I have duty again within the hour, so I have to go and eat.
You—no, I guess you do not want any food, do you?" She
shook her head.

"Not yet." Her throat was still tight and her breath came
in chest-hurting little gasps.

The other three Pairs were still asleep, and around them
the Dyaddi who had kept the late night watch at the gates
also slept. The length of the room away, men in widely scattered clutches of five or so slept, or lay with their heads
close together so they could talk without disturbing the others. She let Tarpaen walk with her over to the hospital barracks, waited while he spoke to one of the men on duty. She
lost track of time. Tar gave her a gentle shake.

"He says Creos is near the back, straight in, one of those
inside will take you if you want to go."

"I don't want to," Breyd replied truthfully. "But I will.
Niv needs someone."

"Yes. I—Breyd, thank you." His voice sounded strangled.
Breyd looked up at him, shook her head. "For doing this. I
don't think I could."

"Oh." On an impulse, she laid a hand on his face. "I think
if you had to, you could. I think we have all misjudged you,
Tarpaen." He flushed and mumbled something. "Don't mis-
judge yourself." Before he could think of anything else to
say, she squared her shoulders and went inside.

12

The guard Tar had spoken to eyed her warily as she passed him. The white-haired, withered old man who came to lead her to Creos stopped in his tracks when he saw the distinctive Dyaddi armor and the red cape, and for a moment she thought he would turn and bolt. "It's all right," she said wearily. "I won't touch you. I know the difference between my own and the enemy." Had he even heard her? But finally he turned and gestured for her to follow him.

The hospital barracks were like other buildings around the courtyard—low and long, not well lit; this had fewer windows than the messes. The ancient was a shadow moving across the dimly lit antechamber; he opened the thick inner door and went through it. She followed.

The smell and noise hit her like a blow: Someone was screaming mindlessly at the far end of the room, someone almost at her feet moaned continuously. Hands reached for her, catching in her cloak or her legs. A frantic, shrill boy's voice: "Mother? It's you, isn't it, Mother? I can't see!" She freed her cloak, but hands caught hers and held them desperately, almost pulling her down. She gasped with pain and shock: Blood-matted hair hung over thick reddened bandages covering most of his face. Most of his teeth were broken; blood ran from the corner of his mouth. The old man came back and pulled the hands from hers. "Pull the cloak in to you," he hissed. She nodded, wrapped it around her arm, and hugged it to her. Another hand reached for her—a skinny, beardless boy with his sling still attached to his wrist. The sling hand gripped his thigh around the cut-off shaft of an arrow. "Water? Someone, please—water! Tell them to bring me water!"

I can't bear this. She felt for her water gourds; they were back in the barracks. The old man turned to glare at her. She shook her head helplessly, whispered, "I'm sorry," and moved by him. Behind her, she could hear the boy sobbing.

The horrible mindless shriek stopped abruptly; someone else began to wail and his voice soared: "No, don't, don't touch it—don't!" He, too, was suddenly still. Someone very close by was crying steadily and hopelessly; she couldn't see who. The reek of blood was so thick she could almost taste it, and so many had been sick her own stomach was threatened. The soles of her sandals stuck to the floor where it had not been freshly sanded. Torch smoke and the harsh odor of soporific steam caught in her throat.

Creos had been laid near the back wall a little apart from the others. The smell of pitch overwhelmed everything else here. Niverren crouched next to him, a wad of wet cloth gripped in one hand, a wooden water bucket at her elbow. Her hair had been pulled roughly back and thrust under a black scarf whose ends dragged in the dirt; the cloak about her shoulders was the green one Breyd had worn over her priestess robes.

"Niv?" She went down on her knees next to her sister, touched her arm. Niverren's face was waxy and yellowish; the corners of her mouth sagged and her gaze scarcely focused. She had not wept, so far as Breyd could tell. "Niv?"

"He's too warm," Niverren whispered frantically. She turned away to dip the cloth in the bucket, wring it out, and pat it lightly against his forehead and cheeks. "Much too warm, Breyd; he'll die."

"Wait." Breyd laid one hand against her own brow, her other against his forehead, and then at his throat. Beard prickled her fingers. Niverren gasped and started as Breyd touched her face. "He's only a little too warm, Niv. You're cold. Here, give me your hand. Oh, Niv, it's like ice."

"That must be the water," Niverren said dully. "They told Tar to fetch the bucket and some cloths when he brought me here, they haven't enough to spare for everyone." She stared blankly for one moment, drew in a shuddering breath and went back to sponging Creos' face and arms with the wrung-out cloth. Across the room, Breyd could hear the blinded boy screaming for his mother. Niverren was oblivious to everything but Creos. "Tonight, after dark, they'll send him home with me."

Breyd stared down at his gray, gaunt face, then looked at

Niverren in horror. "Tonight! Oh, no! Niv, they can't do that! If he needs——!"

"They cannot do anything else for him here." Niverren concentrated on dipping the cloth, wringing it, refolding it carefully so the surface she touched against his throat was smooth and clean. "There is nothing anyone can do, except watch and care for him, and be there when he finally wakens. That is for me to do, Breyd. He can't wake up in here, I couldn't bear it."

But Mother—when she sees this— Breyd closed her eyes, swallowed past a tight throat. "You're right, of course. That was horrible enough for me, just now."

Niverren sighed again. "And there are so many injured. Some they can help, but not Creos." She sat back, cloth dripping into her lap. Breyd took it from nerveless fingers, wrapped an arm around Niverren's thin shoulders. Niv leaned against her gratefully and fetched another shuddering breath.

She couldn't think of anything to say, except, "What can I do to help you?"

Niverren withdrew from her embrace and sat back up, eyes fixed on the unconscious man before her. "Nothing. Be here, a little, if you can."

"I can do that."

They sat together quietly for a long time. Niverren finally roused herself. "Nidya said she would come later, if they would let her. But Mother—she was on the roof near the street, getting something of Tar's for the wash and she heard them shouting down in the street—something about the Pairs fighting—I forget."

"Oh, no." Breyd let her head fall into her hands. "She knows we're all right?"

"Tar told her; he said he'd seen you coming back, you were fine." *Oh, Tar,* Breyd thought and the thought warmed her. *I owe you a great deal for that lie.* "But for Mother," Niverren said, "just knowing you had been out there—it was awful. I don't know how she got down from the roof without breaking everything. She wouldn't let Niddy give her anything but plain wine, because Father said you'd both come, and she was terrified she'd miss you."

"He went home when I came here."

"Oh." Niverren frowned uncertainly at the cloth, finally dipped it into water, wrung it out and laid it lightly against

Creos' brow; he moaned and she snatched her hand back, leaned forward to watch him anxiously, but he was quiet again. She retrieved the cloth and blotted his face with it. "Ina is preparing our old room; I can care for him better there." She sat back on her heels. "It leaves you no place; I just realized. Oh, Breyd, I'm sorry!"

Breyd shook her head. "Don't be. I have a place here, for now anyway. Don't worry about things that aren't important, Niv."

"Oh. Yes." She was quiet for some time; Breyd sat cross-legged next to her, her knee just touching her sister's hip. Creos stirred a little now and again, but mostly lay so still the only sign of life was the slow rise and fall of his breast.

Breyd looked down at him and tears dimmed her sight. She hadn't really ever thought about Creos. He was special to Niv, but not to her mind particularly handsome or special—just rather nice-looking, friendly—always pleasant to his wife's younger sister. Pleasant to everyone. *How could this happen?* Her own leg ached horribly everytime she looked at his. *How will he manage? They'll stare at him and pity him. I would hate that, and Niv will hate it for him, it will make her bitter and he'll hate that.* But something cold was forming deep in her belly. *How dare they do this? Creos and Niverren—they were so happy and now look at them.* She shut her eyes. *I hope Haffat dies in worse pain than this; I hope everyone he loves dies before he does and he knows that it was all his fault; I hope he weeps, and cries for his mother and for water and only then dies in agony.*

Well along the wall, someone began to scream and another voice roared out: "Hold him down! Don't let him move like that!" The scream soared, cracked shrilly and fell into choking, wracking sobs. Niverren started and caught her breath in a little shriek of her own; the cloth fell from nerveless fingers and splashed into the bucket. She began speaking again, rambling on almost to herself. "Mother spent most of last night in the courtyard, praying or weeping or both at once. I don't think poor Niddy got any sleep either and she looked so old and frail this morning, it just terrified me." She peered at her sister uncertainly. "Breyd, what would we do without Nidya? Mother would not go to sleep all night long, would not let Niddy talk sense to her. Oh, Breyd, I am sorry. As if you don't have enough to be worried about." She fixed an anxious gaze on her younger sister's face. "Did they really send you out to fight—really fight? You don't look as afraid as I would be. Are you all right?"

Breyd smiled and hoped it looked more reassuring than it felt. "They really sent us out to fight, Niv. It wasn't so bad, but you know how awfully steep the road is. I'm a little tired from the climb back."

"You look tired. Is Father all right?"

"Of course. He's gone to see Mother."

"Oh—of course. You said. She was so frantic when I left, I almost didn't know what to do, Breyd. I was afraid to go with Tar and just leave her with poor Niddy and Ina, but—"

"I know she's upset. Poor Mother, hearing about us that way. Father will take care of things, he always does." Her sister's tense shoulders relaxed a little.

"Of course he will," Niverren said. Creos made a tiny, fretful sound and she bent over him anxiously. "They said he was given something to put between him and pain. Oh, goddess, if it should wear off now!" But Creos fell silent once more and after a long, quiet moment, Niverren sat back on her heels once more and fingered the green cloak. "I wore this, it was all I could find."

"It's a better color on you, keep it," Breyd said. "I have a newer one anyway, remember?"

"I suppose," Niverren said doubtfully. She swallowed hard. "His father was here all night, they said. I saw him when Tar brought me. The look on his face, Breyd! He was coming from in here, and I saw his face. He won't want Creos like this!" For the first time, there were tears in Niverren's eyes, and one made a grimy streak down her face.

I can easily believe that. But how dare he let Niv see that? Does he think he's the only one who hurts? She shook her head. "Oh, Niv, that must be shock. He won't hold to that." Niverren looked at her dully.

"You do not know his father," she said with finality. "He sees only a cripple. As though that—that—" She momentarily couldn't go on, couldn't manage the word, flung out a hand toward the bandages instead. "As though *that* were all that is Creos, or it were his wit or his manhood or his father's manhood—!"

"But if," Breyd began. She bit her lip, shook her head as Niverren looked at her questioningly. "Nothing; I forget what I meant to say," she finished lamely. *What if Creos feels the same way?* But she couldn't ask that.

She might as well not have spoken; Niv did not seem to have heard her. "A leg is flesh and bone, only a very small part of Creos, nothing that matters if the rest of him survives. And he *will* live without it. I will tolerate nothing else."

There was no answer possible to that. Breyd patted her hand and sat back to wait with her.

Tarpaen made himself eat, though later he couldn't remember what he had eaten. Other men from his company came and went. When he first sat down, someone touched his arm in wordless sympathy, but no one actually said anything to him and he was grateful for that. He ate quickly, then went back to the darkened barracks to rest. Any time at all with General Piritos was as exhausting as full duty under anyone else and the general wanted him back later. He picked out a pallet at random, lay back atop the rough woolen cloth, his own cloak folded under his head for a cushion, and closed his eyes. Someone nearby snored gently, and two men against the opposite wall were speaking in very low voices; it wasn't enough to keep him awake.

When he woke, the men had gone, the snorer was still at it—or someone else was—and a handful of pale, mud-dabbed and utterly exhausted men now slept heavily all around him. He eased quietly onto his feet and went outside. A horn called the hour as he emerged into the last sunlight. He still had time before next duty; he ought to fix the loose horn strap. He needed to find Menlaeus or Breyd.

He probably should have gone home earlier. *But Father will have told Mother what he could; he can calm her better than I can.* It was hard for him not to lose patience with his mother lately, worrying about him the way she did. As if he were in any danger! *Only if they come here.* He could never say that.

What will Niv do if Creos dies? But how will she manage if he lives—like that? And how can Breyd and Father bear it, knowing they will have to go back out there to fight as they did today, and then see what they did? I could tell by her eyes, Breyd knew what she had done and she hated it. I am glad that I am not down there, in the midst of the fighting; what I could see of that, what they told me—I couldn't, ever. I am glad to be safe here—unless the Diye Haff come within the walls.

He wondered at himself a little: *Have I changed as suddenly as I think I have? Or does it mean I was a coward all along because I don't want to kill or to die in horrible pain—or come back maimed like Creos?* Menlaeus would deny that. Of course, his father would say that no matter if it was true or not.

Those who fought never seemed to worry beforehand about such things: Breyd had looked only a little tense this morning, nothing else, and if Creos had thought of it that last morning, he had never said. And yet Creos was such an ordinary person.

Tarpaen blinked and stretched hard; he'd been in sun and now most of him was in shade. He looked up and froze where he was; Laius stood in the middle of the yard, fists on his hips, and he seemed to be glaring up at the wall by the main gates—possibly at someone there. *I had better tell Nabid about him,* Tarpaen thought suddenly. *About this odd dream of his especially. Nabid can do nothing worse than to tell me they already watch Laius and that it is none of my business. But if I tell him, then it's his problem.* While he was deciding this, Laius turned away with a loud oath and strode off toward the gates. Tar drew a relieved breath and slipped into the messes.

But he couldn't find Nabid or Mip; he was frustrated and angry with himself for wasting what little free time he had by the time the hour sounded.

Laius had come back at some point and was already in place on the inner wall, but he sat cross-legged, drum balanced between his knees, eyes fixed on the prince's palace or a point beyond it. His face was expressionless and if he saw Tar, he gave no sign of it.

Tar felt a sudden, overwhelming pity for the big man. There were no companies going out at this hour, no traffic in or out of the gates, nothing for the inner gate drummer to do until nightfall—and Laius would be off duty at sundown. Before he could go over to talk to him, General Piritos came up from the barracks and clapped him on the back in passing. He didn't smile; he never did, and his eyes were already studying the plain as he mounted his low block and began firing off orders. "To the royal chariot, draw back across the Alno. To the phalanx at road's base, under Edrimon, tighten ranks. To the slingers under Frewis, go east to the river." Exacting, high-speed work; Tarpaen set aside everything that had worried him to concentrate upon what he did.

He needed every bit of that concentration: Just at sunset, Diye Haff heavy infantry launched an attack on a Ghezrathi company trying to pull back near the road for the night. Before they could retreat any further, cavalry came up behind them, where they were most vulnerable.

Tarpaen could see little of this disaster for all the dust and the distance. Men over by the barracks were shouting in amazement or anger, until one of the general's aides ran down to shut them up. Silence, except for Piritos' even, expressionless voice: "To the common chariot, go north to aid the phalanx under Virtun." The call was picked up below and sent on, but too late; before the cars could even be turned, the enemy horse were already galloping back toward the sea, leaving at least a hundred men dead or dying. "To the common chariot," Piritos said flatly. "Go to Virtun and remain there until aid is sent." He glanced westward, then gestured an aide to his side. "Tell me tonight, that we must back the infantry with chariot or horse, to guard against such a disaster as this." The sun cast his shadow across Tarpaen; a moment later Atos sank into the sea and the wind fell away to nothing. The plain was all shadow now, and most of the Diye Haff had pulled back across the Oryon. The general watched them go in silence for a moment, then said, "Tell me tonight, to suggest to the prince such companies of horse for the future—and such maneuvers as that one." Fires sprang up on the west bank of the Alno and upon the east bank of the Oryon; at a drumbeat from the inner wall the gates opened and men took wagons out to bring in the dead and wounded. *There will be many of those tonight*, Piritos thought grimly. "Tell me tonight, we must find a company, perhaps light infantry to go mounted down there. Send Rup to make an inventory of horses that could be available and bring the numbers to me."

Tarpaen undid the straps that had held the horn to his lips the past hour, and rubbed sweaty cheeks. Piritos glanced at him. "You did well, Tarpaen. I shall ask for you at fourth horn tomorrow, if you are still willing."

"Sir." He must have been staring. Piritos dismissed the aide and looked down him.

"You think me hard, or indifferent? All those dead and I

stand upon the walls, moving men here and there or talking about numbers and companies?"

Tarpaen could feel the blood mounting his cheeks. He shook his head. "I—sir—"

Piritos held up a hand for silence. "Consider this, before you judge. What if Piritos stood here, with so many eyes on him, and showed whatever rage or grief or fear he felt— what would it do to those who must fight—or those inside who wait for the fighters?" He sighed heavily, shook his head. "Perhaps you thought nothing, and I only read in your eyes what I should find in my own, if I stood where you stand, to look at a man like myself. Go, Tarpaen. Ready yourself for tomorrow."

"Sir," Tarpaen said, and fled before the man could say anything else.

The general watched him go and sighed faintly again, then turned his eyes toward the eastern ridge. He could just see the edge of black cloud beginning to boil above it. He smiled grimly. *So the priestess perhaps manages my storm after all. The Diye Haff caught us by surprise just now; well, they will have at least one special surprise coming to them tonight.*

Tephys lay at full length upon the stone floor, upturned hands cupped to hold water. But tonight, only her own attended her: Eyzhad who crouched at her left shoulder, a jug of water balanced upon his knee; Meronne knelt at her right shoulder. The young woman named Tephys' successor a scant hour earlier sat cross-legged at her feet.

Denira wanted to weep, but she was too numb: Her mind had finally gone blank and she stared into the distance. Only the cold stone under the thin, ancient storm-gray robes passed from heir to heir, and the rough skin of Tephys' feet against her fingers linked her with the real world. Outside this silent, shadowed shrine, Atos must be sinking into the sea and the first stars in the east; in the lower temple there was no sound but Meronne's whispered, repetitive chant and the drip of water, as Tephys petitioned Denota for a great storm.

It was unnervingly silent in the messes; the Dyaddi who were not on duty sat together and ate, and watched as a dusty company of slingers staggered in and crossed the room, followed by ten of the common chariot. Breyd and Lochria eyed each other in rising anger as men checked when they saw the Pairs, then carefully found someplace well across the room to sit. Bechates came in behind the chariot, sat heavily, and murmured something against his Secchi's ear. Lochria leaned close to Breyd. "Father was in the yard just now, with Akeros and Xenia, when the chariot came in. All three of Akeros' older brothers were part of that company."

"What word?"

"Two dead for certain," Lochria said. "The other missing. His uncle was one of the captains; the horses ran him down. Father says his ribs are broken and he's coughing blood; they doubt he'll live." Her voice was expressionless, but her eyes were all pupil and her face was pinched. Breyd caught her fingers and squeezed them. "He says they're making room in there for more wounded; he saw Niverren, just now, leaving with Creos."

"Now? She wasn't alone?" Breyd started to her feet.

Lochria tugged at her hand. "Sit, eat. That boy and your brother were with her."

"Oh. Good."

"Yes." Lochria was breaking bread into small pieces. "There is a vigil at the House of Warriors tonight."

"I know, Father said." Breyd nibbled at her bread; it was newly made, still soft and warmly fragrant, but she had no appetite. She swallowed, tore another piece from the flat loaf and turned it over between her fingers.

"There is also a vigil in Denota's courtyard," Lochria said. "Father thought perhaps the Secchi should go."

"Why?" Breyd set the bread down carefully and shifted so she could look squarely at the other woman; she could feel color mounting to her cheeks and the sudden surge of anger edged her voice. "The men who died out there today—they don't worship Denota. And why should we be separated from the Primes?"

She felt Menlaeus' hand on her arm and shut her mouth. Lochria shrugged. "Well, that is one of the mysteries of Secchi, isn't it? Women and not women, warriors and not warriors."

"The Primes won't be allowed into the Temple itself anyway," Menlaeus said softly as she frowned and tried to find the right words. "We are as much Denota's as you Secchi

are, you know. So if we are let into the courtyard to pray for
our dead, then you should be also."

Breyd picked up the bit of bread she had torn off and ate
it. It had no taste. *It will give you strength whether it tastes
or not. Eat.*

Lochria leaned over to talk to her Prime, then said, "All
right. If Menlaeus is willing, and you will go, we will come
also."

In the end, twelve Pairs left the barracks at the next horn
and went to the long temple set between the inner and outer
walls. Lamps flanked the entry to the narrow courtyard and
the double doors of the distant temple. Men stood in the
courtyard, waiting to enter the temple or waiting for others
to come out; a few sat on the ground next to the inner walls.
Several men near the low gates looked up as Menlaeus
spoke to the priest stationed there, then stared at the Secchi
as the priest waved them on. Breyd tried not to see as men
swallowed, or licked their lips and backed cautiously away
from them. Menlaeus led them into a deserted corner of the
courtyard where they could see the face of the temple. He
knelt and the others knelt around him.

There was a pedestal inside, Breyd knew, and upon it a
sword twice the length of even a very tall man. *It is all right
to tell you that much*, Menlaeus had said earlier. *In this
place, you must try to see the sword in your thoughts, and
think about that thing you desire, and the dead warriors you
pray for. But be careful what you ask. The sons of Denota
are fond of irony, and they may grant what you ask but not
the way you ask it.*

It seemed terribly simple—if deadly—compared to the rituals she had participated in. But when she had asked, "That
is all?" he had shrugged. "It's enough."

Now, in the dim lamplight, surrounded by other Dyaddi,
she felt curiously at peace. Perhaps it was enough. She
closed her eyes, and thought of swords—the god-sword of
the temple.

She had feared to think about swords initially. *If that vision should come back here, now*—Time stretched, one of
her feet went numb. *I should pray*, she thought but her mind
was blank, and she was suddenly afraid. *Denota chose
me—or Tephys did. If I create some disorder here*—No. She
would pray, for Creos, and Akeros' kindred, the man who

died with them, fighting that ambush. *For the ones—the ones I killed.*

It was very quiet all around them—so silent she heard the low growl of distant thunder, and the answering thump of blood in her temples. And another prayer came to her, all at once. *If we are to die as I saw, he and I, then do not let me die before I make them pay dearly for him.* Her mind emptied completely. It was enough.

Outside the city, clouds spilled across the ridge and towered above a white-crested sea, and now the lightning and thunder came closer together. The wind rose from a faint breeze to a high-pitched shrilling that tore at tents and banners and sent men on both sides of the river scurrying for what cover they could find, others to hastily put out cooking fires.

In the city, men and women scrambled down from the roofs with bedding and other things the rain might ruin or wash away, or to drag down wildly flapping awnings in the market. Xhem ran back and forth along the roof, throwing things down for Ina to gather up; Tarpaen and Nidya dragged cushions and chairs inside and covered the brazier so the coals wouldn't be put out.

On the west bank of the Alno, a small company of royal chariot had set up camp in a narrow defile; they hastily moved up to high ground for the shallow gorge would turn into a torrent when rain came. A company of light infantry moved from under the tall cedars where they had been sheltering.

I did not want this; I do not want this. Denira's eyes were fixed on the bare soles of Tephys' feet, on the fingers holding the woman's heels. No one in this still, darkened cavern had moved in a very long time, and she wondered dully if Tephys still breathed. She could barely remember waking in her own house at dawn this same day; it might have been years instead. The look on her mother's face as she stepped aside and the High Priestess swept into the narrow courtyard, Meronne at her heels. She had still been stupid with sleep, but her mother must have realized at once. Tephys brushed past her mother, took both Denira's hands between her own, then laid open palms against her temples. "She is the one." She spoke so softly that only Denira and Meronne could hear her words, then raised her voice enough so everyone in the household could hear: younger brothers and sister, a widowed sister of her father, her mother, all crowded anxiously into the doorway of the courtyard, staring at the priestesses. "Priestess and apprentice and Heir I name you," Tephys said formally. "Denota's own chosen daughter. You will come with me, now, at once. You must learn as quickly as I can teach you; there is much to be done this day."

There had been no time at all; somehow she had found herself clad in the novice white and green, the shock-silenced household and her weeping mother behind her; a bewildering series of ceremonies, words, and passwords, a small ceremony in the lower temple and then in the little clay house; another in the open courtyard, an exchange between herself and Tephys of bites of ripe fruit and three dry, choking heads of green grain. A very small cup of wine so bitter she wondered if it had been poisoned. One strand of her hair had been cut to her scalp and placed in a box, and her novice green and white had been taken away while she stood naked and shivering; they were replaced by these dreadful, worn gray things, and a pair of sandals which cut too tightly across her toes.

Tephys led her through the streets and into the palace, into a small and windowless room where the prince sat. When she would have knelt to him, Tephys caught hold of her arm and shook her head. Pelledar had completed her confusion by kneeling before her to touch her feet. And then they were in the street again, passing silent people or being passed by them; Tephys had come straight down to the Cleft and the lower temple, and began this seemingly endless ceremony to bring about a storm.

Her legs had gone completely dead, but her arms ached fiercely. At one time, she had been hungry, but her stomach seemed to have gone numb as well. *Why a storm?* she wondered. Of all the things they had told her over the course of this endless day, only one stayed with her: *You will learn the ancient paths beneath the temple, the entries and locks and chambers, how to raise Denota's protective barriers that separate this place from even the palace and how to lower them; the places where food is kept, the wells and cisterns; and if the hour comes, you will bring Queen Ye Sotris and her babes to this safety, and serve them.* Until? She had not asked that, had not dared ask any question. The answer to

that was clear, at least: Until the Diye Haff went or the city
died—until Ye Sotris dies or you do. For as long as it takes,
if it happens.

A lifetime—however long or short that lifetime might be.
At the moment, she seemed to see years and decades of
darkness cut by dim oil lamps, silence broken only by whispers, three babes grown to two men and a woman—herself
to withered, gray-haired and bent age. Denira swallowed,
fixed her eyes upon her fingers, and tried to think of nothing
at all. In the silence, she could hear the distant drip of water
and, just perhaps, the low growl of distant thunder.

High above the Cleft, the city streets were slick with rain;
the few banners on the outer walls flapped wildly in the
gale, and it was very dark indeed as clouds muffled the last
stars along the western horizon. Occasional flashes lit the
plain and the walls, and made a pale, gleaming snake of the
road joining the two.

The parade ground and courtyard of the barracks were
nearly deserted, only a few men hurrying between the hospital barracks, the gates and the messes; the streets beyond
were empty for the first time in several days.

Niverren lay on the very edge of the pallet she and Breyd
had shared for so many years and listened to her young husband's labored breathing, audible at least to her even above
the sound of the rapidly approaching storm. It was blessedly
silent in the courtyard, with Nevvia forced inside; with any
good fortune at all her mother slept over there; with Tar and
Xhem had the main room for the night, and she could just
make out a dim light still burning in there.

Creos was quiet, save for his breathing. Be grateful, she
reminded herself. She still had him; the barracks physicians
said he had as much chance to live as anyone, and her father
said such men did not offer soothing lies. Though nothing
was certain, no physician needed to tell her that.

The enemy had pulled him from the sea instead of leaving
him to drown; they had kept him alive and tended to his leg
so he did not bleed to death on the deck; they had given him
whatever things they had to keep him quiet for a little; any
sleep he had before the pain tore at him would surely be a
blessing.

Nidya had her own medicines, and knew how to use them;
not all women had her skills.

Nidya had offered to sit with Creos, had offered her valerian; Niverren had refused both. *If he wakes and I am not awake to reassure him; if I slept and did not hear him waken, or if he died and I did not know it until the valerian released me and I woke....*

She tensed and held her breath as Creos murmured something in his drugged sleep; he turned his head fretfully from side to side and she came cautiously up onto an elbow and gazed down at him, then laid a hand against his cheek. He subsided at her touch and became still again. Niverren lay back down once more.

In the main room, Tarpaen wedged his dagger in a block of wood, moved the small lamp to cast its reflection against the wall, and sat back. Xhem looked at the makeshift shrine, at his companion, then crossed his legs so his posture matched Tar's as closely as possible. "I do not understand," he said finally; his voice was not much above a whisper. "Why do you not go to the temple, instead of making your own here?"

Tarpaen shrugged. "You know what I am, little brother. The temple of warriors is no place for me." Xhem stirred indignantly, and Tar smiled at him. "They would not let you enter, anyway, because you are not yet old enough—and I would not go without you."

"You are as much a warrior as the general," Xhem said proudly. "The general stands upon the wall just as you do; he does not go down to fight."

"I think it is a little different," Tarpaen said and he smiled again. "But never mind. The gods who guard the temple of warriors will not care that we make our own shrine here; they will care only that we pray to them." Rather self-consciously, he drew out a second dagger—one that had been part of Menlaeus' father's small store of weaponry—and laid it on the floor in front of his knees. Xhem, who was watching him closely, carefully and exactly copied the gesture, drawing the prized small blade Nabid had given him and which he wore on a narrow leather baldric just like Tarpaen's. Tar closed his eyes; Xhem closed his own and tried to think of a suitable prayer. *Let my brother Tar somehow fight for the city as he wishes; but keep him safe, if he does.* But there was dreadful Creos a room away; Xhem swallowed, opened his eyes to gaze anxiously at the little shrine, then closed them again, and tried to think of nothing at all.

At his side, Tarpaen held his fingers against the knife blade and prayed, *Let nothing else come against this family, no other tragedy beyond Creos—for I do not think I can bear to see it.*

Their movements hidden by storm, a small company of Ghezrathi crept up behind Haffat's light chariot camped by the mole on the sand. The fighting was brief and extremely fierce; the Diye Haff were caught badly off guard and made only a little resistance before most of them turned and fled on foot. Someone uncovered a lantern and ran onto the mole to wave it; a messenger waiting on the main road turned his edgy horse and galloped back to the city.

More men ran onto the mole then, and readied ropes while one of them stripped, tied one end of a long rope about his waist, put the other into the hands of his captain and let himself be lowered into rough water. The captain paid out rope, and then he and the silent company waited what seemed a terribly long time for the tugs on the rope that would tell them the swimmer had accomplished his goal; men laid hands upon the rope and drew it in, dragged the exhausted man onto the mole and wrapped him in a cloak. Two of his companions lifted him bodily then and bore him from the mole, back across the sand and into the shelter of a low bank and overhanging bushes. "You succeeded?" one of the men asked as they settled out of the wind.

The swimmer drew and let out several deep breaths, finally nodded. "I couldn't find the plug, to draw it, but I holed the ship at arm's length under water, near the stern. It will not last the night." Men surged to their feet as voices rose suddenly above the sound of the storm, topped and drowned by the clash of weaponry, but the sound could have been near or distant and could have come from almost any direction and rapidly faded away.

In his small cell, Septarin was unaware of the storm, or of anything save his own misery. Food had been shoved through the door twice, water once apart from that. No one had spoken to him, and he had seen no one save once the back of a man in his father's colors, striding down the narrow and dimly lit hallway. The bread was stale, the fruit overly soft; the water faintly leather-scented as though it had been held in a bucket for some time. He ate and drank to ease the gnawing pain in his stomach, slept on the cold stones of the floor, or, like now, simply sat with his back to a wall, staring blankly at the faint light coming from the hall beyond that locked door. He was no longer certain his father would send for him, and, at the moment, too desperately unhappy to care.

The streets and alleyways of Ghezrat ran with water; the lightning had passed over some time past, though now and again those in Denota's courtyard could hear the mutter of thunder away toward the isthmus, and even more seldom against the utter black of the night sky, the least pale blue flash well down on the western horizon. The stones of the courtyard were dangerously slick, the walls and Tephys' small thatched shelter dripped water. A circle of women ignored the chill in the air, the occasional gust of wind and the water thrown onto them from the trees that overhung the walls. Ten novice priestesses in white with green sashes—all that remained with one of their number a Secchi and another clad in the subdued gray of Tephys' heir. Interspersed among them were the twelve older women who ordinarily only came to this place in their dark green upon the four corners of the year. In their very midst was a wreath of new grape leaves, dried grains surrounding a cup of wine, and, floating upon the surface of that cup, a lit wick which flickered faintly.

Tephys, her face as gray as her new apprentice's robes, her sagging body held upright only by will and by Meronne on the one side and Eyzhad on the other, stood just beyond the circle of women, arms extended as she chanted the prayer. The wick flared very brightly, three times, then sank without trace into the cup. The women took up the chant, repeated it thrice, and turned to face outward. Tephys gently shook off her supporters and stepped between two of the white-clad girls, bent to take up the cup, and drank. She let her head fall back, grateful for the chill, damp breeze, and waited for the goddess to fill her.

Shoulders set, face turned toward the gates that led to the street, Khadat stood very still and silent, waiting as the others did for Tephys' words. When they came, they made little sense to her and gave her no comfort.

But there had been no comfort for her all these past many days—little since Perlot had died and Hemit returned as he was; even less now, with all her family in Merikos dead or scattered, what family she had here lost to her as well.

She had gone in search of Apodain this evening just at sunset and found him in the room which had been his father's and still held Perlot's chests of parchment books, his father's panoply, the chair that had been Perlot's favorite. He had simply looked at her inquiringly, no sign of discomfort at being found in this room, though for many years she had forbidden it and he had never come here that she was aware. "I must attend a ceremony in Denota's courtyard," she had said flatly. "You will come with me." But he had simply shaken his head and turned away from her.

Only that. For some reason, it had shaken her more than argument or passionate refusal or anything else he might have done. She had not known how to go on. In the end, she had turned and left without saying anything else. *Denota give me back at least this son, if you will not give me Hemit,* she prayed silently. But perhaps she had lost Denota as well; behind her Tephys still spoke and still the words made no sense. Khadat let her eyes close.

Haffat

The sun had set and clouds were boiling over the eastern sky and the sea, bringing a chill wind with them. The Diye Haff camp, set as it was along the eastern bank of the Oryon and within the shelter of the ridge, was mostly protected from the wind, but men nearer the river worked feverishly to move tents and horses farther back from the water, and to get as much of the camp as possible out of the wind.

Haffat stood under the canopy of his tent, gazing after Knoe who was searching out another sacrifice of some kind. The priest vanished behind a line of chariots—all they could rescue earlier from the marshes between here and the sea, where this river broke into smaller and smaller streams and finally into a vast and reedy swamp. His eyes shifted, watching his soldiers securing the camp against the oncoming storm. There would be other men as well, to prepare the company that would cross the river under cover of full darkness. Haffat eyed the coming storm and nodded in satisfaction. He himself would lead that company—in a simple but highly successful maneuver he had used when he was still a company captain in his father's armies. It would be a harsh night, and if this goddess had sent the storm, then it would serve her fair to have it used against her.

More than fair. *What horror was that this morning?* He had no clear picture from the men who came back—even the normally phlegmatic captain of chariot had babbled something about red-clads, a bloody aura that enveloped everything, men screaming and falling—blood and limbs and shattered bodies everywhere. *Two hundred and forty-seven dead. They will pay for that.*

He turned abruptly from the entry as two of his personal guards came to pull the long poles and lower the flap before the wind could pull it down. With the entry shut, it was close in the tent; humid and overly warm, particularly with so many lamps hung over the long, narrow table where they had been at maps for so much of the late afternoon. He signed to the one servant who remained, settled back in the deeply cushioned leather chair while the man damped the wicks of all but one lamp, and finally gestured for him to leave.

The young man perched on the edge of the table stirred restlessly; subsided as Haffat signed him to silence until the servant was gone. "Now, Hadda. Your news of yesterday—I wanted to thank you for that, but there was no time."

Hadda eyed him warily; Haffat's color was blotchy and his eyes smoldering black, a dangerous sign. *But he would not harm me.* "Mere luck, Father. Your priest is not pleased."

Haffat sighed and now he looked merely tired. "It is not safe for you to pester Knoe, my son; he controls powerful forces."

"Or is controlled by them," Hadda said. Haffat compressed his lips, but finally nodded.

"Yes. Or is controlled by them. In either event, I have better use for you than a sacrifice to Knoe's temper."

"Father, believe this if nothing else: I do not like your priest, but I do not deliberately bait him, either. The man frightens me. Does that please you?"

Haffat studied him for a very long moment. "I would be happier by far if you and he could cooperate, rather than this constant nipping at each other. You remind me of two dogs, necks all hackled and growling."

"No, Father; I do not growl at Knoe," Hadda said softly. He shook himself. "Was that all you wished to say? I am glad I learned something useful, but it was merely odd fortune that I chanced to be with the Mirikosi."

"All the same. But that was not why I waited until Knoe was gone, or why I wanted to speak with you. This city." Haffat waved a hand vaguely southward. "Your uncle may recover from his wounds, but it will be a long time before he is able to govern Ghezrat, when she is mine. That being so, it may be he will remain behind when I take Ye Eygar; I may go on to Rejnikh and then head west to Gryptis. If I do that, I think I will return here, and take up residence for the winter. In the meantime, you will govern Ghezrat for me." He sat back and folded his arms; Hadda stared at him blankly. "You are not pleased by that?"

"Father, you cannot!"

"Cannot? Even you dare tell me what I can and cannot do," Haffat replied and he laughed, but his eyes were dark.

Hadda swallowed nervously. "I? Father, I did not mean— but Knoe, he said that Heliar, the prophecy—"

"Yes, the prophecy," Haffat said evenly. "But that made no mention of Heliar's injuries. I think perhaps this was meant all along, as a sign to me that I must eventually talk to the god directly and decide such matters for myself. Not through Knoe." He fixed thoughtful eyes on his son, who had gone quite pale. "I have long had it in mind, there was a very important reason I must keep you at my side, Hadda. And more than once I have dreamed of you, that you served a great purpose in my empire. Again, three nights ago, I had this dream, and I saw you in that palace, looking over the plain. Understand, I am sorry that Heliar is hurt, and I will be greatly saddened if he dies. But if the god uses his death to further my vision—"

"But—"

"It has always been my intention that you learn the pleasures and responsibilities of ruling. When I must give over Diyet and dodder into my grave, you will be prepared to take her and to oversee this vast empire that is already mine, and all that is still to come."

"Father, please." No sound came. But Haffat's eyes softened as he looked at his son.

"I know, my poor son; you have friends in Diyet and a pleasant life there. There are none in the camp or the armies who fill the void left by these friends, none your equal in rank or wits. Knoe may see that as a sign of some weakness, but I understand it. You are a young man, handsome and clever—no soldier. Why should you be happy in the company of soldiers?"

"I have failed you."

"No. I am a soldier and son of a soldier, but this does not mean I see all men as either soldiers or as nothing. Not everyone is made for this life. When the city is taken, and you have its palace, you may send for your friends, as many of them as you wish. There is a gift for you. Will it suit?"

Hadda bowed his head; his shoulders sagged and he nodded once. *No land withstands the emperor; what chance has a mere son?* Haffat got to his feet, came over and wrapped an arm around him. "Even—Jerred?" Hadda whispered.

"Whosoever you wish."

"Then—whatever *you* wish, Father."

"Good." Haffat clapped him on the back and picked up his heavy, dark cloak. "I must go, the company should be ready to cross the river and I have final instructions to give. Remember tomorrow, before sunrise; I want you at the pyre, with me."

"I . . . all right. Take care, Father."

Haffat paused with the flap in his hand. "I never take great chances," he said with a faint, sardonic smile. "And those I do take bind the men to me. Good night to you."

"And to you, sir." Hadda dredged up a smile; it vanished the moment the flap slid into place behind his father. He began to shiver violently. *Knoe will kill me!*

He got to his feet and paced around the long, narrow trestle table. Wind shook the tent and, dim as the inside light was, he could see occasional flashes of lightning through the coarse canvas fabric, could hear the sharp crack of thunder and the scream of frightened horses, the shouts of men dealing with them or with flying tents that had not been properly secured. Someone nearby was screaming for help; one of the cars had been bowled over by the wind and had gone end for end into the river. He sat down at the table, and buried his face in his hands.

He could not send for Jerred, or anyone else: The soldiers virtually worshiped Haffat and half of *them* were terrified to be so far from Diyet. He himself was dreadfully unhappy. It was not just these fool's tales of great snake-monsters in the deeps, or demons lurking in the caverns and beneath the overhanging rocks in the deeper parts of the river. Just—the distance from a pleasanter clime, from wines that were pale and sweet and meats that tasted of the delicate herbs grown in Diyet, of a land where snows came of a winter and there was none of this flying dust and sour red wines, that nose-wrinkling yellow powder mixed with boiled pots of grain and goat meat, the evil infections that set upon the least scratches and made gaping wounds of them.

No, Jerred would not come; none of his friends would, unless commanded by his father—and where would be the pleasure in friends who must see themselves as no longer friends, but slaves, to be forced to come to Ghezrat?

Those in the city would not see him as friend, either, however they accepted the new rule in Mirikos or any other captured city. Here, he would be forever enemy. These were not like the Mirikosi or the Idemitans. Everyone said so.

And Father will set me to rule them? In preparation to rule all his empire? But he dared not refuse. The look in his father's eye just now: "He has attacked men for less, with no warning at all, and tonight he is possessed of a fury." *He is angry because so many died—but those Pairs, Raej was there, he said they killed like crazed beasts.* It was a god-thing, Knoe said, and their gods would be cast out when Ghezrat was taken. But to be there, inside those walls with—with *girls* who could do that. "I am dead no matter what I do," Hadda moaned and buried his face in his hands. "I can't rule anyone, I don't want to."

But he would be quit of Knoe if he remained here. The lion-priest terrified him more and more of late; why could his father not see what the man was? Knoe would sacrifice anything—anyone!—use that gruesome gold-handled knife on Haffat himself, if his Lion demanded it. *Fanatic.* And to bring in these Ergardi: Knoe believed he controlled them, that he could twist their fatalistic beliefs and their dread powers to his own ends. Even now he had them working to shape new and horrible weapons of Gryptiosi Fire. It was even whispered one inhabited a prisoner's body.

Any man could be Ergardi, in a stolen body. He was shivering violently. That servant of his father's, even. If Knoe knew what Haffat planned—*If he came here, with the blood of his sacrifice still wet on his hands. They say it was a man Knoe slew outside Mirikos.* Hadda shuddered, shoved his way past the now soaking wet flap, and ran out into the storm.

13

The sky was a pale, rainwashed blue when Piritos mounted the outer wall and gazed out across the plain—or what of it he could see. Atos already warmed the heights and the gates, but down there everything east of the Alno was still deep in shadow. Water still slicked the outer parapets and lay in puddles everywhere; out on the ledge, muddy rivulets cut new rills in the dirt and deepened the ruts beside the road.

The storm had been all he could have desired, but it could have been disastrous for them. Across the Alno, men shifted through the wreck of brightly-colored cars—all that was left of the company of royal chariot that had camped there by the river the night before. His face remained expressionless from many years of habit, but he was truly furious. *Ten cars missing, and their horses gone; nine drivers vanished and seven dead, and four of the royals.* A chariot lay on its side, half buried in mud, and nothing but the underside of another could be seen above the water midstream. On the near side were two dead horses, and as he watched a man's body was pulled ashore and laid on the bank.

"We should have known. I should have," the general growled. They had expected enemy sorties during the storm; one of the Ghezrathi companies had surprised several Diye Haff trying to break a dam west of the Alno and taken them prisoner. But that had all been early, and once the storm passed they had apparently all withdrawn across the Oryon. Near daybreak, while the drivers were harnessing the last horses and the fighting men eating their bread and readying their weapons, a large company of Diye Haff broke cover and fell on them from three separate directions. They had speared men still stretched on their sleeping mats, slaughtered unarmored men, killed weaponless drivers, and taken whatever cars were ready in a stunning, lightning raid, and were gone before the few fighters still on their feet could regroup.

A clever enemy; a well-planned maneuver, Piritos thought grimly. *And for all the undoubted damage we did last night during Denota's storm, this is a terrible loss. More bloody-handed and daring than any I conceived. But so stupid—not to keep watch while they readied! And now someone will say, "But they weren't supposed to have been there!"* He closed his eyes very briefly. Like those poor boys trying to hold the jetty, half of them unable to swim. "Because they were going to retreat onto land when the time came, because nothing else was supposed to happen, and men died for our blindness." He was muttering to himself, he realized and drew himself up sharply; someone would hear him. *The gods take you all, my heroes.*

He squared his shoulders, drew a deep breath as footsteps scrunched along the rain-washed sand and rubble of dirt and small stones that always littered this edge, however often it was swept. An aide came with messages from the prince and from the captains. Piritos glanced through the bits of parchment, listened as the aide passed on what Grysis and other captains had to tell him. "All right. To the prince, we shall need his son; he will suspect as much if he has been told about the destruction out there. Send word to the palace by messenger, to have the boy given back his panoply and escort to the messes. Tell the prince his general begs him to say nothing to the boy, we will tell him what he must hear. To Brysos, to meet the boy at the barracks and warn him that the least breach of orders on his part will see him back in his prison cell for good, if not to the top of a pyre tomorrow at dawn with the other dead. To Grysis, that he again send Pairs with Kroserot. To Edrimon now on the road, if they ask for a prisoner exchange today, we will grant it but in the same place. This time they will not try to surprise us as they did yesterday." He smiled grimly. "To Nabid, send me young Tarpaen for three hours if he is able. To Nabid also, commend Tarpaen for his skill and wit yesterday.

"To Prisno, has he found men and horses and have he and Apridos planned how to use them to protect the infantry against slaughter like yesterday's? To Prisno, continue to enlarge the horse company and plan further maneuvers; we will meet at ninth horn so I can see what he intends. To Nabid, to meet at ninth horn with us so horn calls can be de-

vised for them and whatever Captain Prisno names." He
paused, thought. "That is all; come back at third horn." The
aide turned and hurried off. Tarpaen came onto the wall bare
moments later; the horn swung loose in his hand and he was
out of breath.

Piritos laid a hand on his shoulder. "I need you for three
hours; can you manage?"

Tar nodded immediately. "I can do that, sir."

"Good. Good lad." Piritos mounted his block; sunlight
was spreading across the plain; behind him a drummer beat
out the call for companies, first horn sounded and the outer
gates were opened. Messengers galloped down the road, followed more slowly by a few common chariot and a partial
phalanx of heavy infantry, the five Dyaddi marching by twos
along their right flank again. *Father—Breyd.* He thought
they must be the first Pair; he still couldn't be certain. *How
can they go back out there, after yesterday? But I saw those
men yesterday, they were terrified of the Pairs—terrified of
my father!* He had heard and seen them in the messes late
the past night—men glancing nervously over their shoulders
as they whispered to those huddled around them. He drew
one last deep breath, adjusted a strap and set the horn against
his lips, and waited for the general's first order.

He sent two quick signals and waited again, but there was
a lull and Piritos was listening to some message from the
high priestess. Had it really only been two days since he'd
come to the general's attention? Yesterday, he'd been a mass
of nerves, but today—odd, how little time it took for even
something like this to become comfortable.

But a lot of his fear had gone last night, when he and
Xhem made their shrine.

He straightened the horn as Piritos snapped off another
order—to royal chariot, return to the city. *To what was left
of the chariot, rather,* Tarpaen thought grimly. It was all the
talk. Fortunately, it gave men something to do besides
spread terrified rumors about the Dyaddi. Better, it made
them angry when they heard how Haffat's men fell on them
like men hunting birds, slaughtering unarmed and sleeping
men with as little feeling. They already said down there that
Haffat himself had led his men, the lion upon his breast
gleaming like a target—but no one had been able to reach

him. *They would say that, though. Those nobles cannot bear thinking common men could do such damage.*

All the same, that raid even overshadowed Demorian's swim through the storm to sink a Mirikosi ship full of men and supplies. Tarpaen looked toward the sea but he couldn't make out the stub of mast they said you could see above the waves—the sun reflected off the water blindingly, but he couldn't have seen anything so small at such a distance.

But that doesn't matter, not to the general. Somehow in the last day or two days, he had also stopped caring that his eyes were so bad. He had no place out there and a man who went out to become a hero as often came back on his shield without the chance to kill a single enemy. *But I can do this, and do it well; this is useful.*

There was another lull; companies moved onto the plain; Haffat's infantry had not yet crossed the river, though they were thick on the eastern shore. *That ridge was not rich farmland, but it fed our goats and cattle.* With such a vast army camped there, it would be turning to a sodden mess of mud and flattened grass. Garbage would be everywhere—broken weaponry and harness, the ends of meals and other, less pleasant thing.

Laius was tapping at his drum again, tightening the screws and muttering to himself.

The man worried him, enough that he had finally gone to Mip this morning and unburdened himself. Mip had listened, but all he said was, "I know, he's been odd. His blood, of course—but he's not acting so strangely he can't follow orders, and he knows the signals. He's the best we have for the inner gate." He ran a hand through short-cut, graying hair and sighed heavily. "You did right, telling me; we'll watch him."

Tar glanced over his shoulder; Laius was standing and glaring out toward the eastern ridges. The general's aide stood above the inner gates, and there didn't seem to be anyone else nearby. *Maybe they just don't want Laius to know he's watched.* That would be prudent, he thought; he turned back as the general sent another order.

The drum clattered out a pattern behind him; gates opened and a small company of royal chariot came out. Tarpaen stared in astonishment: The prince's heir rode in the third car! *After what he did?* But there was no swagger in

Septarin just now; he gripped the rails to keep himself upright and his head was bowed.

General Piritos spoke; Tarpaen shook himself and concentrated on the task at hand.

Septarin felt giddy with so much sun and fresh air, weak as much from relief as from lack of food. At first he had wanted to shout or laugh, to run screaming through the palace halls, but the men who had collected him and his weaponry were the same two who had thrown him in the cell. He bit his lip, reminded himself of conduct becoming a warrior, stood still while they put his armor on him, and went quietly with them.

The barracks had been full of grim-faced men and hardly any of them paid him the least attention. *What has gone wrong, why do they look like that?* Had they only brought him here to be part of a surrender? But the talk was all royal chariot—wounded and dying. And Dyaddi, though anyone who said that word was glared into silence.

His father's men brought him to the messes, where Brysos was talking to some of the company, then turned and left him. *Have I become invisible?* Septarin wondered. But one of the drivers had seen him; he touched the man next to him and both turned to look. Septarin made himself stay where he was, and ignore them. *They can't glare at a prince! Who do they think they are?* The way they had looked at him. He ran his fingers along the pleats of his linen while Brysos read the list of dead and missing, the names of those injured in the morning's predawn raid. *So that is why I am here; not because they've seen sense, but because they need men.* Well, it was an insult, but the result still put him here; he would accept it.

Brysos finally set the lists aside. "Go and get ready." But as Septarin began to edge away, Brysos stepped in front of him. "You will stay." Septarin swallowed and schooled his face so nothing would show while Brysos berated him; he nodded or shook his head as necessary whenever the man paused, but he actually heard very little. *I know what he would say, anyway; the general said the same things the other night.* At least Brysos was not bellowing at him, and no one paid any attention to them. Brysos folded his arms finally, and said, "I trust you understand all of that."

"I do, sir." He bowed his head. "Thank you, sir."

"Good." Brysos turned without further word and went back into the messes. Septarin looked around for his car and wondered who would drive it today. Since Loros—was it Loros?—was dead.

But he didn't dare think about Loros. *He had no right to disobey me, it was his own fault, not mine. If he had done what I ordered him to do, the car would not have sat still for so long—he would not have been where he was when that arrow was shot.* Septarin gritted his teeth, lowered his eyes until he could get his temper under control. A commoner, daring to argue with a prince! It must have been fate guiding that arrow. *They would do well to remember that.*

But he had promised himself he would not dwell on what was past. And he dared not be angry here; if Brysos or Piritos knew, they would send him back, he would be shoved back into that dreadful hole.

And Father will let them. What manner of prince is he, to let these men dictate how he treats his heir? But Pelledar—he had been a stranger, a dreadful, cold stranger. *As if he was ashamed of me.*

They would go soon, he had better make certain his car was ready. But as he started across the fighting ground, someone slammed into his shoulder, knocking him off balance. *That was no accident.* He clutched at his belt for the dagger, but his hand was grabbed; and he looked into the eyes of his cousin Ryllan.

"Now, then. You will listen to us, little cousin," Ryllan said very softly. *He hates me,* Septarin thought in astonishment; he suddenly realized there were men all around the two of them—other members of the royal chariot. And they all looked at him with the same cold contempt. "Little cousin," Ryllan said once more. "You will close your mouth and listen for just this once. This is not the palace. And your father and mother and your tutors—all those who kiss your feet or your backside—they are there and we here. And once the company drives beyond the outer walls, they are even farther from you than we are. Do you hear what I tell you?"

"I hear it," Septarin said evenly. He drew himself up as tall as he could, but still had to look up to meet Ryllan's eyes. "Do you actually dare threaten me, here in this courtyard, before all these men?"

"I tell you something *practical*," Ryllan countered, even more softly. "To which you will listen, little prince. Out there, rank is nothing, a driver's blood is as red as that of any noble or prince who rides behind him. What you did is inexcusable; your father should have had you flogged in the square for it." Septarin flushed deeply and clawed for his sword, but someone gripped his upper arms bruisingly, tightening enormous, hard hands until he gasped and subsided. "That is better. Stand still, and be still, and listen. Your father has indulged you shamefully; the general indulges both you and the prince, and it would seem we are to suffer for that, and to suffer with you. But we see it otherwise. What you did out there will not happen again. You will do nothing—*nothing*—which is not ordered by the general or Brysos—or myself. Do you understand what I say to you?" He waited until Septarin, his eyes black with fury and his face still very red, reluctantly nodded. "You will do exactly as ordered, not from fear that your *father* will put you in a cell, or that the general will slap your hands, or that your mother will weep over you, or that the goddess will condemn you to the outer darkness between worlds if you do not. You will do exactly as ordered, because one of us will ride close to you whenever you go into battle. Think yourself above orders at any time, and you will find yourself in the thick of the enemy, weaponless and afoot. Because if I am near enough, I myself will hurl you from your car."

"You would not dare," Septarin whispered; he was so shocked he could not have raised his voice had he wished. He knew it must show, that it must be in his face for he had felt the color drain into his feet; they could all see it, and he hated each one of them for knowing they had frightened him.

Ryllan smiled, and it was not a pleasant smile. "I would not only dare, princeling," he said flatly. "I would do it gladly. And so would any of these around me, including Gos who drives you this day."

That stung him where nothing else might have. His voice went high. "You tell me that a common would dare!" He squeaked and then fell silent as the hands dug into his biceps once more.

"But who would believe it?" Wordoron said softly. "That a commoner would dare assault the son of his own prince? Or that any of us, noble as we are, would throw the son of our prince from his car? And who would take the word of an overimaginative boy, however royal, against that of a trained company of fighting men? Do you think we would not swear as one that you make this story up to call attention to yourself as any child does—the way you have always done? And if you die out there, we will swear that you let go the car at the wrong moment and fell from it."

"Think on it, princeling," Ryllan said quietly. "Think on it, and learn prudence and caution—at least for this day and however many more they send you into battle with us." He paused, gave Septarin a searching look and seemed satisfied by what he saw. "Learn, or die," he added, then nodded to his companions.

One day, when I am prince, they will all suffer for this! Septarin thought furiously as the men walked away. His knees were shaking so he dared not move just yet. They had threatened his life! And they had made it so he would not even dare go to Brysos and tell him what they had said! *But if I went to Brysos, or to Piritos*— He could never talk to Piritos, anyway; not the way the general had looked at him that night, spoken to him, and in his father's very presence. Piritos would laugh to see how those men had frightened him; he would laugh and tell Septarin he had been made the butt of a soldier's joke. Whether he believed his prince's son told the truth or not, Septarin decided bleakly. *But if Brysos believed, he would not let me back out there to fight. And I want to fight.*

Was it worth even this? He knew the answer to that. If anyone—any single person thought he hid in the palace behind his mother's skirts, as Apodain skulked within Perlot's walls—"I would die first. I am no Apodain, I could not live with such shame." And those few moments on the field—he had felt himself truly part of the company, and then, when he had fallen upon the Diye Haff and watched their surprise that a slender youth could command such a car—their fear when they saw that youth was a true fighting man, who could wield a spear or a bow as well as any other of the royal chariot. *Better than most,* he tried to assure himself, and the tightness in his throat began to ease. *Does not the son of Atos drive a warrior's car from which to smite his enemy, and is he not depicted as a youth at the finest hour of golden youth?*

This was but a setback, a small one. His father had again relented and sent him out here to rejoin the company and to fight. Pelledar must have been miserable, thinking all his waking hours upon his son, his own part in that son's unjust punishment. His father would not immure him again, and so long as his son wanted to fight, Pelledar would surely never deny him.

All the same. *Until I can find the way to revenge myself, I will not jeopardize my place in the royal chariot. Not for them. They would like it if I left, they would win. And they must not win.* So for now at least, he would do exactly the least thing ordered. *You had better,* a small inner voice reminded him. *Or they will kill you.*

It was quiet at the base of the cliff; Breyd could hear the creak of leather armor, the scratchy noise of bronze plates rubbing over each other, the labored breathing of someone in the third rank.

Water pooled beside the road, and still ran down among the rocks; the road itself smelled of wet rocks and mud. But it was drying rapidly now the sun had cleared the eastern ridges. A light breeze ruffled the puddles.

Companies moved past them on the way to fight; a gray-faced man stumbled past the phalanx leading his limping horse up the road. Two messengers passed him going the other way at full gallop. She wouldn't look at the man standing beside her, and after a while stopped looking at those going by. *They think we will go suddenly mad, without cause, and kill them all.*

If the Diye Haff attacked this position again—She bit her lip and remembered what Menlaeus had said this morning before they joined the infantry. *They will not simply throw men at us again; if our own men fear what we did, think how their men see us.* But sooner or later, they would have to fight. *For Creos, for that boy who cried for his mother— Haffat will pay for what he has done to us.*

She glanced up. What was left of the royal chariot was coming slowly along the road, men leading lame or exhausted horses. She fixed her eyes on a spot just above the approaching men. *There will be wounded and dead in those cars, and I do not think I can bear to see them.* And it would do them no good. But she could still hear: The clunk of a wheel hitting stone, and someone's agonized, shrill panting. Someone moaned steadily; another man was talking to him, his voice low and soothing. She couldn't make out the words; she doubted the injured could hear him. Burned wood and burned wool assaulted her nose; the smell of blood left a foul taste in her mouth and for one desperate moment she feared she would be sick again. Menlaeus laid a hand on her wrist. She tried to concentrate on breathing deeply, the way he had told her, on holding the air, letting it out slowly. It didn't block her senses; it did keep her from vomiting. And then they were gone, moving slowly up the road.

The Diye Haff stayed well out on the plain all morning. She walked about and stretched when Kroserot allowed it, then came back into formation and watched distant, tiny figures of men running one way, others galloping toward the road. There was no dust at this hour, but no pattern she could make out down here. She could hear Tarpaen up on the wall. His bright, clear horn was easy to tell from the others, and the crisp way he sent out the calls.

She was proud of him. Proud of Tar, but he'd only been hard to live with while he was close to Laius; before that he'd been all right. When she was little, he'd watched out for her. *Tell him this afternoon, when we return to the city— before anything happens, and I can't.* Menlaeus stirred. *He knows when I worry. He knows I cannot let that particular worry go. But it's wrong of me to worry him, he has enough to bear.* She managed a smile for him; he smiled and turned his eyes back to the road. Breyd went back to her study of the distant companies, and waited for the signal to end their watch.

Back in the messes a horn later, Grysis came looking for them. "They want a second watch of pairs where you were for the late guard and an additional company halfway up the road. Kroserot's twenty will take that second position, so you'll be out there until sunset. But there'll be leave after that for you until midnight."

"Good." Menlaeus picked up his bread and wine and got to his feet. "We'll need to choose the additional pairs. Do you have the time now?" Grysis nodded and they left together.

Breyd went over to join Lochria and Xera. "I'm looking for my brother Tarpaen. Have you seen him?"

Both Secchi shook their heads. But one of Kroserot's men at the next bench said, "I saw him just now. The signaler with the clouded eye, isn't he, up with General Piritos most of the time? I just now saw him on the wall."

"Do you need him?" Lochria asked. "Maybe someone could get him for you."

"It isn't as important as that." She edged her way onto the bench, took a swallow of the wine. An evil taste filled her mouth; she spit it back into the cup, and Lochria laughed.

"Yes, isn't it wonderful? All that rain last night and you'd never know it by the barracks well—it's worse than yesterday. Here, eat some bread, it'll take away that taste."

"Oh, that's just awful. How can they do that to even the wine *we* get?"

Xera wrinkled her nose. "It tastes like bad eggs smell; did you ever pick up an old one and have it explode on you?"

"I hadn't thought it through so carefully, thank *you*," Breyd said pointedly, and set the cup at arm's length. Xera grinned at her and then all three were laughing.

"Hush," Breyd said finally. "They all think we're dangerously mad anyway; we don't need to sound crazed, too."

"Do what Eriana is doing," Lochria said; she was still giggling. "Bring some from your neighborhood well and tell the boy at the hatch to leave your share unmixed."

"That's a clever thought," Breyd said. She bit into the bread, tucked the bite into her cheek so she could speak around it. "So, how did Eriana ever think of it?" Xera spluttered, and it was enough to set the other two off.

But they weren't alone, Breyd suddenly realized. The entire mess was on edge, men laughing at horrible things or for no real reason at all. *Better than weeping. But we all sound half mad.*

Menlaeus came back to find them sitting together in the shade near the front gates. Lochria and Breyd were working on Lochria's leather arm brace; the other three Secchi leaned against the wall and were half asleep. He stood watching them for a few moments, then sat down and held out his hand.

"If I might. You have to rethread it. Like this." He reworked the straps, handed it back to her. "Try that." Lochria slipped it on.

"Better. Thank you." She took it off and stuffed it in her quiver. "Father said we may not be done for the day."

"No. They want us on the road again, but this time half-way up. Next horn."

"I had better go find him, then," Lochria said, and got to her feet.

"In the messes, with Akeros."

Menlaeus got up, helped Breyd up. "Xhem brought a basket for us from home. Nidya sent a flask of broth and another of herbed water for us to heat this evening. I left it in the barracks, under my cot. I told Tar we'd have leave but not to tell your mother; we'll surprise her. Niv says Creos spoke to her around midday, and even drank a little of Niddy's broth."

It was hotter than ever when the phalanx went out, but people still waited as near the gates or the barracks as they were allowed. A woman scrambled back as the Dyaddi passed her, and a group of soldiers who were standing next to the gates moved off abruptly as the company came up.

There was a delay at the gates. Breyd glanced up at the walls, though she had little hope of seeing Tarpaen. From the street, the outer wall wasn't visible. But Laius crouched next to the inner gates, drum balanced on his knee, and he was glaring down at them, teeth bared. His gaze raked across her face, moved across the phalanx. He gave no sign of having recognized her. *His eyes!* she thought, and shivered. *Why are they keeping him up there? He looks half mad.* But his signal came crisp and loud. There was nothing wrong with that. The outer gates were cleared and they started forward. Breyd blotted damp palms against her cloak and put Laius from her mind.

It was hot and windless, even so high above the plain, but the sun was sinking toward the west and would draw the heat with it before much longer. She slid the heavy wool off her shoulders and tugged the neck as far from her throat as much as she could. Kroserot ordered a halt at the top of the precipitous first turning, just short of the long, straight haul to the gates. "We'll watch from here. Loose formation; I want eyes on the lower road, the base of the cliff on both sides of it and the rock all the way up to here, both sides of the road."

They can't expect a sneak attack like yesterday's, Breyd thought in sudden panic. *Not here!* But a quick look around reassured her. She had climbed the rocks lower, as a child, but up here the drop was sheer all along the road right to the city; even if men could somehow clamber up the dangerously steep and unstable cliffs to this point, they'd never find a way onto the road. But they'd be seen long before they could get anywhere near the road, particularly from the general's vantage. *Perhaps they expect a suicide attack.* But Haffat could not be that desperate yet.

Not your business why, she reminded herself. *Watch.*

The first warning came some time later; one of the men clear across the road shouted, "Enemy, well down—there, sir!"

"See them," Kroserot shouted back. "Arrows—two volleys, fast!" At such a distance, they wouldn't be accurate. It was enough to discourage the Diye Haff, who retreated immediately. "Fools," Kroserot grumbled. "Utter fools. As you were, keep your eyes open, all of you."

Shadows were lengthening as the afternoon wore on; it must have been difficult for men trying to see movement off the left of the road, but Breyd could see clearly. The ground out there was rough and very steep, in places almost sheer. Where it wasn't, boulders littered the ground and broken stone lay everywhere. There were a few places a single man might hide, but he would have to reach them first. She would have seen.

A ragged double line of slingers toiled up the road; they were covered in mud. As they neared the phalanx, the captain glanced up, looked to both sides, and slowly edged his men to the other side of the road, away from the Dyaddi. He slowed as Kroserot came over.

"What news from below?"

"Hah." The captain spat noisily. "No one knows what we're supposed to be doing out there; we were nearly run down by our own cavalry."

"Must have been in a hurry."

"Someone's decided they have to either get that ballista back or burn it where it sits. No reason to take out your own men going after it. And then someone said it isn't even where they thought it was."

"Where is it?"

"Who knows," the captain growled. "Come on, lads. Nearly there."

* * *

There was no movement on the road for some time after that; Breyd could see the other phalanx at the base of the road, where they'd been all morning. There was too much shadow down there to make out much of the plain; probably the Diye Haff would begin to pull out soon. Her legs ached. Breyd looked out across the cliff face again. Shadows were longer and deeper; there wasn't anything else. No pattern to anything down on the plain. Two Mirikosi ships sat just off the jetty, out of arrow range; there were men all up and down the road. An empty wagon waiting with the other Dyaddi, down there. *For the wounded.* She swallowed and turned to look along the top of the eastern ridge, back toward the city. Tarpaen's horn was hardly ever quiet. *The general must see more from there than I can. And make more sense of it.*

Seventh horn was long past; a light wind came up, just enough to dry her sweaty face. Earlier there had been more foot soldiers, now she saw mostly chariots and horse. She drank a little water, tucked a bit of bread in her cheek. Kroserot clapped his hands ringingly. "All right! Break formation, walk a little." Menlaeus stretched, rubbed his shoulders, and went back to talk to Lapario. Breyd dug her fists into the small of her back and turned to say something to Lochria, but Lochria had her hands full at the moment with Bechates; he was clenching and unclenching his hands, sure sign of distress. *All this waiting.* She walked up the road a ways and back down. Menlaeus handed her his bottle and some dates.

Kroserot clapped his hands again. "All right! Open formation, and eyes open, all of you!"

A high, desperate blare of horns echoed from the cliffs above them; Breyd spun around and stared. The rock ledge east of the city had come alive. Men spilled recklessly down the rocks, leapt to the ground, and raced for the gates. Men were shouting, screaming curses, and the sound of swords clashing into shields rose above everything. A single horn rose above the rest—Tarpaen's signal.

Kroserot swore wildly. "Around, now! We guard against attack from down the hill, nothing else!" Another signal, picked up by another horn and then another, echoing across the walls and all around the city. "Enemy at the base of the outer wall," Kroserot interpreted for them. "The Dyaddi hold and they're being backed." Breyd was trembling; *she* knew the Dyaddi up there were fighting, she could feel the edge of their killing fury. "You Dyaddi, hold here, that is an *order!*"

He barely had the words out of his mouth when a clatter of rocks on both sides of the road and just downhill of them brought him back around. The captain stared blankly. "How did they get there? How did they get so close, and we didn't see them?" With a shout, men threw themselves onto the road and up it, short spears at the ready. The phalanx tightened and set its spears.

For Creos. And for all of us. Breyd let her spear fall, drew the sword and set her back against Menlaeus'—and welcomed the goddess' fury.

General Piritos swore furiously under his breath, then pointed at Tarpaen and raised his voice; he had to, to make himself heard above the fighting down there. "To the light infantry under Iltiar, out by the north gate and the main to trap these. To Dyaddi in the barracks, ready. To the company under Edrimon, maintain your position." Tarpaen nodded and sent the signals; Piritos glared down at the narrow ledge and then along the road. Tar jumped as the general began to swear aloud. He had never yet heard Piritos angry, and this frightened him more than the sudden attack on the gates. *But how did they get there?* he wondered.

Piritos must have been thinking along similar lines. "They must have climbed onto the ridge last night and waited until this hour, when we would be tired and not expect such an attack. But why would Haffat send them? He must know they will never breach the gates. He can see Dyaddi—he intends something else while I am distracted." He frowned, tugged at his beard, and laid a hand on Tar's shoulder. "To the commander upon the southern walls near the Shepherd's gate, watch for enemy coming across the plateau—wait."

"I haven't such a call," Tarpaen began unhappily, but Piritos was already shaking his head.

"To a runner, to come and carry word." But one of the two aides at Piritos's side was already shouting that command; across the gate, one of the messenger boys jumped up and sped off, along the inner wall. "Another messenger, quickly: To those inside the city who wait with the old men, to all those who are to come onto the wall and hurl the stones, be ready. Two hands of them between the walls at the ladders, two more hands waiting along the inner wall—and two in the street below." He was tugging at his beard once more and scowling ferociously.

Laius' drum beat out an order—*too fast,* Tarpaen realized. But Laius would be affected by all the fighting, so close that he could hear men screaming. *If he could see, down there*—He didn't dare look; the Dyadd at his feet was a blur of blood-red smoke and impossible speed. No one could move that fast! Dead men lay everywhere, all around them. He swallowed, looked the other way as the gates opened just enough to let a small company of light infantry edge through. "Get down to those who guard the avenue," Piritos bellowed at his aides, "and get the civilians out of the street! Clear the whole area!" He swore so suddenly and shockingly that Tarpaen would have dropped the horn had it not been strapped to his lips. But he had cause. The phalanx at the base of the road had been engaged by an overwhelming company of foot and cavalry, and well back of them, he could see the captured Ghezrathi ballista.

"To the phalanx under Edrimon—no, cancel that; Edrimon will hold, he must. And he has Pairs. Ah!" he added and he sounded grimly satisfied. "I knew it; there is the rest of it. To the phalanx under Kroserot, men climbing the ledges upon both your flanks!" Too late for that warning, though Tar sent it anyway; the middle phalanx was already engaged. But a company forced its way past the men at the base of the road; the Dyaddi were surrounded, the rest of the phalanx overwhelmed, and two full companies of horse shoved through what was left of Edrimon's men and came on at a gallop.

Something crashed to the road high behind the middle phalanx and rolled away, dropping from the steep side and vanishing in shadow. "To the phalanx under Kroserot, ballista." Another stone, at least the size of a man's head, slammed into the road and rolled crazily down and then slid from the road in a pile of rubble. Kroserot waved his spear to acknowledge the warning. Two of his men fell to enemy spear, vanishing as had the stones into shadow and rubble.

The ballista sent stone after stone, without much effect; one or two fell among their own men, driving them into the Dyaddi. "They try to adjust it, to make certain of the range," Piritos muttered. He glanced down, looked along the wall both ways; he could barely tell which were his and which enemy, except where the Pairs were. *He thought that if he threw more men against the Dyaddi, they would be over-borne? This day will cost him dearly.* He looked up as the ballista began to work once more and a stone came whistling down to the left of the road, short of the upper phalanx and offside. "They do not get any better." Piritos smiled grimly, but the smile was wiped from his face a breath later as a horrid blast of sound slammed into him. A sheet of flame roared up from the rocks where the thing had fallen. The men nearest it were thrown back into their companions and several lay where they had fallen.

"Dear goddess," Piritos breathed. "They are using Gryptiosi Fire! There is an Ergardi down there!" He stared down the hill, but could see nothing of the ballista for the fighting this side of it. "Find a boy, at once, send him to warn Tephys. No, bid her come this instant! Tell the boy say this also, if she argues: Ergardi." He had not taken his eyes from the road; Tarpaen stared at him. The general's face had gone gray.

Another stone, this one of plain rock—but the one immediately after exploded, directly behind the phalanx. For one heart-stoppingly long moment, he could see nothing of Kroserot's company, only oily black smoke and a sheet of flame. *Father—Breyd!* He couldn't make out red anywhere, where were they? The general touched his shoulder. "Boy," he said urgently; his eyes remained fixed on the fire down there.

"Sir?"

"To—I cannot think! To the barracks, whoever commands, heavy infantry and a company of slingers to cover that phalanx, and to Kroserot," he drew a deep breath and let it out in a hard gust, "bid him retreat, but in good order."

"Sir." Tarpaen swallowed; for one horrid moment, he could not think either. He closed his eyes, sent the first command, then began the second; someone down in the street shouted, "The surrender! We are surrendering!" A woman's voice topped his hysterically and someone shouted them all to silence. The general turned to bellow an order at the aide on the inner walls. Tarpaen jumped back as something whistled between them; Piritos staggered into his signaler, then clutched at his leg; Tarpaen stared in shock. *That is an arrow, someone's shot him!* Another slammed into the general's shoulder, and he sagged at the knees and fell. "Sound the call!" he managed between clenched teeth and bent forward to grip the shaft in his thigh. Tarpaen gasped for air and began again.

Stars exploded in his head—something heavy and ungiving had slammed into his head, but from behind him. Laius' huge hands gripped his shoulders and kept him upright; Laius' voice grated against his ear. "Traitor! You and he both, to all of us! You cannot sound the surrender before we have cause!"

"Laius, it isn't!" Laius tore the horn from his face and threw it aside. "Laius, you aren't supposed to be out here, go back!"

"Aye, you would like that," Laius hissed; his eyes were all pupil, his teeth bared. "All the glory for you and your sister—and none for Laius, is that it? Well, if you want glory, have some now!" He lifted Tarpaen as though he were no weight at all, took the two short steps that would bring them to the wall, and threw him over.

"You fool!" A pained whisper; General Piritos dragged himself to his feet and leaned heavily against the stones. "He called the retreat for one company only, what have you done?" Laius did not seem to hear him. "Look out there! No one has laid down his arms, no one retreats but those on the road! Those before the walls—do they retreat?"

Laius looked down the wall. There were bodies everywhere, blood smeared up the wall and splattering the stones; men screaming and women's shrieks and curses. *They all fight,* he thought blankly. He glanced down the road, to see a few men edging slowly back up toward the gates, dragging other with them. A stone hit the road and rolled down into their pursuers, who leapt wildly back. "They all fight," he whispered. He looked straight down. "And I have killed my friend." But Tarpaen lay on a sprawl of enemy dead. He looked stunned, as though he couldn't remember how to breathe. No one had seen him there yet, even the Pair had moved away from the wall to attack men backing toward the ridge. But others came running from the other side of the gate, bloody swords and spears ready to kill.

Tarpaen rolled over and tried to sit up; Laius heard him yelp and he fell back. "What have I done? Tar—Tar, I didn't mean—!" Tarpaen could not possibly have heard his voice above everything else; he was struggling to free his dagger.

The newcomers halted and one pointed a sword; they had seen him. "No!" He stared wildly around him, then snatched the general's sword from its scabbard and leapt from the wall.

Tarpaen shook his head to clear it. Something had happened to his eyes, all he could see were red shadows and his face was sticky. He drew an arm across them and it came away red. *Blood. Mine or someone's.* He stared at the point of his dagger blankly, then jumped convulsively as something landed hard next to him. Laius lay very still, his head bent at an impossible angle. His eyes stared blindly above his friend's head, his teeth were bared. Tarpaen cried out, then turned sharply. Someone coming—he couldn't see! *Ours, theirs! Oh, Laius, you great, damned fool, what have you done?*

He crawled awkwardly, backing away, hands outstretched for balance; his palm fell across a sword. Somehow, he caught it up, brought it around, two-handed, got it in front of him as he backed more, and finally found his footing. It hurt to stand, and every breath tore something. *I am already dead, then.* He swallowed. *All right. But I will not go alone.* He set his shoulders against the wall, rubbed his eyes with the heel of his hand and gripped the sword two-handed again and bared his teeth at the Diye Haff, who leaned on his own sword and grinned at him.

Tar lunged; the sword's point caught on armor; his left leg gave out; the Diye Haff grabbed his shoulder and flung him back into the wall; brought his sword up and swung it backhanded across Tarpaen's exposed throat.

General Piritos lay facedown upon the low pedestal where he had been standing. His sword lay on the ground, under his dead signaler.

Another ball of Gryptiosi Fire slammed into the road, a little behind the company and just off the road; Menlaeus was thrown into Breyd by the blast, and both fell. He landed on top of her, a dead weight.

No—not that, not this. Her eyes were full of dirt or cinders; black smoke covered everything. It was suddenly deathly still, except for a faint ringing between her ears. She could not even hear the horn sounding the retreat. She tried to drag herself up, then to one side or the other; her hands were bleeding from a hundred little stinging scrapes when she finally dragged her feet loose and tried to sit.

Aroepe lay facedown an arm's length away; her hand clenched convulsively, began to feel blindly around her for something; just past her was one of the phalanx. His eyes were open, staring through her. Thrown across him, facedown—she couldn't tell who it was; Xera sat up and began to crawl across the road, her mouth open as though she must be screaming in pain. A flame leapt up behind her and went with her; Duplos threw himself on his daughter and began to beat the cloak out with his bare hands. He was screaming, she could see his mouth move frantically, but still couldn't hear anything.

Father! *They'll come for us, now, while we're helpless, they'll kill us all!* But Jocasa and her Prime stood back to back in the middle of the road, between the company and the Diye Haff and the least red haze lit their faces. What was left of the enemy stepped slowly back—they feared the Pair, but perhaps they also feared their own ballista.

She wanted to scream and swear, she would have wept from fury, but there were no tears left in her. *Father. I couldn't save you after all, could I? I'll stay with you, then.* She pulled herself onto her hands and knees and crawled to him.

There was a little blood on his face, running in a narrow trickle down his neck. *A cut, a small stone, nothing more.* But his brow was furrowed with pain and blood stained the hem of his pleats; as she stared at it, the stain spread. *Help. Someone, someone has to help me, he'll die!* They might have already been dead; no one seemed to see them. *Someone—the city, why don't they send us aid? They must have seen—where are they? Why have they not sent down from the gates to aid us?* Kroserot could have said, but she could see Kroserot from here, or what was left of him. She bit her lip, hard, and turned quickly away.

Her hearing returned between one breath and the next: Xera's high, thin wail; Duplos shouting, "Hold still, let me get it off!" Someone in the other direction was coughing.

"Father." Her voice sounded odd; too high, tremulous. He shifted uncomfortably, opened his eyes, and found her hand.

"So. I guess after all we could not cheat your vision," he whispered.

She shook her head wildly. "No! That isn't true, I

won't—I won't have it!" But he squeezed her fingers and shook his head, a little.

"I can't move. And my leg—ah! Don't!" He was panting, gasping for air. "Don't—don't touch it, don't look, I can tell, it's bad. Don't remember me by that. Go, daughter; save yourself."

"No." She clung to his hand. "No! A Secchi does not leave her Prime!"

"That is not what they taught us."

"I don't care. They'll send someone, I'll keep you safe, until they do."

"No. If you die—"

"I will not leave you. *This* Secchi does not leave her Prime." He sighed a little and his eyes closed, but his fingers gripped her hand, hard. She bent to set a kiss on his brow.

She was never certain after whether her lips touched his face, or if the next explosion separated them before she could reach him.

14

General Piritos fought air into his lungs, then gasped as someone caught hold of his arm and the arrow in his shoulder shifted gratingly. One of his aides knelt beside him, staring at him anxiously. His face rested on the stone where he ordinarily stood. He frowned; he couldn't remember how he had gotten there. "Sir?" The aide's face was almost white. "Sir, how badly are you hurt? We must get you down from here at once." But Piritos was already shaking his head.

"It is not so bad." He edged himself back from the stone, then hissed through clenched teeth as his hand hit the shaft of the second arrow. The aide stared at him in shocked disbelief. "Truly." It was only half a lie; both wounds were beginning to throb wildly, but neither was immediately life threatening, and he hadn't bled very much. "I dare not leave, think of the panic among the companies out there, if they could no longer see me on the wall. Wait." He drew a deep breath, a second, then nodded. "I can bear it. At least—here. Cut the shafts. Be careful, they aren't bleeding much at the moment and I would rather you did not start them again! Leave more shaft; I want no surgeon digging for the points." The aide eyed him doubtfully but did as he was ordered. "Good." Sweat ran down the general's face; the aide blotted it. "Now. Help me to my feet, where I should be. I—yes." He set his teeth once more. The landscape faded very briefly, stabilized as he drew a deep breath. "I fear I will need you to stand there, where I can lean against you. Can you do that? Get help if not. My signaler—" He sent his eyes sideways, then remembered.

"He—down there," the aide nodded toward the wall. He looked sick. At that moment, Nabid himself came pelting along the wall, horn in hand. Piritos waited until the captain of the signal company had caught his breath a little and nodded he was ready; he swallowed bile, fought his mind clear of everything save what truly must matter, and said, "To the phalanx under Kroserot, retreat at speed." He took the cloth another aide held up, blotted his brow, then took the cup a third man brought. "Thank you, all of you." His eyes were back on the battlefield. "To the common chariot, turn east toward the river, attack comes." Nabid, his mind reeling and his heart sick, concentrated upon the complex pattern of calls. If the general could manage, he decided grimly, so could he.

Tephys came up the ladder from the street; she was breathless and utterly white. "How close are they?" Piritos frowned, momentarily unable to remember why he had sent for her. "Ergardi?" Tephys prompted. She seemed to see him for the first time; her eyes widened. "But you have been injured!"

"And men are dead," Piritos interrupted her harshly. "Yes, I know it. I will survive and if I stay here, so may others. There is no time for your foolishness, hold to the point, priestess! Ergardi—yes. Look down the road, below the straight, at what lies there."

Tephys edged toward the outer wall, looked where he indicated, and drew her breath in sharply. Bodies lay everywhere; oily black smoke rose from the road and little fires still burned here and there. "Ah, goddess!"

"Yes. The ballista is down lower."

"I see it. What company is there—ah, no, there are Dyaddi out there!"

"There are dead men and women. And men down there and along the road who came upon us unseen by anyone until too late. Magic, priestess. Whatever you can do to prevent it happening again—do it, go." One of the aides came to draw her aside as Piritos waved a dismissive hand and turned back to Nabid, another order already upon his lips.

"A half-strength phalanx," the aide said, rather apologetically. It was doubtful anyone had ever before seen the High Priestess spoken to as if she were a slack young soldier. "There were five Pairs as part of it. But there are dead enemy out there, too. They let that fire fall upon their own men!"

Tephys laughed mirthlessly. "But to an Ergardi, there *is* no such thing as that: 'their own men,' for they are not men. Didn't you know?" She turned toward the inner wall. "Whatever can be done, I'll do. Tell the general that when he is again among us. See he is tended, we can ill afford to lose *him*."

Piritos gazed down along the base of the outer wall. The light infantry had backed the few Diye Haff still standing down the wall; two Dyaddi clung to each other just beneath him. He shifted his head cautiously so he could look down the road. The phalanx was finally moving again, men carrying or dragging what they could of their company, others limping or walking slowly, leaning upon each other for support. There were red-clads out there, moving toward the city, but his eyes and mind would not function properly; he couldn't tell how many.

Endimion and his phalanx had enclosed what remained of the company which had attacked them; the ballista was burning furiously. A rapidly retreating trio of Diye Haff chariot that must hold the personal guard and the Ergardi who had primed the ballista and covered the attack. "To—" he hesitated. There was no one even close to them, no one who could have caught them or cut them off before they reached the river. And Tephys had not said what fate might hold for any who tried to kill or capture an Ergardi.

He shrugged and let it go, then said to the aide who stood bracing him upright, "Tell me tonight, to ask the priestess how many such weapons the Ergardi may have. Tell me tonight, to ask the priestess how a mortal man may take or slay an Ergardi. Tell me tonight, to decide with the captains how best to take back the fords of the Oryon, and with what company, and when." A shrill, wordless cry broke his concentration; Kroserot's sorely broken and greatly reduced phalanx had reached the gates. He bit his lip. "Tell me tonight, to decide how best to reinforce the road against this ambush, and how to prevent another such surprise attack from the north." His own pain was bearable, if he did not breath too deeply and was careful to move very slowly if he moved at all. *Think what must be done; you have no time for your own pain.*

She must have lost consciousness; there was a gap in her memory. Somehow, she was on the other side of the road, her leg hanging over a sheer drop; something was crushing the breath out of her. A limp arm flopped across her face, and the metal plates sewn to his armor were cutting into the back of her neck. She could no longer feel her hands, but her

lower arms were hot. *Burned.* She had burned her hand in
the brazier once, and Menlaeus had— "Oh, no. Oh, no." She
fought to free herself but whoever lay across her was too
heavy. She moaned. "Someone—please, someone come."
The weight was rolled away from her, a shadow crossed her
face and someone rolled her to her back, caught her by the
armpits and began to drag her. Something wrong with her
eyes—her whole face was sticky and she couldn't see too
well. "Easy, lass, it's your people, don't fight us, it's all
right, you're not bad hurt. We'll carry you, get you back to
the barracks."

Were they mad? She shook her head, fought to free her-
self but whoever held her shifted his grip and held her down.
"Don't, let me go, I'm all right, but Menlaeus was hurt—my
Prime—" She raised her voice. "Father—Father? Menlaeus?
Father, where are you?"

"Lass—Breyd—"

"My Prime—I can't go without him! Father, can you hear
me? It's Breyd! Menlaeus—Father—?"

They were talking just above her; someone else said impatiently, "Look, we can't stay here and besides, he's—" He
was shushed violently.

"He's what—*what is he?*" She flailed out in panic,
shrieked as her forearm scraped across rough cloth. One of
them stooped, picked her up, and began walking uphill.
"Menlaeus is all right, he's fine," the person who carried her
said soothingly. "He's ahead, just up there. There, see?"

She shook her head; she couldn't seem to get her eyelids
apart. There might have been something red up there, but he
was lying to her, "That isn't Menlaeus; he'd never have left
me!"

"He didn't want to, they took him on, it's all right, let's
just get you up there, you'll see."

But the bond between them pulled her the other way.
They were leaving him back there, wounded and bleeding,
with night on the way and Diye Haff waiting. "No!" But the
goddess bond had already sapped her dreadfully, and the
blast had taken the last of her strength. Everything faded.

She woke to pain—hot pain along the backs of both her
forearms. The noise then; men shouting all at once, too
many of them; a woman's high-pitched wail, someone weeping. Her head throbbed and she could not understand what

anyone around her said. Someone dripped cool water on her face and blotted it with a soft cloth; it smelled like the barracks well. She pushed it aside fretfully, opened her eyes rather cautiously, and rolled onto one side to push herself upright. Her arms throbbed furiously. She gazed at them dully: The skin was very pink in two long strips from her wrist nearly to her elbow; the hair was singed away, but it hadn't blistered. *Painful. Not—so bad.*

"Breyd. Are you all right now? There was blood all over your face, but it wasn't yours." She sat back on her heels rather cautiously; her arms still hurt but not as badly. Two of the phalanx crouched beside her, watching her anxiously. They were filthy, so covered in black soot as to be nearly unrecognizeable, otherwise seemingly not hurt. She tried to think who they were but couldn't remember names. "You'll have to get those tended to. Maybe they'll let you go home. The hospital—they won't have room for something that—"

Something missing. His voice ran over her, unheeded. Missing— Someone— *Dear goddess.* "My father—my Prime. Menlaeus. He isn't here!"

One of them rolled onto a knee and stood. "I don't see him. That doesn't mean much, it's mad in here."

"He isn't here!" she shouted, and he stared at her. "He's—he's out there, you lied to me!"

They looked at each other helplessly and one of them edged back a little, but the other reached for her fingers and tried to smile. "I'm sorry; we didn't lie, though, we just had to grab whoever we could save and go, before more of those *things* fell among us. I am sorry, Secchi. But we were almost the last; he might have come in ahead of us."

"No!" she whispered. "He is not here, I would know." She snatched her hand away from him and shook her head wildly. "He's out there, on that road, he was bleeding, barely conscious. They'll take him prisoner, they'll kill him, don't you understand?" All at once she felt a tug on the bond between them, as though it had been stretched even longer. The bond itself held. *Someone has him, has taken him.* He could not have moved by himself, and she was not there to protect him as she had sworn. Because of these. The two men with their sagging mouths, the sorrow in their eyes—or was it guilt? She wanted to throw herself on them, to rend them with her bare hands, her blades; it took an effort that left her sick and panting not to do just that.

They had brought her here. And they were between her and Menlaeus. *This cannot be.*

One of them shook his head. "I am sorry, then. Because if he is not here, it must be—I am afraid—"

"No! He is not dead!" She tried to stand, but her legs would not hold her at first, and the fighting ground faded alarmingly. *I left him out there, I deserted him.* She staggered up, lurched to her feet, somehow stayed upright. "Don't you dare say he's dead!" They stared up at her; she panted, fell back a step, caught her balance again. "You dared separate me from my Prime?" Fury and fear gave her a sudden jolt of strength; her voice rang out across the fighting ground, silencing men nearby. They turned to stare.

"Secchi—Breyd," the man who had held her said unhappily, "the fire-stone from that ballista separated you two before that, and we only did what we had to—what we could."

Someone laid a hand on her shoulder, she turned and shoved him, hard, spun back. "You left him, out there on the road! He'll die out there! I have to go, he needs me."

"No, you can't!" The two put themselves between her and the gate.

"I can—I have to, I can find him!"

"We can't let you. You're hurt, it's dangerous out there."

"Can't?" Her voice rose shrilly, more men turned to stare. "You can't order a Secchi to desert her Prime! I can—he's alive. *You left him!*"

"We had no choice!" One of the two men, finally stung past pity to anger of his own, shouted back at her. "You're mad, girl! You can't go out there. They'll kill you and you're in no condition to go anywhere!"

Words. Meaningless words. They would build a wall of such words if she let them, a wall to keep her in. "Get out of my way!" she said flatly.

"You fool of a girl, you won't get five steps!" the second man yelled at her; his face was deeply red and his eyes hot.

"My Prime needs me, get out of my way!" He stepped forward to grab her, and actually had a hand on her elbow when she drew the dagger and slashed at him; burned skin screamed at her, but she could ignore it for now—she would have to. He swore wildly and leapt out of her way; other men who had come to see what the matter was backed away as she turned round once, to let them all see the dagger. "I will kill the first man who tries to stop me. Move, all of you. Menlaeus is out there, somewhere, he's been hurt. He's bleeding. I will go find him, alone, if you are all so cowardly!"

Someone swore and snatched at the knife; she spun into him and slashed out. He yelped furiously and fell to his knees, clutching his hand to his chest. "Put down that knife, girl!" someone roared at her.

"Come and take it!" she screamed. "But get out of my way! My Prime is out there—he's been hurt, he's bleeding—he will *die!* Don't you understand that?"

"Lass, no." That was Ridlo—she remembered the name now, the man who had carried her. He took one small step forward, hands spread wide, his voice and face both full of pity. "You cannot know how bad it was out there, you were not sensible. Truly, he will be all right if he was only injured."

They were wasting time, and she had none to spare. She held the dagger between them, point toward his belly and bared her teeth. "I am not a child, nor a lass to coddle; I am Secchi and that man out there my Prime! How *dare* you have separated us? How *dare* you have brought me and not Menlaeus, and if you could not bring him here, how *dare* you have brought me? No!" Her voice rose to a near-shriek. "Lay that hand upon me, Ridlo, and I'll cut it from your arm. *Move aside!*" She leapt toward him. Startled, he gave back, and men on both sides of him fell away. She could see an opening, there; she shifted her grip on the blade slightly and began a sideways stalk, but none of the men nearest seemed to wish to test her. And then someone came straight through the crowd, scattering men and swearing furiously. She spun around, but Grysis slapped the knife up and gripped both her elbows.

"What is this? *What is this?*" His face nearly touched hers; his grip tightened until his knuckles were white, and the dagger fell to the ground. She felt him kick it aside.

"Let go of me! My Prime is down there!"

He was shaking her fiercely. "And this is how you shame him, and the bond and yourself?" That reached her where nothing else could have; she went suddenly limp in his grasp. He waited, she shook her head. "He is outside the city, you say? And alive? You are certain of this?"

"He was—was bleeding," she whispered.

"Never mind that. You know whether he is alive or dead, you can tell so much, because of the bond. Is—he—yet—alive?" He spaced the words carefully, waited until she managed to nod, then nodded in turn and gave her one last little, almost gentle shake. "All right. Then wait a little, let me deal with this." He glanced behind him, jerked his head. One of the boys came forward, a cup in his hands. "I will settle this, you drink."

She was shaking her head once more, half-frantic already, panic threatening to swallow her whole. "I don't—no, I don't want—"

"I did not ask!" Grysis snapped. "It is an order, *Secchi!* Drink!" He released her and stepped back cautiously, as though ready to snatch at her once more, but she let the boy hand her the cup. He waited until she had swallowed. *Horrible; someone let the wine sour.*

"If I drink all of this, I cannot—"

"All of it," Grysis said inexorably and folded his arms. "And yes, you can. You are First Secchi, and a brave young woman; you can do whatever you must." He deliberately turned his back on her. "Now, then, who can tell me where the First Prime was out there? Who saw him last?"

She drained the cup and licked her lips. They were numb. She touched them with her fingers, patted her cheeks—they were numb, too. *He dosed it—I trusted him, and he's ruined everything.* Her knees gave and she sagged; Grysis caught her and lowered her to the ground. The cup rolled away. She swallowed dryly, looked up; Grysis knelt over her. "What have you done? My Prime!"

"I am sorry, Breyd," he whispered. "But I have no choice, any more than you have. You are hurt and so weak, you would die trying to find him—if they did not kill you first. But no one can go out of the city alone, you know that."

"I have to." He was fading away, everything was blurring, red; her voice faded. He touched her face, turned away, and got to his feet. She couldn't move, but she could still hear him, shouting at the men around them.

"Stupid fools! Don't you know better than to cross a Secchi in such a state? Don't you realize *this* is how those tales of unstable Secchi came about—when one is torn from her Prime?"

* * *

The air was cool but windless; she could smell Nidya's heavily spiced lentil soup, and someone was weeping. "Shhh." Niddy's voice. "Daughter, please."

Nevvia's voice was thick with tears, and shook so she could hardly understand the words. "I'm—Mother, I'm all right. I won't leave her. I can't leave my baby."

Breyd blinked, hissed as something cold and sticky was laid over her left arm. "Breyd? Baby—baby, I'm sorry, I didn't mean to hurt you."

"Mother, please, help me to sit up."

"Oh, no. Mother, tell her she can't!"

"It's all right, Nev. Breyd?" Breyd nodded and Nidya wrapped an arm around her shoulders. She drew a deep breath, a second, and cautiously sat up. Everything receded alarmingly; she let her eyes sag shut and took in more air. "Here, hand me that, Nevvia. I have her, it's all right. Bring me another piece of linen, it's on your chair. Child," she added gently, "I've put my yarrow salve on your arms and I have wraps for them. It will ease the pain." Nidya was gentle and the salve was already helping a little, but both Breyd's arms were throbbing wildly by the time the last end was tucked in place.

"Mother?" she whispered. Nevvia stood in front of her, her face swollen with weeping; tears ran unchecked down her face. "Mother, it's all right, see, it isn't so bad? I'm not—I'm not really hurt. And Father—"

Nidya got up and wrapped her arms around her daughter; Nevvia was sobbing, trying to catch her breath, and Breyd wasn't even sure she'd heard.

The pain faded a little, the hammering pulse in her arms eased, but the panic was rising again. *He is alive, the bond still holds, I can't—* Her mother was still weeping wrackingly, it was cutting her like knives. *She can't—she has to stop, I can't bear this.* Father. How long had she been here, how much of his time had they wasted? *I have to go, he's out there, I have to find him.* She shifted her weight cautiously. *If I can just get my feet under me.*

Niverren came running from the room she shared with Creos. "Don't—you'll fall, you're swaying where you sit!"

"I—Niv, help me," she whispered. Niverren's face was blotchy, her eyes swollen and red. "Creos—he's not—"

She shook her head wildly and buried her face in Breyd's shoulder. *Not Creos. It's Father, she's afraid for him too. But*

I can find him, he isn't—! Her fingers felt swollen, they
wouldn't close; she patted Niverren's hair. It was tangled
and matted, and felt awful. She couldn't have even washed
it or oiled it since Creos came home. "Niv, help me up, I
have to— Father's still alive, it's all right, but I have to find
him."

"It's Tar," Niverren whispered. "Tar's dead."

"Tar? No! No, he can't be, what fool's rumor is this? He
was on the wall this afternoon, I saw him up there—I heard
him!" Nevvia drew a shuddering breath, tried to say something, but her voice broke and Nidya drew her close once
more. "Niv, there's some mistake, there was fighting before
the walls, but nothing on them." They had gone mad out
there, all of them.

"The men who brought you home said," Niverren whispered dully. "They found him out there, by the gates." She
shook her head helplessly; Breyd patted her hair. "They
couldn't tell us anything else. Not why he was there, not
anything!" It was a mistake, that was all, Breyd thought. A
horrible, tragic mistake, but such things did happen, another
man of similar body type, possibly another horn signaler.
Her heart sank. Xhem came slowly from the storage into the
dim light. His face was pale, his eyes puffy, and he was
trembling violently. *Oh, goddess. If Xhem—* He was always
there, in the barracks or around them somewhere. He would
know. She held out a hand, but he didn't see it; he dropped
down next to the fire, hugged his thin legs to his body and
screwed his fists in both eyes.

My brother—oh, Tar. She swallowed. No. It had to be a
mistake; they wouldn't let him out there when things were
calm, and in fighting— But he served the general, Piritos
wouldn't have let him go. *I'll find out; someone will know,
when I get back to the barracks. After—*

"Niverren, please. I'm all right, you have to help me up."
Her sister stepped back and looked at her blankly, then slid
her hands carefully behind Breyd's elbows and held onto her
until she stopped swaying. Breeze rattled the woven leaf
sleeping canopies on the roof, lifting damp hair from her
forehead and chilling her breast. "My armor— Niddy,
where's my armor?"

Nidya pointed toward the main room. "It's in there; you'll
have to sleep in there." Her voice was husky. "A little soup
first, then—"

"No. I'm all right. Niddy, I have to go, Father's alive, he'll be all right, but I have to go to him!"

Nevvia pushed away from her mother and threw herself desperately at her youngest daughter; Breyd staggered back into Niverren. "No! *Don't go! Don't leave me!*"

"Mother, I have to, he's out there, beyond the walls. I can feel him, don't you understand that? They don't know where to look for him, but I do, I can find him!" She wrapped her arms cautiously around her mother's shuddering body and looked desperately at her grandmother. "Niddy, tell her, help me! I can't stay here, the bond is still there."

"You're hurt," Nidya said; she came up and took Nevvia's shoulders, but Nevvia shook her off violently and tightened her grasp on her daughter.

"No! I won't let you go!"

"Father's hurt, too! Niddy, I *can't* leave him." Nevvia was sobbing wildly. Breyd swallowed, plucking at her mother's arms. *She's trying to hold me, she's between me and Father, he'll die!* "Niddy, I almost killed a man in the barracks," she lowered her voice to a frantic whisper. "Because he wouldn't let me. It's not just *me*, it's this—what the goddess did, I'm *him* as much as I am me, and I'm what she made me, *I can't help myself!* Get her away from me, before—take her, let me go!" Niverren blanched and her mouth sagged; she set her jaw then and caught hold of Nevvia's near arm, Nidya took the other. Breyd was trembling almost as wildly as her mother now. Nevvia fought them both wildly.

"Don't leave me! If you go, I know I'll never see you again!"

"Mother—I *have* to. I'll find Father, I'll bring him home to you."

"Breyd!" Nevvia went limp and fell into Niverren's arms. Nidya let her go and came over to grip Breyd's shoulder.

"I won't try to stop you, I know a little about this, remember I had a friend who was Secchi. But you aren't strong enough to help him, and you'd never get past the gates, even if you could walk that far they'd stop you, and they won't let you back in the barracks—they said. Here, come with me." Breyd tensed, but the older woman turned her and helped her into the main room. "We'll manage here. Can you control this at all, child?"

"I don't know," she whispered. "Grandmother, don't try to stop me, please don't get between me and that door. I know what I did, why they won't let me back in the barracks. I'm—not safe."

To her relief, Nidya simply nodded and said, "I understand that. If I let you go, now, what will you do, though? You're weak. Go to Tephys," she said suddenly. "She did this, the things that made the bond. You'll tear yourself apart like this, Breyd, go to her, see if she can help. Will you do that?" Breyd swallowed, tried to think. *Tephys. She's powerful, she meets with the general and talks to the prince; she has to help me.* She nodded finally.

"I'll go to Tephys. I swear it, Grandmother." *Tephys will help me. She and Denota both owe me that.*

"All right, then. Your armor and your cloak are there, everything you had on or with you when they brought you. I'll help you as best I can; let me get you something to drink first."

Drink. I won't drink, Breyd thought, but she nodded again and Nidya left her. She found the cloak, the armor, the greaves sitting inside her shield. Her arrows were gone, but the javelins were still fastened to the inside of the shield, and her sword was still in the baldric.

Nidya came back with a cup and held it for her to drink. "Don't look at me like that, it isn't drugged," she said crisply. "It's water, with a little of the vineyard common red, and you know *I* would never lie to you. Drink."

It was cool, familiar; it soothed her throat and eased the muscles a little. "Thank you, Grandmother."

"Of course."

"How long have I been here?"

"It's not quite ninth horn, almost midnight."

"Too long—it could have been worse. Tell them—" She couldn't say that. *But I will find him.* "Tell them I'll find out about Tar. I'll—I'll come as soon as I can. I swear I'll come back, tell Mother that."

"I'll try. Here, how do you put this thing on?" But a small, thin voice behind them said, "I know. I can do it." Xhem took the breastplate from his grandmother and helped her into it. Small but capable hands separated the straps. Nidya gripped his shoulder, leaned over to kiss Breyd's cheek.

"I'll go back to your mother. Child, be careful." She turned and was gone before Breyd could say anything.

Xhem worked in silence, snugging the breastplate, and the

greaves; he helped her settle the weaponry where it belonged. She took the helmet from him. "Thank you. You did that very well."

"They won't have you back. They said so." His wavery voice caught her at the door.

"Won't?"

"Cannot. The hospital barracks are full. There isn't room for any more."

Hospital— She shook her head sharply. "I won't go there anyway."

"But you can't fight like that, they said so. I heard when— when they left the barracks with you, earlier. They—my brother, Tar, they won't bring him home."

"No. Of course not."

"Grysis and—and someone else, one of the general's aides, they were arguing about it. About you."

"Grysis," she spat.

"No, B–Breyd. You have him wrong, truly." His voice was gathering strength as he talked. "He wanted you to stay among the soldiers, those who would understand you, but they said—the aide said it wasn't safe, and that man—"

"I know. I—hurt someone."

"You were burned and it wasn't safe for you to stay, so he had to send you. I came, when they brought you. I thought you might want—might need—" He swallowed, fell silent rubbed his eyes with his fists.

Breyd look down at him. *Tar. I can do this one thing for you, can't I? I can take care of the boy for you.* "Thank you, Xhem. That was clever of you." *Tephys—I promised I would go to her, and I will. But not now. Grysis knows, he—he said he understands. If he was really arguing for me, like Xhem says—if he can help, right now. I can't waste any more time!* "All right. I cannot even go into the barracks, it seems. But you can." *Why does that sound familiar?* She set it aside, unimportant. Xhem sniffed, hard. "If you mean what you said, I can use your help, Xhem. If I have not already ruined my chances with Grysis."

"No. I heard him telling them all, he was so angry with them, even the man you—even him, for not realizing what they did to you."

"He'll help me, we'll go. Now."

"Are you sure you can walk that far, Breyd?"

"I can. I can do whatever I have to do." He smiled in turn,

though his eyes were still dark with misery, then edged past
her to pull the door ajar and let her out. As he followed, the
door was pulled from his fingers. Niverren stood there, her
face gaunt, a wet cloth dangling from her fingers. "You cannot go! Breyd, you're hurt, you can barely stand up!"

She sighed wearily. "Niv, please. There isn't any time,
and I can't stay. Father is not dead. I *know* how to find him.
And I *have* to." She gripped Niverren's fingers. "Go back to
Creos, take care of him. Try to tell Mother it's all right. I'm
all right. If I can't come right away, I'll send word with
Xhem."

"Breyd." Niverren's fingers tightened on hers. "Breyd, do
not do anything foolish. Be careful, please."

She can't hold me, I can't let her. "All right." She freed
her hand. "I will."

The narrow alley was deserted, and only a few people
were in the wider streets. She saw none of them and when
two older men near the main square drew sharply away from
her, she ignored them. The inner gates were closed, the postern closed. Three men with drawn swords stood by the
gates, ready to open them for the change of guard at ninth
horn. She looked away quickly. Three men and a closed
gate, Menlaeus beyond it; her heart thudded in her ears.

Xhem left her leaning against the wall opposite the barracks gates, and sprinted between two small companies of
light infantry. Once they had passed, she could see open
ground all the way to the messes, but no sign of the boy. She
drew her arms in close, under the cloak. They hurt whenever
she moved her hands or her wrists particularly; throbbed
wildly when anything touched them. *They are not bad, nothing to endanger life. I held a dagger in the barracks.* She
could fight if she had to. *Once I have Father back.*

It seemed forever; ninth horn finally rang out. Four Pairs
came from the barracks and went down the avenue; she
shrank back into shadow, unwilling to let them see her. But
Grysis was right behind them; Xhem led him across to her.

She had expected him to be angry, even afraid. But he laid
a gentle hand on her shoulder and said, "Here, sit on the
curbstone, you're all black eyes and nerves."

"I'm all right, sir."

"Your arms?"

"Tended."

"Good. They worry about burns, you know that, how bad they can turn. They won't let you back in the company to fight yet."

"I understand. But my Prime—"

"There was a search, along both sides of the road. We did not find him, but you know that. Two other men and a Pair are missing."

"He's alive," she insisted. "Still out there!"

"I know. I believe you. But it has been taken from my hands. They tell me the Diye Haff were hidden from you until they came onto the road—they could be anywhere out there, still unseen. The general's ordered there will be no more searches."

"I—I can't." She drew a deep breath and clenched her hands on each other. Pain flared up her arms, cramped her hands. It cleared her mind just a little. "Grysis, they'd can't *order* me like that! You saw what I did, in there! I could feel it, what I'd do; my *mother* was trying to hold me, I didn't dare stay with her! I can't leave him! And I'm dangerous to anyone who comes close to me!" He gripped her shoulders, pulled her close. "I can't be the only Secchi this ever happened to; they have to have told you what to do. Grysis, help me, please."

"I'll help you. However I can. But I don't know what I can do, they've made orders. Remember if you are able that Menlaeus is a sensible man."

"He's also bonded," Breyd whispered.

"But by that, he'll *know* you are safe; it won't be as hard for him. Other men are also missing, another Pair, did I say? One of them must have found him, they must be taking care of him and waiting until it is safe to show themselves."

"I— all right. Perhaps."

"Good girl. I will see if I can talk to the general, but he was wounded this afternoon. He'll live, they say, he's not bad hurt, but none of the captains has been allowed to see him yet."

The general—and Tarpaen was with him. She didn't dare think about Tar yet, not until she could think about Menlaeus without her breath coming short and desperate. Grysis gripped her shoulders.

"I will reach him for you somehow. We can protect you better in the barracks, and once your arms are healed—no, you can't accept that, can you?" She shook her head.

"I—think I will go to Tephys. This—it isn't weapons, is it?" She laughed shakily. "Sir, will it be all right, if I go?"

"You have leave, Secchi," he said formally, and he let her go. "Report to me in the messes when you return."

"Thank you, sir."

"Can you control this? At all?"

"I will try."

"Good. Go." Breyd watched him cross the avenue and enter the barracks; he walked slowly, as if very tired. *He has lost today also; those who fight for him and men he has known all his years here.* "Xhem."

"Breyd?" Tears still edged his voice, but it no longer shook as terribly.

"I must go up there, the temple. But I am not certain I can walk the whole distance without aid. You'll stay with me?"

"I will stay with you," he replied softly, and came over to wrap an arm around her waist so she could lean against him. He was surprisingly strong for his size, she thought. He needed to be tonight. The streets were dark, deserted, and very steep. It seemed to Breyd she had never walked so far in all her days.

Women filled the upper temple: minor priestesses, a few of the green-clad older women who ordinarily served four days a year only, and each of them seemed to have some urgent task. It was some time before Breyd could find anyone who would carry her message down into the Cleft for Tephys. Two of the girls who had been her one-year companions led her and Xhem off to the base of the wall next to the red clay building, brought two deep cushions for them, and went back to their duties. Xhem curled into himself and stared blankly at the vine-roofed little shelter where Tephys conducted public ceremonies. Breyd settled her pulsing wrists carefully on her knees and tried not to think how much distance was between her and the gates.

She felt frighteningly weak, all at once, and everything was beginning to ache.

The novice came back quickly. "The High Priestess cannot come now, she is deep in some rite. She said she would send instead her heir. Breyd?" The girl stooped and peered a little more closely. "I—oh, Breyd, I did not know you!"

"No." Breyd tried to smile; she couldn't remember the

girl's name. "What are they doing, so many people at this hour?"

"Everything is upside down at the moment. I must go, I am needed by the gates. Blessings," she added hastily and scooped up the long robes so she could run. Breyd bit her lip. *What use will this be, if Tephys will not come? Some new heir—* She thought about simply leaving. *I could attach myself to the end of some company going out, it is dark down there, they might not see me.*

Soft-soled sandals scraped across the clay floor of the little temple; Breyd squared her shoulders. *I will not be put off; she will have to go and tell Tephys.* The thought broke and she stared blankly at Denira, who knelt before her and gazed at her in wide-eyed shock.

"Denira? They did not say it was you."

"Breyd—oh, Breyd, you're hurt!"

"No, don't look like that. Denira, I need Tephys. I *need* her."

"She isn't here," Denira said reluctantly; her eyes went beyond the wall, to the palace. "The prince—" Breyd bit her lip and tried to stand; Xhem scrambled to his feet and helped her up. Denira stared up at her. "Breyd, you can't! They won't let you in!"

"They will. They'll have to." Denira stood up, would have taken her arm, but something in Breyd's eyes stopped her. "Don't—please."

"Be careful, Breyd," Denira whispered.

Careful. She could have laughed, but she wasn't certain she'd be able to stop. "Take care, Denira," she said finally, and let Xhem help her across the courtyard.

15

Fortunately, she had Xhem with her; he came here often enough that the guards outside the palace and those in the hall simply looked at him and his red-clad companion, and let them pass.

At another time, she might have wondered at her nerve in coming here at all—let alone unasked, and probably unwanted. At the moment, this was only a hall, with Tephys at its end. She followed Xhem the length of the main hall to a curtained entry, where a palace guard stood; as they came up, he moved to block the opening and set his spear across the opening. But he had a smile for the boy. "Xhem? They have you out late tonight. The prince is occupied; is your message urgent?" His eyes darted in Breyd's direction; he looked away at once.

He is afraid—if he only knew, he has reason for that. Remember where you are, she told herself. *The least man here has more rank than you—any of them can send you away, and they will not let you near the prince if they think you are dangerous.* "It is my business," she said softly. "With the High Priestess. Sir, is she here?"

The guard looked at her, searching her face carefully. He shook his head finally. "I cannot answer your questions, Secchi. You and the boy had better leave, wait for the High Priestess in her temple. The prince cannot—"

Another barrier, Breyd thought bleakly. But she could hear Tephys in there, talking angrily and rapidly to someone. "Tephys!" she called out sharply; the guard swore and lunged for her but snatched his hand back at once. "Tephys, High Priestess!"

She stepped back; the guard seemed to be at a loss what to do with her, and definitely uncomfortable about drawing his sword against her. Before he could decide, the drape was swept aside, and Tephys stood in the doorway, her face white and her eyes icy. "You. I knew the voice. Who else would it be?" But her eyes focused on Breyd and the anger left her abruptly. "Your arms—oh, beloved Denota, *you* were out there, today. They should have told me! Your Prime? No, don't say, say nothing, wait. Wait for me here, I'll come."

"Priestess?" A voice echoed from the far end of the room.

"My prince, I'm sorry, it's one of the Secchi."

"Don't be sorry. Bring her."

Tephys laid both hands on Breyd's cheeks. "You're hot, and your eyes—"

She shook her head. "I'm not. He's not dead, and they—"

"Wait, he's asked for you, tell it once. Can you manage to control yourself in there, can you bear this?" Breyd nodded. Tephys looked at Xhem and frowned. "Is the boy—?"

"The boy is a messenger, he's come here often. And I need him. He comes, too."

Tephys sighed heavily, then nodded and tugged Breyd's cloak straight, tugged the helm from her hair and thrust it into Xhem's hands. "We waste time I don't have. Come, then."

Breyd followed the priestess into a long, low-ceilinged room brightly lit at its far end. There were no guards inside, no one but the prince, who sat in a low, deeply cushioned chair, and an aged scribe at his elbow.

The prince had been resting his chin on his hand, eyes closed while he listened to the scribe finish reading something. Tephys left Breyd and the boy a short distance away, and went to join Pelledar, who shook himself and sat up straighter.

He looked very tired, Breyd thought, and hollow-cheeked, as though he'd lost weight. She went to one knee and bent her head as Xhem bowed deeply.

Pelledar broke the silence. "Secchi? Come here, to me, child." Breyd stood cautiously, walked across the smooth floor and stood beside his chair. "You look terribly exhausted, and you've been hurt. Ghoric!" He clapped his hands and a thin old man came from behind draperies at the end of the room. "Bring a stool." *I can't*— There wasn't time for this! But she couldn't simply run from the room. *You came here for help, and Tephys is here.* And Menlaeus was— She made fists of her hands, under the cloak; pain set a wall between her and panic. But she could still feel the

mindless fear trying to drive her out, into the night to search
for Menlaeus, the bond between them pulling at her.

The stool was brought, a cushion placed on it; she let
Xhem help her down onto it. "Thank you, sire," she whispered. Her legs were trembling.

Tephys knelt beside her. "Tell me." Breyd glanced nervously at Pelledar, then fixed her eyes on the High Priestess.

"I—they put us on—the road, late." The first words
caught in her throat, but after that it was easier; they poured
from her. She clasped her hands together and stuffed them
between her knees so they wouldn't shake so. "He's out
there," she said finally. "They found me, but not—not Father. He was injured. And then, they wouldn't let me go
back, and I couldn't stop myself, I wanted to kill them all
for standing between us, and now, even my family." She was
gasping for air, shivering violently now; she turned from
Tephys and slid onto her knees at the prince's feet. "Sire,
please, you can help me. I can find him, if they'd only let
me go. You can order them to let me out of the gates. I
know he's alive, but he could die out there if he isn't found
soon!" Tears spilled down her cheeks. "If the Diye Haff
came back, and they found him like that— He can't defend
himself, they'll kill him!"

"But, if they did come back," the prince broke in gently.
"They would have you, too. And you aren't well, child, you
could not fight for him like that." His sympathy was harder
to bear than all the anger and fear in the barracks earlier; she
shook her head, fighting not to weep aloud. In the short silence, she could hear Tephys chanting a prayer.

"I could, if I had to," she whispered. "Please."

"Breyd," Tephys said flatly. "Look at me. Now!" she
snapped. Breyd turned; Tephys took the bonding cord by its
outside knots and pulled it from her forehead.

"No!" She snatched at it desperately, but the priestess had
already risen and stepped back from her. *The bond! Father!*
It was there but no longer the same: a vague sense of him—
somewhere. The tie between them was gone. She stared up
at Tephys. *She looks upset with me. Angry.* "What have you
done?"

"I have done what I must to ease your pain and his,"
Tephys said softly.

"He'll die!"

"Perhaps," Tephys said. "I told you once before that nothing was certain. But he would not like it if you died trying to find him. Would he?" Breyd opened her mouth, closed it again.

"Secchi," Pelledar said gently. "You're injured, burned, and I can see you're exhausted and in pain. You can't go out of the city like that. You'd die to no purpose, and be of no use at all to your father. A father would hate that. They'll search again, when it's light—as much as they dare. Perhaps he'll already have made it back to the road."

Perhaps he'll be dead by then, she thought dully. The raging purpose that had filled her was gone with the cords. *If I can't find him at all now, because of that— I was wrong to come here. I could have—I think I could have controlled it; now I have nothing, even the chance of finding him.* She could have wept out of fear and frustration both. The prince was speaking again; she bit her lip and tried to pay attention.

"You should be sleeping at this hour; your arms will need care. Your captain will arrange leave for you so you can stay with your family until you've healed."

The blood left her face. "Sire, please," she whispered; in another moment, she'd be weeping again. "You can't just send me home, I can't leave him! Please, sire, just let me go back to the barracks, back to my company, Grysis knows, he can—" She bit her lip. She was babbling; he'd think her hysterical and deny her, perhaps simply have the guards take her panoply and send her home for good. *With the Prime gone, and the cords gone*—Tears blurred her vision.

"But you cannot fight like that," Pelledar said. "You would put yourself and those around you in danger. And your Prime might have already found his way back to the road."

"He was hurt. I don't think he could—could walk." She swallowed, shook her head.

"And if it is safe, as soon as it is safe, there will be men out there searching for our people." *Safe.* She shook her head again. "Priestess, help me convince this poor child!"

"Sire, it is not that easy," Tephys said. "She was put through extremely intensive training; the goddess has put a duty upon her and bound her to her Prime. She cannot dispute the bond, Denota is stronger than a mere Secchi, and the bond says she must protect her Prime and be with him—at whatever cost. She has confronted enemy soldiers and killed them. You cannot expect her to put that aside and be once more an innocent child. Ask your general about that, he will know."

"The general will know—exactly what, priestess?" General Piritos stood in the entry, an aide at his side.

"You should not be here," Tephys said. "You were wounded."

"I have no choice; Ghezrat does not have two generals. What will I know?" He came into the room slowly; Pelledar's servant was summoned and sent for a chair. Piritos sank into it with a faint, tired sigh and let his aide blot his forehead, then leaned forward. "Secchi," he said. "Let me see you." She turned around slowly, wincing as she put weight on her hands. "You are Breyd, Menlaeus' daughter. It was bad out there, I am sorry you were part of it."

"Sir." She gave him a salute; he returned it wrong-handed. His other arm had been bandaged, she realized. *When Tar was killed*— But she couldn't think about that, not yet; not with Menlaeus—

Fortunately, Piritos didn't give her time to think about her brother. "Your captain spoke to me just now; I see you found the priestess." He looked up at Tephys. "There is a problem here? Other than her missing Prime?"

Breyd bit her lip. Tephys said, "I have taken the binding cords from her—for now, Breyd," she added. "When your Prime returns, I will give them back to you. But I think you must see the sense of that now?" She nodded. "Good. But she does not see the sense of letting those arms heal before she goes back out to fight. And the prince would have her go home to her mother and simply wait."

"I see." Piritos was silent for a moment. "My prince, it would be wrong to waste this soldier's skills—even if we could afford to send an able-bodied fighter home to her mother, she would be shamed by that. You cannot take from her mind everything she has been through by taking away her weapons. You cannot remove the burden of that bond from her; you would only make it worse by trying to keep her from trying to find her Prime." He turned back to Breyd. "I saw what happened when they tried to keep you in the barracks. Don't look like that," he added quietly, "I don't hold you responsible. Grysis says the men have learned caution."

"I'm sorry, sir," she began, but he waved that aside.

"They told you it was too dangerous to search out there,

and so it is." She stirred, and he held up a hand to silence her. "As soon as it is day, there will be men out there— looking for enemy and for anyone of ours, including your Prime. I will not lose any more trained and experienced men than I can help, you have my word on that."

"Sir, I could help."

"Secchi, you were out there on the road, and you fought a long and hard battle; you were burned. I know, if you do not, what can happen to injuries like yours if they aren't allowed a little time to heal."

"But—" She caught her breath and looked down at his feet so he wouldn't see her weep.

"But. I agree with your captain. You are better off in the barracks and with your own company. Your family would care for you and love you, but the Dyaddi will also understand better what you are going through. Isn't that so?" She nodded, surreptitiously blotting her eyes on the cloak. "Unless you would prefer to spend the next days with your family?" She shook her head. "All right, then. A bargain between us: You can remain with your company; in return, you will promise to stay in the city until your captain says you can fight again."

He had given more than she could have hoped for, still less than what she wanted. *They will not give me what I want.* "Sir," she said. "You—you swear they'll look for him?"

Tephys made a displeased little noise, but Piritos said, "I swear that, Secchi Breyd. Your promise?"

"Yes, sir. I promise."

"Good. Go on, then; Grysis will be waiting for you." His eyes fell on Xhem as the boy got up and helped her to her feet; he gravely returned Xhem's salute. But he was already on another matter by the time Breyd and Xhem reached the door. "I am a tired man, priestess, and not entirely comfortable. So tell me how we stop these Ergardi, and use short words so we can be finished here in short order." The heavy drape fell across the door behind them and muffled Tephys' response.

Piritos sighed and let his aide put a cushion behind his shoulders. Prince Pelledar settled into his own chair and the old servant came with wine. Tephys took the stool where Breyd had been sitting. "How to stop them— I don't know,

General. If I did, I would be doing something about it. Kill them—they can be killed, and if you kill one, it's said the rest are weakened by his loss. For a little."

The general smiled mirthlessly. "Yes. Tell me, then, how we are to kill them."

"You are the warrior, not I," Tephys said. "But it is said they are like all magicians—they cannot work spells at any distance. The chariot bearing their lion-priest was kept from sight because there was a magician in it. I wager there was an Ergardi among those men who came onto the road today, or very close by, though unfortunately not near enough for one of the Dyaddi to sense him out there."

"It doesn't matter how close they are. You can't spear what you can't see." Piritos slapped the chair with the flat of his hand, then looked around for his aide. "All right. Tell me when we return, to discuss this with the captains."

Pelledar was watching him anxiously. "General, I didn't realize how badly you'd been hurt. You should have sent word."

"Well, I am here now, my prince. It's not so bad, really. Uncomfortable, of course. I am angry enough with myself just now, I don't feel much pain. Priestess, do the Dyaddi sense these magicians well enough to guard a search of the ground on both sides of the road? We are missing seven men, the First Prime and another entire Pair."

"I know that."

"I will not abandon them. It is bad for morale, and we cannot afford to lose men or Pairs."

"If the Diye Haff took them," Pelledar began doubtfully, but Piritos shook his head.

"No. Their own dead and wounded were left out there. They had no time and I think they feared their own ballista as much as the Dyaddi."

"The Dyaddi." Pelledar set his untouched wine cup aside and got to his feet to pace between his chair and the great circular hearth. "General, are you certain that was the right thing to do just now? That child—"

"I am certain, my prince. That child, as you call her, killed at least twenty men in the time it would take you to walk from here to your throne room." Pelledar closed his eyes and shuddered. "Yes. The goddess granted us a two-edged sword in the Dyaddi. You cannot remove that battle from her mind by taking her from her company and giving her back to her mother. And it may come to a point when we need one more fighter before the walls, to fend off Haffat. You would shame her to send her away. She has earned better from us than that. And if Haffat somehow came into the city—which is better, and more honorable: for her to die fighting before the walls, or defending herself and her mother from Haffat's soldiers with clay pots and the kitchen knives?"

Tephys stirred. "Her Prime is alive and the bond between them is still very strong. If he had died out there, it would be gone as though it had never been; if he had come back to the city too badly injured to fight again, I would have removed Denota's compulsion from both of them. The goddess did not ask me to do more than take the cords; Breyd is still Secchi, and *must* fight."

Pelledar looked very worried still, but he nodded and let it go. Piritos let his aide take his cup and help him to his feet.

Breyd was leaning heavily on Xhem by the time they reached the square before the main gates. She had stopped twice and here she stopped again and leaned back against the wall. "I'll be all right here," she said finally. "Go, find Captain Grysis, then come back and tell me where he is. I don't want to have to look for him. I'll be fine, go." He hesitated, eyed her uncertainly, then nodded and sprinted off. She gazed blankly in the direction of the main gates. *I cannot look weak when I go in there, not as weak as I feel, at least. They might send me home anyway.* The hammering pulse in her arms eased; she drew a deep breath and let it out cautiously. Father— She had the general's word and the worst of that deadly panic was gone, but the desire to go to Menlaeus was still overwhelming. She looked away from the gates; they were shut tight, heavily guarded. She couldn't go that way and it would drive her mad, if she let it.

The general had been so pale and moved so slowly. *If we had lost him today, what would the city do?* Tarpaen— She swallowed, scrubbed her hand roughly over her eyes. Someone in there would know what had happened, how he had died. *I will kill them for this; for my brother.*

The slap of sandals on stone roused her; Xhem came running up. "He's in the messes; he's waiting for you."

"All right." She eased herself away from the wall. "I can walk—I think. You go ahead, I'll follow."

She couldn't remember much of those last moments on the fighting ground—enough that she looked around warily for Ridlo or anyone else from that company as she neared the messes. Xhem took her hand and led her around a handful of men with torches, on their way out. Smoke trailed behind them, thick and sooty. The smell of pitch was briefly terrifying; she could almost feel the road under her, the body on top of her—she shuddered, shook her head hard to clear it. Xhem gripped her fingers tightly and led her on.

The fighting ground was nearly empty, but there were people everywhere over by the hospital barracks. Two women came past her, scarves drawn down over their faces; they were holding each other up and one was weeping.

Grysis was inside the messes, talking to Edrimon, whose hand was wrapped in a bloodstained bandage. He held up a hand, said, "Wait a moment," and got to his feet. He looked at her searchingly for a long moment, finally laid his hand on her brow. "She hasn't—what did she say?"

"General Piritos said I could come back, sir. Not to fight yet."

"Good."

"Sir—my brother. Who would know—I have to know what happened."

"His captain—someone from the signalers. I don't know if Nabid is still awake, but I'll pass the word on for you." He waved a hand in the direction of the Dyaddi bench. "Two of the Secchi said they'd wait, in case you came back; they'll help you to the barracks."

She opened her mouth, closed it again without saying anything. *He hasn't time for problems like this.* She looked down at Xhem, who was fighting tears. He must know something; she couldn't bring herself to ask him. *I don't know if I can manage to walk from here to the end of the messes, and then back to the barracks.* But Xhem blotted his face on his cloak and said, "Captain Nabid just came in. Your captain is pointing this way."

She turned; the messes swam and she clutched at the boy's shoulder. The normally expressionless signal captain looked as if he'd been violently sick and the smile he gave Xhem was ghastly. "Xhem: How are you, lad?" Xhem bit his lip and nodded. "Secchi. Tarpaen has been brought in and—and readied, in case any of his family wishes to see him. They've put him and the other dead in the south end of the hospital barracks. If his mother wants to see him a last time—"

Mother, in that place, seeing all those injured, hearing—? "No," she said, so sharply Xhem jumped and Nabid stared at her in surprise. "Mother is not strong and Tar was her only son. And if—if what they said, his injuries—" She drew a deep breath and when she went on, her voice was steady again. "They say his head was nearly severed." Nabid compressed his lips. After a moment, he nodded. Xhem moaned softly, stuffed a fist in his mouth, and bit down on the fingers. "Do you know—how he died?"

Nabid gave her a look she couldn't interpret. *As if he's afraid to say, or so upset by it that he can't.* After a moment, he shook his head again. Breyd swallowed. "I will go. And Xhem—if he wants to, and if you will permit it." Nabid looked at the boy rather doubtfully, but finally nodded. Breyd went to one knee and gripped his arm. "Can you bear it, Xhem? You need not, you know."

"I will come with you," he whispered. "I—I want to."

"We will both go."

"The pyre will be lit tomorrow at dawn," Nabid said. "The families won't be let out there because of the danger, we sent word of that. You are certain his mother—"

If he had seen her tonight, he wouldn't ask that. With any luck at all, and enough of Nidya's dosed wine, she would be deeply asleep by now and wouldn't waken until late the next morning. "I am certain, sir."

He eyed her critically. "You don't look very good, Secchi. Are you certain you can walk that far?" She nodded; he gave her one more doubtful look but turned and led the way. There were few companies going out, at the moment, just some men standing here and there, little clutches of them. Someone down by the sleeping barracks laughing a little too loudly; men near the messes talking in low, worried-sounding voices. A few men coming from the gates looked as though they had fallen in the river; one leaned heavily on another, who was talking animatedly, and they all laughed. Nabid led them past the main entry to the hospital barracks, where anxious, silent women and old men stood or sat, waiting for some word, or to be allowed in.

She realized she had been holding her breath, bracing herself for another trip through that entry. *But they would not carry the dead in there; there is barely enough room for the living.*

Very near the south wall, Nabid pushed aside a rough wool curtain and held it for her. Xhem shrank close to her side; his fingers slid into her hand. The smell of blood was almost palpable here; the sense of death overwhelming. Two small oil lamps burned against the back wall and a little brazier holding cedar. She could smell it; it wasn't enough to overcome the smell of blood. Men lay upon the floor, pressed closely against each other; there was barely enough room to walk. Others lay upon boards set on trestles against the walls. Nabid took up a lamp from a niche by the door and led the way.

Tarpaen lay on a pallet near the back wall. Breyd squared her shoulders, drew a deep breath, and looked down at him.

They had rolled a cloak tightly and wrapped it around him so his head was held in place; a long, trailing end of his own cloak lay across his throat, as if it had fallen there by accident. His skin was marble-white and when she touched his hand, it was nearly as chill as stone, and as hard, but his face was peaceful and in the uncertain light, he almost looked asleep. Xhem choked, squatted beside the body and buried his head in his hands; his thin shoulders shook. Breyd wrapped her arms around him, pulled him close, and let him weep.

She could not cry. She looked down at him for what seemed a very long time and couldn't even feel anything. *My brother. He was not armed, and Haffat killed him. He could not have fought, could never have defended himself, and Haffat killed him. I would cut his throat slowly and watch him bleed, I would kill him a little at a time and I would be glad to see his pain.*

She laid a hand on his breast; but there was nothing of him there, only a cold, hard shell that had once held Tarpaen. *I will make them pay for this, Tarpaen, I swear it. And tomorrow, when your soul flies free, let it go to the House of Warriors—and let them welcome you freely as a brother and a hero. And do not doubt your right to a seat among them.*

She stood, leaving Xhem still crouched at his brother Tar's side. "Sir, where is his panoply? Such as it was— surely there was no time for them to strip it from him?"

"It is here, set aside. Grysis suggested perhaps you could say for him where it should go. If he had a son, of course——"

"He has Xhem."

To his credit, Nabid merely nodded and knelt beside the boy. "Xhem? Tomorrow, Tarpaen's panoply will come to you. As his heir, you will be allowed to attend the lighting of the pyre. I will free you from duty to accept his arms." Xhem got to his feet carefully, cast one last tearful glance at the fallen Tarpaen.

"Thank you, sir," he whispered.

Nabid patted his shoulder. "Go home now, sleep. Mip will be here at first horn; he will teach you the words you must say out there." Xhem rubbed his eyes with grubby fists and left. Nabid watched him go. "Your brother *should* be proud of him. And for what he himself did, seeing worth in a green young peasant and helping to shape it."

"I know it," Breyd replied. She stood looking down at Tarpaen for some moments, and Nabid stood with her. "Do not send for his other women; it would distress my grandmother unbearably, to see him like this and this place would haunt our mother for the rest of her days. His other sister is wife to Creos. It would be terrible for her to have to come here again. I am here for them. But he knows that."

"There is his horn," Nabid said.

"Xhem can take that to my mother—to my grandmother, Nidya, to give to Mother." She freed a thin leather cord from the belt at her waist and drew her dagger, knelt to cut one long strand of curling hair from just behind Tarpaen's ear. Nabid watched in silence while she tied the end of the curl, then knotted the ends of the cord together and hung it from her neck. She stood, tucked the hair between armor and linen. "I have that, to remember him by, sir. It will be enough."

She followed Nabid from the room with the dead in an exhausted, pain-filled daze. Just outside, Jocasa and Aroepe were waiting for her. Jocasa said, "Sir, Captain Grysis sent us to take care of Breyd; he said you're wanted in the messes." Nabid left them. Aroepe wrapped her arms around Breyd's shoulders and held her for a long moment; Jocasa hugged them both and said, "Come on; Breyd, can you walk, or should we get Father?"

She shook her head. "I can walk; I don't want anyone carrying me. But I think I'd better lean on you." It seemed to take forever to get across the fighting ground and later she couldn't remember it at all clearly; she barely recalled them easing her down on her cot, being held upright by Jocasa, who sat next to her while Aroepe undid her armor.

She ached all over and one knee was stiffening; dull, throbbing continuous pain under Nidya's bandages—the yarrow ointment was wearing off. But even the constant pain didn't keep her awake. Jocasa tucked the cloak around her legs; Aroepe kissed her cheek. "We'll be right here, if you need us." She nodded, closed her eyes and slept.

Tenth horn: The messes were half empty, only a company of light infantry just come from the plain near the Oryon, and several men in still-damp tunics, their hair stiff with salt water who were laughing and drinking and swapping tall stories in a corner. The officer who watched over the messes left them to it: After all, they had swum out against a hard tide just before midnight, and despite close watch by Diye Haff on the mole and on the ships out there, had sunk one and fired another.

In the darkened barracks, Breyd slept heavily; Jocasa and her Prime on one side and Aroepe and hers on the other. Five empty cots against the wall: Menlaeus—Lochria and Bechates who had vanished at the same time, without trace. Duplos, who had burned his hands beating out his Secchi's cloak and Xera who had refused to be parted from him.

A distance away, General Piritos tried to sleep; an aide dozed at his side. He had refused a soporific, fearing they might not be able to waken him if he was needed. At the moment he was sorry he hadn't taken the dose: The wound in his leg had not been deep, but the arrow had cut a long gash before finally embedding itself in muscle and it stung; his arm throbbed. His mind scurried from one problem to another: *That drummer—why did they allow him in a company at all, let alone on the walls? Why hadn't anyone set a night patrol along the ridge, men who know the ground enough to walk it in the dark and find anyone hiding there? Boys and men stuck on the jetty who couldn't swim and why?* They always said the same thing: "It wasn't supposed to happen that way." Or, "They weren't supposed to do that." *Every war or battle or skirmish I have ever fought, at least once someone has said that, over some utterly appalling, stupid thing!* "Each time we underestimate an enemy, or judge him by what *we* would do—and men like Tarpaen die for some-one's *stupidity*. Are we so blind as that—so stupid we cannot see our enemies for the cunning men they truly are?" *Perhaps the gods mean it as a test—whether we can see how we continually sacrifice soldiers to hidebound ideas, and find a way to rise above such stupidity. Or perhaps it is simply our fate, to fight the same battles over and over, and let people die because this new enemy was not supposed to do anything but what we intended for them to do.*

Somewhere between one gloomy thought and the next he dozed off, but he moved so restlessly the sleep did him little good, and he emerged at first light looking old and gaunt.

Pelledar remained in his small hearings room until tenth horn, trying to make sense of things. These Ergardi, this cer-emony set for dawn, to burn those who had died in the past two days. *So many bodies.* His son, out there in the barracks, that Secchi probably somewhere close by. He looked one more time at the small square of parchment folded into his hand. Apodain's petition. But he had already sworn to Khadat; and Brysos had turned the youth down; his message had come via one of Piritos' aides: "Send him back to us if you will or if you find you must, prince. But think on this first: His repute in the barracks is sullied by the charge of cowardice, and while the royal chariot would mostly wel-come him, there are some who would not, and many men in other companies believe the rumors and gossip. These are companies which must back the royal chariot or assist it, or be assisted by it—men who might not actively do Apodain harm but who would not move quickly to aid him, if there was need." *They would kill him, given a chance, and let the Diye Haff take blame for it,* Pelledar realized bleakly. *What-ever their commanders told them.* "Also, consider this: That if Apodain returns to the royal chariot, having left as he did, men will see it as proof that we are in a truly terrible strait—to take any man, even a proven coward, to throw him into battle in a last desperate attempt to rout the enemy. Much as I would personally like to have Apodain back in my command, I cannot risk the rumor his presence would start, or the danger to his person—and so I told him. Tell him whatever you will, of course, but take my warnings into account when you make a decision, I beg of you."

There was no choice, not really. Pelledar rose, walked over to the brazier and opened his hand above the coals.

There was a brief odor of burnt hide, the fire flared momentarily, and Apodain's note was gone. The prince stood looking down at the little twist of ash. "One day, young cousin Apodain," he said softly, "I will tell you of this, and why I chose as I did. And I will apologize to you, I swear, for having done this." He sighed and turned away. It was very late, and enough smoke from the brazier had drifted back into the chamber to give him a headache. He would go join Ye Sotris and try to sleep. *For who can say that there will be another night after this one, for us to share?*

Apodain sat upon the roof amid the tangle of vines and plants that had once been a fine garden, and gazed out across the city and the barracks, past the walls to the plain which was dotted here and there with fires. There, the Oryon, and there the Alno—not properly visible, of course; but the large cluster of fires to the east showed where the Diye Haff camped just across the Oryon, the smattering of small blazes upon the plain those of the Ghezrathi, and then total blackness to mark where the Alno ran, because any fires had been built in the swales or under the shelter of groves or orchards.

The kitchen servant Isra had had no difficulty in avoiding Khadat and reaching the barracks in secret with his message to Brysos. Of course, Khadat had been at her self-important busiest: Her duties to Denota; her duties in the cellars storing foodstuffs and making certain of the cisterns; the hour or so in meeting with the prince's council; and then back to the goddess' temple to aid the High Priestess in some gambit or other against the enemy gods and the enemy magicians.

He shrugged that aside as unimportant. They had Gyptiosi Fire, everyone knew that; he himself had seen the clouds of oily smoke in the late afternoon. Not unexpected in a Haffat, who would surely use whatever means necessary to subdue Ghezrat, particularly now. "His dignity has been affronted, that the city dare hold out against him so long," he murmured.

His own—but he had no dignity left. It had taken all the courage he could gather, to send that message to Brysos. To crawl, and crave pardon, and none of the fault his to begin with. Brysos' reply had been polite but firm: There was no place for him. It had been a kind note, for all that. Apodain found that somehow more shaming than if the man had brusquely turned him aside.

The message to the prince had been even harder to write, and to that there had been, as yet, no reply. *He will not answer,* Apodain realized suddenly. *Mother has some hold over him, or uses her wealth and Father's power and position and that of her Mirikosi family, to keep Pelledar to his vow.*

He should get up and go down to his couch, he thought. Rest, if not sleep. It did not seem to matter much.

Everyone else slept at this hour, Nidya thought with relief. Finally, they did: Ina and Nevvia and Creos heavily, a cup of wine heavily laced with valerian to each; Niverren because she was so exhausted she could not have remained awake another moment, and finally fell over fully clothed next to her husband. Xhem—he might have been asleep; at least he was quiet, Nidya thought. "Poor child. The young take it so hard to see life go; they do not realize it is a natural thing." And yet, how natural was it, that the young died and the old like her lived on? "My son by marriage bond, Menlaeus. Breyd says you live, and I must believe it. My poor spoiled Tarpaen. It was no more your fault than your mother's. She never meant to ruin you. Or to try. Because you rose above all that; you were beginning to turn into someone I liked very much. The boy was partly responsible for that, but he only provided the means for you to prove yourself." She folded her hands neatly together and let her head fall back so she could look into the night sky. "The gods will know how to judge you, young Tarpaen; they will see the good hidden deep inside you, and the hero who was there all the time. And if not that—why, then the good man who might have been, if there had only been time. Go in peace, my grandson; we will meet again."

Haffat

Across the Oryon, the Diye Haff camp was brightly lit, and most men gathered around large firepits to roast meat and drink; they laughed, and listened to other's exploits from the day's fighting. The injured had been taken out to ships anchored just off shore, the dead to the other side of the ridge, where a few men were readying the pyre. Two of Knoe's priests had gone with them, to anoint the dead and prepare the rites; others were with the wounded. Knoe himself sat in his ritual tent with the Ergardi.

Five small dark men knelt in a half-circle before him, so close together their shoulders touched. Knoe took their hands and clasped them all together above a gold sacrifice knife, its blade engraved with a lion. "You will remain here and nourish each other tonight, and rebuild the strength you expended in battle. The god is pleased with you, and your accomplishments this day. As proof of this, he has brought you alive and unhurt from the thick of fighting, and he has given into your hands two who are one. He will ask more of you tomorrow, and the day after, until this city is his, and then he will reward you with new flesh to house your true selves. He gives you now his strength and his breath." He blew gently on the clasped hands. The Ergardi looked at him, old and knowing eyes in young nomadic faces, and as one replied: "To the god all honor, and His Will our command." They bowed low over the clasped hands, heads very close together. Knoe stood and left the tent at once, before the aura created by their oneness touched him; it could not take him, but it could make him ill. *It is all very well for them to blend their own way with the lion's; they are powerful but only in service to another.*

He paused before the smaller tent that ordinarily housed priests, and smiled, hesitated with his hand on the flap. No, he decided. *Let them stay there a while, and wonder what I will do to them.* He turned away.

"Knoe!" One of the priests came running up. "Master, the emperor sent a man, just now, commanding you to come." He was panting, his eyes wide and frightened. "He commanded, and that soldier looked—"

Knoe held up a hand for silence. "I will go to him. He will not harm me."

"They—I have heard the way men talk, out there, because those five died of Fire. If the emperor is as angry as they— Master, what would we do if you could not lead us?"

"The lion would lead you, as he always has," Knoe said sternly. "Compose yourself. Go into my tent, and sit before the shrine, and pray to Axtekeles for strength."

He walked quickly through the camp, ignoring the grim looks cast his way, or the men who laughed too loudly or fell silent after he had passed. *Haffat would not harm his priest; he knows that would bring the god's wrath upon him.* But perhaps not. More and more the past days, Haffat dared to contradict something his priest said. *As though he believes himself directly in touch with the god.* And there was Haffat's temper; he had been so full of himself after he and his raiding party came back with all those horses and the chariots—moments later he had nearly attacked the Mirikosi who came to tell him about the sunken ship. Fortunately his son had been there; Hadda was one of the few who could draw Haffat from that wild mood. The Mirikosi had been hustled from the tent almost before he realized his danger. *Grateful to Hadda? I? The world is indeed turning upside down.*

He hesitated just short of the emperor's tent, then shrugged and went in. *The god will protect me, if he wishes me to live.* And so would Haffat.

Haffat was listening to two of his captains argue over some position on the maps; he looked up as Knoe came into the light and frowned. *If even Haffat blames me—* But the emperor waved him to a seat. "Priest. Wilus, you know what to do, assemble the men in camp and tell them I will come out shortly. Then I want the hospital tents and all the wounded but the most serious, moved to the other side of the ridge. The noise and the stench damage morale. We have enough problems without that. The worst of the wounded to the Mirikosi ship in the bay where we first landed. See it is done tonight. Req, those who will prepare the pyre—make certain they know it is not to be seen from the city walls. If they would count our dead, let them send spies. Keep the guard ready, in case they do. Go." The captains bowed and left quickly. Haffat frowned at the map, then shoved it aside. "Priest, there is an ill mood out there because our men died under that ballista. No," he waved a hand as Knoe stirred. "Wait. Say nothing. I was responsible for the troops, you for the ballista, so if you are at any fault, then so am I. That does not matter. We damaged their morale badly, hitting them like that; we took prisoners and killed many, and there is report from several different men that their general was wounded. It was more than worth the loss of five men, but the men see only the dead comrades and fear they may die the same way." He got to his feet. "Come with me." Knoe bowed his head and stood up.

Men stood in the track running past the emperor's tent. Knoe could see some who were merely curious, many more who glared at him or looked at him with open loathing, and some were muttering, too low for him to catch the words. But Haffat held up his hands and got silence. "You men fought well today; because of your courage and your skills, we killed many Ghezrathi and even took the fight to their walls! This paid them in part for all those who died yesterday at the foot of the cliff, against those red-clads.

"I have heard the grumblings; there were men of ours lost this afternoon to our own ballista. I have dealt with this; those who fight out there tomorrow and the days after will have new commands, so they know when to pull back and let the ballista do its work. Follow those orders, and you will be in no danger from the Fire.

"I have also heard from the officers that some of you men would have us do away with the ballista and the Fire—and with the Ergardi and even with my lion-priest and Axtekeles himself. I will not hear such talk from you. Think instead what we gained from that attack! Because of the magicians, we approached the very city walls and fell upon them unseen; because of the ballista, the red-clads on the road had no real chance to attack. If they cannot be killed hand to hand, then we will kill them from a distance.

"They know this; they have cause tonight to fear us because we have the means to destroy their paired fighters." He paused, a few men cheered. "And we will!" A louder cheer. Haffat held up clenched fists, then turned and ushered Knoe back into his pavilion. Once inside, he resumed his chair and motioned for his servant to bring wine.

Knoe drank and set the cup aside; he suddenly felt weak. *I did not really think he would kill me, or feed me to his soldiers. But I did not realize how glad I would be to still be alive.* The silence stretched, but it was a comfortable one. Haffat drank his wine and scowled at his map, finally drove a dagger through the center of it to pin it to the wood. "You will still use the Ergardi?" Knoe asked finally.

"I meant what I said out there," Haffat replied. "And they all saw you at my side; they know this means you are still my close ally, and that I have not turned from Axtekeles."

"Thank you."

"You know your god, Knoe, and I my men. But next time, the Ergardi stationed with the ballista will wait to launch Fire until the machine is set for range and the signal given. Another such disaster might prove ill for him, and there would be nothing I could do save punish his murderers. You cannot tell soldiers to let their own die and do nothing to avenge them—not in the heat of battle."

"I understand." He didn't, even after so long at Haffat's side. He knew men committed such acts, and only thought what might come of their actions later, if they thought at all. *Like beasts; how can they bear it, to have no control over themselves—or do any of them see what low creatures they are?* "I ask that you remember, my emperor, the damage it would do all the Ergardi if one were killed. You know how useful they were today."

For one long, still moment, he wondered if he had gone too far. But Haffat finally said, "I know it. That is military business, priest and I am dealing with it."

"And it is my business," Knoe said softly, "because the Ergardi are under my protection."

"Of course."

"Do you require anything else of me?"

"Not just now," Haffat said.

"The dead will be burned at midnight," Knoe reminded him.

"Come here first; we will go together." Knoe bowed. *So. He is not certain of my safety.* It was not a comforting thought. *But it is all before the lion; if he still needs me here, then I will live.* He had his hand on the flap when

Haffat said, "I have heard you took prisoners today, lion-priest. Why was I was not told about them?"

"You were busy, my emperor," Knoe said. General Jemaro pushed the flap aside, checked as he came face to face with the priest, then stepped around him and bowed.

"My emperor, there is—the enemy has somehow evaded our men and attacked the ships just offshore." Haffat swore furiously, jumped to his feet and followed Jemaro outside at a dead run. Knoe followed, more slowly.

Men were shouting and running in all direction; a company of horse galloped by. The south sky had turned ruddy and smoke billowed toward the clouds. Knoe pushed his way through to the river's edge, where he could see. Somewhere near the end of the main road, he thought, off that jutting stone wharf, the silhouette of a sailless mast, shorter than it should be and tilted at a crazy angle, stood out sharply against flames. Tiny black shapes—men were running on the shore and out on the mole, running across the decks to fling themselves into the sea. He shook his head and turned away. *That will not do much for Haffat's temper. But it will distract his men from those five men, and from the Ergardi—and distract Haffat himself from my prisoners. At least for now.*

He walked quickly between a long line of tents, past a double picket of horses; skirted men who worked by torch and firelight to prepare captured Ghezrathi heavy chariots for their own men to use. *After Idemito, they would have left off whatever tasks they did, whenever I passed, and bowed to me, and to the priests who served under me.* It was a sign, he thought: A sign he must find a way to turn the emperor back to his own homeland, to persuade him to govern his empire from Diyet, once he took Ghezrat. "Find a way to return Haffat home, and his priest with him," he whispered. The Ergardi worshiped Axtekeles by fasting and long vigils, but the god did not deny wealth and comfort to his servants. Just now, Knoe thought, he had had enough of dust, and dirt, and hard pallets on stony ground—enough of battle and dying men. "Better to end my days in plenty and wealth, and great honor, at the emperor's side, many long years from now."

There had been other faint signs recently; Heliar, dying of wounds—the god had named him to rule Ghezrat and he never would. And vague dreams from which he woke edgy and exhausted, soaked in sweat. The earth goddess had so far proven much stronger than he had thought possible.

But perhaps I finally have the lever to topple her. He pushed aside the flap and let it fall into place behind him, stood still until his eyes adjusted. There was no light here but that of torches in front of his own tent; the smell of pitch was very strong. Against the back wall, two cages had been built, and set as far apart as possible so the two in them could see but not touch each other; in one a thickly bearded man of middle years, and in the other a black-haired girl. Both wore full panoply and red cloaks, though the wool was so filthy it had been difficult to tell the original color when they were brought in. Fire had burned the man's beard, the cheek above it was blistered. One of the girl's hands was badly burned, but none of the physicians would go near her to tend it.

Knoe came forward and folded his arms, and gave them his most arrogant glower. They stared back, both without expression, and waited. After a very long silence, Knoe finally spoke. "The innermost guard of the city, the great mystery of Denota—and yet, nothing after all but an aging male and a virgin. Or, more likely among soldiers, merely a young female." He waited again; no response of any kind. "You are dead, both of you," he sneered. "The lion of Haffat devours all things in his path, and crosses over the land as *he* wills, not as the land itself would choose. Your earth goddess cannot touch you here. You have lost, two who are one. Lost your city, and your honor—and soon your lives." Another long silence. The male—that was an experienced fighting man, and would not be easily baited; but the girl showed no more fear than he did. *What manner of girl child does this earth goddess consecrate to her service?* But he knew part of the answer to that: Two who could become one dreadful death-dealing force. Dangerous. All the more so because they served an earth goddess. *She blesses the crops and the lambs, and sends forth maidens to make slaughter for her—it turns everything on its head and makes no sense!* What manner of females lived in that city, if these came out to do battle? *The lioness serves the lion, knowing he is greater than she and more powerful, that he will kill her and her young if she tries to rise above him, but these females—* She was still staring at him and it made him uncomfortable, all at once. Knoe turned and left the tent.

Bechates and Lochria watched him go, and heard his footsteps crunching away across loose sand and dirt. When he would have spoken, she held up a hand for silence, so she could listen. Finally, she let down the hand and nodded. "That one is gone, Prime. Speak low, and be careful what you say. There are more of the priests about and one may be outside listening to us."

"Secchi." Bechates nodded. They had been warned not to name themselves, not to call each other anything but Prime and Secchi, if they were taken. *Even the Mirikosi do not know the exact nature of it,* Tephys had said. Bechates swallowed. *If they try to learn from her, or from me— If they learn she is my daughter, and use that knowledge to pressure me—* He could no longer feel the pulse hammering in his hand, the fingers twitching—her pain; that had been instantly reft from him when they were caged, along with every other sense that had come with their bond. The smell of burned hair was stronger in his nose than even the pitch; a muscle in his cheek jumped now and again and his eye watered constantly.

"Your face, Prime."

"I can bear it," he said. "Your hand, though."

"I could still use a sword, if I had the chance; my dagger hand is not burned, just scraped." She was quiet for a moment. Her lips trembled. "I did not think they meant to trade us tomorrow. I fear that priest plans to— I think he will kill us, Prime. But he might keep us alive, to find a way to use us against the city."

"Yes." Bechates swallowed. *I know she is terrified, but if she does not let it show, I dare not.* "I know. And he is curious—you saw that." She nodded, bit her lip. Bechates set his back against the wall of the cage and pushed at it with his arms, and then his legs. Nothing moved. "It isn't just wood, there's a spell of some kind. But we must get out of here. Somehow."

"I would like that," Lochria said steadily. "But if we can't— They can't learn what we are." She closed her eyes for a very long moment, rested her forehead against the cage. When she finally looked up, her face was set. But he already knew what they would have to do. His hand moved as hers did, took hold of the red binding cords. "Prime."

"Secchi," he whispered; they gripped the cords, and pulled them off.

It felt no different, and that, he thought, was the most frightening thing of all. "I knew from the first," he whispered, "I knew some dread thing would befall us, you and I. When Tephys chose us, I saw—not a specific thing, but I smelled death and pitch. But I cannot bear to think it will be a priest's knife."

"No!" Lochria whispered fiercely. "Denota will not desert us, we'll find a way to escape! But we can't just give up!"

He sighed; his burns hurt and he was dizzy with exhaustion. If she could remain defiant, though, so much the better. He looked down at the circle of cord, then began to undo the knot she had tied. She had already undone his knot; the cords dangled from her fingers. After a moment's thought, she wrapped them around the now swordless baldric. "We won't give up. Test the walls of your cage, watch the priest—be ready to take any advantage of any mistake they make."

She nodded. "You rest first, I'm not as tired as you. I'll wake you if there's need."

He twisted his cords around his belt, then eased himself down into a corner, pulled the scorched cloak around his shoulders and closed his eyes. Lochria leaned against her cage, eyes fixed on the closed flap, the fingers of her unburned hand exploring the woven wall as high as she could reach.

The ship was still burning, but flames no longer colored the clouds. Only a few men still stood or sat around the fires and none of them paid any attention to Knoe as he passed. He hesitated outside Haffat's pavilion. Light shone through the cloth and he could hear many men inside; Haffat's voice, too low for him to catch any words, an angry Wilus complaining bitterly about the loss of the food aboard both ships. Someone else closer to hand talking about some maneuver that made no sense to Knoe—but such things never did. He was about to go on in when someone broke into laughter: Hadda, and from the sound of things, rather drunk. *And what is he up to just now, I wonder?* Knoe looked around quickly, then stepped off the track and into the shadows so he could listen.

"So tell me, Nayasi," Hadda asked cheerfully. "How did it feel, fighting girls? Did you not bring back one single long tress as a badge of honor? Or did they all squeal and flee

when real men came upon them with real blades?" The
laughter was abruptly cut short, and Knoe saw shadows
against the pavilion wall; Nayasi had Haffat's pet son by the
throat, and his voice was deadly serious.

"You listen to me, prince. Next time we battle the Dyaddi
you go and fight them—or better yet, go with the carts to
help pick up the dead they leave behind. Go test your own
bronze against theirs. But do not laugh when you speak of
them, not to me and not to those very few men in my company who engaged them and lived to tell of it." He stepped
back and walked away. Hadda's bewildered voice followed
him.

"Nayasi, by all the gods, it was a jest!" Knoe permitted
himself a small grim smile, but it was carefully gone when
he stepped around the corner of the pavilion and the foot
soldier held the flap aside for him.

Haffat had stripped; a pile of wet linen lay at his feet and
his hair was plastered to his skull. A servant was rubbing
him down and another unfolding a fresh tunic. His mouth
was set and his eyes grim but as Knoe came up, he was saying to Wilus: "The ships can be replaced, and the goods they
held. Send to Herric in Mirikos and tell him we must have
wheat and beans, rice, whatever he can provide. The
Ghezrathi will pay for those ships." His eyes found Knoe.
"Priest. I am told you have taken a Dyadd. But you did not
tell me. Why is this?"

"A Pair, my emperor. But when was there time to tell
you?" Haffat let the servant towel his hair, settled the dark
blue cloak across his shoulders, and sat. One of his servants
handed him a steaming cup. "It was cold out there, priest;
one ship was holed and the other fired. I lost enough food
for seven days, enough metal to rearm four phalanxes, and
fourteen men."

"I am sorry," Knoe said. "A Pair was found just off the
road, unconscious; the Ergardi who shielded your men had
them bound and brought them."

Hadda had been on his way toward the flap; he turned to
gape at the priest. "You brought a Pair here? After—
everything they say the Pairs do, all they've killed?"

"They are under a special guard," Knoe said evenly, "and
surrounded by Axtekeles' power. They are both injured and
they have been disarmed. They are no danger to you." He

added angrily, "I would not have endangered the emperor by bringing them here if I could not control them!"

Silence. Hadda licked his lips nervously. "What will you do with them?" Haffat touched his son's arm, but Hadda shook him off. "Look at him, Father. They are prisoners for Knoe and his god." His voice had gone dry and he looked very frightened. "What will you do with these, priest?"

"What has this to do with you, prince?" Knoe replied softly.

"It is everything to do with me, priest. You mean to kill them, don't you?"

Haffat touched the priest's hand to get his attention. "Yes. What will you do with a Pair? Will you tell me Axtekeles asks you to shed the blood of a maiden."

"A maiden?" Knoe laughed. "That maiden looked at me just now with my death in her eyes. Ask anyone who was out there—before the walls and on the road—ask them how many died on the swords of these Pairs, who were spitted by such *maidens!* Their goddess fights through them somehow, my emperor!"

"But—!" Hadda protested.

"I did not say I would kill them," Knoe said sharply. "But if I find the way to separate them, and make this one again two, and helpless—does my emperor really wish to see men slaughtered by these Dyaddi? Or does Hadda only weep for an enemy who has killed his own men, simply because that enemy possesses breasts and might bear children?"

"And once you have learned all you can from them, or made them helpless—what will you do with them?" Hadda asked. "My Father accepts your god's word, to sacrifice this bull, or that bird—this man." He swallowed. "You will kill them. But if the goddess Denota calls them hers as the Mirikosi say, she may take revenge for them."

"You know nothing of such matters, prince," Knoe said flatly. Hadda shook his head.

"I know nothing of *your* god; that does not mean I know nothing of gods. If Denota were roused to full fury because you killed her own fighters, she might bring together all the gods worshiped in this land: we might all die here, because the sun and moon, the very land, the sea and all things between were set against us!"

He is a fool, and a soft fool—but he is Haffat's son, Knoe reminded himself. He sent his eyes toward the emperor.

Haffat actually looked proud of the boy for such a ridiculous notion. He swallowed a sharp retort he wanted to make and said, "It is a point and I shall ask the god."

"Hadda is right," Haffat said evenly. "I would gladly see every last red-clad slain in battle, but I find it disturbing to think of them slaughtered like beasts."

"They will not die, then," Knoe said quietly. He looked up at Hadda, who was watching him suspiciously. "There, does that please you? They shall remain where they are, and I shall learn whatever I can from them, and once I have done that, they will remain here—at least until the city is taken."

"It pleases me, Knoe," Haffat said. "Hadda?" The prince nodded but reluctantly, Knoe thought. *Add more guards to the tent, that Hadda does not get himself killed by that female, attempting to save her.* He got to his feet.

"It is nearly midnight. I must go if the dead are all to find release before day comes."

"I will come with you," Haffat said. "A moment." He drew his son aside and said quietly, "That was well thought, my son. I am proud of you."

"Thank you," Hadda said. When his father let go his arm, he filled his cup and walked away toward the rear of the tent. *I can almost hear them, out there: Knoe thinks me a fool, Father sees me as brave, and both for the same act. Why does neither of them see Hadda, who wants only to go home where he belongs?*

16

Breyd woke hot and disoriented in the predawn hour, alerted by the first hour horn, frightened without quite knowing why. It smote her between one breath and the next and she forced herself to lie quite still. *You will not panic; you will not! He is still alive, nothing has changed since you slept last night.* The bond between her and Menlaeus, stretched to cobweb thickness as it was, still held. Nothing else mattered; for now, she would not let anything else touch her. *Unstable Secchi. They were afraid enough of me, out there; now no one will dare come close to me. My repute is graven in stone among those who were in the courtyard last night. And any they spoke to after.* Which probably meant every man in every company by this hour.

He is there, he is still alive, someone will find him and bring him in today, she told herself. Slowly the fear faded, enough that she could function this morning.

Her face was hot, her mouth dry, and her arms ached. *I must not let them know,* she thought. If they thought her feverish, or ill, they would send her home. *And I must be here, for Father.*

For the Dyaddi. Things Jocasa and Aroepe said at some point last night began to come back to her: Xenia's Prime Akeros had burned his hands putting out her cloak and they had sent him home; no one thought he would fight again. Eriana and her Prime both hurt in the fighting before the walls; they would not leave the barracks today or the next, possibly more. Two missing: Lochria and Bechates had simply vanished, like Menlaeus, and no one could remember when they were last on the road with the rest of the phalanx. *Goddess, keep them safe, if they live; keep them close if they are—if they are dead.* It would make her weep, if she thought about them; she could not afford that weakness this morning. *Do nothing that will make them send you away.*

You must be there for Xhem, and for all your family this morning, when they light the pyre. But sensible Lochria, of all the Secchi, would understand why her friend did not weep for her.

She finally rolled over and very cautiously sat up. Nidya's burn ointment had dulled the pain in her forearms and the sleep had helped though they still ached constantly. But as soon as she moved them, pain flared; it was agony to use her hands or straighten her arms. *They will not know this. They will not send me away.* It took all the determination she had to simply get to her feet and walk from the barracks. She stopped just outside to lean against the wall and catch her breath, to gather enough strength to walk across to the messes.

Men and the few women filled the long room and both hatches were open, but it was quiet this morning; even the nervous laughter was gone and the small company which had created such havok among the enemy ships sat near the door, heads low and close together, faces grim as one of them spoke quietly and urgently. She could see Nabid and his second Mip just beyond them, surrounded by horners. Nabid was pale and gaunt in the flickering lamplight, and Breyd wondered as she passed him if he had slept at all. Xhem was there, too—skinniest of the messenger boys clustered off to one side. His face was white, his eyes puffy and red-rimmed; he was staring blankly at the bread in his hands.

She got bread and a cup of wine, a handful of rather dry dates and went back to join her company. They looked up. Silence fell over the bench. Jocasa raised her eyebrows; Breyd nodded once and Jocasa turned back to her Prime.

Xenia sat at the end of one bench, eating bread as though she knew she must eat but had no heart for it. She cast little nervous glances from one to another of the other Pairs, bit her lip, tore another small bite of bread loose. She started and caught her breath in a little squeak as Breyd eased herself down onto the bench across from her.

She is afraid, like I am; fearful for her Prime—afraid they will send her back out to fight and even more afraid they will not. "Did you sleep?" Breyd asked softly. Xenia nodded. "You had better have more of that bread, you haven't eaten enough to keep a mouse alive." Xenia managed a turning of lips that tried to be a smile, then obediently tore off a piece of bread and ate it.

She swallowed, sent her eyes sideways. "I—I do not belong here," she whispered urgently.

"Then I do not, either," Breyd whispered back. "But I intend to stay, and so will you. They need us." She turned to her own food. *I can't eat this.* But Xenia was watching her anxiously. She took a bite of bread, washed it down with the wine. It hurt her hands to hold the cup, but the wine eased her stomach and she made herself finish all of it.

Xenia was still watching her. "Eat," Breyd urged her. "If I can eat, you can eat. Do it for your Prime." Xenia looked doubtfully at the bread; Breyd waited until she had put another bite in her mouth. "Good. Did they let you see Akeros this morning?"

"They took him home already, Grysis came to tell me when I was getting my food. His hands—they looked so horrible! All blistered and puffy. He won't fight again, not soon." Xenia looked at her with wide, tear-filled eyes. Breyd closed her own eyes, shook her head.

"Don't—it's all right, Xenia, don't. If I weep now, I won't stop."

She looked up as Xhem came over. "Niddy asked me to thank you for telling her what you are doing; she will send you oil and peppers tonight, and fresh water to mix with your wine. She gave me more stuff for your burns." He handed her a leather wallet that reeked of the ointment. "Aunt Nevvia said you must be very careful for her sake, and promise you will not go outside the gates. She wants you to come home and stay. Niddy said you and I must pray for—for Tarpaen, this morning, since the family cannot go outside the gates for the pyre." He blotted his eyes on his cloak and sniffed hard. "Niverren says think of your mother; Niddy said also if you need anything else, tell me so I can fetch it for you." He drew a deep, shuddering breath. "Niddy says because—because she could not leave Aunt Nevvia, she did not come to—she could not come to see Tar—"

She laid a hand on his shoulder. "Don't, I know what she means, and I understand. It's all right, Xhem. You and I saw him last night. And we will be out there, for all his family."

He nodded. "Captain Nabid said to tell you, they will light—the pyre soon, if we are to go—"

"We'll go." She managed to get to her feet without much

fuss and no one seemed to notice how much weight she put on Xhem's shoulder. *I am tired, a little weak; they must not see that, and send me away.* She walked through the barracks without his help, but as they turned to go up the main avenue that led past the temple and the prince's palace, her courage nearly deserted her. *I cannot walk so far; I can't do it.* Xhem looked up at her anxiously and wrapped his arm around her waist. She brought her eyes down from the top of the hill, set her jaw and picked out a jutting wall. *Twenty steps; that isn't much. You can walk twenty steps.* They passed the wall; she looked up a little, found cracked stone steps. *Thirty paces, no more than that. You can walk that far.*

She leaned against the temple wall at the top, enough to catch her breath; her vision swam and everything ached. *It was only yesterday you were thrown across the road,* she told herself. *Of course you ache, of course your burns are painful. Do this, and then you can sleep a little. You must be strong so Grysis will let you out with the phalanx.* She held out her arm and Xhem placed himself under it once more.

It was very cool outside the south gate, and still dark save for the ruddy line of predawn against the eastern ridges and a few torches. Priests from the Temple of Warriors poured sweet oil on the wood; other priests walked around the pyre to bless the soldiers who had come to bid farewell to their dead comrades. There were no women and children, only a few old men huddled near the gate, protected by several men with drawn swords. She was the only female in sight, Xhem the only boy. Nabid came from the city and stood with them as the last bodies were brought from the barracks and laid upon piled wood.

Where is Laius? He should have been here. Did Tar matter so little to him? She looked at Nabid, but his eyes were closed and his expression withdrawn. *They have not even told me what happened. Enemy just outside the walls—the general wounded—did they kill an unarmed man to throw the companies into chaos for the loss of a signaler? Or was he trying to protect the general?* She swallowed. *I was hurt and half-mad last night, but someone should have told me. Nabid should have said when he took me to Tar.*

The priests had emptied their flasks of oil and stepped away from the pyre; others came forward with lit torches. *I cannot even see which body is his. Oh, Tar! Haffat will pay dearly for this, I swear to you.*

One of the priests raised his voice in the final prayer. "Let these honored dead be welcome at the great feast; let Atos take them to his bosom, and call them kindred. Let each hero who lies here shed his flesh so he may join the gods and call them brothers. Let the warmth and light of Atos fill those they leave behind, and grant them peace." A silence; the priests took up the torches and set them to the wood. Fire roared up.

Peace, Breyd thought bitterly. *Atos, if you are here, waiting to gather up my brother Tarpaen, do not give me peace until Haffat is dead and his armies destroyed! Give peace to my poor mother and comfort to my sister and grandmother; give peace to Xhem. Give me instead strength and courage; do not let me fail my city or my father. Make me worthy.*

She gasped, clutched her hands together; heat filled her breast and burned her cheeks. It was gone almost as instantly as it came but her hands still tingled. Silence all around her, save for the crackling of flames.

The priests walked slowly around the circle a last time, well away from the pyre which now burned high and hot. When they came to Nabid, they halted. Nabid knelt and gathered up a bulky bundle wrapped in a dark cloak. The head priest laid his hands upon it. "Blessings to the man whose armor this was, courage and strength to its inheritor." Nabid knelt and offered Tarpaen's panoply to Xhem. The priest laid one hand on the boy's head. "Take this weaponry and this armor and with it courage, for one day you will be called upon to defend your city and your prince, as did your brother."

Xhem's fingers trembled, but his voice was steady as he repeated the ancient response: "I take the panoply of my brother. No dishonor will stain it, or my brother's honor. And when the time comes, I shall put on my brother's armor, and take up his sword, to defend my city and my prince." Nabid patted his shoulder. Xhem gave the brightly burning pyre one last miserable look, then turned away, and they joined the others who were going back into the city.

It was a little easier, going back downhill. Nabid had offered to leave a man with her, but she'd refused. *I saw how the men out there looked at me when they went by, when they thought I was not watching.* When they stopped so she could catch her breath, she flexed her hands cautiously; the palms still tingled but her arms barely hurt. *Something—what I said out there, something happened.*

She was still very glad when she made it back to the messes.

Grysis—at the captain's bench by the hatches, and for a rare moment alone. She caught her breath and went over to him. "Sir."

"Secchi. Should you still be on your feet?"

"No, sir. I'll go back and sleep soon. But I have to know. My brother—no one has told me how he died." He looked up at her—warily, she thought. "I *have* to know," she said. "And our mother—"

"She may learn eventually," Grysis broke in flatly. "I do not think you will want to tell her."

"What did he do?"

"Nothing wrong," he assured her quickly. "The drummer went mad—General Piritos said the man thought the surrender was sounded. He—threw your brother from the walls." He grabbed her as she swayed and thrust her onto a bench. "Here—wait, here is my cup, drink."

"Laius." She shoved the cup aside and tried to get to her feet. "I will kill him—Laius!"

"He did that for you himself!" Grysis almost had to shout to be heard. She stared at him blankly, shook her head. "He is already dead. He stole the general's sword and jumped from the walls and broke his neck when he fell."

"And—and Tarpaen."

"Nabid can tell you better, he saw it. Your brother took up a sword, he said, and fought, but of course he could not hold out long." *Tar. Oh, my brother.* Tears spilled down her face; Grysis wrapped his arms around her and held her in a crushing grip while she clung to him and wept. "Here, Secchi," he said finally. "This is no place for you just now." He pulled her to her feet, kept an arm around her while he looked around the messes. "There—Mibro, you and Jocasa, come here!" He patted Breyd's cheek awkwardly as the Pair came running. "Go, get some sleep, Secchi. Don't look at me like that, I have not forgotten your Prime and I will not, but *you* will not go anywhere looking like that. The general said men will be allowed to search once it is light and the company in place to guard them. You cannot do anything to help your Prime except sleep, and get back your strength, and the use of your arms so you can fight again. Jocasa, you and Mibro help this Secchi back to her cot; stay with her until she sleeps."

She was so exhausted it took both Jocasa and Mibro to get her upright and keep her on her feet. People must be staring, she thought dully; they must have stared as she wept, they must have thought—but she no longer cared what they thought.

The sky was pale blue, Atos not yet risen; a cool breeze blew up from the south, bringing the smell of wood smoke. She shuddered; Jocasa gripped her shoulder in wordless sympathy. *They understand.* Her family, the prince, Tephys—even Grysis—none of them could possibly know what she felt just now. These knew.

At the doorway into the barracks, Jocasa looked up and stopped short. "Father! Over at the hospital barracks, that is the prince's chair!"

Mibro looked where she pointed, shrugged and said, "May be. His father came down after we rousted the pirates, made a speech to us, how well we'd served the city. Tough as a spear point, the old prince." He started into the barracks. "Prince Pelledar won't like it in there."

"No one would," Jocasa said quietly. "Breyd? Come on, let's get you flat." She looked at her fellow Secchi thoughtfully. "I wager we won't have to wait long with *you*. None of us looked as gruesome as you do, even after that first fight at the foot of the cliff."

She dredged up a smile from somewhere. "You always say *such* nice things, Jocasa." Jocasa laughed. Her eyes remained gravely concerned. They eased her down onto the cot; Breyd remembered one of them removing her sandals, someone tucking the cloak around her feet, nothing else. She slept heavily, and did not waken until nearly first horn the next day.

Prince Pelledar stood just inside the hospital barracks with four of his personal guard. *My father came here when there was battle. I cannot simply sit in the palace and hold myself apart from those who battle for the city—for my throne.* He had wakened early, uncertain at first what had roused him. The smell of burning wood and oil— He sat up and buried his face in his hands. *They burn the dead outside the city walls.*

Ye Sotris slept heavily. He eased himself from the couch

they shared and threw a light robe around his shoulders, tip-
toed from the chamber, and climbed onto the roof. He could
see the outline of the ridges and distant southern mountains
against the eastern sky; flames and smoke rising from beyond the wall. *They told me the numbers of dead and
wounded, how many missing. I cannot remember.*

Because you are afraid to remember, an inner voice said.
Because it will shame you, knowing how many men die.
How desperate the plight of the wounded. Somehow, it had
all crystallized; he must come here. And now he stood very
still and listened to the muted shrieks and wails, the sound
of many men shouting, or crying out or weeping, and he was
not certain he could force himself to move. *Even the old
man who guards the door has more courage than you!* He
swallowed, and walked into the large room.

His vision blurred and he wanted more than anything ever
in his life to simply turn and flee. He was rooted in place,
staring in horror at men who lay upon pallets or on the floor,
or on trestles against the wall. Flies hung in a black cloud or
clustered in men's wounds; the sharp smell of urine caught
in his throat. A woman not ten paces from him crouched
over her man, shrieking and tearing her hair; he lay with
fixed, blank stare and sagging, blood-covered jaw. Beyond
them, a beardless boy had torn the bandages from a stump of
arm and clawed at the pitch spread over what was left. A
voice rose to piercing, momentarily blanking out everything
else: "Someone, anyone—a dagger! Bring me a dagger, I
cannot bear any more!"

Pelledar caught his breath in a faint shriek; a heavy hand
fell on his shoulder. He spun around and stared into the eyes
of his general.

"Sire," Piritos said softly. "Come with me, now." Pelledar
trembled. "Let us get you out of this place." Piritos was
pale, his face streaked with runnels of sweat, his hair plastered flat. He wore nothing but a loincloth and fresh bandages on his shoulder and his thigh. Pelledar swallowed,
blindly turned from the wounded, and let himself be led outside. "That was a brave deed, my prince," Piritos said as the
door closed behind them. "Very brave. But you will do yourself no good coming here. The men in there are the most
badly injured. They will not know you or be aware of the
honor you just did them."

"Honor," Pelledar whispered. Bile flooded his mouth and

for one terrible moment, he feared he would vomit. The sickness receded, a little. Enough.

"It was an honor. I do not fault your heart for sending you here but—my prince, if you cannot disguise your horror at what you see, then I must beg of you, do not come into the barracks again. It will weaken your resolve, and your people cannot afford that. Worse, it will distress the soldiers who must go out to fight, if they see you as you look now. They will think we are already doomed."

"I—am sorry," Pelledar said.

"My prince, no." Piritos stepped aside so his men could see him into his chair. "You meant well and I salute you for that. It is not your fault that you could not face that." He gestured toward the barracks. "You are not the first or the only one to be sickened by it. But we cannot afford your pain or your pity. Please, go back to the palace. Forget what you have seen, and remain strong for all of us." Pelledar nodded; his face was utterly white and he was trembling violently as they handed him into his chair and carried it back to the palace. *Men dying and dead—and they have done nothing to bring this on themselves!* He moaned and clutched himself, and bit his lip so the men carrying him would not hear him weep. *All those brave men, those boys— that woman wailing for her dead husband. Ah, Denota and Atos both, what have I done? Haffat will not give over until they are all mangled and dead, and I go headless to my own pyre, with their shades to weigh me down forever.*

He caught the side of his hand between his teeth and bit down, hard. He could not emerge from this chair weeping and ill, his servants and his household guard would panic; his young wife would learn of it and— *No.* Somehow he got himself under control just as the chair was carried into the courtyard, somehow held his face expressionless and walked steadily up the steps and through the halls and up three flights of steps to the windowless clerk's closet off the great throne room. One inside, he leaned back against the door and let his eyes close.

It was still dark outside when Breyd woke, only a few dim oil lamps in the barracks to let those on duty at first horn see their way between the rows of cots and pallets. She yawned, stretched cautiously, rubbed her eyes. Aroepe sat on the cot next to her. "Breyd? How do you feel?"

"Mmm—tired still."

"You've slept almost a full day. Even through all the yell-ing in the courtyard at midday." She held up a handful of linen strips. "I thought I would unwrap your arms, make cer-tain everything was healing. But look." Breyd rolled over and sat up, held her left arm to the light. "I thought—they said you were burned! But I can't see anything."

Breyd touched the skin gingerly, then ran her fingers lightly from elbow to wrist. There was still no hair where it had been singed away, but no other sign of fire on her. She flexed her hands with care, then clenched them.

Aroepe was staring at her; as Breyd met her eyes, she managed a weak joke. "Your grandmother's ointment must be wonderful stuff. Or maybe the legends are true, that we—heal faster, because of the goddess."

Breyd shook her head; she felt rather dazed. "They don't hurt at all." Aroepe unwound the long strip from her right arm. The skin was paler than the rest where she had been burned, nothing more. *I prayed to Atos—is this his sign?*

But the sun god's anger was a hot fury like the Pair fury, when Denota's bond took them. She felt cold, filled with chill purpose. *If Haffat had not come, Father would not be out there, and Tar would not be dead. I will kill Haffat. Somehow, some way. I will kill him.* She bent over to pull on her sandals, and to get control of her emotions. When she spoke, she sounded only a little breathless. "Help me with my armor, Aroepe, will you?"

She could not find Grysis; Kroserot was dead. But Evrikos came into the messes as she was finishing her food, an officer's cloak slung across his shoulders. She went up to him, wordlessly held out her arms. Evrikos looked at the pale streaks, then studied her face for a very long moment. He finally shrugged and said, "The phalanx leaves as soon as I speak with Nabid. Go."

The sun rose as they marched from the gates, the phalanx, three Pairs, Breyd and Xenia. Xenia was subdued, pale in the early light; Breyd felt naked without Menlaeus at her right shoulder.

There were black oily patches on the road, but no other sign of the fighting two days earlier. A priest stood in the midst of the stains, guarded by archers as he chanted, other men were working out from the road, searching among the rocks. Breyd clung to her spear and fought for control. Menlaeus. He was out there, somewhere—still alive. Someone behind her was grumbling to his neighbor. "The Diye Haff could have climbed into the rocks out there after dark. If the magicians hide them again—"

"Why do you think that priest is out here?"

"But he may not be able to see them, either. Why are they still searching? No one could still be alive, and dead—there would be vultures—"

Breyd dug her fingers into the spear and briefly closed her eyes. *I will murder him with my bare hands!* "Silence back there!" Evrikos shouted furiously. He turned as one of the man scouring the east bank came back with a dagger.

"Ev—sir. I found this among the stones, just out there."

Breyd pushed forward and held out a hand; it shook. Her mouth had gone dry. "It is Father's, I helped him wrap the haft. Where—where was it found, Morius?"

Morius turned to point. "Just there, where the rocks form an overhang."

"I see." Evrikos looked thoughtfully at Breyd. "You think your Prime is still out there—they told me." She nodded, unable to speak. "You think you can find him." She nodded again. He waved a hand. "I did not take you back into the company for that purpose. Look out there, Secchi, you can see what it's like. Anyone could be out there, and he could be anywhere!"

"I know, sir." She hadn't expected they would let her join the searchers, but her heart still sank.

"He is not in the open; but other men are still missing. They were not returned with the prisoners yesterday, either."

"Sir," Morius said. "I also found this, in the same place." Breyd took the rind from him; it was fresh enough to still be pliable, and release a little tart, oily fragrance when she bent it. "There was blood by the knife, but not very much."

Breyd shook her head. "Father had no fruit with him, but he never eats these."

"Then I tell you what I think," Evrikos said. "My missing men found him; they may be out there somewhere, but they're hiding. Perhaps they've found a cave. They'll come in when they can, or when they dare. Or one of them will come for help. With the Diye Haff moving around out there and us not able to see them, it's too dangerous for them to do anything now—or for me to let you out there." He eyed her warily.

Breyd bit her lip, then turned to look out across the cliff face. It was at least a full *ciph*, top to bottom, and it ran most of the way around the city. *What use is it, to know Father lives, but not know where he is, or which way, or how far?* He could be anywhere out there. Evrikos was right. She touched her fist to her breast and went back to her place in the line.

Moments later, the priest walked back toward the city, his guard close around him. He was shaking his head and muttering to himself.

Xenia glanced at Breyd as she came back; Breyd shrugged, then shook her head. Xenia turned back to look down the road.

There was dust everywhere this morning; Breyd could see little of the fighting and none of it made sense to her. *I can only tell theirs from ours by the direction they leave the plain: to come this way, or cross the Oryon.* Horn signal from the walls, someone sending out the general's orders. *But not my brother.* She turned hot eyes to the Diye Haff camp. Across the Oryon, they were building another ballista, and men came across the ridge with a cart of fresh-cut logs.

By Haffat's orders. Who is he, to come here and covet what is ours? Xenia touched her arm and whispered, "Breyd, you're trembling. Are you certain you should be out here?"

"I am fine," Breyd whispered. She forced her eyes from that camp, looked out to sea instead. Foam capped the waves and the water was steel-gray this morning; waves dashed high against the shore and the stone mole; two ships anchored well offshore rocked wildly. Not far away, she could see what was left of a brightly-painted Mirikosi trading ship, heeled over so far to one side its decks were awash.

The mole itself was deserted; it would be dangerous to try to bring a ship in with the tide running west to east. The Mirikosi know that, Breyd thought angrily. *The Mirikosi were our friends. They have always traded with us, walked our streets, eaten our food and drunk wine with our men— and now they lick their conqueror's sandals!*

At third horn, they drew into tight formation and marched down the road to cover the base of the road, while Edrimon's company went back inside for food and rest. By fourth horn, with the sun nearly overhead, there was dust everywhere—clouds of it where men fought. She could hear the clashing of metal and the cries of the wounded. A company of enemy horse galloped up the road and turned off eastward, toward the Oryon.

But chariots came up the road right behind them. The cars were pulled to a halt a distance from the phalanx, and men jumped from the cars with javelins and bows. Breyd could see the red haze rising around the Pair in front of her; the edge of the bond rubbed her nerves. But the company was not closing with them, and Evrikos shouted: "Wait!" The Dyaddi edged forward a pace, two paces. *They cannot help themselves,* Breyd realized. *They will throw themselves at those men, and the enemy will hold their distance and shoot at them. Unless they have protection they will all die!* "Shield them!" she shouted. Evrikos turned to shout her down, then realized what she had said. "Shield wall!" he bellowed in turn. "Cover them, front rank, hurry!" Breyd grabbed Xenia's arm and they ran forward, shields high, to help cover the Pairs, who were racing down the road. But other Diye Haff came running from the west. "Third and fourth rank, quarter turn to meet them, go!" Evrikos shouted.

An arrow slammed into Breyd's shield and bounced away; a spear struck the ground in front of her feet. But many of the men were backing away now, climbing into the chariots and trying to turn them. The Pairs fell on the rest.

Breyd brought her shield arm down and freed a javelin; Xenia drew her sword and set herself against Breyd's shoulder. Behind them, enemy were screaming and trying desperately to escape the Dyaddi. Evrikos and the rest of the company killed or wounded half the foot soldiers before the rest turned and ran. The chariots were all jammed together as horses shrieked and fought to free themselves; a car splintered and the driver went down with it. Breyd threw herself into another car and killed the fighter. The driver leapt from the car and fled. Two more horses went down, and several cars finally broke free, their horses galloping wildly down the road. A car went over, throwing the passenger and then the driver. The rest who could ran, leaving behind their wounded and dead, and the rest of the chariots.

Jocasa and her Prime sat in the dirt, clinging to each other; Aroepe and Laprio held each other up somehow, but both were shaking. Xera and Duplos sat a little apart from the rest, on the back gate of an enemy chariot, staring dully at the ground.

Breyd knelt to rub her javelin in the dirt to clean the point. She looked at the boy she had just killed with it; he was huddled in on himself, his face still contorted with pain. His beard was nothing but a few straggling hairs on both sides of his chin. *He is dead, and I am alive.* He had followed Haffat and he was dead. She turned away from him, and felt no pity for him—nothing but that cold anger. *I did not ask him to come here; Haffat did. I did not seek his death, Haffat brought that about.*

She walked over to Aroepe and her Prime; they would need help; all the Dyaddi would. Men stood guard around them, while others dragged the enemy bodies away, and retrieved whatever weapons they could.

"That," a man near Breyd said quietly as he took back red-stained arrows, "for Kroserot, who was my captain and my friend."

"For Kroserot," another said as he wiped his sword a last time in the dirt and sheathed it.

"Yes," Breyd replied as softly as she accepted three javelins with her particular leather wrappings. "And for my brother, and for my Prime."

"That for my father." Xenia said flatly, and resheathed her sword.

They took one of the whole chariots to transport the Dyaddi and sent a man to lead it; six men came down from the phalanx at midroad to replace them and not long after another company came out to relieve them and to bring up the horses and chariots which could be used. The rest of the cars were set afire.

Xenia was covered with dust and darker runnels where sweat had plowed through the dust. Breyd knew she must look at least as bad and even her teeth felt thick with grit. With luck, the women might have access to the baths next to the hospital; if not, even a bucket of cold, rank-smelling water from the barracks well would be better than nothing. *Ask Xhem to ask Niddy for body and hair oil.* The road seemed endless; the backs of her legs ached fiercely.

Eriana was waiting in the far end of the barracks where the Dyaddi slept, with three wooden buckets of water and cloths. Someone had strung two cloaks up, to block the corner. "I already asked. Grysis says we women can have the baths but not until eighth horn. So I had water brought. It's—from the well here."

"Yes," Breyd said. "I can smell bad eggs from here. Bless you, though. I could not have gone for it."

"I know," Eriana said. "Nor me. *We* were all the way down the road earlier, remember? Grysis found a messenger who was off duty and willing to be useful."

Breyd sponged off her face and the back of her neck. "Ahhh. That is wonderful, reek and all."

"I thought you were burned," Eriana said curiously.

"I was; it wasn't as bad as they thought," Breyd said and bent down to remove her sandals and shake them out.

"Oh. Well, I am glad to hear it. Did you hear, my betrothed came earlier and left me oranges. I'll share."

"Oh, lovely," Jocasa said. She was still pale and exhausted from the fighting, but she accepted a wedge of fruit with a smile, popped it into her mouth, and spoke around it. "Mine has gone to see Mother and come to the gates to walk me home twice, but he never brings gifts."

"Someone's gave her a silver brooch," Eriana said, "but I wasn't supposed to say who."

"Breyd?" Aroepe asked. Breyd looked up, laughed briefly and without humor, and went back to tugging at the greave straps.

"I think Apodain has forgotten all about me. I don't think about him, much, either."

"How can you not think about someone like that?" Xera asked. "He's just so beautiful—I've been madly in love with him ever since the first time I saw him win the footraces at midsummer. All that lovely browned skin—" She sighed happily.

"Wonderful," Breyd said. "He's yours, then."

"Oh, I wish, I really do," Xera said. "Jeplo is nice enough, but he's short and a little chubby—not at all as nice to look at."

"Yes," Eriana said. "But you have to remember, with Apodain comes Khadat. Breyd, how can you bear the thought of living with that woman?"

"I won't," Breyd said firmly, she looked up to see all the other Secchi staring at her. She managed a grin and added, "I think I shall abduct Apodain, and we shall seek our fortunes elsewhere."

"Oh—? Oh," Eriana laughed. "You're joking, aren't you? It's too bad anyone so pretty and wealthy has to have a mother who could turn you to stone with a look."

I won't have him at all, let alone her, Breyd told herself firmly. *Even if I survive this war, whatever comes, it won't be Apodain.*

When she looked back later, the days all ran together, and she could find little to separate them: Menlaeus's knife, that shield wall, Eriana's oranges. Another day, long after, when they let her go home for a little; Creos was barely conscious and raving, in constant pain. Nevvia had hacked her hair short and clung to her daughter frantically. She had come back to the barracks shaking and sick with worry, and been almost grateful Grysis had not let her go again soon.

Another day, and another: She could not separate them. Nidya sent messages and small corked jugs of oil and hot peppers, fresh water from the fountain near the house.

She appreciated the water even more than the peppers, though the bread was tasteless—they were conserving the salt. But the water level was falling as midsummer neared; even after she had rubbed herself with scented oil, she could smell the faint odor of sulfur.

Another day, following a very black and cloudy night; the orange ball of Atos rose as the silver rind of Atelos sank into the western sea. *An omen,* said many of the older men; others like Captain Frewis laughed or jeered at them. But as the sun lightened the eastern sky, battle hardened veterans of the Diye Haff came from clefts and folds in the upper ledges behind the city to the south, to attack her walls at an hour and place unexpected.

Apodain came abruptly awake as horn cry shattered the dawn. For one long moment, he lay stunned, but the call shifted to one he knew—*Enemy at the gates*—and he leapt to his feet, caught up his brother Hemit's bow and arrow case, and pelted to the roof. He shivered a little—he was clad only in a thin tunic—and scanned the land beyond the walls anxiously. There. Men had been working to build yet another funeral pyre; the enemy would know by now that the gate was opened at this hour and somehow they had climbed from the far side of the Oryon to wait their chance.

*How could they have managed such a climb in full panoply,
in the dark?* Apodain strung the bow and tested the string.
He himself had made that climb in daylight, years before
and never since. *But there will be fewer of them to climb
back down.* He set an arrow to the string and waited; from
this roof, he had a clear view across the funeral pyre toward
the nearly sheer eastern cliff face. Diye Haff were running
from the cliffs toward the outer wall, speeding toward the
gate and some of them he thought, carried grapples. *There
are not enough men along this part of the city to stop them;
they must send others to guard the wall!* But horn cry rose
from the main gates again: They were attacked there, and
along the west end of the walls.

Apodain drew the great horn bow and smiled grimly. He
could have hit half those men from a moving chariot; here,
above them and on solid stone, he could not possibly miss.
He let fly a long silver and black-flecked arrow; a Diye Haff
commando stumbled and fell. Apodain already had another
arrow in place.

Out on the city wall, someone turned to see who was
shooting; he turned away at once. Apodain set his lips in a
tight line and felt for another arrow; another Diye Haff fell,
another. There were only a few shafts left, but now men
came running along the wall from the main gates, and old
men and boys had already climbed up by the Shepherd's
gate to throw stones. The southern gate was shut tight.
Apodain drew back and sighted once more. His right arm
wanted to tremble with the effort of staying straight against
the pull of the unaccustomed heavy bow.

A shriek brought him around, arrow still nocked on the
string; Khadat stood in the middle of the roof, a cloak
clutched around her and her hair all in disarray. "Give me
that at once, and get below, you stupid young fool! Did I
save you from the chariot only to lose you here?"

He swung back around and loosed the arrow at random
and shouted, "Get off this roof, Mother!"

"Reott, take that bow from him!" Khadat screamed.
Apodain glanced over his shoulder. Reott stood just behind
Khadat, clad only in his underlinen.

"Reott, there are enemy out there, and she is in danger.
Get her down from here!"

"He will not!" Khadat shrieked in a wild fury; the words
were cut off as her voice spiraled. "Let go of me—let *go* of

me!" Apodain's eyes were fixed on the enemy beyond the walls. He kept them there until the last enemy had been cut down or fled, and he had used the last of Hemit's arrows.

He remained on the roof for some time, watching as men cleared away the enemy bodies; watching as the priests and comrades of the dead went back out and the pyre was finally lit. When he finally unstrung the bow and went indoors, Khadat was nowhere in sight.

She returned at fourth horn, clad in Denota's green and carrying a spray of wheat to hang across the outer lintel, but her face was as grim as if she had participated in some dark rite of Atelos. Apodain was loitering in the hallway. He waited until the servants had put the grain in place, then stepped into the light where she could see him.

Khadat stopped and set her lips in a hard line; she tried to brush past him, but he stepped in front of her. "We will talk, now," she said flatly, "in my accounting room."

He shook his head. "We will talk here, Mother."

She folded her arms across her chest and demanded furiously, "How dare you take Hemit's bow?"

"Because you hid mine where I could not find it," Apodain replied evenly. "And I needed it this morning."

She glared at him, but Apodain returned the furious look with an expressionless one of his own and waited her out. She sighed deeply. The anger died out of her face, and a little frown puckered her brow. She laid a trembling hand on his arm. "My son. Why must you still fight me, every finger of the way? I kept you alive, are you no more grateful than this? The prince tells me that the boy who once drove you is dead, but you live. If you are not pleased to live, then can you not at least be glad for me?"

Loros died because I stood aside and let Septarian kill him. "And now you are alive. Your body is still your own, not a plaything for the Diye Haff—are you not grateful?" Khadat's face went very deeply red, then almost as suddenly white as she took his meaning.

"How dare you speak to your mother in such a way?"

"You made me what I am, Mother. I will not let you die by their hands; I will not die that way either, if I can prevent it."

"We will not—"

"Mother, we are close-kin to the prince. If Haffat takes the city, how long do you think we will live—once the prince is murdered?"

"I warned Pelledar not to anger Haffat!" Khadat began in a furious whisper.

"Yes. But that is in the past, and it doesn't matter which of you was right." He drew himself up and she stared at him as if he had suddenly become a stranger. "I swore a shameful oath to you, under dreadful pressure. I have kept that oath. But you will not order me to stand still and let Haffat kill us all, Mother. I will do what I must to keep this house safe. You will not stop me."

Khadat gripped his arms; he took her hands and moved her away from him. "You ungrateful, wretched boy!" she shouted. "I—I will—"

"Do whatever you choose, Mother." He turned away from her and started to walk away. "I no longer care." He turned back then, as if he only just remembered. "Tell me where my panoply is hidden." She was staring at him blankly. "My panoply."

"I will not have it," she whispered. He could not be certain if she replied to him, or to some dreadful inner thought. She turned, one shaking hand holding onto the wall, and went into her accounting chamber.

Reott came up behind him as Khadat closed the door. "Sir. Your panoply. She will never tell you where your arms are. But I will."

Thirty-seven days since he had been wounded; Piritos was angry with himself. His thigh was nearly healed and clean, but he had reopened the shoulder twice and this time it wasn't closing neatly. *An older man does not recover so quickly from wounds as did the youth who swam the isthmus with Perlot and his son.*

His mood hadn't been improved when he looked into the enemy camp this morning. The ballista were both nearly finished. *They deliberately built them where we could watch.* But they were right in the camp, heavily guarded; he could not send a raiding party to destroy them.

Piritos let an aide examine his wound and help him wash and put on clean linen; he drank his wine but could barely force himself to eat plain bread, and fell asleep in his chair. He came awake at his aide's touch, tired and disoriented from the unexpected and too-short nap. "Sir, the captains." The aide eyed him doubtfully. "I can send them away."

"Bring them," he said shortly. He waited as they were seated and wine brought, tried to control his temper. *It is not their fault I am tired. Or that I once again hurt.*

Brysos looked around the table and finally spoke up. "Sir, for tomorrow—we have an idea."

Piritos listened in astonished silence until the captain of royal chariot was finished, then shook his head. "Are you mad? Take back the mole—for what purpose?"

"A raid," Frewis replied at once. "It was my thought first, sir. If we can hold it, they won't be able to land any more ships. And it will hearten the men, even if we can't hold it for long."

"And how heartened will the men who die out there be?" Piritos inquired sarcastically. "And their families?"

Frewis eyed him sidelong, but Brysos said, "We will put a half company of royal chariot out to protect their flank, picked men. But that is not all of the plan. If we attack the mole, perhaps fire another ship, or fire the camp out there—Haffat will come from the main camp across the Oryon, as he did before. We can send archers on our best and fastest horses, with pitch-tipped arrows to fire the ballistas."

"You've all gone mad," Piritos said flatly.

"Sir, no," Nabid said quickly. "We've worked it out; there are men who know the river banks and the open land this side of the Oryon; we have men who can hit anything at the farthest range of an arrow. A target as large as a ballista would be nothing."

"But—to take the mole." Piritos shook his head. "We couldn't hold it before, and we've lost men and horses since then. Too many to risk such a thing."

Frewis stirred. "But General, it isn't necessary to hold the mole for long, and this time it will be seasoned men backing us, not wild boys. We badly need that raid, though, sir. And if we can, somehow take out one of those ballistas, or even both of them, before they are completed. We cannot afford another one of their attacks like that last one."

He was right about that, Piritos thought bleakly. And his captains needed that raid as much as any of the companies. They were losing heart, and he could not blame them. It made a man feel hopeless after a while, fighting such an endless war. All the same, he might have won against the commanders, but against the commanders, and his own pain and exhaustion—he had no last answer for them. "All right. We will send out a hand-picked sortie to take back the mole, a full phalanx to back them, and mounted archers ready to fire the siege machines." He got to his feet, swaying slightly; an aide came over to support him. "I am going to my couch. Go over the maps one last time, and make certain there is nothing left to chance. You will hearten no one if your plan fails."

But the raid was in trouble almost from the first. Haffat let them overrun the shore and take the mole unopposed; he drew back the company that had camped on the sand and doubled the guard on the ballista. The men who rode out to fire it did not return, and no one ever knew what happened to them.

Late the next afternoon, Piritos watched Haffat's chariot and cavalry sweep across the thin line of Ghezrathi noble chariot and back through it once more, cutting off the mole; a slender warship came in the other way, and men leapt onto the stone wall, capturing the Ghezrathi. Haffat's crack horse split, some going to secure the mole; most turned left and drove the fleeing Ghezrathi royal chariot before them.

By day's end, fully half the plain between the Alno and the Oryon was controlled by Haffat's men—from the stone mole where ships anchored and men unloaded them, most of the way to the cliff. Five of the city's most experienced—but thinly stretched—heavy infantry companies were ranked against them.

Piritos closed his eyes and turned away; Atos dropped into cloud cover. As night came on, a hundred or more of Haffat's fires spread across the plain.

They won back a little ground the next morning, lost a little by nightfall.

"The general has ordered us to stand only half-length duty out here from now on." Evrikos was very pale and his broken left arm had been bound close to his body. He was clearly in considerable pain, but the only officer of any kind left to the phalanx; Edrimon had been pinned to the ground at the base of the road the day before by at least ten enemy spears, the rest of his company wounded or dead.

Breyd stood with Xenia and Akeros and tried to pay attention. Akeros' left hand was still heavily bandaged; he had bound the spear to his right wrist because his hand would not hold it for long at a time. Xenia's face was pinched with his discomfort.

Breyd was giddy from exhaustion; whatever sleep she got never seemed to be enough. The bond between her and Menlaeus held, but she was beginning to wonder if it was only her mad desire that kept it alive.

Two other Pairs completed this partial phalanx: Jocasa and Aroepe, and their Primes. Eriana—poor, silly Eriana would never tease any of them again. Eriana and her Prime Lotros were gone, killed two days earlier when the ballista lobbed Fire into their midst. Poor little Eriana would feel very out of place at the feast-board of heroes. In spite of her weariness, Breyd smiled. Unless, of course, some hero already there paid court to her—or unless Xera was already there, awaiting her friend.

Poor Xera. *No, pity Duplos, and the poor woman who wed Duplos and bore him only Xera.* Breyd had herself been wounded when a single ball of Fire fell among them, but she had somehow put that aside in the urgency of the moment, had helped dazed and frantic Duplos pull his daughter from the fray, but too late. Xera had died that night of dreadful burns, without knowing any of them—her family or the remaining Dyaddi who gathered nearby. Her mother— *I will not think of her,* Breyd told herself. There was no point; one more woman with her hair hacked short for grief, her gown rent by her own nails, her voice already hoarse with shrill wailing. They could not help themselves, any more than Nevvia could, but it did no good to the living in the hospital barracks, or those who must somehow find the courage to go back out and battle an enemy seemingly without end. *Goddess, keep them from us, these women who can do nothing but bewail their fate and their dead, and so distract the living from what tasks remain to them before they themselves are killed.*

The Diye Haff had the mole and everything across the Alno. Perhaps they camped in Nidya's vineyards and ate her grapes while they bragged to each other about their kills.

She shook herself; Evrikos was still speaking. "Ridlo, you will hold the middle road, I will take the lower. At third horn we will be relieved."

But long before third horn, Evrikos was overwhelmed; Ridlo's company held against the men who swarmed up the road, but more came up from rocks on both sides of it. The remaining Dyaddi made one run at them, but the enemy merely pulled back and sent archers to the front of the ranks; Ridlo's company had to grab the Pairs and haul them back into the relative safety of the company.

They were outnumbered by at least seven to one. Ridlo waved his sword and the company began to retreat toward the gates.

Ridlo was at her left arm, Duplos at her right, and the three of them killed and stabbed and cut wildly at the enemy, but more came. Others were always there to leap across their fallen comrades and fight. Somehow, finally, the walls were close, the road level, and Breyd heard the loud creak of a gate being swung open. Strong hands dragged them inside.

"All theirs," Breyd whispered; there were tears running down her face, but when she looked, Ridlo also wept, and so did Duplos, and all the men of the phalanx who had made it back to the city. The two Pairs clung to each other. A horn cry alerted them, a shouted order followed. "Move, now! Back to the barracks, to make way for those who follow!"

"Those few who follow," Ridlo whispered.

"I know," Breyd replied; they wrapped arms around each other, and held each other up. A horrid blast threw them to the ground again; Breyd pushed herself up on shaking arms and stared in horror at the gates. They were twisted and half off their hinges. Another blast and then another, somewhere outside the city. She blotted her face; her nose was bleeding.

Someone on the wall bellowed: "Aid to the general, now! And someone else, "They have a ballista south of the city!" Flame shot skyward not far off. *Mother, Nidya!* Horror blocked her throat; she would have bolted for home, but her legs wouldn't hold her. Someone on the inner wall was screaming and men came running along the inner wall. "The Temple of Warriors! It's—it's gone, all gone, all of them! There's nothing left but fire and a hole in the outer wall!"

Horn cry silenced them. General Piritos, his face bloody and his cloak rent, stood above the inner gates, leaning heavily on two of his aides, but his voice was still strong. "The street will be cleared, to make room for those who follow! The companies will go to the barracks and tend whatever wounds they have, and hold themselves ready!"

* * *

At midday, the order came and within the hour, she watched from the roof above the barracks with the twelve Pairs, the other fourteen single Primes and Secchi. What was left of Evrikos' phalanx and all the other companies waited on the inner wall and the fighting grounds as a pale Prince Pelledar climbed the steps to the inner wall and crossed to the outer, Piritos close behind him and trying hard not to show the weariness and pain every man and woman in the barracks knew plagued him. Behind them came Tephys, Meronne, and four priestesses, but not the successor who had been her shadow for so many days.

Before the wreck of the main gates stood a chariot—a Ghezrathi royal chariot newly painted with golden lions and flying truce flags. The driver held matched stallions in place; a hard-faced man of middle years with chill eyes and a gold lion about his neck gazed up. Behind the car, twenty mounted men wearing black armor and gold lions.

There was a long silence, which Haffat finally broke. "I call upon my brother, Pelledar, and ask him this last time: Shall we have peace?" He swept his arm wide. "My army holds your plain, all the outside world is mine—you sit behind these pitiful stone walls and you are alone. Do you think stone shall crush the lion? But other cities have hidden behind such stone walls, and in the end it has cost them all.

"Is this your choice still? There is a ballista south of you, another to the west. And there are trees still to be turned into beams for another ballista and another. We have already breached your walls. Will you let others continue to die, while you cower in your palace?

"Or will you yield? For I said at the first that you had one chance and no other, to avoid Haffat's wrath, but I am not an evil man and the Lion is generous. We take pity upon your people, led astray by swaggering generals and arrogant princes and superior priests! But this is the last time; there will be no other. Will you yield?

"If you do, Haffat will allow no further harm to your city and your crops, your vineyards and your ships than you yourself have already caused to be made. Haffat will take your word that he and Pelledar shall be brothers, and shall join together thereafter in the fight against our common enemies.

"Say yes, and there will be peace between us."

Pelledar looked down at him; he might have spoken, but

Piritos leaned forward and whispered, "Wait. Hear all of this pretty speech."

Haffat waited a very long time, and when he spoke again, his voice was harsh. "Or shall we have war again, and more war, until there are none left but women and their infants to man the walls? Until you have eaten the rats and then the babes themselves, while Haffat's men sit before your gates and grow increasingly angry? Do you wait and wait again until the gates are taken despite you, and the fury of Haffat's men pours through them—for know this, my brother, I can say to these soldiers now: 'Those brothers you lost upon the plain, they are avenged by those you have killed.' Continue to deny me and to keep them waiting before the gates and what man could control their fury? What man would?

"Both rivers are now mine; your stone mole has been mine for many days. Your entire plain is mine, to burn and pillage or to leave much as I have found it—and the fault yours for whatever damage has been done these past days, for *I* surely did not wish it!

"Give over the fighting," Haffat said quietly into a very deep silence. "You can go nowhere, you have no allies. There are none who will march to Ghezrat's rescue, however long you hold out against me and mine, none which are not already my lands or which will soon be. The ballistas stand ready with Ergardi to control them and Fire to send against you."

A very long silence. The streets were jammed with anxious people, the barracks roofs and the fighting ground full; the inner walls all around the city covered. No one spoke.

Haffat stood in his chariot and gazed up; Pelledar squared his shoulders and brought up his chin. "I must talk with my captains, and with my council," he said. "Give me until this hour tomorrow, to bring you an answer."

I have him—I have them! Haffat thought jubilantly, though he kept it from his face by main effort. *Else he had never said such a thing!* "Granted," was all he said; he touched the arm of the driver, who turned the car about and drove it at a gallop back down the hill.

Pelledar leaned heavily against the wall. Piritos touched his shoulder and he shook his head. "I am sorry, General. I could not send him away angry once more. It is enough; enough men have died, enough young women. It—it is enough."

General Piritos blinked rapidly, and when he spoke his voice was rough. "You did right, my prince. But come; there is not much time until he returns, and you have much to decide between now and then."

17

Pelledar turned from the wall and was surrounded by his household men, led across to the inner wall and down to his enclosed chair. He looked at no one; in the streets, people stared after his chair and began to whisper. A woman burst into tears and was held by her husband, but tears ran down his face as well.

Tephys came across the square moments later, her priestesses around her. A woman clutched at her robes. "Priestess—Tephys. They say he'll come in and kill us all!"

"He's killed everyone in Mirikos," another woman cried out and someone beyond her whispered, "He'll send his sorcerers with that fire!"

"He won't," Meronne said softly. A young woman with newly hacked hair knelt on the cobbles, clutching her three small children and sobbing hopelessly. A girl of perhaps four clung to her leg and wept because her mother did, knowing only her mother was afraid; a stony-faced boy only a little older held his sister and stared at his mother. Tephys went to her knees and touched the woman's hair, then set a hand under her chin. "You must not weep," she whispered. "These babes need you strong." She got back to her feet and raised her hands, cutting through the rising hysteria. "The prince has not given the city to Haffat!"

"Yet!" a man's voice bellowed from deep in the crowd. Tephys turned to glare in that direction.

"Go to your homes, all of you," she shouted. "Pray to the goddess for courage and strength! There was nothing decided yet; Haffat came to ask for surrender, but he did not get it. The prince has gone to consider with his council what is best for all of you. You all know his love for the people of Ghezrat, he will never abandon you to the Diye Haff!" She heard grumbling back in the crowd, but the young widow crouched at her feet had stopped weeping. "Spread

that word around the city, if you will do something useful."
She let her hands down and led her priestesses back to the
temple.

Piritos listened to Tephys, then turned so he could look
out across the plain—where one now very distant chariot
was being driven at full speed toward the southern crossing
of the Oryon followed by his royal escort. Men stood on
both sides of the crossing holding Haffat's banners and those
of Axtekeles. Piritos sighed faintly, crossed the narrow
bridge between the walls and walked toward the barracks.

He could still hear the weeping and nervous voices in the
avenue as he walked away, but none of what people were
saying. Just as well, perhaps, that he could not.

On the fighting grounds, the companies were drawn up in
formal ranks, the captains standing with them. But the ranks
were badly depleted and some companies had lost half their
number or more. It sickened him. *All that waste of good
lives, and for what?* His leg still ached when he climbed; the
long cut had healed, but the muscle was still weak. His
shoulder burned, and he'd come awake twice this last night,
rolling on it. He'd stayed awake the last time. *Only a matter
of time before Haffat came to the gates. How many times has
he written or given that brave and ringing speech, I wonder,
since some scribe wrote it for him?* He must have thought
himself a true Great King out there today, Piritos thought
sourly, with his chariot and his gold ornament, and his escort
of royal sons and cousins.

Pelledar would accept Haffat's terms, though he had not
said so. He might not think yet that he would give in, but he
had no choice; Haffat had left him none.

Piritos reached level ground, and the leg tried to give way
on him. Some of the nearby older men—heavy infantry and
a few of the common chariot attached to that phalanx when
their captain was killed—eyed each other sidelong. He bit
his lower lip to hold back anger, for he knew what they
thought: *The wounds must be worse than we are told; he will
die of them.* Not two full moon-passings, and he looked like
a wreck of an old man. *That things come to this pass, that
Ghezrat's general excites pity among those he leads!* He was
upset with them—more with himself, for hating their pity.

He turned to face what was left of his army. "You heard
the words of Haffat. He offers us surrender upon good terms,
no injury to property or further loss of life, if the prince

gives over now. Now, should Pelledar refuse that—*kindly* offer," he emphasized sourly, and scattered sardonic laughter answered him, "I suppose we shall all die, one way or another—by slow starving, or Fire—one by one fighting from street to street or slaughtered in our homes defending our families.

"The prince will accept, I think." He paused, waited until a low murmur of comment died away. "Even if he were a warrior king of three hundred years ago come back to life, Haffat still holds all the plain. And if we surrender now, we still have something: Our families and homes. Our pride. No one else has withstood Haffat as long as we did.

"But if we surrender now, there is a chance we might one day take back Ghezrat. I tell you this, knowing some of you will say we quit too soon, or that we must keep fighting, must kill whatever enemy we find in our streets. You will remember this single act of our prince is not the end of everything. You will not act recklessly, or give the enemy cause to exact vengeance against your women and children.

"If the prince says, lay down arms, I will obey that order; so will you all. But we are giving *in,* not giving up!" He paused; a shout of approval answered him. "Yes!" He held up his arms and waited for silence. "This will not be an easy time for any fighter. It may be as long as a season, or a year—it may be longer still, before we can reclaim our city.

"Enough of that. Remember what I have said, do not lose hope entirely; this is not the end of everything.

"Go to your homes now. Tell your families that their prince will not simply feed us all to the lion. You know the horn call, if I send for you at any hour, you will come at once." He looked around the courtyard, nodded. "Whatever I learn, whatever I can tell you, you will know." He spread his arms wide; tears filled his eyes. "If I could do more for you, you know I would. Whatever can be done to salvage eventual victory from this black hour—that we will all do, you and I, and the prince—every one of us. The gods give you strength." He turned and walked away quickly, making his way diagonally across the ground toward his small set of rooms. Behind him, there was utter silence for a very long moment, then men near the gates began to chant his name. Other men and a smattering of women's voices took up the chant, and it spread until it seemed to him the walls shook with it. He turned in the doorway of the chamber that served as the meeting room for his cadre and held up both arms in salute, then went inside. His shoulder was bleeding again, just a little, his vision blurred, but that was emotion. He blotted his eyes carefully, eased his tired body down into his favorite chair, and waited for the first of the captains to come.

Behind him, the Dyaddi embraced in one tight knot all together; beyond them, an older man wiped his eyes and sniffed loudly. At his side, a boy turned to his neighbor and asked in a small voice, "He doesn't really believe Haffat won't kill us all, does he?"

"He put a good face on it," the neighbor said softly. "But it's a choice between the ballista and a sword across the neck, *I* think." The slinger behind them snorted loudly and said, "They're fools. We could have held the city against Haffat; he's lost enough men already and he is so far from home, it wouldn't take many more deaths for them to turn on him."

The sedan chair stopped at the base of the broad steps leading to the palace; Pelledar took the steps by twos, hurried down the hall and went directly to the roof garden. Ye Sotris was there, seated on her favorite bench; the younger boys were nowhere in sight. Pelledar skirted the pool and knelt next to her, wrapped his arms around her waist and let his forehead rest against her knee. It was a very long moment before he recovered his breath enough to speak. "I feared you would be already gone."

She laid a hand on his hair, stroked it back from his ears gently. "No. I would not have left you without—saying good-bye. The steward told me where you were. I hoped you would come back, and that there would be a—a little time for us. It is—quite bad, isn't it?"

"Haffat has all but the walls now. And he has breached them badly; the Temple of Warriors is—is gone. All of it. We have lost everything outside. He threatens us with siege."

"Do not tell me all he threatened," Ye Sotris whispered. "And I will not ask. I was in my father's court the winter the pirates came to offer such terms as fighting men name; I know the bloody words they use."

"I asked time to consider," Pelledar said. He sat back and looked up at her. "I have until this hour tomorrow."

"But you will take his terms," she prompted after a moment. He turned away from her and nodded.

"As many of them as I must. But that will be all of them, or nearly all."

She laid a hand under his chin and turned his head so he had to look at her once more. Her eyes suddenly were brimming, and her lips trembled. She looked down at him for a very long time, then slipped from the bench to kneel beside him and bury her face in his shoulder. "Come with me, with us—underground. Don't leave me down there, alone in the dark with your children. They—Haffat will kill you, husband!"

He shook his head, patted her shoulder. "No. He will not do that."

"Don't *lie* to me!" She pounded her fists against his chest. "He will kill you, and I will—I cannot face years of dark and silence, not without you!" She gulped, pressed her face against him to blot her tears, then looked up at him once more. "Please. I planned this hour, so many times, how brave I would be for you. Now it's here—oh, Pelledar, beloved, I can't!"

"Ye Sotris," he said softly, and bent down to kiss her. He sat back on his heels and sighed very quietly. "All right, beloved. When could I ever refuse you? I'll come—but later, once the terms have been set." He managed a shaky laugh. "They've all been at me to go and hide if this hour came—Tephys, my general, all the council."

"You'll come? You swear it?"

"I swear it," he said. *Goddess, keep her and my sons safe, and forgive me the lie,* he thought urgently, and kissed her again.

She looked beyond him and blotted her eyes on his shirt. "Your youngest sons come," she murmured and brought up a smile. "Look boys, who has come to see you." Pelledar smiled at her and kissed her fingers, then turned and held out his arms.

Two women clung to each other in the middle of the market and wept while others walked around them, white-faced and silent. Two men fought for the last loaf at a bakery; another woman bought oranges and dates from a stall, and as the owner took her coin, she gripped his fingers. "You'll be here in the morning—or for another hour tonight? My ser-

vant will come back, if you'll wait—we'll buy whatever rice
you have left. When Haffat comes—"

He freed his fingers and shook his head. "I only have a
little left, and my own household will need it. I'm sorry."

Her eyes filled with tears. "But—but, you'll be back?"

He shook his head again. "If Haffat comes, maybe none
of us will." The woman gathered up her oranges and dates,
turned, and fled.

Piritos woke just before sixth horn as he had ordered himself, but for a moment or so he could not recall why he slept
so early in the day, why it was so quiet outside his chambers. His head ached fiercely. He'd reopened the wound in
his shoulder once more this afternoon. The whole arm
throbbed when he flexed his hand and he gasped when he
touched the bandage. He sniffed cautiously. It didn't smell
yet. If it did, they'd warned him he'd lose the arm and probably his life if he wouldn't stay still long enough for it to
heal completely. *I have no time for this,* he thought angrily.
He felt old, tired despite the sleep. "You have no time for
that either," he told himself as he sat up. The room swam
momentarily and he clutched at the wall to steady himself.
"Not yet."

What he must do now was to get himself on his feet, before one of his aides came in and found him in such a sorry
state. Not that any of them would gossip, but word would go
around somehow, as it always did. The gods knew how bad
morale must be just now; this would make it even worse.
When Haffat came riding into the city, morale would plum-
met. Those who already prepared to take back the city
needed to know that their leaders could still lead them when
the time came. *If I am still alive,* he thought. Haffat would
most likely kill *him* as soon as the outer walls were secured.

Sixth horn. Piritos sighed and got to his feet. An aide
paused in the doorway; the general mustered up a smile that
must have reassured the man, because the aide smiled back
and moved on. Moments later another came in with a cup of
mixed wine and warm bread, a small dish of olives and another of fruit.

He let himself down into the chair, let the man set out the
food for him. The smell of wine twisted his stomach, the
food held no interest for him. He picked up the bread, broke
off a large piece, and made himself eat it. "We will go

soon," he said. "I will need you and Berdris to come with me, to remind me of everything I need to tell the prince, before he makes his final decision. I will need a horse." He took another bite of bread, managed a sip of wine. Pushed the rest aside then, with a would-be casual laugh. "Not too hungry just now, must be the extra sleep and all this fuss with that son of a camp follower out there."

"Of course, sir," the aide said. *He does not believe me. I cannot blame him, if I look half as exhausted as I feel.* "Shall I send Nufia to help you dress?" The general nodded; the aide gathered up the remaining food but left the wine cup. Piritos waited until he was out of sight before he took up the finger-cloth to blot his forehead. It was getting warm in here.

Fortunately, old Nufia was his usual deft self; he got his general into clean linen, buckled the freshly burnished armor into place and set the cloak over all with a minimum of effort. He was also, fortunately, not the type to fuss; he merely clucked over the general's shoulder, put a clean cloth pad on it, and bound it up once more. He stayed with Piritos when the general went into the courtyard and waited until the general got up on his horse before he mounted his own.

There were still a few soldiers on the fighting grounds, others in the messes or around the entry; men in the hospital barracks and anxious relatives and friends hovering there. Other men near the gates, standing in groups of three or four and talking in low voices. Beyond them, a few old men standing together in the square, several younger men outside a nearby wineshop. *The rest must be home, waiting for the sky to fall upon them,* Piritos thought grimly; he dredged up a smile and a raised hand for those he passed.

Four young men forced their way into the crowded wineshop near the main gates and gloomily eyed the solid block of men between them and the counter. "What is this, Frin, the fourth we've tried?" Frin shrugged, shook his head. The gray-haired solid men still in old-style hardened leather armor shoved past them.

"I told Frewis it would come to this," one of them snarled. "Comes of having a soft boy for a leader; he'll sell us all to the lion tomorrow."

"Ahhhh." His companion spat noisily. "Old prince would've told him to jump off that ledge out there, or come on inside the gates if he had the nerve and see how many it cost him to smoke us out. Maybe the general can talk sense into Pelledar."

"The general." The first man turned in the doorway. "You saw him today, I'm surprised we couldn't smell that arm when he went by. Man's half dead already. Come on, let's get out of here." They walked unsteadily into the night. Frin looked at his friends, eyes wide with dismay. One of them gripped his shoulder and the four went back outside.

Grysis stood outside the messes and looked up at what could be seen of the walls. In twos, men patrolled all the circuit of the city this night, watching anxiously for some surprise raid on Haffat's part. The torches they carried turned the low clouds a smoldering red.

He drew what remained of Eldrimon's phalanx inside with him—only fourteen men alive and still on their feet out of an original eighty. The remaining Dyaddi sat in a subdued huddle at their usual benches. Grysis waited until the others had found places to sit, then settled himself on the table, feet on the bench, where he could see most of them. "The general has just gone up to the palace; when he returns, I think we all know he'll have the bad news for us."

"We can't simply give up now!" one of the phalanx began, panic edging his voice. One of his comrades gripped his shoulder and Grysis held up a hand for silence.

"It isn't so simple as all that. They can spend us to the last man, and leave our families with no shield against Haffat's wrath. In that case, we've fought for nothing. In some lands, men set their jaws and say, 'do your worst' to someone like Haffat. We all know what follows: such men *do* their worst, and burn the cities to the ground, kill all the men, throw the boy children from the walls, steal the king's gold and gems, and take all the city's women to their own distant lands as slaves.

"You don't want that for your women, or your children—or yourselves, do you? But that isn't the way our general thinks. Or our prince. Or the way you must think now. You fought for your families, now you must live for them.

"You of Edrimon's company: They want watch all night, in case Haffat decides to jump us tonight while we're off guard. You'll go up there and patrol by twos from eleventh horn until first. Pair yourselves off however you are most comfortable; Captain Frewis will be in the messes when you come back. He'll know where to put you. Go to your families first; keep them calm if you can. Ridlo, I need to get numbers from you, for the general." Ridlo nodded and dropped back to the bench. The rest of the phalanx left.

Grysis waited until they were all out of sight, then drew the Dyaddi in closer. He looked at Ridlo and said, "I think I know you, Ridlo. But if I have misjudged you, you will not leave the barracks alive tonight." Ridlo eyed him warily. "Because I will tell you things that must not be general knowledge." Grysis turned to study what was left of his fighting Pairs.

"When Haffat comes to take our weapons, there will be no Dyaddi out there. The other captains have already told their companies that the Dyaddi will vanish; that the goddess creates Pairs in time of need, and takes them away when that need is over. Any man who speaks of Dyaddi to the enemy, or names aloud one who was a red-clad will suffer the wrath of Denota."

"We can't just vanish!" Jocasa said. "Can we?" she added in a small, worried voice. Aroepe threw an arm around her and drew her close.

"You will not vanish. You will hide your red cloaks, your bronze and your weapons—some in Denota's Temple, others in secret places beneath the barracks. You will speak of them—and of what you were—to no one. You Secchi will wed those men to whom you were promised, and you will go to the homes prepared for you." Sharp movement at his side; Grysis looked at Breyd; her jaw was set and her eyes angry. She looked away from him. "To all appearances you will be young wives of wealthy merchants, or the fathers of such girls. That is *all* the Diye Haff must be allowed to see.

"Because you Dyaddi will form the innermost circle of a new army—a secret army protected and guided by Denota. One that will hide in plain sight among the people, study the enemy, find his weaknesses—that will plan, and carefully add to its numbers, and wait for the hour it can rise up and take back Ghezrat." He paused, looked around the bench; Ridlo gaped at him and the Dyaddi were stunned into silence.

"The goddess demands this service of you; Tephys bid me say that, and remind you of your duty to Her." He paused;

silence. Mibro looked sidelong at his daughter, who cast up her eyes. Grysis saw the exchange and laughed shortly. "Remember that the priestess is under great pressure just now and her temper is short; also, she does not serve Denota the way you have.

"Ask any man out there this afternoon: most would tell you they'd go on fighting if there was a way. You all know how it feels to battle for so long, lose so many friends and companions, and then simply—stop. Well, the fight will go on: In secret.

"You Dyaddi were joined as a company at the same hour, forged and bound by Denota herself. Of all the city, only you can be trusted to keep this secret, no matter what. The bond between you would never let one of you betray another."

Ridlo shook himself. "If Haffat learned what you intend—"

"Then he would take the city apart until he found every man or woman who might be against him. But he won't learn, until it is too late, until the secret army is well established.

"That is one reason I chose you, Ridlo. I know you, we fought together against the Bejinis. I would trust you with my life." He considered this, shrugged. "Obviously, I do. I don't know the other men in your company nearly as well. But you know them.

"I want you to choose men you trust: some who will live beneath the city while they clear passages and entries that have not been used in a hundred years; some to gather food and other supplies. We also need men who know the alleys and passages between walls. Men who know how to hunt, who can stalk, and kill, and not be caught at it."

Ridlo shook his head. "But Haffat will take our weapons, and everyone knows about the caves beneath the city! The cisterns, the drainage tunnels that come out by the road."

"There are more passages and caves underground than that, some known only to a certain few. And Haffat will take our weapons, but he won't get them all. Most of us have swords and spears from our fathers which were only set aside for newer; the Dyaddi will have their weapons, and we'll siphon off whatever we dare besides that. The Diye Haff know we have suffered heavy losses; they've seen bodies, they've brought us back our sorely wounded and our dead. They have seen the pyres. They won't have any accurate count of our numbers, or know how many Pairs we had originally. When Haffat's captains count our armed, they will find fewer armsmen than were on that fighting ground this evening—and not a single Pair."

"He'll learn eventually," Ridlo said doubtfully.

"Perhaps. By the time he does, we will be organized and in place. But that doesn't matter, this does: If some of us don't take the fight underground, then we will truly have lost everything."

"The captain is right," Laprio said suddenly. "We can't give up; Haffat has the city now, but he won't hold it forever. Not unless we let him."

"It isn't necessarily safe," Grysis said. "But we aren't safe under Haffat, either. For now, go home. Say nothing to your families of this, but calm them if you can. Return here at second horn tomorrow. I will have more to tell you then." He leaned forward to grip the hands of each of his company and clapped Ridlo on the arm. "Sleep if you can; tomorrow will be long and hard. Breyd—stay behind, please." The others filed out; Breyd watched them go.

Grysis seemed uncertain how to begin, or possibly unwilling. He finally sighed and squared his shoulders. "I saw the look on your face, just now, when I mentioned the marriages. Do you want to talk about it?"

"There is nothing to talk about." She set her jaw. "I will not marry Apodain."

"You haven't any choice," Grysis said flatly. She shook her head. "Breyd, listen to me."

"I am listening." She stared stonily toward the doorway, where the royal chariot still sat.

"If all the rumors about him bother you—"

She waved a hand dismissively. "It isn't that. I decided long before this—this *taking* by Denota, even before I was made one of Tephys' priestesses, that I would not marry. But I have another task, one given me by Atos himself." She turned to look at him, as though daring him to laugh or even doubt her, he thought. She thrust out her arms. "I was burned, do you remember? When Father—when he disappeared. Not as terribly as Duplos, but painfully enough."

"I remember," he said quietly.

"I prayed to Atos over my brother's pyre that morning.

Not for peace but for vengeance. Atos took away my injuries and in return gave me a purpose: Kill Haffat."

He stared at her, looked away and tried to think. *I knew she was different, changed somehow, but I thought it was because of Menlaeus!* "I see," he said finally. "Do you plan to run up and stab him as he rides into the city, or something even more stupid?" he asked brutally. "You'll be killed before you can ever reach him. There's a better way."

She laughed; there was no humor in the sound. "What—marry Apodain? How convenient!"

"Marry Apodain," he agreed, as though she had meant it. "A common young woman wouldn't get close to Haffat; the young bride of a man of royal blood might." She blinked, stared at him as if he'd gone mad, and suddenly let her face down into her hands.

"I'm—I'm sorry, sir. Sometimes, it seems that's all I can think about—killing Haffat. Planning how I'd do it. Or I think of all the men I've killed out there. After Father vanished, I'd look at dead, mangled men, and I knew I had done that, I'd killed them, and I didn't even *care!* I'd just—I'd tell myself it's one more small piece of Haffat. I didn't think—I never thought I could hate any man the way I hate him. Anyone who followed him here."

Grysis was quiet for a long moment. He sighed finally. "I argued when they first sent me Pairs, that the young women must know what it was to kill men in anger, in war, in cold blood—how it would be looking back later. They told me, 'There is no time, you train them in weapons, the bond will take care of such things—blur them over—and the Primes will manage that problem, if there ever is one.' " Breyd looked up at him in wonder, but Grysis now stared beyond her, or through her.

"The first enemy I ever killed in battle was a gray-haired man with blue eyes—out on the isthmus, after Perlot died. I can still close my eyes and see him. The second, and the ones after—I remember how angry I was, we all were. We worshiped Perlot, you young ones don't know what he was like." He looked at her and smiled. "A little like Menlaeus, really: He knew us all, he knew how to get the best from us; we'd have died for him." He shook himself, came back to the moment. "I hated the Bejini—the damned jins—I still do. Because they coveted what was ours, Perlot died, a lot of us went under with him, and Hemit—but you've only seen what he is now. He was my friend, my sparring partner out there in that same courtyard where you learned to fight.

"I had it easier than you, Breyd. A straightforward enemy that we routed and sent home with depleted numbers. They say the king of the jins was assassinated by his own guard late the same year, because of what we did to his army. I only had to come home once they were gone, and adjust to ordinary, plodding life. But you—"

"Me! Me what?" Breyd asked after a little silence.

"We need you there. In Khadat's house. We'd want someone there anyway; but you're pledged to him, and by Khadat's own doing," he said. She shook her head, not understanding. "Apodain never knew; she made a secret bargain with the prince and had his panoply and his horses brought from the barracks and only then told him. If she knew how men would see it—but she didn't care about that. She is like that, you know: It is whatever Khadat wants, and nothing else matters. Her family, the ships they own, Perlot's wealth. Rumor already circulates among her household, how soon she will approach Haffat and strike a deal with him."

"Oh, no." Breyd had gone utterly white as he spoke. "The things they say—about him. How can he bear it?"

"He does what he must," Grysis said. "Because he has no choice. Any more than you have: We must know what Khadat is up to, especially once Haffat holds power here. What her household does. We already know which of the servants are still loyal to Perlot's memory, or to Apodain; which care more for Hemit than Khadat; which would support her in anything she did.

"But of all the Secchi, only *you* were pledged to a royal or a noble house. Not all of that class are as self-centered as Khadat, but aside from Brysos, none of us know the nobles and certainly none of us are invited into their homes or even speak with them. And even Brysos is a commander, not a friend or an equal.

"We must know who thinks what, how they deal with Khadat and with Haffat. Which of them can be trusted later. Everyone says Khadat would do anything to keep her sons alive. We need to know if that includes making bargains with Haffat. Because Apodain is eighth in line for the throne; Haffat kills such men."

"I—" She swallowed dryly. "I can't—"

"You can. If you could walk up in the street," Grysis said

brutally, "and stick a knife in Haffat's guts and die for it, you can do this. It isn't so much, after all. Deceive Khadat, and wed Apodain; listen and watch. And pass word on to those who will bring it to me."

As much as she has always hated Khadat—if Mother ever knew, Breyd thought. She swallowed. "But if—if something went wrong, my family—my mother—"

"If you murdered Haffat, would they fare any better?" She looked down at her hands; he waited. She shook her head. "This way, at least you can do something to help overthrow Haffat and take back the city. If he is gone, then your mother is safe, isn't she?"

She drew a deep, shuddering breath, let it out slowly. "My poor mother. She has always loathed Khadat. She will hate having to send me there."

"But she's known it would come to that, one way or another, when the Pairs were dissolved. And remember Perlot would have been just her age, if he'd lived," Grysis said. "When he was young, he looked very much like Apodain, there wasn't a girl in all Ghezrat who didn't adore him. Imagine him wed to Khadat."

"But why would he—?"

"Nobles aren't like the rest of us, you know that: All those laws, to keep the blood pure," Grysis said sourly. "Why do you think Apodain didn't simply take his panoply and his car and return to his company? He is *owned* by his mother until he is twenty-two! As was Perlot. And his father chose him Khadat." He was quiet. Breyd gazed at him wide-eyed; he couldn't tell what she thought. "Khadat must be very worried just now," Grysis went on thoughtfully. "Because we know Haffat killed the King of Mirikos, and all his family; he did this in Idemito and all the other lands he's conquered—or so I'm told. Once he is in control of Ghezrat, he will most likely kill Prince Pelledar, and then begin to eliminate his heirs."

Her stomach dropped. Breyd stared at him in shock. "Our—but the prince will go into hiding, won't he? With Aroepe and the others!"

"No. The queen and her sons may already be hidden, but the prince will stay. He dare not vanish, because Haffat will know there is something afoot. He'll turn the city inside out until he finds the prince and if he can't, he'll kill and torture until someone tells him about the secret places under the city."

Breyd swallowed. "He'll find Ridlo and kill him, and those men Ridlo chooses, take all the hidden weapons. Everything will be lost.

"How long do you think I will have, before they come to kill Khadat and her sons?"

"We don't know. But I don't ask you to martyr yourself, young Breyd. We will set up a way for you to escape the palace, if your life is in danger."

If I learn about it in time. But what if Khadat finds me out, or Haffat does—and they take my family! Her heart banged painfully against her ribs. To face the enemy unarmed, to speak with such men—even Haffat himself. To hide her hatred and anger, and pretend to be only a simple common woman recently wed to one of the city's nobles. *If they learned what I was doing—Father might be afraid to do what I must. But if he was afraid, no one else would ever know it.* She dug her nails into her leg; Grysis was talking once more. "I know Khadat's stablemaster; he has served that house since Perlot's day and I would trust him with my own life. He will know what you are besides Apodain's bride, and he will show you the hidden ways from that palace.

"That is another thing we'd like you to do: We know one tunnel goes beneath the prince's palace, another comes out in the city cisterns. Khadat probably knows very little of them, except those that are part of the palace; Apodain should know more, because he's a royal son, and that's something passed from father to son, and to no one else. If possible, learn from him all you can about those passages; they could prove useful to us." Grysis looked at her; all at once he looked very worried indeed. "Will you do this?"

Breyd met his eyes levelly. "I will do this."

"Knowing the risks."

"Knowing a few of them, at least. I will do it." She managed a shaky laugh. "If you will make me wed Apodain anyway."

"Give Apodain a chance. Did you never meet him?"

She shrugged. "Upon the palace steps, and once in the courtyard, out there. He was so worried about his driver, I don't think he even knew me."

"Give him a chance," Grysis reiterated. "Now. The boy

Xhem will serve as go-between; anything you want to reach me, you will tell him. Nabid already spoke to the boy, and he's willing."

"I am glad," Breyd said softly. "For his sake. My brother—Tar thought of Xhem as his younger brother. I've grown fond of him myself. But won't it be dangerous for him? I mean, if they caught him—"

"No one will look at a boy like that and realize what he's doing. And we won't be putting him in danger. After all, he's your little cousin, of course he'd come to see you. Go to your mother now, go and sleep." She slid from the table and set her fist against her heart. Grysis got to his feet and returned the salute, then, to her surprise, he placed his hands on her hair in a father's blessing.

It weakened her dangerously, as nothing else could have, and she thought she might weep on him as she had when Tarpaen died. *Do not; he must not think you are afraid. He will worry that he chose wrong, and endangered everything.* Grysis patted her shoulder and left her. She stood where she was until the moment passed, and she could pass the men by the door.

The fires between the inner and outer wall had died down near sunset, but it was nearly midnight before the stones cooled enough for men to clear a path to the ruin of the Temple of Warriors. The low wall that marked the entry to the courtyard was still intact, but beyond that, a rubble of shattered stone filled the courtyard. Two priests and several supplicants were found crushed beneath the pillars of the temple itself, which had fallen across the stairs. The entry to the temple had fallen in and what little could be seen of the interior glowed red-hot. The sunpriest Vertumnus, who had come to help sift through the courtyard, finally drew the searchers aside. "No man could have lived through that, even with the gods' protection." He knelt to begin the prayers for the dead.

Denota's courtyard was full of women, despite the late hour: Frightened, weeping women, some clutching small children. More stood in the avenue outside the walls, waiting for the opportunity to go inside and seek what little comfort the goddess could offer them. The priestesses conducted prayer after prayer, and spoke to as many of the women as possible; Meronne finally came from the Cleft and addressed all of them. "The goddess did not say victory would come at once, or easily! But she did say it would be ours! She will not let harm come to you! Pray for courage and calm to meet the days ahead." As she returned to the Cleft, an old woman whispered to her neighbor. "No harm to us. But what of all those already dead—wasn't that harm? And my son Bechates and my granddaughter?" The neighbor shook her head and burst into tears. The old woman primmed her lips angrily, got to her feet, and walked away.

Tephys stood with her toes against the very edge of the Cleft, inhaling the steam. Now and again she raised her arms, or spoke; Denira, who stood at her side and a little behind her, could not hear what she said. The high priestess spun away from the gaping hole and opened her eyes. Her breath came short and there was strain in her face. "I have made a temporary opening in the barrier around the palace; you will go at once and bring back Queen Ye Sotris and her sons. As quickly as you can. I cannot hold this for long."

Denira turned and walked toward the two lamps, lit a third from the wick of one and stepped around the low shelf and the priestesses who guarded it. The opening behind them was invisible unless Tephys herself willed it seen; it was so narrow, she had to turn sideways and hold her breath to fit through it. *Fortunately the queen won't need to come this far,* she thought. She held the lamp high: Tunnels went off in every possible direction. Denira chose the righthand-most and hurried along it.

Back in the main cavern, Tephys waited until Meronne came down to join her. "It is panic up there," the older woman said sourly.

"They have cause to fear Haffat and his lion-priest," Tephys said. "Forget them for now; the barrier upon the outer walls must be renewed and we must take up the part of the Warrior-Priests in strengthening that barrier. The Ergardi must not come into this city, or I fear all truly *will* be lost."

The night sky had clouded over thickly, but small oil lamps had been set in the niches along the main avenue, and to illuminate the crossings. Piritos rode slowly, grateful that the poor lighting forced the horses to go at a walk; anything more jolted his shoulder almost unbearably. *That is new.*

That is—not good, he thought vexedly. But, this night of all nights, he must reach the palace in a condition to think.

The avenue was deserted. By what could be seen down the smaller side streets, there was no one abroad at all, save a few soldiers near the palace and a very few supplicants outside Denota's gates as well as the men who walked the slow circuit of the city walls, to make certain Haffat intended no sneak attack, even though he must know those walls were his. *His for now. For a little while only,* Piritos told himself grimly.

Nufia maneuvered the horses over close to the steps, to allow the general a shorter drop to the ground. Somehow, Piritos managed to dismount without shaming himself before so many, to climb the broad flight of stairs unassisted. Pelledar had been closeted with his council for hours in the throne room, but for this final, long meeting, he had chosen to use the small room. *Thank the gods for so much.* He could never have managed those three flights of stairs tonight.

Pelledar was waiting for him; a fire had been built in the brazier and one of the servants was setting sticks of cubed meat and olives in the coals. Septarin sat with his back to them all, two of the skewers in his hand, his attention apparently all for the meat. He glanced over his shoulder as Piritos and his aides came in, smirking disagreeably. Piritos suddenly wanted to smack him, hard. Septarin turned his back on the general, got to his feet, and bowed jerkily in his father's direction.

"You swore to me," Pelledar said mildly.

"All right, I swore." Septarin sounded very sulky, and he sent sidelong angry glances in the general's direction. "Have I time to eat this, Father?"

"You have time. Here, or in your rooms—or you can have food brought to the family hall. So long as someone knows where you have gone for when the priestess sends for you. Remember!"

"I know, yes!" Septarin snapped. He pulled a chunk of meat from one of the skewers, popped it into his mouth and passed the general chewing noisily, eyes glowering and fixed somewhere beyond him. Piritos turned to watch him go, then looked at his prince, eyebrows raised in question. Pelledar shrugged.

"I have told him he must go into hiding with Ye Sotris and his brothers, and he is displeased. But he was already angry with me." He gestured; servants brought chairs for the general and one of his aides. "I did not know if you or your men had time to eat yet. I have not, and so—" He waved a hand toward the brazier.

"Thank you, sire." Piritos said. Fortunately, he thought, the smell of the meat was not very strong where he sat. But perhaps his stomach could accept a little food. Certainly, when a prince honored a general by offering meat, it would not do for a mere general to insult him by refusing it. He beckoned one of his aides. "Why don't you and Nufia help with that? Roast some for yourselves, the prince has given you leave." He waited until the two men had settled next to the coals, then eased his back into the cushions. "Angry—I see. Septarin thinks you should have had Haffat speared as he sat before the gates."

Pelledar actually managed a laugh at that, though his eyes were still dark with worry. "He did not *quite* say so! But he does not understand—"

"He is young," Piritos said as the prince hesitated.

"Yes. And I fear that before high summer, he will be prince—even if he does not sit on this throne because Haffat's man does."

Piritos accepted a cup of wine from one of the servants; it was warmed and spiced, barely watered—soothing to his queasy stomach. He drank one long draught, wrapping his fingers around the cup to hold in the warmth. "I will not give you easy lies, my prince. I fear you are right. But if you also hid with Ye Sotris, we could persuade Haffat that you somehow escaped the city."

"What," Pelledar asked dryly, "between this day and tomorrow?"

"It would not be impossible," Piritos urged, but the prince was already shaking his head.

"With a very pregnant wife and small babes—Haffat would never believe we got through his guard. If he did, he would send men on his fastest horses along all the roads, for what car could carry such a fragile burden anywhere but the roads? Such a car could never move quickly; he would learn almost at once that you had lied to him." He sipped cautiously from his own cup. "And then he would search—until he found us." Piritos sighed, closed his eyes and shook his head. "Please, my friend. I have already been through this.

With Ye Sotris. I do not think I can bear to refuse it a second time."

Piritos looked at him for a very long moment. "Then I'll let it go. But it seems such a pointless waste!"

"What? My life against all those others?" The prince sent his eyes sideways toward the brazier, back the other way; there were no other men in the chamber but his servants and the general's men about the brazier, and they were talking together in low voices as they turned the skewers and dipped bread in oil. "All those others," Pelledar went on in a low voice, "who may yet pull some victory from this defeat?"

"It does not follow that your life balances theirs—!" Piritos began, but Pelledar shook his head once more, silencing him.

"We have not underestimated Haffat and yet he is within a day of taking the city's walls. It will not do to underestimate the man once he comes here. He is clever and cunning both, and he will know at once if he has been duped.

"Ye Sotris and the babes are already safe; Septarin will be safe. Those who prepare against the day Haffat drops his guard—they will not be safe, but at least *I* will not be the cause if they fail. Not because Haffat tore the city apart for me, and discovered them."

Piritos sipped his wine, waited to answer until one of the servants had placed a small table at his right elbow with bread and oil, and refilled his cup from a steaming, fragrant ewer. "So you are clear in this; that Haffat will have the city."

"I asked for a day, knowing we must have whatever time could be bought to prepare for his entry," Pelledar said. "But I knew when they took back the mole this last time that it was a matter of when, not if. And so did you."

Piritos nodded heavily. "I knew it."

"I will tell them tomorrow, when he sends for an answer—though he must already know what it will be. I will ask three more days, to let us ready for him, and prepare the people, and make sacrifices."

"Yes, do that. He may deny you, but he may not. He can afford to be generous now. They say he puts great store by the appearance of generosity." Piritos took another sip of his wine, accepted the skewer of meat from Nufia with thanks and waited until the man had settled next to the fire once more.

"And then he will kill me. And—I would not willingly choose to die."

"What man would?" Piritos asked wryly.

"You yourself," the prince reminded him quietly. "You do much the same thing as I do, don't you? You offer yourself to Haffat out of the same motives. He will not keep me alive long; my claim to this chair is seven hundred years old and his numbered in days and written in blood. He must hate you: the general who thwarted him for so many days. At least he will be circumspect in my death—but I fear he may behead you with your own blade before the main gates."

Piritos laughed quietly; the prince stared at him. "They say it is not such a painful death. But Haffat will never make a public martyr of *me;* he is too clever for that. Besides," he added somberly, "he needs only to look at my scars and my face, and see the easiest way: to let it out days from now that Piritos died of a suppurated wound. Who would doubt it?

"Of course, he might let me live—a crippled general with no army—but I do not expect such fool's compassion from Haffat."

The prince set his cup aside. "I am sorry."

"No. Not for me. I have had a long life and an honorable one, and perhaps it is better to die before I see what an enemy does to this city and her people. But I am a soldier; I have lived most of that long life knowing the chance of death by violence. I do not fear it now."

"You do not welcome it," Pelledar said.

"Of course not. But just now, I am tired, and I hurt, and I ache for all those men and boys—those young women!" He slammed his free fist against the chair arm. "I am sorry. But all those who fought so hard for us, and for themselves and each other, and who lived to see this day, and fear what will happen or see the waste of lives—"

Pelledar drained his cup, held it out for the servant to refill. Piritos let the man add to his, to warm it. Pelledar finally broke the silence. "*You* could go into hiding, you know."

Piritos shook his head. "Haffat would know something is afoot. It is my place to be at the gates when Haffat comes, to set the proper example for my soldiers. And if I surrender my sword as token for the city, then I will save you from that ordeal, my prince."

Pelledar looked down into his cup, moved it to swirl the liquid. "What will you do with the army, when he comes?"

"That must depend on what Haffat demands. I would prefer all the companies to line the avenue and the way into the barracks, with the remainder inside—to make certain none of the people turn violent. Haffat might agree for that reason." He shrugged. "We will know soon enough. Ask him tomorrow, when you and he talk again, what his plans are to disarm us."

Pelledar nodded. The servant filled both cups, and brought more bread and oil. Pelledar ate very little; he drank his wine and talked about Ye Sotris and the younger boys. Piritos picked at his meat, sipped his wine, and listened. The servants cleared away the skewers and empty oil dishes and brought dates and sectioned fruit, and more wine. Finally Piritos set his cup aside and got to his feet. The wine had not clouded his mind very much, but it had taken the edge from the pain in his shoulder.

To his surprise, Pelledar stood and came over to lay a hand on his good arm. "Today I let Haffat call me brother, and speak to me from that chariot as though we were both Great Kings and equals. Only for Ghezrat did I refrain from telling him again what he truly is: an upstart, son of a soldier and a common woman, an emperor by conquest and not by true greatness. I do not call him Great King to myself, or brother, and I swear to you, I never will.

"Perhaps I am not much of a Great King myself, after all. But I know true courage when I see it—a man who faces certain death to ease the way for an entire army, and for all those who love him. And I would call *you* brother, now."

"My—my prince." Piritos gazed at him, stunned. He shook himself. *To set aside a life of comfort, and a fair wife and babes—I never had a wife or children. How can he face losing so much, beyond all we both lose—and with such dignity?* "My brother," he whispered, and gripped Pelledar's arm. Pelledar managed a very shaky smile and turned to walk quickly away. Piritos was still staring as he slipped through the draperies that hung behind his throne.

In the darkness of the porch outside the throne room, Septarin leaned against the rough stones of the outer wall and pinched his nose to keep from sneezing as another gust of greasy smoke drifted past him. He looked carefully all around, made certain there was no one nearby, then slipped into shadow. Pelledar could order whatever he chose; Septarin was not about to go cower in a cave with his mother and the babies and all those women who served a goddess. *My father is a fool and coward, to hand the city tamely to that Haffat and his! But I have known that for long, just as I have seen through the general from the first. For Father to call a man like that brother? He must be drunk! Piritos is a commoner; he had me shoved into that reeking little cell for daring to prove myself a hero against the enemy.*

Where could he go? He hesitated in deep shadow, eyed the open gates dubiously. He could not stay here, someone would find him and either send him in disgrace to that Tephys or they would shove him back in the cell as his father had threatened earlier. He dared not go to the barracks, Piritos or one of the others would send him home—and so would the father of his boyhood friend Imbro.

What was that he had heard the two saying, though? Something about men gathering in hiding, to fight back and take the city from Haffat? *I could be a part of that—they will need leaders, men who are not afraid of these Diye Haff and their horrid god. And after all, I am a prince—I am the heir, and if Haffat kills Father as he kills all the kings, why then I am Prince of Ghezrat, and the city* must *obey me. But they will want to, because I am all they have, the best they have! As my uncle was when he fought the Bejini!*

Heady thought. Now, how to find such men?

Those in the barracks would know, of course, but he could not go there just yet. Later, perhaps. For now— He nodded, and slipped back along the wall as Piritos and his men rode out of the courtyard. "Food first." He had barely eaten in there, for anger and dismay. His stomach growled as he worked his way toward the kitchens, where he knew he could filch bread and dates without being caught. And then, a warm and very plain cloak and some coin—both of which he could most likely find in his tutor's chambers. *They will not see me go, will not know where I have gone. But one day very soon, everyone will know.*

Piritos let Nufia help him down from the horse. His arm—he wouldn't think about the damned arm. He stood very still, hands clenched in the riding pad, until the world stopped spinning around him, then straightened up so he could walk to his quarters. But as he stepped away from the horse, men came from the dimly lit messes. "Brysos? Frewis—Lodis, what is this, all of you here at such an hour?"

"It is later than we had thought," Brysos admitted. "We had to know what was decided." Piritos bit back a sigh and came into the light; Brysos eyed him in dismay. "But you do not look well, sir; we can wait. Better if you sleep."

"Yes." The general did sigh this time, very quietly. "I think that might be best; it's been a long night." He managed a smile. "I am sorry you had the wait for nothing."

"Well, sir," Grysis stepped back into the messes and one of the other captains moved a bench up, "we had things to discuss, too, you know. But we thought—since it might be the last opportunity we have for a while—" He floundered, finally, looking appealingly at Brysos.

"Sir, we thought you might drink one last cup of wine with us."

"One last cup?" Piritos laughed dryly. "Do I look that dreadful?"

"Of course not, sir," Frewis replied bluntly. "But we fear what Haffat might—" He bit his lip and fell silent.

"Yes," Piritos said gravely and let himself down onto the bench. "Haffat might, as you say. Let us face that when we must and not before, if you don't mind. Better to save what wit all of us have left for more important matters."

"Sir," Frewis said. One of the other men set a jug and cups at the end of the long trestle and poured, passing the cups down. He brought the last of them and handed one to the general, who held it up and smiled at them all.

"Do not look so unhappy," he said mildly. "Drink instead: to those of us who had the honor of fighting for this city in her most desperate hours, at the head of such brave soldiers."

"I shall drink to that," Brysos said. "And to my own captain." He drank deeply. Piritos wrinkled his nose. This was the plain red of the barracks, a little sour and very strong—if they had mixed it, there couldn't be more than a drop or two of water.

Fortunately, they hadn't given him much. He drained the cup and set it aside. "My good friends," he began. The wine took him between one breath and the next and his eyes sagged shut; Brysos and Frewis caught him before he could fall over.

"Here, hurry," Lodis said urgently; he pushed forward with poles and a heavy blanket wrapped over them.

"No great rush," Grysis said. "It was a strong enough dose that he will not waken before midmorning—and by then he will be long since below the barracks and safely out of the way." He glanced up as Nufia came forward to kneel beside the general. "You are positive he was not seen from the walls this afternoon?"

"My life on it, sir," Nufia said quietly. "I myself could just barely see this Haffat, and I stood higher than the general. But Haffat's eyes were all for the prince."

"Don't be too certain of that," Brysos said. "And we still haven't worked out what to say tomorrow, what are we going to do?"

"Don't panic, for one thing," Nabid said. Brysos glared at him.

"Tell them he was in the Temple of Warriors," Frewis said angrily. "How will they prove otherwise?"

"Because the entire army saw him here this evening," Brysos reminded him.

Nabid shook his head. "Each of us can speak to his companies tomorrow, and tell them—"

"The truth? Everyone? What kind of secret is that?" Frewis laughed sourly. "No. Tell them all he died late tonight, just before first horn, that we took him to the Temple of Atos and they burned him in secret. Everyone knows how dreadful he looked all day today."

"Morale—" Brysos began anxiously.

"Morale!" Frewis spat. "If he is executed by Haffat tomorrow, what does that do for morale? But if the blood in his shoulder is poisoned, we may lose him yet." He looked down at the sleeping general and touched his fist lightly to his breast. "Sir, we would do anything for you, anything you asked. But we will not let you die."

Brysos looked around for Nufia. "All right, take him. And take good care of him." But as Nufia knelt by his master, and the other captains turned away, Grysis spoke against his ear. "Take him—but wait down there for me. I know a place where he will be truly safe."

Haffat

All across the Diye Haff camp, men celebrated, even though
the victory was not yet complete. But Haffat listened to his
general and his captains and finally shook his head. "Let
them celebrate. The Ghezrathi are finished; they know it and
so do I. At most they will try to delay me taking the city.
Mix more water with the wine if you fear there will be battle
tomorrow, but those men have earned this hour."

He himself sat before his pavilion, a cup cradled between
his hands and a man at his shoulder to refill it. It was mostly
water, but no one would know that; they knew only that
Haffat drank with his army, and it pleased and honored
them.

He had emptied the cup twice and the sky was completely
dark when Knoe came and knelt at his side. Haffat signed
the servant to bring another chair and cup for the priest.
Knoe took both gravely, held the cup briefly aloft in salute,
then drained it. They sat in a companionable silence for a
while, looking across the river and up at the city ablaze with
torchlight all along the outer wall. Beyond that, other
lights—the upper windows of the palace itself, Haffat
thought. *I will like the view from those windows, I think.
Hadda will enjoy it very much.* "Just as the god foretold," he
said with satisfaction. Knoe glanced at him, turned his eyes
back toward the distant city. "I am grateful He did not warn
me how much time it would take, or how many lives,"
Haffat went on thoughtfully. "More of my captains would
have argued against it in Mirikos, had they known."

Knoe glanced at him once again, but was reassured by
what he heard and saw. He sipped his wine and settled his
shoulders more comfortably against the chair. "Perhaps one
reason the god was reticent." Haffat eyed him sidelong and
Knoe smiled; the emperor laughed. "But my emperor," Knoe
went on, "perhaps it is time for you to think beyond the next

city and the next. Before long, you will run out of suitable relations to set upon these thrones."

"I suppose you are right, Knoe." He stared at the distant city and sighed very quietly. "Do you know, for all my vast empire—for all the strength of my army, I could see it in Pelledar's eyes today. An upstart, he thinks; a common soldier, daring to name himself Great King."

Knoe shifted his weight and moved the chair so he could study the emperor. "But you are a Great King. Because it was not his father, but his many-times great ancestor who conquered this land does not make Pelledar any greater than you. You have taken and you hold an empire so vast that—of course you are a Great King. Why should it bother you so, what a man like Pelledar thinks?"

Haffat sighed. "It should not, put that way. This afternoon—Pelledar's face was the color of parchment, he looked like a blubbering child. How can he bear himself? How can his woman bear his touch? And yet, they say he has made three sons on her, and that she is near time to bear him another."

"But she is Eygari," Knoe reminded him. "I have traveled through that land: They are singers and dancers, they make better lyres than bows—they create tales and sing them or stand upon stages, masqued, to play them out."

"Feeble. Like Pelledar. It should make me sick if he did call me brother—or Great King, the same as himself. And yet—"

Knoe snorted. "The men who rode with you today and listened to you said you sounded like a true Great King. Could Pelledar have made such a speech as you do, to frighten brave men into tears? Is that not enough for you?"

"I forget how practical you are, Knoe."

"Yes. One reason I would have you consider whether you have enough empire. It may not be—practical for you to go much farther from Diyet. Particularly as hard as this victory came. Your men—"

"I know. If I were not Haffat, none of those men out there would have come as far as Mirikos. They begin to long for Diyet, and some of their captains echo them."

"And suddenly, I am tired, Knoe. Sometimes it seems I have never had a life that was not this constant riding, and meetings with my staff and my officers, and fighting and death and blood and more fighting still." He drove a hand through his hair. "And supplies, and lists, and how to transport them or obtain them." He lifted his cup, found it empty, and held it out for the servant to refill. "I know," he added tiredly, "Wilus tells me as often as you do: Let those responsible manage. But if we had landed here without grain for bread, or wine, or enough horses or spears—who would have blamed Wilus?"

"They would, if you let them. I have consulted the god just now," Knoe added in an abrupt change of subject, "and he bid me say you have done well in defeating this earth goddess. He bid me to warn you however that a man of Diyet knows how the earth dies when winter comes, but it lives again each spring. By this he tells you, do not underestimate Denota or any who follow or serve her! He bid me say this, also: Think upon all the lands you have and what matters to you; think what you would still have." Haffat frowned and shook his head. "By this, he means, you have taken Ghezrat and now you must choose: Are you a conqueror or a king? Are you satisfied, or are you hungry for more? What does Haffat truly want above all other things? Think long and carefully. Do not decide in haste."

"Yes. All right." Haffat contemplated the distant city walls and brooded for a while, then shook himself and said, "Ghezrat—I wanted it so badly and I still do: to ride through those gates and into that palace and know it is all *mine*. It would be good to look out over the sea from those windows; to bear the winter rains here rather than snows and chill wind in Diyet. And yet—" He sighed. "I think of my Empire and it seems to me Ye Eygar would make a better outer boundary than Ghezrat. It has a long coast upon the Great Sea, it has heavy trade in tin from the north and ivory from the south. And I must take the forts at the isthmus in any event, and so we will be partway to Ye Eygar when they are mine." He leaned back, slouched down in the chair and rested his chin on the lip of his cup. "And, of course, Pelledar's wife is Eygari. They did not come to his aid against my army, but they might think it safe to come against whatever force I leave with the city. And they might hope to rescue—or avenge—Ye Sotris."

"Risk a kingdom for a woman?" Knoe laughed and shook his head.

"Ah. But they think highly of their women in Ye Eygar,

don't you remember when I sent emissaries to bring me a princess?"

Knoe shook his head again. "That was before my time. They refused you?"

"Flatly," Haffat said. He brooded on the contents of his cup. "That woman's father said Diyet was too far and too minor a kingdom to bear the honor of one of his daughters."

"An insult," Knoe said.

"Yes—but not so much an insult as it would be today: I was young and my empire considerably smaller." He considered this, smiled and let his head fall back so he could gaze up at Ghezrat through half-closed eyes. Knoe felt the most immediate of his worries slip from his shoulders. Haffat had been overly burdened these past days, others beside his lion-priest must have felt his temper. *I thought myself out of his favor; more fool I.*

Haffat stirred, sat up a little straighter. "You must tell the Ergardi I am pleased by what they did today. They will be well rewarded—in this city, if they desire."

"If they are able," Knoe said. The Ergardi had been utterly exhausted when they returned to the camp—something, they said, to do with the walls, the earth itself. *Once the city is ours we will find a way to change all that.* They would have to: The Ergardi refused flatly to go anywhere near those walls just now, but Haffat might want one of them to take over Pelledar, or Denota's priests once the goddess was properly neutralized.

Haffat had no such doubts. "They have already served me well; I will not be ungrateful. But I will certainly want them to bring the ballista against Ye Eygar—if I decide to take it," he added quickly.

I think he will never be satisfied. But that could wait. He thought he knew the answer to his next question, but he asked it anyway. "Who will take Heliar's place in Ghezrat, if you do not remain here?"

Haffat eyed him sidelong and did not answer at once; it occurred to Knoe he was either embarrassed to admit his choice, or simply uncertain how the priest would receive it. But he finally pressed himself upright in the chair, held out his cup for another dose of well-watered wine and said, "Hadda, of course. He is of limited use in a campaign and Ghezrat will be a good test for him, if he is to rule all the empire after me."

"All the empire," Knoe said blankly. *This is against everything—is he mad?*

Haffat glanced at him. "Of course! Who else would be my heir? Oh, I know he might find Ye Eygar more to his tastes—"

"Is this wise?" Knoe asked, and momentarily wondered if *he* was wise to ask such a thing. But Haffat merely shrugged.

"It will make him strong. Why else do you think I insisted he come with me? If I had left him behind to keep pleasant company with his friends, what possible good would have come of it? I would have returned to find my son the center of a society of useless, foolish young men, and himself the greatest fool. Hadda would have learned nothing. Here, at my side, he has at least learned how to hold his tongue when he must—and how to stand up to overwhelming fear. I should apologize, I suppose, for letting him thwart you before so many people the other night. That Pair, you remember."

"Oh?" *Does he possibly apologize to me for his son?* Knoe's heart lifted.

"You know I do not like sacrificing men; but you and Axtekeles know I accept His will. I would find the sacrifice of a young woman—unpleasant, let us say. But if Axtekeles asked it of me to keep and expand my empire, I would sacrifice anything. Anyone, even those dearest to me—holding back only Hadda."

"Yes," Knoe said neutrally.

"Yes. It cost *you* nothing, and it served as a forge for my son, that he dared stand up to you. You surely know that he fears you above anything else in this world—or above or below it."

"If you are pleased, my emperor, then I am also pleased. But I do not intend the sacrifice of those two," Knoe said softly. "And the god does not ask it of you—or of Hadda. He tells me instead to bring them into the city when it is yours, to keep them caged as they are now, but in some secret place—separated and so two who are *not* one ever again. Fighters, but kept forever weaponless. This the god has shown to me, and he tells me the city will remain weak, even as they do."

"Subtle, priest," Haffat said, as softly. "Do it." He looked back at the city. "For of all things I now own, and those I may yet gather to me, this is the one I will *not* lose." He gazed at his new conquest. "They call her Ghezrat of many walls," he whispered. "Ghezrat of many gardens and temples—Ghezrat the high and wondrous. And look, Knoe: She has fallen to a man whose father was a soldier and his mother a camp follower—or so Pelledar told me, the first time we met." He contemplated the brightly lit city. "Fallen to an upstart who is now Great King because he is emperor of the dread Diye Haff. Of Diyet and Idemito, bright Mirikos of fair harbors—and now Ghezrat the Broken." He drained his cup. "Ghezrat, which has surely fallen so low in the minds of its people and its prince that it will never rise again."

18

The avenue in front of the barracks was still being held clear, and in the square itself seven men stood guard, keeping a few curious boys away from the damaged gates. The men and women who waited for some word from the Temple of Warriors had been moved back into the high street leading toward the palace, or the side streets. Breyd reached the square before the gates quickly, but as she edged into the street that would take her home, men came out of the nearby wineshop, and women who had been hovering in anxious little groups nearby mobbed her, clutching at her cloak, at her arms. "Secchi, what are they saying in there?" "They say we will all die when Haffat comes here!" "What word from outside, my son was there!"

She tugged at her cloak, patted a woman's hand, raised her voice to be heard: "I don't know who is left outside, I'm sorry but none of us do yet! We won't die, they are making terms now to keep all of you safe, I don't know anything else!" She pulled her cloak free, wrested her fingers from another woman's crushing grip. "I haven't been home myself yet, my mother doesn't even know if I'm alive. Please, I have to go!"

The women nearest let go of her hand, stepped back, and turned to shout: "Step aside, the poor girl's mother—"

"Poor girl!" some man back in the crowd growled. "She's a fighter, why should the woman expect any better than we get?"

"Breyd!" She turned her head; Ridlo and two other members of Evrikos' phalanx were fighting their way toward her. Ridlo got her between them and shouted: "She knows no more than any other low-rank fighter, let her go! No one will learn anything else tonight, not until the prince decides what to do and how best to do it. Go home, people!" No one moved; Breyd clung to Ridlo's arm and let him and his friends bull their way through the crowd. A little beyond the wineshop, it was suddenly easier to walk and five or six shops down the street there were only a few people standing in doorways or crowded around a pool.

Ridlo stopped. "Thank you." Breyd shook out her cloak. "Need an escort the rest of the way?" he asked.

She shook her head. "I don't think so. You've important things to do."

"Making sure you don't get trampled is important," he said. "Oplo, why don't you and Xhenon go back, talk some sense into those old men if you can? I'll be back as soon as possible. Come on, Secchi."

She opened her mouth to protest, closed it again. There was the corner by the bakery, it would be as bad as this if not worse because the Temple of Warriors was so close. Her own narrow little alley could be impassable.

Women and a few older boys clustered around the bakery; people stood around the fountain in her own street. Ridlo called out what little assurance he could as they passed people: "We don't know anything yet! You'll find out as soon as any of the fighters do, but the prince won't abandon you!" Breyd stayed close to him. She could hear muttering as they passed the fountain—three of the old men who gossiped with Misso and her sister. *They think we should have stayed out there until there was no one left to fight.* But it would do her no good to argue with them.

Ridlo waited until Ina opened the door for her. "You were right," she said. "I'd have been trampled; thank you." He nodded and left. Breyd drew a steadying breath and followed Ina into the house.

The main room smelled musty, as though it had not been aired or used in some time; in the courtyard, she could smell cedar smoke—Nidya burning incense, as she had when Tar was ill once.

Nevvia was huddled in her favorite chair, Nidya sitting next to her, coaxing her to eat but not getting very far; Xhem tended the brazier. She could not see Niverren, but an almost continuous, low-pitched moan came from the room where Creos had been put.

She paused in the doorway and stared at Nevvia. *Oh, Mother.* It had only been a few days since they'd let her come home, but Nevvia seemed thinner and more fragile than ever. What was left of her hacked-short hair hung lank to her shoulders; her face was pale and gaunt, the skin under her eyes smudgy. *She could—she could die.* Breyd stepped back into the main room to divest herself of the sword and her armor, set the cloak aside, and walked into the open.

Nevvia held out trembling hands. Nidya got up and hugged her granddaughter; she used the opportunity to whisper, "Breyd, get your mother to eat." Breyd nodded, then knelt at her mother's side.

"Oh, baby," Nevvia whispered. "They couldn't—even Xhem couldn't tell us anything, and then I saw the fire and the whole house shook, I thought they'd killed all of you."

"No, it's all right, I'm here now. Shhh." Breyd sat back and laid a hand against her mother's cheek; Nevvia held it there. "They have a ballista."

"I know," Nevvia whispered. *Of course she knows. Because of Father.* Breyd swallowed. "They did some damage with it, but I wasn't near that. They had to—there was a lot to be done before they'd let me have leave." Nevvia's hands tightened on her free hand. "It's all right. I won't be going back outside."

"We've lost, haven't we?" Nevvia asked; there was very little sound behind the words. Breyd nodded, unable to speak at all suddenly; Nevvia's eyes sagged closed. "Your father—I kept hoping—"

"No, Mother!" She freed her fingers, wrapped her arms around her mother and drew her head close. "He's—Mother, I would never lie to you, he's alive. Truly."

"But it's been so long. And if Haffat comes—into the city—"

If she believes that, I don't think she'll survive it, Breyd thought. Her heart sank. *She'll give up.* She shook her head. "Haffat might come in, but he won't stay here long; he'll leave someone behind to—to help the prince govern for him. He'll go away, find something else to conquer. He won't—"

"I don't think I can bear any more," Nevvia said flatly.

"Mother." She swallowed, cupped her mother's face between her hands. She could feel the fine bones of her jaw; her shoulders were birdlike, they were so thin. Tears filled her eyes. "Mother, please, don't. You're frightening me. It will be all right, I swear it will."

"You sound like your father."

"It *will* be all right. I need you, Mother. And—and Father

will, when he comes home. Please. You can't—you're wasting away, Mother."

"I can't—"

"You can, please. You have to." She picked up the bread, broke it in half, and tore off a bite for herself. "Here, we'll share this."

Nevvia shook her head, but when Breyd held up the bread, she took it. "I can't—I think about Tar and I can't—"

"Oh, Mother. Tar would hate it if he thought you had done this to yourself for him. You know he would. Father would hate it. Mother, I'm so worn out from the past days, all the fighting, everything. I just couldn't bear it if you made yourself sick. I need you. After all that—everything out there, I need things like they were. Even a little. Please."

Nevvia closed her eyes and shook her head, but after a moment she bit into the bread, chewed, and swallowed. "I'm sorry, baby, I didn't realize. Of course, you've had an awful time of it." Breyd looked around, found her wine cup and handed it to her. "I didn't mean to be so much trouble."

"You're never any trouble, Mother. It's just—you worry me because you're so thin. Come on, eat some more."

Nevvia ate two more bites of bread, a few dates, drank wine. "There. Happy?"

"Of course." Breyd drained the cup Nidya brought her.

"You won't go back again?"

"Tomorrow, for a little. Not very long, and mostly to get rid of the armor, Mother. Not to fight. That's done with."

"Oh." She clutched her daughter's fingers once more. "Then, they'll send you to Khadat!"

"Not right away. I'll have some time here, for you. I promise I will." Breyd pressed lank hair off her mother's forehead. "You look tired, Mother."

"I am tired," Nevvia said fretfully. "Your grandmother doses my wine all the time."

"Well, you need the sleep, don't you? Let me help you."

"It's all right, Ina is used to putting me to bed." Nevvia managed a faint smile for her. "I don't need my children taking care of me like I used to tend them. I'll sleep a little. You'll be here?"

"I'll be here." Breyd kissed her mother's cheek, helped Ina get her to her feet, and watched her go. Nidya sat in the chair where she'd been. "Oh, Niddy—she looks terrible!"

"I've done what I can, it's all this worry. You must be

easy on her, Breyd; she cannot help the way she is, and she cannot help herself thinking your father won't return. Whatever you tell her. And Tarpaen—"

"I know. There are days I hardly think about him; and then, when I do—isn't that awful?"

"You have had other things to think about," Nidya said. "Once you're a mother, you'll understand better." Breyd bent over the dish of dates, scowled at her hands. *What— bear grandchildren for Khadat? Not likely!* But Nidya was saying something else. She looked up, shook her head. "I said, you're about to fall over, child; you're swaying where you sit. I've told Niverren you're here, but she can't leave Creos; besides, she gets snappish with everyone when he hurts like this, and I don't think *I* could bear you two bickering. Go on, get out of the rest of that. I had Ina clear the couch in the main room for you earlier and put fresh blankets and cushions out; I'll bring your old blue."

She was tired, all at once; blindly exhausted. She set the dish of dates aside, somehow got to her feet without help, and hugged Nidya without leaning into her. *Even Nidya feels so thin; has she always, or am I so used to the muscle in a Secchi's shoulders?* "Thank you, Niddy."

"Mmmph, *feel* you, girl; you're nearly as hard as that armor was! Go on, shoo. I'll be right in."

The last watch of the night was a chill one; Ridlo paced back and forth near the gates, cloak pulled tightly around him. The wind came from the north, across the water, and swirled around the walls so there was no protection anywhere.

It was truly black across the plain, except where the Diye Haff had lit their fires—in that enormous camp beyond the Oryon and all along the ridges, a few in the very middle of the plain next to the road.

So far they had not destroyed anything across the Alno. If they spoke the truth about Haffat, his conquests of other lands, perhaps he would leave things as they were. *He will, if he has any sense—they say he is a sensible man. If he does not gut the city, he will want her as a source of tribute.* He would take the isthmus, of course; every king who had ever waged war against Ghezrat had wanted the isthmus.

What will Haffat do to us all, when he comes?

Some time after tenth horn, the campfires across the river

began to die down and flicker out; the camp was becoming hard to see. By first horn, there was a little gray light to the east. His replacement would come onto the wall soon. But Grysis came first, and sat on the block where Piritos had stood for so many long days.

"I have talked with the two men you sent me and they'll do. Keep in mind we'll need another five or six to work down there. And another thing, a word in your ear. To be passed on to no one without my saying so; you must swear that." He waited.

Ridlo looked at him but could make nothing from his expression. He shrugged. "All right. I swear."

"General Piritos. It will be given out to the people and to the army that he died this past night from his wounds." Ridlo stared at him in shock. "It is not true," Grysis went on, "though his shoulder is unclean and he has a hard fight ahead of him. Or so the physicians tell me. He is in a safe place.

"Morale will be low enough generally. We can't afford for men like you to feel everything's lost before we begin."

"You're right about that, sir." Atos made a smear of ruddy orange against the ridges, brightness between dark hills and a low line of black cloud. He froze, then gestured urgently. "Come, look."

Grysis leapt to his feet and leaned across the wall. All across the road, near the base of the cliff from river to river, Haffat's army was drawn up in ranks: Phalanx upon phalanx, a thicket of long spears standing high above men's heads; another company and another, and behind the infantry, the Diye Haff chariot, flanked by Haffat's cavalry. Before all, two men who bore the standards of Haffat and of Axtekeles.

Ridlo turned back as someone cried out a distance away, and Grysis clambered onto the general's stone, but he could see little. Word was passed from guard to guard upon the wall, though, and finally came to them. "There are men—a full company at least, two men deep! All along the southern walls, standing and waiting!"

Ridlo stood very still and gazed down from the walls at the assembled force. Third horn sounded; Atos climbed from behind the hills and ridges and behind the heavy clouds. *As though he is ashamed to show his face to us—or ashamed to look upon us.*

* * *

Breyd woke at first horn and for one long moment lay flat, eyes closed. It was quiet out in the courtyard, finally quiet in the street. She sat up, buried her face in her hands. *Everything we did—everyone we lost, and it still wasn't enough.* What more could Denota ask of them? *Spy on Khadat. Marry Apodain and spy on Khadat.* At the moment, that didn't seem real; leaving Nevvia did, though. *I can't leave Mother; she's so afraid of Haffat, so upset by everything. If he comes into the city, she might—* She couldn't complete the thought.

Footsteps came across the gritty courtyard and stopped just inside the room; Breyd looked up to find Niverren leaning against the doorframe. "So, they let you come home." Her voice was husky, as if she'd been crying.

"For a little."

"All that—for nothing."

Breyd stirred and shook her head angrily. "It wasn't."

"It was!" Niverren hissed. "Father gone, all those men dead, and for what? If they'd given in at once, Creos wouldn't—wouldn't be—"

"You don't know that! You weren't out there!"

"No," Niverren said. "And you weren't here, fighting to keep him alive."

No; I fought to keep Xera alive and she died anyway, Breyd thought bleakly. But she could never tell Niverren any of that. Even if she had wanted to, the words simply wouldn't come. "How is he?" she asked finally.

Niverren ran a hand across her head, dislodging the cloth she'd draped across her hair. "He's—this morning he's better. But he's better most mornings, it only gets worse as the day wears on. It hurts him horribly sometimes. He says he can feel his foot, and that his toes are cramping, and *there is nothing there!*" She drew a shuddering breath. "I'm sorry," she mumbled. "Xhem's told us you—were out there guarding the walls, just that, so Mother wouldn't be so frightened. I knew better, even before Father disappeared, I think. But I went to get the bread, a few days ago—they're all talking about the Pairs. How they fought, and how many of the enemy they—"

"Don't. Please. It's all right, Niv. Most days, I didn't have the time to think about what I was doing, or how bad it was."

"The boy came to tell us what happened last night, before you came home. Mother's terrified the Diye Haff will kill us all—or take the women and—"

"Don't," Breyd said harshly. Niverren started. "Don't think such things. It isn't any use. But it isn't true, anyway."

"I didn't think it was. I pray the boy's right. I wish I could be as strong as Niddy; she says so long as Haffat doesn't storm the city and send all the women as slaves to Diyet, she can survive having them inside the walls. Creos—"

"They won't bother Creos, Niv."

"No," she said bitterly. "They'll think him useless, won't they?"

"If he lives, do you care what *they* think?"

"No," Niverren said flatly. "But his father—his father's never even come to see him. Creos *says* he doesn't care so long as we're together."

"Well, then—" Breyd got up and drew the blue tunic over her head. Niverren gazed at her critically.

"You're all muscle, hardly any breast. More like a half-grown boy than a woman old enough to bear children." She laughed sourly. "Khadat will love that, won't she?"

"I don't care if she does," Breyd said shortly.

"You haven't changed at all that way, have you?"

"Why should I be thinking of marriage right now? But would *you* want to go live with Khadat?"

Niverren turned her head. "I think I heard Creos. Don't think of Khadat, it's Apodain you'll be bedding. You aren't putting that short thing and the armor back on, are you?"

"I have to—for now. They need me in the barracks at least once more, before midday."

"Mother won't—"

"*I* know she won't like it!" Breyd said testily; Niverren stared at her and Breyd came over to wrap her arms around her. "I'm sorry, Niv. I know things aren't easy for you right now; my temper isn't any better. I'll try to watch it. All right? Do you think Creos would—?"

"Let me see how he is this morning," Niverren said cautiously. "I'll let you know."

Neither Xhem nor Niverren was in sight when she came into the courtyard. Nidya sat in Nevvia's chair, and she had drawn the other up close. Ina brushed past her on her way into the storage. "Here, child, sit," Nidya said. She eyed the pleats but said nothing about them. "We have food for you, if you have time."

Breyd nodded and sank into the cushions. "I have a little time, Niddy. But I won't be gone long."

"Good. Are you tired of oil and peppers? I don't think you'll see them in Khadat's palace, they're common, you know."

"I'd never be tired of your oil and peppers. Don't remind me about Khadat." Nidya looked at her keenly, finally shook her head. "Thank you, Ina," she added as the other woman brought her bread and oil. She ate. Nidya sat and watched her; the silence stretched. "That was good, Niddy. I'll have to go, soon. I'll learn everything I can for you—but it won't be much."

"I understand that. I'll try to convince your mother."

"I won't desert her."

"She knows that—or she would, if she weren't so upset. She's already lost so much, it's hard for her."

"I know." Breyd dipped the last of her bread in the oil. "I asked Niverren if she'd like me to see Creos. She was odd about it. Did I do something wrong?"

"She's—possessive of him right now. Trying to protect him from hearing anything about the fighting."

"It must drive him mad," Breyd said. Nidya shrugged.

"I wouldn't like to be kept in a box myself, but I'm not Creos; Niverren probably knows better than we do, what he needs."

Creos began to moan once more, a tight-lipped, low, almost constant sound. Nidya continued to drink her wine. Breyd shuddered. *How does she bear it?* Suddenly she wanted to run. With Tarpaen dead, Menlaeus missing, Niverren a gaunt-faced stranger and Creos— She swallowed, bit her lip. *Mother needs me. I have to be here for Mother. And Father would want me to be strong for her.*

The meeting in the barracks was very brief; Grysis looked harried and he had only a few minutes for them. "Come back here at midday, bring your reds. They will be put underground in a safe place for the day you take up arms once more. The priestess is to send word to the prechosen mates, the marriages will take place in secret, down in the Cleft."

"Not tonight!" Breyd gaped at him.

He gave her a stern, warning look and she subsided.

Aroepe gripped her fingers and Jocasa wrapped an arm around her shoulders. "Not tonight. The priestess said she would prefer it, but she has not yet finished protecting the walls and the city so Haffat's magicians cannot enter. We will get word to you.

"There are too many men in the barracks at this hour and we must do nothing to arouse anyone's curiosity. Remember that! And tonight, if Haffat is still outside, come back at midnight, ninth horn. I will show you one way under the city from the barracks and another halfway between here and the temple; I am told Tephys will show you another. You will keep these completely secret; you will not even speak of them among yourselves.

"Once you Secchi are in your new homes, and you Primes back with the rest of your families, you will visit each other just as you would have if no enemy were inside the city. You will be careful what you say to anyone, extremely cautious of who is brought into our circle. If you doubt—even a little—keep quiet. You can always go to Tephys with messages to be passed on; you Primes can go to the wineshop near the main gates, or the old bread and soup house near the Shepherd's Gate; the men who own both places are safe."

Jocasa looked drawn and pale, as though she hadn't slept. "Sir, if Haffat does hold the city tonight—?"

"Then you will dress as ordinary supplicants and make your way to the temple after dark. Tephys will take you below, and I will come there, and we will decide what is to be done." He watched them go, but as he would have gone back into the messes, Breyd came back. He looked at her tiredly. "You do not still fight this marriage, do you?"

"I would if there was a way," Breyd said flatly. "But not just for myself; my mother needs me."

"I am sorry. I wish I could do more for you."

She sighed faintly and turned away. "I know. I'm sorry to be so difficult, sir. I know you have enough to do—and with the general—"

"Yes, we have plenty to do before Haffat comes through those gates." *The general—but there are too many men around; someone might overhear. And her face might show the surprise,* he decided. *Tell her tonight, with the rest of them, when they are beneath the city.* Breyd touched his arm.

"Sir, when did you last sleep?"

He laughed; there wasn't much humor in the sound. "Don't you fuss over an old soldier, Secchi; save that for your mother. If you have anything left in the barracks, take it now."

"All right." She remembered something. "My father's old panoply—"

"The one that's here? Already shifted below, late last night. Along with the leathers you first wore."

"No, I meant—other things we have at home—what Creos had left when they brought him in, the weapons that belonged to my father's father. And Xhem has my—my brother's panoply."

"Bring whatever you can carry, if there's no safe place to hide it at home. But the boy already brought his brother Tar's weaponry, at first horn."

"Good. Thank you, sir."

"Midday," he reminded her. He turned back and walked briskly toward the messes.

There was nothing left in the barracks but the water jug and the heavy goat's hair blanket Niddy had sent. The red cloak had been more than enough for warmth. *Will they let me have it back when everything is over?* she wondered. Had other Secchi from other wars kept any of their panoply? But what use would a woman have for such things? Women didn't pass weapons on to their daughters, the way fathers did to sons. *Or did they? Niddy might know, her friend was Secchi, she said.* But what would a woman do with even the cloak, except bring it out of storage now and again, and remember what she had been—and what she had done? Breyd shuddered, gathered up the blanket and the jug and left quickly.

How can they think we will be able to act like other wedded women—enough to fool the Diye Haff? How could they ask that of previous Secchi—fight, and then come home and forget what they'd done? *Father fought for the city, then came back and left it behind. At least, he never brought it up, all the years I was a child. But that was—what he did fighting for the mole wasn't like what he and I did out there. Forty-seven men dead, just like that. All the others, after—*

It was nearly as difficult to get through the streets as it had been the night before, but there seemed to be fewer frightened or hysterical people—more gloom. Hardly anyone tried to stop her.

Her own narrow street was utterly empty, even the fountain and the covered area behind it. Xhem met her at the door. "Niddy has gone to take a rest with Aunt Nevvia," he said. "She had me empty a chest and we brought it in here for your things."

"All right." She let the blanket fall onto the sleeping couch, sat down heavily next to it. Her clothing and her few personal belongings were stacked on the couch. She fingered a slender belt Menlaeus had given her the previous midsummer, after she'd won so many of the races. *Father. I don't think I can face this. I'm just not—I'm not enough like you; I'm not strong like that.* Xhem eyed her sidelong, then turned and left without another word, but he was back a moment later with a small tray.

"Niddy said to give you this, when you came."

"All right," Breyd said again. A cup, a bowl of cool lentil soup, a wooden dish with a few figs in sweet liquid.

"And to tell you that you must eat it all," Xhem added. Breyd looked at him, dredged up a smile she scarcely felt, and took the tray.

"I will eat it all. I won't bite you, Xhem."

"No, cousin." She didn't think he sounded entirely certain.

"You don't need to be so formal, Xhem. Grysis tells me we're in this mess together. I'll need your help, if I have to go live with Khadat and Apodain."

He sniffed. "My—my brother Tar said that. Not to be so formal."

"He was a good man," Breyd said softly. She put an arm around the boy and he leaned into her. "You're going to be a lot like him, Xhem, I can see it already."

"I am?" he asked in a very small voice.

"Of course you are." For a moment she thought he'd weep. *He'd hate that, weeping in front of me or anyone else,* she realized. She changed the subject. "Here, are you hungry? Niddy gave me enough to keep Grysis going, I'll never finish it." She drank some of the soup and held out the bowl. Xhem took it and gave her a watery smile over the rim.

It was as dark and still behind the Cleft as Denira had feared it would be; fortunately the two young princes had gone somewhere with Eyzhad—exploring, the priest had said. Fortunately because Ye Sotris was having a terrible time controlling her fears. "He said he would come—"

"Majesty, it isn't yet fifth horn. The emperor was to come to the gates at sixth, and the prince will need to make decisions after that." She had already said that; Ye Sotris once again nodded, as she had each previous time. She was still wringing her hands.

"I know—I'm sorry. I'll try to be patient."

They both turned as footsteps came along the passage, but it was Tephys, an oil lamp in one hand. With the light shining up from under her face, she looked utterly ghastly, and Denira caught her breath; Ye Sotris was too lost in her own misery to notice. "I thought you might like more lamps," Tephys said. "It's safe to have light so long as you stay in these two chambers and the halls that connect them. Denira, Meronne needs you for a little." Denira bowed, picked up her own small copper lamp, and hurried off.

"Tephys—" Ye Sotris began. Tephys held up a hand for silence.

"I must go in a little; they will need me by the city gates. If you have any message for the prince, give it to me now, and I will pass it on."

Ye Sotris shook her head. "Only his promise. Remind him." Tephys nodded, turned and left. Ye Sotris sank onto the couch and buried her face in her hands.

"Priestess?" Denira's voice echoed along the passage. "Meronne said—"

"She doesn't want you, I do. Keep a close eye on her; she will be distraught when the prince does not join her." Denira stared at her; Tephys' lips twisted. "Of course he won't. He won't dare put her in jeopardy, and he won't leave the city to Haffat, not willingly. You'll get your face under control before you go back to her."

"Priestess, I can't do this!" Denira whispered.

"You can," Tephys said flatly. "There isn't anyone else." She stepped back a pace, studied the girl. "I was wrong about one thing. You're devout enough, and your love of the goddess true and deep enough. But you aren't—" She broke off abruptly, drew herself up. "You have only to sit and keep the queen company; your friend Breyd will be doing things that will get her strangled or beheaded if she's found out. If she can manage, so can you." She brushed by Denira and was gone.

"Breyd? What is Breyd—?" But Tephys was already out of hearing. Denira stared after her. "What did she mean? And—wrong about what?"

Fifth horn: Grysis went onto the wall with one of the general's aides, to talk where they wouldn't be overheard and see what was going on across the plain. The two ballistas still flanked the city. *But Haffat won't remove those until the walls are his, and he is inside.* The Diye Haff had broken ranks and no longer stood openly outside the south walls. Now, only a few men dotted the landscape, watching the city from a distance—most likely to warn Haffat if the prince tried to flee.

Their camp looked no different; most of the movement was down at the mole, where ships were being unloaded.

"They have been at this all afternoon," the aide said gloomily. "I still say there could have been a way."

"We all say that, friend," Grysis replied. "But what? Fight against that ballista? Those magicians? Take it to siege—but who would come from outside to break a siege? That would only have delayed the inevitable."

"I know, and not for long. It just seems so pointless."

"It's not; don't think that way. How is your man doing?"

The aide's gloom deepened and he sighed heavily. "They can't say yet. His arm's ugly, though. He was awake; he was given the message. I think he's too sick to be angry."

A small silence, which Grysis broke. "It won't be safe for you to come up through the barracks any more. I'll come to see him late tonight, tenth horn or so; I'll bring one of the messenger boys and show you both another way in and out. You'll need to begin learning the passages anyway."

"All right. I'll tell him. And if he— Wait." The aide pointed suddenly. "What's that? What are they up to, out there?"

Grysis looked. A small company of horsemen had just crossed the Oryon, armsmen in dark armor and dark cloaks, two banners, and one man in the very midst of all the rest whose armor gave off fire in the late afternoon sunlight. Somewhere off to their right, a signal echoed across the rocks: Enemy on the way. Another signal came down from the heights behind them. Grysis laid a hand on his companion's arm. "The prince will be here any moment. Stay on the wall with me; you'll be able to tell the general exactly what Haffat's terms are."

The prince's men swarmed onto the wall, the prince in their midst. He looked pale and exhausted in his plain blue and white robes—as though he hadn't slept at all. He looked around, then beckoned to Grysis and said softly, "Thank you for the message about the general." Grysis nodded and moved away as Tephys came up to stand just behind them; she was followed by most of the prince's council; Nabid and the other captains came from the barracks to form a half-circle around him.

Do they expect an assassination attempt? Pelledar wondered dully. *But why would Haffat make a public martyr of me and a rallying point for resentment and possible revolt when he can dispose of me in secret as he did my brother in Mirikos?*

The sound of horses coming up the road brought his attention back where it belonged: Haffat and those men with him had nearly gained the gates.

There were seven of them: Haffat in the middle, his muscled bronze armor burnished so it could have shone by itself. His horse was a finely bred northern black; the household men also rode blacks, and wore black armor. The man at his right elbow was enough like him to be kin, most likely one of his numerous sons. At his other side, Knoe sat and stared avidly at the walls.

Pelledar glanced at the priest, at the emperor, fixed his eyes finally on the younger man. He was older than Septarin, twenty or so. He sat his horse well and there was a tensile strength to him, little bulk in contrast to Haffat, whose bare arms and legs showed good corded muscle. Like Haffat, he was beardless, but unlike the emperor, he shifted on his saddle pad and looked very out of place. His eyes darted from the wall, to the guards surrounding the prince, to the gates, to one or another of his companions; his hands played with the reins, or with the various straps depending from his baldric and his belt, or with the horse's mane.

Haffat stared up at him; Pelledar continued to study the boy next to the emperor. *That is the one who will sit upon my throne.* He looked at the rest of the small company: That dreadful priest Knoe, with his black, intense eyes and hairless head; Haffat, who looked as though he had slept well and deeply the entire night—who now smiled as expectantly and eagerly as a child given wondrous gifts.

Pelledar could not remember ever being so tired. *I could sleep for a thousand years.* But there had only been an hour before dawn when he had been able to seek his couch: Before that, there had been Septarin; a quiet hour with Piritos. *I am glad we had that, he and I.* The council, those letters. Khadat. He had wanted to wipe that arrogant smirk from her face. *How long before she sides openly with Haffat?* His mind reeled with all the instructions his council had given him; all the argument; the things his captains had told him.

The men grouped around him were worried, he knew; worried that he would somehow say or do the wrong thing, and give to Haffat some advantage that would be hard to overcome. *And yet, he has every advantage already,* Pelledar thought grimly.

Haffat held up a hand. "How says my brother now?" he asked. "Shall we make a peace between us?"

Pelledar held up both hands, and Haffat fell silent. "We shall have peace. I have spent many of the sons and daughters of my city; I will not spend women and children as well."

The men behind Haffat stirred and looked at each other, but Haffat held up a hand once more and drew his horse to one side. "Then I ask of my brother, come down and walk before the gates with me. We two alone will discuss the terms." Someone behind him hissed a warning, but Pelledar was already shaking his head.

"No. Give me the terms, and I will discuss them with my council. Haffat may be emperor and absolute ruler of his empire, but that is not how princes have ever ruled in Ghezrat."

Haffat frowned. "Does my brother fear I shall kill him? Does he think me such a fool?"

Tephys touched Pelledar's arm. "Sire, may I?" He nodded; the High Priestess stepped to his side and glanced at Haffat, then fixed her cold gaze on Knoe. "The goddess will not allow her prince to leave the city while Ergardi magicians sit outside the walls."

Haffat laughed suddenly. "Ergardi? But there are no Ergardi among us here!" He spread his arms wide, taking in the small mounted company. "Surely the servant of the goddess is aware of that."

Just as she is aware they have not gone very far, Tephys thought grimly. Knoe still studied her, his eyes intent. *Yes,* she thought. *You know your own enemy, don't you, priest? But your magicians cannot come here—and if you enter this city, you will learn that lions are not creatures of streets and alleys. Try yourself and your god against Denota, and see what comes of it.*

He couldn't have heard that, but his eyes were challenging, and he brought his chin up to glare at her; he turned away then, as if he'd lost interest. But she could feel his thoughts on her, and knew his curiosity was high. *What have you done with our missing Dyadd, priest? And what do you plan to do with them?* She had hopes. *Bring them; see what comes of that, priest.*

She stepped back as Pelledar folded his arms to wait.

Haffat finally broke the silence. He sighed a little and said, "If there is peace between us, there must also be trust. But if you will have it this way:

"The city gates will be opened at this hour tomorrow. In return, I will bring only this escort and fifty soldiers hand-picked by my own general. Your general will surrender his weapons to me, personally, and he will accompany Jemaro to the barracks where what is left of your army will give up its weaponry. There will be no violence, no challenge by any soldier, or Jemaro will be forced to make reprisals.

"But we will not speak of reprisals, or anything else but peace and friendship.

"The city will remain under the protection of the prince, no property inside or out will be taken from the people. Your temples will remain untouched, though I would place one small temple within the walls for Axtekeles, and leave priests to care for the altar.

"My son Hadda will live in this city with you, and serve as my agent since Ghezrat is now a part of my realm; a small garrison will stay with him.

"In five days, at midsummer, my men will celebrate with games; the Mirikosi tells me Ghezrat also holds games at midsummer. We will hold them together, as a sign of peace and friendship between us. What say you?"

A silence. *Does he really think footraces and wrestling will bring us together, after so much death?* Pelledar wondered. He finally said, "I need three days, to ready the army and the people, to be certain they accept—"

"No!" Haffat snapped. His son touched his arm, whispered against his ear. The emperor subsided, but his expression was still dangerous. "Do you seek to somehow put me off entirely?"

"I seek what I have said," Pelledar replied evenly. "And to meet with my council and discuss these terms."

"And for that I offer you one more day," Haffat said flatly. "You know what I offered, if you refused me. Delay will do you no good, and will only serve to anger me. I fought for this city and I won it from you. Now I wish to enjoy what I have won; it would be foolish of you to deny me—to attempt to deny me."

"I do not deny you," Pelledar said. "But I will not simply open the gates. The terms must be put into writing, so that both sides know exactly what they are. Not only Haffat and Pelledar, but all Haffat's people and Pelledar's. My people must be told what to expect, and when; the army must be given orders. If you truly do not wish to speak of reprisals, then give me the opportunity to see there is no need for them!"

Haffat listened as his son said something, and his priest spoke against his other ear. He turned to look out across the plain and there was a long silence. Finally, he turned back. "You think you need three days; but it is my experience that people think whatever *they* will choose to think. In three days those who have fears now will have horrors, and those who are angry now will be possessed of furies then. Better to give them a little time only, and then let them see that the anger is for fools, the fear pointless. One day. At this hour tomorrow, I will return with the documents you ask, my general and my soldiers. Do not seek to again delay me." Haffat turned his horse and rode away without another glance at his new city; Knoe gave the priestess a long look and a knowing smile before he drew his mount around to follow; the armsmen came after.

Pelledar stood above the wreckage of the gates and watched them go. When the emperor and his honor guard were down below the first turn in the road, the captains came over to him; Pelledar's hands were clasped together so tightly the knuckles were white. He sent his eyes sideways as Brysos came up beside him. "I am sorry," he said very softly. "I do not think I can move just yet."

"Stand then, my prince," Brysos replied quietly. "Here,

lean upon my arm, if you will. To argue terms with that man took courage."

"Perhaps," Pelledar said, but some of the terrible tension left his face. "He can break those terms whenever he chooses, though. That boy at his side—I think you have seen your new prince."

"Perhaps not," Grysis said. "Games! Is the man mad?"

"It was my thought," Pelledar admitted. Silence. "I can stand now. Thank you, captain." Brysos bowed; the captains went back along the wall and down to the barracks. The prince turned to look at the men and women who had come with him; at Tephys, who was still staring after Haffat and his escort. *Which of them, I wonder? Which already hate me for giving in to the enemy? For handing him my city and my people as a most costly host's gift? I knew it would give me great pain to do this. I didn't realize how unclean I would feel.*

"It would have caused me great pain to do what you just did," Tephys said quietly. Pelledar turned to stare at her. She was still gazing out across the plain. "But you did the right thing. And your people will know that one day, if they do not already realize why you have done this."

"Some will." Pelledar shook himself. "Give my love to my wife. Tell her—I have another long night, and a longer day tomorrow. Tell her I will come when I can."

"Yes," Tephys said.

"You know—"

"I know; I will not tell her. But do not despair, Prince Pelledar. The goddess has not yet deserted us; she will bring victory from this yet."

"You—see this."

She glanced at him. *Tell him the truth? But that is my burden; I know victory will come—not when or how.* "I see it," she said calmly. He eyed her sidelong, but she thought he was satisfied.

Word spread rapidly throughout the city: the prince's councillor Polyos spoke to an anxious, silent crowd before the palace walls, Tephys to another within those of the goddess', the captains to their companies. By seventh horn the bare terms of surrender were common knowledge.

* * *

Far below the barracks, General Piritos shifted uncomfortably and opened his eyes. There was a low, rough-hewn stone ceiling above him, a small, flat oil lamp with a very short wick set in a niche near his feet. Sweat slicked his face and chest, and ran down his sides; his whole left side throbbed. He could not think where he was, or why at first.

But he knew this chamber. It was one of those underground with a hidden entry known only to Ghezrat's general and a very few of his aides or captains. He closed his eyes and groaned, then whispered, "Who has done this? Who has dared?"

A voice spoke against his right ear, "Sir." Nufia sat cross-legged upon the floor on a thick cushion; his face was so haggard Piritos guessed he had not slept in at least a day. "Sir, pardon it," Nufia said softly, and ducked his head. "Captain Grysis knew the way into this place, but we all knew the plan. The captains, those who care for you—even the priestess sent word to us that you must not die, but we would have done anything to keep that from happening, even without her say.

"Captain Brysos sent a message down for you from all the captains, for when you woke. He says, 'We have lost our city for now only. A city is a thing that can be lost and regained, but not a man, and we will not let Haffat kill the one man who can lead us to final victory. Nor will we lose the general beloved of all who serve under him.'" Piritos stared at him, and Nufia stared back; there was a long silence, which the aide finally broke. "Those were his very words, sir."

"Brave words," Piritos said finally. "And daunting. One man—no one man can be all those things. And what will they do when Haffat finds himself cheated of my head?"

"He will not, sir; they have named you dead, and with good cause," Nufia replied and let his eyes fasten on the general's shoulder; the wrappings had been removed, the wound reopened so it could drain. It looked and smelled unclean. "Sir, you must listen to Captain Brysos."

The general considered this, finally let his eyes close. "The gods aid them in the days to come. But Nufia, I fear what they did will be of little use, and the rumor they spread only premature."

"You will not die, sir. We will not permit it."

"Oh." The faintest of smiles touched his lips. "Well, then.

I will not die, if you are so insistent; perhaps I will sleep again instead."

Apodain sat on the edge of the roof, gazing out across what could be seen of the city and the distant fires of the Diye Haff camp. There were a few fires behind him, strewn across the southern highlands; he did not bother to look at them.

His mother had been summoned to the palace hours before midnight and had still not returned; if he stood, he could see lamplight shining from the window of the prince's throne room. *What could they still find to talk about?* he wondered. *Haffat has won, we have lost; what can they hope to salvage from this?*

Half his old company was dead, General Piritos said to have died during the night of festered wounds—as many as half the Dyaddi; Khadat had sourly informed him the Secchi he was to wed had not been among them, though her Prime had. *Poor girl. It was hard for me as a boy, to lose my father; how much harder would it be to lose both your closest fighting ally and your father—in one man?* How soon would they set the ceremony? In the past, they had wed the Secchi as quickly as possible, but how would that serve a young woman who had barely had time to weep for her father?

But everything had changed; would the ceremony still stand? He had heard enough from his mother about how Haffat had left traditions alone in Mirikos and other places. He thought about it for a while. Better than almost anything else he could think about at the moment. He was not certain he could remember anything about her from that one meeting, save the red tiara and the startled look on her face. Even from the step below her, he had been taller than she—a small young woman, then. Very much a commoner, from the way his mother spoke about her. He didn't remember a peasant, though. Just a small, surprised looking girl.

He tried to imagine Khadat sharing the palace with her son's wife—with a son's wife of any rank or class—and failed utterly. *Think of her as a grandmother, myself as father.* Even more impossible. *But why should I wed? They will only kill me, sooner or later, and if I have a wife, they'll kill my wife. Why should I be responsible for that girl's death as well?*

Why even wed? He had never known Perlot before his

mother came, of course—but some of the royal cousins had. Even Khadat had seemed shy and sweet at first, they said. *Will the girl change when she knows we are bonded for life? Ah, why even bother! So Mother will eventually have a grandson, so her wealth stays with her blood?* But he no longer cared for her family wealth and her precious ships, if he ever had.

Footsteps crunched across the crushed stone path and stopped just behind him. He suppressed a deep sigh and asked, "Mother?"

"I thought I would find you sulking here," Khadat said briskly. She had not known about his request to Brysos and the captain's refusal to have her son back in the company, but she was aware of his returning depression and had taken advantage of the change in him. "Come below at once, to my accounting. Pelledar had many things to say, and you should be apprised of them." He turned to look up at her.

"Why?"

"As my son, and your father's heir." It hurt her to name him that, in Hemit's place; he could see it in her face. "And as eighth in place after Pelledar for the throne, of course."

"Of course," he echoed. It had never sounded remotely real. But Khadat would bully him until he gave over and went with her; better to simply go, and at least appear to listen, and be done with it. *I won't have much longer to listen anyway.* He got to his feet, followed her down the broad stone steps and into the small, overly close accounts room. Khadat took her usual place behind Perlot's small table and waved him to a seat.

"I sent for food and wine," she said as she settled a cushion against her back and let Perlot's cloak slip from her shoulders. "Now. Haffat had two letters delivered a while ago, written by the Mirikosi to be handed to Pelledar when the war was over and matters ready to be settled. They give me some hope." She looked at him; he shook his head. "Hope." She waited as a tray was brought and set on a little claw-footed table next to the desk. Khadat waited a moment longer to make certain the servants were out of hearing. "Pour wine for both of us, son. Take bread and fruit, and eat; I know you have not all day. And don't tell me you aren't hungry. There is much to be done these next days if we are to salvage anything and set ourselves as high as possible with Haffat's man."

He obediently rose, poured wine in two cups, and set a dish of flat bread and sectioned oranges between them. Khadat took her cup but waited pointedly until Apodain took a bite of bread and ate two pieces of orange. *She has already betrayed Ghezrat,* he realized bleakly. But Khadat was Mirikosi by birth and by family, and by holdings. Perhaps it did not seem to her treachery, to side so quickly with a conqueror. *No, it would not; if I taxed her or any man ever does, she will laugh that sour little laugh of hers and say she is practical. Sensible.* The bread stuck in his throat; he kept his face impassive somehow, drank a little very watered wine. Sat back and waited.

"That is better," Khadat said. "Now. They say Haffat does not put his stamp upon conquered lands and the letters from Mirikos agree with this; the city's temples were left intact, the nobility are unscathed, and my family ships were not taken—well, other than those Haffat brought here, but they say he paid for the use of them and their captains."

"And you—" He couldn't say anything else; fortunately, Khadat was too pleased by this last news, at regaining what she had thought forever lost, to even notice his distress.

"Trade will resume when Pelledar comes properly to terms with Haffat's man—his son Hadda, I think they said—and if I understood the prince properly, there will be no impediment other than perhaps a small tax above what the city already puts upon goods."

"Nothing," Apodain echoed. *They will kill Pelledar, too; and she does not see it, or does not care.*

Khadat drained her cup and let her son refill it for her. "The prince says once the soldiers are disarmed, there may be a call for other weaponry to be turned over. That sounds sensible to me. If the Diye Haff come here, we are to give them what we have."

The bread fell from nerveless fingers. "Give them—!"

"You will not be foolish about such things, Apodain," Khadat said severely. "You will do what is asked of you. You will keep in mind what is important: Swords and armor are *nothing,* particularly not against free access to my family's trading company!" She folded her arms. "You should be grateful; you have your life, your health, your family—and that family's power and wealth as near intact as no matter. Unfortunately," she added acerbically, "I could do nothing with the prince on the subject of this Secchi you are to marry. He put me off, claiming more important matters to deal with, and I finally had to let it go. You may have to marry her after all."

"Yes."

"Do not look so distressed." Khadat leaned across the table and gripped his hand. "She is nothing and nobody; I will be able to have the marriage voided, especially once Haffat comes. And remember that young wives are not always long-lived."

"No." He did not dare let himself think what she meant by that. *Mother will be difficult if she cannot put the marriage aside, but she would not actually hurt anyone. If I could simply not marry the girl.*

"I have kept apprised of her situation for you. Her father is dead, of course."

"Yes, I knew that."

"Oh?" She eyed him curiously, finally shrugged and went on, "Her brother is also dead, her sister recently wed to man crippled out there. Her mother has no wealth or power and apart from her mother, she has an aged grandmother who owns a few vines, some distant cousins—none of them important." Khadat sighed gustily. "Well! Enough of that. Do not worry about this Breyd, I will take care of that for you."

"Thank you, Mother."

"Haffat is a practical man, they say. Now, he has already used our ships, he knows they are among the best and fastest. Once I have the opportunity to talk to him, I can show him there is room for all of us to profit."

Apodain ate another piece of orange, another bite of bread, finished his wine. "Was anything else said?"

"Nothing important," Khadat said dismissively. "You look tired. Why don't you go and get some sleep?"

"Yes," he said and got to his feet; somehow managed to keep his face impassive as he came around to kiss the cheek she proffered. When he glanced back from the doorway, she was already deep in her accounting books.

19

At third horn, the city gates were opened to a company of fifty mounted and armed men led by a grizzled captain with a heavy beard, at their head the emperor's personal guard of seven, surrounding Haffat and his son; three black-clad priests rode behind Knoe.

Just inside the square stood the Ghezrathi captains. As the mangled gates were thrust aside and the Diye Haff rode through them, Brysos came forward with an unsheathed sword held between his hands. He knelt; Haffat dismounted and took it gravely. "This was the weapon of our general, who is dead the past two days of wounds he had above those gates," Brysos said. "He would have given it to you himself otherwise, in token of the submission of his army."

"My thanks to you, and to the shade of your general," Haffat replied. He handed the sword to Hadda, who would have passed it on to the captain of Haffat's guard, but the emperor touched his hand and shook his head minutely.

Brysos swallowed and went doggedly on. "The prince awaits you up there, upon his steps. If it—if it will please you to enter Ghezrat."

Haffat let his head fall back so he could look up: at the walls where no guards now stood; at the distant, tall palace, its white limestone walls brilliant against a bright blue morning sky. He smiled and said, very softly. "Oh, yes, it will indeed please me, captain." He remounted; Brysos would have stepped aside, but Haffat said, "Stay with me, please, captain. As my guide through these streets, for I do not know the way." *As my shield against the populace,* Brysos heard behind the spoken words. He bowed deeply, laid a hand upon the neck of the emperor's horse. Haffat touched his heels to the animal's black flanks and rode slowly through the broad square.

Xhem stood at the southernmost end of the square, where

these enemy would pass to ride up the avenue toward the palace. *I must remember everything, for Niddy and for Niverren—and for Creos, who asked the duty of me first. For Aunt Nevvia, but I think she will never ask; for Breyd, who must put her armor away and wait in the house. How can they ask that of her?* She had talked about it last night, after Nevvia went to sleep and Niddy to bed. He could understand how she felt—as though she deserted all of them, even though she would continue to fight and most of them would not. But she would not have to look the enemy in the face in her own barracks, and hand them her sword.

For his own father and his siblings, who would not come out here today—even for his mother, should she ever ask him about this hour. Though it seemed to him the last two times he had gone to see them, she had nearly forgotten him. *As though I were grown and living with other soldiers in the barracks,* he realized. But he had Niddy to mother him, the others to help—Breyd, who had begun to talk to him, not like a little brother as Tar had, but more like an equal.

For himself above all, he must remember, so one day he could tell his children and his grandchildren. *If I live as long as that.* Just now, he could not believe the city would ever win over this shining man who rode brazenly into the city with armed men at his back and the general's sword lying crosswise and apparently forgotten upon that chinless boy's knees. *Doesn't he know whose blade that is? Doesn't he care?* But what was Piritos to them, save a dead enemy? *But he was my general; I could kill them for dishonoring him!* It was just as well the rest of the army was kept away from this moment; Xhem knew plenty of men who would be furious enough to kill for the general's honor and his sword.

But that sword was already dishonored by Laius, when he stole it and leapt down to fight the enemy. Not to protect my brother Tar as they try to tell me; Tar was already dead thanks to Laius. At least no enemy had stolen the blade; someone had found it out before the walls that night. Xhem turned away briefly to blot his face on the edge of his tunic.

There were people everywhere, several deep; silent, watchful, wary people. Old men and women, some children, a few mothers with the little ones, but no young women anywhere in sight. But they said the women were terrified what the Diye Haff would do to women, and any young men who had survived the war were in the barracks, awaiting the arrival of

Haffat's company. They would wait for some time, it seemed, since that company rode toward the palace with Haffat. The emperor smiled at people on both sides of the avenue and held up a hand in greeting as his horse passed at a walk; Hadda smiled, too, though his smile was not as warm as his father's, and did not touch what seemed to be worried eyes. *Does he think we are stupid enough to kill them?* Xhem wondered.

He watched as Haffat's company rode past and his heart sank. *A year ago—even this spring before my brother Tar came—I would not have seen the difference between these men and ours. I would have seen only bright armor and swords and spears.* The last of them passed and he turned away, sickened. Men and women all around him spoke to each other in low, worried voices. He ignored them all and forced his way through the milling crowd to reach the barracks. Nabid would be there; Nabid would need to know what he had seen.

Pelledar stood upon the highest step of the long flight which led from the horse-forecourt to his palace; partly so people in the street beyond his walls could see him, and see the meeting between the two men. *Partly so Haffat must climb to the highest point of Ghezrat to claim her,* he thought wryly.

That did not matter, of course; it was unlikely Haffat would notice that subtle point—or care, if he did. What matter five steps once he dismounted, or one, or twenty, if the prize he desired lay at the end?

As for the people—Pelledar gazed across the wall to the silent, tightly packed crowd lining the street from the main gates and standing at least twenty deep on either side of the palace gates. Perhaps it was foolish, to care whether they saw what he did or not, when he gave over the city to Haffat. *But one day, when they rise against him, they will remember this moment.* Or so Brysos had said. If it served as a goad to one person out there, or as a shameful memory which must be held onto until it could be forever banished. Just now, he scarcely cared. *My people already know what I am,* he thought bleakly. Whether any of them saw beyond his surrender to the cause for it—well, that was what princes were for, to keep their people safe. *But at this moment, I could greatly envy my brother of Idemito, who sleeps the great sleep with his gods and his men.*

He remembered Ye Sotris then—somewhere below the city in Tephys' care, somehow coping with the boys, with the child she would soon bear him. With Septarin, who must be a maddening handful by himself. *Unfair to my Ye Sotris, to think of death when she has so much life to tend.*

He had promised her he would come; but she must have known it was a lie, and that their new son or daughter would already be fatherless.

Polyos came forward and pulled him from unhappy thoughts. "Sire, they come. See you?"

"I see them," Pelledar replied steadily. He glanced at Polyos, at Potro beyond him and the priest Vertumnus at his shoulder; the other way, then. Tephys at his shoulder, her face giving away nothing; Eyzhad, whose face was gray and whose lips and chin trembled. Khadat, who wore robes of fine cloth and a gold fillet across her brow, as befitted a princess of two cities; her chin was high and her expression cool, but her face was pale and the skin under her eyes a smudgy purple despite the cosmetic she had used. She met his eyes, shifted hers at once. *She is angry because I would not have Apodain here, at her side.* But Apodain was not a member of his council. And whatever Khadat intended, however she planned to salvage her personal affairs and wealth, he would have no part of it, nor in bringing young Apodain to Haffat's attention. *Let Khadat do that, if she is determined to see the boy dead; or let Apodain himself, if he is so foolish.*

The remaining two members of his council, both older cousins whose sons were part of the royal chariot, stood quietly beyond Khadat. They seldom spoke during council meetings, unless their prince asked it specifically. They would doubtless not speak today, and possibly could have been left out of this sad ceremony, but Pelledar had asked a specific favor of them—to watch Khadat, and keep her from doing anything foolish, if that was her intention.

I wish Haffat joy of that woman, he thought grimly. And then he could hear horses coming up the stones of the road, could hear the murmur of voices as Haffat and his company rode through the palace gates. The fifty armed men stayed on their horses and fanned into ranks five deep, ten across; Knoe's priest escort moved off to one side. Knoe dismounted and came over to hold the bridle of his emperor's horse. The personal guard dismounted; one held the horses and another came to take the sword from Hadda so he could dismount. Hadda looked uncomfortable; the honor guardsman had to nudge him to get his attention and return General Piritos' sword to him. He took it but seemed uncertain what to do with it. Haffat smiled at him and beckoned, then looked up the stairs and included Pelledar in that smile. He and Hadda ascended together. At his father's gesture, Hadda stopped a stair below the prince. Haffat mounted the final step.

"My brother," Haffat said quietly and held out his arms.

Pelledar brought up a smile he scarcely felt and extended his arms. He suffered himself to be embraced, let Haffat give him the kiss of equals, and stepped back. Haffat was frowning. *He realizes I will not treat with him as an equal. Not unless I must, to keep my people alive. But never for only myself.* Haffat shrugged then, and gestured; Hadda came up to stand between them.

"This is my son and heir," Haffat said. Pelledar inclined his head; Hadda sent his eyes sideways, toward his father, as if to say, *What next?* Haffat reached across his shoulder to take the sword from his son, and then pressed the younger man between them so Hadda could embrace Pelledar, who again let himself be clasped close. "Hadda will stay here, with you, my brother, in your palace. Solely," Haffat added quickly, and with a pleasant enough smile for all the council, "as my go-between, so that you and I may truly understand each other at all times, and Ghezrat may take her place among the other lands without undue difficulty. Since I may not remain here in person for long—well, we all of us know how distance and barriers of language often cause problems where none are intended. Now, we do speak a common language, but Diyet and Ghezrat are separated by enough distance that there might be misinterpretation of certain phrases or words. Do you not agree?"

"Certainly," Pelledar said carefully. "And he is most welcome to stay at my side and aid me in the days to come." Haffat nodded; his smile was warm, the eyes coolly appraising. The prince indicated those flanking him. "These are my council, and you shall meet them all later, if you wish. They, also, shall welcome your son, and have spoken to me their willingness to make you and him comfortable among us."

"Why, then," Haffat said and gave Hadda a look, and then a nudge.

"My thanks." Hadda's voice sounded strangled; the smile was forced. Haffat laid a hand on his shoulder, as if to reassure him; Hadda glanced warily at the hand, then fixed his eyes on a spot beyond the prince's shoulder, shifting his eyes once more when Khadat moved so he must gaze upon her. Haffat looked up as she moved; she smiled and he looked rather startled.

"Is this—?" He looked at Khadat again and just caught himself. "I do not see your queen here, my brother, to greet us. Though the Mirikosi tell me she is soon to bear you another child. Are she and your sons awaiting us within?"

Pelledar shook his head, and it was no difficulty at all for him to look very troubled indeed. "She is gone, she and all my sons with her, and I do not know where."

"Gone?" Haffat's voice went hard; but immediately he was smiling, and Pelledar was left to wonder if he had seen the dreadful fury in his eyes. "Surely she has not fled?"

"I do not know where she has gone," Pelledar repeated—exact truth, just as Tephys had told him; he spread his arms in a helpless shrug. "I went into our bedchamber three nights ago, and she and the babes, and my young heir—they were every one gone, and much of their clothing, and no one in the palace could say when they had last been seen, or where."

"But this is dreadful," Haffat sounded anxious. "For my brother to be reft of his lady so. I do trust that you do not suspect I am somehow responsible . . . ?"

Pelledar shook his head. "Of course not." He hoped he looked sufficiently worried. The goddess knew he *felt* it.

Haffat was still watching him, but a little of hardness left his eyes. *He believes me,* Pelledar thought, and the thought nearly overbore him; his knees wanted to give way. He forced himself to again pay attention; his conquerer was speaking again, and there was definitely relief in *his* voice. "Well, then. Now, my brother, I would have sworn no one could have left your walls without being seen, but perhaps she took your sons and tried to reach her father. Would she do this?"

"I—I don't know."

Haffat laid a hand on his forearm. "Well, if she has left the city, we will find her. I shall send men out by the main

roads, especially between here and Ye Eygar; we shall find
her and return her to you. But any man can see this distresses you, and to no point, and there is much else we must
discuss. Shall we take your council and my son and go inside, my brother?"

"Yes." Pelledar looked out across the gathered people and
across his city. *Perhaps for the last time,* he thought, *but it
is no longer my city.* Fortunately, those who stood outside
the walls and waited were too far away to make out individual faces; they must hate him for this day, and he knew it—
but he could not look at their faces, and their anger. He
turned away and walked steadily into the palace. Haffat
whispered to his son; Hadda turned to smile and wave at the
silent people and followed the prince; the council followed
him. Haffat gestured to the captain of his personal guard and
went into the palace. His captain sent most of his companions back down the steps to join the fifty armsmen and
Brysos, and with a word for Brysos, reformed the horses
into long lines of two. The priests and Knoe remained behind, in the courtyard, but the rest of Haffat's men rode back
out of the gates, down the street once more, this time bound
for the barracks, and Brysos went with them.

In the fighting courtyard of the barracks, the Ghezrathi
army waited—less than two-thirds its original strength. Before each phalanx, its captain stood, except for the royal
chariot, where Brysos' second held the place for him. That
company was well under half its numbers: Many had died or
been too badly wounded to return to the ranks; Septarin was
gone, and the royal cousins were at the palace. Seven drivers
and twelve riders stood near the front of the companies. The
Dyaddi and their red cloaks were notably missing; the general's remaining staff filled in the space where they would
have been.

The Diye Haff general wasted no time in Haffat-like
pretty speeches and gestures. He rode to the fore of the companies, dismounted and stood facing them, fists on his hips.
Men in the rear ranks grumbled and shifted as much as they
dared: Haffat's captain was a squarely built, powerful man,
but so short that few of them could see him. His voice carried, echoing across the courtyard. "I am Jemaro, the
Symatarch of the emperor's armies in the field. We are all
plain fighting men here, so I speak bluntly to you. In a little,

I go with your Captain Brysos into the barracks and there you will come, a company at a time, with your weaponry. The emperor permits that each man retain his panoply—but all blades, bows, and shaft weapons will be left today, and we shall hold these barracks.

"Now," Jemaro's voice lost a little of its bark and he began to pace back and forth before them, "you men know, there is no sense to more fighting. We are practical, after all, we warriors. The emperor has drawn up a list of reprisals for crimes commited by any Ghezrathi, but I shall not even speak of them. You men have more sense than to throw away your lives and those of your loved ones for a fool's notion of vengeance.

"Of course, in any army one finds fools, and so I agreed when the emperor said we must take weaponry. But your swords and spears and all the rest will be kept as you leave them, by company and untouched by any of the Diye Haff, so that if Haffat needs you to protect Ghezrat, or fight for him elsewhere, you can take back what is yours.

"So let us do this and be done! The emperor has commanded me to say, if any of you will join our army now—speak to me when you come into the barracks. This has been done by men in every land so far. Those of you who are soldiers and upon whom peace would hang heavily, do not feel it strange to join with us; we understand that this is what you do, what you do best. You are fighters. Also, the emperor bids me tell you, there will be celebration in five days time and games, to honor the longest day, your gods, and ours." He turned and beckoned to Brysos. "Captain. I shall be inside. Send in the companies, then dismiss them to their homes." Brysos set a clenched fist against his breast and turned to face the army as Jemaro stalked across the ground, seven of his men behind him. The rest stood or sat their horses near the entry.

Brysos squared his shoulders and raised his voice; the murmur of voices which had begun when Jemaro left them was abruptly silenced. "You have heard the—generous terms the general and his emperor give us. You will not shame your city, your prince, your families, or above all the shade of your own general; you will enter by companies and tamely hand over your weaponry, and then go to your homes and your families.

"I myself will attend these games the emperor plans,

though I fear," he added wryly, "that I am a little old and fat to strip off my tunic and enter the races." A little humorless laughter greeted this, but some of those in the front rank looked less tense than they had. "I won't order; that isn't my place any longer. But we must have healing now, if not open friendship with those men." He gestured toward the gate. "At least we must have no hostility. Such competition as games provide, and such pleasures as a celebration allow— that is a beginning." He paused, sighed gustily, and pointed toward the royal chariot. "The general's staff first, to represent him, and then the royal chariot. And then each company in turn. I shall remain at the entry to the barracks; the rest of you will go to your homes at once when you are done in there." He stepped back, let the twenty men who had served Piritos in one way or another pass, and fell in behind them.

"Games." Ridlo glanced at the man next to him; he was muttering to himself again, and the look in his eyes was worrying. Men straggled past him; Piritos' aides and servants, heading for the gates—the company of royal chariot in three neat ranks, going into the barracks.

A pause, and then men began coming out a few at a time. Ridlo waited. Finally, no more men came out. He looked over at Brysos, who glanced inside and then nodded. Ridlo held up a hand, turned to face the dreadfully depleted company, and said, "Let us go and be done with this."

Strange—he would not let himself think *unnerving*. Weapons were already piled against the far wall and there were no Ghezrathi inside the barracks but themselves and Brysos at the door. That square stone block of a Diye Haff general— Jemaro. His gaze was penetrating. Ridlo set his sword and a bundle of spears on the bench and saluted, fist to breast; Jemaro returned the salute. He pivoted on his heel, squared his shoulders, and walked swiftly toward the courtyard, but just inside the entry he had to stop and hang onto the wall, to hold himself upright until the world around him stopped spinning. He drew one final deep breath, shook his head, hard; Brysos gripped his elbow and got his attention. "Are you all right?" He nodded, looked at Brysos sidelong, then away; he could feel the color mantling his cheeks. "Don't look like that, young soldier!" the captain said testily. "You are not the only one who held up well before them only to have it strike you here, what you had done. It took half the general's men just so—and me as well," he added gruffly, "if you would know." He clapped Ridlo's shoulder hard enough that he would have gone staggering if he hadn't still been holding onto the wall. "Go on, go home, you did well—all these past days and particularly just now. Be proud of yourself."

He doesn't know us common soldiers one from another. Still, such praise from such a highly-placed captain. Ridlo hadn't expected that. "Sir, I am proud—of every one of us." He drew himself up, saluted Brysos, and strode from the barracks, past the remaining companies, across open ground and past the Diye Haff.

Apodain had been upon the roof when Haffat entered the city, and had watched in silence as the emperor and his fifty men, his guard, and his priests came slowly up the hill from the gates to the palace, until he had lost them behind the prince's walls. He had seen Brysos leading them afoot, and he had felt shame for his former captain's dishonor.

His mother was there, somewhere, with the rest of the council. He was grateful that Pelledar had—for whatever reason—refused to let him stand with Khadat, for he doubted he could have found the strength to refuse her. *But I could not have survived that, being named twice traitor.* How she could be so blinded by ships, and gold, and trade, that she did not see how she had tainted herself already. . . .

He turned and left the faded roof garden abruptly, decended rapidly to his rooms, where he had transferred his own panoply when Reott had shown him Khadat's hiding place for it. The chest ordinarily held his clothing; now it contained the cloak and fine tunic reserved for banquets atop armor, helm, weaponry, and the cloak of a royal charioteer. Surely the Diye Haff would come in search of other swords once they had taken the weaponry of the army. They would not have his, nor would they have the best of his father's. Hemit's—well, there might be little time before Khadat returned, there had been few enough opportunities of late when he might hide his things without her knowing. Whatever weapons Khadat knew about, she would certainly give to Haffat when he came as a sign of her good intentions toward them and as surety for her family's precious ships. So if she had Hemit's panoply to give them or show them, and certain of his father's less useful things, it might be enough to keep them from searching too deeply.

He slammed his hands against the carven head of his couch. "Is she so much a fool, or so greedy? So blinded by gold she can't see anything else?" No answer, of course; most of the servants were in the streets or at the gates, waiting and watching with everyone else. He didn't have much time. He took the fine feast garments from the chest, gathered his armor, helm, and sword in the cloak and carried them into the passage, down the steps, through his father's room and into the little garden behind it. There was a stone out here, and under it an old storage area that he did not think Perlot had ever shown Khadat. She had certainly made no use of it in those dark hours when she was having the siege jars filled and set in the hidden passages below the cellars.

The stone was one of several that made a path from the room where Perlot had entertained his friends to the gate he himself had used to escape the household the day Khadat had bribed a prince and stolen back his commission. He tightened his lips, set that thought aside, and stepped into bright afternoon light.

It would be difficult to see into this small triangle of a garden from anywhere save his father's room; the wall was high and there was an aged, spreading olive tree blocking the rest. But Apodain set the panoply down by the hearth and came out into the open to look cautiously all around before daring to pry up the stone. The space beneath was filled with one enormous jar; the scent of damp dirt was faintly overlaid with spice. The jar had once held grain, he thought; it hadn't held anything in the nearly seventy years since, and by good fortune the stone lid fit across it well enough that the interior was dry. He went back for his bundle and placed it inside, replaced the stone with great care before returning to his apartments for the bundle of javelins that had been hidden between the woven frame of his couch and the cushions—and had made for very uncomfortable nights.

Perlot's things, then: The ceremonial sword he had left behind the night he and Hemit had gone to take back the isthmus forts, the sling and bag of copper stones graven with curses. He took out one, read it and smiled: "An enemy's gift," it said. He could just remember Perlot reading the curses on the stones to him, and him laughing at the things they said. Haffat would not have these either.

Perlot's good armor had gone down with the ship he and Hemit had ridden and so had the beautiful dagger with the hunting scene that Perlot had so often let him handle, much to Khadat's dismay. "Men with swords and spears and shields hunting a lion," Apodain murmured as he let the chest lid fall on the rest of his father's and grandfather's panoply. "That would have been a properly symbolic thing to have." By now it had surely long since rusted through; but wherever he was, Perlot's shade carried it, shining and sharp-edged as the original had once been. Apodain gazed down at the chest. "Father, I wish just this once I could have you here—not for a father's companionship or love but for a soldier's advice. They will not have me in the barracks and Mother tells me nothing, I do not know what or how they plan—or if they do—but it doesn't matter since I have no part in any plan." It almost choked him; he swallowed, went on. "Have I done right? Because I swear—I swear by your shade and by your honor they will *not* keep me from whatever fighting comes." He gathered up the sword, the sling, and the bag of stones, and carried them out to put in the jar with his own panoply. He had never felt so alone since the dark hour when Septarin came to smirk and tell him he had been pulled from the royal chariot. Now he was truly alone and could only do what he hoped was best.

Two days. There was less confusion in the streets and more despair or resignation.

Nidya sat in the storage watching Ina measure out lentils and rice for soup. It was quiet, the chamber barely lit and the only sounds the *chuff* of the wooden scoop going into the jar, the whispery sound of the dried stuff spilling into the big pot. Ina forced the stoppers back in the jars, drew the lid back over the hidden storage, climbed laboriously to her feet, then bent down to pick up the pot. She eyed the storage area critically, finally shrugged and turned that same critical glance on the older woman. "Are you all right?" she demanded gruffly.

Nidya nodded. "I am all right, Ina, don't fuss over me."

"You did not sleep well last night."

"How should I have, worrying whether the Diye Haff would send for Breyd?"

"But she said they would not know."

"Bah," Nidya said tartly. "Everyone in the city knows who was First Prime and his Secchi; someone will surely speak names, and then—but how would you know whether I slept or not? *You* snored most of the night!"

"Aha!" Ina said. "I told you!" She settled the pot on one hip, slapped the side of it. "Are you coming?"

"In a little. It's cooler here than elsewhere. Did the boy bring the water for the soup?"

"Breyd did," Ina said shortly. "When I asked."

"Oh."

"She'll be all right," Ina said, but she didn't sound as sure of herself this time, and Nidya didn't answer.

Breyd sat in the courtyard in the cushions that she had always used, ever since she could remember; everyone still slept but Nidya and Ina. Nevvia had taken valerian-tinctured wine and wouldn't wake until at least third horn.

She hadn't slept; there didn't seem any point. *They all surrendered, but I sat here, cowering behind Denota....* Breyd fixed her eyes on the cold ashes scattered around the brazier and thought dully, *Someone should have cleaned that, the fire won't burn right.* A moment later her thoughts drifted, her eyes fixed on the opposite wall, and she had forgotten the brazier. Forgotten almost everything.

She still wore her old blue, sashed with the belt Menlaeus had given her. Ina had come out earlier to make vexed little noises over her bared arms and shoulders, at the contour of them. A faint, sardonic smile touched Breyd's lips. *What could she or anyone else expect, after so much weaponry? The goddess didn't provide against muscle, did she—or take it back when the need for it was done?*

Sounds of low-voiced conversation brought her back to the moment: Niverren's distraught voice, Creos trying to sound reasonable and soothing and merely sounding harassed. *I would sound more than simply harassed, if Niverren fussed over me as she does Creos.*

In a way, Niverren had; but with Creos requiring so much of her attention, Niv had her hands full. *How awful, to be grateful for Creos and his needs.*

Other voices: Ina and someone—possibly Nidya, more likely Xhem from the way Ina was talking. She spoke to her mistress as though the older woman were an errant and none-too-bright child; to Xhem—particularly now—she was unfailingly kind. *That would send me mad also, I think.* But Ina was kind to Breyd these days, too. *Perhaps he doesn't notice any more than I do.* She shook her head, let her mind drift.

Some time later, at least by the way the shadows had shifted, Nidya came out and sat in her daughter's chair, and cleared her throat. "Breyd. Breyd?"

She blinked. "Niddy, I'm sorry, I was—"

"Yes, all right," Nidya said. She patted the arm of the chair invitingly. "Come here, child, talk to me a while. It's boring here for an old woman, your mother is still asleep, Ina won't fight with me and no one else has ever dared." She smiled; in spite of herself, Breyd smiled back. She got up, scooped up cushions, and brought them over, settling her shoulder against the chair and letting her cheek rest on her grandmother's knee. Nidya gently eased a strand of hair out of her face. "Xhem says there are to be games, in three days." It was all she could think of to say.

"Yes. *They* told us. I should be doing something to ready for them, I suppose."

Nidya looked at her sharply. "Will they let you join them?"

"I think so." Breyd sighed faintly. "Everything they have done so far says they will let the city go on as it has, but I've been ordered to."

"Ordered?"

Be careful; say nothing. "Well—asked, by the man who was my captain." Nidya snorted angrily; Breyd looked up at her and managed a faint smile. "You know Haffat leaves a green boy in the palace and a few men to keep the green boy safe from all of us. And he leaves a few of those priests to found a cult of the lion, if only for the green boy and his soldiers. But nothing else." *At least for now,* she thought grimly, but she had kept all such thoughts to herself around the household women and would continue to do so.

The silence stretched. Nidya finally broke it. "Ina says you brought water this morning. That was good of you; I know how you dislike it when people stare."

"They probably still do," Breyd replied vaguely. "I didn't notice." She sighed and roused herself with a visible effort. "I am sorry, Niddy. It's just so—" She shrugged helplessly.

"I won't say I understand," Nidya said, "because you

know I don't really. My friend would have, but she died in childbirth years ago. I think if you could just talk about things, instead of keeping them inside as you do, it would be better for you."

"It might," Breyd admitted. She considered this, shrugged again. "Niddy, I don't really understand myself."

"I know," Nidya agreed.

"When Denota chose me—oh, I don't *know!* Maybe Tar was right, that I gave myself airs and kept things to myself that didn't need to be secret."

"No," the older woman broke in, very firmly. "That is not like you, and I remember better than you do. I also remember Tar as he was then, not as he was near the last."

Breyd thought about this. "All right, he was horrid about it, jealous or spoiled or both, and I wanted to strangle him. But after the goddess warned us, and then everything. . . ." Her voice trailed away. Nidya sat very still and simply waited. Breyd finally cleared her throat and went on in a husky voice, "It's all been too much, too quickly, and it's not done yet, and Niddy, everything is *stuck* in there. Even if I wanted, I couldn't find the way to just talk about things."

"Then don't," Nidya said softly. "If you want to, or need to, I am here. Don't feel you must bare your soul to me, or to anyone else."

Breyd nodded and got to her knees so she could wrap her arms around the other. "Thank you, Niddy."

"Well, of course, child. Here," she added tartly and gave her granddaughter a little shake, "have you eaten anything yet today? Anything since last night? Wait," she added as Breyd eyed her sidelong, "and let me save you the trouble of finding a lie for old Niddy. Take the chair, I'll go and make you something."

"Niddy, I can—"

"Yes, but you won't," Nidya retorted. "Besides, you know it's always been the rule in this household, to do the thing you are best at. Well, I am best at food and you have done your share and more lately. Sit, be quiet, and I shall bring you something."

"Yes, Niddy," Breyd replied meekly, and as Nidya looked at her with close-drawn suspicious eyebrows, she even laughed.

"Better. Are you yet bored with oil and peppers for your bread?"

"Never."

"Good. We have plenty of oil and too many of the peppers; they'll never keep." Nidya got to her feet and walked back to the kitchens. Breyd eased into the chair and slid down, legs sprawled before her. Her mother would be distressed with her for sitting so; she must remember not to give Nevvia a hard time this way, not to sit like this in Khadat's house, when she went there. But it was comfortable, particularly in this chair with its high back and all those cushions for her shoulders. She could not recapture that pleasant blank, nonthinking state she had fallen into earlier; Nidya had reminded her how long it had been since she'd eaten and now her stomach was telling her. "Traitor body," she mumbled sourly. "To keep me here and aware of you and of things around me."

She could hear raised voices in the room that had been hers and her sister's: Niverren's ragged-edged, Creos laughing a little, though he sounded upset. She couldn't make out the words. And then Niverren herself came practically running out of the room, and Creos called out, "Niv! Oh, Niverren, I only meant it as a jest!"

Niverren stopped dead in the center of the courtyard; her color was high, her hair all undone and she had made fists of her hands. "You were so quiet, Breyd, I didn't know you were here," she said flatly, almost accusingly. "Look at you, Mother would die to see you like that, sit up!"

Did she think I was sitting out here listening to them? Breyd pursed her mouth. "You are not Mother. How does she like seeing you look the way you do, or listening to you? And I do not wish to sit up." Niverren's eyes filled with tears; she brushed past her sister and ran for the kitchen. Breyd pounded the arms of the chair and swore under her breath.

Niverren hurried past her moments later, a cup and one of the small winejugs dangling from her fingers; she went into the room without a backward look. Nidya came out a moment later with a small tray and set it across the chair arms. She sighed as she stepped back and sent her eyes toward the room where Niverren could be heard arguing with Creos in a low, urgent voice. "And what have you done to upset her? Or she you?"

Breyd rolled her eyes. "A little of each, perhaps. Don't take sides, please, Niddy."

"I don't intend to," Nidya said crisply. "It is more than unpleasant and tense enough here, without that."

"Oh, Niddy. I'm sorry." Breyd held out a hand; Nidya took it, wrapped it around bread and patted her knuckles sharply.

"Don't be sorry, eat. It will sort itself out."

"Yes." *Everything will be all right.* Menlaeus would have said that. Menlaeus was not here. She closed her eyes, bit off bread, and chewed it carefully, aware of Nidya standing and watching her, to make certain she ate. Her grandmother walked back toward the kitchens finally. Breyd dipped bread in the hot, flavored oil, ate it, washed it down with the very watery wine. Before she could get up and take the tray away, Ina came to get it.

She sat for some time after that. Niverren and Creos were—not exactly arguing, but only because Creos, like Menlaeus, wasn't much for arguing. But Niverren wasn't ordinarily, either. Finally she heard Niverren's exasperated, "Oh, all *right!*" And her sister came out to stand in the doorway. Breyd looked up to see Niverren eyeing her uncertainly. "Creos—wants to come out a while; I can't manage him alone."

And you can't bear to ask me, any more than you can let Creos try on his own. "I'll help." She got up, took some of the cushions from the chair and, dropping them nearby, came over and followed Niv.

The room might never have had anything to do with her: The bed had been shifted so Creos was against the far wall. Both of Niverren's good oil lamps were in here and lit. The room smelled of pitch and stale bodies and sickness, like the barracks hospital only worse because the room was so small—and the smell partly her normally fastidiously clean sister's, mostly the equally fastidious Creos.

She hadn't spoken to him or even seen him since they'd taken her weapons and Grysis had sent her home. She didn't even recognize him at first. His hair had grown and was flattened to the sides of his head, his beard had grown in very thickly. He was much too thin, his face pinched and pale against the dark of his beard. His eyes were fever-bright. But the voice was all Creos. "Little sister," he said warmly. "My wife tells me you will help her serve as my missing leg for a few steps."

Niverren made an unhappy, vexed little sound but Breyd

held out her hands and smiled at him. "I will be glad
to, brother. You must feel like a bat in here, it's a cave. Here,
can you edge this way? Niverren, why don't you let me?
There isn't enough room for both of us, you can get under
his shoulder when he and I get him upright."

"You don't—" Niverren began, but threw up her hands
and stepped back with an exasperated sigh. Creos pressed up
with his arms and eased his body sideways until he could
twist around at the edge and slide his legs over. "Breyd, let
me—"

"It's all right, love, she's got me, Niverren," Creos said.
Breyd had already knelt by his left side and come up under
his arm, bringing him upright with her.

"But you'll need—" Niverren said anxiously.

"Over by the door," Breyd ordered. "You know I'm stronger than you, Niv; we'll hurt him if we both try to move in
here with him between us."

Niverren gave her another anxious look but Creos smiled
and nodded. He was too short of breath at the moment to
speak, and Niverren backed away, eyes on him the whole
time, until her heels caught on the wooden door frame and
she nearly fell. She turned then and ran into the courtyard to
ready the chair, then ran back as Creos and Breyd paused in
the doorway for him to catch his breath. Niverren slid under
his other arm and wrapped hers around his waist; the three
made their way slowly across the short distance to Nevvia's
chair and Creos sank into it with a little sigh, closing his
eyes. Niverren knelt to stuff pillows around him and to lay
a hand against his brow. He looked at her, smiled, took hold
of her fingers. "It's all right, love; I'm just not used to being
so much upright."

"If it's too soon," Niverren began anxiously; Creos shook
his head.

"I've been too long abed, if anything. The sun and fresh
air feel very good." He glanced at Breyd. "Thank you, little
sister. If I'd known you were that strong, I'd never have
teased you back before Niv and I wed."

Breyd managed a laugh for him. "You know very well
that's all recent."

"Well, yes. You look magnificent."

Niverren made a fastidious little face. "It's—not wom-
anly, all that."

"It must be, since it's hers and she's not become a man

overnight," Creos said. Niverren merely shook her head. "Do you know what I would like? I would like oranges. I have thought of nothing else for days."

"Oh, Creos," Niverren murmured, "you should have said. I can—we haven't any, I am sure we haven't, but the market—"

"I wouldn't want you to go alone," he began. Niverren waved that aside.

"I can take Ina; Niddy said something this morning, that if the bakery still had bread, we should buy that instead of using our own grain. In—you know, in case."

"Why don't you do that, then? Oranges," Creos said thoughtfully. Niverren went into the kitchens and came out shortly with Ina and the market basket.

"Will you be all right here? Breyd, you'll stay with him, in case he needs anything?"

"I will stay with him," Breyd said and Creos said at the same moment, "I will be all right, Niv."

"I may be a little longer," Niverren said doubtfully. "I have not been to the temple all these days. I should go, I think. Take something for the goddess, for bringing you back."

"Do. If I need to lie down again, we'll manage." Niverren gave him one last worried, harassed look; Ina tugged at her tunic, and she went with the older woman. Creos slumped in the chair and sighed. "Poor Niverren; this has all been dreadful for her."

"I know." Breyd took back her own cushions and settled nearby.

Creos eyed her thoughtfully. "None too easy for you, either, has it?" She shook her head. "Talk to me a little, Breyd; Niv won't tell me anything about what's happened. The boy would, I think, but Niv is always there when I talk to Xhem and she doesn't want to hear any of it." Silence; he waited. She sighed faintly, shook her head. "I know it was bad," he added quietly.

"We lost," she said finally. Hard to get that much out, at first, but after that, it was not as difficult. Unlike Nidya, or Nevvia or Niverren, Creos had been out there and he understood. And he simply listened as she talked. "And so," she spread her hands in a wide shrug. "And so, they offered terms, and the prince took them, and now Haffat is there."

She gestured toward the palace. "His men hold all the plain."

"And yet, we didn't lose all we might have," Creos said.

"No. But—"

He was silent; she couldn't go on, finally shook her head and swallowed. "But it hurts to surrender, doesn't it? Don't try to tell me different. I know. I recall jumping from the mole that night, I was one of the last and I waited out there in the rough salt water with the cold seeping into my bones and my guts, waiting for the last of the men to decide if they would jump or not—those who swam little or not at all, so those of us who could swim could help them. But by the time the last of them did, I was so cold I could barely remember how to move my arms and legs and then the side-swells caught me and, well," he sighed. "I think it must have been most of the night, hours and hours, that I tried to fight my way to shore. It felt like that. The last thing I remember is a ship, and men with Mirikosi accents shouting down at me to surrender. I couldn't answer, I was too chilled by then and I'd swallowed enough salt water my throat didn't work properly. But I think I would have said no, even so, and tried to swim away. Perhaps I did. They tell me I got between the ship and a boulder somehow, I don't remember that. Nothing until I woke here, with Niverren washing my face." Silence. Breyd looked up at him; he looked at her. "I would have died of the shame, I think, if I'd had to surrender to them. At least I was spared that."

"Yes." She sighed and some of the tension went out of her shoulders. "But they will pay for it, Creos. One day, they will pay." She looked at him, defying him to laugh, but he nodded.

"Yes. How or when, which of us can say? I will surely have no part in it, and I am sorry for that, and a little ashamed."

"Why? Because of that?" She indicated his leg.

"All right, I know. It's a stupid thing to feel."

Do I dare tell him? she wondered. Grysis had given her a free hand in naming anyone she thought useful to the secret war to come. Who would ever suspect a man with one leg? But Niverren would be horrified, and she couldn't be certain Creos would keep the knowledge to himself; he might grow feverish again and talk in his sleep. Or *they* might come and take him to question, or threaten to take Niverren, and he would tell them anything to have her back. *No. I won't let them do that to any of my family; I won't tell any of them.* She looked up to see what Creos had been doing while she considered this problem; he had fallen asleep in the chair. He was still sleeping when Niverren and Ina came back with bread, a basket of dates, and a few undersized oranges.

20

Breyd got quietly to her feet and followed Niverren across the courtyard; her sister turned back at the entry to the storage. "I'll get his bread and oranges ready if you'll stay with him a little longer." Breyd nodded, and her sister managed a smile that fell far short of worried eyes. "Thank you. I didn't want to leave him alone. But he looks happy." She held up one of the oranges and made a face at it. "Awful, isn't it? They were the best anyone had. Our new lord and his men have taken most of the rest."

"Taken?" Breyd asked sharply.

Niverren's mouth twisted. "Oh, they *paid*. Not full price, certainly, just enough that no one can honestly say they stole them. And then they stand about the market, those men, and *smile* at us, as though we should *like* them for what they're doing. They—they don't bathe, Breyd. They smell like stale sweat and too much garlic and they looked at even Ina like—oh, I don't know, but they've taken our city, and now they're stealing our food. Breyd, that's an *army* out there! If they take all our food, what will we have left? Is it better to starve us than to kill us at once? Horrid, smug, smiling—oh, I hate them! I hate all of them!"

Breyd gripped her sister's arm. "Niv, don't. It's no use to get yourself upset like this, it only makes things worse for you, thinking about it. Letting it eat away at you." Niverren stood very still for a long moment, then nodded. "Of course they aren't like us; they're northerners. And they're *enemy*. Niverren, you don't dare forget for a moment when you're out in the market, or anywhere else. Be polite."

"I can't! Are you mad?" Niverren demanded hotly.

"I didn't say make friends with them! Don't be rude, or offensive. You don't know what will set someone off, Niv." Niverren was staring at her; she bit her lip. "Tell me you'll

be careful, when you go out there, Niv. Promise me you
will."

"Oh," Niverren said bitterly, "I smiled. I thought of poor
Ina trembling at my side, and Creos." She shook her head
angrily. "I remembered, and I smiled and went about my
business as quickly as old Ina could move."

"Good. I'm glad you remembered. Remember Creos;
think of Mother. Smile if you have to, avoid them if you
cannot smile. At least keep the anger to yourself. Swear to
me."

Niverren was startled and showed it. She shook herself,
set the orange back in the basket, and in a subdued voice
said, "All right. I'll remember. And I swear I'll be careful."
She leaned against the wall and blotted her forehead against
her tunic. "We didn't even try to go to the temple; those men
were everywhere on the main avenue. I'm exhausted. The
heat, all the people out there—it's been so long since I
walked that far, or that quickly." She managed a faint smile.
"Next time I'll send you to get Creos oranges. You could always move faster than anyone else." She started into the
storage, turned back. "I just remembered. Have you heard
this emperor of *theirs* plans games?"

"Ours. Remember to say that, Niv, whatever you think. I
knew about the games."

Niverren looked outraged. "Does he think we'll just accept him and that army because he gives us *games?* He really thinks we'll all just go out there and watch his horrid,
smelly soldiers strip and run?"

"Shhh. Remember! But they say he's held games elsewhere; his way of honoring his lion god, perhaps." She hesitated, then said, "I already told Creos about the games. He
wants to go."

"Oh, dear," Niverren said fretfully. She glanced in his direction. "How could he? Oh, Breyd, I wish you hadn't."

"But he'd know about them, sooner or later. And sooner
or later the barracks physicians will have time to make him
a brace so he can walk on that leg, and with a crutch he'll
be able to get about—some, anyway. At least, he will if—"
She hesitated, glanced at Niverren, and plunged on. "He will
if he hasn't lost all faith in himself." Silence. Niverren had
gone utterly white. "I'm sorry, Niv. It's not my business to
interfere."

"It's all right. I know what you're trying to tell me."

Niverren let her eyelids sag shut. "I try so hard, Breyd, I swear I do! Not to coddle him, treat him like a child. But something like this—it's so hard not to fuss over him, not to worry over every least thing he does." She sighed and continued in a small voice, "He was so awfully ill, I thought he would die every minute of so many of those first days. And then, so much pain and he's only just started to be—be Creos again the past five or six days, it's taken that long, and it still hurts him. He tries not to let me know, but I can see it, I know when he wakes in the night and can't sleep for the pain."

"Oh, Niverren, I know you're doing your best not to baby him. So does he, if he hasn't said. If that helps you."

"He told you that?"

Breyd nodded. "He said. He understands how hard it is for you, Niv, truly, but he's getting frustrated. His leg should be healed enough that a careful ride out there and back won't do him any harm, Niv. But why don't you send Xhem to find his captain—it's Frewis, isn't it?" Niverren nodded cautiously. "Ask Frewis if one of the barracks physicians can come. They should have a little free time now, with no more injured coming in. They can tell you if he's healing all right. They say Frewis is one of the better captains; I'll wager he'd do that, and find men who could carry Creos to the gates. The prince has always had carts for the games, hasn't he? To transport the people who don't want to walk that ghastly road—or can't." Silence. "I'd like it if he was there; if some of the family came."

"You aren't— Breyd, you can't!"

"I *have* to. There are reasons; don't ask, I can't tell you." Niverren was silent so long Breyd began to wonder how deeply she had offended her sister.

Niverren finally shook herself. "All right. I suppose. I can't hate his father for thinking he's a useless cripple and then say he's too crippled to do anything." She managed a weak, watery smile. "You know, the first thing he and I said to each other was, that it didn't matter, the important stuff of Creos is still here. He's alive."

"His father is a fool," Breyd said flatly. "Creos is fortunate to have you, Niv."

"Well—yes, of course. I'm luckier, though. Stay with him, will you?" Niverren added. "I'll ready his food and be right back."

* * *

Xhem came in as Niverren settled down next to the chair to feed a now-awake Creos bits of orange; Breyd had to turn away to hide a broad grin at the disgusted look on Xhem's face: Niverren putting segments of orange into her husband's mouth, Creos taking them and kissing her fingertips before he ate them. She tended to forget how very young the boy was. He came over to her and tugged at her belt, then murmured against her ear, "Grysis sends word, 'Tell Breyd the marriages are tomorrow at midnight in Denota's Cleft; no one except Pairs and prechosen.' He says to tell you he is sorry, but Tephys is afraid so many all at once will give the secret away."

"I understand," Breyd whispered. *Poor Mother! And poor Niddy! Not even to see me wed!*

"Grysis says, tell you when they are gone the city will hold a great ceremony, the marriages, the victory—and real games."

"I'll remember that. If—you see him, tell him Breyd says thank you, and I'll do my best out there."

Xhem nodded gravely. "Um—just now, I saw a man looking for this street and this house, and asking people where Breyd, daughter of Menlaeus might be found. I think—I think he is one of the Lady Khadat's household."

"Oh." Breyd looked up as Nevvia came into the courtyard, Nidya's arm around her; she was rubbing her eyes and yawning. *I haven't even had the chance to just—just be with Mother; I can't leave her yet!* She got to her feet and managed a smile. "Mother. You look wonderfully rested."

Nevvia wrapped her arms around her daughter's shoulders and hugged her tight. Nidya went back into the storage. "You're still here. I was afraid—"

"Shhh, it's all right. I'll stay with you as long as I can."

"Well." Nevvia leaned back to eye her doubtfully; Niverren moved so her mother could have the second chair and Breyd helped her down into it. "But, you know, you *are* promised to Apodain, precious. We women don't have much choice in these things."

"I know."

"Does he still look like Perlot? I remember him at the games last year at midsummer. He looked so much like his father. Such a wonderful wrestler, too."

"He *looks* lovely," Breyd said darkly.

Nevvia shook her head. "Oh, child, you aren't still being difficult about marrying, are you? It isn't as though he's another Laius." She sighed, let her forehead down onto her hand. "Do you know, Laius has never come to visit me?" Niverren made a shocked little noise; Breyd glared up at her warningly. *They didn't tell Mother; somehow Niverren's heard, though, and I wish she hadn't.* She crouched down to place stuffed cushions around Nevvia, who smiled faintly and protested, "You're treating me like an invalid!"

"I am not! I'm spoiling you, and you deserve it," Breyd said, would-be severely.

At the same moment, Niverren turned from Creos, eyes shocked, and said, "Mother!"

Nevvia looked up and met Creos' eyes instead. She smiled at him, and Creos smiled back. "Why—look who's come out and stolen my best chair, it's Niv's man." Her eyes crinkled and her mouth quirked. "And here I thought you were hiding from *me* in there, all this time."

"Mother!" Niverren stared at her aghast.

Breyd wanted to step on her sister's foot and shut her up; better yet, to shake her. *Can't you see how hard she's trying to be normal for us? What it's costing her?* Breyd smiled at her mother and patted her fingers. "Don't be silly, Niv, you know how Mother likes to tease."

Niverren frowned and might have answered, but before she could say anything, someone pounded heavily on the outer door and without waiting for a response, pushed through the main room and came into the courtyard.

He was tall and heavily built; his face seemed to be set in a permanent sneer; he wore fine-woven silk caught to his waist with a broad, soft leather belt, and on his feet were soft sandals. He glanced around with obvious distaste before announcing generally, "I am Emyas, cousin to the Princess Khadat. She bids me tell Breyd, Welcome, daughter. The marriages of Secchi to the prechosen are to be confirmed by the goddess tomorrow, but Breyd is to come with me now so the princess may see her clad in a manner suitable to the house of Perlot. And to properly meet her prechosen mate. The princess bids me say to Breyd, let her Prime come with her so the Secchi may pass from Prime to husband if she wishes—but to waste no time."

Niverren flushed a deep and mottled red; even Creos looked quite angry; Nevvia would have risen but Breyd laid

a warning hand on her mother's shoulder. Nidya, who had
come into the courtyard at the sound of a loud and unfamiliar voice, set her fists on her hips and demanded, "What is
this? Shall we have no time to ready this daughter of
Menlaeus ourselves?"

"But what can *you* do for her?" Emyas looked around the
courtyard and his lips twisted. "You have nothing save
things of your kind and class. Princess Khadat reminds all of
you this girl will wed into the royal family, for she was wife
to Perlot, brother of Prince Pelledar, and she is also daughter, sister, and cousin to the royal family of Mirikos. Her son
Apodain is in the succession."

Breyd stood up and closed the distance between them.
"We know who Khadat is, and who her son—like everyone
else in Ghezrat." She lifted her chin; he looked down at her
and his mouth quirked with distaste. "How dare you come to
this house," she finally asked, very softly, "and enter as if
you walked into a stable? We are not noble here, but even
our prince would not fling his way inside a common man's
house as you have! How dare you or the princess *order* me
to come to her now? I was not *bought* to tend her son! I am
Secchi to the First Prime, and I paid the goddess in *blood* for
this marriage!"

He had let himself forget what she had been—that she
was anything but common; she could see the sudden, wary
knowledge in his eyes.

She could feel how warm her own face was; anger tightened her stomach. *How dare she send for my father, as if she
didn't know better?* "You will go back to the princess and
tell her—*remind* her that my Prime cannot stand for me.
And tell her this: My mother lost her only son in battle; her
husband is still missing and no one knows where he has
gone. The princess will understand what it is to lose so
much. But I will not simply walk away from my own mother
without a proper chance to say farewell."

Emyas was bright red. "You common—you—!"

"Secchi," she reminded him softly. "They have not yet
lifted the goddess bond from us. Remember that, Emyas.
Tell the princess I shall come tomorrow, at this hour. For
now," she added flatly, "you may go right back through that
room where you left the door wide for all the street to enter."

Emyas gave her a chill look, turned on his heel, and went.

Breyd glared at his back. Nevvia came to her feet and stared after him. "Oh, no," she whispered. Breyd turned around and hugged her close. "That—*awful* person! Oh, Breyd—baby, what have they done, sending you there?"

"Mother, it's all right, he was just trying to be important and he's not. Don't worry about me."

Niverren was staring at her. "You terrified me, talking like that! Breyd, you can't—you can't just say things like that, not to anyone—but never to a nobleman! And that Emyas looked so dangerous when you told him to go. A cousin of Khadat's! Remember what you said to me? It isn't safe for you to do things like that!"

Breyd settled her mother in the chair once more and scowled at her sister; her eyes were still hard and Niverren retreated a pace, but Creos took his wife's hand and squeezed her fingers. "Nonsense!" Breyd said forcefully. "Emyas is a *servant*. He makes certain Hemit's linen is changed and helps carry him around."

"He's noble," Nevvia began anxiously.

"He is also Khadat's servant; he's Apodain's servant, and he will be *my* servant." She slewed partway around to glare at the entry to the main room; it was quiet in there, the man had gone and actually shut the door behind him. As she looked, Xhem came out, nodded and silently mouthed, "He is gone."

She was still furious. *How dare Khadat send such a horrid person to just collect me, as if I were a shipment of goods? How dare he come here, now, when things were just beginning to feel normal once more? Smug, snotty creature. And now Mother is all upset again.* But Niverren was right in a way, even though it was maddening to hear her say it: She couldn't fight Khadat and that household the way she'd gone for the Diye Haff. She drew a deep breath, letting some of the anger go with it. "Mother, don't look so anxious," she said softly. "It's all right, I know something about Emyas. He's a bully; nothing more. He didn't best Apodain in the barracks, and he won't have any better out of me."

"No, child, don't say such things," Nevvia whispered urgently. "You must not—mustn't treat Khadat like an enemy, it isn't safe. Women of our class—we don't belong up there, we don't understand them, Breyd. And Khadat *is* dangerous." Her eyelids closed, she bit her lip and shook her head. "Perlot was so—lovely; like Apodain. There wasn't a girl in

all Ghezrat who wouldn't gladly have wed him, even those
of us who would never have been considered. When his father brought Khadat here, we were all heartbroken. She was
always that hard, that cold—just like she is now.

"One of our cousins—Belo, you won't remember
him—he served in the kitchens up there in those days, so
sometimes we heard things that weren't common knowledge. He said at first Perlot tried to make the best of things,
but she was just horrible, whatever he did; she hated it when
he did anything she couldn't control. She wanted to own
him. She'd be angry when he had parties, because it was
something apart from her—even plain, quiet parties, only
wine and some friends and poetry, like those your father
gave, you remember?"

The two of them might have been alone; Breyd smiled. "I
went with him to the market and he let me pick the wine
jugs last time, remember, Mother? And the wine cups to
match, plain, cheap stuff but it had that pretty band of blue
around the rims. And then we went out to Niddy's vineyards
to get the wine." She did remember, suddenly: She could see
herself and Menlaeus, laughing over some silly thing, trying
to hold the donkey while the tenant farmer and his wife
loaded the jugs; they'd gone flying when the stubborn little
beast yanked free and ran away. And Nevvia later, laughing
at them covered head to toe in red mud. . . .

"You looked so outraged," Nevvia said. "And I kept trying to convince you the mud was good for your skin."

"It wasn't good for that new Eygari cotton tunic, Mother."

"I know. I saw that long red stain the last time it was
washed, even through the blue dye. But you should have
known not to wear white to the vineyards. I should have
done a better job of convincing you, though. One time,
Menlaeus was coming to visit me, not long after our fathers
decided we'd wed. I wore pale blue, terribly expensive; but
he was so lean and dark, so handsome, and I didn't know
him then, but I wanted him to like me; not think I was odd
and foreign."

"Oh, Mother!" Breyd whispered. "How could anyone
think that? You're so lovely."

"Exotic, Menlaeus always said." Nevvia smiled; her eyes
were unfocused. "So I wore the pale blue and Mother fussed
with my hair for the longest time and Father fussed at both
of us for bothering since the contract was already made. And

then the pigs got loose in the vines, and Father was bellowing, we all had to help catch them before they stripped the fruit."

"Oh, *no*," Breyd said softly.

"Oh, yes. I fell, of course; I was utterly filthy and I smelled like the pigs and the dirt of the vineyards; my hair was down all over my shoulders and there were bits of leaves in it. I couldn't stop weeping. But he—Menlaeus looked at me that hour like—as if he'd never seen anything in his life more beautiful, and he was so *kind*. You can't think how wonderful that was." *I won't ever know, either,* Breyd thought grimly; somehow, she kept it from her face. "You have it, too, Breyd—Greatgrandmother's southern blood—but more than I ever did."

Fortunately, before she could say anything, Niverren broke it. "All that story about the pigs and Father, you've told that a hundred times, Mother. But I've never heard this about Khadat. What about Prince Perlot and his parties?"

Nevvia closed her eyes briefly. "Your father never brought anyone here but other men—from his company, or other friends."

"Well, of course not!" Niverren said indignantly.

Nevvia shook her head. "Of course not. Belo said Perlot still paid girls to come and play the pipes and recite poetry, but he didn't—he—well, he only *listened* to them after he married." Her cheekbones were pink. "But one of the girls died a few days after such a party. Belo said later, the servants all knew the girl was fond of Perlot, and that Khadat found out."

Silence. Niverren broke it. "Mother. Are you possibly telling us that—that a noblewoman murdered a *pipe girl* for flirting with her husband? Things like that don't happen!"

"No?" Nevvia asked tartly. "They aren't like us, Niv. And Khadat—"

"But why haven't I heard any of this before?"

"Because," Breyd reminded her, "no one would spread gossip like that against a noblewoman, not over a pipe girl. It wouldn't be safe."

"What little scandal there was got hushed up at once," Nevvia said. "But Belo said Perlot stopped having parties."

"Oh, *Mother*," Niverren said in exasperation. "No one does things like that! Not even Khadat would—"

Nevvia didn't hear her; she had Breyd's fingers clasped in

her own, and she gazed anxiously into her youngest child's eyes. "You'll be careful? You'll remember?"

"Mother. Of course I'll be careful." She wasn't certain *she* believed the story any more than Niverren did, but their mother clearly did. *It certainly explains why she hates Khadat, anyway.* "I won't do anything to upset her, Mother. I promise."

Nevvia was asleep by full dark; Creos and Niverren at least in their room and quiet. Xhem was running errands for Grysis. *I don't care who or what Khadat is; I don't care about Apodain.* But by midnight, Breyd found herself pacing the floor of the long room. She'd sworn to Grysis; Tephys had already put the bond on her—she could not face that palace: Chill Khadat, horrid Emyas. And who *really* knew what Apodain was like? *Mother needs me here, I can't leave her. And what do they really think I'll do up there? Grysis was saying what he had to, so I'd marry Apodain. . . .* She finally wrapped herself in the dark green cloak she had worn as a novice priestess, let herself quietly out of the house, and walked as fast as she could, through nearly deserted streets, to the temple. *Tephys must see me; she will not dare deny me. She'll help, she has to.* She hurried down the main street, toward the square. A few of Haffat's soldiers stood watch by the gates; she thought there were others down by the barracks, in shadow. One thick-set, bearded man looked up as she passed the wineshop. His eyes gleamed and for one moment, she thought he would say something. *A girl abroad at such an hour, with enemy in our streets—I must have been mad! I should not have come out,* she thought in sudden panic. But he turned and went back inside. She held to the shadows after that and practically ran the rest of the way to the temple.

The high priestess was standing at the foot of the steps, a chalice in one hand. "I haven't much time—but I expected you. Before this."

Tephys, I'm afraid. She wanted to say that; to cling to the priestess. But Tephys wouldn't understand; there was no real comfort here. "Khadat has ordered me to come to her tomorrow."

"And you are surprised?" Breyd shook her head. "Your captain tells me you aren't resigned to this marriage. You surely haven't come to ask me to set it aside?"

"I—but you wouldn't, would you?"

"No. Even if I wished to, the goddess would not let me. This was no casual decision on my part, Breyd. You should know that."

She stared down at her feet. "I know it. And I already told Grysis I would do what he asked."

"I know what he asked. I am as much a part of it as you, Breyd. Remember that, if you need help in the days to come. If you cannot reach Grysis for some reason, Khadat will never stop you coming to me." She studied the girl; Breyd bit her lip to keep herself quiet. "It's not really about Apodain. It's your Prime, isn't it?"

"Tephys, I can't marry! You know Father's still out there, somewhere. If I marry and Denota dissolves the bond completely—"

"Control yourself!" Tephys snapped. Her face softened at once, and she laid a hand on Breyd's cheek. "I am sorry; I have had a long and hard day already, and I am tired. I know this is difficult for you. I wanted more time to prepare all you Secchi, but that wasn't how things happened, was it?" She sighed faintly. "The Diye Haff are still with us, the task given you is not completed, and your Prime still needs you. If you were thinking properly, you would realize that. The bond between you and Menlaeus will not be taken away when the others are dissolved."

She wanted to weep, as much from relief as Tephys' unexpectedly gentle touch. She swallowed, nodded. "Thank you."

"Thank Denota before you go home tonight, and again tomorrow," Tephys said crisply. She removed the hand and folded her arms again.

"It's as much my mother. She's lost so much already."

"Your mother and all of us. Send her to me, if she worries you so much, and I will ask Denota for strength for her. Remember her in your prayers, it will help." *It will not be me at her side, though,* Breyd thought. "Bury your resentment; the goddess does not serve only *you* or yours."

"Yes, Tephys."

"That is better." Tephys gazed at her thoughtfully, and finally said, "The bond between you and your father will not prevent you from being a true wife to Apodain. Don't look at me like that, as if you'd never thought of such things. After tomorrow night, you and he—"

She could feel herself flushing; her face was hot. "No."

"Don't be silly, girl. Your father wouldn't ask you to deny the boy after you wed him; you need not deny him because of what you do for Grysis and the city, either. Do nothing to arouse anyone's suspicions in that household; take the boy to your couch or go to his."

"Tephys—I—"

"Think about it," the priestess said sternly. "Ask Denota for guidance before you leave here tonight."

She wouldn't get anything else, Breyd realized bleakly. She bowed her head. "I will. For the other—thank you, Tephys."

"You are welcome. Don't leave here alone, either, not at such an hour. I will send Eyzhad with you. Remember that you are a young girl, not a fighting woman, that the men out there are not all ours, and not all protective of our young girls." Breyd flushed deeply once more and her eyes were hot, but she simply bowed, turned and climbed the stairs.

Nevvia was surprisingly calm the next morning. *She is trying to be brave, for both of us.* Breyd swallowed her own dismay and managed to eat a little while Nevvia talked to her. "I knew you'd have to leave this house when you married, sweetheart, whoever he was. I know Apodain will be very good to you, and he'll let you come visit us." Neither of them mentioned Khadat. "I'm just sorry they won't let family come tonight."

"I am, too, Mother. If you want to get word to me, anything at all, send Xhem." Nevvia nodded. Breyd hugged her hard and kissed both soft, thin cheeks. She had already gone in to say good-bye to Niverren.

Nidya held her for a very long moment and whispered against her ear, "I'll take care of her." Breyd nodded. "Tell Xhem if they do let you run in Haffat's games; we'll all come and cheer you on." She nodded again, suddenly unable to trust her voice.

Xhem was waiting for her by the door, her small chest at his feet. He opened the door for her, picked up the box. Fortunately, it wasn't heavy; Xhem would be mortified if she tried to take it from him.

She braced herself for another long walk past the main gates, past even more of Haffat's soldiers; but Xhem turned the other way at the bakery and led her along the back side of the city, close to the west wall and through the craftsmen's market, up a narrow alley between two rows of tall, thin houses, and finally brought her out on the back side of the temple. "I'm amazed, Xhem. You know the city better than I do."

He looked back at her and she thought she'd pleased him. "The other messengers have shown me a lot of shortcuts; I've found others by myself, though." He set the chest down just short of Khadat's gates and blotted sweat from his face. "Grysis said to tell you this morning, come late to him, whenever you can, but be cautious. I will visit Nessa in the stables every day if I can, and there is a girl in the kitchens, Sapha. You can trust her, Grysis says. If you can't come outside, she will get word to Nessa, and he'll tell me."

"Sapha. Nessa," Breyd repeated. She held out her arms and he came into them; thin, hard arms wrapped around her neck. "I'll miss just having you around all the time, Xhem. Come when you can, but don't arouse *her* suspicions."

"I won't," he said confidently. Breyd patted his shoulder and walked up to the gates; Xhem picked up her box and followed.

She had been afraid Emyas would be waiting in the courtyard; that she would have to ask him to take her to Khadat. But the woman stood in shade at the top of the shallow steps, waiting, hands clasped before her, her face expressionless. Breyd came up the steps, stopped before her and met her eyes, then bent one knee—enough to show respect, no more. Khadat touched her shoulders with fastidious fingers, brushed her cheek with cold lips and let go of her.

She was taller and heavier than Breyd remembered, very elaborately dressed. *To point up the difference between us,* Breyd through sourly. Her hair was pulled back and up in many curls and coils, held in place by metal pins and several fine bands. Her tunic was simply cut, but the fabric was the finest silk Breyd had ever seen, a subtle shade of amethyst that changed as she moved. She wore massive gold and amethyst earrings, a heavy collar necklace with an enormous pearl and amethyst medallion swagged below it from a number of fine chains. Her hair and body smelled of expensive oils; her skin was extremely white and very soft.

Her eyes had narrowed as she stepped back, her mouth pursed. "Let me see—as I feared."

"Yes," Breyd replied softly. "Such things happen, Princess, when one is given no time to ready." Khadat gave her a startled glance, then thinned her lips and turned away.

"You will come with me. Rooms have been prepared for you and new clothing. My tirewoman will come to dress your hair, and you will take supper with my son and me at sixth horn." She said nothing else, simply went up the steps and down an open, airy hall. Breyd followed.

The walls of the hallway had been painted in bright colors: the sea, dolphins, and fish—ships with brightly colored sails scudding across the water. A smiling man in the stern played pipes, another in the bow leaned over the rail to touch the water. *Oh, how lovely. Think how wonderful that would be—such a ship, with the wind in my face. Free of land. Almost like a bird, flying over the water. . . .* But Khadat was halfway up a broad flight of steps. Breyd hurried past the mural and caught up with her.

Ships. She had seen them all her life but never until now thought about them. *This is what it is to be wealthy; to have such wondrous things as that painted wall.* But Khadat did not even look at it.

A cool breeze came down the steps and along a smoothly tiled floor. There were more painted walls here: Fantastic flowers in rainbow colors rose above her head. Khadat paid no attention to those, either; her back was utterly rigid. *My son. Not, your future husband. Not Apodain.* No, there would be no warmth for her here. But she didn't want warmth. *That is not why I came, to marry Apodain, to sit and wait for his mother's ships.* Khadat had stopped near the window opening at the end of the hall; she stood aside and indicated an open door. Breyd stepped into a light and airy room easily the size of Nidya's entire house, including the courtyard. The walls were white, unfigured except for the carved blue rosettes at the corners of each window and the doorway. The air was cool and fresh. *Creos would like this.*

But Creos would never see it; Khadat would surely never permit Breyd's family inside the palace walls. When she turned back toward the door, Khadat was gone, and a boy in servant's unrelieved white was bringing her chest through the door. An older woman with graying hair, in servant's white sashed in deep blue stood in the doorway, arms folded across her chest. She waited until the boy had set the chest down at the foot of a wide and finely carved sleeping couch and gone away. She came into the room only then and walked around Breyd, her displeasure at what she saw visibly deepening by the moment. Breyd set her jaw and kept her peace.

"Well! My princess was right. But there are possibilities. I am Pria, the princess's personal woman; I am here to see what we can do to make you presentable."

"We will not do anything," Breyd said flatly.

Pria stared at her; her eyes narrowed once more. "The princess had *ordered*—"

"I am here, by her order and Denota's. I will wed her son. If she has plain clothing for me, I will accept that, but I will *not* weigh myself down with oils and cosmetics! I will not bury myself in jewels or let you burn my hair to make it curl. I am not noble, and I will not pretend to be." She glared at the woman who glared back.

The silence stretched; Pria finally broke it. "All right, be that way. The young master will see you for what you are and that will be the end of the whole sorry matter." She turned and walked quickly from the room.

Breyd glared after her. "Let him see me for what I am, and let Khadat—and let them both choke on it." She turned away and walked over to the nearest window. "Horrid old creature," she muttered. A sheer, gauzy curtain rippled with the afternoon breeze; as she had hoped, there was a narrow balcony beyond it, overlooking a very small and neglected garden. Beyond that, the palace walls cut off most of her view of the city, but by leaning out a little, she could see the eastern walls and beyond them, hills and the high, precipitous ridge.

She stood there until the shadow thrown by the inner walls across the courtyard told her she should go in. Someone would have to show her the way to dinner; Pria would probably be angry again if she weren't in plain sight. Breyd sighed. *Save your strength for Khadat, this woman is merely another like Emyas.* She brushed the curtain aside and came back into the chamber.

Her heart lurched painfully; someone had come into the room and stood there, watching her; compared to the balcony, it was dark and she couldn't see anything but shape. *How long has he been there?* She blinked rapidly. *You must expect this,* she told herself angrily. *And not leap from your skin. There is no door, and in a house like this, servants come and go.*

But as she blinked the last of the sunlight from her eyes, she could see this was no servant: Apodain came into the light and stopped a few paces away from her. "My—my mother told me you had arrived," he said finally. "I thought someone should come and properly welcome you."

Oh. How beautiful he is! But his eyes, why does he look at me so? But it could not be her, she decided. He had sorrows that had nothing to do with her, enough unhappiness to darken his eyes more than they were. *He has just never met your eyes before.* He was still looking at her—*waiting for you to say something, while you gape at him.* "Thank you."

"It must be strange." He stopped abruptly.

He is embarrassed, The thought surprised her. *But why?* "It is strange," she said finally. "But this is a lovely room. Not like my home, or the barracks." It was her turn to stop sharply; she bit her lower lip and his eyes fell. *You don't need to remind him!*

Mother was so angry just now, I could hear her and Pria. But she's lovely, just like this. Those huge eyes—they really do tip up at the ends, just a little; all that wonderful, thick hair. But she's so tiny, so exquisitely small, how could she have fought? That low, resonant voice. He remembered it, all at once. "I remember you—your voice. You were in the courtyard of the barracks. You and other Dyaddi. I heard, about the road, your Prime." He drew a deep breath, let the words out with it in a rush. "We have something in common, you and I. I lost my father."

"No!" She had to fight herself, not to shout at him. "No. My father is still alive!"

He turned away. "I didn't mean— I wasn't trying to hurt you. I'm sorry."

He was being kind; she hadn't expected kindness and didn't want it, not from him. *I can't afford to be weak, not in any way. But why is he being so nice to me?* He was being forced to marry her. Khadat didn't see the honor of an alliance with a Secchi, why would he? *Forget that. What he thinks doesn't matter, except that they must not suspect you. Remember what Grysis told you, do not rouse suspicion.* She drew a steadying breath and said, "You didn't hurt me, it's all right. I understand what you meant to say . . . I think."

Apodain turned back and gave her a tentative smile; even that warmed his face wonderfully, but it was gone at once. "This ceremony tonight. It isn't much time to know each other, is it?" She shook her head. "They tell me the Diye Haff plan a celebration—games, in two days."

She nodded once more. "I heard that also. Their general told them in the barracks, when they took the weapons." She felt the blood heating her face. "At least we were both spared *that*," she added flatly. He waited. She turned away from him. "I'm sorry."

"It's all right," he said quietly. *I would have hated that, to be pulled from my company and hidden while they faced that ordeal. To be part of a company for so long, then pulled from it at such a moment. Like I was when—* He couldn't say it; she would hate him for even thinking they had *that* in common.

But she was speaking again. "A celebration," she said. "To honor their lion god with games as well. Like our own Midsummer games, as they keep telling us. I . . . had thought . . . my captain thought I would be part of them."

Apodain stared. "I *do* remember you! Last year, the foot races!"

She shrugged, looked faintly embarrassed. "That was me; I won every event, except one. My best friend Denira beat me."

"That was you." He looked at her in mild wonder. He looked all around the empty room, glanced at the door opening a second time, then closed the distance between them and said quietly, "You must know how my mother runs this house and all within it. She is very displeased that—well, never mind. You will find life easier if you manage to avoid her whenever possible." She looked up at him. "She has a temper," he added. "I annoy her as little as possible; I avoid her when she's in a—a mood."

He can't be warning me against her, can he? Breyd looked at him, but his face gave away nothing. *Or does he know more of that tale of Mother's—a dead pipe girl and poison?* But she would never be able to ask him that. "I served Denota for a time," she managed finally. "I have been around your mother, though she would not remember me. I do not expect her to clasp me to her bosom and call me daughter."

Apodain shook his head; his eyes remained dark and worried. *Afraid—for me?* But all he said was, "No, she will not do that. Mother is not—not a warm woman, save toward my brother." He walked past her to the window, brushed the curtain aside and gazed down into the courtyard. Breyd came out and stood next to him. "I would like to say this—and then I will go." His face was averted, his eyes fixed on the little garden. "I would have fought with my company. I don't expect you to believe that, you must have heard the things they say about me. But—that was *my* enemy. It is still my enemy, to fight somehow. In these games. Any way I can." He looked past her, out across the city. "I didn't mean to tell you that. But the look in your eyes when you said— the surrender. I thought—never mind." He spun away from the window and strode from the room. Breyd turned and watched him go and couldn't decide what to think. *He's complex; not just a pretty form and a handsome face, whatever is under that.* She turned back and stood where he had, looking down into the small garden, until sixth horn sounded and a servant came to take her down to dinner.

The dining hall was long and narrow, the walls painted with magical creatures in a border at waist height; the table a richly polished black wood; chairs of the same wood were cushioned in fine silk. Apodain sat across from her, Khadat reclined at the far end upon an ornate couch covered in leopard skins. She watched them both closely as Breyd was ushered into the room, but Apodain greeted his betrothed distantly, and as if for the first time, and thereafter applied himself to his food. The plates were golden, the cups long and pointed, held upright in ornate gold wire frames. Breyd stared into a silver goat's face with red stones for eyes; Apodain drank from a golden ram's horn. Khadat's cup was as ornate as her couch, leaping beasts balanced on the wire frame that held a gold coiled snake.

The bread was made of very fine flour, sweetened with honey; there was spiced oil to dip it in; oranges already sectioned and a cool soup. She couldn't decide what was in the soup, the flavor was so subtle, but it was good. She drank it all in cautious sips, very much aware of Khadat's narrowed eyes. *She must think I do not know how to conduct myself at a table.*

The fruit and soup were taken away; a roasted fish brought. Khadat watched her closely the entire time, as though willing her to create some kind of disaster. The fish was taken, a dish of figs and another of dates set in its place.

Finally Khadat cleared her throat. "You, girl. My son tells me you have participated in the games before. I have already decided Apodain will enter them; are you as good as he says?"

"I win them," Breyd replied quietly.

"That is good," Khadat said. She did not sound particularly pleased. "Such a female must be good for something. My son makes a good point, though: Haffat will find people in this city opposed to him—openly, or in ways they deem subtle. Now, this Haffat is no fool and he is proud; he will realize he's being snubbed and eventually, he will be stung to retaliate. If we approach him with open good will, however—" She paused; Breyd looked up to find Khadat watching her closely. "Did you wish to say something?"

"No, madam."

"Good." The woman looked gratified. "He is here; what is, is. Since he is here, only a fool would attempt to undermine him, to sneak behind his back. If the army could not rout him, then ordinary people are not likely to send him away because they do not like his soldiers, or are openly rude to him or his heir. But I will not let my family's wealth and all I have worked for since to be taken away because I closeted myself with a grudge. Those who are practical and sensible can salvage something from such times. And what do you say to that, girl?" she demanded suddenly. "You fought these men. Do you have enough wit to see the time that is over? For I warn you right now, I will not tolerate any actions by *anyone* here that Haffat might take wrong. Not from my son and certainly not from you."

Breyd spread her hands, and said quietly, "Why, then, madam. What can I say? But I am also a practical person. Besides, I am within your walls now; I must do as you bid me." Khadat narrowed her eyes suspiciously, but Breyd simply looked back at her.

"That will do. Apodain, I will send a message to the prince that you and she will participate in the games."

"Thank you, Mother." Apodain picked up the bowl of dates and held it out. Breyd took one. It was sticky, very fresh, almost too sweet for one used to the dry and often brittle dates from the barracks or the leathery ones her mother bought. Khadat got abruptly to her feet and walked out. Apodain sent his eyes sideways, warningly; Pria stood just inside the door, her back to them, seemingly interested in something down the hall. *Listening to us, for Khadat,*

Breyd thought. "More cheese?" he asked. Breyd shook her head. "Have you seen all the palace yet?"

"Just this room and my own," she said.

"Then, if you are done, why don't I show you? It is a good hour for the roof gardens." He stood up and came around to help her to her feet. Pria stepped aside as he ushered Breyd into the hall and started to follow them, but Apodain turned around and said pointedly, "Mother said she would have a loom and wool found, so my new wife has something to occupy her spare hours. Why don't you help with that?" Pria mumbled something but went down the hall and down some stairs. Apodain touched Breyd's arm and led her in the other direction.

"Mother seldom takes meals with anyone, even me; I doubt you'll have to go through that again soon. But I will eat with you whenever I can, if you don't mind," he added quickly. She paused between one step and the next, looked up at him.

"I don't mind." *What does he want? A young girl's eager response? Some sign of pleasure?* She couldn't tell by his face; he looked troubled, but he could be thinking anything.

She realized she was staring at him, still standing upon the steps, Apodain's eyes still fixed on her face. "Are you all right?" he asked finally.

She made herself move, and somehow managed a smile for him. "I am all right. And I will be glad to spend time with you, Apodain; whatever time you can spare."

Pelledar sat upon the throne in his ground floor chamber and watched men gathered around the hearth, laughing and joking as they toasted meat on sticks. *Haffat's men. My own seem to be fewer every day.* It sometimes seemed he could go for a full horn without seeing anyone in the halls that he knew.

Haffat made no comment upon the dwindling number of Ghezrathi in the palace, or the corresponding increase in the number of Diye Haff. At least they hadn't replaced his personal servants. *But that will be next.* He was a little surprised to still be alive. *At least all my family is safe.*

He had not talked to Tephys in some days; this afternoon he would see her for the first time since the Diye Haff came into the city; she had sent word asking his presence for a ceremony of blessing, to honor the dead and restore harmony to the earth.

He wondered if he would have a moment to speak to her. He had no time in private with anyone, anymore.

Haffat looked up and waved a laden stick at him. "Is my brother certain he is not hungry?" he asked. The prince shook his head, managing a faint, rueful smile in token apology. Haffat shrugged, pulling the meat free with his fingers, and ate it quickly. *He has no more manners than my son, when he was a baby,* Pelledar thought sourly. Breeze blew through the windows, but the chamber still reeked of men who did not bathe and oil properly; who ate onions the way civilized men ate dates.

Beyond Haffat, an empty skewer dangling forgotten from one hand, Hadda stood staring into the courtyard, or perhaps beyond it. He was a moody young man, Pelledar thought; he and Hadda had exchanged very few words. *What a wonderful prince he will make here when Haffat goes—a petulant boy with his father's blood and his own sullen attitude.*

But so far, Haffat had not said when he would leave, though he talked often with his men about the campaign against Ye Eygar and the supplies he would need for it. His vast army still camped on the far side of the Oryon, except for the companies who had gone to take the isthmus. He was waiting, or so Pelledar gathered, for more supplies to come from Mirikos and the lands beyond.

He had not directly questioned his "brother." Pelledar expected that hourly; already Haffat knew Ye Sotris had not gone to Ye Eygar by the main road, or southwest toward Iselik or Meliawusa. He must already suspect they had not left the city. Pelledar swallowed and tried to think of something else. *The priestess was right. I am glad I do not know where they went.*

In the meantime, Haffat was deferential, and polite—and he paraded Pelledar at his side constantly. By the time these games were over, there would be no one in all the city who did not hate their prince as a traitor.

You knew this might come, if they did not kill you before the palace that first day. You knew it when you gave in to Haffat. But however Haffat persuaded the city, he would not shield Pelledar from the goddess; Denota knew his heart and her judgment must be the one that counted. *Though I am*

*sorry to have it said that Pelledar was a coward and that he
sold his city to Haffat out of fear.*

Fear. His eyes went to the lion-priest, who sat at the
hearth next to Haffat. He was neatly pulling bits of meat
from the skewer and popping them in his mouth. He hated
the way Knoe looked at him, those knowing eyes under hairless brows. *As if he has already found out my secrets, and
the city's secrets, and wishes to let me know it.* But that was
a dangerous thing to think, it would weaken him when he
could not afford it. *Priests learn that expression, to daunt
those who are not priests.* Tephys had given him such looks
once or twice, when he was younger and full of questions.

What would he dare ask Tephys this afternoon? *Wait and
see,* he decided.

Knoe declined Haffat's invitation to come with them;
Pelledar thought he looked uncomfortable, but all he said
was, "I have important things to tend here." In the end
Hadda remained behind also, but Haffat came with him, and
several of his personal guard.

"The Mirikosi tell me this Denota is your chief god. Perhaps why your city has such fine fields and flocks. But it
does not explain your warriors. Is that Atelos, the moon who
cares for them?"

Pelledar shrugged and chose his words carefully. Haffat
must know this already; he was trying to secure some bit
of information for Knoe. "Denota is chief of all, but no one
in Ghezrat worships Atelos. Atos is a warrior god, of
course."

"Your Temple of Warriors—my men are down there helping the priests clear the stones away so it can be rebuilt.
They tell me there is a place, another gate just beyond that
where another shrine could be built between the walls for
Axtekeles. It would be a good gesture on your part to do
this; Hadda and the men I leave with him must have a place
to worship."

"I will ask my council," Pelledar began. Haffat waved
him to silence.

"Why should you? There will be wrangling and to what
point? You understand the value of such a gesture, and I
would like to see the first stones laid for the shrine."

In other words, agree to this or I will do it anyway. And

yet, to let his lion inside the city. But that was a matter for Tephys. *Tell her today what he asks, if you can.*

The guard remained outside the gates; the two men went through and descended into the Cleft. Tephys stood alone, a dark shape outlined in steam. Pelledar glanced at Haffat. His companion seemed to be having a little trouble breathing, all at once. Tephys strode forward. "My prince, thank you for your time." Her eyes went to Haffat. "Emperor. In Denota's place and in Her name I bid you welcome." Her voice was cool. Haffat nodded shortly; sweat beaded his forehead, despite the almost chill air.

He drew himself up with a visible effort and replied, "Thank you."

"My prince," Tephys turned back to Pelledar, "if you will come." To Pelledar's surprise, Haffat made no effort to come with him, or argue when Tephys bore him off. Tephys knelt facing the steam, looked up at him and mouthed, *Kneel.* She bent low over the steam, then picked up a cup, held it over the steam and murmured over it, drank and passed it to Pelledar. The prince held the cup to his lips, and around it whispered, "He plans a temple to the lion god."

"We know." Tephys took back the cup, held it over the steam again, drank and gave it back to him. "Ye Sotris sends her love, but wonders why you have not yet sent Septarin down to join her?"

Pelledar blinked, held the cup to his lips and tried to think. "But I—he went—I sent him before Haffat came!"

Tephys eyed him sidelong. "All right. He isn't there; we will deal with it. Here—do nothing to let that man see we are not conducting ritual over here!" Pelledar bowed his head; Tephys bowed hers very briefly, hissed at him, "Stay there until you can control your face!"

"Yes." Tephys got to her feet and carried the cup over to a niche near the ever-burning lamps. The prince remained on his knees, head bowed. *The young fool! I should have known he was not resigned to my order, I should have made certain someone remained with him!* He drew a breath, let it out slowly, and much of the anger went with it. *There are only a few places he can go, and no possible harm he can do. Tephys will find him.* He sighed. *I am so very, very tired.*

He got up and walked slowly across the cavern. *Keep it from your face,* he reminded himself. But Haffat was not paying any attention to him. His face looked absolutely green and he was gasping for air; as Pelledar came up to him, he turned and felt blindly for the steps, and bolted up them.

"Yes." The prince jumped; Tephys had come up behind him and she looked grimly pleased with herself. "I did not think he would care for Denota's welcome." She came around him and laid her hands on his shoulders in blessing. "Go. Do what you must; I will send Ye Sotris your love and we will find your foolish boy." Pelledar merely nodded and went up the steps.

Haffat stood near the gates; he was still rather pale and his breath came too quickly. As Pelledar came across the courtyard, he blotted his face on his cloak, then turned to lead the way back to the palace.

Down in the market, a few women stood and spoke together in low voices or bargained for what fruit was still displayed. There was less every day, it seemed; less reaching the stands because the Diye Haff bought it before it ever came into the city, or because it simply was not on the trees or the vines when the women went out to harvest it. There was still bread, but the cost of that had gone up and many of the women had begun to break into their own carefully hoarded stores of grain to bake their own.

Several boys ran through the street, laughing and chasing each other; one of the women yelled at them sharply and they took off, vanishing into one of the narrow alleys that honeycombed the area. Only after they were long gone did one of the women reach down for her knotted bag and find it missing.

At the far end of the alley, two boys stepped back into shadow as the rest pelted into the street beyond. "Septarin? Are you all right now?"

Septarin nodded; he had already opened the bag, pulled out bread, and stuffed it in his mouth. He chewed hastily, swallowed and took the jug the other handed him. "I am fine, Imbro. I didn't expect to need so much silver. I have to be careful with what I have left."

"Everything is expensive now," Imbro said. "I'm glad you came to me for help, though."

"My friend for so many years," Septarin said expansively. "I thought of you at once."

"I am sorry I couldn't simply have you to stay," Imbro said. "But Father would send you back to the palace at once; he's afraid of *them*." Septarin shook his head, bit off more bread and washed it down with another swallow of wine.

"So is my father. But I wouldn't want to get you into trouble."

Imbro looked less anxious than he had. "If you come back tonight after ninth horn—remember the time when we ran off, after your tutor took us to temple, and stayed out very late? And how I got inside without Father catching me?"

"Over the inner wall and onto your roof, I remember," Septarin said promptly. "If I have no other shelter by ninth horn, I'll come." He gripped Imbro's arm and gestured toward the street with his chin. "You had better go, they're looking for you." Septarin waited until they were all out of sight, then sighed, leaned back against the wall, and finished his bread. It wasn't the best he'd ever eaten; there were husks in it, an odd mix of grain, and it hadn't even been sweetened. Much worse than the stuff he'd had to eat in the messes, which had been bad enough. The oranges he found in the bag under the bread were green and small; they puckered his mouth. The wine Imbro had bought for him was fortunately well mixed because it was a dark red and very sour.

Had he only been out here two days and two nights? It seemed much longer, but if he had been missed yet, word hadn't reached the market. But he had to be careful: gossip was so thick down here, that if one of those market sellers recognized him, or one of Imbro's friends did, everyone would know. And then, Tephys would come and get him. . . .

Much as he hated to admit it, even to himself, it had scared him, being out here and on his own—not daring to trust anyone. Yesterday, he hadn't even eaten until full dark, when he'd finally worked up nerve enough to go to one of the smaller winehouses close to the barracks. It had been dimly lit, the wine dreadful, but it had only cost one small silver and there had been bread and a thick soup to go with the wine.

It was the kind of place soldiers went for drink and talk with their own kind. A few of Haffat's men had occupied one corner the previous night, a few gray-haired Ghezrathi men who looked like heavy infantry huddled in the opposite corner, casting occasional glares across the room and mumbling to themselves. But Septarin had felt comfortable here;

these were soldiers, his own kind. Men he could lead, once he had the opportunity to sound them out. They wouldn't betray him.

There had been plenty of low-voiced and careful talk like that he'd heard in the market: *They hate Haffat for what he is doing; some of them even begin to hate my father, for letting him come in.* It made him uncomfortable: He was still angry that Pelledar was trying to treat him like one of the babies, and for that horrid, dark little cell. But to hear people talking that way, about his father. . . .

But if his father went about publicly with the emperor, then he deserved such talk.

By the sky and by the horn that had just sounded, it would be dark soon; he finished the bread. There would be more bread at the wineshop; probably a thick, peasantish stew to go with it. And who would expect to find a prince of Ghezrat in a wineshop where the Diye Haff went, planning their deaths under their very noses?

At full dark, he walked back down the alley and stepped into the open. A glance across his shoulder—there was a light in the palace window, in his father's throne room this night, as there had not been the two previous nights. *Celebrating with his new friends,* Septarin thought sourly. He drew the hood up and forward to shade his features.

The barracks were nearly dark, the gates pulled almost closed, one of Haffat's men leaning against the wall next to them with a long spear in the crook of his arm. Septarin walked by him, shoulders tight, half expecting the man to call him to a halt, but the Diye Haff merely glanced his way and turned back to his study of the opposite wall.

It was odd, the deep silence down by the gates and beyond the barracks wall; only a few men walked abroad at this hour, and he had not seen a woman or child anywhere since before sundown. *They will be glad when I deal with Haffat,* he told himself.

The man who tended the pots merely glanced at him, took the coin he held out, handed him a small jug and a cup and said, "The woman will bring soup and bread shortly." He nodded and turned away.

The shop was crowded, but there were no Diye Haff here yet. Septarin looked around, finally found a bench against the wall where the light was especially dim and settled down with his wine. It was more of the overly sweet red, not nearly as watered as he would have liked. He made a face but drank deeply; it would take the edge from the taste of the food.

The bench rattled as someone dropped next to him. Septarin glanced up, met dark, keen eyes, looked away at once. Silence. Then his neighbor nudged him, held up his cup and said, "Here's to our new emperor." Septarin goggled at him; his jaw dropped as the man added under his breath, "May he rot for ten thousand years!"

He swallowed; his voice didn't want to work. He pulled back as the other tried to peer under his hood. *This is how it begins,* he told himself firmly and took a deep swallow of his own wine. "Aye, may he rot."

"You're one of ours, then?" A quick, low voice; no sound of drink in it.

"One of—of course I am," Septarin said indignantly. His mind was working furiously. "I had to make certain of *you,* though, didn't I?" He flinched; a square, scarred hand caught hold of the hood and pulled it away from his face.

The man nodded, let go of the cloth; Septarin pushed it up so he could see out. "Yes, I thought it was you, by the voice. But what is a—a man like yourself doing here?"

It wasn't what he said, but how he said it. *He knows me, but he won't come out and say. Subtle,* Septarin thought, and was pleased with himself for working that out. "What is any man with any pride doing? Avoiding *them,* of course."

"I see. Shhhh," he added sharply. A moment later a thin rag of a woman came by bearing a pot, a skinny boy in tow with a basket of cups. Septarin's nose wrinkled at the smell of the food, but it was thick and hot and he was hungry. He accepted the cup, took a heavy wedge of bread to go with it, and ate. The man at his side ate quickly, went for more wine and another cup of stew. "You've left there, have you, then?" He picked up the conversation where they'd left it a while earlier; Septarin had to think for a moment; he finally nodded. A very low voice against his ear: "Rumor says the emperor holds the queen and her babes, and *you* also—so the prince will do what he says."

Septarin shook his head. "Of course not!" he said flatly, and went on very rapidly, "I am here, and I *know* where Mother is, but *they* won't bother her, especially once we rise up and drive them into the sea and—"

The man shushed him vigorously; Septarin realized his voice had gone up and the men all around them were staring. He reddened. "You have to be very careful, even here," the man murmured. "They can't put spies among us. Anyone can tell one of us from a foreigner, after all. But they come here, and they could listen from outside, perhaps."

"Well, of course," Septarin said with as much dignity as he could summon. He drained the winecup to cover his embarrassment; all around them, men went back to their eating and drinking. When he lowered the cup, his companion was looking at him thoughtfully.

"So you've left them. Could be I know people who will hide you, keep you safe."

"My *father* wanted that," Septarin spat; he only just remembered to keep his voice down. "I want—I won't cower with the babies, not from them."

"I see. Wait here." The man got to his feet, took Septarin's cup and his own and brought them back filled. "All right. Perhaps I know people who could help you with—whatever it is you want." He held up his cup, touched the rim to Septarin's and met his eyes meaningfully. "To those who see what needs doing—and do it."

"To the downfall of the Diye Haff, and the death of Haffat," Septarin whispered. Heady words. His companion looked truly impressed and that, too, was a heady experience. He drank deeply. The taste of the red wine brought him back to earth with a thump, and left him coughing. His companion patted him roughly between the shoulder blades. "Here," he said, "that's bad stuff they serve here. You take mine, and go on out, I'll meet you, bring friends. Do you know the niche along the inner wall opposite the Goat Gate?" Septarin shook his head. "Do you know the Goat Gate?"

"Of course!"

"They don't patrol the entire wall, they only keep a guard on both sides of the main gates. Go there now, it'll be safe for you to wait for me there. I'll come as soon as I can before ninth horn. I'll bring—well," he added in a very low voice as a handful of men crowded into the wine house, "You know what manner of men I'll bring." He looked at the newcomers. "You had better go, sire. Don't talk to anyone between now and then, just go. For your safety."

"Certainly," Septarin said grandly. *He called me sire.*

Even with the heavy soup and the bread filling his belly, he felt a little light-headed. But those who had just come in spoke with foreign accents—Diye Haff. He picked up the jug the man had given him and edged around the side of the room to slip into the night once more.

"Ridlo?" Captain Frewis came over and sat as Septarin went out. "Who was that?"

"You'll never believe it. That was the prince's heir."

Frewis turned to stare toward the door. "Are you serious?" he whispered. "What is he doing out here?"

"Hoping to lead us to holy victory."

"Dear goddess, we don't need this, not now! We can't have him running about the city babbling such things! You'll have to go get him."

"He's meeting me at the Goat Gate, ninth hour. That will give us time to get some men together, grab him, and get him below before he ruins everything."

"Before he gets himself killed."

"That too. But I'm not worried about *him*. He's dangerous; he can't even keep a secret as important as his own mother's hiding place!"

"If he knows where she is! But if he suspects there is a resistance—"

Ridlo shook his head. "I gave him a flask of wine, told him to go now and wait for us. He's no head for wine, anyone could see that, he'll be sound asleep long before we get there. He won't be any trouble."

"I don't like it. Go find a couple of men now, and get over there; as soon as he shows up, grab him." Frewis set his lips in a tight line. "He'll find the underground, all right. And he won't see the light of day again until it's safe for us to let him out."

Haffat

Knoe was furious. He had warned Haffat to stay away from the goddess' temple! And now look at the man! Haffat had been practically staggering and his skin was an unhealthy gray still, even after a cup of good wine.

He had to leave, before his temper exploded. "Goddess," he mumbled to himself angrily. "She is the lock and those two I hold the key—and I cannot set one to the other!" He could not remember ever being so frustrated, not since the Lion had first breathed on him and taken him for His own. "What is that priestess up to?" But Tephys had not come from her temple in all the days he'd been inside Ghezrat—and Knoe dared not go there.

Not yet. "Once I unravel this great mystery. . . ." But whatever he did, the two who became one withstood him. He had threatened, described tortures with loving detail—had even threatened her virtue before his eyes, his life before hers. They looked at him with that cold, distant stare and never spoke, not one word in all the time he had held them. *How can they remain silent in the face of all that?*

Haffat still did not understand why it was so important to break these two, to learn their secrets—*there* was the difference between a plain fighting man and the chosen representative of a god, Knoe thought sourly. Even after he'd explained—break the bond between these, learn what it is, you break the power of the earth goddess and the city will never rise again; defeat Denota and Ghezrat is crushed for all time.

"But defeat Denota," he whispered to an empty corridor. "Break into her mysteries and grind them into the earth. Defeat her and give her deepest secrets to Axtekeles and the god will know you for his most faithful servant ever, and he will reward you." Enough power to stand against any earthly force, any prince or emperor. . . . *They will worship*

Axtekeles from here to Diyet and beyond, and into the lands where the Ergardi once dwelt, and beyond the great sea to other lands yet unknown—because of Knoe.

How long did Haffat plan to remain here, playing with his precious son and this weakling prince? He must return to Diyet or go on to conquer Ye Eygar; he had no other choices. But Haffat looked almost ... comfortable in this palace. And he was already talking about wintering over in Ghezrat, with Hadda.

I knew it was a mistake, to let him name that dreadful, weak boy his heir! There must have been a way, I could have foreseen it somehow, prevented it. He is stepping away from the path the god chose for him; why can I not make him see how dangerous this is? For both of them—for all of them. There might be the key: Haffat would listen if he thought his actions might harm his precious son.

"He won't even listen when I warn him about Denota. He knows the Ergardi cannot even come near the gates, but does he worry about it?" He should; such things were symptoms, like sweating to mark the onset of fever. After his experiences today in Denota's Cleft, though, Haffat might prove more sensible. If he wanted to use the Ergardi against Ye Eygar, he had better pay closer attention to their concerns; they were not ordinary humans, like Haffat's soldiers. "I have done all I could, to bring them to Axtekeles, but they are still a—thing—apart."

The key to controlling Haffat must be Pelledar, and the secrets *he* concealed. He knew about these two who became one, these Dyaddi; he knew where his woman was. Knoe was certain of it, and even Haffat was becoming impatient with his "brother"; just now, he'd actually said, "If you would have something gainful to do until we leave, priest, find me the queen and her progeny. Find me his heir; I cannot dispose of the prince if his son lives."

Knoe hesitated, looked around the hallway to make certain it was otherwise deserted, then went down into the storage cellars and through the door at the end, into the wealth of tunnels and passageways that had been dug beneath the palace. *As if they had been meant for me, waiting for me to come and make use of them.* His two were just this way, along a dark corridor, behind two separate locked doors, hidden by the god's power. A pinch of Axtekeles' powder, perhaps: it could keep a full-grown man from fighting the sacrifice knife as it had in Mirikos; it could give the Lion access to a child's tongue as it had outside Idemito. It could kill, or persuade or weaken at need. Knoe smiled grimly and plunged into the darkened tunnel. They would not deny him this time—even if they tried to, they would not deny the god.

Several long, grueling hours later, Knoe wrapped a deeply hooded cloak around his body and strode down darkened avenues to the outer walls. *I swore to the god I would serve Haffat, when the god asked it of me; I swore I would protect him and see his empire was everything he could wish—for the god's glory.* He turned into a narrow side street. To see all that fall into nothing, because of Haffat's pleasure in taking this city and placing it like a great gem in his son's pampered little hands! The lion-priest ground his teeth and strode on.

It was not that thought which had him so upset at the moment. *I placed the powder in my own mouth and breathed it upon them. The lion's breath has never failed me in all my years of service, and yet, they stood in those mean, dark little cells and stared at me, and would not answer whatever I asked them.*

It was impossible! "Denota," he whispered. "You cannot prevail, not against the Lion's power. Remember what Haffat said to your people's prince and tremble, knowing what I will do, and what Axtekeles will do, if you do not yield now." No answer; he hadn't really expected one. It was an arrogant earth goddess. *But she will learn. In time.*

Perhaps in a way it was his fault, the way Haffat was acting. "I set deadlines for Denota, and when she does not respond I shake my head, and set another deadline. Bah." He spat. "And Haffat—he places a deadline before Pelledar and when that is not met, he steps back, and sets another. . . ."

He paused as a horn call floated over the silent city, worked out the meaning. Eighth horn. Not as late as he'd thought.

In one sense, at least; in another, it was all too late. Haffat *must* leave Ghezrat, soon; he must attack Ye Eygar before the next dark moon or the city would never fall. There was some danger Knoe could not see clearly—smoke and steam and a high-pitched wail. . . . He knew only that Haffat must march just as soon as these ridiculous games were over.

Somehow, he found himself near the gates a while later; one or two fading torches marked the outer postern and the two men who watched over it. He considered going out of the city and at least partway down the road, then decided he did not want to talk to anyone—not even to name himself and pass the guard—and went on. There were steps a short distance away, more a ladder leading onto the inner wall, and a thin stone bridge joined it to the outer wall. He climbed across to the outer wall and leaned against the parapet for a while. The air was still and biting and he could see a little fog down on the plain, marking the rivers and the swamp, pooling in the low places.

Fully half the emperor's encamped army was lost in fog, only a little hazy, ruddy light marking where fires burned nearest the water. Two ships' masts rose from fog; that must be the mole, and those ships the Mirikosi ones whose captains owed allegiance to this arrogant Princess Khadat and her family.

Haffat had actually laughed when Knoe tried to warn him about this Khadat. "Let her be; let her reestablish the shipping and the trade as it ought to be, she has that talent. And she may prove useful to me—a woman and ambitious. Besides, I've seen the way she looks at me—haven't you?"

"I would deal with her now, with a blade across the throat," Knoe growled. He knew her sort: Arrogant females: They sought to hold power over men with their faces, or their bodies—or both. In the case of this one, by means of her family wealth and connections. Haffat might be emperor of a vast realm, but with his pitiful concerns about which weak king called him brother and what peasant with a crown named him Great King, Haffat would be an absolute innocent, wet clay in the woman's hands.

Knoe turned away from the view and moved slowly down the outer wall, toward the south. There would be little or nothing to see out there tonight, but it was pleasant up here, even with the scent of scorched stone and wood, the increasingly unpleasant odor of unburied bodies that came from the collapsed Temple of Warriors. Still—he seldom had any place all to himself. A distance farther on, beyond the next two gates, there would be small houses close to the inner wall, people sleeping on their roofs or in the courtyards. He had gone that way the night before and heard low-voiced conversations, the heavy snores of men and the lighter ones of women. A few more steps along the outer wall, then, no more than that. He wouldn't walk that far again. And perhaps if he returned while Haffat was still awake, he could find opportunity to persuade him more to adhere to the god's plans for him. Haffat seldom slept more than a few hours very late at night and he was usually quieter after dark than when he first woke. It was worth a try.

Knoe stopped. Just up there, he could hear someone talking—to himself, or to someone else? He took a quiet step, a second, stopped once more and held his breath.

It was a boy, he thought; by the voice, it had to be a boy. A very drunk boy. He pulled the hood of his robe back a little, but not so far as to expose his brow or his head, since even the drunkest or most foolish of Ghezrat knew who *he* was. Opened his mouth to speak, but the boy's next words froze him, speechless, where he stood. "When I lead all those men—my army against that emperor, against that green Hadda, then they will know I am a true prince of Ghezrat. And my father will look at me and he will know then what *he* is, and what I am, and—" The sound of a bottle sloshing. "Better save that—last swallow. May need it later. But he will know, Father will know, and he will be so sorry that he tried—" He hiccupped loudly. Knoe cleared his throat, and Septarin—it must be Septarin—spun around and flung himself unsteadily to his feet. "Who's there?" he demanded in a penetrating whisper.

"A friend," Knoe replied softly. "Were you not awaiting a friend?"

"Maybe," Septarin said warily. "Maybe I was. Whose friend are you, though?"

"Not the friend of a prince who betrays his city and gives his soldiers and their swords into the hands of their enemy," Knoe said. His accent was not Ghezrathi, even if it was not as strong as the northern accent. But Septarin had drunk an unaccustomed amount of wine, and he was beyond noticing anything of his new companion save the words he spoke. He laughed once, delightedly, then clapped a hand over his mouth and drew himself up with what he must think was dignity. Knoe smiled grimly himself and took a step toward the young prince. "We have many things to talk about—haven't we, sire?"

"Well, of course," Septarin said loftily. "I have come to lead you, like I told that man tonight. Against the emperor and his underlings. You have things to tell me also, haven't you?"

Knoe nodded, began to walk slowly forward. Septarin turned unsteadily and fell in beside him. "Once I am certain you are who I think you are. There are Diye Haff everywhere, you know." Hints and riddles: Was the boy really part of some underground movement? Would the men of this city dare? Or was it all in the boy's mind, or his own? Perhaps this skinny slip of a boy somehow could be made to serve Hadda, without even knowing what he did? Knoe considered the possibility: It would be an elaborate plot, but this was a fool of a green boy—a princeling off his tether for the first time in his life, clearly one who had no head for wine and entirely too great faith in himself, who had listened to too many of the tales of heroes, and saw himself as the greatest of those. Such a boy would believe anything, if it was presented properly. Such a boy would tell everything he knew, without knowing he'd done that.

But if there was such a secret movement afoot in Ghezrat, it was very well hidden, for even Knoe had not heard of it, and he heard everything the men who walked through the city reported to the emperor, as well as everything his own priests overheard. There had been such an attempt early—was it in Righ, that men had tried to bide their time and finally rise up against Haffat's emissary and those men he left behind? But such men bristled with self-importance; Knoe knew the urge they had to talk—to families, to friends, to others in their former companies—it was nearly irresistable, They never seemed to understand the nature of such secrets: A secret shared is no secret at all. By the fourth day, it had been common noise about the Righ market, even the children knew of it.

This Septarin—it must be all wind, for no one else had so much as breathed a hint of conspiracy and underground. Besides, even in Righ where men were all fools, who would have trusted such a green and self-important boy with any least, single secret? *Learn what he knows,* Knoe told himself. *If he knows. And then . . .*

"I know that there are Diye Haff everywhere," Septarin said impatiently. "That was why I was sent here, instead of meeting you in that winehouse earlier. They told me you could take me to meet those who would aid me in taking back the city."

So much for that notion, then. The winehouse by the gates was frequented by Haffat's men; no one would be fool enough to start a conspiracy *there*. Someone was having fun with this fool of a young prince—or simply getting rid of him. Knoe sighed very softly. First in succession to Pelledar—the second and third, and possibly fourth were mere babes and could be found later, they were no threat. The rest could be taken as they fell into his hands, or into Haffat's. "My prince; sire. I can do what you ask. First, though, let us drink a toast—to the downfall of the Diye Haff and to the victory of our fine young prince." Septarin fumbled with the skin and held it out. "I brought wine," Knoe said. "Wait, let me loosen it, it is tangled in my baldric." He drew the stopper quietly with his left hand and with the right stealthily drew forth the little clay flask of the god's powder.

He freed the wineskin, emptied the powder into the liquid and held it to his lips, then passed it over with a flourish. Septarin stopped, swayed a little and took the skin.

"To—all that you said," he replied carefully, tipped his head back and drank deeply.

He froze. Knoe took his upraised hand and drew it down, gently freed the wineskin. Septarin's eyes were glazed, his expression vague. Knoe backed toward the sheer edge of the outer wall and glanced over; the space between wall and drop here was negligible, even narrower than most places around the city. He began to chant. "Axtekeles, the power and the strength; to the Lion this royal sacrifice; from the Lion power to his servant and glory to the emperor."

Septarin's face changed subtly. "Axtekeles." His voice was low, resonant—it shivered the stones beneath Knoe's feet, and the air that came from the boy's mouth was hot. "To my priest Knoe, well done. But beware the land, and the hills of this city, the earth and its protectress."

"And in the end?" Knoe asked softly.

"In the end—honor to Knoe and to his emperor, if that emperor is brought back to the way of the Lion. Ahhhhhh!" Septarin's voice spiraled; Knoe clapped his hand over the boy's mouth and held him; Septarin had come back to himself, however briefly, and his eyes went wide in horror as the Lion let him go. He fought wildly to free himself. But for a priest who had subdued and carried young bullocks, a mere boy was no burden at all, and his goddess had abandoned him. "But you abandoned Her first, fool of a boy." Knoe laughed wildly, caught the struggling Septarin up by shoulder and knee and raised him overhead, then threw him down into the darkness. There was no sound for a long time, and then a distant soft *thud*. A clatter of loose stones. Knoe smiled, brushed his hands down the outside of his robe, and felt around for the wine flask.

There hadn't been enough of the boy to make his heart beat rapidly.

He pictured telling Haffat, Haffat's expression of surprise, then shook his head. Let them wonder—let them *all* wonder who had done this, including Haffat. As for the men who were to have met the boy—but why worry about such—possible men? Figments of a child's wine-flown imagination; or else angry and defeated men playing with such an imagination. No such man would come here this night or any other. Knoe shoved the stopper back in his wineskin and walked briskly back toward the main gates.

21

It was very dark between the walls near the Goat Gate. Ridlo eased the hood from his lamp briefly, shook his head and covered it once more.

"Sssst! Ridlo!" One of the men he'd found to help him grab Septarin came up beside him. Any sign?"

"Prosan? No, nothing new." They had found the empty wine flask on the outer wall, a torn piece of leather tie a few steps away. But that was at eighth horn.

"You think they got him?" Prosan looked up sharply as ninth horn sounded.

"Don't think so." Ridlo sighed. "We've been out here long enough to use up our own luck. Go back below, tell Grysis we couldn't find the boy. I'll come later and apologize for not sticking close to him."

General Piritos' aide Nufia had come over to join them. "Don't be so hard on yourself. This is Septarin, after all; he might not have let you. We'll get someone up here at first light to finish the search; you get back to the wineshop and keep an ear open. If he's taken, it won't stay a secret long." He hesitated. "You don't think he knew enough to—?"

"To be dangerous? Not to us. But half the men in that wineshop heard him say he knew where the queen is."

"Our men," Prosan reminded him.

"There were Diye Haff in there, far corner, like always. But I'll wager anything you like it's already spread: someone's told his woman, someone else a friend. You know how something like that gets around."

"You could hardly stand up and warn them all to keep quiet about it," Nufia said. He patted Ridlo's shoulder and vanished into the darkness between the walls. There was a hole up there, between the walls and against the back wall of the Temple of Warriors; Nufia said he'd had to crawl a ways, but the opening was still there, still hidden, still usable. Prosan went with him.

Ridlo stared after them gloomily. *The stupid boy is dead, and it's my fault.* Stupid boy—Prince Pelledar's heir. "I should have gone with him, I could have found a way; or I should have followed him immediately. Instead, I get two men out with me and put them—all of us—in jeopardy and we still don't know what's happened."

Drunk as he had been, Septarin had most likely fallen from the wall. Ridlo made his way along a dark and deserted alley and came out on the street that would take him back to the wineshop. He would sit for another horn or two, nurse a cup of wine and listen, but he didn't really expect to hear anything.

Ninth horn: Denota's courtyard was empty except for two young priestesses refilling the oil lamps and putting fresh straw beneath the woven canopy. Down in the Cleft, Tephys walked from one newly joined couple to the next, touching the joined hands of each with a flowering branch. The Primes stood behind her, Meronne with them. There was no one else in the cavern except for the girls who tended the lamps.

Breyd stood next to Apodain, her hand clasped in his. She eyed him sidelong; he was pale, his jaw set. *Is it such an ordeal for him?* But she herself had trembled when Tephys began the short ceremony and once nearly moved to tears. *She spoke those same words over Creos and Niverren. Niv was so happy, and Creos never stopped smiling once.* But this was not at all the same thing; she could sense haste and fear, Tephys' need to perform this rite quickly and in secret and have them gone. *And Niv has always known Creos. I know nothing of this man, except that he is noble and beautiful, at least to look at—wealthy, or anyway, his mother is. He was kind to me when I first came, but I still don't know why; I can't guess what his thoughts are now.* She swallowed, clenched her free hand. And she was wedded to him.

On her other side, Jocasa and her shipmaster's son leaned against each other, her head on his breast, his cheek against her hair. *Denota, let them hold onto that happiness. Let at least some of us be truly rewarded tonight.*

She looked up as the sweet, fresh scent of flowers reached her. Apodain held out their joined hands and Tephys laid the

branch across them. The blossoms were trembling. "Find joy
in each other and pleasure, be fruitful. The goddess' love
bind you forever," the high priestess murmured, and moved
on. *Fruitful.* Breyd bit her lip; Apodain's fingers were suddenly a little damp.

Tephys was standing before them once more, branch upright before her. "Go home," she said softly. "Remember
who and what you are, and what you will be—but do not
speak of it. Denota's blessing upon each of you."

"That's . . . all?" Breyd whispered dazedly. Apodain led
her across the floor, past Tephys and Meronne who stood at
the base of the steps to bless each couple a final time as they
left. They climbed in silence. Apodain kept hold of her hand
as they crossed the courtyard and slipped into the shadows
along the wall, but she thought he had forgotten it, and her.
He seemed very distant, lost in his own thoughts. She decided to be grateful for the silence and for a moment to mar-
shal her thoughts before they went into the palace; Khadat
might be waiting for them. *To see us to his couch, or
mine—or perhaps to separate us?* Her mouth was very dry.

The courtyard was dark and empty. Apodain drew her
aside as they passed the gates, just into the stable where it
was very dark. "I wanted to tell you this. Please, just hear
me out."

"All right."

"I know Mother would be pleased if I stayed away from
you. She wanted someone noble, preferably Mirikosi—
you'll have gathered that, though."

"Yes." She eyed him warily, but couldn't make out his
face at all.

"Her reasoning isn't mine, or her prejudices. I wouldn't
avoid you because she said I must, or because you aren't—
aren't good enough. But I understand this is strange to you."
He shook his head, drew a deep breath and said, very rapidly, "If you wish to remain virgin, that is your decision; I
would never force you. Because of what you've been
through, because of your Prime, because you aren't ready—
whatever your reason."

For one stunned moment, she could only stare at him,
what she could see of him. *To have realized how I felt, and
then to find the courage to say that. . . .* She blinked aside
tears and said, "That is the kindest bride-gift you could give
me, Apodain. Thank you." She hesitated, then impulsively

added, "It isn't—it's not you, personally. It's Father, I can still sense him. Tephys said—it wouldn't matter. But if she was wrong—"

"Don't. It's all right." He laid his fingers against her face. "We should go in. These games tomorrow—you'll need sleep."

The palace was quiet, Khadat nowhere in sight. Apodain left Breyd at her doorway and went down the hall to his own apartments.

Xhem could hear Nidya rustling about in the storage, measuring the contents of the jars and muttering to herself again, as she seemed to be doing whenever he saw her the past few days. He found her bent over a jar of rice. She sat back on her haunches with a groan, panted a little, then saw him and smiled. "This cold floor is hard on an old woman's joints," she said. "How is my grandson this morning?"

"I am fine, Niddy. I have errands, though. For Captain Nabid—about the games," he added hastily as she gave him a sharp look. "And I thought I should make certain that Captain Frewis has men coming here to carry Creos. . . ." His voice trailed away. Nidya eyed him a moment longer, enough to make him nervous. *I wasn't careful enough!* His grandmother must not know what he was up to, she'd be afraid and make him stop.

But she relaxed all at once and shook her head. "I really can't blame you for wanting to be out and about, boy. I appreciate the news you bring in, we all do." She glanced behind her grandson and lowered her voice so her words barely reached Creos, who was propped up in Niverren's old chair close to the low inner wall, with pillows piled under his leg. "Thank you for listening to Creos just now. He needs someone to talk to besides Niverren, but I know he's poor company for a young boy."

"He knows interesting things," Xhem said. "And I like my cousin Creos."

"And we all like you," Nidya said warmly. "Go on, then. I don't know if Khadat will let us talk to Breyd today; she may plan on keeping her well away from her low beginnings. So you bring her to us if you can, but if not tell her that we love her and miss her. Will you do that, boy?" Xhem nodded, then turned and hurried back into the open. Creos was asleep. Xhem opened the door and looked out cautiously before he let himself into the street. Misso and her sister were down near the fountain, talking to a young woman holding an enormous baby. Misso hissed, "Hey, Boy!" at him and her eyes were avid, but he was already running as he passed her; he shook his head and picked up speed. She shouted something rude at his back.

He cut from street to side street, through narrow alleys and small shops that opened on both sides, always as quickly as he dared. There were people nearer the main gates, lots of them; Women coming from shopping or going to pick over what might be left; men in short linen pleated kilts standing close to the barracks, eyeing the Diye Haff who guarded the inner gates and the barrack gates. They were men who had been soldiers, ready for the games. They didn't look happy; Xhem didn't blame them. *To have to pretend to enjoy this, like I had to when Mother set me to watch my little sisters and told me how privileged I was to be trusted with them. She would have beaten me for getting above myself if I hadn't pretended. And Nabid says Haffat would be very angry if at least some of us didn't go.* He edged between two such groups, conscious of warm, tense muscles, scented body oils—the smell of garlic as one group of relay runners shared a fat bulb. *They say the best runners eat garlic every day.* But his brother Tar had said Breyd was the best in all Ghezrat, and he never saw her eat it, or smelled it on her.

He avoided a few armored and armed Diye Haff at the upper end of the square near the gates and pelted off a side street. Two of them were eating oranges. Niv would be furious if she could see the size and color of those oranges. He had to step aside for several carts heading toward the square, then sped up again, haring in and out of foot traffic all the way to the market. He slipped into a narrow alleyway, leaned against a cool, shaded wall to catch his breath, then looked around cautiously. The small sandal stall of Inhada— who was husband to Nabid's sister and so someone they could trust—was just a little farther on. He had to be very careful from now on.

It was hard to see where he was going, with so many people in the market: He finally darted between Inhada's stall and that of the blind old woman who sold dyes. Inhada was arguing price with an old man; he let one hand down out of sight and wiggled his fingers briefly as Xhem dropped to his

knees and eased under the aged boards. He felt along the
ground, located the opening at the base of the high stone
curb, forced himself into it feet-first, and squirmed down until he hung at arm's length.

It was barely a drop at all; even Breyd might have been
able to stand on tiptoe and touch the opening ordinarily
screened by well-fitted stones. Now that Inhada's stall was
blocking it, the heavy stones had been set aside. Xhem
rubbed his ribs where he'd scraped them and leaned against
the wall to catch his breath again. Breyd might have been
able to reach that opening, but she would never have fit
through it. He couldn't reach it from down here, but fortunately he wouldn't have to. There was another way out.
Many of them.

It was cool down here, dark except where light came
through small holes in the paving or other openings—farther
along, it shone through gaps in the cliff. Some of the others
said there were caves out beyond the walls, and more in
here, too—caves and passages and narrow tunnels that connected the whole city from beneath.

Ordinarily, he would have been wild to explore, but just
now, he had many more important things to do. To remember things he'd seen out there, to recall the messages he had
to pass on, word for word, just as they'd been given to him.
And Nabid would worry if he was late.

He had reached the damp places: There were openings to
his right, where the city cisterns had been built. Tar had told
him about those, how they were carved out of stone during
another war, ages ago, because the city had suffered so many
sieges.

Ten long steps past the last opening, another five short
ones; it was nearly dark here, and the tunnel was no longer
smooth stone but crumbling dirt and small rocks, deep rubble to catch in his sandals if he wasn't careful, and send him
sprawling. Fourteen steps; there was a little dusty sunlight
here to show the branch to his left; it had been cut by men
through the smooth green stone that made up so much of the
city. A little beyond that, he came into the low-vaulted cavern where the cisterns were, beneath the barracks. His nose
wrinkled; the smell of the sulfury water was very strong and
he wondered how Grysis and those other men could live
down here. *It would be worse than my cousin's hut beyond
the ridges, the old one who sleeps with his goats in winter.*

He edged around the pool of steaming water; it had intrigued him, but Nabid warned him boys were not permitted here. Some special place for certain fighting men who served Atos and Atelos, he hadn't understood it, but then, Nabid hadn't said much, either. Lights were kept burning all around the water's edge and Xhem could see daggers—hundreds of them—wedged into the ragged stone wall behind the pool. He averted his eyes. Perhaps it was not good for a mere boy to look at it too closely.

This place could be reached from somewhere in the hospital barracks and from a place between the walls near the messes. Xhem knew only that much; those entries were out of reach for now, anyway, since the enemy had taken over the barracks..

A single oil lamp smoked fitfully beyond the steaming pool, just barely showing him the path between fallen stone and mud spills, and then he was hurrying across a flat, smooth stone floor. Torches fluttered, there was always wind coming down from the city. The light was strong here, though: He could see from one side of the long, low cave to the other. Benches lined one side, some piled with folded blankets and cloaks; cots and pallets were stacked near an opening and a faded curtain that had once been a rich hanging had been draped across a cleft in the stone. General Piritos was in there. Xhem had carried a message back to Ridlo the day before that he was sleeping most of the time, that his shoulder was being tended, that he still had a good chance.

Nabid and Grysis sat under a torch across from the general's chamber; nearby three other men were honing swords. Beyond them, visible only now and again as the torches flared, were piles of spears and shields. Grysis had a flat box of wet sand in front of him and was drawing lines in it with a long, narrow stick as Xhem came up; Nabid pointed at one of the lines and shook his head.

"Good lad," Nabid said softly. "What word?"

Xhem drew a deep breath, closed his eyes and began to enumerate, turning down his fingers one at a time as he spoke. "From Ridlo: Prince Septarin was found upon the rocks, dead, just before second horn. I suspect magic in his death, and will talk to you at the games or below the barracks tonight. From Frewis: Seven of our men were seen drinking with the Diye Haff last night. They are older infantry, none we would trust anyway. Names and companies—I have that list here, captain." Xhem drew a small piece of hide from his belt and passed it over. "Also from Frewis: We will not speak other than casually at the games, I think someone followed me from the wineshop last night. From Potro of the royal chariot: Haffat has set a quota for rice and other grains to go with his men to Ye Eygar. The council argued with him last night as much as we dared that we have none to spare, but Haffat only smiles, and listens—and then reminds us his ballistas have not moved and the Ergardi are still in his camp. We have no leverage against him. From Potro again: We must convince as many of the people to attend Haffat's games as we can. The emperor becomes angry when anyone even suggests that the people might still fear his men. But Khadat says her son and his new wife will join the games. The emperor is pleased at that and says this is a true test for all of us, whether we are friends or not. Khadat meets Haffat's eyes very directly and smiles at him, we must watch the woman." Xhem thought for a moment, finally nodded. "That is all, sir."

"Good work. What from the streets?"

He had to think again, to remember such things as he had heard, out there. "Our people worry that the Diye Haff will take all the food; already there is not much and the best is taken away. I heard one enemy bragging to his friend that he would easily win the tossing events today, but the other didn't want to shed his armor in such a crowd. Another grumbled about the heat and the dirt, many of them do that, and complain how the market smells strange, and how everything is oily. They do not like our food, except for things like oranges and dates. Near the barracks, I heard a guard telling another guard how his son had just begun to walk when they left Diyet. They both sounded angry and they looked very unhappy, sir.

"Most of the gossip this last time I came through the market was about Prince Septarin. I heard many women and some men say the Diye Haff have killed him, that they will kill the prince and all his family so the emperor can put his son on the throne; they talk very quietly and speak of other things when the Diye Haff are anywhere near. The Diye Haff did not speak of it where I could hear them."

Nabid pondered this; Grysis shoved his tray aside and said, "Good job. Keep your ears open at the games, and when you find your cousin Breyd, tell her to watch for me at the far end of the courses, near the sea. I will find her, or if I can't for some reason, expect Nabid. Remember the signal?" Xhem nodded and rubbed the bridge of his nose with his finger. Nabid clapped him on the back.

"Here, you're too thin by half, boy; I've got an extra round of bread that won't keep."

"Thank you, sir." He ate quickly; the captains went back to work on their map, but as he was getting up to leave, Grysis pushed it aside.

"Carry a message to Ryllos, Xhem: We need a royal who knows the passages beneath the palace. And tell Ridlo we need more men down here to shift stone." Xhem nodded and hurried off.

At third horn, the city gates opened and people began to pour through them: many of Haffat's men, followed by Diye Haff in loincloths or woolen short tunics, Ghezrathi in short white linen tunics or pleats—the actual participants. Other Ghezrathi followed, some in bright clothing, carrying flowers or grain sheaves, the kindred of the participants. A crowd after them, but not as many people as had come to watch in previous years. A chariot for a gray-faced Prince Pelledar; the emperor, his son and his personal guard rode beside it. A few of the Diye Haff who had been living inside the barracks came next, followed by wagons and carts, and some of the common chariot to carry anyone who needed to ride down to the plain: the very young, the old or infirm. Creos sat in one of the carts, flanked by two of his friends. Xhem, who walked alongside, thought he had not seen Creos so happy in a very long time. Niverren sat in the cart behind, where she could keep an eye on him without appearing to fuss. Nevvia, a scarf draped across her hair, was between her daughter and her mother.

"I didn't see her," she whispered; she was craning her neck in an attempt to see farther down the road. Nidya held onto her arm so she wouldn't fall as the cart jolted down the road.

"She is all the way forward. We'll see her."

"I know," Nevvia whispered. She swallowed. "The stones are all black out there; they were never like that before. I—is this where—when they were out here and Menlaeus—"

"Shhhh," Nidya said softly against her ear. "It could be. But don't, you'll upset yourself for no good reason, and

Breyd will worry about you. She can't afford to worry right now, so you have to be strong for her."

Nevvia blotted her eyes with trembling fingers. "I'm trying, honestly."

"I know you are." But as Nevvia edged forward on her seat to see if she could find Breyd, Nidya looked at the rock beside the road. After a moment, she closed her eyes and turned away. When she looked the other way, toward the city, she could see the end of the procession—those of some rank or standing like Khadat, who were carried in enclosed chairs.

The land on both sides of the road from the city to the sea had been set aside for games for at least two hundred years; no crops were grown or beasts permitted. The grass and flowers which were ordinarily thick here by midsummer had been badly damaged by the fighting, and great ruts cut through the ground where the ballista had been dragged, but the broken weapons, shields, and other litter of battle had been cleared away, and there was grass still for people to sit on. Courses had been newly marked out for the foot races, others for throwing contests and wrestling. The Diye Haff had their own additional competitions: a long course that crossed the Oryon and went down to the sea for horse races, and for another race where two men alternately rode a horse and ran against other such teams.

A woman across from Niverren set her lips in a tight line as their cart passed the start of that course; the Diye Haff were getting ready, stretching and rubbing down their own legs and the horses'. There were no Ghezrathi competing against them. "This isn't a day for horses!" the woman muttered. "They should know better. Games are for people, to honor Denota!"

Niverren caught her eye and minutely shook her head. "Don't," she said quietly. "Don't show such open anger toward them. My sister already warned me, it isn't safe."

Several Diye Haff were hard at work setting up the platform for Prince Pelledar and the emperor, some bringing chairs and cushions, setting small tables between them, while others raised an awning to shelter them from the sun. As Xhem ran alongside the cart where Creos rode, he heard someone spit loudly, and another said, "They think *this* is all it takes? Give us games, and we'll forget about our dead?" Someone else shushed him urgently.

Grysis walked slowly from one part of the field to another, now and again he brought up a bland smile as he saw someone he knew, but so far as he could tell, no one else was paying any attention to him. A woman's angry voice stopped him. "My son is wrestling today." He paused to look around, as if he'd lost someone. A short woman with a deeply lined face was talking to another who carried wheat stalks. "Or I wouldn't *ever* have come." Two Diye Haff stripped to loincloths came striding across and knelt next to the circle. The women eyed them, wrinkled their noses, and walked away.

Grysis bit back a sigh and walked on. The two men were to all appearances intent on the coming matches and hadn't noticed the snub.

Well, men who had fought as long as these knew the people they'd fought wouldn't change overnight; they wouldn't expect immediate friendship. He wondered whether Haffat was as sensible: Whether he was sincere when he offered games as a rite to join them all, or simply made a gesture and hoped for a good surface, whatever seethed underneath. *Someone who could get close to Haffat and learn what he thinks, what he says, what he means by it—* Yes, he thought sourly, all we need do is subvert Khadat from Khadat's side to ours, and persuade her to seduce Haffat. Because I will swear she is more like him than she is like any of us!

"Look at that," an older man growled to two companions, as they walked by one of the carts Haffat had provided for the games, to give free Mirikosi wine and sweet, honeyed loaves to any who wanted it. "They've brought us free wine and loaves. D'you feel as grateful as I do?"

"Makes you want to go find that general of his—Jemaro?" his companion replied sarcastically, "and tell him you're ready to join up."

Breyd smoothed down the lightweight linen undertunic and tried to calm the nerves that plagued her every time before a first race. The blood was pounding in her temples; her stomach ached and it was still early enough that none of the other women had come to look over the course and ready themselves. *Deep breath; another. Remember this goes away after you run once. Remember you promised Grysis you would do well; you can't do well if you pay attention to anything else. Deep breath.*

But it was impossible to ignore the Diye Haff. They were everywhere—men standing all around, laughing a distance away, walking back and forth and setting wagers on the women's races.

I will hear those voices in my nightmares, years from now. I thought it would get easier. It still hasn't. How dare Haffat do this to us? One of these men killed my brother, and he's probably walking around—probably out here! Does he really think I can set that aside? She bent over to stretch out her back. *I never hated anyone before Haffat, or as much as I hate Haffat. For what he did to all of us—but mostly for this.* She could see him, if she straightened up and turned around. He was on a low platform with his cousins and brothers and that son around him, Prince Pelledar at his right elbow. The prince sat in the same fine, high-backed and deeply carven chair he'd always had brought down to the games; Haffat and his men sat on plain chairs, with his son Hadda at his side and the lion-priest just behind him. *He must think we are all truly stupid, to look at that and believe our prince rules Ghezrat and accepts him and his as friends!*

Three men crossed behind her, slowed, and looked at her thoughtfully. She bit her lip and stretched her shoulders back and forth to loosen them. *Ignore them; don't let them see anything.* They walked on a moment later, and one of them laughed jarringly. "Too small and brown," he jeered. "Don't they make real women this far south?"

"Hah," his companion said. "Woman that size in a footrace? Don't waste your coppers."

Fury possessed her. *I wasn't too small when I killed your kind!* She spun around. No Diye Haff there; they'd already vanished into the crowd. The few people nearby weren't paying any attention to her; too busy gossiping or arguing. "Too small," she hissed. "You filthy, laughing—" She couldn't get any more words out. She turned on her heel and strode down the course toward the sea. *They'll pay for this; pay for all of it. And you, you loud, vulgar beast with a pocket full of copper—you'll swallow those words before the day is over!*

Apodain had come down from the city at Breyd's side, among the other athletes, but he'd left her almost immediately. She was tense and withdrawn. But he ran also; he could tell what she felt by the way she rubbed her muscles, the way she continuously stretched one thing or another. Knew what it was like before that first race of a games, she wouldn't welcome company any more than he did. He was to wrestle first; he would be much more relaxed by the time his first race came.

They were nearly ready to begin; Prince Pelledar's steward was speaking to him, pointing out things. The prince looked ghastly. *To lose a son, though—even one like Septarin. But Pelledar truly was fond of the boy.*

Haffat was relaxed, even smiling as he looked over the crowds—a man taking pleasure in his most recent acquisition. *It is not his. We are not his, and never will be! To send his army against us, to kill and maim so many of ours and pretend it never happened? To hold games for his own men would have been bad enough. To make such a mock of our own games is unspeakable.* As unspeakable as kill a boy and sit next to his father, and pretend he had no part in it. Apodain's hands clenched into hard fists. *He thinks to win again today. By everything holy, he will not!*

Horns sounded; Pelledar got to his feet and stood at the front of the platform. The prince held up his hands, people began to kneel or bow, until only Diye Haff stood; Apodain saw Haffat come partway to his feet and gesture sharply with the flat of his hand; his men knelt, and a few prostrated themselves on the grass. The prince looked out across the games field.

"My people, my Ghezrathi. I make you a gift of these games, which have been given to me—to all of us—by the Emperor Haffat. Let us thank him by a fair showing in all the events, and with pleasantness on the part of each of us to all of his men, when we meet them or compete against them." A rumble of response; under cover of that, someone behind Apodain muttered, "A pleasant dagger in the gut—" Someone else shushed him hurriedly.

"As a token of his vow not to interfere with our lives," Pelledar swallowed and went doggedly on. "As a token of that vow, the emperor has asked us to order the games we always have. We have done this; there will be wreaths for the victors at day's end. For now—those who participate, I wish you well; those who watch, I wish you pleasure. To you all, these games." He resumed his throne. Those nearby broke into nervous, wary applause that spread across the field. Frewis came forward then.

"Those of you who have participated in the past will know where to go and when; anyone who does not know, those Diye Haff who compete against—compete with us, come to the first footracing course beside the road, there." He pointed. "Someone will be there to tell you." He jumped down into the crowd; people immediately began to scatter, and next to the road, several skinny young boys lined up for the first race.

Khadat's servants had put her chair where she would be visible—not that she cared what the city people thought of her presence, or Apodain's. "All the same, they will see that some of us are wise enough to put a good face on this event, and go on from here." She eyed the platform thoughtfully. From this vantage, she had a clear view of everyone, and she was near enough to make out their faces.

Pelledar looked dreadful. *I could have warned him it would lead to no good, indulging that wretched boy.* Septarin dead would foment distrust, she had already heard a handful of wild rumors about what the boy was doing outside the palace and on that wall—drunk, some said—at such an hour. *Snooping, prying, getting above himself and putting all of us in jeopardy.*

Some of them said Haffat had done it himself, luring the prince out there and killing him. *They are fools; he has not won an empire the size of Diyet by acting so stupidly.*

She turned her attention to Haffat and gazed at him thoughtfully for some time. He was not as attractive as Perlot, but Perlot had been weak, something of a disappointment. Certainly not what she had expected in the brother of a king. Haffat was powerful, confident enough of that power he did not punish his enemies. *He gives them games and comes to watch them, and acts as though things are right and good so they will begin to accept him. He's a subtle man, and a clever one.* But most of all, powerful. Even so, he was far from the base of his power and money, they said his supply lines were stretched very thin. *I have ships, and wealth. And I am still a handsome woman.* She leaned forward a little and smiled as his eyes moved across the crowd.

Apodain turned away from the platform and went in search of his first match. To his surprise, he found Breyd there. "I didn't expect you. You don't have to watch me, you know."

"I know that," she said. Her color was high, he realized, her voice flat with anger. She looked up at him and managed a smile that turned her lips but didn't reach black eyes. "I was drawing attention over there. But I thought. . . ."

He stepped close to her, laid a hand on her arm. "You're all right?"

"I'm so angry right now, I could spit!"

"I know," he said quietly. She looked up at him, startled. "I understand. All of this, all these men. We can't let them walk over us out here, Breyd. Use that anger, channel it. Show them they didn't take the spirit out of us. That they can't."

Grysis will have my ears for this. But she'd taken fire from his words; she gripped his arms, hard. "You're right. We'll show them!"

He shifted his hands to her shoulders and impulsively asked, "The last race of the afternoon, the two-relay for men and women. Will you run that with me?"

"I never have, but I will." She smiled suddenly; it warmed her eyes and caught at his breath. *How lovely,* he thought. It wasn't just her face, it was the feel of muscle in her shoulders, the curve of her arms. Just now she wore only a thin, plain tunic and sandals, her hair was bound loose at one shoulder—no hint of cosmetic, no fragrant oils.

He was staring; he let go of her and managed a smile. "I never have run it either." His eyes went beyond her. "Here comes Grysis. I think he is looking for you."

Grysis was looking for her; he was smiling broadly as he came up and set a father's kiss upon her brow. "How fine you look together," he said cheerfully, and leaned across her to clasp hands with Apodain. "And I've just put a wager on you, Apodain; don't let me down."

"I'll try not to, sir."

"Ahh, none of that sir stuff. All plain folks these days, aren't we? But particularly today. Here, girl, word in your ear about this young man of yours." Breyd obediently leaned close to him. Grysis whispered, "Your family is partway down, on your left. Find a way to go down to the end of the course after, I have messages for you."

"Yes," she whispered; as he straightened, she added aloud, "I hope you plan to watch the women run."

"Have to, I know half of 'em." Breyd blinked at him. "But I've put my money on you again, of course."

"Of course," she echoed blankly. Grysis slipped around them and into the crowd.

Apodain's first match was against a tall, skinny Diye Haff who was cheered on by a crowd of his fellows, but not for long; Apodain pinned him immediately.

Breyd joined the cheer for him, then left him to collect the clay token for his next match and walked as quickly as the crowd would let her, down to the start of the main race course. Seven other young women stood at the starting flags or walked back and forth nervously. Breyd removed her sandals, stretched her arms and neck, and eyed the course with misgivings: The larger rocks had been pulled to the sides to mark the course, but there were little bits of sharp, newly cracked stone everywhere and ruts from chariot wheels. Those who didn't plan two steps in advance, or those who couldn't see where they were going would have bleeding feet. Stay out front, she thought.

She turned to look over her competition. *No wonder Grysis said he knew half of us!* Aroepe and Jocasa had put themselves next to her; two of the other Secchi were at the far end of the line. And between them, Denira looked up and gave her a nervous grin, then turned her attention back to the course.

Why is Denira out here? Breyd looked up as Apodain moved to the front of the crowd where she could see him, then bent down to massage her calves one last time. Denira had always run, of course; she and Breyd were close competitors. But she was the heir to the high priestess now, and Tephys had never let any of her priestesses participate in the games; she never came down to bless them.

She and Denira finished almost together; Jocasa was right behind them, but Aroepe had pulled up early and the others had not made good time. "Hah!" Denira's eyes were gleaming and her breast heaved; she wrapped her arms around Breyd, who hugged her back fiercely. "You forget—how wonderful—that feels. Breyd, your arms, I can't breathe!"

"Sorry."

"It's—all right. I have to find Mother, I don't get to see

her enough, but I'll see you in the next level, at the *start* of
the race."

"Only because you'll never catch me once we start,"
Breyd retorted. Denira laughed, brushed damp hair from her
eyes, and went. Breyd gazed after her and felt the race-high
drain from her. *I almost forgot—but that was Denira and the
racing, I forgot how it boils the blood. Denira isn't safe out
here! Tephys shouldn't have let her outside the walls, where
that lion-priest could—* She couldn't complete the thought.

"Well done." Grysis spoke from behind her and she
jumped. "Here, I found a boy with water for you." Xhem
handed her an enormous, dripping sponge. She ran it over
her face, pressed it against the back of her neck, and sighed
happily. By the time she was done, he had a cup of water for
her.

Grysis drank in turn, leaned across her to hand the cup
back to Xhem, and said very softly, "I have a gift for you;
for your wedding."

"Grysis, I don't need a gift—not from you!"

"Wait, hear all of it, then decide. I spoke very late last
night with one of the men who disappeared when your father
did. He's alive." Her lips moved, but no sound came; he
tightened his grip on her wrist and whispered urgently,
"Here, bend down, inspect one of your feet as though you'd
hurt it, until you can control your face!" He knelt beside her,
peered closely at her toes and kept talking. "They are still
outside the city, we talked through a hole way down past the
barracks area. Your father's leg was broken, but he's much
better now. I don't know much else except that they somehow wound up farther down the cliff and well around it
above the Oryon. You know what that's like over there,
sheer in most places and a nasty climb over solid rock in full
sight of the enemy camp. So they got sensible, and stayed
put; they found a cave for shelter, there's plenty of water on
that side, of course, and they snared birds and the like. Your
father says he's thin, and he says his leg's still a problem,
but he's alive."

She stared blindly toward her foot, at nothing. "When—
when will he—"

Grysis shook his head. "Not sure. They're stuck right
now; can't go back the way they came because there was a
rock slide, haven't yet found a way under the city. There are
men below the barracks right now, working to expand that

hole or find another way in for them. They've got food, though. We shoved small bags of bread and dry fruit through with a spear. Menlaeus sends you his love." She sat very still for what seemed a lifetime, and tried to think.

"Mother—"

"Xhem will tell your grandmother tonight so she can break the news to your mother. He sent her a message also."

She blinked furiously, blotted her eyes on the sponge Xhem handed her. "Tar—does he know?"

Xhem turned away; Grysis said gruffly, "He asked how his son was. I had to tell him. But he'd already suspected— the horn signals; he said he could hear them out there, but it was never Tarpaen." He looked at her searchingly, then shook her arm. "Here, did I do wrong after all?"

"No. It's just— I *knew* it, but it's been so long, I began to doubt myself. I should have known him better." She bit her lip, blinked rapidly. "Give him a message for me, if you can. My love; and tell him I'm waiting, so we can fight again. But this time we'll win."

"I'll tell him; remember where you are, who you are."

"I am Apodain's wife, at Haffat's games. I won't forget."

"No." He gripped her arm again then let it go as he got to his feet. "I know you won't." He left, taking Xhem with him. Breyd looked back up the long course, at the sky. Time to get back to the start; she would have to run again soon and Apodain should have his first race before much longer.

She passed Creos and some of the other men of his company not far back toward the start of the course: The woven branch side of the wagon had been taken off and propped against the wheels. Several men leaned against it, enjoying its shade, but Creos was on the side, his leg dangling, laughing with two of his friends. There was no sign of Niverren. She waved at him and when he beckoned, shouted, "You're busy, anyone can see that! And I have another race, I'll come after that!" Nearer the start but not as close to the platform as Khadat, she finally found her family: Niddy and Ina seated in the shade of another of the wagons, Niverren breaking up a loaf for them; Nevvia was seated on a small blanket on the grass.

"Mother." Breyd knelt to kiss her. Nevvia held onto her fingers.

"You shouldn't run so fast in this heat, you'll hurt yourself."

I fought in worse heat, she thought, but carefully did not say. She managed a smile and shook her head. "You always say that, Mother, but I do it every year anyway."

"You were very fast," Niverren allowed. "Here, can you eat? This is theirs, but it seems only fair we eat their free bread, as much as everything else costs now. Wasn't that Denira? I thought she'd been chosen for the goddess, to succeed Tephys. Her mother hasn't stopped bragging about it since Tephys barged into her house and took the girl away."

"I think Tephys sent her, to show up everyone else."

"You mean—*them?* Or you?"

"The women don't run against the men in Ghezrat, you know that, Niv. But Denira isn't fast enough to beat me," Breyd replied. "Niddy, you look comfortable, how are you doing?"

"Well as ever, child; where is your Apodain?"

"He isn't—well, yes." She blinked rapidly. "I suppose in a sense he *is* my Apodain."

"I should hope so," Nidya said firmly.

Nevvia was watching her face anxiously. "You don't look very— Breyd are you all right in that house?"

"I'm fine, Mother. His mother isn't a nice woman, but she hasn't eaten me yet."

"Oh—*you.*" Nevvia laughed weakly. "You and your terrible jokes."

Breyd patted her hands. "Someone has to make them. I'll come by after the next race, if there is time. I'll bring him to meet you. Apodain and I are doing the two-relay also, but that will be much later."

Nidya indicated the wagon and settled her shoulders against the woven branches. "We are going nowhere until you are done for the day, and until that cart goes," she said. "How pleasant it is out here, and how odd that it should be. But it is strange for those of us who saw none of the fighting. Do you know, when we left the city this morning, I saw the Diye Haff tents for the first time?"

"Mother, let's not talk about that," Nevvia said quickly. "Breyd won't want to."

"No, it's all right, Mother," Breyd said quietly. "I don't mind. But don't upset yourself thinking about them, and I won't either. Not for this one afternoon." She leaned over to kiss her grandmother, old Ina, and her sister, then hugged her mother. "Next time up, if I have a moment, I'll stop again."

Her father alive. *I wish I could be there, when Niddy tells Mother,* she thought wistfully. She worked her way through the crowd.

She passed Khadat at a distance. The woman lay well back in the shaded chair, eating dates, Breyd thought. Her eyes were fixed, but when Breyd turned she didn't see Apodain as she'd half expected. *What is Khadat looking at on that platform?* she wondered. The prince, who sat very still and tried to contain his grief? All the men around the emperor, or perhaps the emperor himself? She froze briefly. That priest; that hairless, dreadful horror of a man with his black, quick eyes stood between the prince and Haffat. For one awful moment his eyes touched on hers, but they moved on at once. She looked away quickly, and melted back into the crowd.

Snatches of conversation as she passed some of the city people, a few of Haffat's men standing close together and grumbling. *Who cares how foreign you think this place—and us?* she thought sourly. *Go home, then, every last man of you!* Men she'd seen in the barracks who eyed the Diye Haff sidelong. A few of those awful old men who'd been fighters for all their long, long lives—they glared openly at the Diye Haff; but they'd glared at her, too.

Stay away from them. Grysis warned you, you can't trust them, they see things as they always were, as they should be, and nothing else is good enough for them.

She made her way to the beginning of the course, where some more young boys were gathering for the next race. A familiar face came between them and her; she had to think hard to realize who it was, though: Lochria's prechosen, the merchant. He looked nearly as gray and wan as Pelledar himself. *He really does care for her. And she's been gone as long as Father.* "You are Breyd, aren't you?" he asked doubtfully.

"Yes. I—" she couldn't say she was sorry; she would hate it if he or anyone else said that for Menlaeus. He looked down at her.

"You would know, I think," he said. "They said you knew—a little about her."

"I knew what most of the company knew," Breyd said gently. "Here, we can't stand here talking like this, people will stare and my legs will stiffen, let's walk a little." A clear place well away from anyone, she thought. Particularly from the Diye Haff. "What have they told you?"

"Nothing," he said dully. "They told me she and her father disappeared, nothing else. But I . . . couldn't ask."

It appalled her. He was heartstricken, and no one had done anything for him, talked to him—anything. *As if I had asked about Tar, and no one had said.* She looked around cautiously; no one. She lowered her voice anyway. "I was out there, with them; there was an ambush, both sides of the road, we were fighting and then the ballista threw stones at us."

"There was fire, thrown from below, I knew about that."

"She and her Prime were taken by the Diye Haff. They were still alive, a few days ago, the general's spies could tell us that, but not much else." He looked at her blankly and she stared back, aghast. "*Surely* someone had told you she was alive still?"

"I think they said—they thought she and her father were captured. But no one has—if they weren't returned to us by now, then—?"

"They were still alive and being held by the lion-priests." He paled; she gripped his arm. "I'm sorry, there isn't an easy way to tell you these things, and it isn't safe out here to talk about them; *they'll* see, and they'll wonder what we're up to. Wait, walk a little more with me, let me think."

He was a son of one of the wealthy merchant families, Lochria had said. Just now she couldn't remember which family. His family didn't matter so much, though: Anyone could see he was suffering. *Grysis told me to trust my judgement, bring in men who could help us. This one has an ear to a class I do not—either by Father, or by Apodain.* She thought a moment longer, tried to find a reason to keep quiet. There wasn't any. "Here. Are you listening?"

"I am listening, Breyd," he said obediently.

"Good. Say nothing to anyone else, do nothing. Walk down toward the sea, where the races end, and wait there. Someone will come to talk with you; he will say two things, my name and hers. By that, you will know I have sent him. Will you do that?" He nodded; she let go his arm and he walked away without saying anything else. *Dear goddess, what have I done?* But it *was* done, beyond recall.

She had to run again soon; Apodain was supposed to be

at the javelin competition. *I wonder they trust us with such things.* But Haffat was doing a thorough job of it.

There was a good-sized crowd over here, as many Ghezrathi as Diye Haff. She worked her way toward the front; stopped as a voice somewhere to her right growled Apodain's name. "Yah," another said. It was an older man's voice. "What's he doing out here, away from his mother? Think he'd be ashamed to show his face!" She turned; she couldn't see who was talking, one of the royal chariot was between her and whoever it was. *How dare they?*

Before she could say or do anything, the noble said very clearly, "You two, hold your tongues. Apodain was a member of *my* company and a braver man than *you* know. Ask any of the drivers, if you don't believe me. But don't dare talk about him like that, we won't put up with it." He turned and walked away. Breyd stood very still and waited. After a moment, the two men turned to gaze after him; they were heavy infantry, older than her father, more of the type Grysis warned her about.

"Think he meant that?"

"Who knows? They'd all stick up for each other. Still. . . ." They walked off. Breyd scowled at their backs and turned back to find a way to the front. A loud cheer went up. By the time she emerged from the crowd, Apodain was holding his javelins above his head; his face was flushed and he was smiling. The match was over and the applause had been for him.

22

Sixth horn: The afternoon air was thick and the wind died. The crowd thinned as people sought shade; two wagons carried the very old and a few mothers with small babies back to the city. Breyd ran her last race against four other women, but only she and Denira finished and Denira was staggering as she crossed the line.

She was surrounded; people grabbing her hands, cheering, patting her back. Grysis pushed his way through the crowd and shouted, "Back up, let the girl get some water!" Breyd found Denira, threw an arm around her waist and brought her with them.

"How do you bear the heat?" Denira panted.

"You do what you have to," Breyd gasped. "But you know it's never bothered me."

Denira laughed and shook her head. "I know. I'd have beaten you—if the wind hadn't gone." She drew a deep breath, expelled it in a rush. "Ah, goddess, but it is hot out here!"

"There was a boy here, with water."

"I saw him earlier—the one who lives with your grandmother, isn't he?" Breyd nodded. The crowd was breaking up rapidly. Denira glanced cautiously around, then lowered her voice. "Tephys sends you a message, Captain: Prince Septarin was murdered by the lion-priest."

"How certain?" he asked.

"We were brought to the palace to pray for him; I saw only a horribly broken body, but she told me after that she saw the mark of Knoe's power on the boy's lips. She said tell you, and tell you also that our time is not as distant as you may think. She has seen this, and Knoe has hastened it by what he did. She said, tell you and the general that Knoe is spending a lot of time under the palace."

"If he finds a way into the caverns," Grysis began, but Denira shook her head.

"She said to tell you the goddess' walls are very strong, around the palace and around the temple. Knoe is not powerful enough to break through them, and down there, he and his god are both weakened. But she says he has not tampered with the walls; she does not think he is properly aware of them." Grysis still looked worried, though, and a moment later he left them.

Xhem came running up with a two-handled cup. Breyd drank and passed it to Denira. Xhem wrapped his arms around Breyd and hugged her hard. "You won! I knew you would win!"

Denira finished the water; Xhem took the cup back and ran to refill it. "Oh, Breyd," Denira said wistfully. "This— right now, that race—us—it was just like before, like last year, wasn't it?"

She could see one of the horse races finishing by the Oryon; the Diye Haff out there watching it. Two of them walked by and looked the two women over curiously. *Dare to look at me, you*— It wasn't the same; it couldn't ever be like that again. But poor Denira looked so miserable, all at once. And for the brief span of the race, there *had* been nothing but the race itself. "It really was," she said gently. "I'm glad we had that race."

"Before anyone comes, Tephys said tell you, she has reminded Khadat you were a priestess; Khadat will not suspect anything if you go to the temple daily."

"Thank her for me. Tell her I'll come soon."

"She needs you, Breyd—as a go-between for her and the general. Boys like that one of yours don't come to the temple ordinarily, it might look suspicious if they began to. And the palace overlooks the courtyard. But she can't go under the city or send anyone, either, because we don't dare let down Denota's walls."

"All right. Tell her I'll come tomorrow."

"I will; I'll have to go, she needs me back there. She really only let me come so I could tell them about Septarin. And to find out anything I could." Breyd hugged her hard.

"We'll come out of this," she whispered fiercely. "We'll beat them."

"I know we will," Denira said and her face was suddenly very calm. "Denota promised us."

Denira drank a little of the fresh water Xhem brought, then left them. Breyd finished it and knelt beside him. "How is Creos managing?"

"Niverren is with him; he's asleep with his head in her lap."

"Good. Mother's still here?" He nodded. She thought for a moment. "One final race of older men, the last for the girls, and then the paired relay. I have time."

Ina slept with her head on Nidya's shoulder. Nevvia was peering toward the sea, clearly waiting for her. Breyd dropped down, kissed her cheek, let her mother blot her forehead. "You look exhausted," Nevvia said.

Breyd smiled. "I should; I won." Nevvia smiled and patted her face.

"Well, of course you won! But are you really going to run again? In all this heat?"

"I promised Apodain we would. But I'd like to." *The two of us taking the wreaths, instead of Haffat's men getting either of them.* She wanted that badly, and winning this last race would make it certain.

"Well, if you're sure you can—oh," Nevvia said suddenly, and her eyes went wide. Breyd turned to see Apodain coming toward them.

"They said you were here." He knelt beside her and smiled at Nevvia. "You must be Breyd's mother; you're very much alike."

Nevvia's cheeks were pink. "And you're Apodain, of course." Breyd watched him while he talked to her, to Nidya. *He doesn't act at all like Khadat would.* The way Khadat behaved, she might have no family at all. He was kind, not overly familiar or condescending; Nevvia was visibly charmed by him. "You're really running again this afternoon?" Nevvia asked finally. "I'm worn out simply watching you."

"I think it's harder sitting out here in the heat than moving around in it. Breyd? We'd better go."

As they walked off, she said very softly, "Thank you, Apodain. That was kind of you."

"I like your mother."

"I'm glad." She glanced toward the platform. Prince Pelledar was sitting in shade, eyes gazing out toward the distant ridge beyond the Oryon. Haffat sat next to him, smiling and talking about something; Pelledar nodded his head but didn't seem to be paying much attention and Haffat didn't seem to care. *He only cares that we see him there, on a level with our prince.* "He only cares for the appearance," she said softly, but when Apodain turned back to ask what she had said, she merely shrugged and motioned him on.

Frewis and two of his men, and three of the Diye Haff were in charge of the last races; she took the ceremonial dagger from one of them and looked at it thoughtfully. The blade shone like a mirror but the edges were dulled; the handle was inlaid with shell. Apodain took it from her and led her a little away from the others. "You run out and back, and pass this to me. There will be a barrier across the course halfway down. Have you done this before, do I tell you what you already know?" She shook her head. Her skin was beginning to tingle and the knot was back in her stomach. "Hold the knife by the cross-grip when you run, so you won't drop it; when you get—there," he pointed down the course about four long strides worth, "transfer it to your other hand and hold it by the blade, as far out as you can. All right?" She nodded. "Ready?"

"I'm ready," she whispered; he smiled and gripped her arms; his eyes were as bright as hers.

"Yes, I can see it. There isn't anyone here who can beat us today."

She could hear shouting down the course, coming nearer, then all around them as four men hurtled across the finish. Loud argument broke out immediately: the Diye Haff judges converged on Frewis, while the other two judges tried to separate three of the men who were rolling on the ground, clutching and clawing at each other. Apodain drew Breyd back onto the road.

A woman behind her snorted. "I knew this would happen. They're no better than animals." The woman she spoke to murmured, "I think—maybe we should go, now. Before—I think we should go."

The fight ended abruptly; the Diye Haff runners stalked off and were surrounded by other Diye Haff. The Ghezrathi glared after them, then turned as one man and went the other direction. Frewis looked around, found Grysis and went over to talk to him; Grysis nodded, glanced at the platform and went after the disgruntled Ghezrathi.

Breyd glanced at the platform herself; Haffat had come halfway to his feet; he and his lion-priest were watching closely. The girls' final race was lined up quickly and sent off; there were few people around the start now, and they were subdued.

All the other women in the two-relay were Secchi. Breyd felt her heart lift: Xenia at her right side, and beyond her Aroepe and Jocasa. On her other side, Ris and Morosa, Atrea and Kyris. *For all of us—against them,* she thought, and saw the same intent in Jocasa's eyes.

She nearly forgot to transfer the dagger and shifted it awkwardly at the last moment, but he must have been prepared for that; he snatched it from her and was gone. Breyd stumbled back out of the way, as Xenia came in beside her, then turned around to watch and catch her breath. Xenia's new husband was gone, and now Jocasa's, but Apodain was far ahead of them.

The noise was deafening; people packed the sides of the course once more and they were screaming, cheering on the runners. She was cheering herself, screaming Apodain's name as he pelted toward the finish. No one else was even close to him.

"We won!" She threw her arms around him, and he caught her up, swung her in a circle and hoisted her above his head. People were cheering wildly, screaming out his name and hers. Hands caught at her, pulled her from his grasp and she caught hold of his fingers, but then he, too, was raised above the crowd and borne to the prince's platform.

Prince Pelledar stood before his chair, the emperor and his son at his shoulders. He held up his hands for silence and got enough to say, "To the victors!" More cheering as Breyd and Apodain knelt to let the prince put the wreaths on their heads. He took them by the hands and brought them to their feet, turned them to face the crowd.

But when Apodain would have led her down from the platform, Haffat stepped forward. "In Diyet," he said, "there are other prizes besides a garland of leaves. And so I give each of you this." He gestured; Hadda stepped forward and gave each a pierced gold coin; a lion pulling a chariot ran around the outside of the hole. She made herself smile; kept the smile in place as Hadda eyed her warily.

More applause as Apodain handed her down from the platform and jumped down himself. The crowd was already thinning out, though, as people began to walk back toward the city and the wagons were filled. Breyd caught her breath; Khadat was waiting for them, next to the platform, arms folded across her chest, eyes narrowed, but she smiled at Apodain and straightened the wreath. "That was excellently done, I am proud of both of you," she said. "I am going now, to see the meal is ready; come soon so you have time to bathe." She glanced up at the platform, then turned and let Emyas make a path for her.

By the time Apodain got her back out to the road and into the open, Khadat's sedan chair was gone; Emyas was gone. "Why don't we find your family again, so you can show them that, and say good-bye?" he asked.

"I'd like that, thank you." She sighed. "Does Khadat think I'm too common to know how to bathe? Even my grandmother's tenant farmers bathe, you know."

"I know. So does Mother." He laughed sourly. "It wasn't you; she did that for Haffat."

"She's—" She bit her lip. There were people everywhere, pushing past them, standing close by; this was no place to talk. And if she missed her family out here, she might not have a chance to see them any time soon.

The wagon was being packed, the side replaced by the men who drove it; those who had ridden waited nearby. No Niverren; but there was Nevvia. "Look what I have," Breyd said.

Nevvia threw her arms around her. "Oh, we saw! You both ran so fast and then, up there with the prince! You both looked so happy, I was so proud of you. But what did that— what did he say to you, after?"

"He gave us these," she said, and held out the coin. Nidya picked it up, looked at it closely and gave it back to her.

"Save that," she said crisply. "It will impress your children. Look, they're ready for us. Nevvia, we have to go now."

"Don't—come as soon as you can, baby," Nevvia whispered. Breyd swallowed, nodded.

"As soon as I can, I promise."

Men came to help Nidya and Ina into the wagon; Apodain hesitated, then kissed Nevvia's cheek. She smiled at him, hugged Breyd a last time, and went. Breyd kept a smile on her face until the wagon was gone. A moment later Creos and Niverren went by, but his eyes were shut and hers fixed anxiously on his face.

Breyd looked up at the city and sighed. Apodain glanced at her. "I know; that road. We could have gone with them."

"No. There wasn't room, really. And we would never hear the end of it, winning that race and then riding back with the old women."

"A point," Apodain said gravely. "Do we fight the wagons for the road, or wait until they're gone?" He smiled and waved as another wagon passed them and someone inside shouted, "Wonderful race!"

Before she could answer him, a chariot drew up. "Apodain!" Ryllos shouted. "I knew you'd take that race! Here, they haven't left the heroes of the games to walk back, have they?" Apodain looked startled, Breyd thought, but pleased, too. *Look at all the people staring at them. Ryllos is making certain everyone knows he's still one of them.* "You don't walk, not today," Ryllos added firmly. "Come on, in you come—it's a big car and the horses need the work."

"Oh." Breyd let Apodain hand her up, took Ryllos' extended fingers, and smiled at him. "I've never ridden in a chariot before." Apodain vaulted in next to her, wrapped her hands around the rail, and put his arm behind her.

"Well—we can't let them out, unfortunately."

"It's all right." She let her head fall back; let the air flow over her and dry her forehead. It was heady; standing and being carried along the road. "It's wonderful."

Ryllos let the horses out just a little, drew back on the reins as they caught up to one of the wagons. "Word in your ear," he said softly. "It's nearly certain Haffat had Septarin killed. A few of us are trying to find a way to get hold of Pelledar and get him hidden before *he's* killed. After all, once he's gone, Haffat won't have any reason to keep the rest of us alive, will he?"

"He won't if Pelledar's dead, either," Apodain said quietly. "But you'll never get close to him."

"We might. His bedchamber, late tonight. Haffat hasn't that many men in the palace. We need someone to warn him, though."

"I don't know if—"

"They'll want you up there, both of you, wager anything."

"It's possible. If I can, I'll tell him."

"If you can't, send word; Potro's on the council, he said he'd find an excuse to see the prince if he had to. But he's got children to worry about, and he's nervous anyway these days."

"All right."

"Haffat has sent a lot of the prince's servants away and brought in more of his own men than we originally saw up there. But so far he hasn't barred the council." He swung the chariot out around a line of wagons, put the horses to a gallop and only reined them back as the road started up the slope. He glanced over at Breyd. "Still all right?"

"Wonderful," she replied. The ride was; the talk was worrying. *Is Ryllos part of what we're doing, or is this his own scheme? And—he knows Apodain, but he doesn't know me. How could he just—talk like that, without knowing if I'm safe?* Maybe he did know; maybe Grysis or his own captain had told him so. But she wasn't going to trust that. She'd have to let Grysis know what was going on, right away.

Pelledar went to his own apartments so he could bathe. Haffat and Knoe stood in the hall and watched him go, then Haffat beckoned and went up to the roof. Knoe followed.

The emperor stopped next to the pool and stared down at the fish for a long moment. Eyes still fixed on them, he said, "Knoe. You did me a good service last night and you'll be well rewarded for it. That priestess, though—are you certain she didn't suspect anything?"

"If she did, it didn't show. If there had been a way to keep her away from him—"

"There wasn't, you know that." Haffat looked out across the city. "This is a fine garden; look how far you can see to the north. Even in the middle of winter, the Mirikosi say the water is warm and there are flowers. Not like Diyet."

Knoe eyed him warily. "Do you plan to live here?"

"Plan?" Haffat turned to look at him; after a moment, he shrugged. "I haven't planned anything yet, except to take Ye Eygar. But it would be pleasant to winter here, this year. I think Hadda would like that, and it would give me time to show him more about ruling."

If he hasn't learned that yet, he never will, Knoe thought sourly. But Haffat would never see that.

"And I was thinking. That woman—the one on Pelledar's council, did you see her today?"

"*That* woman?" Knoe stared at him, aghast. "Khadat? The woman who was married to Pelledar's brother?"

"She was a princess in Mirikos, before she became one by marriage here," Haffat said. He thought about this and smiled. "A noblewoman twice over. And they tell me Perlot has been dead for many years. But I could have guessed that, the way she was watching me today."

"You can't—" Knoe pulled himself together with an effort. "My emperor, that woman isn't any more capable of lust than she is love! I have seen her, I know what she is."

Haffat laughed. "You are a priest, Knoe; by your own admission you have never set the god's path aside long enough to look at any woman."

"I don't look at this one as a woman, either. She is drawn to what you can do for her, *what* you are."

"Well? What's wrong with that? Knoe, you act as if the woman were dangerous!"

"She is the wife of a Ghezrathi prince and her sons are in the succession," Knoe said. "We're already rid of the crown prince. That puts her sons one step nearer the throne."

"Mmmm. You think she isn't aware of that? She's noble, she's well connected. She is also a priestess, if I heard right. She is more use to us alive than dead, Knoe."

Silence. Knoe finally sighed heavily. "If you say so. I would still watch her, if I were you."

Ryllos brought them right to Khadat's gates. "Remember," he said; Apodain nodded and lifted Breyd out. He stared after the chariot until it disappeared behind a turn of the wall.

Someone had filled her jars with cool water and left her new drying cloths and a fresh long gown; there was food on a small table next to her couch. She washed, dressed, and ate cold rice, sweet bread, fruit, then wandered over to the window and looked out. She could hear voices: Khadat's angry, sharp voice, Apodain's flat reply—nothing of what they said, except Apodain's, "I will *not!* Whatever you say, Mother!"

She stood quite still and watched them go, Khadat striding furiously across the courtyard, Apodain just behind her. "What won't he, I wonder?"

They were gone. She hesitated, then crossed the room quickly, and hurried out the door. She paused at the foot of the steps, but Pria was nowhere in sight and there were no other servants around. She ran down the steps and walked swiftly across the courtyard, stepped into the stable, and waited by the door for her eyes to adjust to the gloom. "Nessa?"

"Saw you coming," he said. "Something up?"

She told him, added, "They may already know what Ryllos is up to. If not—well, I've told them. But there isn't much time."

"No. I'll get it to them myself if I have to. The princess and Apodain went up to the palace; you were asked for, too."

"And Khadat told them no," Breyd said.

"No—he did. I could hear him when they went by, told her flat he wouldn't have you brought to that man's attention again."

"Oh." She considered this, turned, and left the stable and wandered slowly back toward the palace.

There was still a little daylight left, and the loom had been set where sun would fall over her shoulder and onto the fabric. She walked around it, fingers trailing across the smoothed wood. "Niverren should have such a beautiful loom." She picked up bundled wool from the basket beside it, set it back again, and walked onto the balcony. The eastern hills were ruddy with Atos' last rays, the walls very red. Two of Khadat's kitchen servants stood against the stable wall, talking to Nessa. *One of them must be the woman Xhem said was safe. But I forget her name.* Out in the city, she could see men and women walking along the inner walls, taking the last light.

She shook her head and turned away. "How can it look so normal, out there?" But what was normal any more?

She went back into the room, walked around the loom again, finally carried the basket of wool over to her couch where she could sort through it. Bundles of yellow—a gaudy color, it would look awful on anyone. An enormous wad of fine-spun white under that, but the bottom of the basket was lined with bundles of a very bright, thick blue. She freed a strand of it, ran it through her fingers, and held it up to the fading light. "This would make a warm winter cloak for Apodain." It would be fitting, for her first weaving in this house to go to him as a gift. A gift in return for today.

It would give her something to do; better yet, if Khadat saw she was busy with a large project, she might not keep such a close eye on her son's new wife. But there was no

point to starting today; she was still too keyed up and it was
rapidly growing dark. Besides, there was only the one small
lamp in this room. She must ask Khadat for more lamps and
brighter ones. She put the wool back in the basket, and
shoved it under the loom.

Khadat had stopped Apodain on his way up to his rooms.
"Wash, put on the clothes set out for you. Pelledar has sent
for you and the girl."

Ryllos was right, he thought. "All right. I will not bring
her with me, though."

"You won't tell me what you will do or not do!" Khadat
thundered. Apodain merely shook his head, turned, and went
up to bathe. When he came down some time later, she was
still angry. "The emperor has asked to see you both; you do
not want to displease him, Apodain, remember he holds our
future!"

"I will come with you, I said so; she will not. We can
stand and argue until tenth horn, if you like, Mother."

At that, she turned and stalked off across the courtyard
and down the avenue toward the prince's gates. But just
short of them, she stopped and smiled. It made him nervous;
what was she up to? "All right. I would have preferred for
him to see for himself what Pelledar has done to you, marrying you to this common, little— But he already saw her
out there, didn't he? Sweaty and covered in dust, her hair all
limp hanks and those dreadful arms!"

"Mother!"

"Be still, I am thinking. Yes, this is much better." She
turned to look at him. "You know I will not tolerate that
child in my house much longer, Apodain. It is up to you how
she leaves it."

"What do you mean by that?"

"Mean?" She widened her eyes at him, as if in surprise.
"You tell the prince to set the marriage aside, or I shall. Or
you persuade the girl to go back to her mother. Or I shall
make her life such a burden, she will go of her own free
will. What did you think I meant?"

She will kill Breyd. His heart sank. *She will have to go, at
once, tonight.* He realized Khadat was watching him through
narrowed, thoughtful eyes, waiting for some response. He
must not let her even think that he cared the least bit for
Breyd. *I never believed those stories about her—until now.*

She *could* kill—a pipe girl, a newly made wife—anyone. And never feel the least remorse.

Pelledar sat on his throne, ran the red sash through his fingers, and stared dully at Haffat. The emperor was seated on the deep sill, looking out to sea, talking to Hadda who slouched in a chair close by. He looked away, finally let his eyes fall to the sash. *Token of mourning for my son. For myself also, I think.* Haffat had no reason to keep him alive except Ye Sotris; he must realize by now that Pelledar had no intention of telling him where the queen was.

But he hadn't asked in some days, either. Maybe he had accepted Pelledar's early suggestion; that she had somehow evaded his horsemen and reached her father after all. It might not be likely; it wasn't impossible. And there was no trace of her anywhere in the city.

Septarin, his young body shattered on the stones out there. *My poor son. In the dark and the cold, all night long, before anyone found him.* It hurt more than he would have ever thought it could, almost as surprising as the intensity of his grief. *I thought I had already accepted he might die in this war, that it would not touch me if he did.*

Haffat's voice broke into his thoughts. "My brother is sad. I am sorry to see this." Pelledar looked up; Haffat's eyes were stormy. Hadda was prowling the chamber, his shoulders tense, his face set and now and again he cast nervous glances in his father's direction.

"I have lost a son," Pelledar said. "If you forgot that, I did not."

"I did not forget," Haffat replied; his voice was low, gentle—at odds with those black eyes. Hadda gave Pelledar a frightened look, shook his head minutely. *He is warning me,* Pelledar thought suddenly. He let his eyes close. When he opened them a moment later, Haffat had turned from him to stare out the window once more. "The games went very well. One argument in an entire day—in Diyet there would be more fighting than that."

Pelledar roused himself with an effort. "You did well, making the preparations in such short order."

"Yes. The boy who won the wreath. He is your brother's son, I am told. And the other winner his new wife."

"Yes," Pelledar said warily.

"And his mother that woman on your council, the

Princess—Khadat? Khadat. I took the liberty of sending for them—in your name, of course—to come here so you could congratulate them." Pelledar gaped at him; before he could think of anything to say, though, a servant showed in Khadat and Apodain.

She is mad to bring him to this man's attention. And that girl, that fine young Secchi— Khadat swept in, her hair dressed in high curls and gold bands; gold bound her wrists and lay against her throat, hung from her ears; she smelled of jasmine oil and her cheeks were flushed under the pale cosmetic. Apodain wore nothing but a white tunic sashed in unfigured dark blue and sandals. His jaw was set.

Haffat smiled widely and came forward to greet them. Khadat returned the smile and inclined her head just enough for courtesy as among equals. She hissed at Apodain, who had gone to one knee; he glanced at her, shrugged, and got back to his feet.

"Well!" Haffat took Apodain by the shoulders and then clapped him on the back. "That was a splendid display this afternoon. And your young woman—lovely, wasn't she, Hadda?"

Hadda pursed his mouth but dutifully said, "Lovely, of course."

"But I don't see her here; I thought you would bring her."

Khadat spread her arms expansively, but Apodain spoke first. "She was—very tired, Emperor; I don't doubt she fell asleep in her bath." *He doesn't believe that.* Apodain met the emperor's eyes squarely. *But he won't challenge me; it would interfere with his pleasant facade.*

"Since we are here," Khadat broke in firmly, "perhaps we could discuss a matter close to my house—and of some urgency?"

Pelledar looked at her for a long moment. *Arrogant, dreadful woman. How could my brother have ever made sons on such a creature?* But if he could turn the attention from Apodain, and that Secchi. . . . When he spoke, his words were clipped and he knew his loathing of her must show. "Yes, my dead brother's wife. Tell us about this— urgent matter, why don't you?"

Khadat looked startled; she sent her eyes sideways toward the emperor and his son, then drew a deep breath and plunged into her set speech. Pelledar had heard it before and let most of it wash over him; she was concerned about the trading contracts between her family in Mirikos and the house of dead Perlot. *Let Haffat deal with this, and with the woman herself since he or Hadda must from now on,* Pelledar decided grimly. Khadat paused for comment; Pelledar looked at Haffat.

"Emperor, you know more about this matter than I; after all, Mirikos is in your control . . . also." Haffat's eyes narrowed, but he came forward to take Khadat's hands and he was smiling. Khadat fixed her eyes on his face and smiled back.

"Princess Khadat, yes. Some of your family's ships will be here in a day or so with supplies for my army. You and I can talk then. But, you know, I would like to establish a closer link between your houses here and in Mirikos—and my own. Some of the profits would go to Diyet, of course, but the overall profit will be higher since you would have direct access to northern goods. And of course, once the isthmus is opened and certain of the lands beyond joined to my empire, we can consider other agreements concerning that. It will take a certain strength, I think, on your part, to persuade the Mirikosi branch of your family to accept such a link, but I think you are a strong enough woman to manage them."

Khadat's cheeks were very pink now, and her eyes bright. "Why—I know that I can. Of course, there are those in this city and even my family who do not want to accept how things have changed, and they see all change for the worse. But I think you will find, sire, that I am not such a person."

"Why, no," Haffat said smoothly. "I do see that."

Pelledar glanced at Apodain. He held himself utterly rigid, and his face was set. Pelledar shifted his hand a little; Apodain glanced at it and then at the prince; his mouth quirked humorlessly.

Haffat released Khadat's fingers and she turned to Pelledar. "A final matter. I know you claim again there is no time, but we are all here and I would have the problem solved and behind us. This—" she gestured with a jerk of her head to indicate Apodain. "This marriage, my son and that dreadful Secchi."

Pelledar sighed heavily. "Khadat, can we not leave this for another time?"

"We cannot," Khadat began angrily, but Haffat stepped close to her and laid a hand on her shoulder.

"What is this of Secchi? I've heard that word."

"Commoner," Pelledar said flatly.

"It means commoner," Apodain said a half breath behind him. He had never thought so fast or clearly in his life. "But the kind of girl who runs, hunts."

"Huntress. Commoner," Haffat said thoughtfully. "Oh. Of course. That girl with you today at the games." He smiled pleasantly in Apodain's direction. "That is a Secchi, is it? I like that. And I was very impressed with you and your Secchi, that final race was no contest at all."

"We were fortunate, sir," Apodain replied softly as the Emperor waited for some reply.

"Fortunate! Yes, well. Hadda, come here, you must meet this young man properly, but of course you remember him from the platform."

"I remember," Hadda said warily. Haffat said something against his ear; Hadda stepped forward and embraced a startled Apodain. Pelledar saw Khadat poke him in the ribs and he returned the embrace.

"Here is a gift for you, Hadda." Haffat smiled at them impartially. "A man of about your years and your class, and possibly of similar tastes. You must get to know my son, Apodain. After all, he will remain here to aid your prince—your uncle, I suppose I should say—and he will have few he can call close friend when I am gone."

"I shall be pleased, sir," Apodain said in that same soft, expressionless voice.

"And I shall also." Hadda's eyes moved rapidly. His father was waiting for him to say something more; Khadat was watching them both. "That was your new wife, that—that little girl I gave a gold lion?"

"It is that we must discuss," Khadat broke in as the two young men looked at each other and found nothing else to say. "Sire, she is a commoner, a person with nothing to recommend her to a boy of such high rank as my son. She does not look or sound right, she does not speak properly, she does not know how to dress—she is not one of us. Apodain was put into this marriage against my better judgment and against my will; now that I would have him out of it, the prince avoids me and puts me off."

"And what do you say to this, Apodain?" Haffat asked. "I thought you made a delightful pair; don't you like this girl?"

"Sire, with respect," Khadat broke in vigorously, "this is not a matter for a mere boy to decide, whom he shall marry!

Nor does liking come into such things! But in Mirikos a marriage between royalty and common is not binding. The common wife may be set aside, or another wife be brought into the house to keep the blood line pure. It was once that way in Ghezrat; doesn't that hold true in Diyet?"

"But your son is no mere boy," Haffat said quietly. Khadat eyed him sidelong and closed her mouth. "And I am not the man to ask about such things . . . Princess. After all, my own mother was a commoner." Khadat stared at him in horror, too stunned to keep control of her face. "How do you feel about the girl, Apodain?"

She will not dare harm Breyd now, and she knows it, he thought jubilantly. "I like her. Very much." Khadat turned that horrified look on him; he gave her a cold smile in reply. But it wasn't just a knife through her pride, it was true. *I—I really do like her; she isn't 'one of us.' She's not like anyone else.*

Khadat blinked and closed her mouth. Haffat said smoothly, "When I return from Ye Eygar, perhaps we can talk about this again. But I am disposed to leave such a marriage alone because I know how important new blood is in royal families—look what my mother's did for my house. But surely the princess knows," he added pleasantly, "that it is my policy never to tamper with local custom or something that already exists."

Khadat had to try twice before any words came. "Sire, of course, whatever you wish," she muttered.

"Yes," Haffat said mildly, but Apodain heard the metal behind that single word, and those black eyes were hard as they moved from his mother to him. The smile that went with the chill stare was a wide flash of teeth, rather unnerving. "My son will expect you, and whatever other friends you can find for him, Apodain. He is particularly skilled at soldiers' board games, and carries a fine matched set with him. He also breeds horses."

"Of course." Apodain looked at Hadda. "I play *at* such games, but I'm not very good. I know others who like them better. I have seen some of the northern horses at a distance, I'd be interested in handling yours."

"Of course." Hadda glanced toward his father, but Haffat had beckoned Khadat over to the window. He turned back to Apodain and shrugged. He looked and sounded extremely uncomfortable and there was a long, stiff silence between them. Hadda shrugged again and made a visible effort. "I have seen your chariots, they seem much more practical than ours, particularly in uncertain ground."

"Yes." *You have certainly destroyed enough of them, did you never see one whole?* Apodain swallowed rage; he could feel his mother's watchful eye on him. *Does she really think it will matter how much this Hadda likes me as a friend, if his father plans to kill us all?* Did she really think he would spare her and her family—and her precious ships—if she flirted with him, or even took him to her couch?

Hadda was watching him uncertainly; he brought up a vague smile and wandered away. Apodain sent his eyes sideways to meet Pelledar's, and he said very softly, "Uncle. Listen carefully; Ryllos and certain others plan to come tonight and rescue you, your bedchamber, late. Do they guard you?"

"They—no," Pelledar whispered. He bit his lip, sent his eyes cautiously toward Haffat, who was engrossed in conversation with Khadat, to Hadda, who was well across the room. "You be careful, Apodain; don't risk yourself and that girl for me, I know what—what I'm doing. But I would have spared you this time and place, and Haffat's attention. Remember that."

"I will remember, Uncle. It isn't my doing, though, and Mother's already put Breyd at risk tonight. All of them."

"Yes. She knows something he could use against us."

"I know. She's very angry with him now for denying her, and it must have half-killed her to hear he's not pure." Apodain's mouth quirked.

"She puts a good face on it."

"She still wants those contracts. But so does he; she won't have to bribe him with—with Secchi for her family's precious ships. She'll hold that for a more valuable bargain."

"I'm sorry, boy."

"Not your doing, Uncle. Be careful," he added as Haffat leaned out and called to someone down in the courtyard. Khadat looked over his shoulder.

Careful, Pelledar thought bitterly. But his nephew meant well. "A word of warning; Haffat is using your mother right now; he wants to be certain people in the street see her there, with him."

"I know what she is," Apodain replied softly. Haffat shouted down to the courtyard again, turned to say some-

thing to Khadat, who laughed. "The gods guard you and
care for you," Apodain added hastily. There was no time for
anything else; Khadat came swiftly across the room to collect him, only just remembering to sketch her prince a bow.
Hadda came away from his window and held out his arms to
grip Apodain's shoulders.

"I look to see you soon," he said, but he sounded doubtful. *Surely he does not expect that I will say no to him and
his father. Does he think I'm that foolish?* Apodain merely
nodded and caught hold of his upper arms in turn. They
were surprisingly well-muscled, strong under the fine cloth.
Not all he seems. Tell Ryllos that. Apodain knelt before his
prince, then followed Khadat out.

There was a very long silence in the throne room; Pelledar
listened to the familiar slap of Khadat's sandals in the hallway, the fading sound of her footsteps clapping loudly
against each step in turn as she descended. No sound from
Apodain. *Dear goddess, why did his mother bring him here?*
he thought. The woman constantly amazed him; nothing had
ever seriously threatened her, and she thought nothing
could—not even Haffat. Stupid, stupid creature.

He looked cautiously for Haffat. The emperor was gazing
toward the window above the temple grounds, apparently
without seeing it. Hadda had gone over to peer out the window where his father had stood. "There are more ships coming in," he announced.

Haffat seemed to come back from a distance. "Yes, I
know. Wilus was down in the courtyard just now, he brought
me word they had been seen from the mole." He clasped his
hands behind his back, turned on Pelledar so suddenly the
prince started in surprise. Haffat smiled and it wasn't a good
smile. "I have not much more time to spend in your company, my brother, before I leave for Ye Eygar. I know you
will be sorry to see me go." His eyes were very intense,
fixed unblinking on Pelledar's. "But first you will tell me
two things." He straightened up and shouted, "Knoe!"
Pelledar jumped, turned as the lion-priest came through the
doorway. "You heard that woman? What she said?"

"I heard her," Knoe said softly. He fixed the prince with
a chill stare of his own. "These Secchi—that word has nothing to do with *common,* does it?"

It caught him by surprise. "The Secchi? They *are* common, athletes."

"They are part of a fighting elite," Knoe broke in flatly. "You know what they are—and where they are. Those red-clads—"

"We had red-clad fighters, only a few, and we have none now. They're dead; why do you think you prevailed out there?"

"Lies!" Knoe shouted. Haffat touched his shoulder and he subsided.

"Lies," Haffat echoed softly. "But you lie easily, don't you, my brother? Your wife has fled the city, with the babes, and you do not know where? You know where she is. And you will tell me, now. You knew she had not gone to Ye Eygar; you know she is here, in this city. I will find her eventually, you know; why don't you tell me now, before I grow angry?"

Pelledar looked from Knoe to Haffat, and back again, set his lips in a tight line and said nothing. "Would you not like to be reunited with your queen?" Haffat asked softly. "They tell me she is a fair lady, and a gracious one, and your two sons are very young. They must miss you very much, my brother. And I also hear that Ye Sotris will bear you another child very soon; will you keep yourself from her side in such an hour? She will curse you, brother, and your young sons will weep for you, that you do not come to them."

A long, chill silence. Pelledar drew himself up and squared his shoulders. "No. But she would curse you, if she knew what you had done to her first-born." He turned his eyes toward Knoe. "You did that, somehow. And my son is dead. Did you really think I would give my wife into your hands, to murder as you murdered my Septarin?"

Haffat's knuckles stood out white; one hand gripped the other and he stood motionless for a very long moment. "I will not leave this matter unfinished! You will willingly tell me—now, this moment—where Ye Sotris has gone to ground, or I shall wring it from you!"

Pelledar's hands trembled; he laid them carefully on the graven stone arms of his throne to still them and looked into Haffat's suffused face. *Goddess, guard my Ye Sotris, and my babes—and judge me well.* "You never will. My *brother!*"

Haffat said something under his breath, so quietly Pelledar could not understand him; he turned away. Pelledar was halfway to his feet when Haffat spun and pounced; his hands locked around the prince's throat and he dragged him from the throne, threw him down, and fell on him. Pelledar gasped and tore at the hands, but they might as well have been stone; he couldn't breathe and then he couldn't see. For one still, blessed moment, he felt nothing at all; then pain exploded white-hot behind his eyes and everything was gone.

"Father, no! Don't—you're killing him! Knoe, help me!" Hadda had one of Haffat's arms in both his hands, but he couldn't move it; Knoe came across, grabbed the emperor of all Diyet around the shoulders, and dragged him back. Pelledar came partway up with them, fell back as Haffat's hands released him.

Haffat swore furiously. "Let me go, I will be done with this Great King of Ghezrat, this—this wretch of a prince!"

"Father, no! Listen to me!" Hadda shouted. Haffat turned on him; Hadda was white to the lips but he kept hold of his father's arm and Knoe still held him.

Haffat drew a deep breath, turned his head and spat across the polished tiled floor. "What—first that Pair and now this prince? Are you as soft as he is?"

"I am not soft, my emperor," Knoe said against his ear. "And I also say, do not kill him . . . yet."

Hadda licked his lips and stared at him. "If I—if I let you go, Father, will you listen to me?" Silence; Hadda glanced down; Pelledar's breast rose and fell rapidly. Haffat nodded finally; Hadda cautiously let go of his arm. Knoe released him and stepped back, but Haffat ignored him; his eyes were fixed flatly on his son, who gazed levelly back at him. "If I were soft, I would never dare confront you when the black mood takes you. Pelledar can still be persuaded to speak—whether you are here or halfway to Ye Eygar when he tells us where his wife is, what does it matter? And this matter of Secchi—do nothing for that dreadful woman before you leave, make her no contracts, offer her no assurances. Give her time to think while you are gone. She will tell you anything you want to know when you finally return, to gain back what is hers."

"Perhaps," Haffat said warily.

"Not perhaps."

"He is right," Knoe said, and Hadda looked at him in surprise. Knoe flashed him a very sardonic smile. "The woman can be left for later, if we need her. But the prince has the answers."

"He will not tell us anything. He's weak and stubborn both, you can't persuade people like that," Haffat said flatly. But Knoe shook his head.

"That was before—" He glanced down at the unconscious prince. "He has expected to die at any hour since we came. You attacked him, but he will waken and find he is still not dead. It will break him. But if it does not, *I* will break him." Hadda glanced at him, licking his lips, but said nothing.

Haffat stood very still, stared at the far wall, then walked over to look down at Pelledar. "All right. Take him, get him out of sight. Give out that he's taken ill, fever, and cannot see anyone for fear of spreading it." He eyed his son thoughtfully. "You realize what this means for him. I will not be here many more days. Are you strong enough to accept what Knoe does? Not to deal in torture yourself, but to know that *he* does?" Hadda shrugged.

"I don't know. But it doesn't matter; Knoe doesn't answer to me anyway."

"I don't," Knoe said calmly. "But think about what this means to us all, Prince Hadda. This of Secchi. It has to do with these fighting Pairs, with the female of them—and the goddess hides the rest from us. There were Pairs, and now there are not. There are two who become one, and then they do not, and the man who finds the key to that holds the key to Ghezrat. The army has laid down its weapons and the walls are ours, but Denota's power is still upon those walls, I can feel it under my feet when I walk there and the Ergardi dare not pass the gates; Denota's strength still holds Ghezrat together. *She* is the reason this city has held itself together for seven hundred years! Break her, and Ghezrat is yours forever."

"That is your task," Haffat said evenly.

"Yes."

Haffat turned to his heir. "You will leave all that to Knoe. Remember that *you* must distance yourself from Pelledar's death, Septarin's death—any other deaths in the royal blood line."

"Yes," Knoe said softly. "You must be able to look even that gimlet-eyed priestess in the face and say you have no knowledge of these things; put them from your mind, put even Knoe from your mind. I have set aside a place for myself beneath the palace; we need not even deal with each other and perhaps it is better if we do not."

"Yes," Hadda said. His mind reeled. Haffat strode from the throne room. Hadda knelt beside the prince, laid a hand against his throat. The pulse was rapid but steady. He got back to his feet; Knoe picked him up and walked out. Hadda stared after him for a very long time, then shook himself. He was alone in the throne room. "This is my chair now. This my room. That my city. This my palace." *Words. Empty words—you know it and even if your father doesn't, Knoe does.* He turned away from the empty throne and wrapped his arms around himself to keep from shaking.

23

By the time she reached the outside steps leading down to the horse-forecourt, Khadat was in a towering rage; she swept out of the palace grounds, across the avenue, and up the side street, into her own horse-forecourt; Apodain eyed her back with resignation and kept up with her.

She kept quiet most of the way, but once she had passed her own gates began to mutter under her breath. Apodain was near enough now to catch most of it; she was furious with Pelledar for putting her off, furious with Haffat for not supporting her against the weak Pelledar. "What does he think he is doing? Who does he think he is? Does he not realize how good a catch my son is? I had thought even a daughter of his own, but then to learn from his own lips what he is, and he is *proud* of it! And you!" She suddenly turned on Apodain at the foot of the steps. "You might have aided me, back there! You could have backed me when I told them what that girl is, that she is inferior, that you would prefer a woman of your own class. You *could* have been more friendly toward his son, by all the gods at once! Do you not understand even yet, Apodain, that these men represent our future?"

Apodain shook his head. "Why should I have said anything? He will kill us whether I am nice to him or not. Now that Septarin is gone and once Pelledar dies—"

Khadat held up a warning hand, and he shrugged, fell silent. "You will cease this kind of foolish talk immediately, Apodain; I will not hear it again! Those two men who sit with Pelledar now are our future; they are not such fools as to mouth the words and thoughts of others, as you are doing." She gestured sharply for him to follow, led the way into her accounting. "They are a very long way from Diyet, and they clearly plan to keep Ghezrat as she is, as an outlying state. As they have done with Mirikos and Idemito and all the others. If they are to keep the people here from causing trouble for them, of course they will keep trade the level as it has always been. They have no one here save that boy of Haffat's, and their soldiers. They must depend upon our kind, to help the lower classes and less clever of our own people to see Haffat means them no harm, and that if they simply go on with their lives, they will prosper as they always have." She narrowed her eyes. "Are you listening to me?"

"I am listening to you, Mother," Apodain replied wearily.

"Do not take that tone of voice with me! Listen, and pay close attention. I've done everything, all of this, to keep you alive. To make certain we retain this house, and the wealth and rank that goes with it, that there *is* such a house and such wealth and rank to pass on to you once I am dead—a good many years from now, before you say or think it, and upon my couch, not at Haffat's hands!" She folded her arms, leaned against the wall and waited.

"Yes, Mother. All right."

"Better. Now. Surely Haffat would have no reason to invite you to become friends with his son *and* heir if he meant to execute you tomorrow, would he? You will accept this offer of friendship in the manner in which it was made, that is to say, openly and with pleasure. Whatever friends you have, you will do all you can to persuade them to be friendly toward Hadda also; if the boy is kept happy and occupied, he will have less time to get into mischief; also, he will need advisors and a council of his own. A boy like that will not want Denota's priestess, or old men or women like myself; he will want others of his own age and kind. Do you see this?"

"I see it."

She had fixed her eyes on some distance, across the small room and probably well beyond that plain, whitewashed wall, and no longer paid much attention to his responses. "You will stay away from that Breyd, unless Haffat or his son commands her presence. You may think I was not aware of you out there at the games, but I saw you, and I remember what you dared tell Haffat. There is no point in your forming an attachment with her, because I *will* find a way to break this marriage."

"Yes," Apodain said quietly. "I think you probably will. But not by killing her."

Khadat stared at him for a very long moment. "Where did you get such an idea as that?"

"That's not important. Haffat plays that game better than anyone, Mother; whatever you did, however you accomplished it, he'd know—and he'd hate you for it." He met her eyes levelly; after a moment, Khadat shrugged and looked away. *As if it wasn't important. But I've won this point, and she knows it.*

"Tephys says the girl served the goddess this year, among the novices. If that is true, then she was already promised to Denota, and Pelledar had no right to pledge you to her." She considered this, nodded in some satisfaction. Her eyes came back to him. "All right. I will be watching you closely, Apodain. Remember what I have said to you, and do not try my patience. You are underage, you have no rights whatever; and you may have subverted half the household servants but my cousin Emyas is loyal to *me*. Disobey me, and you might find yourself confined to your apartments until your beard turns gray."

He bowed his head over her hands. "Yes, Mother." Khadat withdrew her fingers from his with a curt nod and left him. Apodain followed her slowly, into the hall, then began to climb the stairs in her wake. Going to remove her fine gown, no doubt, so that she could spend the rest of the day in her accounting, poring over figures. He sighed, wondered if he dared speak to Breyd yet or if he must wait until Khadat had gone back down. *Wait. And remember to watch for Pria. Or Emyas.*

But as he reached the top of the stairs, he heard Khadat's shrill, furious voice coming from Breyd's rooms. "You stupid, common little wretch! You do not dare stand upon that balcony and show yourself to the world out there—as if you were selling your personal wares! There is a curtain, why do you think it is there? If you have nothing better to do with yourself than to peer out of windows, you will stay behind that curtain, and goddess help you if I learn from anyone that you have ignored me! You have a loom and all the wool any young woman could ever desire; you will apply yourself to that, and make yourself of use!"

He stepped back into the shadow of his own open doorway as Khadat stormed into the hall, but she had no eyes for anything just now. She turned on her heel and strode back to the stairs, mounted them with sharp little clacking noises from the hard soles of her sandals. Her own apartments and Hemit's were up there. Apodain edged into the open, stood at the base of the steps and held his breath so he could listen, but he could hear nothing.

No Khadat ordering Emyas down here to keep an eye on him or on Breyd, which was what he had feared. She might yet do that, after she had changed clothes. He heard her distant shout for Pria, heard the woman's sandals scuffing across the smooth tiled floor; he exhaled gustily and practically ran back down the hall.

Breyd sat at her loom, staring toward the window; when he came near he could see her face was extremely pale, her mouth set in a hard line, and her eyes furious. She did not move until he came into her line of vision, then her eyes flickered his way, back again. "Why are you here?"

"To—"

"Your mother has said I am not to welcome you, to this room or to my couch—had I intended that," Breyd said evenly.

"I heard her. She's angry because Pelledar won't dissolve the marriage and Haffat won't either."

"Oh." She looked up at him. "I don't know that makes it any better."

"It doesn't. She shouted at me first, down there."

"I know. But—"

"Because I didn't support her. She—" he glanced over his shoulder. Khadat's voice, still muffled by distance but she was out in the hall, he thought. "I'll come later, tell you then. I just wanted you to know, you're safe for now." She came partway to her feet, but he had already turned and left the room. Scant moments later she heard Khadat at the steps, shouting for Pria, the clatter of her sandals going down stairs.

Tell me what? "Safe?" she whispered. She clapped a hand over her mouth. The very notion was laughable; but if she started laughing, she wouldn't be able to stop. Finally she sat back down and turned back to the loom. The warping was done, the first two rows of deep blue weft run. She felt for the pick and forced herself to concentrate on easing the tines between the warp threads, to compress the blue.

Three quiet, long days went by; she warped the loom and finally wound blue yarn onto shuttles. By the third morning, the fabric was as deep as her stretched hand and as wide as the loom. She leaned back; one hand massaged the back of her neck absently. Everything was stiff but particularly the muscles sweeping out across her shoulders.

Khadat could not fault her for shirking the loom, though it wasn't really much length compared to what Niverren could have done in three days. But Khadat wouldn't know that. Pria would merely think her clumsy-handed.

Pria had brought her the lamps she'd asked for; she'd also spent much of the day after the games on the stairs, or in the halls—watching, Breyd realized uneasily. But this past day, Breyd hadn't seen the woman. *They both think me beaten. That's good. I need to get out of here tonight, an hour or so.*

She had gone to the temple each morning; Khadat encouraged that. But Tephys had nothing to tell her the first day, and she had nothing to tell Tephys.

The priestess surprised her the second morning by leading the way into a narrow passage behind the altar with the oil lamps—she'd never known it was there. "It goes in an almost straight line to Khadat's undercellars." She gestured with her lamp and the flame trembled. "Just now you can't pass that way, because of the barriers I have put around this place. I will lower that one, if you think it will be useful to you. But you will damage the fabric of it, so use it for nothing short of disaster. That," she indicated another opening, "comes out beneath the palace."

Tephys was—different, she thought. She'd always been dedicated to Denota, to the exclusion of everything else; it blinded her to people and what they needed or wanted that didn't have to do with the goddess. But in just a few days since the marriages, she had become grim-faced, fixed rather than simply dedicated, as if her whole being had been focused on one thing so tightly nothing else existed. Breyd's fingers burned for the rest of the day after they brushed against the high priestess' arm. *Denota is filling her, as she did us. Arming her for the day we take back Ghezrat.*

Apodain hadn't been able to come back that first night, as he'd said, for Emyas had been prowling the halls and steps most of the night. The second was much the same. She scowled at the loom and got to her feet.

* * *

An unfamiliar horn call brought her around and over to the window. But she couldn't see much of the city or the plain from this chamber, unless she moved to the far right side of the window and stood on tiptoe. Even then, she couldn't make anything out at first, certainly nothing new. And then, movement in the distance—thin, fine, almost invisible against the bright blue of the sky and the deeper gray-blue sea. "Masts," she suddenly realized. "Masts. Ships. Haffat is moving." He must be; there were at least fifteen masts she could see, all moving. And now, just tantalizing glimpses of mounted men, an honor guard bearing Haffat's banners. More horns rang out.

She gazed toward the sea until her neck began to tighten once more and her head to ache in earnest. She couldn't *see*. But voices filled the air and the courtyard was full of excited men and high-voiced women. She pulled back a little as Khadat strode into the courtyard and shouted for order. "All of you, back to your tasks, I will not tolerate this behavior! Nessa, have my chair brought!" Moments later, she was handed into the curtained chair and carried into the street; Emyas rode at her side.

Footsteps sounded in the hall behind her. She turned sharply and moved away from the window, but it was Apodain. He was breathing hard, and the breast of his tunic was damp. "She's gone down to see her ships off, her cousin went with her. Pria's gone on an errand for her. I'm sorry I couldn't come sooner."

"It's all right. Tell me about it." It wasn't, but it wasn't his fault, either. She sat at her loom; he walked over to the window and looked out across the city and told her.

She stared at him after he was done, uncertain what she could possibly say to all that. He glanced at her, looked away again. "Haffat is on his way to Ye Eygar; he's taken most of his army with him, but there is still a full company of fifty in the barracks and several hundred more out on the plain. He took the ballista from the east wall, but the other remains; rumor goes both ways as to whether he took the magicians also, and whether Knoe remains with Hadda or has gone with Haffat.

"He even has a prize catch: Twenty-seven Ghezrathi, older men—you know the kind, we fight, this is all we've ever done, it's all we can do—they've joined one of his companies." He stared out the window, then turned and left.

* * *

That night, at ninth horn, she wrapped her dark green cloak close around her, picked up her sandals and stole from the room, down the steps, through Perlot's room, and into the triangular garden with its olive tree. The gate gave easily and silently and she slipped into the street, hugged the wall, and walked quickly until she came to the inner wall and the Shepherd's Gate. *Four steps, feel the wall until you locate the pattern of three pushed-in stones.* She had repeated Grysis' instructions to herself faithfully each night, but at the moment she wished he'd been able to *show* her instead. Her fingers slid across air, found the pocket. Down. . . . The opening was well hidden, particularly for a woman with no light; she felt along it doubtfully when she did locate it. "Go," she ordered herself. "He said there would be a lamp each night, in case. It won't be dark down there."

Her hands were damp and slipped on the stones; fortunately there was no real drop. Darkness pressed thick all around her; the breath caught in her throat, but her eyes were already adjusting; there was a hint of light—that way. She kept one hand on the wall and edged slowly forward.

Seven steps, a bend. Just as Grysis had promised; and the lamp was right there, on a flattened outcrop of stone. She waited until her hands stopped trembling and her chest had quit hurting, picked up the lamp, and went on.

Forty-five steps, a branch—take the left. Ninety-two steps, another branch, take the right, and just beyond that a cavern. Straight across, take the way marked on the roof with soot. Two more caverns, another long passage. The distant drip of water and then the unmistakable smell of the barracks well.

Grysis was sitting on a blanket, talking to Frewis and three tired-looking dusty men she didn't know. He must have been watching for her, though; he jumped up and came over to take the lamp and wrap an arm around her shoulders. "We were getting worried; Nessa said he'd seen you at the window, but he'd heard Khadat the night of the games."

"I'm all right; I couldn't get away."

"I won't keep you long, then. What's the woman up to? Besides the obvious—everyone's seen her with Haffat—up in the palace or today, riding down to the mole to see him off." She gave him what Apodain had told her.

"Most of the servants look up to Apodain and despise his

mother; Nessa must have told you that, though. Emyas is another Khadat, and Pria sees nothing but whatever Khadat wants. Nessa told you about Ryllos?"

"He did—too late for us to stop them, but three of them got in and out somehow without getting caught. Unfortunately, the prince wasn't in his bedchamber. He's disappeared and they couldn't find out anything from his personal servants because they've all been sent away."

"They've killed him, then," she said flatly.

"We don't know. We have to assume that. This evening they gave out that he was taken ill. But we can't get into the palace to search for him; Hadda's there and there are Diye Haff soldiers everywhere. Ryllos is lucky to still be alive."

She felt sick. "It's—" She shook her head; Grysis gripped her arm.

"I know. It's not right. He knew, we all did, but it doesn't make his death easier to bear." He shook himself. "Anything else?"

"No."

"All right. Find out from Apodain if his father showed him the king's passages beneath the palace."

"King's passages—what if he asks why?"

"He probably will ask. Their existence isn't common knowledge and the passages themselves are only known to the prince and his close heirs. Pelledar hadn't even shown them to Septarin yet. Perlot knew them, we thought Ryllos or one of the cousins did, but apparently not. Apodain might have been too young when Perlot drowned, but ask him. Tell him that Grysis needs to know. And tell him why."

Her mouth was suddenly dry. "You think I can trust him?"

Grysis laughed shortly. "I've always thought that. In every sense. But he has something I wanted from the first: A way to Haffat."

"All right." She got to her feet, hesitated. "About Father—you said he was—was close."

"He was; they were digging out the hole yesterday and it collapsed on them; we couldn't get any more food through. They said they'd find another, we're trying to map things and figure out where they are—he's all right. He just isn't—"

She swallowed disappointment. "Just isn't here," she finished for him.

"They had plenty of food for a couple days, and water. They'll be all right."

"I know. I'll come back tomorrow or the night after, as soon as I have anything useful to pass on."

"Good. Take care, and don't let that woman catch you."

She managed a smile for him. "I don't plan on it."

She came back up to the street just before tenth horn; it was very dark and still. She got back inside the walls, crossed Perlot's room and regained her apartments without anyone seeing her. She sniffed the green cloak, but it only smelled like clean wool—not sulfur, as she'd half feared, or even dust. Pria would notice something like that, she'd tell Khadat. *I don't think I can remember all these things by myself. I know I can't watch my own back.* Too many things to remember and all of them common and frightening at the same time. She finished undressing, pulled her old, familiar blue over her head and fell onto the couch. A moment later she sat bolt upright. "I forgot to ask him; if Knoe was out there when they went." Knoe. She wouldn't let herself think about the lion-priest. Exhausted as she was tonight, *he* would keep her awake.

Apodain stood at the edge of the roof and watched men ride up from the plain—more Diye Haff from the small camp next to the main road, coming in to the barracks. Six—seven days since Haffat left Ghezrat; he'd be past the isthmus by now, well on his way down the southern coast of the great sea. He turned away and started; Breyd had come up behind him so quietly he hadn't known she was there. He looked at her for a very long moment; something about her face, or the way she walked. Something different; he couldn't decide what.

She walked past him to look down at the enemy camp. "You can see farther from here," she said finally.

"Yes."

"Don't go." She caught hold of his wrist; her voice was very low. "Your mother just went out, she took Pria with her."

"I know. I saw her." He looked down at her. "She's up to something; I don't know what. She doesn't trust me just now." Another silence; this one stretched. "I . . . was awake last night, I saw you go out." She went very still; her eyes were still fixed on the Diye Haff camp, but he didn't think she saw it. Finally she turned her head and looked at him. "I know it isn't my business," he said slowly. "But if Mother knew. . . ."

"I know. But you don't know it isn't your business," she said quietly. "I have a message for you—from Grysis."

He went cold all over. *If Mother knew, she'd kill her right then! Or give her to Hadda, or—* He couldn't complete the thought. But she knew what she was risking; her face told him that. Finally, she finished speaking. He looked out at the enemy camp, at the palace. At her. "Tell Grysis I'll do it," he said abruptly. "I'll lose board games to Hadda and learn what I can from him. Tell Grysis—" He hesitated. Breyd shook her head.

"Come with me tonight," she said, "and tell him yourself."

There were more of Haffat's soldiers in the streets and in the market, Xhem thought, with the emperor gone. It had only been—twenty-one days?—but things were very different already. The son did things his own way, or he did not know how to give orders that his men would obey. There was less food in the market; Nevvia was all bone and huge eyes; Nidya looked pinched and worried of a morning when she measured out the grain. Niverren never went to the market any more unless one of the neighbor men could go with her, not since she and Ina had had an uncomfortable encounter with some of the soldiers. She hadn't even said much about it to Niddy, and he hadn't understood everything Ina said to her later. All three women had made him swear repeatedly that he would never say anything to Creos. *As if I would,* he thought angrily. Creos would be angry for her and then ashamed for himself, that he could not go to the market and protect her.

Creos had been quiet since the games and he hadn't tried to go out since; he hadn't even talked about it, though now and then the two men who had come for him would bring wine and bread and spend an evening with him. Niverren visibly disapproved of the wine, but she didn't say; she stayed with Nevvia in the courtyard and let Creos and his friends take over the main room, as Menlaeus had done.

Xhem was increasingly uncomfortable anywhere now but beneath the city, with what there was left of the army. Down there, things were more straightforward. Men got angry when passages or a low ceiling collapsed or when a tunnel didn't lead the way it should—when the numbers didn't work out right and there wasn't enough food. Tempers flared, but it was over quickly.

It was much easier for him to slide through the opening beneath the sandal stall these days, and when he stripped off his tunic for the night, his ribs stood out as they had not since he was a boy of seven, the year there was a late frost and the grapes died on the vines. He ate—Nidya fed him, and he suspected she fed him some of her own portion because her face looked so thin and he could see the bones and the blue lines in her hands; Creos shared his bread whenever Niverren was not around to catch him at it; Nabid fed him whatever could be spared down below. He was always hungry, and it seemed he was always running.

It surprised him, that none of those soldiers realized what he was up to. They had grabbed a few men in the market only a day earlier, and the night before that, took away men who'd done nothing worse than stand outside the winehouse by the barracks. The men in the market had their heads close together and one of them had been whispering—it seemed to be all that was needed for Haffat's soldiers.

But there was reason to whisper: The food disappearing, other things vanishing; the prince gone, except they still said he was ill.

Xhem slid under the sandalmaker's stall and into the lower passages, hurried down to the cavern under the barracks. It would be the last time he could come this way; there was no more leather for making sandals. They must find him another entry to the underground, but two that he knew of had been opened in the past days.

General Piritos was finally on his feet; he was overly thin and his hair grayer than it had been, but he no longer limped. The arm was bound close to his chest. Today he was pacing, dictating orders to an aide as he had upon the wall but he stopped as Xhem came near. His eyebrows went up. "Grysis, how many of these children do you have out there?"

"Five boys, counting Xhem," Grysis replied. "Xhem, how are you lad?"

Xhem ducked his head in the general's direction before

answering. "I am fine, sir. They are dismantling the sandal stall at sunset today; I can't come that way any more."

"All right. Frewis, you know the entries better than I, and where the boy's house is; think of one that will be safe and close by. What from Ridlo?" He held up a hand. "Here, you'd better sit down first, you're all out of breath. And let me see if there's any bread." He got up, went away and came back with a wedge of flat bread and a little oil to smear on it. "Eat first, then tell me."

"Thank you sir." Xhem finished the bread quickly, organizing his thoughts while he chewed. "From Ridlo, they took Lortis, Werin and Lodis. Lodis has already come back and said he was asked about what other men had said in the winehouse. He claimed to have drunk too much to know anything, and they let him go; Ridlo is bringing him down later, to stay. He saw Lortis being taken into the barracks; he has not seen Werin at all. From Ryllos, his cousin did not suicide, his life upon it. From Potro, Prince Hadda has taken two of his children, which means there are now eleven noble children in the palace. He says he has men he can trust to help take the palace, but he won't dare act if they can't discover where the—where the children are kept first. From Breyd, she will come tonight, but says Tephys tells her the Pairs must be assembled here, seven nights from now and she will come also. From my cousin Creos, his friend Idron and twenty others he can vouch for are willing to help, when the time comes."

"You spoke with Creos?" Grysis asked. Xhem eyed him sidelong, finally shrugged.

"He asked me. He said he thought I might know something he didn't. I didn't say anything, but he said that if I ever saw his captain—"

"There is nothing wrong with Creos." Frewis had come back unnoticed. He sat down cross-legged on the stone next to Grysis. "He is part of a leg short, but it didn't affect his wits. And they were good ones when he served under me. Anything else?"

"From Nessa: Apodain went to the palace again last night; Prince Hadda acted more oddly than usual, and Apodain could smell his mother's oil on the prince's tunic. He'll tell you more tonight, though."

Grysis ran a square hand through his hair and said, "To Ridlo, stay low and out of that winehouse by the barracks.

To Creos, tell his friend to come to the Goat Gate, where the back wall of the Temple of Warriors was, at ninth horn; tell him to be ready to give names to the man he'll meet there. They'll be told what to do, and when."

"Yes, sir."

"Here, Frewis, did you find a new path for our young friend?"

"I'll show him."

"Frewis," Piritos said gravely. "A word against your ear before you go." Xhem anxiously watched the two men walk away, then turned to Grysis.

"Sir, I saw how he looked when I came in. He's not going to tell me to go home, is he?"

Grysis thought about this, finally shook his head. "Don't worry, boy. I don't think he would; he knows we need you, and grown men couldn't do what you're doing out there."

"Thank you, sir."

Across the cavern, Piritos drew the other man to a halt. "I trust you only with this, captain; get another man or two to help you if you must, but no more than that, and keep the matter to yourself as much as you can. I want you to bring me one of Haffat's men."

Frewis considered this. "An officer?"

"Any man will do, I think—preferably one who will not be much missed. We are running out of time; and I need to know more than that boy can tell us."

It was very dark and quiet in the cavern below and behind the temple cavern; no sound but the occasional drip of water into an unseen pool, very little light. Denira fought despair as best she could; she needed to put on the best possible face for Ye Sotris, who had her hands full with her two boys and her own fears—the growing discomfort of her pregnancy, rapidly nearing its end.

It was increasingly difficult for her to remember anything from outside; the games, Breyd—the two of them laughing as though nothing had changed. She had told Ye Sotris everything she could recall of the games so many times that they had become more like a tale than anything real: What races there had been, who had won them; how Pelledar had looked, what he had worn.

The queen listened, or played with her sons, or recited

them verse and stories from her own childhood. If she wept, Denira never heard or saw her.

Fortunately, Denira thought, there was no reason for *her* to hide. She was allowed a little freedom, though usually she only came up into the temple courtyard very late at night, after the queen was asleep.

She looked up as shuffling footsteps sounded on the gritty stone; Eyzhad came now and again to take the boys for walks. She would have known his particular pace anyway, but the two young princes were already running to greet him. He squatted down to be on eye level with them, and held out his hands. A small, neatly made reed ship lay across them. He looked up as Ye Sotris came over and said, "I thought they might like this." He addressed the children. "When I was a boy, I went up and down the river with my father in a boat of reeds very much like this. Perhaps my young friends would care to come with me and see if this one will float?"

"How kind of you," Ye Sotris exclaimed. She laid a hand on one curly head and then the other and said, "You may go with Eyzhad if you like. Do not get completely wet, and pay close attention to what he tells you!" She watched them go, waved as her sons turned at the last moment to look at her, then sighed. "Poor children." She looked up, tried to smile, but her eyes were somber. "And poor Denira."

"No—"

"It is a kind lie," Ye Sotris began, but she broke off and turned to peer in the direction Eyzhad had come from. "Someone else is coming, I think."

Denira was already past her, gesturing urgently for the queen to step back into shadow, but it was Tephys, her first visit to this cavern in several days. Her face was very grim and Denira could feel her heart beating a little faster, matching itself to Tephys'. "Ye Sotris, will you mind if I take your companion aside for a little? I won't keep her long."

Ye Sotris was pale and Denira heard her swallow, but her voice was steady. "Is it—is it Pelledar?"

"No. Something else." She turned, gestured for Denira to follow, but stopped again in the outside passage. "Take my hands," she said softly. Denira steeled herself; Tephys' touch was a sometimes painful thing these days. This time warmth ran down her fingers and pooled in her palms briefly, faded almost at once. Tephys held the joined hands high and began to pivot slowly, bringing Denira around with her. She stopped suddenly. "There—there. Can you feel it?"

"I can't feel anything. Wait." She closed her eyes. Something beating—a low, slow, heavy beat. "What is it?"

Tephys shook her head. "The barrier inhibits, but it shouldn't block you since you're not fully initiated. Can you tell which way the sound is?"

She edged around a little, stopped almost at once. "That way—where I'm facing. What is it?"

Tephys' eyes were very bright. "It's a heartbeat. And it belongs to the lion-priest. Knoe." She let go Denira's hands. Denira stared into the darkness.

"He's not—he isn't—?"

"Contain yourself. He's beyond the barrier, weren't you listening? I can't tell what he's doing, and I can't find him alone, but I know where he is. One more vigil, tomorrow night. A last purification. You'll be ready?"

She couldn't remember the last time she'd slept all of a night; after the past four nights, she was giddy with lack of sleep. "I have to be ready, don't I?" she asked softly.

"Go back to Ye Sotris. Ask her what she knows about the passages under the palace. Come later and tell me."

"She'll want to know why. Do you think the prince—?"

"I don't know what to think," Tephys replied grimly. "Ask." She turned and went quickly the way she had come.

In a long, narrow, and dimly lit tunnel beneath the palace, Knoe looked up and went very still. Someone out there had thought his name—that earth-priestess, it must be. He closed his eyes, thought of nothing in particular. It was very silent down here, no sound but his own heart. The sense of notice faded; he raised the small, flickering lamp and continued down the tunnel. These man-made passageways seemed to go all directions; even after so many days, he couldn't get a grasp on direction and couldn't be certain he'd found all the tunnels—he hadn't found any that went very far. He'd found a small cave his first day down here, but it was shallow, the ceiling solid; he'd gone that way twice since, or so he thought—he hadn't found it again.

It intrigued him; it must be Denota's power he felt in the walls, a faint sense of *something* that left him aware of the patterns on his fingertips when they brushed the stone. But it was so weak! An ancient spell, he thought; something that was weakening. Easily broken, if only he could get a grasp on it and find out what it *was*. Knoe cursed as he stubbed a toe already sore from previous stubbings. He stared at the lamp in his hand, as if he'd forgotten momentarily what it was, then blinked rapidly and turned to go back the way he'd come.

The Ergardi would have been useful in such a task, but he had not been able to bring them into the city and they had gone with Haffat anyway. That barrier on the outer wall—when the wall was broken by the ballista, the barrier should have fallen, Knoe thought angrily, but it hadn't. Pelledar had denied knowing anything about it; the Pair wouldn't speak about that or anything else. He couldn't ask Tephys because the priestess would not come out of her temple—and he could not go in.

He laid a hand on the wall, then felt as high as he could reach. Nothing, except the pulse in his fingers.

"You become obsessed with this," he growled. "She cannot prevail, in the end. But this is not the key, out here; they are."

He must remember to send down to the camp, for one of his followers to bring him more powder. This last box must have lost its potency, he had given it to the Dyadd and nothing at all happened.

The silence was suddenly oppressive; his ears rang. He shook his head to clear it, walked a little faster. "They are the key," he said aloud. The words were muffled by the narrow stone walls.

Pelledar had proven more stubborn than he would ever have suspected, but he did not always seem to be fully conscious, or aware of where he was. The Pair—he began to wonder if he ever had reached them, even in the beginning. He'd heard often enough what they did in battle; perhaps she took everything from them and left only shells of men and women.

Many of them had died, but Pelledar lied when he said all were dead. He *knew*.

He leaned against the wall, brought a foot up, and examined his toes. They were sore; one bled. He blotted it with his fingertips. The fingers went very cold, then hot. *Something is wrong here—with me,* he thought uneasily, and for the first time in days wondered what he was doing in this place. He scrubbed his hand down his robe; the discomfort faded. He blinked, raised the oil lamp above his head, and set out again.

The Pair was where he had left them; he on his back, arms folded across his chest; she curled on her side, hair spilled over her face. He drew it back and looked closely at her; her eyes looked into his indifferently. He set his lips against her ear. "The man is dead," he whispered. "But he has told me what you are, Secchi. You will tell me where the rest of the Secchi are, and who they are." No reaction.

He tried again, finally let the hair fall across her face again and went over to him. His eyes were half-closed, his face sunken, but his chest rose and fell. "You are not yet dead," Knoe whispered. "But your Secchi will die before the sun sets. She has told me what she is, what you are. Now you will tell me where the other Secchi are, where the Pairs hide, or I will set the god's mark on you, and you will watch her die by your own hands, and by the knife that I give you." His eyes flickered; Knoe leaned toward him and held his breath, waited. Nothing. Finally he stepped back from them, then walked over to the wall and watched them from shadow. No movement except the shallow rise and fall of his breast, an occasional, faint movement of her hair or her shoulder to show she lived.

Hadda stared morosely out the window of the throne room, across the plain toward a vacant mole and smooth sea beyond it. He had the chamber to himself, for once: Apodain had come earlier and brought another of his royal cousins, but they had left after only a short while. The boys his father had made him bring into the palace were elsewhere, doing whatever children in this end of the world did. "I do not know, I do not care to know," he told himself firmly once more. Young boys with their direct stares, their whispering, and sullen looks behind his back—they were not happy here, any more than he was pleased to have them. And he did not share his father's conviction that they helped him keep peace.

He lifted the gold-rimmed cup and tasted the wine; Khadat had been right, it was more to his taste than the red stuff they drank here; good enough it didn't need water. She had sent him two large clay jugs of it and he was grateful for the gift, but the woman made him nervous. She came too often, always with some gift, or some question for him; with questions to ask of Haffat, when Hadda sent him messages, some information on shipments of grain or metals. *Is she trying to seduce me?* he wondered. It was a terrifying thought.

Hadda sighed and let his forehead rest against the cool stone wall. His father *might* have waited until he had Ye Eygar so he could rule there, if he must sit on any throne. They had music in Ye Eygar, good food, bards who sang ancient tales or made plays of them.

He walked back over to the throne finally and flung himself into it, smoothed the parchment he'd wadded in one hand and reread it. "To my son and my brother, Great King of Ghezrat." Hadda snorted aloud; it sounded just as ridiculous as it had the first time. "It has been twenty days since I left Ghezrat; perhaps twenty-five by the time the messenger puts this in your hands.

"I have sent an ultimatum to the Eygari king and he has refused it; the city is no Ghezrat, however; I do not foresee more than five days of hard fighting before it is mine, after which I will return to Ghezrat—at least for a while." The rest was instructions: remember this, do that, don't say this. Hadda scowled and flung the parchment aside. Twenty-five days out. Then five days of fighting. Another five, to settle matters, twenty-five to return. It felt like a lifetime.

Tenth horn: Wind blew down deserted streets; a little rain had fallen earlier, just enough to slick the paving stones of the square. The winehouse near the barracks was full of off-duty Diye Haff. The gate guards looked over curiously as voices rose angrily, and someone came flying out as though he'd been booted. He flailed for balance, caught himself and turned with great care toward the barracks. After a few steps, though, he was turned halfway around and heading straight for the wall. He vanished in shadow; they could hear him muttering and stumbling around for a time but the wind picked up again and drowned out everything but loud, angry voices in the winehouse. "Only Ildun," one of the gate guards muttered. "Drunk again."

"Drunk as usual, you mean," the other said. "Suppose someone should go get him?"

"Why? Man like that leads a charmed life."

Ridlo looked down a short distance along the inner wall and smiled grimly. One man, alone and very drunk. . . . He waited for a gust of wind to cover any noise his bare feet might make and ran.

Apodain snuffed the lamp and stood very still; Khadat had come this way much earlier, paused to look into his room and then in Breyd's doorway, before she went on upstairs, but he couldn't hear anything now. The hall was empty, but a lamp still burned in Breyd's room.

She was sitting at the loom, eyes close to the dark fabric, running her fingers along the upper edge and pressing it here and there with the long-toothed comb. She was smiling, he thought; hard to tell, it was so dark in there. As he moved, she glanced up. "Apodain," she whispered.

He came over and touched the fabric. Soft, thick wool. She would be warm in that, or under it, this winter. "It's quiet out there. I can go for you tonight, if you'd rather."

"I'll go; my fingers are numb from keeping at this so long. You're certain all those boys—?"

"All being held in the queen's apartments. Hadda was upset this afternoon; a little too much wine, and another letter from his father. All I had to do was lose one game to him and sound sympathetic. It poured out. Tell Grysis I'll come when I can."

He went back to his room and stood back from the doorway, watching as her light went out. Moments later she went by, the least of shadows in a very dark hallway; her sandals made very little noise, and she'd wrapped herself in the dark green wool.

Moments later the lower hallway erupted: Breyd's startled shriek, Emyas shouting at her, and then Khadat thumping down the stairs. "What are you up to, at such an hour and dressed like that?" she bellowed.

Apodain came out into the hall and part way down the stairs. "I worked on my wool so late," Breyd said defensively, "and all at once I realized I was cold and hungry, and I thought—"

"A cloak like that—just to sneak into the kitchen?" Emyas demanded.

"I was cold," Breyd repeated and now she sounded sullen. Khadat looked at Emyas, Emyas glared at Breyd; neither of them noticed Apodain, motionless on the stairs and Breyd was staring at her feet. Khadat finally sighed heavily.

"All right. Go. I'll be here when you come back." She folded her arms across her chest and stared down the hall thoughtfully. "Emyas. I don't like that girl. I didn't from the first, but that was because of Apodain. Now. . . ."

"She's lying," Emyas said flatly.

"I don't know . . . perhaps. Something—I'll find out. Go on back to Hemit, he's had a restless night." Apodain retreated silently up the steps and across the hall to his rooms. He heard Emyas' heavy tread on the steps, then Khadat talking. To Breyd, or to herself? he wondered. A moment later, he heard Khadat's sandals and retreated to his couch. Breyd went by, something clutched in her fingers, his mother right on her heels. Khadat paused outside his door, finally shrugged, and went on. Moments later he heard her climbing to her room.

Xhem paused to catch his breath in the shade of the wall opposite Khadat's gates; it was hot and the air thick, but he was tired most of the time anyway. His stomach ached. *There will be bread when I see Nabid,* he reminded himself, and he had only this one final errand before he could go below. He clutched the little clay jug to his chest, crossed the deserted street, entered the horse-forecourt and ducked into the stables.

A woman's harsh voice stopped him in his tracks: Khadat had come up the street from the direction of the temple and he hadn't seen her—but she'd seen him. He stood very still, uncertain what he should do; Khadat was walking toward him. She would never catch him if he ran. But he had messages for Nessa and something for Breyd. Khadat was suddenly between him and the gate. "What is a street boy doing here?"

Dear goddess, Xhem thought fervently and clutched the jug even more closely. As if in response to that prayer, Nessa came into the courtyard, leading one of Apodain's horses. He stopped short. "Princess, this is my small cousin, I did not think you would object if he brought me news of my family."

"Family?" Khadat's brow furrowed. "I thought all your family was outside the city."

"Oh, yes, Princess, across the Alno. But some of them

stayed in the city after Haffat came; the boy brings me the gossip from the market."

"Oh." Her eyes fastened on the jug. "And what is this?"

"Um, well, the grandmother of Breyd sent this for her. A gift, oil and hot peppers for her bread."

"You are also Breyd's kin?" Khadat demanded suspiciously.

"Oh, no, Princess." Xhem bobbed his head, then looked at her with very wide eyes. "My mother knows the cousin of Breyd's grandmother."

"Yes, yes, never mind," Khadat put in hastily. "Well, then. A gift? Had you thought to bring this to her yourself—perhaps with some message?" Her eyes had narrowed once more, but Xhem shook his head.

"Oh, no, Princess. I would never go *there;* I came here, to hand it to my cousin Nessa so he could give it to one of the servants to give to her. Is—is that permitted?" he asked in a small voice. Nessa stood very still, one hand on the horse's nose and the other wrapped in the lead.

Khadat held out her hand. "I will take this to my daughter. I am certain she will be glad to have the gift." She turned and walked back to the palace, jug clasped tightly in one hand.

Nessa touched Xhem's shoulder and indicated the interior of the stable with a jerk of his head. "Quickly, lad, in here." He stopped just inside the door, turned and said rapidly, "Give me whatever messages you have, and then you had better not come back again. She remembers everything; also, she tells everything to the emperor's son."

Xhem bit his lip. "If I got you into trouble with her—"

"That could come at any time, it's not your fault, boy. What messages, before she sends Emyas or Pria to make certain you're gone, or to overhear what we say."

"From Nabid, Apodain is to learn what he can from Hadda in the next two days; he has no more time than that. To tell Breyd tomorrow, ninth horn, beneath the barracks, all the Pairs and herself. To yourself from Nabid, go yourself, no later than tomorrow night, you know where, he will meet you, and he has you a place to sleep."

"Good. Tell him I'll come."

Xhem glanced out the door; his jaw was set. "Tell Breyd from me about Niddy's peppers; that horrible princess took them only to throw away. Make sure Breyd knows Niddy sent them."

"I will do that. Go now. I will see you later, in that other place." Xhem was already gone, haring across the courtyard and out of sight past the temple. Nessa sighed, led the horse over to his stall, and began rubbing him down. It wouldn't be long before Khadat's cousin or her personal servant came to pump him for information; with luck, Reott would come first, or perhaps Apodain.

Khadat stood in the center of her apartment and gazed at the little jug she still held. She smiled gently. "Oil and peppers for her bread—peasant food. I don't know what that wretched child is up to but she is doing something. Here and there, where she shouldn't be, gone from her rooms at odd times. But it can't mean anything good for me. And last night. . . ." She hadn't slept, trying to puzzle it out. Something to do with Denota—she had served the goddess, as a priestess and as Secchi. *Secchi.* Haffat had asked her about them; his priest had. Secchi—Haffat?

She stared at the opposite wall. "If Haffat were here—but he won't return for some time, his priest is no good to me, and his son even less useful. There's no one to give her to, no place to keep her here." She pried the cork from the jug, sniffed gingerly. "They say the hot peppers cover the taste of bread made with inferior grain, though; or the taste of meat which is not good." She smiled unpleasantly, pushed the cork back in place, and went in search of her servant.

Breyd wove the last ends in on the blue wool and rolled it up. She hadn't been able to sleep after Khadat brought her back to her apartments, but at first her hands had trembled so she couldn't weave either.

She stood and stretched; seventh horn had just sounded. *I should have saved some of that bread.* She looked out into the hall; Apodain was coming up the stairs.

"Mother sent me to bring you down to eat." He laid a hand on her cheek. "You look like you didn't sleep."

"I didn't."

"Can you manage this?"

She shrugged. "I'm hungry."

Khadat sat on the edge of her couch; Pria watched as one of the girls set jugs of wine and water and a wooden bowl of bread on the table, then began to serve her mistress. The girl went out, came back with two painted bowls of olives and the yellowish oil Khadat favored for her bread, and then another bowl with a small clay jug sitting inside it. Breyd looked at it and went very still. When she looked up, Khadat was watching her narrowly.

"That was brought for you today." She drew a deep breath, folded her arms and said, "You should have said something to me or to Pria—to any of the servants, if you did not have enough to eat. We are not so poor, we cannot afford to feed another mouth. But the wife of a nobleman does not wrap herself in wool and sneak down to the kitchen like a common thief—she has bread and fruit brought to her in the evening, so it is there for her, or she tells a *servant* to bring her something at a later hour. You will remember this."

"Yes, madam," Breyd murmured. "I'm sorry, madam."

"So you should be," Khadat said flatly. She settled back on her couch and picked up her cup. "The boy who brought that said it was a gift from your grandmother; when Pria took it, she said she could smell peppers."

"Oh." *Niddy sent me oil and peppers.* Breyd blinked rapidly and drew the bowl toward her. "It is oil and hot peppers, Princess."

"Well." Khadat pursed her lips and finally said grudgingly, "Go ahead and eat them, if you want."

She hesitated, then slipped the cork from the opening and poured them out and inhaled deeply. The smell took her back to Nidya's kitchen. *Oh, wonderful.* She tore a piece of bread in half, dipped it in the oil, held it carefully over the bowl to drip. Khadat was watching her closely, waiting for some dreadful, messy blunder on her part; she wouldn't give the woman the satisfaction.

Apodain's voice startled her; she dropped the bread and it fell back in the oil. "I'm sorry, I only asked if you would let me try them."

"You don't eat such things!" Khadat said sharply. "I have never fed you such—such things!"

"But they have them in the messes, I used to eat them there, Mother." Something in his voice, the set of his jaw warned her. Apodain turned his head and met Breyd's eyes squarely, then let his dip toward the bowl. Her fingers froze on the bit of oily bread she had just fished out of the bowl,

er heart began to pound so loudly surely Khadat could hear
t.

Somehow she managed a smile and slid the bowl toward
im; Khadat watched, seemingly turned to stone, the smile
orgotten on her lips as he tore his bread in two and dipped
t in the oil, catching two long strips of bright red pepper in
he fold. But before he could shake the spare drops back into
he bowl or transfer the bread to his mouth, Khadat leapt to
er feet and slapped the bowl away, sending it flying across
he table and onto the floor. The bread he had been holding
and the bowl of bread went with it. Khadat stared at him.
"Are you mad?"

Apodain came around the table. "I am not mad, Mother,"
he said flatly, "but I think you must be. What was in that oil,
besides hot peppers? What did *you* put into it that her grandmother did not think to add?" Khadat gaped at him, then
urned and stormed from the chamber, shouting for Pria.
Apodain ran out behind her, but he ducked back inside immediately.

Breyd sat and stared where Khadat had been a moment
earlier; Apodain caught hold of her wrist and pulled her to
her feet. "She's gone, and I don't know where she went," he
said, "but she just sent Emyas to the palace. You have to be
gone before she comes back."

My peppers; Niddy's peppers. She—"She tried to kill me!"

"Breyd, listen to me! She won't give up because she
failed once, not now; she has nothing to lose. She's probably
on her way to Hadda right now with some tale. He's nervous
enough these days he might have you executed if he even
thought you were a danger to him. But she knows you were
Secchi, and if he learns that—or if she tells Knoe—"

She clutched at his tunic. *"Don't say that!"* The words
sounded strangled; she couldn't manage anything else.

"All right. How much longer until dark?" He shook his
head, drew her across the room, into the hall. "Too long. But
we can't—"

"We?"

"You're going down to Grysis, as soon as it's safe to get
into that tunnel down there, and I'm going with you. I won't
stay here any longer. Now—if we can get out somehow before she comes back—" But Pria was standing in the middle
of the horse-forecourt, arms folded, facing the house.

Apodain grabbed her hand and pulled her into Perlot's

small room, stopped just short of the three-sided garden. "We'll wait here. There's no place to hide once you're past that gate, and between them Mother and Emyas know all the places indoors." Apodain halted just inside the doorway to the garden and backed out cautiously. "You can see in here from the roof and from your balcony—but not under the tree."

Breyd caught hold of his arm and gestured urgently for silence. He listened; Khadat's shrill, strident voice somewhere beyond the low wall. A man's voice, the words indistinguishable. Or maybe two men. Apodain took two cautious steps into the open. The voices faded; he shook his head and came back to put his lips close to her ear.

"I couldn't make out what she was saying."

"Doesn't matter, she's back already, and we're trapped." Breyd's face was pale and her lips trembled. "I'm sorry, Apodain."

He shook his head. "Don't, no time." He hesitated, ran back into the room and came out with two of the lengths of plain dark cloth that had covered his father's couch and wrapped them around his arm. "Do you climb?"

"Climb?" She must have looked as startled as she felt. "That wall? Now?"

But he was already shaking his head. "That tree, high as you can go." He glanced back into the room and added, "and quickly."

She could hear Khadat out there somewhere, shouting for Apodain. *I can't do this; I don't think I ever climbed a tree!* But he looked as pale as she felt. *They'll take me—and they'll take him, too, she won't be able to stop them—even if she wants to. And he knows that.* She met his eyes, nodded once, and crossed the courtyard. Apodain followed and lifted her into the lowest branches.

It wasn't as hard as she'd have thought; the large branches were thick and twisted and wide-spread. Above them, there was less room to move and she was uncomfortably aware of the way the wood shifted under her weight, of the drop. He moved past her and she concentrated on following him exactly. There was just room in a cup of three branches for her to crouch; he lay along one just above her and pulled the loose fabric from his arm. "Take it, cover that white cloth and make yourself small," he breathed. She eased it under her and across her shoulders, drew up her feet, and crouched down. The branch above her trembled, was still. Wind ruffled the leaves and blew hair off her damp forehead.

Someone was standing in the doorway. She held her breath. Pria's voice rang in her ears: "No one is here, and the bar is across the gate! She didn't go this way!" Khadat high above, calling Apodain's name at odd intervals. Silence below, and then Khadat's voice coming from the edge of the roof, her words so clear she must have been leaning over the parapet directly above them.

"She is not anywhere in the palace, and my son is gone!"

Emyas' voice came from Breyd's apartment: "Nothing's gone from in here!" More shouting back and forth. She couldn't make out the words for distance and the northern accent: *Diye Haff.* Khadat was arguing furiously with someone. Finally fading voices. Hadda's men were on their way out to the street, and Khadat went with them.

Breyd shifted her weight cautiously, looked at Apodain who shook his head and mouthed, "Wait." She nodded to show she had understood and settled against her branch to wait for darkness.

24

Eighth horn: The sky had gone dark some time before and there was no sound coming from the palace or in the small courtyard. The wind was blowing fitfully. Apodain edged down close to her, and put his face against her ear. "Wait," he breathed. "I'll go first, in case." She nodded, held her breath as the wind fell to nothing, and listened. Nothing but distant voices from somewhere across the wall. *Khadat could be standing there, just inside the room, waiting,* she thought, and shivered. He gripped her arm, gave her a reassuring smile and worked his way down to the low branches, caught hold of one and dropped.

He waited there, crouched, for a very long, still moment, then came upright and shook his head, beckoning.

Very carefully. She winced as she cautiously straightened a leg. It ached; her hands were stiff from clinging to the branches for so long, and her knees hurt. He glanced toward the house occasionally, mostly kept his eyes on her until she was down where he could catch hold of her waist and lift her the rest of the way. She looked anxiously into the room; it was faintly lit from the hallway beyond. No one was there. She touched his arm. "Go," she mouthed at him. He hesitated, finally shrugged, and came with her.

The gate bar moved smoothly, the narrow, sloping street beyond was very dark and completely deserted. They went swiftly and quietly from Khadat's palace, and from her grasp.

Once they were beneath the wall and past the first bend in the passage, Breyd sagged into the wall and closed her eyes. "I can't, give me a moment. I need to just—catch my breath."

"That was bad," Apodain said. He leaned against the wall next to her. "I don't know quite what to say."

"Don't say anything. You aren't responsible for her. And I knew it wasn't safe from the first, remember?" He wrapped an arm around her; she turned to lean against him, and buried her face in his shoulder. "We'd better go on," she mumbled after a moment. "My knees are starting to shake and I'm exhausted all at once. But we can't stay here."

"No." He kept his arm around her as they walked and held the oil lamp in his other. They moved quietly for some time. Breyd sighed and rested her head against him.

"Thank you," she said. "For getting me out of there."

"I nearly didn't. It all happened so fast, I couldn't think."

"I couldn't believe she'd really done that. I think I would have still been there when she came back with——" She swallowed.

"Don't. That didn't happen, we got lucky. Just a little farther, you'll be able to rest."

"I know. I'm all right now. Just tired. Relieved." She pulled back a little to look up at him. "What were you looking for, in that courtyard just now?"

He drew her around a new fall of stones. "My panoply. I put it in a storage jar, under one of the stones. I wasn't certain the palace was empty, though, or that I could get it out without making noise. Emyas—it would have been like him to move around in the dark, checking all the hidden places down below the cellars and the storage in hopes of catching us."

She shivered. "Don't."

"It's all right, you're done with that. Neither of us will ever go there again. The panoply—well, it's safe there, Grysis can find me weapons—and it wasn't worth dying for. Not that way."

Eighth horn: The air in Denota's temple was thick and still. Denira and Meronne knelt at the ends of the long Cleft, the altar lamps in their outstretched hands. Tephys stood between them, at the very edge of the deep cut, her priestesses and her priest before her. She raised her arms; the lamps flared brightly once, then died.

"The hour has come." Her voice filled the cavern; the stone floor shivered and was still again. "Let the Mother of us all cast off her fair aspect, that the true strength of the Earth be shown. Goddess, to your servant give now the power of these stones, to crush our enemy!"

Green flame roared up from the Cleft. For one blinding moment, the High Priestess blazed with Light; it filled the cavern. Silence, and utter darkness flowed in behind.

Eighth horn: The upper floor of the palace was brightly lit. Hadda paced back and forth between the windows. Knoe stood with his back to the room; he was staring down at the empty temple courtyard and frowning. "Something is wrong," he mumbled vexedly.

"I know something is wrong, priest," Hadda snapped. Knoe turned to look at him. "I didn't send for you to tell me that, I want to know *what* is wrong!" He stopped abruptly. *That is Knoe; you do not cross him, you know never to cross him!* But Knoe was somehow wrong, too: He spent most of his time beneath the city, emerging at odd hours with a vacant look in his eyes. So far as Hadda knew, he had not gone down to the camp in days; or even to the lower city, where the god's shrine was being built.

What is under this palace to do this to him? Or was this part of some subtle plan of Knoe's, against *him?*

Knoe turned from the window. "You are safe enough here. For now."

He caught at that and asked, dry-mouthed: "For now? I can—if I bring in another company—"

"Another company is no use; you have enough men in the palace. Too many, and with too much time on their hands. Even I have heard their complaints."

"They don't—they wouldn't—"

"They are men!" Knoe snapped, silencing him. "Common, ordinary, *stupid* men! They are too many long days' march from their own land and the emperor they followed here has gone on without them."

"He won't! He wouldn't abandon us."

Knoe came across and caught his arms in a painful grasp. "Get a hold on yourself!" he hissed. Hadda swallowed, finally nodded. Knoe let go of him and turned away. "I warned your Father, and I tell you now. It is not a matter of armies and superior strength any more: The city is not truly yours, and never will be, unless this earth goddess is crushed."

"I thought that was *your* task," Hadda replied sullenly. "Or why have you kept that Pair? And why did you take

Pelledar down there?" Hadda bit his lip; Knoe turned on him; his eyes were blackly furious.

"It *is* my task! But this concerns your grasp on Ghezrat. *Your* safety." He came across the room; Hadda swallowed nervously but held his ground. "Somehow she protects them still, even against the Lion's Breath, even so far beneath the earth. . . ." His voice trailed away and he went very still.

Hadda licked his lips. "What? What is it?"

"I must think this through," Knoe said distantly. He blinked and his eyes suddenly gleamed. "But meanwhile, there is something *you* can do. That woman—Khadat. What word from the guard you sent with her?"

"That her son and the girl were already gone. They've searched the palace, the nearby buildings and most of the other noble houses and palaces."

"She's causing trouble; upsetting people. Haffat won't like this. You should have stopped her."

"Stopped her! Stopped Khadat?" Hadda shouted.

"Stopped her! Those are *your* men with her, aren't they? Who orders them? You or that woman?" Hadda bit his lip and turned away from him. Knoe watched him thoughtfully. *Haffat was wrong; this weak creature could be no one's heir. He will cost us all, if I let him. Will cost me all, and I will not have that!* "The girl might have been useful," he said finally. "But she is not necessarily the answer. Send guards, find that woman, and have her brought. She knows about Secchi. And she is a priestess."

"I know that. Why do you think I've put up with her company all these days since Father left? But she only hints at things; she still hasn't told me anything useful."

"She hasn't." Knoe smiled unpleasantly. "But she will."

The cavern under the barracks was full of people: men in armor edged their swords; two of Piritos' aides passed out bundles of javelins. A splash of red against the wall: Four Pairs knelt in a close circle, heads bowed. Three men came from the tunnel that led down from the Goat Gate. Others went out that way, and out toward the Shepherd Gate. General Piritos sat nearby listening to one of his aides; he looked up as Grysis came over.

"I have the newest report, sir; as of now, a full company of Diye Haff holds the horse-forecourt and the ground floor of the palace; another half-company at least guards the third floor and the roof. There may be another half-company inside; it is impossible to get a count now, but there is only a half-company in the barracks and fewer men in the camp than there were. The emperor's heir is seen tonight at the windows of the throne room and nowhere else. The twelve children he holds hadn't been moved from the queen's apartments."

"How certain?" Piritos demanded.

"One of the fathers was let in yesterday to see them. He'll lead the men who go after them."

"Good. What about the outside?"

"Covered. We'll have enough men to block the gates once we get inside and the fighting starts."

"The goddess barrier—"

"Tephys just sent word: The barrier between the city and the palace goes down at first horn. She is sending her heir here, to attend the Pairs."

"Good. Apodain—we need him," the general said flatly. "No one else can get us into the palace from beneath. Even with the Dyaddi rebonded, a frontal attack on the palace would be disastrous for us." Grysis looked troubled.

"I know. No one's heard, but it hasn't been dark that long, they've probably been hiding somewhere. We have men out there looking for them and three of his company have been trying to get their hands on Khadat—last word I have, she's still with Hadda's men, and we can't get close to her."

"She's dangerous," Piritos said. "She could ruin everything. Send word to Ryllos, bring her to me if they can, but if not—kill her."

Khadat's color was high. She brushed past the hall guards and stalked into the throne room. "Why have I been brought here? Those men would tell me nothing. Have you found them?"

The woman towered over him; Hadda dug his hands into the arms of the throne and brought his chin up. "We have not found the girl, Khadat," he said distantly. "Or your son."

"Then why did you send for me? We have only searched the palace and a few of the houses where he might have hidden. They didn't leave the city, your men haven't seen them in the streets, and they tell me no one has entered the temple grounds. Did you have her mother's house searched?"

As if I would send armed guards into that area, Hadda

thought. Even if they didn't create trouble, his father would have his head for it. He wasn't going to tell *her* that, though. "She hasn't been seen," he said flatly. "Khadat, you create resentment out there; my father will be displeased unless there is a very good reason for it. How certain are you this girl is spying on you—and what could she hope to learn?"

"Learn? Nothing! Do you suspect *me* of—don't be ridiculous!" Khadat snapped. She drew herself up, folded her arms and glared down at him. "She's been sneaking around my house and out of it at odd hours! This is a girl of seventeen years, a common girl; however girls act in Diyet, in Ghezrat they do not behave like that, ever! What good could she be up to? There is something going on in this city, I do not know what, but there's something very wrong—and she is part of it."

"Something . . . going on. . . ." Hadda echoed.

"You've felt it—all these men around you, and you said as much yourself, yesterday!" She began to pace back and forth before the throne. "But I begin to see it myself: That scrawny peasant boy who comes and whispers with my servants—Emyas has seen him down in the market, talking to Apodain's cousin Ryllos and I will swear it was the same boy coming from Polyos' villa two days ago. *That* is not normal, all this whispering, something is afoot."

"I—" Hadda swallowed. Nothing else would come.

"And Emyas tells me there are men missing, suddenly, all across the city: soldiers—men who *were* soldiers," she corrected herself sarcastically. "Not where they were the day before. *She* is part of it, whatever it is, and she's involved my Apodain."

"You've heard her, asked him? Khadat, truly, I cannot just. . . ."

"If I had heard one treasonous word from her mouth, do you think I wouldn't have come to you at once?" Khadat shouted. She stared at him, as if she suddenly realized who she was shouting at, and went on in a much quieter voice. "Prince, I apologize. My son is gone and I am gravely worried; this girl will get him killed."

Hadda shook his head. "If you are right, she will get us *all* killed. But, a girl like that, what threat is she?"

"You forget, Prince Hadda. She is Secchi."

"Secchi. Yes." Knoe's voice behind her. Khadat whirled around and stared at him.

"Where did you come from?"

Knoe smiled. "Secchi. I have asked a prince and a Dyadd what this Secchi is. I have yet to receive a satisfactory answer. But I think you might tell me."

"Don't you dare threaten me! I am a personal friend of your emperor!"

"Yes, of course. But he is not here, and I am. And he may not return." Hadda gasped and came to his feet. Knoe glanced at him and turned back to her. "I warned him this weak prince would be his downfall, and so it has proven. Axtekeles has abandoned him outside Ye Eygar."

"That's a lie!" Hadda whispered. He clapped a hand across his mouth and sank back onto the throne.

"The city holds against him, and his army sits between the walls and the sea, in swamp. Men are dying of fever by the tens every day. The Ergardi have abandoned him; denounced the god—they are gone." Hadda shook his head wildly. Knoe glanced at him. "It is true, Prince. One of my priests brought me word tonight, just before your summons came. Why do you think I left my task down there, when it is not yet finished?"

"He—he will—"

"He was still alive when my priest left him and he had already ordered the retreat; his army may be on its way back here by now.

"There is one last chance to save his empire and win back the god's approval to him. Only one: We must break this earth goddess, destroy her power. It is in the Secchi, I am sure of it. And this woman will tell me. Woman, what are the Secchi? You have lived with one, but you are also Denota's priestess, and the Secchi are hers. You will tell me, now."

She had gone pale in the last moments but her eyes were still angry. "How dare you talk to me like this? But why should I tell you anything? I've sworn oaths, I don't dare break them."

Knoe laughed jeeringly, silencing her. "You would have broken them for Haffat before he left—for gain."

"That's not true! Those are *my* family's ships."

"And Haffat offered them back to you; and now I offer back to you something else that *was* yours, woman. Your son."

She stared at him blankly, then turned on Hadda, who recoiled from her white, furious face. "All this time," she whispered. "All this time, and *you* had him?"

"Not that son," Knoe said. "Not Apodain. The other."

"Hemit—no!" She looked at Knoe, at Hadda; her lips trembled. "You can't."

"I can do what I wish, woman!" he thundered; Khadat retreated a pace, a second.

"I just left him, just now, just—You're lying!" She turned and ran.

"You were right," Knoe said. "She'll tell us anything to save this Hemit. Send the guard to her palace, at once, have them bring her and the cripple here."

"Where are you going?" Hadda shouted as Knoe strode from the throne room.

"I'll be back to deal with her. But there is something that I need." He hurried down the steps, down into the storage beneath the palace where he had his pallet, his small altar, his few belongings. *Dread Axtekeles, was it some flaw in Your servant that sent the emperor on this futile quest for one last city? Some thing I did not do, to ensure You received full honor from him? Was it my fault somehow that unworthy Hadda sits upon such an honorable throne? Cleanse me now of that fault, god; that I may enter battle with this goddess purified in Your Breath.*

He knelt briefly before the shrine, but the god remained aloof. *It is the new temple they build to him between the walls, perhaps. If I somehow misread His words, to place it there and so separate the power of the goddess upon the two walls—but I have kept the Pair separated also. Why can I not think!* After a moment, he sat back on his heels. "The powder. That woman would talk for this rag of a son, but Denota may have put guards on her tongue." He found the new box his priest had brought tonight and shoved it into a fold in his sash. The other box must have become contaminated. It had happened before Idemito, and once in Diyet. This was freshly prepared, outside the city, and not by Knoe. *If there is fault in me, Axtekeles, there is none in your other priests.* But the box had warmed his fingers and it now warmed the skin at his waist; this would serve. He got to his feet, hesitated. The prisoners. He must get help, get the three moved outside the city this very night. *You need them, they must tell you—* He shook himself. They could wait. Khadat came first.

* * *

Apodain kept his arm around Breyd as they skirted the ho[w]
pool and came into the light. Someone took the lamp from
him; Grysis pushed his way through the crowd, pulled Breyd
close, and gripped Apodain's arm. "We didn't know where
you were, we've been looking. You're all right?"

"We're alive," Apodain said. "But my mother. . . ."

"I know, we heard; Ryllos says she came into his father's
palace with armed Diye Haff soldiers, looking for you. His
father's livid. Let that go, for now. The High Priestess sent
word not long ago. Everything is ready, and we're moving
up the attack to first horn tomorrow. The general's waiting
for you, Apodain. Breyd, come with us; the company has
your panoply, and the priestess is sending back the binding
cords—but you'll have time for all of that later."

Apodain looked down at her. "Can you manage this?"

She nodded grimly. "We have something to do—to finish."

It was silent and utterly dark under the temple grounds.
The oil lamps with their drowned wicks had been placed at
the points of Denota's Cleft, the cavern emptied of everyone
save Tephys. She stared down into the black gash of the
Cleft for a very long time, then held out her hands. "To me,
goddess, the power of stone: Adamant stone, cold stone—
and stone turned to liquid, purified by Your fire."

Faint light deep in the Cleft turned her robes red. Steam,
smoke, heat rose from deep in the ground beneath her feet.
Tephys held out her hands and flame shot from cupped
palms to relight the lamps. They burned with a high, spiraling red flame; the oil bubbled and spilled over the sides,
running in glowing ribbons down the walls of the Cleft. The
ground shuddered faintly.

Halfway to the cavern beneath the barracks, Denira
paused with her precious bundle. The tunnel shook, was still
again; the air was oppressive and she could *feel* the weight
of the earth and so much solid rock above her. "Denota, the
beloved, the nurturer, Mother of us All," she whispered. It
gave her the courage to go on; it did not change the world
around her.

* * *

Apodain, Grysis, and the general were still talking, their voices too low for Breyd to hear what they said. She sat very still, eyes fixed on Apodain's black curls and the back of his shoulders. At the moment, the brisk, decisive man who ran his finger along Grysis's hide map and argued with Piritos seemed a stranger; this place did. She looked down at her hands. They were no longer as callused as they had been; she could see instead the mark of the shuttle where it had pressed against the base of her first finger and the inside of her thumb. *You must let Khadat go, all of that go. That is past. You are Breyd, Secchi, fighting woman—and the hour has come to fight.*

"Breyd?" Jocasa knelt next to her and wrapped her arms around her shoulders. "Here, Aroepe and I brought your things, we'll help you arm."

Aroepe dropped a red-wrapped bundle and hugged both of them. "We wanted to go out there, find you; they wouldn't let us. I was so afraid."

Breyd clung briefly to both women. "I know, I was, too." She opened out the cloak and began tugging at the dark cloth Apodain had given her. "Help me with this, there isn't time. Fourth horn isn't far off."

Piritos had twenty or more men around him by the time she settled the baldric in place; Jocasa set the cloak across her shoulders, gripped her hand briefly, and hurried back to her Prime. Breyd glanced after her, looked doubtfully where she'd last seen Apodain. No sign of him. But Grysis caught her eye and waved her over. Aroepe shook her head. "We *have* to go, with the other Pairs, the bond—"

"I know, I understand. Go," Breyd whispered. She could just barely sense it, the goddess binding Prime to Secchi and Pair to Pair, the whole together. Aroepe turned and ran.

Seven Pairs now sat in a close circle, hands clasped and heads bowed over them. Breyd turned away. The look on Laprio's face, just now. . . . *Father. She said I would find you—I might find you. But I can't feel you, only them.*

One of Piritos' aides was lacing him into his armor while he talked. "Frewis, you and your twenty: Get into place beneath the barracks as soon as we're done here, they have the passage cleared at this end and there are no obstacles at the barracks end; wait for first horn. You'll have two Pairs sent

to you before first horn. Lodis, you and yours, same thing.
You come up between the walls and attack the men guarding
the main gates, then close and bar both the outer and inner
ones. Ridlo, you come down from the Goat Gate; leave men
at the main gates if Lodis needs reinforcing, and the rest of
you get to the barracks gates and block them. Nabid, you'll
come down from the market, help Ridlo with the barracks.
You've picked archers for the inner walls?" Nabid nodded.
"Good. Use your heads out there, no order is graven in stone
except this one: No Diye Haff gets out of those barracks
alive.

"There aren't a hundred fifty men in the barracks, if that;
Haffat's whelp has moved most of them into the palace and
he's brought more up from the camp.

"Apodain is the only one besides our prince who knows
how to thread the maze beneath the palace and reach the cellars. Five Pairs go with him, myself, a company of fifty,
with another fifty under Grysis to follow.

"Potro, you'll come with us. Apodain tells me there's a
servant's hall behind the apartments where the boys are held,
he thinks he can get you and your men up that way unseen,
but we can't be certain how many men are inside. Use your
head; depending on how things are, you get them out and
bring them out underground, back to here—or if you can't,
bar them and yourselves in. You have enough men with
you?" Potro nodded grimly.

"Ryllos has ten of the royal chariot and another thirty men
waiting in his father's courtyard—any further word from
Ryllos?"

An aide pushed through the crowd. "Just came, sir; the
Princess Khadat had Hadda's soldiers with her, Ryllos' men
slipped out the back way. They weren't seen, Ryllos says.

"They'll come down at first horn, and do all they can to
block the palace gates; Nessa—" He looked up as the
stablemaster came halfway to his feet. "You and your thirty
men go now; be in position behind the old wall opposite the
palace before first horn and wait for Ryllos."

He glanced at the aide. "Any word about Khadat?"

"She hasn't been seen recently, sir."

Piritos frowned. "Tell me again what you saw."

"From the old wall, sir; I couldn't show myself and
couldn't get closer. She had an escort of five—Hadda's
soldiers—when she went inside; she came running out alone

almost at once. Ten of 'em came out just after. Khadat ran in the direction of Perlot's palace, but the kitchen girl didn't see or hear her, and the girl fled out the back way when the soldiers came into the house. We don't know anything else yet."

A shrill outcry high above echoed through the cavern beneath the temple. Tephys turned slowly. A priestess, it must be: No one else could force the entry into the clay room tonight. But who?

Khadat came flying down the steps and nearly fell on the last of them; somehow righted herself at the last moment and clutched at stone; she was gasping for air and her hair hung wildly about her face. "Tephys! Tephys, where are you, I cannot see!"

"I am here, Khadat." Her voice was very deep; it reverberated through stone and the floor pulsed once. Khadat didn't even seem to notice.

"Where is he?" she demanded shrilly. "My son—my son and that low child who was Secchi and priestess! They must have come here, they are not in the palace. We searched everywhere, there is nowhere else save here! What have you done with them?"

"*I* have done nothing, Khadat."

"Where are you?" Khadat whispered. "What is wrong with this place?"

"Nothing is wrong with this place, Khadat. The wrong is in you."

"No! Apodain—Breyd. Where are they? You *must* have them, you must tell me!"

"Why?" The stone in the Cleft churned at the single word; the air went briefly red.

"They—because they—*she* has persuaded my son—because—" She choked, shook her head violently. "They are gone! And when Hadda could not find—could not find my—my son Apodain, and that—that girl, they took *Hemit* instead. They will not return him to me unless Apodain goes to them!"

"Khadat." Tephys' voice reverberated through her; Khadat sucked in her breath sharply and fell silent. "You reek of Lion, Khadat. Why does a daughter of Denota plot with the Lion and his servant to harm Ghezrat?"

"I—I don't, I didn't— Tephys, why don't you listen to me? They have my Hemit, they will *kill* him!"

"And will Khadat sacrifice her whole son to save the husk of the other?"

"Do not say that of Hemit!" Khadat screamed. "Do not dare say that of my Hemit! I will not hear it!"

"Khadat. You will hear me." Tephys walked slowly toward her; Khadat tried to back away, caught her heel on the steps, and clawed at the stone behind her. She fell heavily. Tephys loomed over her. "It is beyond Hemit; you have sold Ghezrat for your father's ships and Perlot's gold."

"No!"

"The goddess knows what you have done; she sees into your soul, Khadat. Be *still!*" Light flared red across the walls behind her; Khadat drew a terrified, shrill breath and fought her way up one step.

"I haven't. I didn't!" She broke suddenly; tears poured down her face and she shrieked, "I didn't tell them, I didn't say anything, I didn't!"

"And you will not," Tephys' deep voice silenced her. "But part of your weakness was your son and because of that, She spares your life. You will not leave this place, however." She raised her hands toward the ceiling, then brought them down across the smooth stone wall. Khadat lay very still, her eyes wide. Tephys stooped and ran her hands down the woman's arms, then turned and walked away.

Behind her, a slab of pale stone blocked the steps to the surface.

One of the royal chariot drivers had found armor for Apodain, a corselet of small overlapping bronze plates and a small oval shield. Piritos looked up as the man edged his way forward. "Go, arm yourself. Come back as soon as you are ready; we must be in position against the barrier when it comes down."

"Sir." Apodain followed the driver back into the open, took the things, and said, "A sword, javelins or a bow— whatever you can find. Bring them, Erius, will you?"

He looked around for an out of the way corner. Red—one of the Secchi was walking toward him. *My Secchi,* he realized with a start. She looked remote, a stranger with her long, thick hair tucked under the bronze-plated helm and the red cloth tiara—even smaller behind all that polished bronze plate. But the steady eyes and their level gaze were the same. "Here," she said, and took his arm. "There is a place over here; I'll help you."

"You don't need to."

"I know that. I would like to."

He stripped off the dark fabric from Perlot's couch and the sash that bound the tunic to his waist, pulled the loose corselet over his head and held out his arms. Breyd began pulling the side lacings snug. She was quiet, remote, as though the Dyaddi armor had raised a barrier between them; he tried to think of something to say but couldn't. The silence stretched. "He—the general said you're going with us—with me," he said finally. She glanced up at him, knotted the leather ties on one side, and moved to the other. Her eyes were fixed on her task; she nodded finally, then looked up at him warily.

"You don't want me there?"

"That isn't it. I thought, because you're Secchi. . . ."

"But I'm not Secchi, not properly." She finished lacing the armor down. "I'm not—dangerous that way, not any more."

"That wasn't my worry," he said quickly.

"No?"

"Not dangerous. In danger—that's different."

"I've been in danger before," she said quietly. She walked behind him, tugged at the shoulders of his borrowed armor.

"I know."

"Apodain, we have to be rid of Haffat's men, now. If it takes every one of us—"

"I know that, too. And you know I understand the need, Breyd. But you—"

"It's my fight, too. Remember what you said when I first came to your mother's house, what we both *felt* at Haffat's games? It isn't done, and whatever fight is left isn't just yours or just mine, it's *ours*. I'm not saying this very well." She knelt to pick up his shield and let him shove it into place, then began working the straps to snug it down to his forearm.

"Tephys tried to explain it to me, before the marriages," she went on, so softly he could barely hear her. "The Dyadd bond didn't break when Father disappeared, because Denota still had use for me. Even after you and I were wed, the bond stayed. Even though it was different, after Father disappeared." She stepped back, glanced up at him. "You aren't like me. Denota *made* me a Secchi, she *made* me fight; she made the bond and I was just an arm, holding the sword, half of a Pair. It wasn't me consciously going into battle. But you—"

He laid a hand on her face; she looked up at him and was startled into silence. "That isn't so. I've never fought an enemy, I've never killed in battle. But you fought all those days without Menlaeus."

She brought her hand up to cover his. "And you would have." Silence. "You won't try to stop me."

"Any more than you would try to stop me. But swear to me you won't do anything reckless."

"I wouldn't—"

"Swear it," Apodain said quietly. "Because . . . I think I could not bear it, if. . . ." His voice trailed away; he looked at her helplessly.

"Oh." She gazed at him, eyes wide; they warmed then, and his heart turned over. "I will swear," she said very softly. "But only for your promise. Because if anything happened to you—" She closed her eyes, then turned to kiss the hand she still held to her face. "Protector and protected, each to the other," she whispered.

"Each to the other," he agreed softly, and kissed her brow. "Grysis and the general need me again, and I don't have a sword yet. And you're being sought," he said suddenly. Breyd turned to look; Denira was walking across the cavern toward them, red cords dangling from her clenched hand.

Denira's face was pale and there were dark smudges under her eyes, but the eyes themselves were steady. "The hour has come. Tephys bid me bring these to you."

Breyd gazed at them blankly; fear and remembered panic tightened her stomach. "I . . . can't." Denira waited. "You saw me the night Tephys took them away! Denira, I can't!"

"She said you might tell me that; she sent this message, to remind you that—"

"Does she think she needs to remind me of anything?" Breyd demanded fiercely. Denira held her ground; Breyd bit her lip. "Denira, I'm *sorry*. But these—if I put them on, if nothing's changed—"

"Do you think the goddess would do that to you, to all of us?"

"After what She's already done to me? Yes, why not that?"

Silence. "You don't understand Her, do you?" Denira asked softly. Breyd turned away. After a moment, she shook her head and Denira said, "Why should you, though? I didn't.

"She isn't tame, Breyd, like we thought when we served her as novices. Didn't you ever wonder why a goddess of earth would set her temple beneath the ground? Or protect a warlike city built on solid rock? Or warn of war and create Dyaddi to serve Her?

"She's all the things you and I thought, Breyd—spring lambs and new grass and joyful, soft, beautiful things—but she's more: The earth itself can bury you, or break you. Lions kill one at a time, but the earth explodes and hundreds die, it shakes and thousands die. And the Dyaddi are the face of that aspect."

"That has nothing to do with—with those," Breyd said flatly. "Denira, tell Tephys I'm not Hers any more, not like the others are."

"You can't turn your back on Her!" Denira said angrily.

"I'm not. But I no longer serve as Her sword; I'm a fighter—like *he* is." She glanced after Apodain.

"All right," Denira said calmly. "I haven't time to argue, and Tephys said you might be stubborn. Take it with you, then, and don't wear it. Tephys said it may still protect you."

"I—"

"And she said tell you she is certain they are your guide to Menlaeus."

Breyd turned back. After a long moment, she held out her hand; the fingers trembled. "Certain? She said that?" Denira nodded. "Give it to me, then. I won't wear it unless I must. But I'll take it for Father."

Flame-red liquid stone had risen nearly to the top of the Cleft. Tephys stared into the depths. "To me, Goddess, the strength of the earth to move stone, to bury our enemy and crush the Lion." She brought her chin up and raised clenched fists above her head.

In the courtyard high above her, the air was still and thick; the thatched shelter trembled as if in a high wind. Well down the sheer slope, an enormous slab of stone tilted slowly out and fell into the Oryon. The Diye Haff kitchen boy who came for water a little later stared at the wet rocks where there had been a river, then turned and fled back to the camp.

Tephys let her arms fall and stepped back from the Cleft. "It is done," she whispered. The long, narrow cauldron at her feet skinned over with ash. She held her cupped palms out to the lamps; the flame dwindled and became ordinary wick-fire fed by sweet oil. All in readiness, including herself.

"Denira to the Pairs, Meronne to the barrier at the palace. Eyzhad to the walls. The priestesses to walls above each of the gates. And I—" She brought her hands up, gazed at them in wonder. They had taken and cast fire—Denota's Fire, which burned even the cinders and left nothing but white ash—and there was no outward mark upon them. "I remain here."

She let her hands fall to her sides, stepped around the cleft and into the center of the cavern, and sought Knoe. His heartbeat came to her at once—in the palace, no longer beneath it. She smiled and let her eyes close. He had not left those walls, or the city walls; he had not yet realized what held him. He would not realize until too late.

Soldiers milled in the third floor hallway, stood in nervous groups on the steps. Knoe pushed his way into the throne room and growled, "Have you no pride? You are prince here, and Great King. Bid those men act like fighting men! They shame you and the emperor, and the god."

Hadda came to his feet. "What do you think I can do about them? They're afraid!"

"I see that! Why?"

"Why?" Hadda bit his lip. "*I* am afraid, Knoe; if I knew the reason—!" He shoved himself back into the throne and mumbled, "They lost Khadat; the woman never went home."

"She never *what?*"

"Don't shout at me, Knoe!" Hadda yelled. "I wasn't the one who let her go! They were right behind her, but they didn't find— She wasn't there!"

"The cripple?"

"They brought him and the man who tends him, that cousin of hers; she says this Emyas keeps Hemit quiet. They—"

"Never mind all this drivel! Where are they?"

"In with the children, under close guard. Khadat, though—"

"She has no friends in all the city, no other relatives. Where would she go? The temple, of course." Knoe stalked across the chamber and stared down at the empty temple grounds. "What is wrong with the air this night?" he demanded vexedly.

"Rain coming," Hadda began. Knoe snorted.

"From a clear, still sky? There's no cloud in sight, not a bit of wind." He clutched the window ledge, leaned perilously out to stare down. "No wind; and yet, that thatch roof just moved. Why?"

Someone in the hallway yelped; pandemonium broke out. Knoe whirled back to find Hadda on his feet, clinging to the back of the throne and his face was nearly green. "The floor shifted, I felt it!"

"Earthquake," Knoe said contemptuously. "And not even enough of one for *me* to notice. Have you never—" He stopped suddenly. Hadda stared at him, slack-jawed.

"Knoe, don't look like that, you terrify me. *What?*"

Knoe's eyes were looking right through him. "I knew there was something wrong. I could feel it tonight when I came up from the cellars. It was in the air—the very . . . the very . . . stones. . . ." His eyes went wide. Hadda swallowed; his heart was thudding painfully. Knoe whirled around and slammed both hands against the wall. "She has tricked me," he whispered furiously. "All this time—tricked *me*. Deadened my mind with her dirt and stone passages, and so subtly even I did not know!" He beat the wall again, then turned back. "There is no time for this, and much to be salvaged, quickly!" he snapped. "She can still be defeated; but a strong man is needed to hold this city for Axtekeles. Stronger than you; stronger than Haffat." He fumbled at his waist, drew forth a small box. Hadda stared at it, licked his lips. "It's the Lion's Breath, boy," Knoe said softly. "Do you know what that is?"

"You—you put that in—in people and they—they speak— and—and you kill—kill them," Hadda stuttered. He began to back away. Knoe followed, his fingers deftly working the tiny catch; he dipped them into the contents, brought out a pinch of fine-grained red dust. Hadda shook his head wildly. "You won't—I can't!"

"You tell *me* nothing, boy. I can, and you will. Now." He pounced. Hadda tried to leap back, away from him; his sandals slid on the tiled floor and he fell heavily. Knoe was on him before he could move; one hand gripping his jaw, the other dropping the powder into his mouth. He sat back. Hadda blinked, whimpered faintly, and fell back. Knoe watched him for a long moment, then said softly, "You will get to your feet and walk to that throne. You will sit there, and you will wait for me to return."

Hadda rolled over and got to his hands and knees, pushed himself slowly upright, and walked, and sat, hands on the chair arms, eyes fixed on the distant wall. "I will wait," he whispered.

"I have prisoners to retrieve, from down there, before it's too late," Knoe said. "You will wait, until I come, or until I send for you. If I send, you will come."

"I will come."

The new temple of the lion, Knoe thought as he stepped into the hall once more. "The prince is resting; let no one disturb him," he told the door guards. "Bid them quiet out here!" he added angrily.

New temple—yes. He hurried down the stairs. Take Hadda there, where the goddess' power was weakest; let the god speak to him and then give this cracked vessel to the Lion. *Axtekeles will surely tell me then, if I serve him best by taking Ghezrat for myself.* A lion-priest on the ancient throne: Denota would never recover from it; and the Lion alone would be worshiped on both sides of the Sea of Delos.

Denira whirled around and held her hands above her head. The cavern shivered, just once. Dead silence. "The barriers will soon come down, you must go!" Denira closed Breyd's fingers over the cords, turned and ran back the way she had come. As one, the Dyaddi placed the cords upon their heads.

Jocasa and Laprio were on their feet, facing the palace. "They're alive," Jocasa whispered. "Bechates, Lochria!"

Apodain pushed to Breyd's side and gripped her shoulders. "Beloved," he said softly. "Are you ready?" She nodded, her face suddenly pale. *If I lost him now!* Apodain's lips were warm on hers, and his arms went around her.

General Piritos was settling his sword in place as they came up. He held up his hands for silence. "Let us leave this hiding place and take back our own. You all know where to go and what to do." He turned to Apodain. "We've no time to spare if we're to be in place by first horn. Let's go!" For answer, Apodain took the oil lamp an aide held out to him, turned, and led the way across the cavern, into a wide, high-ceilinged tunnel. Breyd ran to take her place at his side; the rest came close behind.

The tunnel led down a steep stone ramp into an enormous cavern, the ceiling lost in darkness high above them. They went along a narrow place passable only by one at a time, then a spiraling climb through tunnels and a long galley open on one side to a sheer drop. Apodain stopped then and gestured for the general to lean close. "Sir, the barrier is just ahead; beyond that point we'll be under the palace. I've warned you what it's like."

Piritos nodded once and turned back to tell one of his aides: "Speak low if you must say anything. More importantly: stay close, anyone lost in there may be lost for good."

They started forward once more, crossed a rough stone floor, then edged down another long, sloping shaft, this one straight but nearly as steep as the road to the main gates. They stopped for a very short rest just beyond that. Apodain held up the lamp and took Breyd's fingers in his free hand. "See, over there?" he whispered against her ear. "That pool of blue water, and the three points of stone beyond it? I last saw those in Father's company; we've passed the barrier."

The passages beneath the palace weren't like the others; Breyd shuddered as Apodain led them up yet another plain, tan corridor; passages cut from stone and earth by men, all alike. Light did not always reflect the same from the walls; there were little currents of air that had no connection to anything, nowhere for them to come from. She felt stifled.

The Dyaddi behind her—she could still sense them, if not as intensely as she had. They were growing strong as they neared the palace; readying for battle, banding together, Primes and Secchi to each other; Pairs to Pairs and all to Denota.

It was dizzying, disorienting atop everything else. When Apodain stopped to consult some inner map, she let go his hand and stepped away from him to rest one hand against the wall for balance; she closed her eyes.

It is very dark here; I cannot see anything, and my arms

ache from being borne so far, but my leg will not hold the weight. . . . She gasped, and her eyes flew open. She spun around, stared at the company clogging the passageway. Piritos looked up, a faint frown between his brows; Grysis stepped toward her, a hand outstretched, but Apodain beat him to it; he wrapped his arms around her and pulled her close. "What? You've gone pale, are you hurt?"

Hurt. I hurt. But she is there, I can sense her. "Father?" She pressed against Apodain's chest and he eased his grip on her. "It's Father!"

"You're certain?" he asked quietly.

"The First Prime?" Piritos asked at the same moment.

She swallowed, remembered to keep her voice down. "I know it's him, I can tell, I can *see*." Almost see. She pushed completely free of Apodain, turned slowly to look at the walls. No sign of anything but the way stretching out behind them, the way ahead. He wasn't behind; ahead, then. But the company was moving again, and she *still* couldn't tell where he was. "I have to go, find him," she whispered.

"Breyd, no!" Apodain gripped her wrist and spoke low against her ear. "You heard what I told the general; it's true! You could wander down here for days—for a lifetime—and not be found. I couldn't even find you!"

"Denira—"

"The goddess doesn't control all of this place; most of it is hers, but there are other tunnels."

Dark, but she is there, not so far away; oh, daughter, I've missed you so! What are they doing, why are we turning? It's another solid wall! But I felt air, there's an opening!

I don't know that I can walk any more, even if they can't carry me. I can't remember my last bread.

"Father." She could feel his pain; his hunger. His despair. She looked down at the cords clenched in her free hand. Apodain saw the look and understood her intent almost as quickly as she did but she pulled her hand free of his and back away from him, just out of reach.

"Breyd—beloved." His face was stricken.

"Apodain. I love you—but he needs me." She pulled the cords down over her brow.

Menlaeus was there—she knew exactly where, now. She ran ahead, staring at the wall, along it—until she found the hole leading into darkness. She ran down it.

* * *

Piritos snatched at Apodain to keep him from following her, but Apodain had not moved; he was staring blankly at the wall. "Apodain? We dare not wait," Piritos breathed against his ear. "She will find us." Apodain turned that stricken look on his general. "I know she will find us," the general added gently. "That is the First Prime and the goddess protects him; but your young woman is extremely resourceful."

"Resourceful," Apodain echoed blankly, but he turned obediently and led the way up the corridor.

Moments later, Breyd came back into the light. "Help me, someone—two of you, anyone—Jocasa, my Prime is there!" Laprio and Mibro followed her at once. The column came to a halt again, Breyd backed into the main corridor, and the two Primes came behind her, carrying a third man; Breyd clung to the hand of a gaunt stick of a man whose wild gray beard and hair all ran together, and whose ragged cloak could just be made out as red; his armor was smudged and pitch-marked. Two others came behind, holding up Menlaeus' companions, both painfully thin, ragged, and unrecognizable behind thick, matted beards.

"Father." Her voice trembled and her eyes were brimming.

"Breyd." Menlaeus blinked rapidly. "This—what Grysis told us of, the last time we could talk to him. Is it already time?"

Piritos gripped his forearm. "Bring the First Prime and his companions with us. It is long past time to take back Ghezrat, Menlaeus; but it is nearly the hour."

Breyd stayed with him and kept his hand in hers; Menlaeus smiled tiredly and whispered, "I have tried so hard to get back; I thought I never would."

"I know. It's all right, Father. You're here now."

They skirted the palace cisterns, passed through several circling corridors until she could no longer even hazard a guess at which direction they were going. Menlaeus' eyes were closed, his mouth set in a tight line. His leg pained him terribly at the moment; it hurt her, too. *Take off the cords,* she thought. But that would be disloyal. She shook her head. He still wore his; the color was just discernible in places. *Oh,*

Father. It tore at her heart, seeing him like this. But Menlaeus surely sensed her worry; he opened his eyes, smiled at her and his eyes were very warm. "Don't worry, daughter," he whispered. "Everything will be all right."

Apodain brought them to a halt; she couldn't tell what was happening up there, but a moment later word came back: Bring the First Prime and his Secchi.

Apodain stood on a low step, the first of seven; a low slab of dark wood covered a hole at the top. "That is the true underground of the palace, there," he murmured to Piritos. "Wait all of you. Potro, you and your men come with me." The tall, gaunt nobleman came forward; twenty men followed. They mounted the steps, edged past the slab, were gone.

They lowered Menlaeus to the first step; Breyd sat next to him and hugged him cautiously. "Father. I was—"

"Shhh. I know." He wrapped his arms around her and hugged back. His forearms were all bone, his hands too thin. She bit back tears and smiled at him. "I thought we would fight together a last time," he whispered. "I dreamed that—I think I did. It's hard to remember."

Apodain was suddenly back with them. He knelt next to Breyd, extended an arm to Menlaeus. "Sir, I'm very glad you're back. Breyd?"

She glanced at Menlaeus, looked up at Piritos, studied Apodain's face, then nodded. "I already said, Apodain. We go together. This is my fight. Our fight. Father—"

He touched his cords, then hers. "I will be with you. Apodain—Breyd. Take care of each other."

She leaned over to kiss his cheek, then got to her feet. Apodain put an arm around her shoulders and drew her close. "General, Potro's men are gone; they should have had time to get into the apartments by now, if they were able. And it's nearly first horn."

"We'll go. Bring these men up to the palace storage, they'll be safer there than here."

Behind them, in deep darkness, Knoe stood and watched them pass. When they were gone, he came cautiously forward, hesitated again. "My Pair—no. The prince—no, again. And I cannot take Prince Hadda now, for the Lion, myself, his father—anyone." He bowed his head and tried to pray, but his mind was a blank. At length he brought his head up again. "There is one way left, if Axtekeles is to have his chief priest still. Go, now, at once. Get from this area into the passage beneath the storage; get into the city by the tunnel that comes up under the old wall; go down to the Lion's temple and gather the sacred hide and the priests and leave Ghezrat. Go into the desert south of Ye Eygar and west of Milawiusa—and seek His forgiveness." He ran light-footed up the shallow steps and edged past the barrier, turned away from the long passage there with its few small, dark prison cells and holes. He had explored the passages down this way often; it would be no difficulty at all to reach the street above, and be gone before those men noticed he was even missing.

Tephys bowed her head and gazed down into the Cleft. "It is time," she said softly. Liquid stone seethed at her feet. She stretched out her arms above the lava, hands down; her hands began to glow, and then her arms. Her hair coiled like smoke above her head; her eyes blazed, and when she spoke the cavern shuddered violently at each word. "Let My barriers beneath and around this city be no more, that My power reach where it will. Let My rock shift beneath the feet of the Lion; let My waters break upon him; and let stones crush the Lion and all who serve him—forever!"

In the Temple of the Sun, Vertumnis fell silent in mid-word as a second shock rumbled beneath his feet just short of first horn. He turned from his altar to the men sitting or kneeling before it. "It is time," he said. His priests came forward with swords and spears, and began to hand them out.

First horn: Brysos stood at the bottom of a long ladder that led up into darkness and into a back corner of the barracks smithy. He turned back and gripped the hands of as many men as he could reach. "Now we make them pay for each of our dead. It is time."

First horn: Ridlo crouched at the entry to the underground, near the Goat Gate; his fingers were dug in stone to keep his balance. "It is time," he whispered, then crawled forward. His men came after.

First Horn: High on the hill behind his father's palace, Ryllos wrapped the reins around his hand a second time and drew his sword. Behind him, a mixed company of horse, men on foot, two other chariots. He held the blade aloft. "It is time," he said clearly, and whipped up his horses.

First horn: The plain shuddered and jolted: two full picket lines of horses pulled free and ran mad, trampling the men who tried to recapture them and anything else in their way. The tents and banners of the lion-priests were smashed into the dirt.

High above the plain, the slab of stone blocking the Oryon broke in half and water exploded down the hill. Two companies of Diye Haff still camped on the east bank were washed away, the black altar tent dedicated to Axtekeles with them.

First horn: The blocks of the half-finished Lion temple collapsed; more stones fell from walls weakened by Haffat's ballista, crushing the priests and destroying the altar.

First horn: General Piritos edged forward cautiously to look out from the underground storage. Terrified soldiers ran toward the entry; others outside screamed in panic as the earth shook again. "It is time," he said quietly, and stepped aside to let the Dyaddi go first.

25

Pandemonium: Men who had been frightened by tremors cried out in terror as the dread red-clad Dyaddi suddenly appeared from nowhere, swords drawn, to cut a swath through their numbers. Men who had stumbled naked and blinking from the rooms where they slept were simply mown down. Three Pairs ran for the stairs, then, Breyd and Apodain and a half company right behind them; the other two Dyaddi chased the men fleeing into Pelledar's small throne room, where others ate and slept around the great circular hearth; Piritos, Grysis and the rest of their men went that way.

Dead and dying Diye Haff clogged the steps; the Dyaddi reached the second floor. As Apodain came up behind them, he raised his sword, turned and shouted, "Half of you, down the hall, that way, go! Clear that doorway and hold it, our people are in there! Breyd! This floor—we have to clear it before we go up!"

"Get in front of them!" she shouted back, and when the men behind Apodain hesitated, she charged around the Pairs, blocking their way to the third floor. "The hallway!" she yelled above the noise. "Jocasa, Aroepe—Laprio! Take the hallway first!"

It isn't going to work, they don't hear me! she thought at first, and nearly panicked, but Jocasa's eyes flickered her way and she turned from the steps; Laprio went with her to attack the men who had formed a spear wall halfway down the hall, and the rest came behind. The spearmen broke before the Dyaddi could even reach them; they turned and fled, but there was nowhere for them to go. Men leapt from the windows or were thrown from balconies and others died by the tens before Apodain drew his company back.

"Up! Third floor next, and the roof!" The Dyaddi were already moving up the stairs.

There had been no more than thirty men in the horse fore-court and none at the gates when Ryllos and his company came down to block the entry. "Half of you on foot and all the mounted. Inside, but stay before the gates!" Men inside the courtyard shouted, drew swords, and came running. They were cut down by archers and javelin. A bare moment later, Nessa and his company came from behind the old wall and across the street. "You men and I—we'll hold the gates—the rest of you, down there!" Ryllos shouted and leveled his spear; men were pouring from the palace, racing down the great stairs, and scrambling from the small throne room—from any other windows they could find. A volley of arrows cut through the air; the stairs were suddenly littered with bodies. Ryllos turned. Twenty or so archers stood atop the old wall and drew down on the next men flying from the palace.

He opened his mouth to call out another order, shut it again; most of his men and all those who had just come with Nessa were already out in the courtyard, engaging the enemy. They wouldn't be able to hear him. A third volley of arrows fell high up the stairs, then no more; when he risked another look, they were standing or crouched up there, waiting for another opening. He waved his spear and turned back to battle.

Diye Haff were shrieking, throwing down their swords and spears, flying wildly down the courtyard from the small throne room. They were followed by grim men who wielded swords and spears and before all a flash of red and bronze in the early light. Two red-clad Pairs, their blades moving faster than anything could possibly move.

"Hold!" Apodain held up his sword, then turned to look behind them. Grysis came up from the first floor with twenty of his fighters.

"First floor is ours!" Grysis called out. Men cheered. "Let's take back the rest!"

The Dyaddi were already halfway up the steps, and now no one tried to withstand them. But as Breyd ran up behind them, an arrow shattered on the stone beside her. "Shields!" she shouted. "They have bows up there, shields to cover the Pairs!"

Apodain was already at her side, his shield upraised to protect her and him; others came to hold their shields above the Pairs. High above them, they could hear men shrieking wildly. "The Red Cloaks! They come back from the dead to kill us all!"

A clatter of wood on stone: Men were throwing aside spears and bows up there; weapons littered the floor. Men huddled at the far corner of the hallway; others lay facedown on the tiles. Those who had tried to fight lay dead or dying everywhere as the Dyaddi roared through them. "Grysis, to the roof, go!" Apodain shouted. He set himself against Breyd's shoulder and she pivoted into him. Grysis and his men were already up the stairs and out of sight.

The Dyaddi cut down the last of the men in the hallway, but now others came from Queen Ye Sotris' apartments and these threw themselves at Apodain and the men with him.

Breyd lashed out, turned, and stepped back as Apodain lunged, brought her sword up. She lost track of time, lost count of men, her own company—anything that was not the fighting. They wouldn't come near her if they could help it, but three at least had been driven within her reach and one of them literally fell into her sword. Behind her, she could hear Apodain: "The queen's apartments! Get that door closed! You by the stairs! Back that way, down the hall, clear whatever is left!" More fighting; she had lost her sword somehow, caught in armor or a body and she couldn't free it. She drew a javelin.

Apodain again: "Grysis!"

"Roof is clear!"

"Good—throne room next!"

Brysos stepped aside to let the two Pairs come forward; his men edged back cautiously to let them to the fore. The barracks were quiet; a few men coming off duty heading toward the sleeping quarters, a few others standing in the courtyard talking. Several horses stood outside the smithy. Four men slept close to the forge, the Diye Haff smith and his assistants, Brysos thought. None wore armor, though swords and leathers lay nearby; the smell of wine was very strong. Brysos motioned for men, drew his hand meaningfully across his throat. Six men drew long daggers and came to join him.

Four dead men; the horses whickered nervously. Brysos drew his company together in deep shadow just short of the entry. "Remember; you men hit the messes, you take the barracks. Pairs to the messes first. We'll watch for any from the hospital barracks. Go!"

Men standing in the courtyard turned and stared blankly as fully armored and armed Ghezrathi came at a dead run, straight for them; they died without raising a hand to protect themselves. Brysos pivoted and gestured urgently with his sword but the Dyaddi were already inside the messes, the others right behind them. Diye Haff were screaming wildly; the barracks erupted. A very few naked men flung themselves into the courtyard but the Ghezrathi were right behind them. It was over almost before it began. Dyaddi came from the messes and charged into the barracks.

A final clash of weapons, then silence. Ghezrathi soldiers from the barracks and from the messes; others came after, half-carrying the Dyaddi.

Brysos looked up as voices came from the gates: Ridlo and his men, and the small company that had come down from the market. He beckoned one of his men over. "Tell Ridlo stay; the others go and make certain the market is cleared. Tell them bid any who try to come outside to stay in their homes until the streets are safe—we'll tell them. Tell Ridlo set his men to secure the gates, then come to me."

Eyzhad looked down from the gates and smiled grimly; there had been ten men here when he climbed onto the arch, where they could see him. The soldiers had come up behind them and killed them almost before they were aware they were being attacked.

He looked across the city. First light; men still fought in the palace and as he looked that way, someone was thrown down from the roof; another clambered from the throne room window and leapt. Upon the circuit of wall, at each gate above the arch, a priestess, her robes reddened by the rising sun.   .

He turned to look out over the plain then: The Oryon had begun to return to its banks; the wreckage of tents and equipment littered the eastern ridge. On the plain, a few men stood in the middle of disaster or walked slowly from fallen tent to fallen man. Horses still ran wild between the Alno and the Oryon.

Behind him, the wild clatter of swords and wailing men ceased; a loud cheer rang out. When he turned his head, Eyzhad could see Ghezrathi upon the prince's roof and oth-

rs at the windows and upon the walls—and no enemy what-
ver.

The sun lay full upon the flat tops of the city walls.
Eyzhad turned to face out and brought his arms up. "It is
ime," he said softly. "To me, goddess, Your power: the
ower of stone purified by Fire." Flame heated his belly,
eat no living man could bear without Her protection spread
hrough his body. He let it fill him, then brought his eyes
lown to the rubble of Axtekeles' temple. Fire roared up
rom beneath. The stones melted into a puddle of glowing
ed but the heat began to lessen as Eyzhad turned his gaze
rom it.

He looked across the plain once more; his eyes touched
he ballista Haffat had left near the walls. It ignited with a
oar.

Below the palace, Meronne stood in deep shadow and
vaited. Knoe stood at the base of the steps leading up to the
alace storage and the prince's cells, and gazed blankly all
round him. With an effort, he closed his eyes, clutched his
ead and dug his nails into his cheeks. "I have lost time,
ow much of it?" he muttered. "They are there—above.
'airs, fighting. The palace is no longer ours, and the god's
emple—" Blood ran down his cheeks where he clawed him-
elf. "Gone. All gone. My prisoners—no. They are not mine
ny longer, but there is no time." He gazed off into the dis-
ance, shook himself again; his voice deepened. "It is Her
nfluence, you dare not stay, Knoe. Go, now, Knoe, salvage
vhat you can to my Honor, go." He looked up, stared wide-
yed all around. "Yes," he whispered. "Up the steps, into
hat passageway and left; I know two ways at least from that
assage beyond the palace walls. I can escape by a south
;ate or an east one, get down to the camp. A horse, whatever
riests are left—go." He turned in a full circle. Hesitated
vith his foot on the lowest step, then turned and walked
ack into the tunnels.

Meronne watched him go and smiled in grim satisfaction;
he made her way over to the bottom of the steps and turned
ack to look at the maze. It would be very black down here
or any who did not have Her gift for this one hour. And she
vould need it. There were three down here, somewhere, to
e rescued. "The heir," she whispered. "I cannot do this
lone, to break the seal Knoe put upon the prince, to find

him and keep him alive once he is brought from Her depths.
The heir must come to me." She stood very still for a long
moment, then crouched down on the lowest step. Denira
would come. She would wait. And they would find him.

Breyd had lost all track of time and place—of everything
except Apodain's presence at her shoulder or her back, of
men driven their way—another sword in her hand, this one
Diye Haff single edged for slashing and too heavy for her
arm. She used it anyway, killed or badly wounded two more
enemy before they were cut down.

Grysis emerged from the queen's apartments and waved
his sword. "Clear!" he shouted. "And the nursery, clear!"

"That way!" Apodain pointed down the hall. "Secure the
king's apartments and the accounting; we'll take the throne
room!"

Breyd blinked. The hall was littered with dead and dying
men. Blood had splashed the walls and obscured the floor;
footing became treacherous. Dyaddi came from the queen's
bedchamber and pelted across the hall, into the throne room.
Apodain ran after them and Breyd went with him.

There had been few men in here, perhaps fifteen in all.
Three simply threw down their spears and ran for the windows, but only one reached it. Someone's javelin bounced
off armor; the Diye Haff under it staggered and caught his
knees on the window ledge, flailed his arms helplessly, and
fell out.

Apodain's shoulder pressed against hers; she used the enemy sword two-handed, slashing at the remaining men who
tried to evade her and Apodain and get through the door.
None made it.

Their men came around them; suddenly there was no one
left standing but Ghezrathi.

"Back into the hallway," Apodain said. "We'll secure it."
But Piritos was coming into the throne room, bringing
Grysis and a few men with him.

Piritos raised his sword for silence. "The palace is ours."
Men cheered. Prosean held his Secchi close and pulled her
away from the window; they slid slowly down the wall and
leaned against it, eyes closed. Jocasa and her father clung to
each other near the door; Aroepe and Mibro crouched beneath the window above Denota's temple, heads close to

gether. Breyd staggered; Apodain's sword arm went around her and held her up.

"You men," he said loudly when the cheer faded. "Make certain there are no enemy left alive in here and in the hall."

"See to the Pairs," Grysis said sharply, and went to help with them. When Breyd would have followed, though, he shook his head. "You're nearly as exhausted as they are. Stay where you are. Apodain, hold onto her."

Piritos walked into the room and gazed into the open, staring eyes of a dead man. "Did we lose any?" he asked generally.

"I saw two men wounded on the stairs; we don't have numbers yet," an aide replied.

"Men to tend them?"

"One of ours stayed behind; Potro brought a physician and so did the men down in the courtyard."

"Good. Any injured up here?"

Apodain looked around. "None of ours, sir, and none of the enemy in here—only dead."

"In the hall?"

His aide leaned out and shouted something to men there, came back in. "None, sir. Only dead, so far."

"Good. Continue to search. The barracks—" He walked over to the window and looked down; black smoke spilled across the inner wall, and rose from what had been the beginnings of a temple, more smoke spiraled up outside the wall as flame devoured the ballista. "Our men hold the barracks roof," he said. He looked down. Ryllos had moved his chariot and his horsemen inside the palace gates and closed them. Dead men were everywhere in the courtyard. His men moved slowly across the steps and the courtyard, rolling over enemy soldiers and dispatching those few who still lived.

Piritos leaned out and waved his sword; Ryllos waved his back and shouted to his men, "The palace is ours!" Piritos waved his sword again and one of the men on the barracks roof waved a spear in reply.

The general came back into the throne room and gestured for his aides. "The men we positioned earlier, send them into the streets to warn the populace to stay indoors until they are told it's safe. Go down, tell Ryllos leave a guard on the gates and ride at once to Khadat's palace. Kill any enemy he finds there, find that woman and bring her here, to me. What is this?" he asked softly, and came to an abrupt halt before the throne.

Apodain turned, bringing Breyd around with him; Grysis came forward with Jocasa in his arms and Laprio leaning on him heavily. The remaining men in the chamber turned and stared. Hadda sat upon the ancient Ghezrathi throne as if he had become stone himself; his fingers were curled into the stone arms, his eyes fixed on the distance.

Brysos stood on the wall by the outer gates and shaded his eyes against the rising sun. Eyzhad came over to him. "There are loose horses everywhere," Brysos said finally. "And men on others now, a few riding toward the Oryon; more heading west toward the isthmus. You were right, priest, they're running—either for Diyet or to warn Haffat—some just running, by the looks of them. Not enough of them, though; there are still at least a phalanx of men and horses." He turned to look along the ridge. "What happened out there, to destroy so much of that camp? It looks as though the river—" He stopped abruptly. "Tell me later—if you can, or will. The walls are secure?"

"We hold the walls," Eyzhad said.

"Good." Brysos strode along the wall toward the barracks and shouted down, "Have you their commander and those four from the messes? Bring them!" He crossed to the inner wall and went down the ladder as five ragged, bloody, and stunned-looking mounted men were led to the inner gates. "You, Req," he said sharply. The man with captain's colors on his armor stared at him dully. "You have seen what happens to men who dare enter Ghezrat with drawn blades. Take that tale to the camp down there. And send word to Haffat: we took back what was ours, the goddess again holds the walls. The Lion has himself become prey. Tell him that and this also. We have Haffat's son. Let him think hard whether he will assault us again; warn him Hadda's life hangs by his actions.

"But tell him this final thing: Come and take the boy, if he will. Leave after that, and we will let you all go in peace."

"He—" Req stopped. "He will not—"

"Take the message," Brysos said gently. "Remember the Dyaddi await you, if you return." He turned. "Open the gates and let these pass!"

* * *

It was very dark beneath Ghezrat. Knoe walked steadily. He did not mind the darkness, but the air bothered him; it was hot, very dry—it bore down upon him heavily. "You have only a few paces to go and you are out," he whispered, as he had for some time now. The curved passage, the branch to the left and a long incline coming out at the base of old wall. . . . He could see light ahead, he thought. He let his fingertips trail across smooth, warm stone and walked a little faster.

The wall disappeared; he walked into the open, frowning. "This is not—this was not here before." Dim red light bathed stone walls or cast black reflections of long stone points across the ceiling. Two lamps burned on the floor a little ahead. It smote him, all at once. "I am lost, but how could I be lost? I went as I always go." He caught his breath sharply; his heart was thudding erratically, much too fast.

"Knoe. Why does the Lion travel beneath the earth?" The voice burned him, vibrated through him.

"Denota," he whispered; he clenched his fists and stared wildly around. "Denota! The Lion goes where he will, in search of prey! Do not stand between him and his desire, or he will—"

"Knoe. You will be silent." Tephys came into the light; he gaped at her. Her robes were red—reflection of the lamps, nothing more, he told himself. *It is a trick. Do I not know all such tricks of priests, do I not use them myself?*

He drew a deep breath; the air was hot: "I will not be silent, woman!" The ground heaved beneath his feet; he looked down at the long, gaping hole before him. Nearly unbearable heat rose from it, and as he looked, the gray stuff bubbled; flame licked the surface. "You have done this, but it is not real."

"Try it on your peril, Knoe. Your temple is destroyed, your priests gone, your own cause lost."

He let his head fall back. "Axtekeles, hear your priest!" But the sound was muted, all sense of the god gone, as if the Lion had never been. *And I am dead. But not alone.* He was still a strong man, strong enough to carry a half-grown bullock, or to fling a prince from the walls. And this—this was only a woman.

The stuff at his feet: *illusion.* But it might not be. He took one step sideways, a second. Tephys stood very still and watched him as he edged around the Cleft and came straight toward her. She raised a hand; he stopped dead. "Lions roam the earth, Knoe," she said very softly. "And they devour whatever they will. But in the end, they die, too, and the earth takes them back." Her voice rose, piercing him. "To Denota, the flesh of the Lion!"

Knoe screamed once. Fire rose from the Cleft and tore from Tephys' hands, engulfing him. It flared, filling the cavern, then faded. Tephys swayed, closed her eyes, and stood very still. All around her and inside her, dreadful heat—she could *feel* heat once more. But it was growing less already. One final thing, before she set aside the goddess' dread aspect—and quickly, before that aspect took her mortal shape as well. *Even You cannot protect Your servant's body from Knoe's end for long; but I am here, Denota.*

She drew together the last of Denota's heat, shaped it and sent it; the altar Knoe had set beneath the palace melted into a shapeless blob of metal.

She opened her eyes to red-spotted darkness. The lamps flickered and began to burn brightly as the air grew cool. A faint greenish steam rose from Denota's Cleft. Tephys looked down into familiar, cool depths, then knelt to gather up a very small pile of white ash. She carried it over and let it spill into the Cleft. "To you, Mother of us all."

For one very long moment, she remained where she was. She looked up then. There was a little daylight at the top of the steps. Sunrise. She brought her eyes down to the stone blocking the steps, then turned and walked into darkness. Meronne would need her, for Pelledar; and Ye Sotris must be told her husband was still alive.

Piritos frowned as Apodain turned and shook his head. "His flesh is cold but not death-cold; he's still breathing. I just can't move him."

"Leave four men to guard," the general began; he caught at the wall and swore as the floor trembled the least bit. "Does She send an earthquake against all of us? Better get everyone out, all our men, those children—leave this wretched creature!" But at that moment, Hadda blinked; Apodain snatched his hand back in surprise, then brought his sword up and grabbed the emperor's heir again.

"No, don't. Don't, please," Hadda seemed unaware of any

of them; his terrified eyes were fixed on the distance and tears ran down his face.

"Bring him," Piritos said disgustedly. "And all of you, downstairs and outside, now!"

"Father!" Breyd whispered in sudden dread; she turned and ran. Apodain thrust Hadda toward one of the general's aides and went after her.

Meronne stood at the entrance to the storage. When Breyd would have pushed by her, she gripped the girl's arm and shook her, hard. "Control yourself!"

"Father—if the palace falls, and he's still there—!"

"That was Denota, bringing down the Lion and his servant!" Meronne hissed. Breyd stared at her. "Did you think She could not control Her own stones? Go. Your father is unharmed and so are the men with him." Apodain came running then; he was visibly short of breath. Meronne looked up at him. "She will be all right in there. Send for one of the Pairs or go and get one yourself. Have them carried if need be. There is a Dyadd beneath the palace; another Dyadd will find them more quickly than anyone could. Then find several strong men who can carry an injured one, tell them bring blankets and poles to transport him. Go," she snapped. Breyd slipped under her arm and vanished into the dark storage; Apodain stared after her anxiously, then turned and ran back the way he had come.

"Father?" He was where she had left him; the men who had been with him for so long slept beside him, but Menlaeus sat with his back against the rough wall, waiting. He held out his arms and she went into them. "We've taken the palace back."

"I know; I could tell," he said quietly.

"Yes. I knew you were there, even when there wasn't time to think." She shuddered and buried her face in his shoulder. "They're all dead up there. We even killed the wounded. Everyone."

"I know. We did that at the mole. It's a dreadful thing." She nodded, then sat up and blotted her eyes and laid a hand on his thin cheek.

"Oh, Father. I—"

"Shhh. Don't. I look dreadful; you look wonderful, child. Has the boy been good to you?"

She brought up a smile. "Yes, of course." She turned as

men came into the hallway, Meronne at their head, and one of the general's aides with long poles and blankets. She got to her feet as Apodain followed, Jocasa in his arms and Laprio held up by another of the general's aides. "Apodain?"

"The missing Dyadd," he said briefly. "They're down there, *she* says. Still alive. Meronne thinks these two can find them."

"I'll come." Breyd set her helm in Menlaeus' hands and said, "I'll be back, hold that for me."

Meronne was already on her way back; Apodain drew back from the stairs as the old priestess came slowly up them. Behind her, men fought to keep their limp burden level. Pelledar's throat still bore the marks of Haffat's attack, almost as if they had been fresh-made; his face was unrecognizable under dirt and dried runnels and flakes of blood. His eyes were sunken and half closed.

"Take him—" Meronne seemed at a loss, suddenly.

"The palace is unfit," Apodain said; his voice gave away nothing. "Take him to my home, if Ryllos has—has cleared it. Give him and the queen my mother's apartments; *she* will not require them."

"Yes." Meronne glanced at him, then led the way toward the storage; the men bearing their prince followed her. Denira came running, scrambled up the steps and hurried after her; her face was white and Breyd thought she had been ill.

Apodain waited only long enough for the steps to clear, then started down with Jocasa. Breyd came on his heels.

It was no longer dark down here: Meronne and those who had carried Pelledar left lamps burning everywhere, and two torches high on the wall nearest the steps flared and fluttered in some unseen air current. "Oh, no. How did they ever find him in all that?" she whispered.

It was a truly appalling sight: Tunnels running in ten or more different directions, some sloping up and vanishing into darkness, others that must dip sharply down, only a glimpse of rough ceiling visible. She looked up at Apodain; his expression was grim. Jocasa lay in his arms, eyes closed, her breath coming still in shallow little pants. But as he met her eyes, his expression softened.

"It isn't impossible, Breyd. He can't have been very far

from here, whatever power Knoe has wouldn't have served him here. He would have been lost forever."

"Oh, no. Father—in all that—" It shook her. *I could have lost him.* Apodain shook his head.

"He's safe now, you found him, you came back."

"I know." *I could have lost you, trying to find him.*

"You can't see all the passages or the entries, but you know that. But Father showed me how they were made, how to find the way back if I got turned around. We'll manage." He looked doubtfully at Jocasa. "When we go in there to find them—"

"I go with you, Apodain."

"I know you do. Stay at my side or right behind me; hold my cloak and don't let go of it. Because I can find my own way in there, but I can't find anyone else. You could—" He shook his head once, hard, as if to clear it. "Swear that."

She nodded. "I won't let go, I promise."

"If I had lost you, back there— Please, don't frighten me like that again, beloved." Before she could say anything else, he set Jocasa on her feet and held her upright.

She stared bleakly at the beginnings of the maze, then turned back to take hold of the Secchi's shoulders. "Jocasa, it's Breyd. We have to find Lochria, you said she and Bechates were alive."

"Breyd?" Her eyelids fluttered. "Tired ... horribly—"

"I know. You fought. We have to find Lochria. Apodain will carry you, but we have to find her." Jocasa nodded again.

"Alive; I felt her, when we put on ... the binding cords." She turned in Apodain's grasp, swayed back into him and brought up a trembling arm. "She's there. Weak." Her eyes closed again.

Apodain picked her up, glanced over his shoulder. "Bring the pallets and hurry."

Twenty steps down the low-ceilinged tunnel, three branches. To Apodain's urgent whisper, Jocasa replied, "Ahead. Straight ahead." Thirty steps beyond that, at a widening in the passage, an enormous flat stone took up the center of the floor. A low-burning torch had been shoved into a hole beside it. Breyd took up the torch and turned slowly; her own binding cords felt warm. "There," Jocasa whispered, and went limp in Apodain's arms.

"There," Breyd said at the same moment, and pointed

with the torch. A narrow opening no different from the rest
except for the feel of the air around it; it hackled the hair on
her arms the way Knoe himself had. *If he is there.* If he were
there, he would pay her, all of them, for what he had done
to Prince Pelledar, she thought furiously. She drew Tarpaen's
dagger and walked steadily toward the opening, but the men
who carried the pallets and the poles beat her to it.

Knoe was not there. The chamber reeked of sweat, blood,
and illness. Breyd stepped cautiously inside and held up the
torch.

A gaunt Bechates lay on his back on one stone bench;
Lochria huddled on another and Breyd could not see her
face for the wild tangle of loose hair covering it. Her arm
hung over the edge, bone clearly visible beneath skin. But as
Breyd stared in horror, Lochria's fingers moved and
Bechates groaned, very faintly. She turned and ran back outside. "They're alive—barely, but alive!" one of the men
shouted. Apodain stood Jocasa on her feet and thrust her at
Breyd, took the torch from her, and ducked into the chamber. Breyd fell back into the wall, held Jocasa close, and
closed her eyes.

She opened them again as footsteps shuffled past her.
Lochria lay very flat and still, the wild tangle of hair pulled
away from her face; her eyes were sunken, her cheeks dreadful hollows. Her breath came in tiny, whistling gasps.
Bechates' eyes were open, unfixed, and his mouth trembled.
"We said nothing," he whispered frantically. "Tell them—
tell Tephys, Piritos—we didn't say anything, we didn't—"
His eyes closed and his head rolled limply. Apodain came up
behind the pallets, torch in hand; he scooped up Jocasa,
looked down at Breyd's drawn face. She nodded; he put her
ahead of him.

Tephys stood at the top of the steps, waiting for them. She
bent over Bechates, brushed loose hair back from Lochria's
face; laid a hand on his arm and then hers. "I cannot be certain. We will do all we can. Bring them, there is a way into
the temple from here." She looked at Breyd, glanced up at
Apodain. "Tell the general I have something—someone he
will want. Tell him to send, but not before fifth horn. I will
need that long to restore her." She looked at Apodain once
more. "Your mother."

"You have her?" His voice was expressionless. Tephys nodded. "I will tell him. Fifth horn."

The high priestess left, taking the men and the two pallets with her, left down the long corridor. Someone had already taken Menlaeus' two companions away and someone else brought Laprio back up the steps; he leaned against the wall, eyes closed, at Menlaeus' side, but as Apodain came forward he pushed himself upright and held out his arms to Jocasa, who sighed faintly and went to him; they walked slowly up the hallway, past small cells and ancient storage pits, through the open doorway to the large storage. Between them, Apodain and Breyd got Menlaeus to his feet, and followed.

Grysis was waiting for them. "The general's gone down to the barracks, but he left word he needs both of you as soon as you can come." He gripped Menlaeus' shoulders, but gently; Menlaeus brought up a smile. "Ryllos has his car in the courtyard; he'd be honored to bring the First Prime."

"Father?" Breyd studied his face anxiously.

Menlaeus patted her arm and said, "Don't fuss, child; I'm tired just now, nothing more. Go; that's a general asking for you."

"He and I will manage," Grysis said. He took Menlaeus' weight on one arm. "Go."

There was no one in the main avenue or anywhere else she could see except soldiers—their own soldiers. Men had thrown open the inner gates and were working on the still warped hinges of the outer gates, others were bringing dead Diye Haff from the along the street where the wineshop stood and setting them in the shade, against the inner wall. The courtyard was crowded, men running in and out or hitching up supply carts to haul the Diye Haff away. Breyd's eyes flinched away from that; from the few dead still on the ground. Another cart stood outside the barracks; men threw clothing and furs, boots and bags into it and other men added to an enormous pile of things by the doorway to the messes.

Piritos came out of the barracks and climbed into the wagon to stand atop the seat; men stopped what they were doing and cheered him loudly. He clenched his fists and held them over his head, finally gestured for silence. "Good work, every one of you, an excellent job! The palace is ours, the barracks ours, and I am told there are no Diye Haff to be found anywhere!" Another loud, long cheer, which he let go on for some moments. He was smiling as he finally went on. "It is now second horn; I have given the order that at third horn, people will be allowed into the streets once more and word spread that we have prevailed here, our prince taken back and the enemy slaughtered! Meantime!" he shouted, and the barracks were quiet at once. "Meantime, we have what is left of a dire enemy camped on the plain, and they are only a very small part of the army still camped before Ye Eygar! The captains have their orders; you will obey them. Set the barracks and the messes in order; other men from the companies will begin to come in after third horn and we must have this place ready for them!

"For now, someone find me a yellow parley flag and set it up by the gates where Haffat's banners were; as soon as it is set, I will go up and wait for their captain." He jumped down; Apodain took Breyd's hand and drew her through the crowd.

They caught Piritos just inside the barracks. "Sir, the High Priestess sends word. She has Khadat, in the temple. She says send, but only after midday." Piritos eyed him sharply, then nodded.

"I don't hold you responsible for anything that woman did, you know that. The prince won't either, when he's told."

"Thank you, sir," Breyd said when Apodain seemed unable to say anything.

"You two—I'll want you up there with me when I talk to the Diye Haff. Find the Dyaddi, do whatever you can to get them on their feet, I want them also. See to that for me." He looked up as Nabid hailed him from the messes and walked off.

The barracks bore little resemblance to the place she slept so many nights, Breyd realized; unfamiliar clothing and armor littered the nearest pallets still, and the air was thick with stale sweat and wine; the floor beneath her sandals was sticky, someone had died here. She caught her breath and turned away. Apodain led her back into the courtyard. "There are enough men in there, you and I would only be in the way." The messes were full of men also, the hospital barracks empty. No one had been in here, Breyd thought, since

he Diye Haff came. There was a deserted feel to the air, and
even with the doors hanging open, a staleness.

In the end, she and Apodain waited by the gates for
Menlaeus and for the Dyaddi. Apodain and Grysis went in
search of bread and wine. The exhausted Pairs sat in the
shade and talked or slept; Breyd used her brother's dagger to
trim her father's hair and beard. Finally, she sat back on her
heels. "You need food and proper rest," she said. "But
Mother won't be so frightened."

His eyes warmed. "How is she?"

"She's been worried about you. I know," Breyd hesitated.
"It was hard enough for me, sometimes, to be certain you
were out there. She didn't have that. And Tar—"

"I know. They told me. But I think I knew, almost from
the first that something had happened." His eyes closed.

"Mother's been so brave for all of us—I didn't think she
could."

"She's never been strong; she's never had to," Menlaeus
said softly. *How thin and pale he is, without all that hair to
hide his features.* Breyd touched his cheek, suddenly anxious; he laid his hand across hers and opened his eyes to
smile at her. "I'll be glad to go home to her." He laid his
free hand on his leg. "I don't think they'll need me here any
more."

Apodain came back with several small, hard loaves and an
open-mouthed clay jug of wine and water. He eyed the bread
doubtfully. "It's stale but all we could find right away.
Grysis is sending men to find better and once the mess captain gets here, they'll start shifting food back up from below.
Meantime—"

Menlaeus took one of the loaves. "Dip it in the wine, it
will soften," he said. "It's better than most I've had lately."

Jocasa ate in silence. Finally, she shook herself and got to
her feet. Laprio stood with her. "The general said he needed
us," she said flatly as Aroepe and the others looked up at
her. "Let's go put the fear of Denota into those filthy little
northerners."

Menlaeus let Breyd and Apodain help him up and walk
him over to the messes, where he could sit in shade—*and
someone can keep an eye on him for me,* Breyd thought worriedly. He was so weak and so thin, he frightened her. But

as she turned to leave him, a small, thin boy came through the entry and threw himself at her.

"Breyd!"

"Xhem!" She knelt and hugged him fiercely. "You're all right!"

"I was afraid, they said *she'd* tried to give you to the enemy!"

"Oh, Xhem! Surely you knew we got out of there!"

He gripped her arms and rubbed his eyes against her cloak. "I knew that, but I couldn't find you last night; and then when I got back, you were already gone and they wouldn't let me follow you and I just had—to wait." He sniffed loudly.

"I know. It's awful, not knowing. Here," she said softly against his ear. "Your uncle Menlaeus—we found him. He's all right, but he's weak. Will you stay with him, keep him company until I get back?"

"Of course." He scrubbed at his eyes with both fists, managed a smile for her. *He's nearly as thin as Father,* she realized with a pang. "Get him some bread if there is any, and help him eat it." He nodded; she hugged him again and got back to her feet.

Men were coming through the barracks gates in a steady stream as word spread, bringing weapons they had held back, and others came up through the smithy as the passage to the lower tunnels was thrown wide. General Piritos came out of the messes with his full cadre about him and a broad, long yellow banner fixed to a spear.

All across the courtyard, men stopped what they were doing and stood quietly; others came from the barracks. Piritos waited while they assembled, then said, "I want every fighting man and woman of you on the outer wall. The Dyaddi will flank the gates; Apodain and his lady, the Secchi Breyd, will stand at my side for our prince. The High Priestess has just sent word that Prince Pelledar will live—" A roar greeted this; he held up his hand for silence. "—but it will be some days before he can do much except sleep. Now! Pay close attention! In a little, I will go up to the main gates with this banner. Those still camped out there will come to learn what has happened. I will speak to them and you will stand where they can see you. We will let them know whose city this is!" Another wild roar of approval. "Brysos, bring the emperor's heir. There are not enough men

eft down there to make an attempt on the walls, but that boy
should keep them from doing anything foolish. The rest of
you, find your captains and make ready at once!"

He stepped back into the messes. Apodain turned and
looked Breyd over critically. "Your armor is smudged at the
shoulder. Here, let me rub it." He straightened her baldric,
stood back and walked all around her.

"Your own armor," she said. He looked down at the borrowed corselet and shrugged.

"There is no time to bring it, but no one will look at me,
anyway; not with so much red on the walls, and a general
come back from the dead."

Third horn: Atos lay full upon the once again summer-
shallow Oryon, the litter of stone and broken trees from high
above, and the wreck of a camp high up the ridges. An already warm wind blew the emperor's banners. Breyd, standing close to the general's right hand and in front of his
numerous aides, peered uncertainly down from the walls.

*How long—thirty or so days—since I last stood on this
outer wall?* The road, the sea, it all looked the same as it
ever had; the ridges east of the Oryon were brown in many
places where they ordinarily would be grass-covered, but
west of the Alno all was still very green. A Mirikosi ship
with bright sails was snugged up to the inner side of the
mole but no one was out there with her.

The Diye Haff camp stood near the crossroads—*almost
where the platform was during the games.* Tents everywhere
down there; but not as many as there had been, and she
could see now many of them had been flattened.

There were banners down there, but only Haffat's—no
golden lions anywhere in sight. As she looked, a small company of mounted men came onto the road and started up to
the city, a bit of yellow fluttering from a tall spear.

It was quiet here, except for the occasional faint creak of
armor or leather, for the sound of the yellow parley banner
snapping in a sudden gust. Men ranged along the wall both
directions as far as she could see; Eyzhad stood on the arch
above the inner main gates and if she looked, she would see
more men all around the city and before each of the gates,
a single priestess, clad only in the simple green and white
robes of Denota.

*Mother, Niddy—Niverren and Creos. What do they think
just now—kept inside their house to wait, not knowing any-*

thing? Had anyone even told Nevvia that Menlaeus was found? She hadn't remembered to ask Xhem; she couldn't remember now if he had been surprised to see Menlaeus there.

She turned her attention to the twenty or so wary men who reined in before the gates and stared up at the walls.

Piritos gazed down at them in silence for some moments, then said, "I am General Piritos. Prince Pelledar bids me tell you we have taken back our city. We hold the palace, the barracks and the walls. Those men we sent to you are yours, the rest are dead. We hold the son of your emperor." He gestured; Brysos brought Hadda where they could see him, then drew him back again and handed him to the men who had been guarding him to be taken back down to the barracks. "I am told the emperor is fond of the boy. We will keep him alive and unharmed until the emperor comes to claim him, if he will.

"What happens next is in your hands and the lives of your men yours to spend or save. We could have come in secret last night and slain you all, as we did in the barracks and the palace, but we did not.

"You are few. Return to your camp, pack up your tents, and leave Ghezrat at once, and we will not try to stop you. Go to Haffat or to Diyet—wherever you will. If you are wise, you will go back to your homes. You have fought long and hard, and lost friends and comrades; it is enough."

The Diye Haff sat their horses and gazed in silence from one end of the city to the other; after one brief glance, none of them would look at the Dyaddi. The man holding the truce flag edged his horse forward. "I am Uboru. I will take your words back to the camp but most of our men have already fled. If I take your message to the emperor, what oath will you give me that you will not kill his heir?"

"What oath would he accept?" Piritos asked. "But I swear it personally, by my own sword."

Uboru looked up at him for some moments, then finally said, "I will tell them what you have said; I will send word or take it myself to the emperor. Whatever he does—but that is no longer my concern. Give us back our dead to burn tonight, if you will, and we will be gone tomorrow." He turned his horse and rode away; his company clattered after him. Piritos stood very still and watched them go.

When he turned back, the streets were full of crying,

cheering people, and the men on the walls cried his name. Piritos came across to the inner wall and raised his arms for silence. "We do not celebrate yet! This was a single trial of strength, not a victory! But your prince lives, and I live, and if the goddess is willing we shall yet prevail!" A great roar went up from the street below; it was echoed twenty-fold by those along the wall. The general held up clenched fists and let them cheer for a very long time. Finally he went back to the outer wall and said to his aides, "Send the wagons down with their dead, but put heavy guard on them. See to it the prince's servants are returned to the palace, and the rooms and halls cleaned; send guards to the temple of Denota at midday and have the woman Khadat brought to the palace, to the first floor where the hearth is. I will wait there for her. A company and at least one Pair upon the walls at all times until those men down there have quit the plain.

"The rest of the men and the Pairs—tell the captains to give them leave until seventh horn, to see their families and tell them we have the city and it is safe for now. To my officers, go to their families if they will but return at fifth horn. We have to begin to plan for Haffat when he returns."

26

Xhem came running up as Breyd and Apodain came down from the walls. "They have taken Menlaeus home already, and Captain Grysis sent word for you—for both of you to go to him, if you like. Aunt Nevvia was weeping so she couldn't speak, but Niddy says tell you bring whatever news you can because Creos is frantic to hear what has happened." He caught his breath and finished in a rush: "And you had better run when you go past the fountain because Misso and her sister have been there ever since people were let outside."

Breyd felt giddy, light-headed all at once. Men all around them were laughing, pounding each other on the back. *When did I last see any of these men smile?* "I'll help you throw them in the water later, Xhem." Xhem's eyes lit. "Tell them I'll come right away; I won't try to keep up with *you*, though."

"We'll both come," Apodain said. Xhem took off.

"Apodain, you don't have to."

"Of course I do," he said; he pulled the helm from her head and ran his hand across damp curls. "There used to be a custom, that a newly wedded husband brought bread to the house of his wife, for luck and prosperity. I haven't done that." Color touched his cheekbones. "I fear the luck may have to wait a little; I haven't any coin."

Breyd found the small bag stitched to the baldric and tipped it into her hand. "Four coppers. We'll buy bread, if we can find any. And as for the luck, I already have mine." She shoved the coins back into the bag and wrapped her arm around his waist.

Apodain laughed suddenly, so cheerfully she turned to look at him. *I have never heard him laugh like that in all the days I've known him; never seen him truly happy.* He kissed her brow and put his arm around her. "So tell me," he asked as they walked through the barracks gates and into the streets. "If the wife buys the bread, doesn't that turn the luck?"

She gave him a sidelong look. "But you and I have done so many things against tradition already. Why should one more make any difference?"

Menlaeus sat in Nevvia's chair, cushions all around him, his leg resting on a folded blanket atop the three-legged table. Nevvia knelt next to him, her arms around his waist; he stroked her hair and looked very content. He was clean, his hair damp and freshly oiled and he wore a tunic of roughspun brown he'd had as long as Breyd could remember. Breyd came over and hugged her mother. "Oh, Breyd, oh, baby; he says *you* found him—just like you said you would."

"Mother, shhh, don't weep. It's all right now. And I've brought Apodain."

"Oh!" Nevvia blotted her eyes quickly on her daughter's cloak and got to her feet. Nidya retrieved the loaves from Apodain, who took Nevvia's hands and bowed over them.

Breyd clasped one of Menlaeus' hands; he patted her hair. "The boy suits you, Breyd. I'm glad." She nodded; Nevvia came back, her face anxious. Breyd kissed her and left them together.

Apodain had gone over to talk to Creos and Niverren, who sat in the shade next to the low old wall. Niverren's loom stood in its old place, a partly finished piece of dark wool on it.

Creos smiled and waved at her; two crutches leaned against the wall next to him and stuck up above his head. *Niverren is being sensible after all.* She went over and let him embrace her, kissed Niverren's cheek, and went back over to sit in Niv's old chair. Nidya brought out the tray with bread, a small dish of oil, raisins and some dry dates, and a round clay cup of broth for Menlaeus.

He fell asleep as soon as Nevvia fed him a little. Nidya took the bowl away; Nevvia laid her head on her husband's knee and closed her eyes. His fingers lay across her dark hair; someone had cut it neatly, but it was still dreadfully short. Menlaeus slept, a faint smile on his lips. "How comfortable he looks already," she whispered. Nidya smiled and patted her cheek. "Niddy, we have to go, it's nearly fifth horn and they need us back at the barracks. Tell Father—tell him and Mother we'll come back when we can." *I will, at least.* Apodain might be kept busier than she; they might send her home to wait for him, though she didn't think either Grysis or the General would do that.

Send her home. She looked at her sleeping father with suddenly troubled eyes. *Home.* Where was that, though? There was no room here, and how could she expect Apodain to come here after that palace with its vast airy apartments, painted walls and servants everywhere? *How could I possibly bear to live in that palace, though—after Khadat?* The barracks—they had been necessary while she fought, she'd been comfortable enough with the other Dyaddi. But with a husband— She swallowed and forced her thoughts in another direction.

Khadat's servants were nowhere in sight but one of the prince's personal men came out of the hall as Apodain and Breyd came up the stairs. "Sir, we've done as the general told us. The prince and his family have the third floor apartments. Most of his servants and some of yours have gone to help clean the palace so we can get him back where he belongs as soon as possible. The queen asked to see you."

Apodain hesitated; finally nodded. "Of course. Tell her we'll come shortly." The man left them in the hall. "Another delay," he mumbled, then asked, "Breyd, will you be all right here? I have to get my weaponry."

She took her eyes from the mural of ships; he was watching her anxiously. She managed a smile for him. "I'm fine, go, do what you must. I'll be—upstairs, in my—my apartments."

It took an effort to walk up those steps and into that room. It was empty, of course; Emyas had strewn her clothing across the floor, but nothing else had been touched; the loom with its thick roll of fabric stood where she had left it. She gathered up the scattered cloth and folded things, set them back in the chest at the foot of her couch. Apodain's footsteps came up the hall, rousing her from a long, blank moment. She turned to see him standing in the doorway, a large bundle in his arms. "I'll have to ask you to help me again."

"Of course." He came across, set his bundle on the couch, and pulled the baldric over his head; she unlaced the borrowed corselet, then fastened up the bronze armor and the greaves. "I nearly forgot. I have something for you." She walked over to the loom; he came behind her, adjusting the forearm bands as he walked.

He walked all the way around it, ran his fingers lightly over the thick roll of finished cloth. "This is—you made this for me?"

"For you."

"My mother never used a loom in all the years I can remember; no one ever made me such a gift." His smile was so warm it caught her off balance.

"I've always woven," she said. "I've always had to." But he shook his head, and held his fingers to her lips.

"All those days, when I thought you must loathe me for being brought here, for the way my—the way Khadat treated you. And you were—weaving this?"

It wasn't just the work, she suddenly realized. *Who ever gave him a gift, since his father died? Who cared enough for Apodain as himself, to give him anything?* "And I will finish it for you," she said quietly.

Apodain touched it with the backs of his fingers. He was quiet for a very long moment, but when he spoke again his voice was troubled. "I don't think I can live in this place again, Breyd. To sleep here—perhaps, if it's this or the barracks, I suppose."

"I can sleep here, in this room, if you can," she replied steadily.

He cast her a grateful look, turned away once more. "I can't take my old rooms; she kept me prisoner there for so long, I couldn't even bear to walk into them just now." He walked over to gaze out the window. "I don't know what we'll do. Where we can go."

"It's all right," she said. "We don't have to live here, there's no one to make us. I'll work the fabric off the loom and then there's nothing here to hold me. We can sleep here, this room, tonight, or as many nights as we have to, until Haffat comes back and we send him away. We'll have time to decide." He turned back and held out his hand.

"We'll stay here, tonight at least. Tomorrow, perhaps—but we'd better go, now; it's growing late and the queen wants to see us."

She had never been in Khadat's apartments: The walls were painted with fantastic fishes, seas and more of the bright-sailed ships; thick carpets and furs covered the floor.

A servant went through the door into the bedchamber, came back with Ye Sotris.

Breyd had never been so near Pelledar's queen; she was abashed when the woman took her hand and prevented her from kneeling. A servant brought her a chair and Apodain helped the man hand Ye Sotris down onto it. She was pale, very pregnant, but her eyes were steady and when she spoke her voice was, too. "They tell me you led the general's men into the palace, cousin; that because of you my husband is alive and those children returned to their families unharmed."

Apodain shook his head. "I led the way in, but I wasn't—"

"No," Ye Sotris said softly. "I have already talked to one of the general's aides, I know what you both did. I am so grateful to have Pelledar back alive, Apodain. And—you are Breyd, I think they said?" Breyd nodded; she was afraid to speak. Ye Sotris' eyes searched her face; she smiled then. "You will convince him; I want to reward you both for what you have done. Something—worthy of saving a Prince's life. Don't say anything now, think about it." She let the servant help her back to her feet and left them.

They stopped in the lower hallway so Apodain could return the jar in the little courtyard to its proper place. When he came back, Breyd was leaning against one wall, gazing at the opposite one. She looked at him and smiled. "You've seen my home. I will never forget coming here—not knowing what to expect. The first thing I saw, after your—after Khadat, was this." She swept a hand. "Ships. I had seen the palace walls, the night I went there, but not really taken it in. This—it warmed my heart, when I thought nothing could. Such beautiful ships." She turned from them, held out her hand. He took it and went out into the afternoon heat with her.

Seventh horn: Some of the remaining Diye Haff were putting together a pyre on the far bank of the Oryon while others brought the dead across and laid them on it. Breyd came onto the walls with Apodain as a message came from the Mirikosi ship inside the mole. "Ask the general whether we will be named enemy for taking away whatever Diye Haff wish to sail with us tomorrow. Remind him that Mirikos was always Ghezrat's ally until Haffat conquered us; that ships' captains have wives and children, as Haffat knew."

Piritos stood on his customary stone, eyes fixed on the pyre; he listened as the message was read, then replied, "Send back to the Mirikosi. Tell him, you may leave without harm and you may even return to Ghezrat and speak to our prince, when he is able to listen to you. But on one condition: You will take the Princess Khadat, her son, and her cousin back to Mirikos with you, and return her to her father's house."

By sunrise the next morning, there were no Diye Haff anywhere on the plain; what was left of the pyre still smoked but not a tent remained. A short while later, Piritos met two closed sedan chairs at the gates. One of the guards accompanying them threw back the cloth and Khadat glared out at him. "I am sparing your life," Piritos said flatly, "because I know the prince would. You have your son and your cousin for company; whatever family ships you have in Mirikos are still yours, but you will sail them out of Mirikos, not Ghezrat. Do not return here, ever." Khadat's mouth moved, but she said nothing; Piritos let the cloth fall and said, "Take them down, wait and make certain they are gone." He turned on his heel and strode back to the barracks.

A short time later, Khadat stood at the end of the mole, huddled in the cloak that had been Perlot's, her eyes fixed worriedly upon Hemit. He had failed again, since Hadda had taken him, even Emyas could not reach him.

It was not my fault! What did they expect, that I would sit and let Haffat take everything? But even the goddess had failed her.

Pria had been willing to come to Mirikos, but no other servants. It took two men for Hemit—Reott had not even replied to Pria's request. There would be men in Mirikos, in her father's palace. Khadat bit her lip. She would think of her father when she must, and no sooner.

They had not even let her go home to pack anything; Pria had gone with the general's men under orders to fill two chests only, one for herself, one for her son. For Piritos to do that—for him to dare pass judgment on her, *he!* A common soldier, and she a woman of royal blood who had joined with royalty! But when she demanded to see the prince, then or after, she had been flatly refused.

But the anger left her at once; she didn't have the strength to hold onto it. She had not slept since they brought her from the Cleft; had eaten very little. She looked across the sea to the north and was suddenly very cold and tired. Movement down the mole; the Mirikosi murmured and left her. She looked up to see Ghezrathi soldiers. *Come to make certain I am gone?* She stiffened. Apodain and that dreadful Breyd were with them, and he had a casually possessive arm across her shoulders; she held his fingers. She turned away from them and fought for control. They had come to gloat, to show her—to see her pain. *She has taught him this. Well, they will get no satisfaction from me.* When she turned around once more, she knew her face was wiped of expression.

Breyd let go of Apodain's fingers as they came up and he removed his arm. Khadat stared at him. "Mother," he said finally and seemed at a loss for words after that.

"I wonder you have the nerve to call me mother," Khadat said flatly. "My son—*her* husband!" Breyd was white to the lips, but her eyes were furious and she took Apodain's hand once more. Khadat smiled unpleasantly. "Well, remember this: It is only because of me you are alive and you have her. Septarin is dead, half the men of your company dead; the prince nearly dead, unless your general lied to me. Most of *her* company is dead—like her Father."

She meant it to hurt, but Breyd brought her chin up. "You know nothing of my father. Last night he sat in his wife's best chair and drank wine with us," she said evenly.

"You lie," Khadat whispered.

"To welcome his new son."

"I shared the cup with him," Apodain said. "Father would have liked Menlaeus."

"Your *father,*" Khadat spat. "Your father was enough like you, of course he would have enjoyed the company of such low—! He never cared what I wanted, I tried to make him strong and it was no use, and you are just like him. *Emyas* is a better son to me than you are!"

Apodain's color was high, his jaw set. "Then I am glad you have him with you, Khadat."

"Yes," Breyd said softly. "You did everything for Apodain. And what you did helped shape him. Thank you, Khadat, for my husband."

She could find nothing to reply to that. A Mirikosi sailor

touched her arm and indicated the ship. Emyas had help with Hemit, another man assisted Pria; the chests were already on board. Khadat turned away and let herself be handed down onto the deck. She stood very still against the rail, her back to them. *They must be standing there, watching.* The oars propelled the ship into deep water, and the sail was hoisted. When she finally turned to look, the mole was very distant and empty.

They moved Prince Pelledar back into the palace five days later; Ye Sotris drew Breyd aside as she left and whispered, "Remember. A proper gift to you both. Allow me to feel I have partly repaid you for what you gave me."

She and Apodain spent much of their time in the barracks or in the messes; they ate in her apartments on a small, plain table that had been Perlot's, and slept together on her couch. She wove the cloak off the loom for him and he wore it, even though the cloth was too heavy for summer.

The general made it clear he would not send her away, but he had no real place for her as he did Apodain. She spent time with the Pairs, but no longer felt part of them, even though Jocasa and Aroepe were still her close friends.

She went at least every other day to spend an afternoon with her family. The Dyadd bond was gone; without it, she felt a little shy around Menlaeus. *I was his child, then his fighting companion. I'm not the second any more, but I can't go back to being a child again.* It would take time, she decided finally. She could only hope she was right.

The rest of them had fallen back into life the way it always had been, or so it seemed to her from outside: Nevvia fussed over Menlaeus, and laughed at his dry little comments at being fussed over. They never talked about Tarpaen around her; she couldn't bring herself to talk about him before either of them.

Nidya fussed over her granddaughter and fed her oil and peppers with her bread. Breyd smiled and ate them and tried not to remember her last dish of oil and peppers in Khadat's house. *That is behind you, let it go.* Niverren was always glad to see her, but she was either busy with her loom or with Creos.

Seven days: She brought fresh bread from the bakery, and news. "The Diye Haff have abandoned the isthmus; we secured it yesterday. The general created a new company, his personal guard; he named Apodain and me the first members."

"Oh." Nevvia caught hold of her fingers. "You won't have to go out there again—to fight?"

She didn't know what it meant, except she was glad for Apodain's sake. She smiled and patted her mother's hand. "I don't think so, Mother. There were messages last night; they say Haffat is very ill and his men won't fight this far from Diyet without him."

"I doubt they will," Menlaeus said. He leaned over to grip her near arm. "I'm proud of you, Breyd. Both of you."

"He should have named you also, Father. As First Prime, and for what you did." But Nevvia's grip on her fingers tightened and she fell silent. And Menlaeus shook his head.

"My leg will keep me from any more fighting. I've had enough of it. I'm happy you were named, but I'm home, and glad to be." Nevvia let out a held breath and smiled at him; her eyes were still anxious. When she went into the kitchen a little later to bring him some soup, Menlaeus said quietly. "You did more out there than I did, anyway; I fought a few battles and broke my leg. I've heard from Ridlo some of the things you did after I was gone."

"Oh, Father, you always talk like that."

"Well, it's true this time. Part of the general's own company. You know, a father likes having children to brag about. It gives him something to bore the other old men he fought with when they brag about theirs."

"Old," Breyd said blankly. "Father, you aren't *old!*"

"I feel it just now. I know, that's the leg. But Niverren thinks I am. She catches my arm when I try to stand; she watches when I walk to make certain I don't fall down."

"Oh, Father! That's just Niverren." She looked past him; Nevvia was still inside; Niv and Creos bent over her weaving. "I haven't had much chance to say, I didn't want to distress Mother. About Tar—I'm sorry."

"Shhh. I know. It's . . . difficult," he said quietly and when she looked at him there were tears in his eyes. "Sons often die before their fathers, especially in war; I just never thought anything could touch him."

Her own throat was overly tight. "At least I had something better to remember him by than the way he and

Laius—" She looked up; Nevvia was coming back, a tray in her hands.

To Breyd's surprise, she merely set it on his lap, kissed his forehead, and said, "Niddy needs me for a little; are you two all right here?"

"We're fine, Mother. Just talking."

She left a while later; Menlaeus had fallen asleep in the chair again, and Nevvia sat at his feet, spinning wool for Niverren. Nidya came across from the storage. "Here, I need water, I'll come part way with you." But she paused with her hand on the latch and turned back to study her granddaughter.

"You look better than your father, but still too thin. And something else—almost as though you felt like a stranger here."

"Truly, it's not that, Niddy. We aren't done with Haffat yet."

"I know that. But it won't come to fighting again, the goddess promised us victory, and now that she's slapped our fingers for being too sure of ourselves, she'll let us have it."

"You think so?"

"I know it. I own a vineyard, child; my mother owned it and hers before her. You ask anyone who tends grapes about how the goddess deals with us. She is generous, loving, caring, but she doesn't ever let the owner of those grapes forget who made them."

"Oh."

Nidya laid a hand on her shoulder. "I'm not surprised you feel strange here; you've gone through a lot. My friend who was Secchi didn't fight nearly as long as you did, or lose so much but I remember what she said, how everyone seemed comfortable, that only she didn't fit. Well?"

"It's—all right, a little of that."

"I know; you never could just come out and say. But you have to think beyond the fighting, Breyd, you and that boy both. You have to learn how to forget things that mattered when they happened, things that don't matter now. You'll wear yourselves to threads remembering his mother, your brother, the fighting. It *was* important, but *it does not matter now!* Go on with your lives and make them count for something. *Do* something. Don't let the past eat you, the way it ate your grandfather." She looked down at her hands and laughed shortly. "All that, and I forgot the jug. Go on, child, back to your man and your new company. I'm very proud of you, we all are. Go."

Prince Pelledar opened his eyes cautiously; the late sun was warm on his feet; he was clean and lay in clean linen. His eyes didn't want to work properly after so long in the dark but surely that was his own familiar ceiling above him. He turned his head a little. Nothing hurt, but he felt terribly weak. A faint sound from the other side of the couch caught his attention; he looked, and found Ye Sotris sitting beside him.

Ten days. Pelledar sat on his throne and listened to his general and his council. "Piritos is right," he said finally. "We have the upper hand this time; we have the emperor's son. He has sick and feverish men, men longing for their own land. He also has those five who survived the barracks and have surely spread the tale by now. There won't be a man among them who won't look at the Dyaddi on our walls and cringe."

He was strong and decisive and something else, Piritos thought, though he couldn't put a name to it. *He is no longer the frightened young man who had no faith in himself—or the man who called me brother. He knows who he is, and what he can survive. I think he may really become a Great King in more than name.*

Forty-seven days. Word was brought that Haffat's ships had passed the isthmus, while other men approached the plain on horse and foot. The next morning, the gates were barred as a ship pulled inside the mole and ran up a yellow flag.

Pelledar came down and stood on the walls next to his general. Men lined the walls and waited; the Dyaddi flanked the gates and the emperor's heir was brought from his confinement in the old queen's apartments. Two men with drawn swords flanked him, but Hadda ignored them; his eyes were fixed on the ship, and then on the company that made its slow way up the road, toward the city.

Twenty men accompanied the emperor, men whose faces were wrapped in thick cloth against the contagion; but Breyd could see sweat on many of them. Incense rose in clouds from braziers and long sticks.

The emperor who had left Ghezrat riding his black stallion now lay upon blankets between two horses. One of Haffat's aides came to the base of the wall and called up urgently, "The emperor has held himself in this world long enough to speak with his son; delay and he may lose that chance. There are few of us here, Haffat's army out there, or what is left of it. But we have nothing left in us to threaten you. Will you bring his son, or send him? We shall swear truce for that long, at least."

Piritos glanced at Pelledar, who nodded at once. "I shall send him; we will make no move against you or the emperor while the truce holds." The aide looked up and met Breyd's eyes; he shuddered and turned away at once, and walked quickly back to his company.

Piritos gestured; the guards took hold of the stunned Hadda, and led him down to the gates.

The emperor was gray-faced; sweat beaded his brow and slicked his hair flat to his skull. He brought out a shaking hand and gripped Hadda's fingers, spoke to him for a very long moment. His eyes closed, the hand fell limp; one of the aides tucked it under the blankets. Hadda turned blindly and came back to the gates. The aide came with him; Breyd could hear him clearly where she stood.

"Your father is not yet dead, Prince Hadda, but he hasn't long to live. He lost four parts of his men in the swamps and marshes at Ye Eygar but even until the very last, he thought this disease would not touch him. And then word came from Ghezrat, and he abandoned Ye Eygar at once. There is a father's love, Prince; that a man leave off the fight for a great land to save his son." Hadda turned away and came back inside with his guard. The aide looked up to the wall. "Sir, we are in your hands now; we could fight again, but to what purpose? They say this fever was brought by the wrath of your goddess. It may be, but that matters little to me, many of the men believe it and they would never fight you. Those who did would die and more of yours—and in the end, Ghezrat would remain yours. Haffat has found his son and seen him safe; I think now he has found his son, he will not live much longer."

"Yes." Pelledar looked down at the haggard face of one who had been an emperor. "We have done enough damage to each other, he and I—all of us. There will be some terms to be set, an agreement to reach, but in the end it will come down to this, I think: You and your emperor go away, and take the boy with you—and we will have peace."

Three days later, a long column of men marched across the southern shore of the Sea of Delos and vanished beyond the high cliffs east of the Oryon. A small company had detached itself from what was left of the army and waited for the incoming ships: Haffat, who had failed alarmingly since speaking with his son, and seemed unlikely to survive the crossing to Mirikos or even to waken once more; his distraught son; his aides and personal company.

Piritos gazed out from the wall; he could not make out which of them was Hadda from this distance. He had wanted to go down there and make certain they were gone, but Pelledar had worried about the contagion, and Tephys had argued with him. *She* has not changed, he thought sourly.

People didn't, though: Hadda would never be a strong king; he'd lose all his father's kingdom but Diyet within half a year of Haffat's death—if he kept any of it, including Diyet, that long. The boy had seen it coming, though, when he talked with the general just before his father's aides came to collect him. "He named me his heir, but I cannot rule an empire, I don't want an empire! I only said I would to ease him, he's so ill. But if he sits in judgment and sees what I do after he dies, what then?"

Piritos had sighed faintly. "Only a wise man knows himself so well at such a young age."

"But I am not wise, sir, ask any of my father's men!"

"They are soldiers, and to a soldier, whatever he holds is a weapon, and anything in front of that weapon an enemy. Remember that, young Hadda, when you deal with soldiers, and when you choose your own council. If you insist upon *my* council, let me say this: You can try to hold together your father's empire, but it won't stay whole long, and it will cost many lives—possibly your own. Or let go all but what is truly yours—Diyet. With the aid of the right men, you might rule well." Hadda had stared at him for so long, he wondered if the boy had heard any of that. Hadda nodded once, then left with the men who came for him.

Breyd watched from the wall near the gate as a dying emperor and a green, terrified young emperor sailed north. Red

nd gold sails bellied in the wind and the early sun shone
hrough them; she caught her breath. "Oh."

Apodain wrapped his arm around her. "What?"

"Ships. Look how lovely that is." He smiled and kissed
her brow.

Pelledar had left word with Grysis to send the two of them
when they were free. He met them in the throne room on the
first floor; bread and fruit had been brought, his steward
came with wine. "Cousin, Ye Sotris tells me how much I
owe you, both of you," he began. "And I thought of something that might serve. Listen, then think about it if you like.
Your mother's ships and the family trading company in
Mirikos won't be welcome here for some time, but we need
that trade. We need someone who can deal with the Mirikosi
and others—Ye Eygari, the northerners. We cannot afford to
let this opportunity pass, Piritos says so and I agree. So
many individual little lands, all separate, there for anyone
like Haffat to pick up, each turned in on itself and concerned
about no one else. We need—not an alliance, there isn't
enough trust among us for that at this point—but trade, and
a start toward building that trust."

Silence. Apodain set his cup aside. "Uncle, there may be
difficulty in building trust if we as Ghezrat ask for it. They
will think you intend to take Haffat's empire over once he's
dead." He looked at Breyd and his eyes lit. "If—if, however,
you were to send out—not a delegation, not a trading company, but enough men and women to form a colony, or take
land for themselves and begin their own city, and *they* were
to propose such trade, set themselves to one side, loyal to
Ghezrat but directed toward seeing peace and trust among
all the lands. . . ." He took Breyd's hands in his. "A gift of
ships," he said quietly. "And men and women to go with us.
There are islands west of the isthmus where men once lived,
but no one lives there now."

"You think you can do this?" Pelledar asked. He looked as
stunned as Breyd felt. Apodain nodded.

"I know we can bring in trade; I have been trained for
that. But the rest—at least we can try."

They set their case before his council the next day. Tephys
watched Breyd closely; her own face gave away nothing.
Denira gazed at her feet or the floor just in front of them.
Apodain talked; after he and Breyd had spent the past near-

sleepless night talking and planning, he was enthusiastic
persuasive. Pelledar finally dismissed them to the third floor
hallway. Less than one full horn passed before they were
called back in.

Pelledar embraced them both. "It is decided. Ships, and
men to sail them. Enough people to begin a land in the islands west of the isthmus and north of Ye Eygar. It will take
a while to decide the details and make out the trade agreements between us. No doubt it will take you time to find the
ones who go with you."

"You have one," Tephys said as Pelledar fell silent.
Denira stood and looked down at the high priestess warily.
"I agree with what you do, if not with all your goals. Denira
will go with these people, to keep them under Denota's protection."

Breyd walked across to grip her friend's cold hands. "We
will be glad to have that protection, High Priestess," she said
formally. She hugged Denira then; Denira gripped her arms.
hard.

Pelledar clapped his hands together once. "Good. That
much, at least, is settled, but Apodain, I know there will be
much more to do. Go, and let me know at once if you need
anything."

Breyd leaned against him as they left the palace. "It's almost as though they were glad to see us go."

"It isn't that."

"But sometimes . . . I don't know. I begin to feel as
though none of it ever happened. Except so many good people are *dead.*"

"My father told me," Apodain said. "People are that way,
once the fighting is over. It was that way after the Bejina
went, it's always that way. Look at your father."

"I know; he hasn't really forgotten, but he's done his best
to put it behind him. Apodain, I wish I could do that, but I
can't!"

"I can't either. It's too soon, there was too much of it.
And everything I see reminds me. And you, too, I see it in
your eyes. Your father is a sensible man; he grieves for his
son, you can see that, but he keeps his pain from the rest of
your family; he eats his meals and drinks the wine Nevvia
brings him, lets his elder daughter fuss over him, and spoils
his young nephew. He may have the same hideous dreams

at bring you awake, but he doesn't keep them with him uring the day."

She led the way into the nearly empty palace, stopped in ne hallway. "He won't come with us, if we go. None of nem will, except maybe Xhem."

"He won't. He's happy here, and that's good. You and —well, at least one of us had the wit to accept their grati- ude while they remembered the offer—and to name a useful ift."

"Ships," Breyd whispered. Her eyes went to the mural. But it's more than ships now: it's a whole new world and new life. Doesn't it frighten you?"

"A little. Not enough to stop me, if you're there. You?" he shook her head and leaned against him. His arms came round her.

It took time, and long wrangling with Pelledar's shipmas- rs and his council; but in the end, they had seven hundred: oung men and their families, a few older men who had erved Khadat's family in Ghezrat—enough people to fill ur ships. Young women who had been Secchi: Jocasa and roepe and their new husbands; Lochria and her merchant. aprio, who had no other family but his daughter. Pelledar ave them free choice of what ships had been Haffat's, as ell as several of his own, and two Mirikosi that had be- nged to Khadat's father. Apodain went over them with the hipmaster and found six that would serve.

Breyd spent what time she could with her family. Menlaeus, as she had suspected, would not leave Ghezrat. "I ave your mother, and Niddy's vineyards to work once my g will let me."

Nevvia wept. Breyd tried to ease her but doubted she'd nade much impression. "Mother, we aren't going that far. t's no farther than Mirikos, really, nearer than Ye Eygar, and eople go back and forth all the time between here and those laces. Three—maybe four days by ship. And we're setting p trade; of course I'll have to come back."

Ten days after the final agreement was signed, and the last ox and crate piled onto the ships, people crowded anx- ously onto the mole and spilled over onto the sand.

Tephys stood on the first of the ships and handed over a undle to Denira, who knelt to take it. "Denota's blessings

go with you and give you increase. Give Her a home among
you, and She will protect you." She stepped ashore and
walked down the mole. Oars came out and the lead ship began to move.

Breyd stood in the stern of the last ship with Apodain; she
leaned against him as it began to move and let his arm
come around her. So many people back there, on shore.
Families and friends of those who were going—Niddy was
out there, somewhere. The curious, as always, stood and
stared; Tephys and her priestesses waited on the sand. The
prince had given them his blessing before the city gates; he
and his council and his general stood up there, on the walls.
Breyd could just make out the bright red banner Ye Sotri
had placed in the throne room window for them.

She looked toward the side; Xhem leaned against the rail-
ing and waved—to his own family, perhaps; more likely his
friends from the barracks, or just people back there on the
mole. He had been surprised, she thought, that she would
think to ask him. *But I am very fond of Xhem.* And he would
have a very bright future with her; she would see to it.

Creos had his friends, his new father to take the place of
the old; Menlaeus his family and his friends, his old company where he was considered something of a legend—to
his embarrassment. *First Prime.* He would always be that,
Breyd thought, not just to her but to an entire city. Nevvia
was happy as long as Menlaeus was, and Nidya had the
household to run for an even larger number of people. They
would miss her, but the household would come together
without her. *And I'll come back, now and again. We will.*

The ships were moving quickly as the sails were set.
Breyd turned in Apodain's arms to look up at the great,
brightly-painted sail, then back toward shore. Already the
mole was distant. Atos touched upon high walls and towers
brilliant white against a deep blue sky—and then the waters
and the wind swept them away, and hid Ghezrat from them.